The Works of George Santayana

Contents

Acknowledgments

The editors are grateful to many persons and institutions for their important contributions to and generous assistance in the preparation of this volume. Members of the Society for the Advancement of American Philosophy were instrumental in starting the project. In particular, John Lachs proposed a critical edition of *The Works of George Santayana*, and Morris Grossman initiated the establishment of an editorial board. Throughout the project Mrs. Margot Cory, Santayana's literary executrix, graciously assisted the editors in a considerate and cooperative manner. Margot Backas, Richard Ekman, Douglas Arnold, Charles J. Meyers, Blanche Premo, and Dorothy Wartenberg of the Research Division of the National Endowment for the Humanities supplied information and guidance. Principal financial support was provided by the National Endowment for the Humanities. Dr. Corliss Lamont, Emil Ogden, and the Comité Conjunto Hispano-Norteamericano para la Cooperación Cultural y Educativa also gave sustained financial support.

Texas A&M University is the center for the Santayana Edition, and the following persons at Texas A&M have given their assistance and support: Donna Hanna-Calvert, associate editor; Robin Baker, Brenda Bridges, and Kristine Frost, editorial assistants; Karen Antell, John Cavin, Denise Johnston, Kara Kellogg, Wayne Riggs, Jodine Thomas, and Celina Villamor, research assistants; Erik Tielking, summer intern; Lori Moore, secretary; Dr. Daniel Fallon, former Dean of the College of Liberal Arts; Dr. Woodrow Jones, Dean of the College of Liberal Arts; Dr. Charles Johnson, former Associate Dean of Liberal Arts; Dr. Ben M. Crouch, Associate Dean of Liberal Arts; Dr. Charles Stoup, Senior Academic Business Administrator; and Dr. Duwayne Anderson, Associate Provost for Research and Graduate Studies. A special note of thanks is extended to the staff of the Office of Interlibrary Loan, Sterling C. Evans Library.

Bucknell University serves as a supplementary location for the Santayana Edition. Editorial staff there includes Annegret Holzberger, editorial assistant, and Chrisanne Curka, Michael Wardell, Sondra Burke, and Kristine Dane, research assistants. Bucknell administrators who have supported the Edition and faculty who have contributed their special knowledge to preparation of the fourth volume are: Dr. Larry D. Shinn, Vice President for Academic Affairs; Dr. Barry R. Maxwell, Vice President for Administration; Dr. Barbara A. Shailor, Vice President for Student Services; Professor Robert L. Taylor, Chairman, Department of English; Professor James M. Heath, Chairman, Department of Classics; and Ann M. de Klerk, Director of Library Services of the Ellen Clarke Bertrand Library, Bucknell University.

    We also wish to acknowledge the invaluable assistance of the professional staffs of the many libraries and archives who have assisted the editors in preparing this volume, and particularly, Roberta Zonghi, curator of rare books, and Mary Francis O'Brien, reference librarian, Boston Public Library; Philip N. Cronenwett, curator of manuscripts, and Joyce L. Pike, librarian, Special Collections, Dartmouth College Library; Nicholas B. Scheetz, manuscript librarian, Joseph Mark Lauinger Library, Georgetown University; Betty Falsey, associate curator, and Jennie Rathbun, Houghton Library, Harvard University; Cathy Henderson, research librarian, Harry Ransom Humanities Research Center, The University of Texas at Austin; Sandra Alston, Thomas Fisher Rare Book Library, University of Toronto; Lynda Clendenning, Laura Endicott, Gregory A. Johnson, Richard Lindeman, and William Runge, Special Collections, Alderman Library, University of Virginia; Susan Bellingham, head of Special Collections, University of Waterloo; Colleen Murphy, Book-of-the-Month Club; and Linda Mehr, director, and Janet Lorenz, National Film Information Service.

    The following have graciously permitted us to print excerpts from letters and from other unpublished materials:

Mrs. Margot Cory
Mr. Robert S. Sturgis
Rare Book and Manuscript Library, Columbia University
Dartmouth College Library
Houghton Library, Harvard University
Rare Books & Manuscripts Division, The New York Public Library,
    Astor, Lenox and Tilden Foundations
Special Collections, Van Pelt Library, University of Pennsylvania

Manuscripts Division, Department of Rare Books and Special Collections, Princeton University Libraries

Charles Scribner's Sons, Publishers

Special Collections, Temple University Libraries

Harry Ransom Humanities Research Center, The University of Texas at Austin

Clifton Waller Barrett Library, Manuscripts Division, Special Collections Department, University of Virginia Library

Yale Collection of American Literature, Beinecke Rare Book and Manuscript Library, Yale University

Special thanks to Jo Ann Boydston for her support and advice concerning textual scholarship; to Charles Scribner, Jr., Chairman of Charles Scribner's Sons, Publishers, for his assistance and cooperation. Other individuals to whom the editors are indebted for assistance in the preparation of this volume include Professors R. J. Q. Adams, David Anderson, Scott Austin, James Bradford, Robert Calvert, Ari Epstein, Morris Grossman, Melanie Hawthorne, Alan Houtchens, Craig Kallendorf, Wolf Koepke, Patrick Laude, John Lunsford, John McCormick, Harrison T. Meserole, Katherine O'Keefe, Paul Parrish, Patricia Phillippy, Kenneth Price, and James Rosenheim; also Helen Osborne, Michael Sims, Betty Stanton, Teri Mendelsohn, Joanna M. Poole, and Terry Lamoureux of MIT Press; Kevin Krugh, Robert Carrick, and Don Cooke of DEKR Corporation; Victor Fischer, inspector for The Center for Scholarly Editions; Robin A. Berry, collator; and the staff and faculty of the Department of Philosophy, Texas A&M University.

This list is inevitably incomplete, and to all those persons whose names are not included here but who helped realize this edition of *The Last Puritan* the editors extend deep thanks.

Herman J. Saatkamp, Jr., Texas A&M University

William G. Holzberger, Bucknell University

An Introduction to *The Last Puritan*

Irving Singer

In a letter he wrote in 1921, fourteen years before he finished *The Last Puritan*, Santayana says that his novel will "contain all I know about America, about women, and about young men. As this last is rather my strong point, I have *two* heroes, the Puritan and another not too much the other way. To make up, I have no heroine, but a worldly grandmother, a mother—the quintessence of all New England virtues—and various fashionable, High Church, emancipated, European, and sentimental young ladies. I have also a German governess—in love with the hero—of whom I am very proud."[1]

The Last Puritan, Santayana's only novel, was an immediate bestseller when it appeared in 1935. Two years later Santayana added the Preface that is included in this volume. In it he discusses the development of his novel over a period of forty-five years as well as his philosophical intentions in this work of fiction. The forty-five-year span that Santayana mentions begins with the period of 1891–1893, which Santayana describes in one of his letters as a "second youth of mine [that] was far pleasanter than my first youth."[2] In 1891 Santayana was a philosophy instructor, twenty-seven years old, living as a proctor in Stoughton Hall in Harvard Yard and spending most of his free time in the company of undergraduates at the Delphic Club. That club was "absolutely my home," he reports, adding that his novel originated as a story that had its setting there. During the twenty years that followed, Santayana may have allowed his novel to gestate but he did little writing on it. Only after he resigned from Harvard and gave up residence in the United States did he find that he could proceed. Beginning with the outbreak of World War I, he lived for five years in England, mainly in Oxford, and that renewed

---

[1] George Santayana, *The Letters of George Santayana*, ed. Daniel Cory (New York: Charles Scribner's Sons, 1955) 190.

[2] George Santayana, *Letters* 303.

association with university life marks the start of consecutive writing of *The Last Puritan*.

Santayana's novel is not a story about college experience or academic adventures. Though the principal characters—Oliver and Mario—are still in their twenties at the end of the narrative, and though the plot centers about their progress into manhood, the book expresses views about life that reached fruition during the years of Santayana's own philosophical maturity. By 1935 he was more than half-way through *Realms of Being*, completing final drafts of *The Realm of Truth* and doing preliminary writing for *The Realm of Spirit*. Works such as *Platonism and the Spiritual Life* had been published in the previous decade. *The Last Puritan* reflects the thinking of a seasoned philosopher, seventy-two years old at the time of its publication, whose ideas were largely formulated even though they had not all been written out. As a work of art, the novel derives its underlying form from the dialectical play between the youthful experience of its two main characters and the accomplished vision of the commentator who interprets it for us.

There are, of course, characters in the narrative who are much older than Oliver and Mario, but their greater age is never presented as giving them access to the philosophic scope that Santayana had himself achieved by the time the novel was finished. Even Mr. Darnley, the vicar who understands the concepts of spirit that Santayana was later to express in *The Idea of Christ in the Gospels*, hardly approximates Santayana's general insight. It appears in the novel as the framework and designing principle of everything that happens to the characters, everything they do or say, and everything that is said about them.

❀

In 1959, seven years after Santayana died, Corliss Lamont published a *Dialogue on George Santayana* to which several philosophers who knew Santayana personally contributed. In the midst of his reminiscences, Horace M. Kallen remarks that the "true image" of Santayana is in *The Last Puritan* rather than *Persons and Places*, which Kallen calls "a shield and a deception really."[3] Later Kallen adds that

[3] *Dialogue on George Santayana*, ed. Corliss Lamont (New York: Horizon Press, 1959) 52.

the novel is "far more authentic than the autobiographical books. Partly because he assumes that it's disguised."[4] If we think of a disguise as a masquerade that does not hide the truth but rather manifests it in ways that are only available to make-believe, Kallen's suggestion may be valuable and is worth pursuing.

In doing so, we are immediately arrested by the subtitle of *The Last Puritan*—"A Memoir in the Form of a Novel." A memoir may be biographical, but it need not be autobiographical. It is an account based on memory even though it is not one's own experiences that are being remembered. To think of the novel as a fictionalized version of *Persons and Places*—which portrays his host the world as Santayana experienced it—would seem to be wholly egregious except for the fact that Santayana's experience reveals itself so fully in this memoir of events that never happened literally in his (or anyone else's) life. Santayana prepares us for the nature of his masquerade by using as his epigraph a quotation from the French philosopher who wrote under the name of Alain. It translates as follows: "It is well said that experience speaks through the mouth of older men: but the best experience that they can bring to us is that of their salvaged youth." The last adjective in this quote is "*sauvée*," suggesting that the best that age can communicate is the part of youth which can be rescued despite the passage of time. Although he gives himself only a cameo role on the peripheries of his novel, Santayana regains his earlier experience in the way that Proust does. Each of them writes his research into past time from the point of view of one who has long since outlived it but now seeks, through re-creative imagination, greater understanding of its inherent meaning than he could have had when he was actually young himself.

As in the case of Proust's masterpiece, critics and ordinary readers alike have wondered how this memorial novel should be classified. It often resembles Santayana's essayistic writing, so much so that Santayana felt a need to justify his making all the characters sound the way he wrote. In the Epilogue Mario complains that "'you make us all talk in your own philosophical style, and not in the least as we actually jabber'" (570). Santayana responds to this kind of criticism in the Preface, and in the Epilogue he insists that, far from writing "'a philological document,'" he was creating a work that would remain

---

[4] Lamont 60–61.

understandable to future readers who may not be acquainted with the idioms of a single epoch. "'Fiction is poetry, poetry is inspiration, and every word should come from the poet's heart, not out of the mouths of other people. . . . Even in the simplest of us passion and temperament have a rich potential rhetoric that never finds utterance; and all the resources of a poet's language are requisite to convey not what his personages would have been likely to say, but what they were really feeling'" (570–571).

This statement should be read in the context of what Santayana says about "literary psychology" in *Scepticism and Animal Faith*. He there argues that no attempt to understand the experience of other people (or ourselves as we existed in the past) can ever have the kind of credibility that science has. What he calls "scientific psychology" seeks objective knowledge by making inferences about the realm of matter out of which experience emerges. To the extent that we think or write about experience in itself—experience as it appears to whoever is having it—we are dealing with immediate qualities, which Santayana calls "essences," that cannot be conveyed in any literal or verifiable fashion. To discourse about essences is to engage in literary psychology, which is fictional and poetic—in an extended sense of these words—regardless of how prosaic our language may be. In other words, a writer cannot succeed in expressing what real or imagined people feel by copying their speech patterns, as a linguist might, or by using any other quasi-scientific device. Instead he must rely upon intuitive awareness that typically belongs to art.

The nature of such awareness had earlier been analyzed by Santayana in *The Sense of Beauty*. In all works of art he detected a capacity for expressiveness that goes beyond either material or formal properties in the aesthetic object. Santayana suggests that art attains its appropriate truthfulness to life through a special kind of "idealization." Through ordinary idealization human beings conceive of persons or events in an abstract and simplified manner that the imagination renders beautiful in some degree. If this occurs through the elimination of individual differences, the characters turn into types and lose their capacity to represent the quality of human experience. In great works of art, however, that does not happen. For there the artist offers to the imagination of his audience something that is "more striking and living than any reality, or any abstraction from realities."[5] Far from being desiccated types, the great characters in fiction give one a sense of individuality that often seems more natural to us than what is found in nature itself. In a passage that foreshadows what he was later to attempt in *The Last Puritan*, Santayana states:

> . . . A Hamlet, a Don Quixote, an Achilles—[these] are no averages, they are not even a collection of salient traits common to certain classes of men. They seem to be persons; that is, their actions and words seem to spring from the inward nature of an individual soul. Goethe is reported to have said that he conceived the character of his Gretchen entirely without observation of originals. And, indeed, he would probably not have found any. His creation rather is the original to which we may occasionally think we see some likeness in real maidens. It is the fiction here that is the standard of naturalness. And on this, as on so many occasions, we may repeat the saying that poetry is truer than history. Perhaps no actual maid ever spoke and acted so naturally as this imaginary one.[6]

In saying that poetry is truer than history, Santayana draws upon Aristotle's dictum in the *Poetics*. But he also goes beyond Aristotle. The latter thought that history is less "philosophical" than poetry because history tells us about particular facts whereas poetry achieves a more universal reference since it indicates what some type of person might have said or done on one or another occasion. This alone would not prove that poetry expresses the truth about human individuality; indeed, it could even be taken to mean that poetry differs from history by giving general information. Santayana rejects any such interpretation: as we saw, he insists that great characters in fiction manifest "the inward nature of an individual soul." In the case of *The Last Puritan*, he thought that duplication of local idioms or dialects would interfere with the proper employment of aesthetic intuition. In order to show what the characters felt, and what they were as human beings, one would have to use an imaginative ap-

---

[5] George Santayana, *The Sense of Beauty: Being the Outlines of Aesthetic Theory*, ed. William G. Holzberger and Herman J. Saatkamp, Jr. (Cambridge, Mass. and London: MIT Press, 1988) 113.

[6] Santayana, *Sense* 113.

proach that probes more deeply into the philosophical ramifications of their human individuality. And that required the language of someone who could analyze their condition philosophically while also integrating such analysis with the kind of inventiveness needed for the creation of a work of art.

In developing this mode of presentation, Santayana successfully challenges many of our preconceptions about the "realistic" novel. Some people have thought that realism involves a search for photographic reproduction; and others have claimed that fidelity to "the stream of consciousness" uniquely demonstrates the nature of human experience. In James Joyce's *Ulysses,* both of these techniques are used to good effect. But do they bring us any closer to "the real world" than Santayana's meditative prose? I do not think so. Once the contents of lived experience are rendered into words, they have already become figments of the novelist's mentality. Joyce's figments are no more reliable epistemically than Santayana's; they merely reflect a different way of perceiving and digesting reality. The great virtue in Santayana's method consists in its exploration of moral and pervasive problems that people, at least of the sort that he depicts, face throughout their existence—whether or not they can discuss such problems as brilliantly as Santayana and his characters do.

❋

These considerations apply not only to the language that the various personages use or the soliloquies through which they voice their introspective attitudes, but also to their individuality within the fiction. In the Preface Santayana reports that his fable mixes historical and imaginary elements. In letters to friends, he states that all the characters are an amalgamation drawn from various people he had known in earlier life. This is the usual procedure in the writing of novels. The models for Santayana's protagonist were several poets in the 1880s and 1890s who seemed to him representative of many intellectuals in America at that time. Though Oliver Alden is unique and imaginary, his story expresses the hopeless plight of other young men whose aspirations found no sustenance in their society. In one place, Santayana says that "all those friends of mine . . . were visibly killed by the lack of air to breathe. People individually were kind and appreciative to them, as they were to me; but the system was deadly, and they hadn't any alternative tradition (as I had) to fall back upon:

and . . . they hadn't the strength of a great intellectual hero who can stand alone."[7]

This much of Santayana's theme is hardly limited to him. It is central in *Roderick Hudson*, the early novel of Henry James, and it recurs as a leitmotif through many of James' later works. Like these Jamesian novels, *The Last Puritan* makes no effort to be sociological. The system that Santayana considered so deadly to his friends was the general atmosphere of American life during those decades of industrial expansion and cultural change. But Santayana gives us only meager glimpses into the social realities of New England or even Harvard. As John Dewey observed in the brief review he wrote soon after the novel appeared, the book includes "extraordinarily little background of scene . . . the scene is scenery; stage setting for the persons who are its characters."[8] To some extent, the characters were chosen as indications of what was happening in America at the time, but we do not see them living or acting as members of a class or major segment of American society. What kind of system, we may therefore ask, is "the system" to which Santayana refers?

For the most part, it was a system of religious and moral ideas related to what Santayana elsewhere calls "the genteel tradition." Throughout the latter half of the nineteenth century, New England attitudes were dominated by attempts to reconcile Protestantism with the romanticism that issued out of German idealist philosophy. Emerson, who was a poet as well as a Christian moralist, had given an example of how this reconciliation might occur. He sought to harmonize a love of nature with a sense of transcendental realities; and he believed that despite the pantheistic elements in this religious outlook it remained faithful to the original teachings of Christianity. When Oliver Alden reaches Harvard in Santayana's novel, he takes up residence in Emerson's former rooms in Divinity Hall. For Oliver, as for the young poets whose history he enacts, the Emersonian influence represents much of the setting for his inner struggle.

In his autobiographical writings, Santayana frequently records his sense of alienation from the Protestant culture of New England. But one has to remember that he was also a part of it. Though his parents

[7] Santayana, *Letters* 306.
[8] John Dewey, "Santayana's Novel," *John Dewey: The Later Works, 1925–1953*, ed. Jo Ann Boydston (Carbondale & Edwardsville, Il.: Southern Illinois University Press, 1987) 2: 446.

were Catholic, he grew up within the Protestant milieu to which his
mother was allied through her first marriage. Most of Santayana's
childhood friends were Protestants, and the manners he acquired in
school were those of a proper Bostonian. In 1950, when I met him,
his accent seemed to me as close as one could get to the way that
Boston Brahmins would have sounded in the nineteenth century.

In saying that the prevailing system of American thought had killed
the promising young poets and intellectuals, Santayana does not
mean that poetry or art or culture in general was scorned by the
society at large. He means that New England, and America as a whole,
failed to recognize that creativity in these areas could be as worthy
and morally justifiable as action devoted to more pragmatic ends.
The works of art that Americans were accumulating with their newly-
acquired wealth were usually the product of Europeans and Asiatics,
an offshoot of Mediterranean and Oriental societies whose ethical
presuppositions were suspect even though they could somehow provide superior access to beauty. In America, as Santayana knew it,
there would seem to be no place for aesthetic or spiritual creativity:
"if a man is born a poet or a mystic in America he simply starves,
because what social life offers and presses upon him is offensive to
him, and there is nothing else."[9]

The "alternative tradition" upon which Santayana could fall back
consisted primarily of the Catholic orientation to which he was introduced as a child. By the time he was eighteen, his belief in Catholic
dogma had largely disappeared, and the atheism he openly professed
in later life was well-developed in him at some point during the next
ten years. What remained, as a constant from beginning to end, was
appreciation of the myths and rituals of Catholicism that could em-
bellish everyday experience by making it orderly, ornate, and filled
with meaning. Moreover, he cherished Catholicism as the living resi-
due of Greek and Latin civilization that had survived in the modern
world despite the inroads of Nordic and Romantic barbarism.

Emanating from this personal background, Santayana's novel belongs to the genre of accounts by a survivor who tells us about some
peril that befell his tribe, and from which only he escaped. There
but for the grace of God go I, the survivor says, because he is aware
of his identity with those who were not as lucky. At the same time,

[9] Santayana, *Letters* 302.

he lives to tell the tale because of attributes in himself that enabled him to get away, attributes that then become essential ingredients in his narrative. Drawing upon the two traditions in his own experience, Santayana puts them in dramatic opposition to one another as a way of showing why and how his friends were destroyed. In the process, he also demonstrates that he himself survived by creatively harmonizing these opposing ways of life. The young poets who were victims of their society suffered a tragic fate because they were unable to make that kind of harmonization.

❋

In various places throughout his novel, Santayana emphasizes that Oliver's history is not only sad but also "tragic." The book has frequent elements of comedy, to which I shall return, but it is clearly intended to be read as a tragedy. In the German edition, the subtitle becomes: *Die Geschichte eines tragischen Lebens* ("The Story of a Tragic Life"). Though this eliminates the idea of a memoir in the form of a novel, it is faithful to the contents of the book. Santayana depicts the tragedy of puritanism as it appears in his twentieth-century hero. The puritanism that Oliver Alden embodies is, however, significantly different from the puritanism of his ancestors in the seventeenth century. He is a descendent of the colonial Alden in Longfellow's poem "The Courtship of Miles Standish," and his first name derives from the puritanical Cromwell who overthrew Charles I. But Santayana's protagonist consistently rejects most of the doctrines his predecessors considered fundamental.

For this reason, Ralph Barton Perry's description of *The Last Puritan* is very misleading—at least, as far as Oliver is concerned. In *Puritanism and Democracy* Perry says: "Santayana's famous book is an account not of the living puritan creed, but of its death; and its death resembles the death of any creed when its subordinations have become negations, its convictions rigidities, and its surviving zealots monstrosities."[10] Oliver Alden is neither a zealot nor a monstrosity. Santayana portrays him as a superior individual, a very good man, a pilgrim hungering for salvation that eludes him throughout life. Perry's comment is accurate about Oliver's bluenose uncle, Nathaniel,

---

[10] Ralph Barton Perry, *Puritanism and Democracy* (New York: Vanguard Press, 1944) 64.

who appears at the beginning of the novel as a satiric vignette of puritanism as it had degenerated in Victorian Boston. At the end, having failed in his attempt to find love or even contentment in the midst of World War I, Oliver partly reverts to Nathaniel. But even then, Oliver searches for a wholesome and sane puritanism that would be suitable for the present and so remain a living rather than a dead creed. He has long since outgrown the Calvinism of his forebears. Like Irma (his German governess) he believes in the goodness of nature, and his religious faith—to the degree that he has any—is closer to Goethe's pagan naturalism than to conventional Christianity.

In calling Oliver the *last* puritan, Santayana does not wish to imply that there will be no others. He originally thought of entitling his book *The Ultimate Puritan*; and in the Epilogue he remarks: "'A moral nature burdened and over-strung, and a critical faculty fearless but helplessly subjective—isn't that the true tragedy of your ultimate Puritan?'" (571–572). In the Prologue the character Mario had already told us that "'in Oliver puritanism worked itself out to its logical end. He convinced himself, on puritan grounds, that it was wrong to be a puritan. . . . That was the tragedy of it. Thought it his clear duty to give puritanism up, but couldn't'" (14).

In conversation Santayana is reported to have said that Oliver is "the dialectically ultimate Puritan, because he's a man who very conscientiously believes he shouldn't have a conscience."[11] But, in the Prologue, Santayana also tells us that Oliver had no "'timidity or fanaticism or calculated hardness.'" He felt "'hatred of all shams, scorn of all mummeries, a bitter merciless pleasure in the hard facts. And that passion for reality was beautiful in him. . . . He was a millionaire, and yet scrupulously simple and silently heroic'" (14).

This being Santayana's conception of Oliver's character, one might conclude that the novel is basically an attack on puritanism itself. For even its flowering in the fine and exemplary protagonist whom Santayana says he loves, and who represents the young poets whose ruin he grieves, results in tragedy and incompleteness. The better Oliver is as a human being, in contrast to monstrosities like Uncle Nathaniel, the more his failure to solve the problems of life would reveal the underlying flaw in puritanism as a whole.

---

[11] Lamont 60.

But though Santayana's motive may have been partly tendentious in this manner, his admiration for Oliver's purity of soul outweighs any desire to demonstrate the futility of Protestant ideology. Oliver is a tragic hero not only because he cannot escape the contradiction of rejecting puritanism on puritan grounds, but also because he is a spiritual man who cannot reconcile himself to the realm of matter without which he could not exist at all, even as a spiritual being.

This kind of self-contradiction does not pertain exclusively to any single religious doctrine. It is not peculiar to Protestantism or to puritanism. It is a paradox experienced by everyone who wishes to rise above his material nature while being constrained, by the realities of life, to make the attempt only as a product of that nature. In the Prologue Santayana compounds the paradox when he remarks that "'puritanism is a natural reaction against nature'" (14). Some of the reverberations in this moral dilemma had already been adumbrated in an essay by William James that Santayana must have read. It is called "The Gospel of Relaxation." Addressing himself directly to the young women in his audience, James encourages them to relax their high-minded intensity and to give their personalities greater access to the benefits of freedom and repose. But then James ends his sermon with the following words:

> Even now I fear that some one of my fair hearers may be making an undying resolve to become strenuously relaxed, cost what it will, for the remainder of her life. It is needless to say that that is not the way to do it. The way to do it, paradoxical as it may seem, is genuinely not to care whether you are doing it or not. Then, possibly, by the grace of God, you may all at once find that you *are* doing it, and, having learned what the trick feels like, you may (again by the grace of God) be enabled to go on.[12]

The tragedy of Oliver Alden consists in the fact that he was *not* able to do it. Having established this, however, Santayana delves into the psychodynamics—or what might be called the ontodynamics—of his failure. According to Santayana, the being of man is divided into elements of spirit and matter. These can sometimes be harmonized— in which case, as Santayana says in one of his letters, "*tutti contenti*"

---

[12] William James, *Essays on Faith and Morals* (New York: New American Library, 1974) 258.

(all's well).[13] But when the two orders of being remain in opposition to one another, the tensions between them create a conflict that is inherently tragic. We would trivialize Santayana's thought if we said that Oliver is a moral but largely repressed—above all, sexually repressed—scion of an overly civilized strand of humanity. More essential in his tragedy, as Santayana portrays it, is the fact that Oliver wants to live in accordance with natural impulses while also seeking a spiritual vocation that would detach him from the vicissitudes of mere existence. He cannot secure the best of both worlds, and he ends up living in neither.

In the Preface Santayana says that Oliver was a spiritual man whose tragedy resulted from his inability to renounce ordinary life, as Christ had done, in order to heed his own calling. When Santayana says that Oliver, like the rich young man in the Gospels, would have given his wealth to the poor in order to follow Jesus but then found "no way of salvation to preach" (9), he renews his point about the aridity of American culture. His major insight goes beyond that, however, for he recognizes that tragedy arises from any conflict within a person's being that prevents him from living in accordance with his own vocation.

In the novel the Vicar speaks of two kinds of tragedy: one of the spiritual man, the other of the natural man. He says that the spiritual man must live a tragic life because "'his flesh and his pride and his hopes'" (247) will have withered early. The Vicar himself is a tragic figure of this sort, and he rightly intuits that Oliver is also one. Other characters have perceived Oliver in the same way: Irma has an image of him as Christ on the Cross, and she identifies his monogram Ⓐ as "the Alpha and Omega of our Saviour" (218); preparatory to rejecting his offer of marriage, his cousin Edith sees him as "'one of those rare persons called to a solitary life in a special sense'" (468); and earlier he had appeared in a dream sequence of his own as Gilda, the tragic heroine in Verdi's *Rigoletto* who gives her life in an act of love and spiritual renunciation.

What the Vicar says about the tragedy of the natural man is also significant. He is talking primarily of his son Jim, whose capacity to enjoy material pleasures had so greatly impressed Oliver. "'The perfection of merely bodily life or of worldly arts is somehow tragic,'"

---

[13] Santayana, *Letters* 410.

the Vicar declares: "'The merely natural man ends tragically, because the spirit in him is strangled'" (246 and 247). As the novel progresses, Oliver comes to realize how sordid and unsatisfying Jim's life really is despite his powers of enjoyment. Though his experience is totally different from Oliver's and the Vicar's, Jim also fails to reconcile the demands of matter and spirit. His failure is symbolized by the image of the black swan. When Oliver first meets him, Jim is the virile captain of the yacht *Black Swan*. He then appears to Oliver as "an ideal elder brother, a first and only friend" (205). By the end of the novel, Oliver suffers not only disillusionment about Jim's character but also grief when Jim is lost at sea. On his way to commiserate with the Darnley family, Oliver is surprised to encounter a black swan in a watery field where none had ever been seen before. What was originally a symbol of beauty surmounting death has now become a symbol of death—in the soul as well as the body—that destroys beauty and does so tragically.

In presenting Oliver and Jim as tragic in these different ways, Santayana scrupulously avoids a moralistic choice between the spiritual and the natural man. These are different options for human beings, but each person must decide which is best for himself. The only basis for a good life that Santayana accepts is the ability to act with self-knowledge about one's nature—one's individual nature as well as one's being as a manifestation of human nature. In the Preface Santayana insists that the sadness of Oliver is not the fact that he died young but that "he stopped himself, not trusting his inspiration" (9). Elsewhere Santayana asserts that death is neither sad nor tragic in itself. What is truly sad, he says, "is to have some impulse frustrated in the midst of its career, and robbed of its chosen object." In the same context, he tells us that the point in life "is to have expressed and discharged all that was latent in us. . . . The task in any case is definite and imposed on us by nature, whether we recognise it or not."[14]

The tragedies of Oliver and Jim thus result from their inability to realize and to fulfill the diverse potentialities within the nature that each of them had. In Oliver's case his failure is more poignant because, almost to the end of his life, he continues to resist his own

---

[14] George Santayana, "A Long Way Round to Nirvana; or·Much Ado about Dying," *Some Turns of Thought in Modern Philosophy: Five Essays* (New York: Charles Scribner's Sons, 1933) 98–100.

spirituality. In a letter, Santayana says that Oliver "was a mystic, touched with a divine consecration. . . . He ought to have been a saint."[15] In making this kind of judgment, Santayana would seem to think that people can learn what their true nature is. And indeed all of *The Last Puritan* can be seen as Oliver's discovery, through painful trial and error, of what he was born to be.

In at least one place, Santayana called his novel the account of a "sentimental education." When the book appeared, critics immediately linked it to *The Education of Henry Adams*. Though it is a tragedy, recording the puritanical self-mutilation that prevented Oliver from carrying out his function as a spiritual man, it also depicts Oliver's progression toward the truth about himself. Having been rejected by Rose because she intuits that he was not made to live in the world like other people and could not love her as a woman wants to be loved, he finally feels liberated from the need to be "commonplace."

In attaining this ultimate awareness, Oliver concludes that there is a divine love to which he can now devote his energies. He believes that it is preferable to whatever earthly love he might have experienced. Without having recourse to any orthodox creed, he sees the direction that his innate calling must take: "'We will not accept anything cheaper or cruder than our own conscience. We have dedicated ourselves to the truth, to living in the presence of the noblest things we can conceive. If we can't live so, we won't live at all'" (553–554).

The "we" here includes his outlandish Uncle Nathaniel, but Oliver speaks as the embodiment of what is deepest and most fully clarified in the puritanism that they jointly represent. To this extent, Oliver's career is not at all tragic. His subsequent death is wholly irrelevant. In having reached a stage at which he can understand the kind of person he is and has become, he attains the type of self-knowledge that Santayana recommends throughout his moral philosophy. Though Oliver fails in life, he has also succeeded: for in knowing himself, he faces up to reality and transcends his own tragedy.

❊

Oliver is not the only character who achieves self-knowledge. Mario also does. Unlike either Oliver or Jim, Mario has nothing in him that

---

[15] Santayana, *Letters* 302.

could be considered tragic. Mario is a healthy-minded man, capable of enjoying the usual animal instincts. He is rational and sensible while also being uninhibited and unrepressed. He is a Cherubino as an adolescent, a Don Juan as a young man, and in maturity a functioning husband, father, and pillar of respectability. Without paying much attention to theological matters, he remains an avowed Catholic and even becomes an official at the Vatican. He has an existence that Santayana considers "natural," and we may take Mario's development as indicative of how a well-attuned Latin can cope with American and European life in the twentieth century. At the same time, he cannot be expected to comprehend the nature of someone like Oliver. Whatever Mario may feel for Oliver as a friend, the limitations in his own nature prevent him from understanding the range of potentialities in Oliver's. To have that kind of awareness Mario would need to be a philosopher, and in this novel the only philosopher is Santayana himself.

In one of his letters Santayana says that Oliver was meant to be unlike him in physical and moral character, but "in the quality of his *mind*, he is what I am or should have been in his place."[16] In his book about Santayana, Daniel Cory—who speaks of himself as one of the prototypes of Mario—also identifies Oliver with Santayana. Certainly they are alike in being scholarly types who pursue the truth and eventually withdraw from routine society. Nevertheless, the differences between Santayana and Oliver are quite pronounced. Santayana regularly enjoyed the good things of this world, and he never claimed to be a spiritual man. In one place he notes that he has "the Epicurean contentment . . . a humourous animal faith in nature and history, and no religious faith. . . . Oliver hadn't this intellectual satisfaction, and he hadn't that Epicurean contentment."[17] From this point of view, Santayana would seem to be closer to Mario than to any of the other characters. Being the older man salvaging his past, Santayana the novelist (like Stendhal before him) appears as the bemused commentator who laughs at his own youthful vitality while also relishing the lovely moments it once afforded. Like Mario, he savored all that European culture had to offer, and he did so by treating his Catholic origins as a resource rather than a burden.

[16] Santayana, *Letters* 308.
[17] Santayana, *Letters* 305.

There is one respect, however, in which Mario is not Santayana, except perhaps as a wish-fulfillment. Mario's sexual orientation is of a sort that Santayana did not have though he obviously considered it entirely normal and desirable. Hardly anything is known about Santayana's sexuality, but the little that he and others said about it would lead one to believe that his erotic life was different from Mario's. One of the rare bits of evidence occurs in a conversation between Santayana and Cory that is often misquoted. They have been reading the poetry of A. E. Housman, and Santayana shocks Cory by remarking:

> "I suppose Housman was really what people nowadays call 'homosexual.'"
>
> "Why do you say that?" I protested at once.
>
> "Oh, the sentiment of his poems is unmistakable," Santayana replied.
>
> There was a pause, and then he added, as if he were primarily speaking to himself:
>
> "I think I must have been that way in my Harvard days—although I was unconscious of it at the time."
>
> He said this so naturally that I was not at all startled. He seemed a little ashamed to confess to having been so innocent. . . .
>
> Santayana then told me that various people at Harvard . . . must have suspected something unusual in his make-up: he felt acutely at times their silent disapproval, and it was one of the things that made him determined to retire from teaching there as soon as he could afford to do so.
>
> "I couldn't stick it any longer than I did. . . . I had even made up my mind that if things got any worse, I would go straight to William James and ask him frankly what it was all about."[18]

In a subsequent footnote, Cory says of Santayana: "If he was a man with the feelings of a woman, he was not aware (until well into middle life) what this might indicate to a Freudian expert. When he did finally suspect something 'unconventional' in his psyche, I am certain it only hardened a predilection to renounce the world as

[18] Daniel Cory, *Santayana: The Later Years. A Portrait with Letters* (New York: George Braziller, 1963) 40–41.

much as was compatible with living a rational life devoted to his labors. . . . He simply considered sex a nuisance; he would never have dreamed of bragging—like André Gide—about an idiosyncrasy in development."[19]

In his recent biography of Santayana, John McCormick makes a concerted effort to show that Santayana was indeed a homosexual. But the information he adduces would seem to prove little more than the possibility that Santayana occasionally had "erotic friendships." Santayana applies that phrase not to any experience of his own, but to relationships within *The Last Puritan*. The word "love" is often used in the novel to describe what Mario and Oliver feel for one another, and also the strong affective bond that ties Oliver to Jim Darnley. There is no suggestion of a sexual attraction between Mario and Oliver. But Oliver's feelings about Jim are presented as an adolescent crush that could well have had physical overtones. In earlier life Jim was expelled from the Royal Navy because of some nameless sexual "immorality" between himself and other sailors. After his death, Jim's father the Vicar says to Oliver: "'Jim has made you suffer a great deal for years. . . . You were more deeply attached to Jim than you have ever suspected.'" To this, Oliver replies: "'Yes. That is the truth. I loved him from the beginning'" (507 and 508).

When the novel first appeared, Santayana expressed surprise to Cory that in the reviews "there are objections repeatedly made to Mario, but not a breath against the ambiguities of Jim. Don't people catch on, or are they shy?"[20] Santayana states in various letters that Jim is modeled on his friend Frank Russell (John Francis Stanley, 2nd Earl Russell). In *Persons and Places* many pages are devoted to their uneven relationship, revealing Russell's emotional difficulties throughout his marriages and love affairs but also portraying him as an aristocratic and forceful man whose erotic appeal entranced Santayana when they first became friends.

These personal details are worth mentioning because *The Last Puritan* has sometimes been called a "homosexual novel," with the intimation that this defines a limiting perspective from which it is written. But that invokes a mode of classification that is too crude, and too imprecise, for this particular work. In the Preface, as in some of his letters, Santayana admits that he is ill-equipped to write about

[19] Cory 43.
[20] Cory 163.

(heterosexual) romantic love; and in fact, his book includes no examples of it, although Oliver woos first Edith and then Rose in his puritanical manner and certainly hopes that sexual oneness will someday develop. It never does in his case, and the heterosexual experiences of Mario and Jim are problematic in ways that I shall presently consider. What remains at the core of the novel is not homosexuality but rather *friendship* as an ideal intimacy. In view of the love that it generally incorporates, it may be called "erotic"; but nothing is gained by reducing it to one or another type of sexuality—whether overt or merely "latent," as Freud would say.

It is evident from *Persons and Places* how much friendship meant to Santayana throughout his life: friendship with women as well as men, friendship with schoolmates or others who visited him in later life as well as friendship at a distance and mediated through letter-writing. Having no family of his own and very little communal involvement, friendship was for Santayana an essential supplement to the solitude he cultivated and needed for his work. As I have suggested elsewhere, Santayana's philosophy of love is at its strongest when he describes the type of bonding which is not marital or sexual or romantic but rather a life-enhancing affection between friends.[21]

Of the many places in which Santayana discusses the nature of friendship, the account in *Reason in Society* is especially useful for understanding *The Last Puritan*. In a chapter entitled "Free Society" some of his comments about ideal friendship resemble what Aristotle says in the *Nicomachean Ethics*. Emphasizing the importance of similarity with respect to social status and moral aspiration, he argues that friendship involves not only personal liking, or even "animal warmth," but also the pursuit of common ideals. "The necessity of backing personal attachment with ideal interests is what makes true friendship so rare. It is found chiefly in youth, for youth best unites the two requisite conditions—affectionate comradeship and ardour in pursuing such liberal aims as may be pursued in common."[22]

In the novel, the moments of greatest vibrancy and vividness occur in the scenes that depict Oliver's growing capacity for friendship: on the yacht or watching a football game with Jim, at Eton and later at Harvard with Mario. Oliver's initial hopefulness with respect to Jim

---

[21] See Irving Singer, *The Nature of Love: The Modern World* (Chicago: University of Chicago Press, 1987) 254–280.

[22] George Santayana, *Reason in Society* (New York: Dover, 1980) 155–156.

dissipates when he comes to realize how little they have in common as far as ideals are concerned. For all its initial excitement, their affiliation is presented as a diminished friendship. In contrast, the intimacy and kinship between Oliver and Mario deepen throughout the novel. Though they are temperamentally very different, their friendship endures and overcomes all obstacles, including the fact that the two young women to whom Oliver proposes marriage reject him partly because they see how inferior he is as a potential lover compared to Mario.

This theme of friendship surmounting the hazards of sexual competition, a theme that Shakespeare exploits in *The Two Gentlemen of Verona,* reaches its climax in the final pages of the novel. Mario visits Rose and her mother in order to communicate the terms of Oliver's will. At one point Rose says that Oliver used to speak of Mario as a lady-killer but that she can perceive from his grief at Oliver's death that "'like almost all other men, you really care for your friends more than for your victims'" (563). Mario restrains himself from replying that "there is a love that passeth the love of women," and he fails to see that Rose is implicitly offering herself as a willing victim. But after he leaves the house, the meaning of her remark suddenly strikes him and he toys with the possibility of adding her to his list of conquests. He finally rejects the idea, and Santayana tells us that "the tag of an old French comedy kept running in his head: *Je ne vous aime pas, Marianne; c'était Célio qui vous aimait*" (566).

The play that Mario recalls is *Les Caprices de Marianne* by Alfred de Musset. It was later to be one of the sources of Renoir's film *La Règle du jeu (The Rules of the Game).*[23] Musset's tragi-comedy has a structure similar to *The Last Puritan*'s: both are based on the contrasting personality of two friends, one of whom is pure-minded and idealistic while the other is a natural man given to the pleasures of lovemaking. The spiritual man having been killed in Musset's play (by henchmen of Marianne's jealous husband), she tells his friend that he is really the one she loved all along. He spurns her, however, with the words that Santayana introduces into his novel. In both works friendship, the true bond between men, prevails over sexual love for women.

Much earlier in the novel, Oliver gives his own ideas about friendship in the brief essay on Plato's *Phaedrus* and *Symposium* that he

---

[23] In Renoir's film Célio—i.e. man of the skies—becomes the transatlantic aviator who is more at home in the clouds than on the ground.

writes for Santayana's course. He insists that in friendship "there may be love, perhaps the highest and most intense love, but there is not a bit of desire." Oliver does admit that desire may intrude upon friendship, but then he claims that this is "mere sensuality" which is driven out "when friendship becomes clear and strong" (420).

Of course, this need not be taken as the definitive statement of Santayana's beliefs. He was a materialist in philosophy who thought that many of Freud's theories about sex seemed quite plausible. He never suggests that friendship can exist without *some* desire. All the same, he generally places friendship and sexual love in very different categories, just as Oliver does. And while some of his own friendships may have been emotionally gratifying, he freely confessed that even his love poetry was based on speculative enthusiasm rather than actual passions. In a letter to an old friend, he says: "Love has never made me long unhappy, nor sexual impulse uncomfortable: on the contrary in the comparatively manageable form in which they have visited me, they have been *great fun*."[24] He then explains that for him love has mainly been "the golden light of diffused erotic feeling" falling upon the otherwise "deadly" world in which he lived.

This attitude toward sexual love is coherent with the thinking of Mario in the novel. Though Mario—unlike Santayana—has enjoyed sexual love on many occasions, he never describes it as romantic ecstasy. For him, as for Jim, lovemaking is a sport that satisfies material appetites. Mario asserts that Oliver's great mistake consisted in regarding all women as ladies without realizing that all ladies are women. He ascribes Oliver's erotic failures to his having had a mother who never loved him and whom he never loved. Mario traces his own success to the fact that his mother has always been the principal object of his affections. He considers this natural since she suckled him and never stopped treating him as her special darling.

That Mario's experience is not the same as Santayana's is clear from those pointed statements in *Persons and Places* about the coldness of his own mother and her inability to love her children. Mario's mother is an opera singer who gave up her career in order to devote her artistic talents to the optimal upbringing of the child she loved so much. Generalizing from her example, Mario enunciates the idea that singing, and art in general, resembles and recapitulates the

[24] Santayana, *Letters* 208.

instinct of love in taking us beyond superficial daily life and enabling us to feel what is deepest in our nature. Santayana had said the same in other books. To that extent, Mario is his spokesman. But, like Oliver, Santayana also suspected that—despite its imaginative power—sexual love might really be "a mere escape and delusion" (396). This ambivalence recurs in all his philosophy.

In the chapter on "Love" in *Reason in Society*, Santayana presents his views dialectically. He begins with a Schopenhauerian reductivism which treats sexual love as an illusory outgrowth of biological imperatives that determine what is really happening in the human organism. He then combines this materialist approach with the more Platonistic one represented by his concept of idealization. He argues that the beloved serves as an image, and possibly a symbol, of some ideal of goodness or beauty that captivates the lover.

By the time he finished *The Last Puritan*, Santayana had already modified this analysis considerably. Mario the natural man sees love as "great fun" and he relishes the play of imagination that it involves, but he does not allow his amatory feeling to become a Platonic longing. He seeks for beauty through civilized dalliance, and is adept at finding it, without having much interest in idealization as Santayana had used that term. Mario is quite different from the courtly lovers whom Santayana discussed in his early essay "Platonic Love in Some Italian Poets." As for Oliver, he never manages to achieve sexual love for anyone. Though he finally realizes the importance of idealization, he assigns it to a divine love that exceeds and defeats whatever hopes he might still have for loving another person sexually.

Oliver's development in this respect is very instructive. For it parallels a progression in Santayana's philosophy. Throughout the novel, Oliver has been shown to be incapable of experiencing what Rose calls "'happy love, natural, irresistible, unreasoning love'" (548). But at the end, he perceives the meaning of another kind of love that takes on greater importance. Having been freed by Rose's refusal to marry him, he concludes that beyond the kindliness he may have felt for the real Rose, or Edith, or even Jim and Mario, his love for these persons was "'only an image, only a mirage, of my own aspiration.'" Though this mirage may differ from the reality of the individuals he has loved, "'my image of them in being detached from their accidental persons, will be clarified in itself, will become truer to my profound desire; and the inspiration of a profound desire, fixed upon some lovely image, is what is called love'" (552).

If we think of the image of one's own aspiration as the instantiation of an ideal beauty that one admires, Oliver's statement would seem to resemble what Santayana had been saying about love as early as *Interpretations of Poetry and Religion*. But actually the conception belongs to the thinking about "charity" that Santayana began to develop twenty-five years later in *Dialogues in Limbo* and would subsequently bring to completion in *The Realm of Spirit* and *The Idea of Christ in the Gospels*.

In turning away from sexual love, in concluding that only divine love could satisfy him entirely, Oliver continues to reject traditional religious ideas about a divinity toward whom that love must be directed. He still believes that the idea of a supernatural being is just another mirage, "'an impossible object.'" But his culminating insight occurs when he concludes that "'the falser that object is, the stronger and clearer must have been the force in me that called it forth and compelled me to worship it. It is this force in myself that matters: to this I must be true'" (553).

Many years before, Oliver's father had told him that friendship was a sentiment that belonged to the boyishness of young comrades discovering what the world is like and that eventual disillusionment would transmute the tenderness of friendship into charity. In his ultimate appreciation of the supervening goodness in what he calls divine love, Oliver finds in himself a capacity for charity that reveals the purity of his own spirit. This is the force that matters. Oliver cannot live in accordance with his true nature, and we are expected to believe that even if he had not died young he would have discovered no way to overcome the crippling effects of his puritan heritage. But he is a hero because he does attain this greater clarification about the nature of spirit and the possibility of spiritual love.

❀

What then is spirit, as Santayana conceives of it? And what can we learn from Oliver's tragedy? There are two statements in the novel that provide some leverage upon these questions. The first one occurs when Oliver recognizes that his aborted love for Rose was a fixation upon an image or mirage within himself. Speaking of all love between human beings, he says: "'And the true lover's tragedy is not being jilted; it is being accepted'" (552). The other comment is given by Santayana himself in the Prologue. He there asserts that Oliver's secret problem "'was simply the tragedy of the spirit when it's not content to understand but wishes to govern'" (16–17).

If we juxtaposed these statements and read them both as reflections of Santayana's own philosophy, we could possibly interpret him as meaning that man's existence in the world is not compatible with the ends of spirit, and that spirit is forever doomed to submission and despair. This mode of interpretation misconstrues the general intentions of Santayana's thought. When he says that Oliver's tragedy resulted from spirit wanting to govern rather than to understand, he refers to the fact—asserted in all his writings—that spirit has no substance of its own. It must always depend on the prior being of matter: it can only arise from material causes that happen to produce it in some animate creature. Spirit exists within the organic and vegetative structure that Santayana, following Aristotle in the *De Anima*, calls "psyche."

On Santayana's view, only psyche is able to effect changes in the actual world. For psyche is itself a part of matter, a bit of living substance within the fields of force that cause all things to be or not to be. As an exotic by-product of psyche, spirit is the light of consciousness or awareness that can reflect about its surroundings, that can attend to qualities or essences presented to it, that can contemplate beauty in all its aspects, that can condemn what it sees and hope for something better, and that can even aspire toward ideal accomplishments. But spirit has no power and remains subject to the sources of power, since they participate in matter as the sole reality that determines the nature of everything existent. Oliver has a tragic life because he cannot fully accept this dependency of spirit. Had he done so, he would have recognized the authority of matter—as Mario does—and felt no need to constrain his instinctual drives or desires.

When Oliver says that the true lover's tragedy is in being accepted rather than rejected, he expresses a despairing sentiment that one finds in other books of Santayana. In *Persons and Places* he states that "*a perfect love is founded on despair*";[25] in *The Realm of Essence*, he claims that "possession leaves the true lover unsatisfied."[26] But these nega-

---

[25] George Santayana, *Persons and Places: Fragments of Autobiography*, ed. William G. Holzberger and Herman J. Saatkamp, Jr. (Cambridge, Mass. and London: MIT Press, 1986) 428.

[26] George Santayana, *The Realm of Essence*, in *Realms of Being* (New York: Charles Scribner's Sons, 1942) 16.

tivistic remarks should not be taken out of context. There is a dynamic within Santayana's dialectic. Far from precluding the human possibility of reconciliation between matter and spirit, he merely portrays the great difficulty in attaining it. This then serves as a preliminary to understanding the true dimensions of that grand achievement. In Mario's ability to sample the varied consummations of life, spirit is also present. It occurs in his playful *joie de vivre*, his imaginative wit, his sensitivity to beauty, and in general his capacity to enjoy the spectacle of nature and materiality to which he is permanently faithful without wholly identifying himself with it. Detachment of this sort, which is essential if spirit is to be free, does not prevent Mario from living in the world and taking action for the sake of what he loves.

I am not suggesting that Mario is Santayana's ideal. He contributes to it in a way that the other characters cannot, but there are facets of spirituality that Mario will never approximate. As a man who has learned to accept his nature within the confines of civilization, Mario has little yearning for purity. Yet spirit, as Santayana interprets it, longs for self-purification. It feels a need to renounce the world that it knows it cannot govern. What Santayana calls "the spiritual life" is spirit seeking to disintoxicate itself from everything that is imperfect in our existence. Santayana is certain that the effort cannot succeed, and he uses the example of Caleb Wetherbee, as well as Uncle Nathaniel and the Vicar, to illustrate the aberrations to which it can lead. At the same time, Santayana also admires the fearless integrity with which these twisted persons crave their own austere purgation. Suffering in a world that spirit never made, the spiritual man responds to the tragedy of human factuality by proudly and defiantly rejecting all compromising imperfections.

The ideal for Santayana would be a composite of Mario and Oliver. For then the two forms of spirit would be united: spirit as an exuberant light that plays upon the waters of natural possibilities, and spirit as the spirituality that seeks purification while beweeping its outcast state within a universe that is ultimately meaningless. Neither is sufficient by itself.

❋

In *The Last Puritan* there is no character who coordinates these different tendencies in spirit. There is none who manifests the total harmonization between spirit and matter. Though Santayana's critics were mistaken in thinking that he considered the purely spiritual life superior to the rational one or that he advocated asceticism and quietistic withdrawal from society, they were right in sensing his skepticism about the usual attempts to resolve basic problems of mankind. Several of the characters in the novel are "good people," as he insists in one of his letters, but none of them fulfills the potentialities of his goodness or appears as a complete individual.

Perhaps that is why some readers have felt that Santayana treats his personages like marionettes that merely express his various views about the world. Santayana declares in several places that the characters are real to him and that throughout the years they have spoken within his inner monologue like separate human beings. This is plausible, and entirely compatible with their being pieces of Santayana's mind. For his mind, and his personality, was radically pluralistic within the categories he imposes. He is not only Oliver and Mario, or each as the alter ego of the other, but also Oliver's father. Peter Alden is a homeless and itinerant aesthete much as Santayana was. He is what Santayana could have been if he had had great wealth, a willingness to make a conventional marriage, and no creative talent. Since these are such vast differences, one might wonder how the two men are alike at all. The point is that, despite his weakness of character and ability, Peter Alden is an enlightened spirit and a naturalist in philosophy who manifests Santayana's pessimism, resignation, and sophisticated detachment. But there is nothing—not even the nothingness of nirvana—in which Alden believes. If Santayana could point to the idealized fusion of Mario and Oliver and say, "That's what I would like to have been in my youth," so too could he say of Peter Alden, "That's what I, in my alienated condition, might have turned into."

On each occasion on which the characters of *The Last Puritan* discuss famous authors and literary works, their opinions are both their own and also Santayana's. Jim and Oliver having the attitudes that they do, the former describes *Hamlet* as "a rum old play, full of bombast and absurdities, but with a lot of topping lines in it" (229–230) while the latter asserts that Hamlet was "tremendously pure and superior to all cut-and-dried opinions of ordinary people and even of science. This was what rendered him unfit for the everyday world" (230). Santayana had taken both positions himself in earlier essays. The same is true of disputes among the characters about Whitman,

Goethe, Homer, etc. In our present age of relativism and deconstruction, this recurrent device will neither baffle nor dismay. But one must realize that Santayana generally agrees with all of the contrasting opinions. The individual ideas distinguish his characters from one another, and yet they are ideas that belong within Santayana's own diversified perspective.

The scope of that perspective is indicated by the fact that *The Last Puritan* is a comedy as well as a tragedy. Though the book is primarily a history of tragic incompleteness, Santayana weaves many farcical and parodistic strands throughout the fabric of this theme. Among the Greek deities, Hermes—god of wit and comic invention—is the one to which Santayana pays tribute most of all in his role as narrator. Santayana's irony and playfulness color every page of the book. Dickens was possibly his favorite novelist. He delighted in the geniality of Dickensian humor mingled, as it is, with ridicule of all pomposity and hypocrisy. In *The Last Puritan*, personages such as Oliver's mother, his governess, and even his father—to say nothing of the lesser characters—often seem to be caricatures, sometimes sketched at great length but for the most part serving to provide comedic vistas into the absurd world through which Oliver must wend his puritan way. The ludicrous, and even grotesque, traits of these characters intrigue us because we see them from the Olympian vantage of Santayana's satire and burlesque. His epigrammatic insights encourage us to feel that we too can share his great amusement in observing, at a comfortable distance, the foibles and stupidities of other people.

In giving us access to this display, which is not always pleasant to watch, Santayana may often seem cruel and possibly malicious. I think he sometimes is. More pervasively, however, tragic and comic elements in his novel emanate from a good will not totally dissimilar from the one that Santayana admired in Dickens. In his essay about him, Santayana states: "Love of the good of others is something that shines in every page of Dickens with a truly celestial splendour. . . . How generous is this keen, light spirit, how pure this open heart!"[27] If we said the same of Santayana's coruscating thrusts, we would surely be guilty of gross exaggeration. He is too severe a critic, and too unrelenting in his delineation of human imperfection, to be called an "open heart." Nevertheless, he is far from being heartless or

[27] George Santayana, *Essays in Literary Criticism*, ed. Irving Singer (New York: Charles Scribner's Sons, 1956) 222.

unfeeling. In his sympathetic but unsentimental manner, he reveals an aspect of spirit that may be taken as the final stage in all his thinking.

I am referring to something in Plato's philosophy that Oliver touches on in his college essay. After having first claimed that Plato "knew nothing" about love, Oliver concludes that Plato may have been right after all in identifying love with desire for the Absolute Idea of the Beautiful—"if this means perfection for every creature after its own kind." Oliver then says, "We can never feel in our own persons the ecstatic bliss of being a perfect porpoise or a perfect eagle. But reason in us may correct our human prejudices, and may convince us that other forms of life are as desirable for other creatures as our own form of life is for us" (420).

What Oliver here calls "reason" Santayana's mature philosophy generally describes as spirit that has reached the ability to love all things as they are in themselves. He does not mean that they are to be loved in their accidental being or for the sake of what they happen to want at any moment. They are to be loved as fellow spirits— however preposterous they may seem—that are striving for some perfection they individually desire, each in its own way and all with an equal longing for goodness. In one place he identifies the acceptance of this universal craving as the spiritual ability "to love the love in [everything]."[28]

Few people in what we call the real world experience that kind of love. The characters in *The Last Puritan* fare no better than the rest of us. Oliver understands the goal but his self-division prevents him from reaching it. The others ignore it or else delude themselves about its implications. I have no way of knowing whether Santayana thought that he himself approached the ideal he had in mind. But regardless of what his own capacities may have been, *The Last Puritan* is an epiphany of his spirit and a testament to spirit everywhere. It is a consummation of Santayana's world, as he lived it in youth and as he remembered it in old age. In its plenitude as a work of art, it radiates the poetic and philosophic genius that appears in all his writings. It reveals, to paraphrase the last sentence of the Epilogue, what the human spirit can "still call its own without illusion."

[28] George Santayana, "Ultimate Religion," *The Philosophy of Santayana*, ed. Irwin Edman (New York: Charles Scribner's Sons, 1953) 581.

George Santayana's Sketch of Oliver Alden.
By permission of Harry Ransom Humanities Research Center, The
University of Texas at Austin.

THE LAST PURITAN

PREFACE

On principle it would seem futile as well as egotistical for an author to explain himself and tell the public what they ought to think of him. He has once for all surrendered his work to their jurisdiction, and even surrendered his own person and private history, which they are now at liberty, if they choose, to make an object of investigation or conjecture: and he cannot be sure, when he thinks their praise or censure to be ill grounded, that after all they may not be right: for who is man, especially histrionic rhetorical man, to see the truth of his own doings?

Nevertheless, in respect to *The Last Puritan* I have been asked for explanations; and in the *Prologue* and *Epilogue* I have already given the critics some hints: rashly, perhaps, since sometimes they have taken advantage of my frankness to exaggerate my limitations. For instance, when I say that my characters all speak my language and are in some sense masks for my own spirit, that is no reason for assuming without examination that they must be a philosopher's puppets and not "living." On the contrary, if these characters are expressions of actual experience, and only dressed, like an actor on the stage, for their several parts, they ought to be all the more profoundly alive, being impersonations of the soul and not sketches taken by a social tourist. When a man has lived as long as I have with his characters—forty-five years—they seem to him to speak and act of their own free will, and without prompting. No doubt this only happens because they are parts of himself; yet these parts were originally contrasted and spontaneous potentialities within him, and by no means vehicles for his own later conventional personality or approved thoughts. If the book is something of a monologue, it is nevertheless *acted* throughout. The *Prologue* and *Epilogue* (and also Oliver's college essay, which has deceived some people) are integral parts of the fable, and written in character, even when, for a moment, that character is a stage-presentation of myself. Indeed, what I am now adding in this Preface, though an afterthought and spoken before the curtain, is also composed for the public, and is no innocent aside. This commentary therefore remains, like the rest of the book, subject to re-valuation and suspicion on the critic's part. In fact, I am more confident of uttering sincerely the sentiments of my characters than of describing justly their place in my own mind. Self-criticism and autobiography, no matter how sincere, are far from being naturally truthful. They belong to a peculiarly treacherous and double-dyed species of the subjective. Perhaps if, as Aristotle tells us, poetry is essentially truer than history, one reason may be that fiction, by an avowed artifice, redresses the balance of selfish illusion, and satirically exposes the dark labyrinths of self-deception to the light of day.

People ask: How much in the story of your Last Puritan have you drawn from real life, and how much is invented? I reply: Nothing is wholly historical, nothing is wholly imaginary. In the first page of the *Prologue* I have taken pains to establish my privilege of hopelessly mixing the two: many of the threads are real but the tapestry is a dream. I actually lived in Paris at the place and time indicated, and in that half scholastic, half cosmopolitan atmosphere. More than one young friend of my Harvard days has rung the bell of that apartment in the Avenue de l'Observatoire, and come to dine with me at a restaurant. Howard Sturgis, too, was really a cousin of my family's, and lived at Windsor, as I describe him: but his halcyon days fell in the 1890's, a little earlier than the events of my story. I laugh at anachronisms, when they are not incongruities. All these real details, however, are transfigured in my fancy and made to dance as they never danced in reality by the imaginary presence of Mario Van de Weyer. Oliver and Mario are the original personages of my fable. In them converge sundry potentialities which from my earliest youth I felt in myself or divined in other people: potentialities not realisable together in a single person, nor perhaps realisable at all in the modern world. Both these figures were self-composed, by an accumulation of kindred traits, as legendary figures take shape in tradition. They were not psychological manikins, contrived intentionally, but true heroes, imposing themselves upon me with the authority of a moral force.

I call this book *A Memoir in the Form of a Novel*, because it was never planned as a story with an artificial dramatic unity, but was meant from the beginning to be the chronicle, half satirical, half poetic, of a sentimental education. In the early 1890's, when I had returned to Harvard to teach but still lived among undergraduates, it occurred to me to contrast the moral development of two friends, one gay and the other demure, who should be drawn in opposite directions, such as to test their mutual affection and lend it a tragic touch. But I soon found that college life hardly afforded occasions even for the slightest comedy. The canvas would have to be filled in with humorous details about the boys' background and families. *How They Lived* was indeed the title which I gave to my first sketches; but the original moral theme tended to be submerged in those miscellaneous episodes, my dominant interest turned to other projects, and the novel lay dormant for years, until the war of 1914, and fresh contacts with university life, now at Oxford, suggested to me how the whole story might be unified and brought to a head.

Meantime a tragic circumstance in the American scene had aroused my special attention: the early death of five or six young Harvard poets in the 1880's and 1890's, all more or less friends of mine, whose unanimous collapse I could not attribute to accident. To what insoluble conflict between the world and the spirit could such failure be due? As I revolved this doubt, the whole nature and history of Oliver began to grow clearer in my mind. My dead friends had all had philosophic keenness and moral fervour; they had all been fearless and independent in mind; but none of them seemed to have found matter fitted for his energies, or to have had the intellectual power requisite to dominate his circumstances and turn what might be unfavourable in them into a triumph of expression. Here, then, was the essential tragedy of the late-born Puritan, made concrete in several instances and illustrated before my eyes. This, added to a certain aridity, difficulty, and confusion which I could feel in the spirits of the elder New England worthies, and in my remarkable teachers and colleagues at Harvard, supplied moral substance for those sketches of manners and types which I could draw from observation.

Old Bostonians will recognise the originals of my Nathaniel Alden and Caleb Wetherbee: yet even these figures have not been copied literally from nature, but caricatured and recomposed with an eye to the general theme of my story. Moreover the original of Nathaniel had no younger half-brother; and the mania for collecting bad paintings belonged not to him but to a different and more amiable old gentleman. Caleb also had not one original but two; and the one who changed his religion had not turned Catholic but Buddhist. For Peter Alden and his wife the models were legion, like those for the Van de Weyer family in New York. Even in the case of Oliver, originals might be found for some of his personal traits or family circumstances. But I paint no full-length portraits from life: I fuse as many sympathetic intuitions as possible into a fiction which might have been actualised as easily as any actual experience, and perhaps more tellingly. My sources for this whole American scene—Oliver's inner life excepted— were diffused widely and observed somewhat externally; for though I was perfectly at home in that life and immensely interested in it, having lived and gone to school in Boston through all the most important years of boyhood and youth, yet I found myself in that world by force of peculiar circumstances of which I felt the strangeness. It always seemed to me a strained, kindly, humorous, somehow fleshless world. Spain, of which I say nothing in this book, was after all my real country: when I went back there, or came across stray Spanish people, I was not happier or better pleased, but decidedly less comfortable physically and morally: yet that old passive passionate way of living, that religion, those very faults and disillusions seemed to me somehow more human, more classical, than all this slavish diligence in modern duties. I could not help feeling that what dominated America was a passing fever, a heresy, a forced enthusiasm, not really satisfying the heart and destined to end in emptiness.

Entirely different was my sentiment towards England and the genesis of my English characters. In England I have never had any home or legitimate stamping-ground, such as my mother's connections through her first marriage had given me in Boston. Perhaps for that very reason my affection for England has always been romantic. From my first prolonged visit in 1887 to the outbreak of the war, when I lived there for five consecutive years, England was the Mecca of my yearly pilgrimage. Physically and morally, I found myself there even more comfortable than in America; all strain was relaxed; the eye and the ear were softly flattered; the imagination was stirred by living remnants of mediaeval Christendom; and something wholesome and Spartan in the air seemed to neutralise the affectations and crotchets of the inhabitants. I could wander about the country in leisurely enchantment. I could live with my scattered but familiar friends in perfect half-silent sympathy. My English characters in this book—I don't know with what success—are therefore evoked poetically. Except Jim Darnley—who though entirely transformed in externals has been recognised by those who knew him most intimately—they are not so much drawn from particular persons as created for me by the landscape, by the voices, by the atmosphere of cool domesticity and indomitable private religion. There was something primitive and sacred here, for instance in the sentiment of my friend Robert Bridges, that escaped me, but that I revered: something at once Spartan, Christian, and feudal, yet merged in the English mist with a profound naturalism, as if the Druid also had survived in the modern man of letters. Was not this the fulness and the happy decline and self-transformation of that very spirit which in my American friends died so hard, or was so cruelly dispersed amongst irrelevant cares?

This brings us back to my hero, who is the hero and martyr of a spiritual crisis. Not all my readers have understood that what we may call Oliver's failures were due to his superiority, not to his inferiority. In the first place, he did not fail altogether, but without breaking away from a social order which violated all his instincts he succeeded in maintaining a perfect integrity and sweetness. He never sought praise, pleasure, or riches. He was faithful in everything and cherished everybody, even his mother, as much as was humanly possible. Charity and insight in him entirely killed personal resentment and even tamed his instinctive moral ferocity. False comforts and false loves never deceived him, so profound was his allegiance to a chivalrous sincerity. Yet he was not perfect; his capacity for perfection was moral only. One is not with impunity an heir to all the Puritans. A certain hardness and egotism limited his comprehension even of the people and things that attracted him most; and with the clearest theoretical intelligence he could sometimes act stupidly. If a thing seemed to him right, he could not admit that other people would perhaps object to it. And in himself he could not be happy. Natural perfection, the witchery of the moment, the irresponsible courage of young life, though he felt their charm, could never win him over to complete acquiescence and inward peace. He had been hamstrung by circumstances. Naturally a spiritual man, he had neither the force nor the time to break through and live victoriously in the spirit.

Satirical reasons are given in the *Prologue*, from Mario's point of view, for calling Oliver the last Puritan, but I had other reasons also in mind. In him puritanism was exhausted, and on the other hand it was surpassed. It was exhausted as a reforming political force, with a secret aggressive worldliness inspiring its iconoclasms. Oliver was "the third sloppy wash in the family teapot", and had neither the robustness to militate in that dubious cause nor the coarseness of fibre to live happy under that domination. But spiritually he was a born puritan, and more thoroughly distilled and refined than his ancestors. If in him the metaphysical austerity of the seventeenth century reappeared atavistically, his late birth relieved him of any horrid uncertainty about the truth of traditional myths and dogmas. Like the Stoics and like Spinoza he found his moral demands face to face with a universe that inspired but did not sanction them. The sea, the stars, the heathen, his own father and his dearest friends set up no such standards as were imposed on him by his sovereign conscience: sovereign over him, not over them. And though this diversity of allegiance condemned him to a secret solitude, he was too rational and generous to blame them, or to think them wrong. If anything, he envied them a little; sighed, like a young heir to a throne, at the limitations imposed on him by privilege: and he admired the grace and alacrity with which Mario, for instance, could rise, without asking questions, to the crest of each successive wave.

Yet Mario, too, like Oliver, was late-born. The two were differently aristocratic, and belonged to the past rather than to the future. Only Mario, being less serious and more adaptable, could make the best of his good luck, and sail before the wind without pretending to have any firm hold on reality. He was healthy and therefore bold, humble and therefore facile. His ability to laugh at everything, including himself, made it easy for him to put up with the mixed loose world in which he lived, and positively to enjoy it: easier, too, than for Oliver, much easier, to put up with himself. People may lead cheerful and prosperous lives, and make wonderful companions, if they can put up with everything.

Oliver was neither humble nor facile; but was he healthy? I have given various indications to the contrary, on which the discerning reader will not ask me to insist. I am willing that amateur pathologists should call Oliver degenerate. But that is not the end of the story. He was a spiritual man, with a divine vocation. On different occasions, Irma, Caleb Wetherbee, and the Vicar compare him with Christ. Now a divine vocation is a devastating thing; and it makes no ultimate difference whether you attribute poetically the mortification and withering up of the flesh to a touch of celestial fire, or cynically regard a high spiritual temperature as an effect of disease. Either way, the spirit burns unquenchably: and the secret of Oliver's tragedy is missed by those amiable critics who write to me that their own sons were just like him, but turned out splendidly; or that if only he had noticed how much nicer Maud was than Edith, or if Rose had only

been less offish and wilful, all would have been well, and Oliver
might have spent a gloriously useful life in the service of humanity.
That is what his mother would have said. I know how readily many
young men with Puritan traditions can be harnessed to the public
coach; and perhaps their hereditary uprightness helps to leaven business, and to make them personally nicer than other Babbitts. But this
solution, which Oliver in his helplessness actually foresaw and was
willing sadly to accept as his human duty, could never have satisfied
him, as it satisfies the normal fleshly and worldly man, who cares for
nothing beyond. For in Oliver there was something else: an inner
inhibition intercepted and waylaid him, as it were, in all his actions,
without availing to redirect his life. He proved inapt, not only in
love-making, but even in those studies, sports, and friendships on
which he had prided himself most. His great error was that he tried
to be commonplace. His vocation remained vague: he had not the
insight or the courage to make it definite. In vain the Vicar reminded
him that Christ had not been a soldier or an athlete or a lover of
women or a merchant or a statesman or even (though the Vicar did
not say so) a professor of philosophy or a believing Christian. All
these sweets are at last bitter to the spirit. Buddha, at the first glimpse
of the truth of life, had abandoned his throne and his young wife
and child, to meditate on the fourfold root of suffering and preach
the way of salvation. Poor Oliver too was ready for every sacrifice:
he was what the rich young man in the Gospel would have been if
he had offered to sell his goods and give to the poor, but then had
found no cross to take up, no Jesus to follow, and no way of salvation
to preach.

It is thought sad to come to an end early, or to come to an end at
all; but such sadness is only the foiled sympathy of body with body,
when motion ceases, and the flesh that was warm and living has
grown stiff and cold. To the spirit, on the contrary, it is glorious to
have finished all there was to do. It would be distressing rather to be
tossed about perpetually from impulse to impulse, where nothing
definite could ever be accomplished, nothing achieved. What was sad
about Oliver was not that he died young or was stopped by accident,
but that he stopped himself, not trusting his inspiration: so that he
knew "the pity, not the joy, of love," the severity of intellect and not
its glory.

On dit bien que l'expérience parle par la bouche des hommes d'âge: mais la meilleure expérience qu'ils puissent nous apporter est celle de leur jeunesse sauvée.

ALAIN.

PROLOGUE

In the first years after the war Mario Van de Weyer was almost my neighbour in Paris, for he lived just where the Left Bank ceases to be the Latin Quarter and I where it is not yet the Faubourg Saint Germain. This trifling interval, with the much greater one between our ages, was easily bridged by his bubbling good nature; and sometimes when in the evening twilight I was putting away my papers and preparing to sally forth to a solitary dinner, the bell would ring with a certain unmistakable decision and confidence, and almost before I had opened the door I was already saying, "Ah, Vanny" (for so his English friends called him), "how nice this is! It seems an age since we dined together." And for the rest of the evening our talk would run for the tenth time over the reminiscences which my old friendship with his family, long antedating his birth, furnished in abundance. Ours was hardly conversation; it was musing aloud; and repetitions troubled us as little in our talk as they did in our memories. Often we would recall the summer day at Windsor on which I had first spied him, still in jackets, gorging strawberry-mess in the garden of my inimitable friend and quasi-cousin, Howard Sturgis, host and hostess in one, who held court in a soft nest of cushions, of wit, and of tenderness, surrounded by a menagerie of outcast dogs, a swarm of friends and relations, and all the luxuries of life. Nor did I forget the reply which the youthful Vanny had made on that occasion to our compliments on the particularly nice curves of his hat. "Prettiest and cheapest topper in Eton; Busby's in the Arlington Mews, 'Whips, 'Ats, & Liveries'; eighteen pence off the price if cockade not required. Groom's hat, that's all."

Then Mario would pick up his thread in our recollections.

"Old Busby looked like Mr. Pickwick; had the breast of a pigeon, and would cock his head behind it to catch the effect of a new hat on the customer. 'Parfect fit, sir; you couldn't do better, sir; thenk you, sir.' We were fast friends from the first day I got a hat there. He was showing me to the door, when I stopped him short. 'I say, Mr. Busby: suppose my people are ruined and I have to look for a job. Do you think I'd do for a small footman?' 'Footman, sir? You, sir? 'Ope not, indeed—I mean, of course you would, sir; the prettiest young groom as you would make; none smarter in London, to jump off the

*box monkeylike—I beg pardon, sir, I mean, nimbly—and hold the door open
for her ladyship.' 'Yes, Mr. Busby, but will you recommend me? She must be
a countess at least,' I added with a wink, 'and young.' And I suddenly grew
rigid and blank-faced, touched my hat with one wooden finger, and left him
muttering. 'I'm blowed if a spry young gentleman like you wouldn't pretty
well find a situation without a character.' But that's all a thing of the past.
Old Busby's gone. Nobody wants whips, 'ats, or grooms any more; and where
there's still a footman, he wears an absurd little motoring cap with a vizor.
And even the Arlington Mews has disappeared."*

"*Never mind,*" I would answer, "*perhaps when the common people set the
fashions, men's clothes may recover their old rakishness. Grooms used to be
more pleasantly dressed than gentlemen, because good form for gentlemen
nowadays is simply to be scrupulously clean, correct, and inconspicuous. Even
your military men hate anything that savours of swagger or aggressive virility,
are uncomfortable in scarlet and gold braid, and take refuge whenever possible
in the blessed obscurity of mufti. Not that the uniform of industrialism absolves
the rest of us drab creatures from self-consciousness or from taking pains. We
mustn't fall short of the right standard or overdo anything; but we compose
our social figures sadly, with fear and trembling, and more in the dread of
damnation than in the hope of glory.*"

"*Not in my case,*" Mario said, smiling broadly and straightening his shoulders. "*I rather fancy dressing up and giving people something to stare at.*"

"*I know; but you're a rare exception, a professional lady-killer, a popinjay
amid the millions of crows. You have the courage of your full human nature,
as your father had the courage of his delicate tastes. To have been emancipated
otherwise, in his day, would have seemed vicious and unkind; and he remained
innocence itself in his person and affections, although his mental enthusiasms
were boundless. That is why we all called him 'dear Harold'. You lost him
when you were too young to appreciate his gifts or his weaknesses. How old
were you exactly?*"

"*About seven.*"

"*When to you he was simply papa, who drew amusing pictures and read
Stevenson's stories aloud, to improve your English. There were many such
Americans de luxe in my generation who prolonged their youth at the École
des Beaux-Arts or at Julian's, confident of personally restoring the age of
Pericles. Even in our Harvard days, I remember how he would burst into the
Lampoon sanctum, flushed with the project of some comic illustration that had
just occurred to him; but the joke could never be brought to have a point, and
the drawing, twice begun, would end in the wastepaper-basket. Later, whenever he despaired of becoming a great painter—as he did every other year—*

he would remember his enthusiasm for the science of genealogy, and would rush to Holland in quest of his ancestors. In that very garden at Windsor where we admired your hat, he had once discovered that in that neighbourhood there lived a well-known family of English Van de Weyers; and nothing would do but he must be taken at once to call on the old Colonel, and be informed about his family tree. But no researches availed to unearth the least connection between that family and the Van de Weyers of New York. Baffled in private genealogy, he would rebound to heraldry in general and to the monumental work which he was always about to compose on heraldic ornament in architecture. His great ambition, he used to say, was to devote his whole life to a very small subject, and heraldry held in a nutshell the secret of all the arts, which were nothing but self-exhibition upon the shield of self-defence. But once having laid down this brilliant first principle, he had nothing more to say on the subject; and the stream of his enthusiasm, rebuffed by that stone wall, gurgled back to the happiness of collecting bookplates."

"No harm," Mario would say, a cloud of gravity passing over his face, "no harm in amusing himself as he chose; only he was a brute to marry my mother and keep her from being the greatest prima donna *of the age."*

"But if your father hadn't married your mother, where would you be? Dear Harold would have loved nothing better than to see his beautiful wife a glorious diva, *treading the boards with all the authority of genius, and borne along from ovation to ovation on an ocean of floral offerings. But she herself and her sensible Italian relations wouldn't hear of such a thing, once her respectable future was assured. In their view the rich young American, proposing just in time, had saved the situation."*

So our talk would ramble on amongst memories that seemed pleasantest when they were most remote; yet sooner or later recent events would intrude, and Mario would tell me of one or another of his friends who had fallen in the war or who were blankly surviving, at a loss what to do with themselves. One evening—when the party of New York ladies at the other table had risen in a flurry fearing to miss the new curtain-raiser at Le Vieux Colombier; *when Mario had seen them to their taxi and had promised to show them Montmartre on the following night after the Opera; and when quiet was restored in the little room at Lapérouse where we remained alone—our talk reverted, as it often did, to the young Oliver Alden, who of all the victims of the war was nearest to us both. He had been Mario's cousin and bosom friend and the most gifted of my pupils in my last days at Harvard.*

"You know what I've been thinking," Mario said after a pause. "You ought to write Oliver's Life. Nobody else could do it."

"Oliver's Life? Had he a life to be written with a big L? And why should I, of all people, abandon philosophy in my old age and take to composing history, even supposing that in Oliver's history there were any actions to record?"

"No actions, but something you might take a wicked pleasure in describing: Puritanism Self-condemned. Oliver was THE LAST PURITAN.*"*

"I am afraid," I answered with a melancholy which was only half feigned, "I am afraid there will always be puritans in this mad world. Puritanism is a natural reaction against nature."

"I don't mean that puritanism has died out everywhere. There may always be fresh people to take the thing up. But in Oliver puritanism worked itself out to its logical end. He convinced himself, on puritan grounds, that it was wrong to be a puritan."

"And he remained a puritan notwithstanding?"

"Exactly. That was the tragedy of it. Thought it his clear duty to give puritanism up, but couldn't."

"Then the case," I said laughing, "is like that of Miss Pickleworth of Boston who declared she envied me for not having a conscience, which I thought rather insolent of her, until she went on to explain, gasping with earnestness, that she was sure *people were* far too *conscientious and self-critical; that it was so* wrong and cruel *to stunt oneself; so* cowardly *to avoid the greatest possible wealth of experience; and that every night before she went to bed she made a point of thinking over all she had said and done during the day, for fear she might have been* too *particular."*

"Good Lord! That's not like Oliver at all. He wasn't one of those romantic cads who want to experience everything. He kept himself for what was best. That's why he was a true puritan after all."

"Quite so. His puritanism had never been mere timidity or fanaticism or calculated hardness: it was a deep and speculative thing: hatred of all shams, scorn of all mummeries, a bitter merciless pleasure in the hard facts. And that passion for reality was beautiful in him, because there was so much in his gifts and in his surroundings to allure him and muffle up his mind in worldly conventions. He was a millionaire, and yet scrupulously simple and silently heroic. For that reason you and I loved him so much. You and I are not puritans; and by contrast with our natural looseness, we can't help admiring people purer than ourselves, more willing to pluck out the eye that offends them, even if it be the eye for beauty, and to enter halt and lame into the kingdom of singlemindedness. I don't prefer austerity for myself as against abundance, against intelligence, against the irony of ultimate truth. But I see

that in itself, as a statuesque object, austerity is more beautiful, and I like it in others."

"I always knew that you thought more of Oliver than of me." Mario had been his mother's darling, and was so accustomed to having women make love to him that he sometimes turned his extreme manliness into coquetry. He liked flattery, he liked presents, and he liked the best cigarettes.

"Certainly I thought more of him as an experiment in virtue. But I prefer your conversation."

"At Oxford, when he had his nursing home, you used to talk with him for ever."

"Yes: but those were philosophical discussions, which are never very satisfying. Have you ever talked with monks and nuns? You may admit that some of these good souls may be saints, but their conversation, even on spiritual subjects, very soon becomes arid and stereotyped, always revolving round a few dulcet incorrigible maxims. Well, Oliver would have been a monk, if he had been a Catholic."

"Yes, and I think he would surely have become a Catholic if he had lived long enough."

"Do you really think so? He, so Nordic, leave the monorail of sheer will for the old Roman road of tradition? I grant you this road is just as straight on the map, or much straighter: but it dips down and soars up so unconcernedly with the lay of the land, like a small boat over great seas; and while the middle way is regularly paved for the militant faithful, there are such broad grassy alleys on either side for the sheep and the goats, and so many an attractive halting-place, and habitable terminus. You might forget you were on a mission, and think life a free tour, or even a picnic.—How Oliver hated picnics, with the messy food and waste paper and empty bottles and loud merriment and tussling and amorous episodes improvised on the grass! Yet, when necessary, he put up with it all gallantly and silently. There was his duty to democracy. No: not a Catholic. His imagination wasn't lordly and firm enough to set up a second world over against this one, and positively believe in it. He distrusted doubleness, but he couldn't admit chaos: and in order to escape chaos, without imposing any fictions or any false hopes upon mankind, he would have been capable of imposing no matter what regimen on us by force. Yes, free, rare and delicate soul as he was, he would have accepted for himself this red communist tyranny that puts a grimy revolver to our noses and growls: 'Be like me, or die.'"

"He wouldn't have found much puritanism among the Bolshies," said Mario, thinking of free love.

"It's a popular error to suppose that puritanism has anything to do with purity. The old Puritans were legally strict, they were righteous, but they were not particularly chaste. They had the virtues and vices of old age. An old man may be lecherous: but that vice in him, like avarice, gluttony, despotism, or the love of strong drink, soon becomes monotonous and sordid, and is easy to cover up hypocritically under his daily routine. The Bolshies have the one element of puritanism which was the most important, at least for Oliver: integrity of purpose and scorn of all compromises, practical or theoretical."

"I don't believe Oliver was ever really in love," Mario interposed, not having listened to my last speech, and evidently reviewing in his mind various incidents which he preferred to pass over in silence. *"Women were rather a difficulty to him. He thought he liked them and they thought they liked him; but there was always something wanting. He regarded all women as ladies, more or less beautiful, kind, privileged, and troublesome. He never discovered that all ladies are women."*

"Yes, and that is the side of them you see; but you forget that many of the ladies whom Oliver knew suffered from the same impediment as himself: it comes from being over-protected in one region and over-developed in another. Sex for them becomes simply a nuisance, and they can't connect it pleasantly with their feeling for the people they love. Therefore sensuality for them remains disgusting, and tenderness incomplete."

"Poor things!" Mario cried, full of genuine commiseration. *"I suppose that's what I never could make out about Oliver, and then his philosophy. Certainly it's you that ought to write his Life. You understood him thoroughly, knew his people and his background, and can toy with all those German philosophers that he was always quoting."*

"I'm not so sure of that. You and I have an immense advantage in belonging to the Catholic tradition. We were born clear, and don't have to achieve clearness. But the light of common day to which we are accustomed may blind us to what is going on in the dark, and the roots of everything are underground. We may be easily dupes of the blue sky and but foolish daylight astronomers."

"Well then, here's your chance of focussing your telescope upon the depths of poor Oliver, until you're used to the darkness and find that there's nothing there. Or rather, you'll find something perfectly commonplace. There's nothing less marvellous than what most mysterious people, especially women, think their secret: only they keep it shut up in a painted casket with seven keys, so that nobody may see what it is."

"To be frank," I replied, *"I think I know what Oliver's secret was—common enough, if you like, and even universal, since it was simply the tragedy of the*

spirit when it's not content to understand but wishes to govern. The old Calvinists cut the Gordian knot by asserting that since the Fall, the spirit had ceased to rule over the world and over their own passions, but that nevertheless it was secretly omnipotent, and would burn up the world and their passions at the last day. Oliver suffered from no such delusion. The holocaust was real enough: it was the endless fire of irrational life always devouring itself: yet somehow the spirit rose from that flame, and surveyed the spectacle with some tears, certainly, but with no little curiosity and satisfaction. Oliver hardly got so far as to feel at home in this absurd world: I could never convince him that reason and goodness are necessarily secondary and incidental. His absolutist conscience remained a pretender, asserting in exile its divine right to the crown. I confess it would interest me to trace in Oliver this purification of puritanism, and this obstinacy in it. But where are the materials? I should have to invent half the story, and I'm no novelist."

"Oliver always kept a diary, and there are a lot of letters. He left me all his father's papers, as well as his own, which I can pass over to you, and we can ask his old German governess for her records, which are surely voluminous and more sentimental than any decent novel would dare to be nowadays. Of course, his mother might help, only she won't. We can't look for anything in that quarter."

"Nor is it necessary. I can easily imagine what she would say. Yet with all the documents in the world, I should have to fill many a gap and compose all the dialogues. I could never do that properly. And how, my dear Vanny, how am I to manage the love scenes?"

"Bah, there are love stories enough in the bookstalls for those who like them. But what is love in a book! This is to be a tale of sad life."

"Think, I shall have to draw the portrait of a lot of living people, and first and foremost of yourself."

"I trust you."

"It will be a delicate task, and perhaps impossible, to find words for tenderer feelings and more varied thoughts than my own. But I will make the attempt. They say we all have a fund of predispositions which circumstances have never developed, but which may be tapped under hypnotic influence. When my intuition gives out, I will summon you to renew the spell, and perhaps I may be able to recover as much of Oliver's thoughts, and of those of all of you, as the world might overhear without indiscretion."

PART I

ANCESTRY

I

A little below the State House in Boston, where Beacon Street consents to bend slightly and begins to run down hill, and where across the Mall the grassy shoulder of the Common slopes most steeply down to the Frog Pond, there stood about the year 1870— and for all I know there may still stand—a pair of old brick houses, flatter and plainer than the rest. They were evidently twins and had been identical at birth, but life had developed them in different directions. The one sister was doing her old-maidenly best to follow the fashions, and had arrayed herself in clean paint, a bright brass knocker, flowering window-boxes, and frilled muslin curtains; whereas the aged Cinderella next door had become more ashen every day. She had long since buried her Prince Charming, and nun-like had hidden her hands in her sleeves and shut her eyes on the world. The wooden blinds were always closed, and the narrow black door, between dusty glass panels, seemed invincibly locked, like the lid of a coffin. A shallow iron verandah, on which only ghosts could step out, since it had no floor, made a sort of grim garland for the first storey, and gave an air of flimsiness to the general decay. You would have thought the place was uninhabited, unless by chance you saw a whistling butcher's boy with a full basket jump from his cart and rattle down the side steps to the basement, whence a moment later he would emerge with the empty basket hooked over his shoulder and rush to overtake his horse and cart that, knowing time to be money, had already started. It was evident that where provisions were consumed there must be human mouths to consume them; the probable rats alone wouldn't have paid the butcher and baker. This inference might indeed have been confirmed by ocular proof, if you had watched long enough. Every Tuesday and Friday at half past eleven the front door opened and gave exit to a lank and rigid gentleman in black, with a small head and pinched features and little steel-blue eyes, blinking. He was young, but had put on old age in his youth, was cautious and nervous in his movements and made sure from time to time that his hat was firm on his head, his scarf pinned, his gloves buttoned, and his umbrella tightly rolled. He always turned to the left, for never, except to funerals, did Mr. Nathaniel Alden walk *down* Beacon Hill. He didn't go out for exercise. The need of exercise, he said, was a modern superstition, invented by people who ate too much, and had nothing to think about. Athletics didn't make anybody either long-lived or useful. An abstemious man could take plenty of sunshine and fresh air by his chamber window, while engaged in reading or writing. And if some impertinent relative wondered how he could take the sun in his house, with the blinds closed, he begged you to observe that all the slats in his blinds were moveable, and that by inclining them inwards, or making them level, he could let in all the light and air desired, without exposing himself to public view. If he went out at all it was to perform some duty, such as to ascertain the state of his financial affairs. An agent collected his rents, but it would have been negligent in himself not to direct his agent's policy, or to be ignorant of the general course of trade and prices. A good citizen must follow the movement of public affairs, so as to cast his vote intelligently, and know whether the party in power deserved his support. If business was good, it did: if business was bad, it didn't.

On Sundays also, weather permitting, Mr. Alden might be seen at church-time issuing from his mansion, but this time not unaccompanied. An awkward youth, evidently uncomfortable in his best clothes, tried unsuccessfully to keep in step with him: Mr. Nathaniel, especially when the brick side-walk was icy, was prudence itself, while his long-legged half-brother Peter was careless and spasmodic. He couldn't resist sliding where there was a clear run of ice in the gutter: and this deportment, undignified for so big a boy on weekdays, was positively improper on Sundays. His eyes, too, even when he tried to mince his steps by his brother's side, would wander absentmindedly to watch the sparrows in the Mall, or to gaze at the familiar fronts of the State House, the Ticknor House, or the Boston Athenaeum. He felt a canine impulse to run down the side alleys, and explore the unsavoury recesses hidden there behind corners. This was hardly a moment when he could indulge so irrational a craving. Yet dogs loved those smells probably very much as respectable people loved hob-nobbing and criticising; and it amused him to imagine the unseemly chalk drawings and inscriptions which he might have found scrawled on those dingy brick walls. Sometimes the demure white shadows in King's Chapel, or the drawling articulation of the minister, shaped themselves in his fancy into the most mocking combinations. Was everything in this world like a puzzle-picture which seen right side up was the lovely Titania and turned upside down became a donkey's head? Perhaps in these musings Peter wouldn't notice, until too late, that his elder brother was bowing and had hurriedly pulled off one glove, before extending his thin hand to a friend—probably a relation—and asking: "May I inquire into the state of your health?" And when in turn he had assured his interlocutor that he was "pretty well, thank you," and both had agreed that it was a beautiful or a windy day, the cold hand—now even colder—was outstretched a second time, the forced smile and stiff bow were repeated, and the social strain relieved. Talk, Mr. Nathaniel Alden had discovered, was chiefly gossip, and gossip encouraged a morbid interest in matters that didn't concern one. Funerals he found the most satisfactory of social occasions, because there you expressed your human attachments without unnecessary chatter. He sometimes went also to weddings and afternoon family parties. He suffered at them, because the tragedy that had darkened his family history, though of course never mentioned, was so public and so painful that it must have been present to the thought of everybody who spoke to him. Why had his father been murdered? Nathaniel Alden knew how deep a lie it was to protest, as everybody did, that the old gentleman had been an innocent victim, who had simply shown firmness in exercising his indubitable right to collect his rents, and had been struck down by a moneyless tenant in a sudden explosion of hatred and despair. Such might well be the literal material truth; yet what were the roots of that violence? That his father had always been a hard landlord and a miser, grown rich on uncertain and miserable payments wrung from the poor. That ultimate outburst of wrath, that one hand raised to smite, had been only a symbol, the fatal overflow, as it were, of all the silent curses and sullen bitterness gathering for years above his head. And the worst of it was, for Nathaniel, that those roots of wrong and vengeance had not been extirpated. He himself was still drawing from them the sap of his own character and position. Yet he couldn't help it: he couldn't abandon his trust and his responsibilities. Unless all his fortune was to be dissipated, tenants must occasionally be evicted and mortgages foreclosed. How horrible that in fulfilling as he must the evident duties of his station, he should never be at ease in his conscience! A scar of horror, if not of guilt, lay consciously on his breast, like the scarlet letter.

In speaking to others, or even to himself, he never came closer to the dreadful facts than to say enigmatically "Under the circumstances," or "After what has happened." But vagueness in apprehension didn't remove his inward unrest; especially as there were other misfortunes besides that major curse in his life: and he trembled at the possibility that some well-meaning aunt or insinuating cousin, perhaps a special friend of his mad sister, might draw him into a corner and whisper affectionately, "Tell me, *how* is poor Julia?" He would wince: and before he could compose an answer, the lady would kindly render it needless by more interrogations. "No change, I suppose? And, at least *physically*, she's quite strong?" And then perhaps he would find himself saying, "Yes, quite strong physically: even in that direction, at present, there seems to be no hope." The kind relative would now wince in her turn. To think the death of a sufferer a blessing might be comforting after the event, but was shocking before.

In this very walk to King's Chapel, Mr. Alden was exposed to indiscretions. Fortunately on Sundays the sanctity of the place seemed to extend throughout the sunken area within the railings, and under the squat granite columns; if acquaintances met there they could decently ignore each other, or at most pass with a mute bow. The blessed silence of the Sabbath saved one, at least there, from the plague of social jabbering. Nevertheless he couldn't help noticing sometimes how, at the church door, some sharp-eyed wife would whisper to her aged husband, or some daughter to her mother, "There goes Mr. Nathaniel Alden with his young brother": and the tremulous lips of the old creature would visibly mumble: "How dreadful that was! What a burden for them always to carry!"

After these ordeals, which duty compelled him to face, it was a relief to be safe within the high enclosure of the family pew, huddled in his cushioned corner (the very one where his father had sat) out of sight of everyone, even of the minister still hidden behind his lofty pulpit, while the organ softly played a few quavering arpeggios. The music was classical and soothing, the service High Church Unitarian, with nothing in it either to discourage a believer or to annoy an unbeliever. What did doctrines matter? The lessons were chosen for their magical archaic English and were mouthed in a tone of emotional mystery and unction. With the superior knowledge and finer feelings of to-day might we not find in such words far deeper meanings than the original speakers intended? The sermon was sure to be pleasantly congratulatory and pleasantly short: even if it began by describing graphically the landscape of Sinai or of Galilee—for the Rev. Mr. Hart had travelled—it would soon return to matters of living interest, would praise the virtues and flatter the vanity of the congregation, only slightly heightening the picture by contrast with the sad vices and errors of former times or of other nations. After church Mr. Alden could enjoy the mid-day sunshine as he walked home to his Sunday roast beef and apple dumpling, confirmed in all his previous ways of thinking. Of course he couldn't deny that he was intellectually more than the equal of his minister. People wouldn't become ministers unless they had rather second-hand minds. Yet a mediocre professional moralist might repeat things which you had never stopped to put into words before. There was plenty of time afterwards for dotting his i's and crossing his t's to your own satisfaction. An Easter sermon on the Resurrection might prudently avoid all mention of Christ or of the Trump of Doom startling the Dead— as Nathaniel Alden didn't wish to be startled—out of the grave. Instead the preacher might blandly describe the resurrection of nature in the Spring, the resurrection of science in the modern world, and the resurrection of heroic freedom in the American character. All that, Mr. Alden thought, was highly suitable in the pulpit: yet he shrewdly added, for his own benefit, that Spring was a dangerous season for catching colds: that ideas revived from time to time in the world were chiefly fallacies, since sound notions, such as that $2+2=4$, never died out; and that the best people in America were not heroes—all more or less spectacular madmen, leading the people astray—but thrifty respectable citizens of the old British stock.

It was a mystery to the town how Mr. Nathaniel Alden spent his time when it was not Sunday morning. Novels he had been heard to condemn as lacerating to the feelings, and he could never bring himself to go to a theatre, even to one disguised under the decent name of the Boston Museum: that, he declared, would be to expose the most sacred part of one's being to artificial emotion. One weakness—or was it his one charity?—Mr. Alden was known to have. He was an untiring patron of all the local painters, old and young. Not that he liked pictures or frequented the society of artists: but once a month he would go into *Doll & Richards'* shop in Park Street, and inquire if they had anything new. It was a public duty, he declared, for those who could afford it to encourage art in a new country. They shouldn't ask whether a struggling painter *deserved* encouragement, but whether he *needed* it. Selfish and worldly people, who considered only their pleasure or vanity, would be quick to buy the good pictures, or those which were called good: an unselfish and public spirited citizen would rather buy the others, which the artist at least probably thought worth preserving. Nobody really knew what good art was; critics and public opinion were helpless shams; the only right course was to aid all devoted artists to paint whatever they chose. In consequence, his house was plastered with canvasses. Even the dark corners of the staircase were packed up to the ceiling with a mosaic of deep gilt frames, each enclosing some sort of painting— landscapes, marine views, studies of heads, happy domestic scenes, and even romantic Shakesperian episodes—everything, in fact, that the ambition of an amateur in those days might attempt except, of course, nudities. The overflow, and especially any large patriotic canvas or battle-piece, which Mr. Alden disliked because (he said) patriotism distorted history, he generously presented to town-halls, schools or museums. The public, he added, *likes* its history distorted. He kept the official letters of thanks on file, to refute any possible insinuation that he was a miser. On this subject Mr. Tom Appleton, then the unofficial Boston wit—the accredited jester being Dr. Oliver Wendell Holmes—proposed a conundrum: Why can't Mr. Nathaniel Alden open the blinds or light the gas in his house? To which the answer was: Because he might see the pictures.

II

One day in June, after his Sunday dinner, Mr. Alden folded his napkin with more than usual precision, as if this time he were not only doing a Duty but doing it under Difficulties. Instead of walking austerely upstairs to enjoy the respectability and privacy of his own chamber, he stood uneasily by the dining-room window, now looking through the upper slats of the blind at the blue sky, and now through the lower ones at the rare passers-by along the brick side-walk of Beacon Street.

"Going out?" his brother Peter inquired, noticing these unusual signs of restlessness and indecision.

"I was thinking of it. It's a beautiful afternoon, and Cousin Sarah Quincy's funeral is at three o'clock."

"But it's in Roxbury."

"I know: a considerable distance and an unsavoury neighbourhood. Cousin Sarah Quincy was in reduced circumstances. We can hardly blame her for dying in Roxbury if she was compelled to live there. Of late I have so far acknowledged our relationship as repeatedly to befriend her financially; I feel that one's conduct ought always to be consistent to the last, and that I ought to attend her funeral."

"How much did you give her?" the boy inquired in a tone between incredulity and congratulation.

"If I remember rightly, ten dollars at Christmas, and this on two successive years."

Peter whistled; and since his brother showed such signs of becoming extravagant, he asked: "Are you going in a hack?"

"I was considering that point, but a hack might seem ostentatious. Besides, they might think that, having taken a hack I might as well go on to the cemetery; and that would be too much. She was only a first cousin once removed."

"Can't be removed again," Peter murmured with a slight chuckle.

"Funeral services," his brother continued, disdaining to take notice of ribaldry, "funeral *services* are elevating, but actually to witness a

burial in the ground can only be distressing to a person of feeling.
That material duty should be left to the undertaker, who is hardened
to it by custom, and comforted by fees. The bereaved family shouldn't
expose themselves to being morbidly harrowed by the ghastliness of
physical death. Physical death is too unimportant. All a dead man's
unselfish interests survive in the living. We throw into the dust-heap
only some outworn soiled copy of the classic text."

Peter was silent for a moment. He had never before quite understood that his brother didn't believe in immortality. Perhaps the other
good people at King's Chapel, who said they did, really didn't. Perhaps immortality in any case was only a figure of speech. What a
relief! It would be so awkward in heaven, after all one had discovered,
to have to put on a perfect innocence.

"Cousin Hannah isn't going with you?"

"No indeed. Hannah is no relation of poor Cousin Sarah's at all.
For a Bancroft to go to a Quincy funeral in that small house would
look like prying."

"Then it's not to be in Church?"

"No, in her own parlour. That's a further reason why I wish to be
there. If I ever go to funerals in church, it's from a sense of duty,
but I don't truly enjoy them. The poignancy of your feelings is
dissipated in so large a place. The public are admitted merely to
crane their necks and to stare: the family marches in the procession,
with everyone tittering about who is present and who absent, and
who is giving his arm to whom, and whether the ladies' veils are long
enough and their moist pocket handkerchiefs bordered or not with
black. And then the expensive coffin and the showy bier and the
display of flowers—how unnecessary and how sensational! In that
theatrical atmosphere you can hardly feel that the deceased belonged
to this every-day world, and was plain Joseph Smith or Betsy Jones.
The corpse might as well be the remains of man in general. Man in
general, Peter, never existed, and therefore never died, and I see no
particular use in pretending to bury him. In a private parlour, on
the contrary, with a simple casket on the centre table, you know that
the bolt has fallen in your private circle, and you have the satisfaction
of realising keenly which of your particular acquaintance has passed
away. Your feelings aren't wasted in vapid emotion, but you readjust
yourself silently to this changing world. Every death loosens a little
the crust of habit, and is a step forward in life. Besides, in this
particular case, by going to Sarah Quincy's funeral I shall be showing

an attention which will be appreciated. Her family and friends will say to themselves: 'Here is one of Boston's first tax-payers'—as a matter of fact I am quite the first for real estate—'and not a very near relation, who has come all this way, out of pure kindness. Probably he was very generous to her during her lifetime.' It will please them: and it won't pledge me to anything for the future. That's an advantage of honouring the dead."

"You aren't going to walk three miles?"

"I had thought of crossing the Common to the Tremont House—the path looks quite dry—and then taking a horse-car; but I hardly know which."

"The yellow one, for the Norfolk House, stops just at the foot of Cousin Sarah's street. I'll go with you, if you'll pay my fare."

"On this occasion I have no objection, since you'll be earning it as a guide." And Mr. Alden almost smiled, walked with unusual briskness into the passage, scrupulously brushed his hat and coat, opened the door, and seeing it was such a glorious day, rolled up his umbrella a little tighter.

The yellow Norfolk House car was already rather crowded, and Mr. Alden was constrained to elbow his way through a group of persons on the back platform, before he could reach the interior. As he brushed past the conductor, he heard that functionary cry behind him in a jovial voice, "Hello, Pete. Going to Casey's Corner?" The words were most distinct, but in the desire to pass on and to find a seat, Mr. Nathaniel was too preoccupied for the moment to take in their meaning. But at once, slowly, deliberately, he heard his brother's voice answering, "No, Mike: I'm going to a funeral with my brother Nathaniel."

It sounded almost like an introduction, and Mr. Alden couldn't help looking round. He saw, under a conductor's cap, some red hair, two impudent laughing eyes, and a grinning mouth; and he saw Peter blushing crimson but bravely clinging to his shame and trying to smile back. Had not the car started and had not Mr. Alden lost his balance and been compelled to seize a strap and hasten to the seat which seemed available at the upper end of the vehicle, Mr. Nathaniel Alden might have found himself "meeting" a horse-car conductor. The fact that there was no room for Peter to sit down beside his brother enabled them to digest their respective feelings for a while in silence. Peter felt the awful nature of his predicament, but he felt the humour of it even more: and it was habitual with him to think himself a hopeless failure, with whom nothing ever went right; in a crisis he was apt to become reckless and to bear down his natural timidity with a mild bravado. He would gladly have hung back and remained with his genial friend on the platform, but to-day duty forbade; and besides in that case his brother might have forgotten to pay his fare; while to have jumped off and run home as he felt inwardly prompted to do, would only have caused the storm to break heavier over his head later. It was the dreadful nature of life, he felt, that if you avoided doing one thing because it wasn't worth while you were thereby caught doing another, which wasn't worth while either. You might as well hold on where you found yourself, and let things rain down upon you as they would. So now he hung to his strap sheepishly, and dangled (he thought) like a man who had been hanged, before his silent brother, who sat on the edge of the bench, looking fixedly before him, with his hands crossed over the handle of his umbrella and his knees pressed closely together in the vain effort to avoid contact with his neighbours. Beside him was a fussy woman with a baby and a large bundle, which—contrary to the principles of a just democracy—kept rolling about and trespassing on his narrow slice of the public space; but unpleasant as intrusion might be from that quarter, the motionless bulk that pressed against him on his other side was even more objectionable. There a huge red-faced Irish priest sat with one enormous paw spread on each knee; he positively exuded animal heat, and a sort of satisfied determination clinched his brutal jaw. What business, thought Mr. Alden, what business have these gross foreigners among us? Didn't we choose distance to avoid contagion and hard work to escape poverty and superstition? He had never, to his knowledge, actually touched a Catholic before. Probably there was little risk for the moment of *moral* infection, but who could tell what loathsome diseases this fleshly monster might conceal under an appearance of robust health? The man looked like a butcher. Hadn't all priests been butchers originally? What evil omens lay in that word! Yet the public danger of Popery and the Inquisition was perhaps a little distant: more immediate was Mr. Alden's apprehension that the poor woman's baby was about to cry, that it might have some scrofulous ailment, and needed a change of diapers.

"Norfolk House. End of the *rout*. All out!" the cheery conductor shouted at last; and as Peter passed him—while the pushing passengers, in as great a hurry as if they were escaping from a fire, or going to see one, separated the brothers a little—Mike whispered, with a poke in the ribs, "Guess that old brother of yours is a stiff all right."

"Not yet," Peter retorted, grimly thinking of Cousin Sarah.

Meantime in Mr. Alden's mind, the indignity of being so rudely commanded by such a low person, and the irritation at hearing a word mispronounced, as it were by authority, and the reversion of his thoughts to the dark problem of Peter's iniquities, all were submerged in a feeling of immense relief. He was now again in the open air, on his feet, and free from personal contact with anybody. And it was almost with relish, as he might have executed the difficult task of carving a duck or exposing a fallacy, that he began the painful investigation which it was now his duty to make.

"May I ask how you came to know this young man, the horse-car conductor? You seem to be on remarkably friendly terms with him."

"Playing base-ball together."

"But how came you to play together, and where?"

"Just by chance, in Boston Common."

"Do you mean that your Headmaster allows the Latin School nine to play on the Common against grown-up working men? That's impossible."

"Oh, I don't play in the School nine. I'm not good enough. Only in scratch games with anyone that turns up. We play just for fun."

"And what is Casey's Corner?"

"Only Casey's Corner Drug Store on Washington Street. There's a soda-fountain, and it's not closed on Sundays like—like other places."

"What *other places*?"

"All other places, except churches." Peter, in saying this felt that he was being flippant and cowardly. It was too late to escape, and he added desperately, "I mean the South End base-ball grounds, and the billiard rooms."

"Billiard rooms," Mr. Alden repeated, as if making up an account, "billiard rooms, soda-fountains, and drugs. Is there nothing else?"

"There's a lamp-post at the corner, and we stand round it. That's all."

"And who are *we*, if you please?"

"I and whoever else wants to stand there. Admission free."

Peter, in his discomfiture, rather enjoyed seeing himself caught, and compelled at last to stick up for his convictions. He hadn't meant to air them, but he wasn't going to give them up. For the moment, he didn't need to explain that, after taking a glass of ice-cream soda, the habitués of Casey's Corner could pass on a plausible pretext through the back-yard into the adjoining billiard room, and that this billiard room was also a bar room where, though the door and shutters might be religiously closed towards the street, drinks could be served even on Sundays.

The brothers had reached the door of the late Sarah Quincy's little wooden house, and Peter already had his hand on the unpleasant encumbrance of crêpe that enveloped the bell; but to brother Nathaniel the investigation of wickedness was even more absorbing than the presence of death, and more deeply satisfying. He stopped, before entering, to have a last word.

"I should like to know," he said icily, "what you can possibly do, standing round a lamp-post with strange youths in a disreputable quarter of the city."

"Nothing, only loafing and joking and smoking cigarettes and watching the people—the girls—going in or out of church, because Casey's Corner is opposite the Cathedral. We'd rather play ball, only we can't on Sunday."

"So there are cigarettes also and you smoke them. I didn't know you had already secretly acquired that habit. But if your time must be ill spent, why must it be ill spent in such a place and with such people?" And Mr. Alden, who read solid books, remembered how a great orator, by a rhetorical exaggeration perhaps excusable under the circumstances, had declared that vice lost half its evil by losing all its grossness.

"I don't know why," Peter rejoined, growing impatient and gradually raising his voice. "It just happens. I suppose I like it. It's easier. It's *more fun*."

He hadn't rung the bell, but the door had been silently opened behind him, while he was speaking, and his last words loudly resounded through the narrow passage, and the adjoining little parlour, darkened and heavy with a religious hush and a strong scent of roses, where the mourners sat waiting in a tense discomfort. Everyone was startled, pained, indignant. Everybody glanced at everybody else, and at the two brothers, Nathaniel very white and Peter very red, as they fumbled in the dark into the two last shaky little chairs that remained near the door. Everyone had also glanced at the coffin, but as no protest seemed to come from that quarter, they all gradually resumed their demure attitudes. Everyone knew that everybody else was trying to pretend that nothing had happened. Yet the muted accents of the minister, after that incongruous shock, sounded more affected than ever, and even Mr. Nathaniel Alden hardly enjoyed that funeral. His dominant feeling, all through the service, was that he wished he had come in a hack. Ostentation would have been better than disgrace. Tragedy, criticism, perhaps punishment had fallen before on other members of his family; but he had always had a premonition that this half-brother of his, whose mother had been a Lanier, and a stranger in Boston, would bring *disgrace* on it for the first time. Even as a small boy Peter had shown a carelessness, a defiance, a secret perversity which marked him out for a black sheep. How often, after being called in the morning, wouldn't he go to sleep again, and come down half awake, half washed and half combed to a cold breakfast! True his mother set him a bad example by not coming down to breakfast at all. Breakfast, with its solemnity, ill humour, and unappetising profusion of food, seemed to cast a moralising and steadying influence over the whole day: it was the improved Unitarian substitute for morning prayers. It incapacitated you, during that day, for doing anything unconventional. Yet in his sleepiness and his hurry, knowing that he would be "tardy" for school, little Peter seemed not to profit by that admirable institution. He would bolt a mouthful or two of oatmeal and, picking up his cap and perhaps upsetting the umbrella-stand, he would run from the house, leaving the front door open, or slamming it, jarring the whole house and sending a dangerous draught of cold air round his brother's thin ankles. How often had the boy been warned that, if he couldn't be punctual, breakfast would be set for half past seven instead of eight o'clock? And when this was actually done, Nathaniel generously sacrificing his own comfort for his young brother's spiritual good, how ingeniously little Peter had perverted that austere measure to evil uses! He had taken to loitering on his way to school, to "cutting" on the sleighs coming down Beacon Street, or to running at full speed down the slope of the Common to the pond, quite out of the direct plank walk that would have so easily taken him towards Bedford Street in time for school. How often had Nathaniel had reason to observe that those who run down hill find some difficulty in stopping half-way. Some day the unhappy child would roll into the pond, and what was the Frog Pond but a symbol for the pit of perdition? Not, of course, that Mr. Alden could entertain any longer the shocking idea of hell; but relief from religious terrors had merely brought the fatal conse-

quences of evil-doing nearer home, and distributed them, most an-
noyingly, among the relations of the culprit.

He wished he had come in a hack: but how, on a Sunday afternoon,
almost in the country, was he to find a hack in which to return? They
would all be already engaged for Irish funerals; the poor, in the
matter of funerals, were so foolishly extravagant. He didn't need to
say to himself that never, never, would he again enter a horse-car:
that determination was too deeply set in his soul to require utterance.
He would *walk* home, since there was nothing else to be done: and
if the effort proved injurious to his frail health, at least he would
have learned the lesson of not frequenting poor relations, even when
they were dead; or if you *must* go to their funerals, at least to go
alone. He would walk home through those three long miles of slums,
most unpleasantly conscious of the silence and of the hanging head
of his brother walking beside him: he would be rescuing Peter, if
only for the moment, from contamination with evil. Little did he
know how far that contamination had already gone.

All the way home, the sense that they were doing severe penance
kept them from speech. Nathaniel hated to walk, and his brother
hated to walk with him.

Explanations were not resumed until after their cold Sunday supper, when by a sort of instinct their Cousin Hannah left them alone
in the dining-room. Not that there were ever wine and cigars for the
gentlemen: but that evening she felt that somehow there would be
wine and cigars in their conversation, and she prudently vanished to
her own room.

Brother Nathaniel, having re-composed himself in his chair (for
he always rose with his fair housekeeper, while Peter opened the door
for her) and having repeatedly swallowed much saliva, then said: "I
think I ought to tell you, Peter, that I don't approve of your intimacy
with persons of inferior education and a lower station in life. Of
course, we all believe in democracy, and wish all classes to enjoy the
greatest possible advantages: but we shall never help the less fortunate to rise to our own level, if we sink away from it ourselves. Your
undesirable friendships have already affected your language and
manners: I had observed a change, without knowing its exact cause.
The same influence in time might affect your morals, not to speak
of your prospects in College and later in the business world. Nothing
makes a more favourable impression on responsible persons than
becoming speech and bearing in a young man. The best nowadays,

I am sorry to say, are none too good. I hope you will promise me to give up all your South End acquaintance."

"No," Peter said sullenly, without looking at his brother, "I won't promise."

There was a long pause.

"If you will not promise, it will become my duty to protect you as far as I can: although I know how little any external protection can help, when the will to do right is lacking. I will consult with the other executors of our father's estate, who are in some sense also your guardians, and if they approve, we will send you away to a distance, where you will be shielded from the worst influences of a large city. I am well aware that no human society is so thoroughly purified that bad company may not be found in it by those who seek it; and I confess I don't nourish much hope of your thorough amendment."

"You'd better not. I like muckers. I like them better than nice people, in many ways, because they are more natural."

"We should not consider what is natural, but what is best."

"One reason," Peter went on, pursuing his own thoughts intrepidly, as if his brother had not spoken, "one reason why a mucker is more natural than a nice fellow is that he can have his best girl."

"At your age any engagement, even a tacit one, would be regrettable. Circumstances will have changed so much by the time you are old enough to marry, that a childish attachment would have become unsuitable and only a cause of embarrassment. I know, of course, boys sometimes have fancies. . . . At Mr. Papanti's dancing class you find yourself surrounded every Friday afternoon by a bevy of sweet young ladies, and if you happen to feel a decided preference for one of them, and fix your thoughts upon her—though the thing is premature—I see no reason why you shouldn't say you have a 'best girl' without becoming—what horrible words you *do* use!—a 'mucker.'"

"I don't mean mooning or fixing one's thoughts or feeling a preference. I mean that when a mucker has a best girl, without ever marrying her, it's very likely that he can have her."

This time brother Nathaniel understood. He opened his mouth wide, as if about to draw some awful imprecation from the depths of his being. But his pale lips closed tight again without uttering a word, and he walked out of the room. In his whole long life he never saw his brother Peter again.

All the next day Mr. Nathaniel Alden in his slippers and wadded silk dressing-gown remained in the little study adjoining his bedroom.

Cousin Hannah reported that he was busy writing letters, and declared himself sadly upset, and had even asked for a glass of her medicinal sherry to quiet his nerves, though his appetite seemed little impaired. Indeed the crisis had brought unwonted colour into his cheeks, and a sense of great responsibilities unflinchingly accepted and thoroughly discharged, caused him to spend one of the busiest and happiest days of his life. On the third morning Peter found the following epistle on his plate at breakfast.

My Young Brother,

   After what has occurred you will not be surprised to hear that your guardians have been in consultation, and have decided to send you for the summer to the Rev. Mark Lowe's Camp for Backward Lads at Slump, Wyoming. Mr. Lowe will arrive in Boston to-morrow. He will immediately take charge of you and conduct you with his other pupils to his mountain Camp.

   In the autumn, if your behaviour meantime has been exemplary, you will go to school at Exeter in preparation for Harvard. Although we foresee the dangers of the liberty you will eventually enjoy there, we think it is right not to cut you off from any Avenue of Repentance, or to deprive you of any reasonable opportunity to retrieve your Character.

   Should we find, however, that you do not profit by this indulgence, we have decided to place you for the next three years, while our responsibility for your welfare continues, in the office of the cotton mills at Pepperel, Maine, where if you cannot correct your life at least you will be earning your living.

Your grieved but dutiful brother,

Nathaniel Alden.

III

The corner of Beacon and Charles Streets was central and respectable. Indeed it formed a sort of isthmus, leaving the flood
of niggerdom to the north and of paddydom to the south, and
connecting Beacon Hill with the Back Bay—the two islands of respectability composing socially habitable Boston. Yet the occasional jingling
horse-car passing in either vulgar direction rendered that corner a
little agitating. Elderly persons would step from one island to the
other somewhat hurriedly, and would be careful to pause a moment
on the kerb and look sharply both ways before venturing to set foot
on the bridge of flagstones that marked off the proper crossing from
the mud of the road. By crossing only with the right-minded file of
pedestrians at the rectangular corners, you might pass unobserved;
while if anywhere in Boston you scurried across a street at an unmarked place and at a rash angle, like a dog or a child chasing a
stray ball, you would set all the heads in all the windows wondering
why you did it: and the inference could hardly be favourable to your
character. Even if you were doing nothing morally wrong, to be
unobserved was always reassuring. It restored to you half of that
negative blessedness which you would have enjoyed if you had been
non-existent.

In the clear dry sunshine of the next Tuesday morning, in that
sparkling month of June, the Reverend Mr. Hart, minister of King's
Chapel, was seen poising his slender form at that very corner. It was
not for him to plunge blindly even into an empty road, without
pausing for a moment to drink in the warm air, admire the blue sky,
and thank God for the green trees. What a privilege to look on these
ancient elms, their drooping branches swaying like hung garlands in
the light summer breeze! He was consecrated to the thought of living
up to his surroundings and of worthily interpreting the refined feelings of his flock. King's Chapel, in its granite simplicity, half hidden
by foliage in its railed nook, amid the already overtopping Babel of
business, seemed to him a symbol of that invisible goodness of heart

and integrity of purpose which would always stand unassailable amid
the ruin of creeds. There was inspiration for him in the Georgian
elegance of the interior, all white plaster, shining mahogany, and
crimson damask. In those high-walled pews, with their locked doors,
every worshipper might pray in secret, as if in his own closet; and he
took care that his own words should never intrude rudely into the
privacy of their sacred convictions. What if, behind those reverently
closed eyelids, recollection sometimes passed into drowsiness? Was
not rest, rest to the body and the soul, one of the first fruits of purity
of spirit? The great error of our forefathers had been to make
religion a subject of wrangling. Controversy might be inevitable in
science, when points of fact were not clearly determined by the
evidence available: but why dispute about faith, about hope, about
love? Why shouldn't each man form his conception of God and of
heaven—if he needed such conceptions at all—according to the
promptings of his own breast?

An earthly voice interrupted these meditations. "How do you do,
Mr. Hart," said an affable gentleman, squeezing the minister's hand
so hard that the pain was excruciating.

"How do you do, Mr. Head," the sufferer replied, trying playfully
to conceal his emotion. "Am I wrong in thinking that you are not
crossing the Common as usual this morning, but going up the hill?
A little bird has told me the reason."

"You are not wrong, Mr. Hart, you are never wrong. You are
guided by Revelation."

"As you by the Law. But allow me to point out the advantage which
you enjoy. The Law lies printed in books, you can quote it in Court,
and the judge must bow to it. Revelation, on the contrary, comes only
to the heart: and those palpitating tablets are in danger of confusing
the divine characters impressed upon them."

"Luckily this time your heart and my eyes agree in leading us to
Mr. Nathaniel Alden's."

"Yes; and on a most important and delicate errand. Isn't that Dr.
Hand puffing up the hill in front of us? I wager he is bound to the
same consultation. He will be the devil's advocate at our council, as
they call it in Rome when they canonise one of their useless saints.
But Dr. Hand's function won't be to point out the imperfections of
our young scapegrace: it will be, I fear, to excuse and almost to
approve them. Medical men take too indulgent a view of human
weakness. If we let them have their way, we might as well expunge

the words right and wrong from the dictionary, and talk only physiology."

"Would that, I wonder, cause more persons to break the law?"

"No," said Dr. Hand, whom they had overtaken, "but it would cause you to expunge more than half the criminal law from your statute-book, so that honest men might obey the remainder."

"Ah, Dr. Hand, I rejoice to see that, although you would throw right and wrong in the dustheap, you would still keep the honest man on his pedestal," and Mr. Hart, conscious of a dialectical triumph, led the others into the Aldens' house.

They were received in the back-parlour, sometimes called the library, because there were two tall bookcases in it with their glass doors locked, and green cambric curtains behind the glass. The books and reviews which Mr. Nathaniel Alden actually read were in his bedroom, and the newspaper never appeared except on a little table by the dining-room window where, after breakfast, he perused it with one eye, while through the gaps in the blind his other eye observed the state of the weather, and satirically compared it with the "probabilities" in the paper, or even took note of the rare passers-by, and judged most of them, alas! to be vagrants unknown, and probably not respectable. It was a sad thought, daily borne in upon him afresh, how seldom in this world anything either great or small, was exactly *right*. Even his own desire to elevate his fellow-creatures had been cruelly hampered by ill-health and horrible accidents. And now there came this new interruption, this almost public scandal caused by the vicious tendencies and unruly mind of his young brother. The back-parlour, which was always used for funerals, would be the *right* place for the meeting that morning. Its name made it seem more private and retired, although in fact it was overlooked by three neighbours in the backyard, whereas the front parlour windows, opening on the skeleton verandah, could have been overlooked at most by the Mall sparrows. Moreover, in the back-parlour there was a large desk, supporting an iron strongbox filled with old letters and documents—how thin, and yellow and meaningless now!—which had once belonged to his lamented father; and also a bronze crocodile for a paper-weight, which in his own childish mind had somehow been associated with Satan, and which now seemed to fall in appropriately into the picture. Sitting at that desk he could preside with more dignity over the momentous deliberations; its protective expanse would conceal his feet and legs, of which otherwise he might have

been painfully conscious. Three arm-chairs had been disposed in a
semicircle for the other gentlemen. They were co-trustees with himself for the boy's property; and since one's property, in Nathaniel's
estimation, formed the chief and fundamental part of one's moral
personality, it had been imperative to consult the trustees about the
education and control of the young man through whom that particular property was destined to exercise its influence for good or for
evil. Their approval, in any case, would buttress his own responsibility, and relieve him of any personal qualms when the ultimate disaster
occurred. He didn't hope to save his brother, contrary to the evident
designs of Providence: but he wished to prove to himself and to all
men that he had done his full duty by the unfortunate boy, who
should be alone guilty of his own ruin.

All this Mr. Nathaniel Alden did not mention in his opening remarks: it could be presupposed; and besides there was something
indelicate, if not impossible, to his mind in formulating anything
ultimate. He only cleared his throat, and in a voice somewhat unsteady at first, regretted to trouble his friends about so painful a
matter, yet desired to have the benefit of their judgment and experience in determining the course to pursue. Peter had fallen into low
company. Evidently, he must be temporarily removed from Boston
and from the strange circles which he unblushingly said he frequented and positively preferred to the natural friends of his family.

"Lucky boy," sighed Dr. Hand, as if thinking aloud, "most of us
would prefer circles we can't frequent, and must frequent circles we
never chose."

The Reverend Mr. Hart felt the unpleasant and unseasonable character of this cynicism, and the duty of smoothing it over. "Our witty
medical friend," he observed archly, "likes to throw a gleam of satire
into the deepest gloom. Even the chamber of death, when he presides
over it, ceases to be wholly mournful."

"I preside over it only before the death. It's your business, Mr.
Hart, to brighten it afterwards."

Mr. Nathaniel Alden coughed, as if to call the meeting to order.
"It is also clear," he said, "that my young brother must not continue
at the Boston Latin School. I see now what an error it was to have
sent him there at all. In the fifteen years since my own time its
character, I am sorry to say, seems to have profoundly altered. Our
democracy has ceased to be ours: it has become more than half alien.
Only a private education can preserve for us the noble traditions

which were once those of our whole community. Next winter, for his
final preparation for College, he must go to some boarding-school;
we can consider later which of them may be the least open to objection
on theological and moral grounds. Meantime, it is impossible for me
to keep him with me at Newport during the summer, where he would
be free to range all day——"

"And all night," chirped the wicked Doctor.

"All day," the other repeated, "without supervision, in a town full
of the frivolous rich, and of their hangers-on of all degrees, even the
lowest. It is a seaport: and I am sorry to observe that my brother's
mind has been poisoned with that strange and false fascination, which
the notion of sea-faring exerts upon some boys. Boating and sailing
are grave dangers, not only to life, but to decent speech and behaviour. Where, then, could we arrange that Peter should spend the
summer?"

"You might," said Mr. Hart with an eloquent gesture which indicated infinite and sacred distances, "you might send him to travel
abroad with a tutor."

"That," Mr. Alden retorted sharply, "might be *possible* if we knew
of any respectable person to whom we could entrust so difficult a
charge: but even then, would it be *desirable*? Why travel, and why
abroad? Is there no suitable retreat in this country, remote from the
perils of the sea and the city? Travelling for two persons, besides the
tutor's salary, would be a serious expense. I should not consider it, if
it were to be at my own cost; but of course the expenses of my
brother's education must be charged to his account; and I hesitate to
make large inroads into an income which was intended to accumulate
during his minority, in order that later, on the assumption that his
character was fundamentally honourable, he might be of greater
service to the community."

Here Mr. Nathaniel Alden became conscious that he was making
a speech, lost the thread of it, and coughed again.

"Do you remember the Reverend Mark Lowe?" Mr. Head asked,
apparently changing the subject. "That tall vigorous parson with a
red face and light hair, who was assistant for a time at Trinity Church?
He had been previously a missionary in India, but now carries on
city missions at home. Last summer he also established a camp for
boys among the mountains of Wyoming. He has sent me the prospectus for his second season, with photographs of the settlement. I
should think it might be just the place for our young friend."

"I too," said the Doctor, "have received that prospectus, and I see it's a *church* camp for *backward* lads. Is Peter backward, or would churchiness be likely to do him any good?"

"A young man, however intelligent, may be backward in some respects just because he has pushed forward too far in others," Mr. Hart observed, a little nettled, "and spiritual influences are never more needful than when we are struggling, as every young man must, against the lower impulses of our nature."

"Ah," sighed Mr. Alden sceptically, "but *what* spiritual influences? Lofty principles or foolish mummeries? Mr. Lowe is an Episcopalian."

"As to religion," Dr. Hand interposed, "it seems that instead of converting the Indians to Christianity he was himself converted by them to Buddhism or Yoga or some other creed which I understand is very hygienic. He is a vegetarian in the tropics, but approves of beef for a cold climate. A sensible fellow. I'm sure his case of religion is mild, and wouldn't be catching."

"My dear Doctor," the clergyman said, conscious that the power of love is irresistible in the end, "you attempt in vain to hide a warm heart under light words, and pretend to be a scoffer; but we know you, and you can't frighten us. As to our friend Mr. Mark Lowe, he has discerned the soul of Christian truth even in those older religions in which so many millions have found comfort. I knew him at the Associated Charities. He may be a little too much of a leveller, but there is something frank and manly about him that must appeal to the young; and slight differences of creed, which he himself ignores, should not stand in the way of our confidence in his good work. He is a thorough modern, full of the spirit of democracy, optimism and service."

Mr. Nathaniel Alden coughed for the third time. Cant, even in his own mouth, made him secretly uncomfortable: it annoyed him, in spite of habit, when he suddenly became aware of it in the mouth of others. Yet he was far too timid to quarrel with the consecrated modes of speech among people of his own circle. When wounded, he shrank: and he had a feeling that this Mr. Mark Lowe, in his own sphere, was also a sufferer. He had not been able to sail before the blast of Phillips Brooks. He had preferred by-ways and obscurity to trumpet calls and dulcification. Perhaps he was, as Mr. Alden imagined himself to be, a deep solitary thinker. All these submerged musings brought to the surface nothing but the question: "Is he not a Canadian?"

"Yes," Mr. Head replied, "by birth: but I'm not sure that he hasn't been naturalised. In any case, there is little difference between Canadians and Americans in the Wild West. His camp is in the United States, and he is quite one of us in heart."

Mr. Alden was far from confident that they were one in heart among themselves. He had certain secret convictions, one of which was this: that human beings could be united only in the common sphere of their actions; they remained for ever separate and solitary in their thoughts—when, indeed, they had any. "It had occurred to me," he said quietly, "that there might be more intellectual refinements in such a place as Concord, or in the home of some professor in a New England College in the country, which in the absence of the students might be an unobjectionable place. The remoteness of Wyoming seems to me unfortunate."

"Unfortunate for us, certainly," said the Doctor, "if we wish to go there and can't afford the trip. But remoteness from the South End is just what Peter requires, and also a change of air from Beacon Street. The farther the better. Youngsters need to have their minds occupied with healthy excitements. Drabness is favourable to vice; and I think a mountain camp, even under a mad parson, better for a boy like Peter than loafing in a sickly New England village biting his nails, and playing billiards in the local bar-rooms."

"You do paint a horrid picture," Mr. Hart protested, shuddering, half smiling, and instinctively withdrawing his hands so that the nails should not be visible. "Your love of picturesque language leads you to exaggerate. Yet the winds of Wyoming, which I am sorry to say have never blown upon me, must certainly be more exhilarating."

At this point the conversation reverted to the weather, and wandered into questions of drainage and vital statistics. Mr. Nathaniel Alden gradually became apprehensive that his friends might remain chatting until it was time for lunch, when at last a higher power would force them to quit. Mr. Head had told a legal funny story: and when Dr. Hand prophesied that before long some Irish Catholic might be mayor of Boston, their poor host's discomfort became intolerable; he coughed for the last time; and as nevertheless nobody moved, he assumed the royal privilege of dismissing his visitors.

"I am much obliged to you," he said, his eyes intently fixed on the bronze crocodile, "for the kind suggestions which you have made, and I will carefully consider them. Should you have any others to offer, or should you learn anything further about this school camp, you would do me a favour by letting me know of it *in writing*." And he removed his chair slightly from the desk, with a movement which, though it left him still seated, caused the others to rise in their places by the delicate power of suggestion.

Mr. Head left the prospectus on the table, which, as Mr. Alden politely held the door open for his guests to march out, blew away and had to be secured under the bronze crocodile. It displayed a view of some rambling log cabins between a pond and a wood, with some suggestion of mountains in the background; also a time table for the boys' daily occupations: 6 a.m., bugle call and first plunge in the Lake; 6.30, the Lord's prayer and breakfast; and so on through a day of which excursions and wood-chopping occupied the greater part. Mr. Hart and Mr. Head walked first down the stairs, already remarking on the fine weather before they got out of the front door, where they smilingly took opposite directions. But Dr. Hand, instead of following them down the steps, turned to his host—who had accompanied them to the street door—with a certain formal air which was not in his customary jovial key. "May I have one word with you? When I received your note yesterday it occurred to me that my advice on this matter might be more useful if I first subjected our young Peter to a medical examination. I therefore sent word to him to call at my office, telling him that I took this step on my own initiative and without your knowledge. He came, and I looked him over thoroughly. He is pale and lanky, like so many of our youths, and his whole organism seems a bit languid, although his muscles are strong enough; but the vital organs are normal, and he is not suffering from any particular ailment whatsoever. What he lacks is spontaneity and a brisk circulation: that would of itself give him confidence and a heartier interest in whatever he may be doing. My advice morally as well as medically, is to give him plenty of rope: he would have a good mind if he found something important to apply it to: but good minds among us, as you know, are apt to remain playful. Our dominant affairs don't require much mind, only sharpness and diligence. Now sharpness and diligence are precisely what Peter lacks: if he is put into the business or professional mill, he will be a failure. To make something out of him you must leave him free to follow his bent; for the moment his tastes seem to be for literature and yachting; by encouraging him there, you may save him from listlessness and dissipation. You have a sloop laid up at Newport, I believe: why not have her put in commission, with a reliable skipper, and let Peter have her to sail in during the summer, with liberty, of course, to take a friend or two with him? The experience would wake him up, I believe, physically and socially. It might help to restore that self-respect which seems to be rather mortified in him, and might set him up like a man on his two legs. We must remember," the Doctor went on, as Mr. Nathaniel Alden frigidly compressed his lips and kept a severe silence, "we must remember that in a few years Peter will have a considerable income at his command. It would be a safe-guard that he should already have been trained in taking care of himself and of his money."

"I quite understand the danger," Mr. Alden said at last, "but if we teach him to squander his money now, how would that help him to use it well later? If we cannot rely on his sense of duty, I am afraid we can do nothing for him. We must allow the laws of life to take their divine course."

Dr. Hand, rebuked, bowed his way out, and Mr. Alden, victorious, closed the funereal front door after him with a certain silent but excessive application of force, which expressed his intense satisfaction; partly at shutting that lewd fellow out and partly at remaining safely locked and solitary within.

IV

If the expedition to Wyoming had been designed for any other
purpose than moral reform, it would have been a great success.
First, the prolonged journey over the prairies by the new Pacific
Railroad, and then another prolonged journey by stagecoach and
cart to the shores of a clear lake, at the foot of pine-clad mountains:
all with the charm of novelty, of small unforeseen adventures, and
of ingenious methods of being civilised beyond civilisation. The camp
life to Peter was a godsend: the wholesome mixture of cleanliness
and roughness: the cooking, which the boys did for themselves: the
few holiday school books, all redolent of the simple life, all breezy
and full of adventure: a little of the Old Testament, a little Xenophon
or bits of the Georgics, with tales of Drake and Nelson and Captain
Cook: miscellaneous talks about India, where Mr. Lowe had
learned—admirable missionary—more than others had gone to
teach; and above all the curious company of the Backward Lads
themselves, odds and ends of maladjusted humanity, especially the
son of an Indian Rajah, who surpassed all the other members of the
party both in backwardness in learning and advancement in experience. "Don't be ashamed," Mr. Lowe would say in his five-minute
sermons before supper, "don't be ashamed of being Backward Lads.
We are all backward lads in God's sight. Be good fools, and brave
enough to be humble, and you will be wiser than most learned men.
Put away human respect. Man is only one of God's many creatures;
here in the wilds you see how little the pride or the welfare of man
count in the universe. Just as a woman is quite as good as a man, if
she doesn't try to be like him, so a Backward Lad is quite as good as
a Forward Lad, or even better, if his backwardness convinces him
that a man can be as near to God in the last and hindermost pew in
church, as in the first stall in the choir. Therefore don't be offended
if this camp is called the Backward Lads' Camp: it is a term of
affection, and there is a sacred text which I rejoice to repeat in secret:
'The last shall be first.'"

This doctrine made a deep impression on Peter. He felt slack and weak, and knew that under the mask of stiffness his Boston friends were weak also. Shams were everywhere: and it filled him with a curious sense of humorous profundity, a sort of charity in sarcasm, to think that perhaps it was the ultimate function of mankind to be a set of ne'er-do-wells in the universe. So, at heart, were these enormous pines, these shaggy bisons, these ferrets and beavers, these trout and these leaping salmon: all making a brave show and just keeping alive, but each of them doubtless a ne'er-do-well like himself in its private destiny. A Rajah was a lord of the earth, and probably quite dazzling on his gilded throne; but look at him here in his little person: unspeakably helpless, amiable only in being shamelessly devoid of any pretence to dignity. Peter was almost reconciled to falseness in others and to helplessness in himself. Circumstances had let him off easily; he was able to be merely helpless, and not false and murderous as well. These Backward Lads were a rum lot, yet he had never felt so free and happy as in their company. The Rajah's son in particular. Peter helped him in his lessons, and learned from him in turn a new theory of morals, with vivid illustrations of how to put it in practice. The scene was not commonly laid in any Oriental paradise, but in Leicester Square. Pagan vices to this dusky youth were splendid virtues; and he confessed to no weakness except that of being incapable of going it strong in all the vices at once. Peter laughed: he was sorry for rich lame ducks, such as the Rajah's son and himself. It was hard lines to be pushed into high places, and have great things expected of you, when by nature you were poor, dingy little mice, only desirous of scampering about and nibbling, and busying yourself in a corner. And were these little hidden pleasures really so little? Where else was there any poetry, any justice, any truth? Was the great public honourable world anything really but pasteboard and trombones?

Genuine cow-boys would sometimes ride into the camp, for a halt or a meal, or for some fresh medicine, of which Mr. Lowe kept a well-stocked chest. Newspapers and magazines were exchanged habitually with two young Englishmen who had a ranch in the upper valley. The cow-boys, and more especially the Englishmen, gave Peter hints which he relished, hints that Beacon Street was not the whole world. It was possible not to have heard of that place, or not to be impressed by it, as the Englishmen were not, even though they had heard of it. Peter had been restless at home without knowing what else to wish for. Sometimes he had ingeniously found his way to India Wharf—you may live in Boston all your life without coming on visible evidence that it is a seaport—and he had wondered what would happen if he should run away before the mast, like Richard Dana. But he was too young and too undecided: and his loose day-dreams had ended in sneaking home again with a vague sense of guiltiness and impotence. Now among the Rockies the map of the world began to take colour in his fancy: the impulse to travel became definite. He devoured Mr. Lowe's Library of adventure: he remembered everything about persons and places that Mr. Lowe himself or the boys, or the visiting neighbours, happened to mention. He remained languid physically, but his eyes and his fancy were brightened: he became, in a quiet way, the wit of the camp, and Mr. Lowe's right hand man; and the report that went home at the end of the summer was so favourable, that the promise to send him to Exeter and Harvard had to be fulfilled.

His brother Nathaniel, after the manner of merchant families, was scrupulously formal in all matters of contracts and promises: on the other hand Peter's good conduct didn't in the least reassure him: the boy was born a black sheep; his mother—their father's second wife— had come from Baltimore, almost a Southerner; and could anything good come out of the South? Therefore Nathaniel instinctively looked about for some honourable means of getting rid of Peter. Peter reformed and conventional would trouble him even more than Peter frankly gone to the dogs; he would have to see him, perhaps to live with him. He would thus himself be a sort of accomplice in the catastrophe which would befall in any case. How much more safely his conscience could watch that vindication of the moral law from a distance! And a means of escape was indeed at hand, no less honourable than convenient. Peter had another relative quite as close as himself, and no less competent to take charge of him: his half-sister Caroline, married long since to a prosperous banker, Mr. Erasmus Van de Weyer. Nathaniel did not visit her, although both families spent the summer at Newport; but there was no quarrel: simply a suspension of intimacy, which was also a suspension of hostilities. He and this lady were no blood-relations whatever. His widowed father had married her widowed mother when the two children were old enough to feel the oddity of suddenly acquiring a new parent and a new brother or sister, almost grown up; and they had always called each other *brother* Nathaniel and *sister* Caroline with an air of mockery.

They were exactly the same age, which made the boy feel inferior; and the girl's capacity for mischief and freedom of speech profoundly grieved his Boston conscience. She put grasshoppers and caterpillars into his bed and tacks in his chair; to which he could only retaliate by severely calling her minx. Luckily she had married very young and had gone to live in distant New York: but now Providence seemed at last to justify her existence in his eyes. For what could be more suitable and satisfactory than that she and her respectable husband should relieve him of the Ishmael?

Prudently, through Cousin Hannah Bancroft, who did visit the Van de Weyers once a year, negotiations were opened. Caroline had received the suggestion with enthusiasm. The family lawyers had arranged the details, and nothing any longer prevented the effective guardianship of this sorry lad, deceptively promising to turn out well after all, from being transferred to the other side of his family. Nathaniel would thus be spared any further immediate contact with evil; while the Van de Weyers, worldly, frivolous, and morally callous as they were, would probably shrug their shoulders when (as would happen) Peter petered out. This was the only pun Mr. Nathaniel Alden was ever known to make, but he repeated it often.

When the return of the prodigal was imminent, Mr. Alden, by appointment, paid a formal call on his step-sister, to make, as it were, an official transmission of the charge.

He was received in a large airy drawing-room, with French windows on three sides, through which the sunlight and sea-breeze, on that warm September afternoon, streamed in only a little softened by wire screens and lace curtains. Beyond, all was green lawn and blue ocean, without a neighbour in sight: and the good gentleman couldn't help breathing a slight sigh, as if all this openness, in filling his narrow lungs, found there some painful obstruction. How different was his own Newport dwelling in the older part of the town, scarcely separated from the main street by a wooden fence and a dusty row of lilac bushes, while behind the house a strip of rough ground sloped shabbily down to the harbour, between a second class hotel and an old lumber yard. For a moment he almost was envious, almost ashamed: yet a second look round the room restored that sense of superiority which was necessary to his moral being. Whatever he had and was *must* be right, whatever he hadn't and wasn't *must* be wrong: else how should he face the universe? This first axiom of his American ethics was at once verified by observation. His own so-

called country-house, viewed from outside, might seem a little smothered, like his life: but what rightness, what austere elegance, what
quietness within! Whereas this wide-open, glaring ostentatious place
was essentially vulgar. The room was littered with little sofas, little
arm-chairs, little tables, with plants flowering in porcelain jars, and
flowers flaunting in cut-glass bowls, photographs in silver frames,
work-baskets, cushions, foot-stools, books, and magazines, while the
walls were a mosaic of trivial decorations, (not the work of deserving
artists, like those in his own house), but étagères with nick-nacks and
bric-a-brac, feeble water-colours, sentimental engravings, and slanting mirrors in showy frames. Could the mistress of such a house be
the daughter—to be sure, only the step-daughter—of his own father,
so single-minded, so strict, so horribly murdered? But here at last
was the lady herself, who had evidently been prinking. He rose stiffly,
and what was his surprise, when before he had had time to observe
her, she seized him by both arms and gave him a warm, soft, frank
kiss on the cheek, with an audible smack to it.

"Nathaniel dear," she cried, "do sit down here beside me, and let
us talk. Now we are more brother and sister than ever. How really
beautiful of you to give me back my young brother! It was almost as
if I had lost him. I feel like Elsa in the Opera, and you are like
Lohengrin or the *lieber Schwan*. You don't *look* like Lohengrin," she
added laughing merrily, till her eyes sparkled with tears, "nor like
the swan; but you are *behaving* like an angel, and that's enough. You
are bringing me back my dear little Peter out of nowhere. Don't you
remember, when he was a baby, how I used to take him in my lap,
better than any doll, and work his arms and legs to make sure that
he had joints? And he liked it. It was the greatest amusement of his
young life. So it's going to be again now. Erasmus—my husband, you
know—Erasmus and I will limber him up. We'll make him dance and
play croquet and polo and run after the young girls, till he forgets
all about that low company which you say he has been keeping. What
has he really done? Out with it! It wouldn't be fair to Rasmy and me
not to let us know the worst, if we are to look after the child sensibly.
Was it gambling, or drinking or women? All three, perhaps. Some
of these boys are so rapid. . . ."

Nathaniel, in his nervous embarrassment, had no time to frame an
answer to one question before she had rattled on to another. He saw
before him a blooming young matron, dazzling in the multitude of
her gauze flounces, all frilled and edged with lavender satin, her

enormous *chignon*, for which several good chestnut heads of hair and a horse's tail must have furnished the materials, her diamonds and laces, and her bunch of pink roses, nestling in a bosom so thinly veiled, as altogether to eclipse them in tender attraction. Surely this spurious sister of his was a dreadful woman. Could any true lady be so bold and outspoken? She wasn't like the gentlewomen of his family, but rather like some bar-maid out of Dickens, or some wicked Duchess in eighteenth century memoirs. Was he possibly placing his unhappy brother among fast, spendthrift, unprincipled people? Meantime Mrs. Van de Weyer was insisting on an answer. No, he didn't think it had been gambling; he couldn't say it had been drink: he wasn't absolutely sure that it had even been—been anything immoral—but . . .

"Then I see. It's been nothing. He went on some lark in the South End. Of course. How old is he? Eighteen? Just the age to be foolish. Young boys underestimate their powers of being agreeable, and look for some easy conquest among maidservants or country wenches. It's their inexperience. I daresay you can remember when you were like that, only you draw a long face now and try to forget it."

"I?" Nathaniel gasped in astonishment. Caroline had a warm temperament, and she was accustomed to gallantry, real or assumed, among her masculine acquaintance. She didn't suspect that it would have required more heroism for Nathaniel to yield to temptation than ever for St. Anthony to resist it.

"No? Were you always absolutely faithful to your young love for me in those old days? How touching! Even after I had left you and married somebody else? How romantic!"

"My—*my* love for *you*?"

"Of course. You don't mean to say that you didn't know that we were in love with each other? Of course we teased and were both insufferable: that's how children show they are in love when they haven't been brought up nicely. Poor mama was so beautiful that she had to neglect us: all very beautiful women are slaves to their looking-glass. But the occasion for you and me was irresistible. No girl of thirteen could possibly have missed it. Two children, utter strangers, becoming suddenly brother and sister in the same house. How prevent an embarrassing passion from springing up? Especially when the hopeless, romantic, illicit attachment could so easily end happily, since after all we were no relations whatever! Nathaniel, why didn't we have our own way and make a match of it? Why didn't we? I'm sure it would have been much better for *you*. As for me, we mustn't say it would have been better, because of poor dear Rasmy, who makes such a good husband. Yet who knows?"

Nathaniel, slowly deciding that it was all a joke, a very bad joke, tried to smile a little, and changed the subject. Being one of Peter's trustees, he wished to ask what allowance she thought Peter ought to receive while under her care.

"How much has he got?"

Nathaniel never could bring himself to mention, and even tried to forget, the total value of his fortune or that of his brother. It would have sounded so large, and yet, as they made use of it, nothing could have been more moderate and simply decent. "Really," he said, "I don't dare trust my memory of the figures, but if all goes well he will some day have a good income, a handsome income. That is not the question now. With his school or college expenses paid, how much should we allow him for clothes, travelling, and charity? Would ten dollars a month be too much?"

"Ten dollars! That's not enough for his washing. I'll ask Erasmus, and we'll let you know. But he must have enough to be well dressed. I don't allow shabby clothes in my house. No: don't become self-conscious and look at your old black suit. It's not shabby, only old-fashioned: in fact rather distinguished. I tell Rasmy his clothes always look too new, as if he hadn't got used to them. You have better taste in old Boston. Only"—and she leaned over confidentially towards his corner of the sofa—"you might have a fresh pair of gloves. Wash-gloves, soft chamois, are better in summer, cooler, looser, cleaner, better for the health, *and*"—she added in a stage whisper, coming so close to his ear that her scented curls tickled his cheek—"*and cheaper*."

He rose and extended a horizontal hand.

"Now, dear Nathaniel, you must come to see us often, especially when Peter is here. To lunch every Sunday, if you will. Let's call it that."

"I thank you, indeed; you are most kind; but my health is delicate, and I never go out to meals. And when Peter is with you, I think it would be wiser for me not to come at all. One can hardly bear to speak of such things, but you know what has happened: the dark shadow that hangs over the recent past, for me and even for him, though at his age such trials are lighter. Our family life has become sombre. With you Peter will start afresh. Let us hope the end may be happy. In any case, for the present, I'm sure his surroundings will be most agreeable, and I should be sorry to cloud them with an incongruous presence."

Mrs. Van de Weyer said good-bye to her step-brother without rising from the sofa, and without again offering to kiss him.

V

For two years—at Exeter, at Harvard, during his holidays at his fashionable sister's, shyly but observantly, playing with her young children, and being humorously civil to her guests—Peter decidedly bloomed. He didn't study very much; a little, with his intelligence, was more than sufficient for the tasks assigned; but he acted in the school theatricals, wrote for the School or the College paper, became the wit of his class, and even played a little base-ball. His languid figure grew somewhat better knit, and his rather pale countenance and irregular features assumed a pleasing expression. To his surprise and positive incredulity, everybody seemed to like him. He in his turn began to cherish certain affections; not so much for people— with all people he was vaguely tolerant and amused—as for books and certain aspects of nature. He went for solitary walks; he read the minor English poets, Thackeray, Montaigne, *Don Quixote*. In his Freshman year he drifted into the company of those precocious rakes who frequented the front row at musical comedies, and the stage door; but he took these pleasures sadly, and in his tipsy moments would call a friend aside to observe that his only real desire was to fade into the midnight with no pain, and that now more than ever seemed it rich to die. Yet on the morrow, looking perhaps a little thin and sallow, he would escape into the country, go canoeing on some sluggish river or deserted pond, and feel that in his heart he was a second Thoreau. So he might have drifted, sentimental and futile until youth was gone, had not a tragic incident befallen.

There was a Secret Society at Harvard to which everybody of consequence belonged; the rites of initiation were prolonged and terrifying, and often included some prank to be performed in public or at the public expense. When Peter was "running"—for the neophytes were forbidden to walk—he was commanded to break one night into the Chapel and purloin the College Bible. The pulpit, where the sacred volume rested on a red velvet cushion, was perched at a great height, and approached by two steep flights of steps with brass railings. In the dark, Peter had felt his way to the summit, and already held the ponderous tome in both hands, when sudden calls from his friends and tormentors posted outside warned him of danger. He listened for a moment: they seemed to be dispersing at full speed; he was being abandoned: should he leave the Bible and try to slip out, or should he carry it away to be hidden in the basement according to plan? At that moment he felt a rough hand seizing him, and instinctively, like a staunch Israelite, he brought down the whole weight of the Holy Scriptures upon his adversary's head. The hand let go; there was some movement, a heavy thud muffled by the carpeted stairs, and then silence. Peter put the book back on its cushion, felt his way unmolested down the steps on the other side, and climbed out of the open window through which he had entered. Outside, in the rarefied wintry night, the coast seemed clear; and he went home to bed.

The next few days were full of summonses, interviews, and secret negotiations. Mr. Nathaniel Alden was again compelled to confer with Mr. Head, Dr. Hand and the Rev. Mr. Hart. Even Mr. Erasmus Van de Weyer appeared on the scene, having actually made the journey from New York to Boston in order to advise Peter, and to exert a friendly influence in the inner circles; for he too was a Harvard man and had belonged to that Secret Society. So, very fortunately, had the local magistrate. The upshot was that at the inquest the night watchman, who was not a member of the town police, was declared to have met death by misadventure. In the opinion of the medical examiners it could not have been a blow on the head given with a soft flat instrument such as a book, that could really have been fatal, but rather an accidental fall against the sharp edge of the brass railings, which had dislocated the vertebral column at the neck. No evidence was available against Peter except his own confession, attenuated as much as possible by the lawyers: of course honour forbade the members of the Society to remember who had received the order to enter the Chapel, or who had given it. The public part of the initiation was suppressed for a year or two: a fund was provided for the widow, and anonymously bestowed; and since many a false or true rumour was current concerning the event, it was thought best that Peter should temporarily disappear, not only from the College but from the country. A tutor was found to take him abroad, and in the first Cunarder that sailed from East Boston, the modest *Samaria* of 3,000 tons, the crestfallen young man, feeling

himself a criminal, slipped away unnoticed and began his long wanderings.

A few months later he reached the age of twenty-one, and came
into his money. Wealth didn't ruin him. The only charm of money
for him was liberty; he hated worse than poverty all the constraints
to which your conventional rich man was subjected: pompous business, pompous society, pompous speeches, and a gold watch-chain
heavily festooning a big paunch. Peter's impulse was to ramble, to
observe, to follow up, not too hopefully, little casual adventures and
acquaintances. But how justify such a life of idleness? His liberty
dragged the lengthening chain of a bad conscience. In vain he alleged
to himself that his health was frail, and rather cultivated frailness. In
vain he made some attempt to serve the sacred cause of science as
an explorer or a collector. He could explore only what others had
discovered, and collect what they had thrown away. His modesty
disinclined him to that voluminous nullity which fills so many books
of travel: yet the side-lights of any undertaking interested him more
than its alleged purpose. He vegetated, physically lazy and mentally
restless; grew stale while still half-baked; heard something of everything and learned nothing well. It was universally agreed among his
Boston friends, whenever they still mentioned him, that he had
turned out badly. Only one circumstance preserved him from complete condemnation: his life in remote parts and even his most ambitious journeys absorbed only a fraction of his income. He was
growing richer and richer; and his brother Nathaniel, beneath the
dead silence which separated them, couldn't help warming a little
towards him on that score. Even the idle rich, if they saved money,
were useful members of society. They were the camel's hump in the
body politic: their function was to repair the waste of a spendthrift
democracy. This public utility might even, in time, restore the truant
to his self-respect; and the most wind-blown character might ultimately reach port if only it had a golden ballast.

Sometimes, at table, on a day when a favourite dish or a rise in
stocks or a crushing defeat of the Democratic party had brought a
glow of suppressed satisfaction into Nathaniel's face, Cousin Hannah
would venture timidly on the dangerous subject, and perhaps she
would say: "This week I have had a letter from Peter. He is in Japan."
And then, if a loud "Hmph" of pretended indifference, ill concealing
a natural curiosity, encouraged her to go on, she would report how
enchantingly childlike and exquisitely sufficient everything seemed

to him in that country; how he had taken a house all made of paper, with little servants who waited on him with the most picturesque ceremony at the lowest imaginable wages; how he slowly boiled himself in his bath, out of doors, during half the day, and spent the other half taking painting lessons or picking up curios in the shops; and how—but here Cousin Hannah would drop her voice, hesitate, and blush a little—how he had married, temporarily married, a little Japanese lady, with her parents' approval.

"Hmph," Nathaniel would mutter again. "Unprincipled people never remember that it's not only on themselves that they bring trouble. Suppose there was a child to this marriage—a coloured child. Could Peter decently abandon it? Could we decently recognise it? And what sort of place could the spurious brat ever find for himself in the world? How often have you heard me warn Peter, when he was a small boy, that crooked ways are always longer than straight ways, and that wanderings, physically, morally, and etymologically, are *errors*? He may now think it a fine thing to be a planet; but a planet never shines by its own light; and it's very little light, and very pale, that it can ever reflect."

"And yet Venus, Cousin Nathaniel—isn't Venus the evening star?— is so beautiful!"

"Hmph," he repeated, "no metaphor goes on all fours. *Peter* was never beautiful, and you'll see what he looks like—a wreck—when he comes home."

Six months would pass, or a year, and Cousin Hannah would seize another favourable moment to say quietly, "There is fresh news from Peter. He has left Japan: his mock marriage is safely dissolved, his little wife and her family showering blessings and multiplying kow-tows on him at his departure. He is in China: has chartered a junk in which to sail up those great rivers far into the interior, while living all the time, so to speak, in his own house. He is seriously studying the language, which he says is not so very difficult if you approach it in the right way, without our prejudices: and he underlines that this time he has *no wife* but only native men-servants."

"They have told me at the office that he's in China; also that he has been drawing out unusually large sums of money. I suppose it was to pay for those kow-tows and for that junk. Let us hope he won't be wrecked in it, or robbed, or—or worse."

Cousin Hannah knew the fatal word he had in mind, now doubly tabooed in that household, and hastened to change the subject to

something pleasant and unimportant. "He writes also that he is collecting ivory carvings, the best of which he means to bring home for
the Museum of Fine Arts. Such things are expensive."

"Undoubtedly he will be paying many times what they are worth.
I know what it is to buy works of art. It would be safer to ask *Doll &
Richards* to send out an expert to buy them for him."

"But, Cousin Nathaniel, think of the pleasure of choosing them
himself! Very likely by this time he too is an expert, and with more
taste than a dealer."

"I daresay. But they'll cheat him."

The news which poor Cousin Hannah had to repeat was not always
pleasant. Expurgate it as she might, she couldn't conceal the fact that
Peter was often ill: now fever, now dysentery, often simply restlessness, tedium, melancholia. He had left China for India, and visited
the native court where his old friend of the Backward Lads' Camp
was now Maharajah: but there the gramophone, the cinema, and the
new-art furniture from Tottenham Court Road somewhat dashed his
dream of Oriental loveliness. Moreover, the heat was deadly, the food
indigestible, and only the religion—Mohammedan—appealing. In
search of a dry climate, the simple life, and Islam in all its purity, he
had passed over to Arabia: was living at Muscat—said to be the hottest
place in the world—in an upper chamber in a great brick tower: was
learning Arabic, was being instructed in the true faith, and riding at
dawn or sunset over the limitless sands, or skimming in a pink-sailed
dhow over the dancing waves of the Gulf of Oman.

But all was in vain. That very tedium, that hunger for something
less disconsolate, which had driven him to such places drove him
away from them. Every country no doubt had its charm, its rightness,
its friendliness to the native mind; yet everywhere the natives suffered and grumbled, everywhere the ruling system was hated and
threatened, while everywhere the solitary foreigner was suspect, inferior, useless, and ridiculous. The East had really little to teach us
which we could profit by learning, and we had nothing good to teach
the East, except indeed hygiene. All the rest which in fact we were
teaching, or attempting to contaminate them with—our industry,
politics, religion, or philosophy—besides being grotesque for them
and unnecessary, was all infected among us at its source, and thoroughly rotten before we exported it. Their own curious tenets and
practices, after the romance of novelty had worn off, he found unspeakably tiresome and foolish, except one only, which rendered all

further religion and philosophy superfluous: namely that there is no power save Unsearchable Power, and that what will be will be. Melancholy gained on him from day to day: any relief to be found in travel or drink or drugs only intensified the gloom and the hopelessness of the next attack. He might as well return home. It was useless for the leopard, or for the piebald cat, to dream of changing his spots, or to prowl elsewhere than in its home jungle. At least the hospitals and insane asylums in America were the best in the world. He would go home and study medicine. But the climate, the voices, the rush, the hypocrisy, would he now be able to stand all that? His courage gave out; he started, but stopped half way. Wasn't Europe "home" relatively? Wasn't the Mediterranean the "home" of our civilisation? And in the next years, if the reports which Cousin Hannah made to Mr. Alden over his beef-steak and boiled potatoes had less romantic interest, there ran through them a certain hopeful trepidation. Slowly, fatally, the truant was coming homewards, the culprit was preparing to reform.

"I have splendid news from Peter," she said one day, "he is settled at Vienna, and studying medicine. He finds it all so interesting, so absorbing, so *gemütlich*! He is going to make a speciality of mental diseases. Think how useful that will be for him when he comes home."

"Eh?" Nathaniel replied, smoothing his thin hair which was now fading from sandy to greenish white. "He will have some difficulty in beating our own alienists. I have just been reading a new book by Dr. Bumstead, Head of the Great Falls Asylum. It is a store-house of profound knowledge. We sane people little know what astounding depths would appear in us if we allowed ourselves to go mad."

"Not really?"

"Yes. *Evil* depths."

"Then," Cousin Hannah gasped, chilled in her enthusiasm, "let us hope Peter will turn to some other branch of medicine. There is such a crying need, for instance, of investigating cancer."

"I am afraid cancer is an evil too."

"But *so differently!*" And the good lady put off further communications about Peter until a more auspicious occasion. Indeed, what further news she received was seldom cheering. There were long silences, when Peter had been ill, or resting torpidly in his yacht in some remote corner of the Mediterranean. Once he wrote: "I am at Nauplia. Near by are the ruins of Tiryns and Mycenae; a castle overhangs the port where was the ancient acropolis; and round the point is Epidaurus, with a steep cockpit of an ancient theatre, between the mountains and the purple sea. How forlorn is all that greatness! How squalid what remains! The sturdy fishing-boats, streaked with blue paint and daubed with ikons, creak against the stone pier; probably not unlike the ships of Homer, even if not wholly 'black.' They may even be called 'swift,' because when you sail in them with a fair breeze, the waves rush by the side with a hurrying music; and swiftness is not a question of miles an hour to a poet, but of quick gain and quick loss. Above all it is this sense of being borne along resistlessly, but insecurely, through a multitude of ephemeral scenes, none very new, some beautiful, many distressing, and all irrevocable."

A year or two would elapse, and he might write from Paris: "Am sitting here by an insufficient wood fire, that is always dying down. I am making vain efforts to forget whether I am cold or not, and to fix my thoughts on the big book before me, and on the sesquipedalian medical terms which adorn it. I long for my boat *Calypso* and the sunshine of the south. Living in houses with a spying concierge and two talkative families on each of the six storeys is distracting to me after the seclusion and discipline of a ship, and the breadth of the desert. Excellent as Charcot's lectures are on insanity, his spirit and outlook are foreign. It is curious natural history to him, not souls undone. I am getting too old to accustom myself to new moral climates. It would be a pity, too, after pottering for so many years over medicine and psychology, to let my studies drop without having an official stamp set upon them, so that at least I may prescribe quinine for my own fevers without committing a felony. Yes, this time I'm really coming home. Don't be alarmed. I shan't invade you in Beacon Street. Doesn't Mr. Morgan in New York live in his yacht moored off the Battery? So I mean to lie at anchor off South Boston or Nahant, and by assiduous attendance to duty, persuade the Harvard Medical School to make me a doctor."

Thus at last, as the rolling ball at a gambling-table runs at first briskly round the outer rim of the fenced circle, and gradually reduces its speed and its courage, until after one or two false rests, it settles definitely into the predestined concavity, so the erring Peter reverted irresolutely to his native shores, turned up his coat collar against the freezing east wind, frequented autopsies and corridors strongly smelling of disinfectants, dined on off nights at the Tavern Club with two musicians, a poet, and some occasional foreigner, and at the belated age of thirty-five received from his old Alma Mater, as

it were *sub rosa*, a higher but imperfect degree, which enabled him
to appear in the Harvard Catalogue and in the Boston Blue Book as
Peter Alden, M.D. He was rehabilitated, re-christened, almost forgiven; but he didn't feel at home.

He never practised medicine, only put to the proof that misleading
adage: Physician, heal thyself. Without being exactly hypochondriacal
or imagining symptoms of strange diseases from which he was happily free, he aggravated his real weaknesses by continually dwelling
on them. He dosed himself cautiously, but indulgently, drank a good
deal, and dismissed, one after another, various sorts of food as dangerous. He even experimented on his own person with certain poisons and antidotes, infections and antitoxins, half in mild scientific
earnest, half in an idle craving for some new sensation, some enormous dream, which he might laugh at the more sarcastically afterwards, the more overwhelmingly real and enlightening the vision had
seemed. He cared little for his life: if things ever went seriously
wrong, he could always put an end to it. Meantime, so long as he was
tolerably comfortable, a certain amused curiosity kept him studying
the world and his own carcase. He picked up a few old acquaintances
and even made a few new ones; sailed to Florida or the Bahamas in
winter, to Mt. Desert or the Saint Lawrence in summer. The Atlantic
Yacht Club elected him a member, and he ceased to be black-balled
at the Somerset Club. His brother Nathaniel, who of course belonged
and lived almost next door, luckily never went there. Peter instinctively avoided passing in front of his father's house. He would turn
by preference into Mt. Vernon Street, because—as a kind female
relation interpreted his action, when one day she found him there
standing almost still and looking about him—because that upper part
of Mt. Vernon Street (said she) was so pleasant and distinguished,
with its great elms and its deep gardenlike grass plots before the
quiet sunny old houses; and a pensive and travelled person like Dr.
Alden couldn't help loving that spot, and walking more slowly when
he passed through it. Yet it was not in fact the trees or the grass plots
that had preoccupied him, but rather this very trick of his in avoiding
Beacon Street and making aimlessly this particular circuit. Was he
morbid? Was he neurasthenic? Was he abnormal? Were there twisted
nerve-fibres and criss-cross sensory-motor arcs in his brain, that
caused him to act like a fool and to feel like a child, and might any
day turn him into an idiot? Hadn't he better consult a specialist, and
protect himself from himself before it was too late?

VI

"Yes," said Dr. Bumstead to his daughter, on an evening when anxious talk had kept them up for a full hour beyond their customary bed-time, "that's how matters stand. Luckily both the boys are doing well; they can almost support themselves on scholarships and odd jobs; yet at a pinch it would be cruel to refuse them a little assistance. There are not many people in Great Falls, Connecticut, who can afford to consult a specialist in their mental troubles. Days and weeks pass without anybody calling at my office. This one private patient from Boston—a millionaire—has been a godsend. For his own good (I say it in all conscience) the treatment should continue. And now that summer is over he oughtn't to go on living in his yacht at New London. It's bleak and lonely, riding at anchor in that broad river, swept by cold winds and rain; and the trip up here twice a week in an open launch involves too much exposure. Besides there are psychological reasons. As a physician, I must dissuade him from staying always on board his own boat, isolated and surrounded only by men, and men who are his dependents. It's one thing to go sailing amid all the variety and excitements of a rough voyage: it's quite another to lie idle and moping in port, without change of scene and without society. Such a life favours regrettable inclinations and morbid thoughts. Once Dr. Alden comes to live with us, I shall be able to treat him daily, watch all his habits, and exert a much more efficacious influence for good. He will be able to take long walks— the best form of exercise for a man of his age with his thoughtful temperament. We have those two lovely wood roads, round the Asylum grounds and over Cemetery Hill. Good heavens: to think that not so many years ago, in my father's time, all that land was ours! And now I've had to sell even our own frontage on Bumstead Avenue. What else can we do? The new edition of my book has had a good press, but the sale is disappointing.—You needn't call him a boarder, except in the census returns. He will be a paying guest, a friend, a colleague, an invalid needing quiet and care; all the more as his residence here won't be permanent—renewed often, I hope, but intermittent. These eccentric private patients require a light hand. They're not like your common run of crazy old dolts huddled in the wards. If you pull such a knowing man up sharp—himself a doctor—he bolts; and it would be a sad thing if Dr. Alden bolted. I must urge him to go this winter on his usual cruise to the West Indies. Then in the spring he will be all the more willing to return to us, feeling that he isn't going to be hoodwinked or confined or hypnotised into giving up his favourite pleasures. Confidence is essential: we can't do anything in such ticklish cases without confidence. You'll see, he is very modest, unassuming, considerate; not forward to criticise anybody; used to all sorts of food and all degrees of discomfort; yet quite familiar also with the best of everything, and withering you with the most merciless underhand sarcasm, if you dare to conceive that your way of thinking or living is better than his. That's the difficulty in curing him. He doesn't love what we call health. He scorns it. . . ."

The next Spring was singularly balmy. Crocuses and snowball blossoms were out in April. New sap seemed to be mounting also into Dr. Bumstead's powerful but battered frame: his affairs seemed less benumbed; in May Peter Alden had returned and established himself in the family: and in September matters had gone so swimmingly that Dr. Bumstead could say to his daughter:

"Look here, Harriet. An idea has occurred to me. It may startle you; but why shouldn't you *marry Dr. Alden?*"

"That idea doesn't startle me at all."

"What? You'd thought of it yourself? The plan doesn't displease you?"

"Why should it displease me? Did you think I was dying to marry some long-haired musician or vulgar commercial traveller? At least Dr. Alden is a gentleman."

"Very much, very much of a gentleman. He's a bit rickety in body and mind; there have been times when he has drunk too much, and indulged in a little cocaine or opium or both; but he's *not* to be regarded as a reformed dipsomaniac or victim of the drug-habit. It has been simply a little deliberate weakness in prescribing for himself what was most agreeable at the moment, without caring for the remoter consequences. He recognises this himself: and his health could be rendered excellent by a regular regimen and by home life.

He's still youngish, hardly forty. A good-looking, strapping young woman like you would be the saving of him."

"You mustn't think that I haven't observed him for myself," Harriet answered. "He is a man of refined temperament who has been unfortunate in his associations, and who under better influences could retrieve himself. A family life is the only healthy one for any of us, as Dr. Alden would have done well, for his own good, to have remembered earlier. My own fault, perhaps, has been to be too much absorbed in the care of others and to forget my own future, when I might remain alone in the world and homeless in my own home. In the end too much sacrifice of oneself empoverishes the character, and diminishes one's power of service. I have no doubt that both Dr. Alden's life and mine would be fuller and richer if we were united. Duty seems to point that way."

"Capital, capital," her father cried. "I'm delighted that you take that sound view of the matter. I will drop a hint to him, and I'm confident that he will end by recognising how much such a solution is in his own interests. But there is one point—a delicate point—that we ought to be clear about before we proceed any further. Dr. Alden—of course partly in fun—often says that he is a woman-hater. His experiences with the fair sex—and he has had them in plenty—have not always been fortunate. He's a little *blasé*. Besides, he has lived so much apart from women, that he is more at home in men's society, and prefers it. A club man, a confirmed old bachelor, and one physically in any case not very vigorous, not very enthusiastic. You, on the other hand, are naturally full blooded; and when it comes to married life, I ask myself whether you would be well matched; whether, to be frank, he could satisfy you."

"Father," Harriet cried, red with indignation, "how *can* you, how *can* you say such a thing? Do you take me for a nymphomaniac? If Dr. Alden prefers the society of men, it's probably because he hasn't ever met any *decent* women. I don't blame him: how *could* he find them in those outlandish places where he has always been travelling? And besides, I can return the compliment. As far as society is concerned and affection and true personal spiritual love, I infinitely prefer my own sex. Who could be dearer and nobler and sweeter and more intelligent than Letitia Lamb? With whom could I ever have a closer union of heart and mind, and one more lasting, and superior to all accidents or moods or conflicts of interest? Only, for family life, such personal friendship and intellectual love are not sufficient. There must be children. But if there are children, do you suppose any woman who respects herself would demand a—a—a useless assiduity in her husband, as if she had married him for pleasure? It's an insult to me and to every good woman."

"All right, all right," Dr. Bumstead said, shrugging his shoulders, and wondering if the course so grandly charted would prove navigable without accident. "I spoke only to make sure. If you are going ahead, I wanted you to go ahead with your eyes open."

"So that's what they're after," Peter Alden said to himself not many days later, after his host and medical adviser had popped the question in the simple words: 'Why shouldn't you marry Harriet?' "The scheme, I must say, is the old man's rather than his daughter's. Harriet hasn't much initiative: which in my view is one of her good points. She merely avails herself of the circumstances; keeps her balance like a stout ship steady on her keel. She would be a fool not to profit by this occasion. And I should be a fool too, if I ran away out of pique, just because they are planning to catch me, when to be caught is perhaps to my own advantage. I have sought everywhere for the kind of life that might really please me: I haven't found it; it doesn't exist; and I might as well accept anything decent that presents itself. If I didn't marry this young woman, probably some day, in a moment of weakness, I should marry another, older, uglier, and less respectable. I don't need women at all sentimentally, to pet and to be petted, and socially they bore me to death; but physically and by a sort of reviving boyish curiosity, I still sometimes fall a prey to them; and I try to make a joke of what is hardly a pleasure. Arrested at adolescence, they call it nowadays; or an old head on young shoulders, as people used to say. Some day, if a fair female—my landlady, perhaps, or my laundress—burst into tears, clung to me as to her saviour, declared that she was about to become a mother, or that without me she would die or starve—I should very likely find myself drying her tears, and leading her to the registry office. Such a marriage might be sordid, but it wouldn't be troublesome; less of a burden for a man of my sort than to set up housekeeping with one of Caroline's lovely young creatures, or with one of my Boston relations, who would require me to preside with her over two great establishments at least, with punctual engagements for every hour of the day and every day of the year, dinners and theatres and concerts and guests and garden-parties and—worst of all—yachting as the gay world understands yachting; or else for a change to be lugged from one European Palace Hotel to another, that she might make a nuisance of herself everywhere and a fool of me. And if, thinking to avoid that predicament, I married a woman of the soulful sympathetic kind, professorial, emancipated, or religious, who would think herself superior to women of the world but in fact would be desperately inferior—then, with her pretensions to understanding and forgiving and directing me, she would drive me mad. I shouldn't be suffered to draw a breath save in subjection and hypocrisy, and no refuge would be left to me but suicide. No: Harriet at least is a happy mean; a point of indifference, a point of rest. I don't ask to be happy; I want to be at peace. If I must let some Juggernaut car crush my bones, let it be the old homely steam-roller of traditional Puritanism. From earliest childhood I know its crunching sound. Conformity to it is easier, and the necessary lies come almost of themselves to the lips. Indeed, lying in this case is rarely necessary, since silence may be plausibly taken for consent. Perhaps I could never be altogether at home with a wife who didn't remind me a little of good Cousin Hannah and of Brother Nathaniel. Harriet is so completely immersed in her local existence, that she hardly knows there are, or ever have been, any other standards; her proud ignorance of history and of the world keeps her content with her one-horse town, her vaporised religion, and her sham mansion. She will never wish to desert them. Her highest ambition is to be the universally recognised first lady of Great Falls, Connecticut: and with a little money, that ambition will be at once realised.

"And this place suits me: remote enough for troublesome friends not to look me up, and near enough for me to reach anybody that I care to see. I am comfortable in this house. The old man, with his professional apparatus and his professional hypocrisy, will quit, and will leave us alone in it. It can be made to look again rather stately. This false classicism pleases me: it is a touching homage to the impossible. If anybody gave out such architecture for a success, it would be ludicrous; but regarded as an intentional failure, as an act of allegiance to a lost cause, it's honourable enough: an aspiration to nobleness. It marks the modern man's hopeless assumption that he is still a gentleman. These lofty square rooms are still inhabitable: we can conceal the radiators, and keep great logs smouldering in the fire. This hall, intended to be monumental, is really commodious; the fountain and marble statue in the hollow of the staircase are at least not an elevator. We can restore the ground floor in the style of the period, and wallow upstairs higgledy-piggledy among our old duds. I will insist on a Chinese room for myself, and Harriet can arrange all the other rooms as she likes them. In walking up and down these dignified stairs, we shall have time to recompose ourselves for the change of atmosphere, in passing from solitude to society, or *vice versa*; I don't mean from sincerity to pretense but only from the illusions with which each probably cheats himself, to the deceptions with which he probably doesn't deceive other people. Let us endeavour to preserve our genteel traditions for one generation more. If I have a son, I should like him to start from there. God knows where he will end.

"As for Harriet herself, she's a first-rate woman: if I tried to fare better I should fare worse. She is good-looking, in perfect health, thoroughly a lady in her punctilious provincial fashion, reposeful yet a good manager, observant yet never nervous, fussy, or meddlesome. Really, for a sad chap like me, there's nobody better. I can stand her mind, or lack of it, because really it makes no difference to me what a woman thinks. I can hold my tongue. God knows I'm weak enough, but somehow I've escaped a weakness which seems to attach to the strongest characters, in that they can't bear it if anybody is not of their own opinion. She may think anything she likes; I shan't mind; especially as I know very well beforehand the sort of thing it will be. I believe I get the best of this bargain.

"As to actual love, and all that, she's a fine female; a little passive, a little sad; somewhat like a blond athlete past his prime, and grown a bit fat, soft, slack, and sleepy. Will she be too much for me? No: a sleepy Juno has always attracted me more and disgusted me less than your frisky flirtatious pouting young thing, or your elderly vampire. She will be indifferent, or will pretend to be so; that tone, at our time of life, is more becoming for both of us. If we have children they will profit by her strong constitution. Her eye is blank and a little cowlike, but her features are noble, and the mouth pure and firm. She hasn't a sense of humour? What does that matter, when what I need and look for is not companionship but peace—something to decide me, to attach me, to render extravagant impulses impossible? Her queenliness is an asset: battered as I am, though only a few years older than she, I feel as if she were the patron goddess who was to receive the defeated hero, and welcome him home from his wanderings. She has consciously undertaken to heal me, to do the mother in the wife. I have never really known a mother, never enjoyed the voluminous soft protection of a wise woman. Caroline was merry and kind, but at bottom too contemptuous. She hated sick children. A boy, especially, must look after himself. She just laughed at me, pushed me into the water, and told me to swim. I didn't quite drown, for here I am; but I swallowed a lot of salt water. A stricter and more prudent woman, a sort of priestess, might have sent me on my voyage better provided: and my boat needn't so often have capsized. With Harriet and the children at home—if we have children—I shall be more safely ballasted. If I still venture sometimes to spread my sails—and why shouldn't I?—I shan't put to sea like the Flying Dutchman, plying from nowhere to nowhere. I shall hail from a recognised respectable port, being duly registered and legally owned, in a word, married; and all the customary currents and trade-winds of the watery globe will lead me round again here. I'll break up *The Old Junk* with her exotic ornaments, and build a clean new yacht to be called *Hesperus*. *Hesperus*, the poetess of Lesbos says, brings all things home: wine to the lip, the goat to the fold, the child to the mother."

VII

Many a time in later years the rich organ of Harriet's imagination, always softly playing, would change its stops, and from the somewhat shrill key of apology and self-justification would drop into the *basso profondo* of an assured happiness. She would cease rocking her rocking-chair, let the magazine she had been holding fall on her lap, draw the folds of her handsome dressing-gown about her large person, and close her eyes, the more luxuriously to re-live the scene which in all her uneventful existence had remained most vividly and most satisfactorily imprinted on her memory. How often she had rehearsed it, how perfectly she knew it by heart, how completely the kindly conspiracy of forgetfulness here and revision and expansion there, had transformed it into a perfect picture of her masterful good sense, her true kindness, her high principles! Again she saw herself sitting idly by the long west window in the front parlour, where Letitia and she always went to admire the sunset: it was rather lurid that afternoon, and the October blast was driving the red and brown leaves rather rudely over the rough grass—not yet that well-mown and well-watered lawn that it had since become. Letitia would soon be there: she said it was so *bracing* to walk up the long hill after working for two hours in the Public Library: and the sunset hour was such a *sacred* time.

"There she was," Mrs. Alden's lips repeated, inaudibly, "I knew her step—and besides no one else would come in without ringing. 'My dear,' Letitia panted, sinking into her chair, 'what a *heavenly* day: almost wintry. And see what a *beautiful* book, on the English Cathedrals, the superintendent has allowed me to take out, although it's starred. Such *exquisite* engravings!'

"'Put it away,' I said severely, 'and listen to me. We have something *important* to talk about. Dr. Alden has proposed, and we are engaged to be married.'

"'Harriet Bumstead,' she cried, 'you don't mean it?'

"'Yes, Letitia Lamb, I do. It will be for the best.'

"'Ah,' she murmured, 'but a *man*! And how *old* is he?'

"'Not *old* at all, for a man,' I replied impressively, 'and we mustn't forget that we're not in our teens ourselves. Of course, Letty dear, if a man had proposed to *you*, I shouldn't have expected you to accept him. But you're so exceptional: you can't eat bread and butter without a fork. And a husband—well, my dear, I know what you are feeling. Men are necessarily coarser than women, and for *you* to have a man near you, even the gentlest, would be distressing. You have so many resources in yourself, read so many languages, know so much about art, and can feel so deeply about Shelley and Botticelli. Besides you are independent. Remember that I haven't been brought up like you in a young ladies' aviary, flitting about as light and free as a canary bird. One grows fond of one's burdens and home has always been everything to me. For years I have had to keep house for my father, and to look after my young brothers, hearing men's talk, and what's more, doctors' talk from morning till night, about all sorts of ghastly diseases. Doctors are always aware of all those horrible organs which we have inside of us, and they must be ready to touch even the commonest people without a shudder. It hardens, but it prepares for life. And after all the life of a married woman is fuller, it brings one so much closer to others, with so many fresh opportunities of doing good.'

"'Ah,' Letitia said pensively, and apparently more reconciled to the idea, '*wealth* does make everything easier—even, I suppose, marriage.'

"'Yes, my dear. And wealth is such a *power*.'

"'And such a *responsibility*.'

"'Of course, but I fully realise it. And in any case I have a sacred charge committed to me already—this wonderful old house, one of the most beautiful in the world, what would become of it if I don't preserve it? It's fast getting out of repair. The paint and even the wood is peeling off on the weather side of our magnificent front columns. The carpets are faded and threadbare, the furniture shabby. My brothers can't live here, there's nothing for them to do at Great Falls. My father has reached the age-limit and must resign; he can be only consulting physician at the Asylum on half salary. We should have had to sell the rest of the land; the trees would have been cut down, the view shut off, and soon the house itself would have to go, for you know it's mortgaged. What would become of us? Poor father would die of it, and I should have to be a school-teacher and live in a boarding-house.'

"'Don't, Harriet, you hurt me. If the worst came to the worst you could live with *us*. Miss Doe's is *not* a boarding-house. She admits no gentlemen and no strangers; has simply gathered a few old friends into her quiet home.'

"'You know you never set eyes on her before you went there to board.'

"'But Miss Doe had been a school friend of Miss Swan's, and Miss Swan is most intimate with Susie Bird, so that there was nothing Miss Doe and I didn't know about each other. You'd love the place, and we'd love to have you. But, of course, now, it can never be.'

"'Not now: but don't think I'm making the thing up. We have actually had an offer for the house, *nine thousand dollars*, for this historic treasure! And that's not the worst of the insult. Mr. Bangs of Bangs' Hotel wants it for a wayside inn for commercial travellers on Sundays, where liquor might be sold after hours and where, as my father says, fat newly-married couples in buggies, and without baggage, might flock to take rooms on a summer evening! What a tragedy! What a desecration!'

"Poor Letty felt the full horror of it. She can't bear to have the truth told plainly. She fell upon my neck sobbing, and we had a good cry together.

"Being the first to recover I said, 'Letitia, don't let's be weak. It's not going to happen. Dr. Alden even intends to buy back the last lot we had sold, and turn that new brick house into a gardener's cottage and stables; and the whole place is to be fenced in and restored in the original style, which is Revolutionary, because of these big white columns like Washington's Tomb at Mt. Vernon; but Dr. Alden calls it Empire, pronouncing it Ompeer, because he rather likes to be French sometimes; and the summer house is to be rebuilt in real marble, just like the one he says it's copied from.'

"'Rome, Villa Borghese, Temple of Diana,' Letitia murmured almost in a trance, 'how well I know it all! How beautifully it will shine on the very summit of High Bluff, among the pines, even if yours are not *umbrella pines*! How classical, how silvan, how Bacchic! What a pity that you'll hardly be able to enjoy it all. You'll have to live in Boston.'

"'I in Boston? What are you thinking of? If I were willing to live in Boston, aren't there scores of other men I might have married? The providential thing about Dr. Alden is precisely that he must live just here, can't bear to go away from this very house where his health has improved so wonderfully under Father's care, and where everything is as he likes it to be. Boston, indeed! What on earth should I be doing in Boston?'

"'Oh,' Letitia whispered dreamily, gazing hard into the sunset, 'perhaps I hadn't understood. Dr. Alden has so much delicacy of feeling. Perhaps he is only asking to become one of the family in order to live here always as a friend. He means that you're to be like brother and sister. Has he positively declared that he *loves* you? Has he kissed you?'

"'Letitia,' I replied crushingly, 'don't be a fool. What do you know about such matters?' Really, I already pitied her from the bottom of my heart. I had almost been an old maid myself. I could make the comparison without prejudice. I could feel beforehand all that a married woman gains in patience and sweetness and dignity, and above all in knowledge of human nature, so that she needn't all the time be talking nonsense. 'Marriage,' I went on, 'marriage in real life, especially between old friends who are no longer very young, isn't like love making in a cheap novel. Did you expect Dr. Alden and me to be spoony? What if he didn't kiss me, provided he gave me a ring like this?' And I showed her the splendid diamond which I'd purposely turned inwards toward the palm of my hand, so that she shouldn't catch sight of it prematurely.

"'Oh!' she cried, positively speechless with admiration.

"'No, Letty dear, men don't give diamonds like this to their sisters. And they don't set out to spend tens of thousands, perhaps hundreds of thousands of dollars in restoring an old place, just to secure a good housekeeper to look after it—for that's all I should be, if I wasn't really his wife. He hopes we may have children—has actually wondered which room would make the best nursery—and of course I hope so too. Think what that will mean to both of us!'

"I saw tears in poor Letitia's eyes, and I took her hand. 'No, dear, don't think that whatever happens you will be less to me than before. On the contrary. As time goes on, if ever you should feel lonely or poor—and I may very likely feel lonely myself some day in this great house—I shall now be able to ask you to come and live with me: or if that didn't seem best as yet, at least I should be able to help you and comfort you much better than before. And you know you have always a home in my heart.'

"And the poor thing kissed me, and wiped her eyes, and hugged her precious library book under her cloak—for lap-dogs weren't allowed at Miss Doe's—and without saying a word began her trudge home in the twilight. It was so delightfully easy, she always said, going *down hill*: and she loved to feel the first wandering flakes of the winter's snow strike and melt against her hot cheeks. I love Letitia; she's a superior person; but she's hopelessly *soft!*"

Thus triumphantly the scene faded from Mrs. Alden's inner vision. She had once more viewed the perspective of her life as she liked to view it. As she opened her eyes, and ran again mentally over the years that had elapsed since her marriage, she couldn't help congratulating herself afresh on her wisdom. How much her influence for good had increased! The Browning Society having become so large and unmanageable, with the Baptist minister and those positively vulgar new women, she had been able to form a select Shakespeare Society to meet in her own house, and have only really nice lecturers: Dr. Alden, indeed, didn't seem to think Browning a great poet at all. And didn't the house and grounds attract visitors even from abroad to admire them, which never had happened in the old days? And didn't the portraits of four generations of Bumsteads—clergymen, lawyers, merchants and physicians—one of them by Stuart—look down from the dining-room walls, three times each day on little Oliver? What a privilege that was! Such noble surroundings must be a daily inspiration to the boy, even if he seemed for the moment unconscious of it: and she must admit without boasting that her own character had greatly developed, and that she could exert a double moral influence on the boy, to make up for the fact that physically and morally his father was not more vigorous. Not that anyone could call him effeminate—an inveterate yachtsman, they said an excellent sea captain, a doctor looking at everything in the cold light of science; but at the same time so quiet, so silent, so secretly sarcastic. It almost seemed that he had a *debased* side, as if nothing could shock him; his smile was like a surgical instrument, half hidden away, not intended to hurt, but yet terrible. He respected nothing; and if he wasn't gross, it was only because he couldn't be. When he pulled the bow of his evening tie—because he *always* dressed for dinner, even when alone, and there was something uncanny about that, like dressing up for one's own funeral—when he tied that neat bow he would laugh at himself in the glass, thinking, she was sure, of all the filthy savages that he had seen running naked, and all the unspeakable practices of the heathen Chinee—and she believed he positively *liked* those abominations, would enjoy defying all Christian decency, if only it wasn't too much trouble. "He longs to escape from us, from everything, from *me*! Only he is too much of a gentleman to show it, when he is here, except by running away as soon as ever he can. What a blessing, in those first days, that we had the house to talk about. In that first winter in California it was the great bond between us; wherever we went we looked in all the antiquity shops for Ompeer treasures; we picked up a lot of beautiful things. They seemed to me extravagant then, I had been so cramped for money. Now I understand that they were good investments, and that we could sell them to-day for twice the cost."

Money was such a comfort. What would have become of the house without money, or of herself, or of little Oliver? Would the child ever have had the energy to push his way undefended through a hard world? And as for Dr. Alden, but for his money he would now be rolling in the gutter.

This sad fact seemed sometimes to cast a shadow on the little boy and to make him melancholy. Yet how could it? Whatever might be said of Dr. Alden (she always thought of her husband as 'Dr. Alden') at least he never interfered with the child's education. In fact the Doctor was seldom at home, and Oliver knew him only as a sort of Saint Nicholas in plain clothes, or a tame pirate out of the works of his namesake Oliver Optic, who turned up occasionally from parts unknown, brought him beautiful presents, pinched his ear, called him 'Sir,' and asked him quizzical questions to which there was no answer. Evidently no depressing influence could flow upon the boy from that quarter. And as to heredity, wasn't she herself the daughter of a physician, a renowned specialist in nervous and mental diseases, and didn't she know perfectly that according to the latest scientific opinion acquired characters couldn't be inherited? Now if Dr. Alden had regrettable traits, they were all due to his own choosing and doing: his family and his inheritance were unimpeachable. And indeed the boy's faults didn't in the least resemble his father's. Oliver wasn't lazy, nor feebly tolerant, nor provokingly humorous. Fortunately he harked back to his remoter ancestors, and took everything seriously. He gave intense attention, understood at once, and never forgot what he had learned: yet he had an odd way of looking at you sometimes as if to say: "And is that all you have to teach me?" She couldn't conceive what was the matter with the child. His little heart always seemed to be set on something else, which nobody showed him.

In any case, it wasn't *her* fault. She couldn't have been Oliver's only parent, though certainly, if nature could have managed it, that would have been the best arrangement. Nothing would have been wrong with him then. But since he had to have some father, what better father could she have provided for him? None: because until Dr. Alden came to stay as a private patient in their house, there had never been any *man* in Great Falls, Connecticut, that a truly refined and cultivated person could think of marrying. The clergymen all had wives, except that sinister curate at St. Barnabas' who believed in celibacy. The young doctors at the Insane Asylum were poor Jews or Irish, and the travelling lecturers never stayed long enough to take notice. Even Letitia Lamb, who travelled so much abroad, and had actually met both Mr. Bernard Shaw and Mr. Bernard Berenson, had remained single. Of course Mrs. Alden might have done so herself, and been proud to be Miss Harriet Bumstead for better or for worse: but in her it would have been selfish. It was imperative not to let the really good old families die out, especially now that the country was being swamped by inferior races. A Daughter of the American Revolution could not prefer her own comfort to the claims of posterity. Posterity was Oliver: and though he might suffer in some oblique way because of his father's weak health and over-refinement, after all he was *her* son: that marked his true place. And indeed he was a good boy, tall and strong for his age (as *she* had always been) and nice looking, though perhaps a little pale and with grey eyes open very wide that seemed to see nothing. Yet in time—for he had a good mind also—he would realise what rare advantages, what splendid opportunities, he enjoyed, and how happy he ought to be. Even on his father's side there was much that was favourable. If the Aldens in recent times had been less pleasantly distinguished than the Bumsteads—with her father's work on Psychiatry world-famous, and so much *sounder* and more *decent* than Krafft-Ebing's—yet the Aldens had genuinely come over in the *Mayflower*, and Oliver had the inexpressible privilege of being descended from those famous Pilgrims, Priscilla and John Alden, immortalised by Longfellow in his household classic *The Courtship of Miles Standish*.

Such were the reflections which often passed through Mrs. Alden's mind as she reclined after lunch in her room, and rested from having done nothing all the morning. Merely to exist and to possess an exacting body that must be washed and clothed and fed with anxious attention is an exhausting occupation enough for a lady in middle life: and Mrs. Alden's happiest days were those on which she had no engagements and could devote her leisure to judicious self-congratulation on her past actions and her present position. In a qualified way she might then congratulate herself also on her young son, and even on her husband. But why couldn't her satisfaction in the latter ever be complete, and why must her reflections always end by confessing that Oliver had been rather unfortunate in his father?

PART II

BOYHOOD

I

The child had been born punctually. This first grave and alarming duty of entering into the world was performed not only unflinchingly but with a flourish: for this thoroughly satisfactory child was a boy. His little organism, long before birth, had put aside the soft and drowsy temptation to be a female. It would have been so simple for the last pair of chromosomes to have doubled up like the rest, and turned out every cell in the future body complete, well-balanced, serene, and feminine. Instead, one intrepid particle decided to live alone, unmated, unsatisfied, restless, and masculine; and it imposed this unstable romantic equilibrium on every atom of the man-child's flesh, and of the man-child's sinews. To be a male means to have chosen the more arduous, though perhaps the less painful adventure, more remote from home, less deeply rooted in one soil and one morality. It means to be pledged to a certain courage, to a certain recklessness about the future: and if these risks are to be run without disaster, there should be also a greater buoyancy, less sensitiveness, less capacity for utter misery than women commonly show. Yet this compensation is sometimes lacking. Mysterious influences may cross and pervade the system, and send through it, as it were, a nostalgia for femininity, for that placid, motherly, comfortable fulness of life proper to the generous female.

Had the unborn Oliver decided to be a girl, he—or rather she—could hardly have been blamed. Such a result would have been equally involuntary, equally normal, equally useful; yet somehow it would have been disappointing. Our admirably gentle and admirably stern Oliver Alden, always choosing the darker and the ruder duty, would have missed existence. Or he would have begun—and how wrong that would have been!—by cheating his mother's hopes. Because while Mrs. Alden always declared that women were intellectually the equals of men and morally their superiors, yet she would have felt that a little girl was only a second-best baby: and how ill that would have gone with her settled determination that everything in her new life—except perhaps her husband—should be absolutely first rate! No: Providence was rewarding her for aiming high.

The child was a fine boy, full weight, perfectly formed, fair-skinned with large grey eyes, and a little fuzz of limp, yellow hair. At the first contact with freedom he wagged his arms and legs about vigorously, experimentally, silently: he seemed ready for everything, anxious for nothing, willing to wait and see. Philosophy possessed the soul of this child from his first breath: inarticulately, of course, as it was destined, at bottom, to remain always; because the words which his education supplied were not capable of uttering it truly. But in action, in determination, and by a sort of inner blind fortitude, his faith was distinctly in him from the beginning. There were good things and there were bad things, and there was an equal duty to pull through both and come out somehow on the further side of all trouble. At least, so I venture to put it into words for him, words which wouldn't have satisfied him; but at this first moment of his existence I may presume to understand him better than he understood himself.

The wisdom of these dumb principles was at once confirmed by the ministrations of doctors, nurses, parents, and officious friends. They all helped him to attain good and avoid evil and to endure beyond, in a slumber full of seething possibilities. The gentle Letitia Lamb was one of the first to take him in her arms, admire his completeness, and sigh a little at the tender, the tragic mystery of life. An experienced nurse, almost a lady-doctor, at once took him in charge. An old iron-handed eight-day clock in a white apron and cap could not have been more punctual. The bath, the bottle, the change of linen, the way of being vigorously tucked into his cot, or strapped into his perambulator, seemed to have been decreed by the Medes and Persians. Experience, duty, and science left little to chance. And life, at least physical life, in the model infant responded perfectly to each appointed stimulus. It was seldom necessary to cry; it was never appropriate to laugh.

His education, in spite of such excellent diligent masters, was carried on exclusively by himself. It consisted in learning the places of goods and evils, and the way they followed one another. That wagging of arms and legs, together with the habit of staring and following the light with his eyes, proved to be very useful for this ethical purpose. Goods and evils turned out to be arranged in a circle or sphere, in what Nurse called his skin, or a little under this, in what she called his tummy; but there were some goods and evils that escaped beyond or came from beyond, such as the bottle when it was not yet or no longer in his mouth; and these potential goods and evils, which Nurse called things, extended very far and had a tremendously complicated life of their own, which Oliver himself afterwards called the world. Even that was not all: for deeper down and higher up than his tummy, there were a lot of other goods and evils, not traceable by the eye, nor possible to run after and take hold of with the hand, when they showed a tendency to run away: and these were himself, his mind, or soul. The mind was the most entertaining and satisfactory region of all in which to keep your goods and evils: nobody else could get at them: and provided the evils were not too violent, like being carried away from what you wanted to do to what you didn't want to do, it was most amusing to have that private world of your own, and talk to yourself about it.

Every day accentuated the difference between himself and what happened to him. Living, real, and self-justified was only his own will, the inner spring of his being, the centre and judge of all that unaccountably went on. The world might sometimes seem obsequious and willing to be commanded: but presently it became tiresome, did what it shouldn't do, and showed itself to be cruelly alien, besetting, and unavoidable. This inexplicable wrongness in the world extended inwards sometimes into his own person, when his hands and feet wouldn't do things properly, or he choked or sneezed; all such interference of himself with himself was most ignominious and discouraging. Yes, and something even worse could happen. Fatality, or alien accident, could invade that secret self of his which nobody else could see, and where at least he ought to have been able to play as he chose. But no: things would sometimes go wrong or run thin even there. The interest would die out, the pictures would fade or become ugly and frightening, and you couldn't stop the silly old words repeating and repeating themselves.

These were private hidden troubles, not frequent or serious: they could be dismissed when you were really awake and doing anything important, such as filling your pail with gravel. Little Oliver escaped almost all the ills of childhood: he was never really hungry or furious, never very ill or much hurt. But when he was hurt at all, he was deeply injured, because his feelings were hurt also. He *ought not* to have been hurt: why then, was he? Even when he grew old enough to understand that sometimes it was his own fault and sometimes other people's and sometimes nobody's fault, but just chance, he was far from reconciled to any of these sources of evil: and he stored up his resentment or his discouragement. Even when things went well, he couldn't be really joyful. They had gone wrong so often, they would probably go wrong again soon. Why make such a show of gladness? All explanations and apologies, all invitations to see how pretty things were, and what fun it would be to play at this or that— though he listened quietly and looked attentively and played as he was told—left quite undiminished and unreconciled the deep displeasure that had sunk into his little heart. It was a proud displeasure, firmly condemning and rejecting everything that was wrong: but though almost everything might be wrong, the inner oracle that condemned and rejected was sure of being itself right, and was not in the least dismayed. Round this coral island, just risen above the sea but invisibly planted on the rock-bottom, the strongest waves were compelled to break: and not only could this young microcosm turn them into a fringe of foam following its own contours, but it could surround itself, within that outer reef, with a belt of calm ancillary lagoons, round which the surf of persistent circumstance might pound all day quite harmlessly, and be muffled by distance when, prophetically, it sounded through the impenetrable night.

Miss Tirkettle—such was the nurse's name—was admirably fitted to look after the baby before he could walk or talk, the first of which he did long before the second: action for him was the simpler, the quicker way of escaping and finding new ground. Yet even action had its difficulties. The first and most serious in his case was to find something to do. There were no other children to play with. The nearest neighbours were not friends of Mrs. Alden's, and their children would not have been well-behaved or well-spoken, and probably rough and dirty. There was Fuzzy-Wuzzy, the gardener's dog: it was Letitia Lamb that had given him that nice name—and nevertheless Fuzzy-Wuzzy would always be running away after the more exciting society of other dogs: because, as Mrs. Alden explained, Letitia Lamb was poor, and though she might give a dog a nice name she couldn't give him any biscuits. Why shouldn't Nurse, then, who evidently wasn't poor, as she always had biscuits in her cupboard, give Fuzzy-Wuzzy a few, so that he might play with Oliver? Because, Mrs. Alden replied (changing, as she often did, the ground of her argument), it was very bad indeed for dogs to have anything between meals. Fuzzy-Wuzzy, however, as far as Oliver could see, never had any square meals, but only bones and rats and rubbish that he could pick up in the stable-yard: and if you never had any meals why should it be so bad for you to have something between them? But Mrs. Alden and Nurse were adamant on the subject of biscuits. They couldn't pronounce the horrid word, but they looked at each other significantly. The dog had *fleas*. He must be severely encouraged to go and scratch himself elsewhere, in the loose company of other measly dogs, or of the gardener's big noisy children, who were too ignorant to know that Fuzzy-Wuzzy was the right name for him, and always called him Yep.

In the absence of a dog, sometimes a sparrow or a butterfly would come hopping or fluttering over the lawn, in that beautifully levelled, watered and mown part of it where Oliver could be taken out of his baby-carriage and allowed to run about free, or even to sit and crawl, after a rug had been spread under him to keep out the dampness. The butterfly or the sparrow might tempt his toddling steps and his top-heavy precipitate little runs: but the naughty creatures would always escape, and sometimes leave him unexpectedly and ignominiously sitting on the ground.

Miss Tirkettle was scientifically trained; she knew no songs, no stories, and no prayers; and Mrs. Alden, if she had ever known any, found them tedious and uncanny to recall nowadays. They were lost in thin ghostly memories of her mother's time; the masculine medical atmosphere of her father's day, and of her own housekeeping, had completely banished them. She had realised how futile and dangerous it was to impress misleading vacuous emotions upon a tender mind. Poetry and mythology and religion and remote history had nothing to do with *life*. Later, when Oliver was older, he might some day come upon songs or stories or prayers in books or theatrical ritualistic performances: and then he might form his own judgment about them, if they interested him at all. His education mustn't begin by stuffing him with nonsense. It must be a direct preparation for right living in the modern world.

All this Mrs. Alden very pointedly observed to her husband. "I don't agree at all," she added, "if you think Miss Tirkettle too old, and want the baby to be handed over to some chit of a silly nurse-maid who would tell him ghost-stories. And next, perhaps, you will be wanting somebody to teach him his prayers. Why should the poor child be made to recite meaningless language like a parrot, and be filled with false religious emotions? In order that some day, I suppose, he may be able to understand better why, in the Middle Ages, they burnt people at the stake. Science has shown how vital these first years are, and how such early morbid impressions warp the mind and weaken the character. The child will have enough to struggle against, with his burdened nervous inheritance. At least, let us not begin by making him superstitious."

"No, no," Peter replied patiently, accustomed as he was to having his wife put words in his mouth which he never uttered, and impute feelings which he never felt. "Prayers and ghost-stories are not what I had in mind; not even fairy-tales. And I particularly don't want a common nurse-maid, quite the opposite. I should like his English to be fundamentally pure: then all the abominable speech he will have to hear will seem to him absurd and amusing. He needn't be troubled by it, and won't imitate it. Did it ever strike you how little we are affected by the servants' way of talking, though we hear it every day of our lives? It's because we recognise it for a dialect apart, which is not our own. That's the way anyone to whom good English is natural must regard the common speech of the day. I suppose it's more important to have the feelings of a gentleman than the speech of a gentleman: but the things are closely allied. No: I want a lady-nurse, a good governess for Oliver, who will play with him and inspire him with good manners and good feelings, not by precept only, but by attraction, so that he may disdain the opposite vices. I want a lively person who will wake up his wits and chase him about and help him build his castles of blocks so high that he will laugh when they topple over. And why should Moses in the bulrushes or Noah's Ark or Jonah or David and Goliath be a whit more religious to a child's feeling than Gulliver or Sinbad the Sailor? They won't be: they will simply fill his fancy pleasantly, and accustom him to enjoy intellectually what is enjoyable in this world—which is mighty little."

"Useless!" Mrs. Alden replied, with an air of settling the business. "I have *tried* reading to him out of that Mother Goose book that Letitia gave him. He wouldn't listen, wouldn't look at the pictures, and was peevish; he wanted to get down on his legs and run after his ball. He seems to be happiest and strongest on the physical side."

"Luckily he has your physique: he is very fortunate there." Peter said this with a little bow. He liked to pay his wife compliments with a sort of playful gallantry. It was an apology, in his mind, for not really loving her: and yet he genuinely admired her in a certain way. She might have been Juno, she might have been Ceres, if she hadn't been Harriet Bumstead of Great Falls, Connecticut.

On that warm September evening they were sitting in the western portico, admiring the after-glow of the sunset between the huge white wooden columns, fluted and without a base, like those of the Parthenon. Here he was allowed to smoke, and he relighted his cigarette before continuing. There was a project he had long meditated, without ever daring to propose it. Why should Harriet disapprove of it, as he felt in his bones she would, when it was so clearly in her interest, in the baby's, and in that of Letitia Lamb, her oldest and dearest friend?

"You mention Letitia. How would it do to ask *her* to look after Oliver? She isn't too young, she is not superstitious, and she's a lady. We might invite her to live with us, and pay her a nice little salary besides, so that she would be laying by a penny against a rainy day. She is fond of the child, and he of her. She could very easily teach him his letters, until we find a good school for him."

"How unperceptive you men are," Mrs. Alden replied in a tone of superior but good-humoured competence. "How could I ask Letitia Lamb to give up her life-work, and her yearly trips abroad?—You know this year she is again chaperoning the Toot girls; such a treat for her, actually taking them to Greece and even to Crete, to see those wonderful excavations! How should she dream of stopping her lectures on Renaissance Sculpture when they have proved such a success, and when she has just discovered how much better a subject for lectures sculpture is than painting, because in showing paintings on the screen the colour is lost and so much detail confuses the audience, while photographs of statuary are perfectly adequate, in fact thrilling and better than if you were looking yourself at the originals in a casual way, as one does in tiresome museums and dark cold churches? You have no idea how hard she works, actually wearing out her eyes, and how she positively delights in the history of art. She *cries* over it. Her lantern-lectures, for a city like Great Falls, are very well attended. Last year she cleared nearly a hundred dollars. And with such a success and such a *vocation*, how do you expect her to sink into a common governess? It would be an insult to propose it. You forget that she's my very best friend."

Somewhat unperceptive, in fact, Peter Alden had been, as he now perceived. If the mysteries of life-long friendship excluded Letitia, what other governess could they find?

"I only wish," Mrs. Alden went on, "that there were a suitable Kindergarten in the neighbourhood. Miss Bibb's is not properly equipped and too far away. I should have to send the child every morning in the coupé with Nannie. That would involve Patrick to drive, and both of them again in the afternoon to bring the baby home. Two servants' time almost swallowed up just in taking a little boy to and from school! I couldn't bear to have such a thing going on under my eyes. It's immoral. Besides there's the horse completely tired out, coming twice up this long hill with that heavy carriage. What's the good of keeping a carriage at all if I can never drive out? You will say: Get another horse! You are so extravagant and thoughtless about money. Letitia wouldn't tell me how much you sent her for Christmas, but I'm sure it was far too much. Very well: suppose I buy a second horse. Then Patrick will complain of overwork and ask for another man to help in the stable. Endless trouble and waste. Children are a terrible puzzle."

Things were in this pass when an unexpected incident gave a Providential turn to Oliver's future.

II

Mrs. Alden's younger brother Harry was at that time pursuing his theological studies at Göttingen, where tepid philosophical currents, set up by the eloquence of Lotze, continued to temper truth to the shorn lamb. Among those red-tiled roofs and modest gardens, he lodged in the house of the widowed Frau Pastor Schlote, whose elder daughter gave German lessons to the foreign boarders. There was also a much younger daughter, Irma, who had recently returned from England, where for some years she had been a teaching pupil at St. Felix's School for young ladies at Southwold in Suffolk. Irma, too, sometimes gave German lessons: but her chief employment was to help in the household. Sometimes she even waited at table; and then, flushed with the heat of the kitchen and the pride of making herself useful, she would sit down at her place at the foot of the board, and enthusiastically and accurately impart all the miscellaneous information which travel and foreign residence had given her. She was just as happy in knowing how to make perfect *Eierkuchen* or to carve a goose, as in knowing the beauties of English literature and even the splendours of English society. A certain sympathy soon established itself between the ardent Irma and young Harry Bumstead, and one holiday, on an excursion to the heaven-piercing ruins of Schloss Hochstein, things came to a head. The two young people, alone of the party, had ventured to climb up into the highest restored turret and most thrilling *Aussichtspunkt* of all, when Fräulein Irma suddenly felt dizzy, fainted or threatened to faint, with imminent danger of falling into the ravine, hundreds of feet below, where a torrent romantically boiled among the wildest of rocks and bushes. It became necessary for her gallant escort, who was a strapping fellow, to detain her in a strong embrace, and help and almost carry her down from that eagle's nest, as the guide book called it; and the expression of trust and rapture with which, feeling herself restored to safety, she slowly reopened her eyes, while her head continued to recline on the shoulder of her protector, left little doubt in his honest mind about the state of her affections. He himself was far from indifferent. Irma, if not conventionally pretty, seemed to him angelic in soul and in body; and with his Christian-socialist leanings he particularly admired her joy in work and her abilities as a *Hausfrau*: while the tenderness of her heart went with a well-informed mind, vibrating to every political and poetical enthusiasm and scrupulously faithful to all the science of all the text-books. What an ideal helpmate for a future liberal clergyman or professor! But alas! it was incumbent on him as an honourable man, to beg Irma the next morning for a private interview. She knew at once by his stunned expression and funereal tone that she mustn't expect, this time, a proposal of marriage. And indeed he began by telling her that his future was not free. Before leaving America he had become engaged to the young lady who gave out the books in the Williams College library. It had been an attachment of long standing, ever since his Freshman year; and on his departure the lady had promised to wait for him as many more years as might be necessary; and meantime she was religiously saving every penny she could spare from her modest salary, in order to help one day to set up their house-keeping. They wrote each other weekly letters, artless and rambling, full of the interests of the moment, and of complete confidence in a boundless and mutual sympathy: more already like the letters of a happy married pair than of separated and pining lovers. It was a sacred engagement. However warm and deep might be the friendship and sympathy which he might find elsewhere, he could offer marriage to no one else.

Fräulein Irma was wonderfully calm, calmer and calmer the further her friend proceeded with his explanations. She felt that she was living through a tragic hour, like the Lotte of *Werthers Leiden*, and that, cruel as this sudden blow might be, it was lifting her to a higher plane of heroic life and giving her a deeper, broader, truer spiritual insight. How much better she would plumb henceforth all the wisdom of that great saying of Goethe's *Entbehren sollst Du, sollst entbehren!* And with what a doubly heart-rending but yet nobler note would she sing hereafter *Es war ein Traum* and *Behüt' dich Gott, es hat nicht sollen sein!* She bit her lips for a moment and then said quietly that she thanked him for confiding his secret to her; understood his feelings; and hoped that their earnest true friendship would always continue as before: and she didn't break down until safely locked in her own little attic, where she could prudently smother her sobs in her virgin pillow. In half an hour she was almost herself again. Her amativeness was generic, and she could easily turn her innocent thoughts upon some ruddy young officer, bursting in his corsets, or some pale poet-like student, in a great slouch hat and goggles, after twice encountering either of them walking round the pleasant circuit of the old town walls. Life was still so rich, so full, so wonderful: and the world was, *ach!* so beautiful!

Young Harry Bumstead, on the contrary, was hard hit. The blooming Irma seemed by contrast to cast a drab and melancholy shadow over the prospect of keeping house for ever with the worthy but not very young librarian of Williams College. Well, that couldn't be helped. He would find courage and happiness now in his work, and later in his home. Yet his inexperience and his vanity, working on a morbid conscience, reproached him with having thoughtlessly caused the lifelong misery of this tender and innocent creature. Would she die of love? Would she ever bring herself to marry anyone else? He wished he could make some reparation—though he had done no harm—and find something substantial to offer to Irma in lieu of marriage. And a postscript to one of his father's letters opportunely suggested what that substantial something might be.

"Harriet," Dr. Bumstead wrote, "asks to be excused for never writing to you. She says she is too busy with the baby. The fact is she is rather troubled about nurses, etc. Mothering is not her element. She is better at introducing a lecturer or presiding at a ladies' meeting to protest against organ-grinders. Even when the child was smaller and couldn't ask questions, it annoyed her if the nurse left him with her for a moment, and she had to pick up his rattle for the third time. Yet in theory nothing is good enough for the kid. They are at their wits' ends to find anybody worthy of bringing him up. They won't put him to school here, because Alden thinks us poor folks too common; and they can't send him to a boarding school, because Harriet says boarding schools deaden the mind and stereotype the character."

Just the thing for Irma: to take charge of a rich little boy's education. The thought no sooner struck the young man's mind than he set himself to realise it. Letters, photographs, proposals, difficulties, finally cablegrams of acceptance passed in breathless succession. It was well, Mrs. Alden had written, that Fräulein Schlote should be young, with experience of teaching, and knowledge of so many languages, and of music and history and science: but wouldn't a clergyman's daughter tend to be bigoted and narrow? However, her brother reasured her, explaining how far Fräulein Schlote, though deeply religious in her feelings, was from forming any *abstract* notion of religion, or seeing God anywhere but in Nature and Society and the conscience of man. In fact, if anything Harriet would find her too liberal, too *pagan*, because she was a great admirer of Goethe, and felt how beautiful a healthy sensuality was to round out the character, and how important it is to develop harmoniously every side of our nature.

"Very well," Mrs. Alden replied. "Let her come on trial. But as to sensuality, healthy or not, let her clearly understand that she won't have occasion to develop it in *my* house."

Fräulein Irma herself was no less pleasurably excited than if her marvellous new life had included the prospect of a husband. In planning and in action, she and her dear friend Harry became comrades once more, and all sentimentality was forgotten in the excitement of adventure. Harry met every objection, got round every difficulty; and when from the deck of the great steamer at Bremerhafen she waved a last adieu to her sister and to her friend, who might so easily have been her bridegroom, her tears were tears of happiness. Alone, yes; but travelling first class—Dr. Alden had arranged all that—and especially recommended to the Captain, by whose side she would sit at the principal table: such a fine old grizzly German officer, portly but vigorous. She was Eva in the care of Hans Sachs. Leaving her Fatherland, yes: but not for the first time. She knew well already, young as she was—only just twenty!—what it meant to live alone in a vast foreign world. Going to live among utter strangers, certainly; but only for six months, unless everything turned out happily. And the little boy she was to educate—here she took his photograph out of her bag and contemplated it for the hundredth time—what a beautiful refined head he had—so Nordic—and what a sweet, serious expression. If she had been engaged as governess to a genuine German Serene Highness—who might have had nasty troublesome older sisters to make faces at her—she couldn't have had a more distinguished-looking pupil. Of course there were no titles in America, so you never could be *quite* sure that you got people just in the order of their real importance. But at least her patron was a Herr Doktor; and what was more, and rare among doctors, a very, very rich man, which nowadays was an equivalent for everything else. And after all little Oliver—what could be more natural?—would one day be President of the United States; and she would go down in history as surely and gloriously as if she had been the beloved teacher and guide of some young Grand Duke or even of some Imperial and Royal Highness.—But she must now go down to her cabin and take her medicine, so as not to be sea-sick; and on the way down she observed that, although all the German passengers she came across seemed to be Jews, one or two of the ship's officers were just as good-looking as the Captain, and younger.

III

The advent of Fräulein Schlote was a blessing all round. Mrs. Alden, on whom everything depended, smiled on the newcomer from the beginning. The first glimpse of her had been a great relief. A foreign governess had suggested so many unpleasant possibilities, even crimes: mightn't she steal Mrs. Alden's jewels, or have some secret paramour, or set fire to the house, out of sheer wickedness? But no: this was no tall, thin, dark, severely critical foreign woman, with aristocratic pretensions; no embittered grand lady, compelled by adversity to become a dependent in a family of rich barbarians, whom she despised. This Irma was all smiling deference and unfeigned admiration; such a little blonde thing, too, looking very young for her twenty years, a mere child, yet not too pretty or well-dressed; not a possible rival or critic at all, but more like a loving pupil or a grateful poor relation. She could be trusted to take entire charge of the baby, without becoming a worse encumbrance herself.

Mrs. Alden liked to be waited on and obeyed, but she hated servants. Servants were alien presences that made her nervous, like a strange cat in the room. She was unpleasantly aware of them passing behind her back, or prowling stealthily about the doors. It was a strain to feel oneself observed by creatures who, however dull they might be and given to routine, were morally independent and probably hostile: automatic creatures that had to be watched, to see if they continued to work normally, and did what was expected of them. The relation between masters and servants seemed to her profoundly inhuman, profoundly immoral: she welcomed every mechanical device, every social arrangement that might eliminate servants. Her tribe had lost, if it ever had possessed, the charitable principle of Christian society, which made possible a familiar union, devoted and merry, between high and low, and freed a motley world from competition and envy. She could never have been with any grace the mistress of a great household, in some castle or palace filled with wayfarers and men-at-arms, craftsmen hammering, old women spinning, fools fooling, maids sweeping and singing, young men carousing, and monks begging. She froze at the touch of difference. Superior power and distinction were insufferable: if she could not imitate them she denied them. And the least degree of coarseness or simplicity beneath her own offended her also. Her moral ideal was democracy, but a democracy of the elect. There could be no oppression in imposing uniformity on people who were really all alike; and such a society exacted from its members only what, if they were honourable, they would exact from themselves. She couldn't conceive life except in a clan, where all the peers should have equal rights and similar virtues. Beyond the pale there could be nothing but outer darkness—an alien, heathen, unintelligible world, to be kept as remote as possible. If they *couldn't* grow tea at home, she supposed they *must* get it from China or Ceylon. And she supposed that if occasionally that dreadful outer world became troublesome, it would be necessary to make war on it and teach it a lesson: but by far the best thing was to ignore it altogether. It ought never to have existed.

Luckily in America the immigrant working classes lived apart in their own districts and tenements, like Jews in a Ghetto. One need have no personal contact with them; and as far as she was concerned—for she wasn't meddlesome—they were welcome to keep up their own ways and religion among themselves, and even their language, if they could preserve it: but as servants in her house they were a dreadful intrusion. This Fräulein was not a servant, but a clergyman's daughter who might have been Mrs. Alden's sister-in-law, but for a lucky accident: lucky, because a *foreign* sister-in-law would have been rather a trial. As a dependent, however, Irma would do nicely, loved the kitchen, which Mrs. Alden abhorred and never visited; loved the pantry and the closets and the trunk-room and the attics; knew very soon where everything was, and how to distribute the clean linen, count and lock up the silver and the good china, and generally so order the business of house-keeping that servants hardly seemed to exist, and when seen looked actually friendly and happy. It was a vast relief to the mistress of the house, a revelation of what comfort meant; her reward for thinking so unselfishly only of what would be best for Oliver, and having consented to admit a strange woman into the home; but providentially this strange woman relieved Mrs. Alden of petty cares, and left her free to devote herself to higher public duties.

Besides, after Oliver had been put to bed, Fräulein could come down again and, sitting on a low stool between the lamp and the fire, could read to her for half an hour—such a rest for the eyes: or could even slip into her room and brush her hair very gently and very assiduously—which was not only pleasant (Mrs. Alden wouldn't have cared much for *that*) but excellent for the scalp, where the hair was getting rather thin, and to keep away her neuralgia. It was most important to preserve her health for the sake of her work. One husband and one child were not enough to fill her life; and she had decided to have no more children. Of course, as a rule, and especially for people of good old American stock, she believed in large families: but in this special case she was sure it wouldn't be scientifically safe. Oliver himself seemed the child of an old man; she had read of grave dangers in that direction—for her, too, child-bearing would be too great a strain. Any woman might bear children; a person who had a mind should be left free to improve it. It was a blessing that Fräulein could be trusted to interview the cook and keep an eye on the gardener and see that the right rooms were swept and *thoroughly* cleaned on each day of the week: this enabled Mrs. Alden herself, after breakfast, when her own room had been done, to retire there and rest a little—somehow one didn't feel so strong nowadays in the morning—with the *Boston Transcript* or *Littell's Living Age* or the *Atlantic Monthly* lying open but unread on her lap—for she thought the illustrated magazines rather vulgar; and as she was sure to *hear* of any new event or idea of importance at the meetings of the Associated Charities and the Art Club and the Browning Society, not to mention Letitia Lamb who brought all the gossip on the other afternoons fresh from the city, she had really no need to do more than look at the headings in the paper, and at the list of deaths, to know everything that was going on. While she improved her mind in this way and by being well-rested kept her interest in everything from flagging, she had the satisfaction of knowing that little Oliver, in the model schoolroom and sun-parlour especially built for him at the other end of the house, was being admirably brought up: better, in fact, than if she had insisted on bringing him up herself. It was simply a fact that young children, however gifted they might turn out to be afterwards, got on better at first with commonplace artless souls like Fräulein, and ran after them as they run after animals, while the ways of serious highly cultivated people put children off. When Oliver was older he would see the difference and learn to rely always on his mother, as was natural, for guidance and affection. But he wasn't ready to appreciate the deeper qualities yet, and he actually profited more by being with Fräulein. "If my friends heard me say this," thought Mrs. Alden, "they would protest that I am far too modest: but all really superior people *are* modest."

Peter Alden, too, who was fond of chuckling in solitude, chuckled at the happy chance that had introduced into the household a person so much to his own liking, and this quite on his wife's responsibility and at the instigation of her favourite brother. Ideally he might have preferred an English or even a French governess, for the sake of a certain refinement and soberness not to be expected of Germans: but Oliver was refined and sober by nature, and perhaps needed more the stimulus of an unfeigned enthusiasm. Enthusiasm Fräulein had, as well as an unusual command of languages: when complimented on her excellent English she would say: "I speak also French perfectly." Her English was British—musical, colloquial, and pure; yet it escaped the hostility which would have pursued it if she had been an Englishwoman: it was set down merely to foreignness. Peter was delighted to see contraband smuggled in this way into his family with the approval of the customs house; sometimes the absurdity of life was its own excuse for being. Perhaps, too, a little Teutonic and Lutheran enlightenment might be more successfully grafted on to the Alden stock than any more delicately shaded or exclusive sentiment: and how stout and self-confident that German culture was, compared with the pale native tradition! Fräulein was a treasure; but Peter from the first carefully avoided any too warm expression of his satisfaction. He was vaguely civil to the young person; and he rather hinted to his wife that he thought German methods and German emotions ridiculous. "If Harriet only knew," he said to himself, "what a balm this Fräulein is to my conscience as a parent, she would send her packing at once." Irma herself thought the Herr Doktor rather cold and sphinx-like, and was afraid he disliked her; until on the first Christmas she received a generous present with a card (from Havana) inscribed to Fräulein Schlote, with thanks for all her skill and devotion. On a separate slip of paper was written: "You may show this Christmas card to Mrs. Alden, but please don't mention the cheque. That must be a little secret between us." The secret, however, was instantly divulged in a letter of sixteen pages to her sister in Göttingen, spotted with joyful tears.

As for the child himself, neither the disappearance of his old nurse nor the appearance of the new Fräulein seemed to impress his young mind. He was accustomed to strangers, and not afraid of them; they all behaved in much the same way; or rather, to his transcendental consciousness, all these bulks moving and doing things, his nurse, his mother, and the rest, were alike strangers, though familiar and harmless, like the elephants in the picture-book: and for some time Irma too was only a different bulk, slighter and moving in a nimbler way. Gradually, however, he became aware of something else in her: her movements were not just motions, more or less necessary and expected, like those of Miss Tirkettle; there was sympathy in them, there was playfulness: Irma was *affectionate*. Her personality began to percolate, as it were, into his own. Discipline was relaxed: it was no longer imperative to play only with clean gravel especially poured out for him: he might now run and dig up his own gravel from the path: but while he readily availed himself of this privilege, he was not particularly happy over it, or grateful to Irma: he simply forgot that the privilege was new, and took it for granted. The routine of life might have become more plastic, making a little room for caprice; but was caprice less tiresome than law? Both seemed to be imposed by some mysterious fatality, or by some contagious will which he made his own without really understanding what he was doing, or desiring it. Yet, though he might sigh a little, sometimes, at the tedium of existence, he would never have dreamt of complaining or resisting. Such was the order of the universe; and his mother said he was much more fortunate than other little boys who were poor and had nothing to keep them busy but must waste all their time playing in the gutter and becoming wicked.

It was a distinct relief to discard the perambulator and to trudge along with Fräulein for a country walk. The confinement of that baby-carriage, and the stuffy luxury of it, had become exasperating. Now at least he was a small man on two legs: yet all was not liberty. Sometimes she insisted on holding him by the hand. In the first enthusiasm of her apostleship she was eager to discover or invent grounds of sympathy with her little pupil. Every pretty flower, every lovely butterfly, every darling bird had to be pointed to, described, and admired. It was good training for Oliver's ear in the German language, and some initiation into the wealth of nature: but he took all this fervid instruction a little sullenly: he would not have been bored running about silently by himself. And sometimes Fräulein lengthened these rambles more than was pleasant for him. He was no baby, to say he was tired, or hot, or wished to be carried: the old perambulator, even if thought of at such a moment, was not to be mentioned. He would rather bear the ills he had, than fly back to others that he knew too well. If a pebble got into his shoe, it might be unpleasant, but he said nothing. Pebbles were not official reasons for stopping or for turning back and going home, as if it had been *time* to do so. Time, the right time for each thing, was the most sacred of the standards one had to live up to. Pebbles were insignificant accidents, like certain needs of the body: and if Fräulein, gasping with intentional enjoyment, said they *must* get to the top of the hill, the view would be so *wunderschön*, the hill must be stoically climbed. The view was nothing to him: but by the time he had plodded bravely to the top, he had forgotten the pebble; and when later, after running down the hill, he felt it again in a different place, he knew that they were going home and that it didn't matter. Such was the nature of country walks; and when he changed his shoes and stockings before dinner, he would shake the pebble out. And if it had *really* hurt his foot very much—the pain, he knew, didn't matter if there was no physical harm done—he would wash it and put a patch on it, as his father had taught him to do; and the next time he would remember to lace both his shoes equally tight, so that pebbles shouldn't get into either of them.

So the young philosopher was educating himself in the essentials: but as to the frills, Fräulein was not remiss in her duty. What better foundation for deep and true learning than a knowledge of the German language? She knew that this was not one of those artificial and accidental languages like French and English, that have grown out of the corruption and mixture of several ancient tongues. It was an original language, a language of the heart: and to teach it the more feelingly and maternally, she would take little Oliver in her lap, and talk to him about the objects to be seen out of the window or in the picture-book lying open on the table. It was not long before he knew the name of everything in German, as well as in English, or better; and what was more, he could recite German verses and prayers (though he wasn't taught to *pray* them) and even to sing little German songs. These last were his favourite amusement, because Fräulein beat the measure like a *Kapellmeister*, and he did the same: and she said that some day he might be the leader of a great orchestra, and instead of only himself singing in time, he would make sixty or a hundred violins and flutes and trombones keep time with him. This was a great thought, immensely invigorating: for Oliver's mind was less perceptive than digestive: contact was nothing to it, incorporation was everything. Anything merely seen or heard remained a picture or a story: that external force, that foreign rhythm, must first pass into him, become a part of his rhythm and of his bent, if ever he was to conceive it clearly or think it important. Once incorporated, once digested, once moralised, the orange was squeezed: its virtue had gone out of it and passed into him: and what the rejected rind or pips or deflated pulp might do or become in that rubbish heap of non-moral abstractions which seems to surround us, left him quite cold. Everything was really only what it was to him and in him; what it was when digested.

Not that his organs of perception were not accurate or retentive: on the contrary, they had all the automatic precision of first-rate machinery, and in later years he was always at the head of the class in school, and the best player, as far as personal skill went, in the field. His senses, his reactions, his memory did everything perfectly for him if he only let them alone. The routine liturgy of knowledge, dates and conjugations, and demonstrations, registered itself early in the passionless upper regions of his brain, to be rehearsed on occasion almost unerringly. Meantime the heart within was asleep, or dreaming of something else. It remained immature even in his manhood. Yet in the midst of that profound indifference, the eye and hand could attend all the more miraculously to the stops and levers of the public world, as if lightly playing a game without a purpose. Material objects were clear enough, and material problems, when once set, were just as clear as the objects: yet everything in that sphere was, as it were, made of glass, perfectly definite, and perfectly indigestible. His masters and friends often wondered how so much competence could exist in one so passive and so little curious. They had not pursued the methods of Fräulein Schlote. How plastic, how digestible, how easily filtered into the heart, were those German words and verses and prayers! How readily they became a part of his rhythms and of his bent, when he sat in Fräulein's lap, and beat time to the measure, like a master-musician leading a choir! Once Fräulein even rumpled up his hair, which was naturally quite smooth and unobtrusive, so that he might look more like a genius. And sometimes, when he was reading or reciting and came to a hard place, she would stroke his bare legs, to help him over the difficulty, and to show that he was getting it right.

One day, without any reason, he climbed up from her knee and put both arms round her neck, holding on very softly and very tight for what seemed to her a long time.

"But darling," she said, smothering her emotions, "why do you do that?"

His German, and even his English, was inadequate to frame an answer, and he merely held on.

"But do you ever hug your mother like that? And of course it would be very wrong not to love her ever so much more than you love me, because she is your mother."

Somewhat slowly and absent-mindedly Oliver let go: he certainly never hugged his mother like that. It was all rather discouraging. Irma felt this too, and never stroked his legs again, and gradually ceased to take him on her lap. "You are such a big boy now," she would say. "You must sit up in your high chair," and she would lock him into it with the oval shelf attached on hinges to the back, which could be swung over his head to form a table in front of him. On this she would lay his brightly illustrated Animal Alphabet from Ant to Zebra, like an open Bible. "There you are, a little angel in a pulpit! If ever you become a pastor—you know my dear father was a pastor—that's what you will look like preaching in a church."

A vague apprehension remained in Oliver's mind that he was destined to be a pastor, and to be locked into a pulpit with a big book open in front of him. A pastor would always look like that and would always feel like that: because the persons he ought to love best, like his mother and God, would always be impossible to hug and it would always be wrong to hug the others.

The high chair was not without a charm of its own, like walking on stilts: and confinement to that pulpit was rather cosy, so long as one's mind was really on the book. Yet after a while for some hidden reason, that perch became uncomfortable. The lesson went on to the end; never did it cross Oliver's dutiful mind to fret or to break off. Life was essentially something to be endured, something grim. There was no reasonableness in rebelling simply because for the moment things might be unpleasant. The digestive mind went on digesting, perhaps rather slowly: and the undigested objects and words would continue to stream by, strangely precise in their strangeness. And when presently the page was finished, the shelf lifted over his head, and he could climb down to terra firma, he did so without hurry, as if exercising the established rights of a freeman. One day his pencil, which he prized because it was blue at one end and red at the other, had happened to roll under the table: and as he crawled after it on all fours, what was Fräulein's astonishment when she beheld the perfect geometrical pattern of the straw seat printed in pink on his little bottom. "What," she cried, "has this wicked chair been hurting my little darling? And why hasn't he told his good Fräulein, who would have made him such a nice soft cushion to sit on? So she shall, this very day."

But it happened to be time for luncheon, and Fräulein, still full of the subject, unsuspectingly mentioned at table the urgent need of a cushion for Oliver's chair, and babbled on about an odd piece of pretty chintz and nice wadding from an old winter jacket with which she would manufacture it that evening, to be ready for pulpit-time the next morning. Mrs. Alden let her talk on; but after a little pause pursed her lips and said: "I don't think little boys ought to be brought up to sit on *cushions*. It is effeminate. The chair comes from the very best makers in Great Falls. I paid a particularly high price for it, and I'm sure it must be quite right as it is—much cooler and healthier in summer than sitting on a stuffy cushion, which is always slipping about and getting tumbled and making one restless. If only Oliver wouldn't fidget, but keep his clothes properly pulled down under him, he would be perfectly comfortable, and wouldn't need to find fault with what is provided for him."

Fräulein, intimidated, didn't dare to observe that Oliver didn't fidget and hadn't found fault with anything. Mrs. Alden being a woman of independent and intuitive mind, unhesitatingly invented the thoughts and actions to be attributed to others: and she was so confident in the truth of her divinations that she didn't hesitate to proclaim them as facts even in the presence of the persons concerned. Sometimes she hit the mark and impressed everybody: and even when she was wrong she made her assaults in so cordial and optimistic a tone, as if what she said was an acknowledged fact, which she generously accepted, that most people hesitated to take offence, or to contradict her. Self-knowledge after all is fallible, and the position of the insulted party is weak, defending himself against cool and smiling injustice. So Fräulein on this occasion dumbly gave up her case: didn't even protest that her cushion wouldn't have slipped about, because she had meant to tie down the four corners to the legs of the chair with four sweet blue bows. But her firmly set little jaw under her snub nose told of an underlying determination to circumvent the tyrant, and spare somehow the tender skin of that innocent heroic child. And indeed before the next lesson she had bound together four thicknesses of blotting-paper with red tape, and attached them firmly to the offending seat. Red tape and blotting-paper surely were not effeminate: they suggested the future statesman and scholar. Mrs. Alden never went into the schoolroom, and need never discover the subterfuge: and in any case it would pass until the cold weather came, with Oliver's fifth birthday, and he attained the dignity and the protection of breeches.

IV

It was on a first day of October, under the sign, as it were, of autumnal temperance, that Oliver had been born: at that turn of the year when the climate of New England, after stimulating the native optimist with one or two blizzards, and trying him with some sudden thaw and spasmodic tropical heats, at last confirms his systematic cheerfulness by settling down to a spell of cool clear weather. Then the sun rides low in the sky, veiled and coloured by exhalations from the damp woods, the sea, and the smoke of cities; while some early touch of frost turns the still vigorous foliage from a harsh green to patches of crimson and russet and glossy yellow. A fresher air fills the human lungs, and the jaded summer boarder returns from weary holiday-making to hopeful business.

It was also during this benign interval that Peter Alden was accustomed to revisit his family. He came usually for Oliver's birthday, bearing some gift; and he departed after Thanksgiving Day, before there was occasion to retract his thankfulness. In the year of Oliver's first cloth breeches the birthday present from his father was particularly impressive, and appropriate to that manly garment: it was a pony to ride. The boy had had no pets: pigeons, and white mice and guinea-pigs, and the rest, his mother said, were so messy: dogs and cats were a nuisance, not to be allowed beyond the servants' quarters; and the horses in the stable were too big and too formidable—A boy at the age of five has a twentieth-century mind: he wants only machines expertly workable; or else living creatures as machine-like as possible, with statistical habits, to be trained and organised to team-work: something with springs and stops of its own, and immense force in reserve, but stops and springs to be controlled by his little master-ego, so that the immense foreign force may seem all his own, and may carry him sky-high. For such a child, or such an adventurous mechanic, a mere shape or material fetish, like a doll, will never do: his pets and toys must be living things, obedient, responsive forces to be coaxed and led, and to offer a constant challenge to a constant victory. His instinct is masculine, perhaps a premonition of woman:

yet he is not thinking of woman. Indeed, his women may refuse to
satisfy his instinct for domination, because they share it; machines
can be more exactly and more prodigiously obedient. Nor will a
parent, a leader, an irresponsible power or sovereign God engage
the respect of such a free agent. He wishes to be the centre of
direction, if not the source of material power. Anything not exactly
controllable he will despise and ignore. The great achievement will
be to harness forces that seemed intractable, and to identify the good
with his own material ascendency.

Oliver, at the age of five, had not yet discovered the tragic error
in such a philosophy, and the arrival of a pony was an excellent
occasion to put the matter to a first test. Fräulein had sometimes
taken him to the stable where he had respectfully admired the carriage horse in the box stall, and the cart horse loosely attached by a
halter to his manger: but he had been rather frightened at their
swishing tails and mouths grotesquely moving, and had been distinctly unresponsive to Fräulein's enthusiasm about the clean stalls,
the neat blankets, the hanging harness, and the wholesome natural
smells. But to receive for his own a live pony, not higher than his
rocking-horse, but with a mane like a lion, was quite another matter:
and when, full to the brim already of a silent intensity, he was suddenly seized by his father and planted on the pony's back, the experience was a revelation. Now he was not in the least afraid. Even
the pleasure of sitting aloft was lost in the impulse to act. His look
became earnest, he grasped the reins tightly with both fists and
pressed his knees manfully against the saddle. Never had he felt such
a sense of responsibility. Of course he wasn't going to fall off: but
the important point was not to pull the bridle too tight, so as to hurt
Dumpy, and yet to pull it hard enough to make him mind. It soon
became evident that the secret of control was not so much force as
suggestion: and for suggestion to succeed the possibilities of Dumpy
must first be consulted. His dumb soul must be solicited and not
outraged; and on this sympathetic basis a firm and thoroughly responsible government was soon established by the child over the
beast, to the latter's apparent satisfaction, and to the very serious
realisation on Oliver's part that it was his duty to rule and that he
knew how to do it.

Dumpy became the symbol of worlds to conquer. It was now Fräulein's turn to find their expeditions too ambitious and to think it
always time to go home. As the interest in managing Dumpy sub-

sided—the lazy thing never *would* trot more than a few yards at a time—his value grew as a seat for placid observation. They could now wander far beyond the Cemetery and the Asylum, down the gentler inland slopes of High Bluff, to the farmers' houses and bits of remaining wood, or even to the babbling upper river and the small ponds. There were cows, there were squirrels, there were ants, there were crows: far from home, indeed, what sights and transformations might not the world afford? Home life, on the contrary, as its circle widened materially, seemed only to extend and intensify its dull tyranny. Sometimes Fräulein would take him to town in the brougham to have his hair cut or get new shoes or try on new clothes at the tailor's. These, too, were festive excursions, because at least he might stand up in the carriage and run from one window to the other and see what was going on in the street. When they got out, he could stop to look into shop windows; and while Fräulein was intent on choosing exactly the right articles, or taking out her purse, opening it, and paying—which always took a long time and much knitting of her brows, with hardly any eyebrows to them—he could notice other children, so oddly teasing, prodding, and chasing one another, and the fat policeman standing in the middle of the street, and the oranges and peanuts for sale at every corner.

Sometimes, more rarely, he drove to town in this same carriage with his mother, always to the dentist's. It was not for nothing that Mrs. Alden was the daughter and the wife of doctors; and while she might wisely or lazily delegate her authority to Fräulein in almost everything else, when it came to matters of health and medical regimen, she resolutely assumed direction in person. A foreign governess couldn't be trusted to feel the immense importance of *physical* care. Foreigners might never have heard of sleeping-porches, and might even retain a sneaking tendency to close bedroom windows at night. The first time that Fräulein knew that her pupil was being taken to the dentist's, though he had only his first teeth and apparently nothing the matter with them, she had innocently blurted out her surprise: as if it wasn't every civilised person's duty to have his teeth cleaned and examined every six months. For Oliver himself these visits to the dentist were solemn occasions: not only were the operations longer and more distressing than at the barber's, but there was a grim array of trays and drawers full of steel hooks, chisels, and lancets, and there were monstrous whirling instruments like the enormously magnified legs of a spider. But first of all there was the

depressing sensation of sitting still at his mother's side in the carriage—the very sensation he had in later years when he sat beside
her in church: for she hated restlessness and vain curiosity and
wouldn't let him stand up and look out of the window. She said there
was nothing to see. There was indeed nothing very instructive in the
long round-about drive down the hill to the city; yet there were
images, there were sensations; and sensations and images were what
that young sensorium craved, without asking whether they were instructive or even beautiful. Merely to watch things flow by was excitement enough. First there were the two granite posts and the two
great elms that marked the turn from their own avenue into the
public road: then you passed the Cemetery gate and the Asylum gate,
where the trolley stopped; and probably there was an empty car
there, screeching round the curves and crashing over the switches as
it turned tail and with much stamping on the gong prepared to start
on the downward trip to the city. Then there were empty building
lots, with great white and black signboards, announcing that they
were desirable and cheap: for the hope that High Bluff would become a favourite place of residence had not outlived the last building
boom, and population had spread into other suburbs. Then you were
at the bottom of the hill and Patrick would loosen the brake, and
begin to trot faster and more securely; unless he had to stop at the
level crossing, where the road was spanned by a long overhead sign:
Look out for the Engine.

Here a negro barber-shop stood on one side and a liquor saloon
on the other: you were nearing civilisation; and from here on the
road was lined with hoardings, vast but a little broken and shaky,
from which, gigantic in size and violent in colour, Corn Flakes, Paper
Collars, Sweet Caporals, and Rubber Heels demanded that you
should buy them. Behind these enormous hoardings you could in
places catch glimpses of lacerated fragments of a scrubby wood,
littered with tin cans, torn paper, broken bottles, and an occasional
old shoe. This was some day to be the Riverside Park: for the road,
on the other side, now skirted the river, reflecting the huge mills and
factories on the opposite bank; and the high smoking chimneys attested how enterprise here had outgrown the water-power which had
first attracted it.

At all this Oliver stared stolidly, without understanding; but his
imagination awoke when they reached the bridge, especially that
shaky middle part of it, which could be lifted to let by the river traffic;

and here, as he grew taller, by craning his neck a little, he could just see the sparkling mill-ponds and canals, and the water gushing from under the mill-wheels, and a bit beyond, the row-boats and canoes moored in front of Murphy's boat-house. What is there in the universe more fascinating than running water, and the possibility of moving over it? What better image of existence and of possible triumph? But that bright vision gone, Oliver would sink again into his corner: the rest, as his mother truly said, was not worth looking at. At the dentist's, however, there were at least steps to climb, bells to ring, a queer chair to sit in, and those great spiders' legs with their quick nerves visible, whirring and whirring.

These drives seemed dull to Mrs. Alden also; for the great transformations which Great Falls had undergone in her time, though interesting to the census-taker or the real estate agent, were matters of course to her: even a little sad and discomforting, as they flooded her little world with an alien population, that did not share her traditions and did not recognise her eminence. Yet a philosopher might gladly have loitered among those scenes, to saturate his mind with the contrasts and superpositions which they contained. Below those new factories and that rickety bridge, which marked the foot of the ancient rapids, now canalised and hidden by buildings, the river widened into a great pool called South Pond; and from this the old village green still rose pleasantly in undulating slopes, traversed in all directions by diagonal paths under the shadow of scattered elms, with a Soldiers' Monument in the middle. This Common was fringed by a semicircle of nondescript buildings: two or three comfortable wooden mansions of an earlier age, painted white or light yellow: two churches, one of red brick with a little domed belfry in the style of Wren, the other Gothic with a great sloping roof and a grey stone spire; the old Town Hall, now a public library; the old Court House, now a second-hand furniture store; and newest and freshest of all, the model High School, with a vast expanse of glass windows and a forest of ventilators on the roof: a place destined to be, a few years later, the goal of Oliver's daily pilgrimage. In the midst of these accretions, the green shaded spaces of the Common retained an air of repose, refreshment and gentility. Here and there a shabby old person was sitting on a bench, apparently willing to do nothing. There were sparrows hopping and twittering. There were dead leaves whirled about, quite as in Homer's time, by some gust of wind; or being swept up into heaps by an aged gardener. After all, here was the heart of that noisy and restless organism which extraordinary circumstances had caused this quiet village to put forth, and clothe itself with, almost to the point of stifling and extinction; yet, here the old simplicity survived, under a crust of bustle and business, of bitter enterprise and bitter commitments. The new world began at the corner, where Main Street and Chestnut Street parted, and divided between them the banks and shops and clanging electric cars of a thriving provincial city. From the same ancient centre a long tentacle had also stretched to High Bluff and to the Bumstead mansion, where three or four generations had already struggled with good and evil fortune, and with a good and bad conscience.

"Mother," Oliver said one day as they were passing the bridge and the boathouse, in front of which Mrs. Murphy was sitting sewing, and holding her youngest sprawling offspring somewhat inconveniently in her lap, "why doesn't she make the baby sit on the bench?"

"I don't know," Mrs. Alden answered without looking. "I suppose the child is too young and can't sit up yet."

"Oh, no; he's almost as big as I am."

Mrs. Alden now involuntarily looked up, a little irritated. But it was a settled principle with her never to show impatience. "Perhaps," she said as if she were speculating on her own account, "he may be sleepy, and she's afraid he might drop off and fall into the water."

While her lips were uttering these words mechanically, Mrs. Alden couldn't help becoming aware that they were nonsense; for that hypothetically sleepy boy would have had to roll twenty feet on a level before reaching the river. Would Oliver notice? For fear he might, she instantly raised the argument to a higher plane, and turned from physical to moral considerations; a great resource when the facts contradict one's convictions. "Very likely," said Mrs. Alden, a little sadly, "very likely it's mere stupidity. Probably that woman can't afford to have a separate chair at home for her little boy, such as you have in the school-room: and so the poor creature has got used to holding him in her lap, even when they are out of doors, and there's plenty of room on the bench beside her. They get almost to *like* huddling together. It's repulsive, and so bad for the little one's health, and so uncomfortable. But ignorant people are like that."

Far, far in a dim past, as if it had been in another world or in a pre-natal condition, Oliver remembered the long-denied privilege of sitting in his mother's lap. It had been such a refuge of safety, of softness, of vantage: you were carried and you were enveloped in an amplitude of sure protection, like a king on his throne, with his faithful bodyguard many ranks deep about him: and the landscape beyond, with its messengers and its motley episodes became the most entertaining of spectacles, where everything was unexpected and exciting yet where nothing could go wrong; as if your mother herself had been telling you a story, and these pictures were only the illustrations to it which painted themselves in your listening mind. But now, in the real world, where you sat alone and were going to the dentist's, the centre seemed to be cold and only the circumference friendly and congenial: an untouchable world where rivers sparkled and flowed, and tugs whistled, and bright brown boats and canoes were moored together to the landing-stage, like bunches of bananas, and Mrs. Murphy sat sewing in the sunshine, and pressing her child to her broad bosom.

V

MY DEAREST LITTLE SISTER!

These last days here have been glorious—I don't mean the weather but the *Eating*! The Doctor, my little Oliver's Father, has been making us a visit. It is better after all that a *man* should be at the head of a household. You know that for the most part the Doctor sits in his yacht, the *Hesperus*, which they say is very beautiful. How I long to see it! Although formerly he had one even more magnificent; only with that strange love of belittling everything which all English-speaking people have—they call it *humour*—he had named his superb pleasure-ship *The Old Junk*, because I believe he had fitted it up as much as possible like a boat he once sailed in up and down the Chinese rivers. What must his life have been, a young man then, alone and rich, in that far country where all morality is so strange and heathen? I dream of it for long, long hours, but I shall never know. He is most reticent; and if I ask him something he puts me off with that cold tiresome American thing, a *joke*! Why *can't* the men here be serious sometimes and tell us, thirsting souls, the truth about something? Lieschen dear, I think I see the reason. It is that they *hate to think*! They are too busy, too tired; or if they half form an opinion in spite of themselves, they won't take the trouble to express it accurately, or to defend it. They laugh at what people *think*, even at what they think themselves, and respect only what people *do*. Yes, my dear, and beneath that horrid cynical scepticism, there is something deeper still. They are *afraid of the truth*! Isn't it dreadful! I want to teach my little Oliver—he is such a brave child, with his silent grey eyes so clear and wide open—not to be afraid of the truth. Of course they are all strictly truthful here about trifles: no little lies, no fibs, no positive deceit. Just icy reticence, and hypocrisy acted out with a life-long reserve. But I don't mean that. I mean loving the face of nature, and preferring to live in harmony with the truth, rather than with what people about you think it proper to say.

But I am wandering from the important point, which is the lovely food! You know how dry and tasteless I usually find it in this house. For two years always insipid chicken and half-raw beefsteak. Seldom veal, seldom ham, and never delicious roast pork. But oh, the change, when the Doctor is here! He is very considerate, and never wants to interfere with Frau Alden's arrangements; but he brings things up from the yacht, or orders them from a caterer's in Boston, as if they were presents. This year he has actually brought his black cook—a native of India, my dear, I have *seen* him!—not to the house, where the servants might object, but to a gentlemen's club in town where they have coloured waiters; and he cooks there, and brings the dishes all covered up in a basket for us at meal-times. It's half an hour in the electric car, and of course the hot things get cold; and Mrs. Alden says it is all useless and troublesome and unnecessary, and that things luke-warm or re-warmed are not appetising. But the Doctor, in his quiet way, laughs it off. "You needn't eat them, my dear," he says, "they are little extras for *me*, because my stomach is so diseased that it can digest nothing but poisons." But she eats them nevertheless, and sometimes is quite mollified, laughs at herself a little, and confesses that they are excellent. The Doctor has a theory about hot and cold things which he calls his Greek philosophy, that people who require things either very hot or very cold have no palate, but only blood-vessels: they want to be cooled when they are warm and warmed when they are cold, but can't taste anything. And he won't have ice in his water or wine, as they have here, and lets his soup and his tea get tepid before he will drink them, because, he says, he wants to know what sort of tea or soup he is taking. Mrs. Alden shrugs her shoulders and thinks he is a little mad, and he takes advantage of being odd (like Hamlet in Shakespeare) in order to laugh at people, and especially at his wife, without offending her too much. You know she is very proud of her family; and though the Bumsteads themselves are not very distinguished, she says her maternal grandmother was an Adams; not one of the Adams's of Quincy, but belonging to a branch of the family joining the Quincy branch earlier. "Yes," the Doctor will say under his breath, "a little earlier: before Adams was spelt with an S." This is an American joke; at first these things had to be explained to me but now I can understand them almost unaided. And although it is a very old joke between them, Mrs. Alden always smiles a little when it comes up again. The Doctor cracks so many jokes at his own expense that he has to be forgiven. And he has such tact! He wished our cook to learn how to boil rice as he likes it, quite dry and soft and not stuck together; so he called on her in the kitchen—I was in the pantry and heard it all unobserved: what luck!—and said that he was never able to get buckwheat cakes except at home, as she made them; but that he liked them so much, with the superior refined maple syrup with which she served them, that he was going to ask her as a favour that she should teach his cook, although he was a Hindu and a little dusky, to make them as she did. One lesson would do, these Eastern people are so intelligent. And Mrs. Mullins, though she thinks it beneath her to talk to coloured people, couldn't help being flattered; and when the sly young Indian came—for he is not more than thirty, very thin with great black and white eyes, enough to scare anybody—she said he was no black man, but more like an Italian, and that she wouldn't have minded actually sitting down with him to a cup of tea. And as he talked very magnificently all the time in excellent English—better than Mrs. Mullins' own—and deftly manipulated the long spoon and the dishes of various sizes, as if he were a magician—she was quite mollified and bewildered; and when he said: "Now, Mrs. Mullins, wouldn't you like to give the Doctor a surprise? Suppose to-day for luncheon you give him some Indian curry such as he never tasted out of India?" And then he proceeded to prepare everything himself, and fetched from a bag he had brought with him, the chutney and saffron and special pepper that were required. And you may be sure the way of steaming that rice remained fixed in Mrs. Mullins' subconsciousness as if by hypnotism; and now she couldn't do it wrong even if she tried: one little heap of rice quite white, one pink, and one yellow; thick curry saturating the bits of mutton cut in cubes; and a generous portion of chutney sauce, to go with it. How it tastes!

But that was only one day for luncheon: the chief feast was to-day at dinner. I didn't know at all what we were to have, because the Doctor had taken charge, saying it was a New England feast and mere Europeans couldn't understand the secret of it. That was also a joke, because he said at the same time that he would take Oliver out on Dumpy, so that I might have the whole afternoon free: and you may imagine that I improved the occasion to go and have a good talk and a glass of beer, with Frau Müller. Well, dinner was served half an hour earlier, now that the days are short, so that little Oliver might come to the table, although he is only six years old. Oysters! You will say, loathsome, slimy, slippery, cold things to swallow raw and almost alive. But wait. Imagine first a plate full of cracked ice; lovely small silver forks like tridents to eat them with; each oyster of the six lying in its delicately shaded mother-of-pearl shell, and not just crudely raw, as you think, but dressed with lemon juice, and a little parsley: and then, entirely to remove that horrid feeling, the Doctor will pass you a beautiful little flask, cut-glass and silver, with a liquid red pepper in it called Tabasco sauce: and two drops of it on each oyster will produce the most delicious contrast between the cold watery substance and the sharp peppery condiment. Then just a sip of old pale sherry—this of course also from the yacht, for at home we keep no wines—and then comes the hot clear mock-turtle soup, with bits of jelly-like meats and slices of hard-boiled egg: so stimulating, so varied: and with it no ordinary soggy bread, but cheese-sticks, and fluffy, puffy biscuits like *pommes soufflées,* and salted almonds. Then another sip of the sherry, or your whole glassful, if you please, because you know there is champagne coming. And now the real surprise of the feast. No boiled meats, no roast joint: instead, on each person's plate, my dear, one entire whole canvas-back duck, larger than a pigeon. You begin to cut it, and to the eye it may seem a little raw; the blood oozes out; but if you take courage and taste it—how marvellous!

And such accompaniments, too; fried crisp bread-crumbs and sweet soothing currant jelly; and fresh cool celery-salad with slightly pungent radishes mixed in! When I exclaimed and clapped my hands, as of course I did, on seeing an entire duck served on my plate, just for me alone, Frau Alden looked at me severely: I mustn't teach Oliver to make gestures or show his feelings: gentlemen are not monkeys. But the Doctor smiled at me, I think he was really pleased, and said: "Take care, Fräulein, you may find little lead bullets in these birds. Bits of metal are rather unpleasant to the teeth, at least at my age, and anyhow not nutritious. Don't think these little duck come from some pond in a farm yard; they are sea-birds bred in the salt marshes which abound along our Atlantic coast: men have to go far out in flat-bottomed boats, and hide behind the cover of rocks or tufts of scrub and tall weeds, so as to shoot them as they fly past: and the fine spreading shot which they use isn't always easy to find or to extract afterwards. When I was younger I used to shoot them myself sometimes for sport: it was a broad primitive life, solitary yet occupied. There is something poetical about those vast expanses of calm water and cloudy skies, and the wild life in them. But it involved getting up before dawn, with poor food and much exposure to cold and damp; and my rheumatism protested. I daresay the young bloods are still at it; but for the most part it has become a business like everything else, and helps the poor whites in the shore villages to eke out a living, at least at this season. Heaven knows what they do for a livelihood all the rest of the year. Probably they are politicians and distil whiskey."

Dearest Lieschen, how wonderful, in the midst of luxury and refinement, with all that beautiful silver and glass on the table, and flowers and lights, and a Venetian lace table-cloth—for Mrs. Alden is very proud of her mahogany table-top, and never lets it be wholly covered, because it belonged to her family, and not to the Doctor—how wonderful to be carried away suddenly into the wild, wild world! I seemed to feel the salt wind blowing, and the birds rising and screeching and spreading their broad hard wings! And then the thought of those dreary back-waters of American life, those ramshackle wooden houses, those gaunt joyless women, those bitter, swearing, hard drinking men! It is not as in our simple countryside, where there is hardship and sorrow enough, God knows, but where everything is well-ordered and healthy and beautiful, and even festive at certain seasons, in the old human pagan and Christian way. Here all is dismal, difficult, ugly, and desolate for the poor. You must be rich here, or your humanity is frozen stiff.

"And how do you like the duck, Fräulein?"

"Oh, very much; but why is there almost nothing to eat in the wings and legs? It seems to be all breast."

"The breast," the Doctor replied, "is the wing-muscle; the more a bird lives on the wing, the more its breast develops. The same thing happens to wild duck naturally which happens to those tame youths who swing clubs at the Young Men's Christian Association: the breast-muscles develop enormously and leave them with spindle legs. You must remember that birds are not mammals, and the breast hasn't the same function in them as in the cow."

Here Frau Alden, who has an ample bosom, blushed a little and said in a sort of whisper: "Really! Isn't this conversation becoming rather *physical?*" The Doctor glanced at me, to see if *I* had any cause to blush, and saw at once that I hadn't. It was the first time he had looked at me as if I were a woman and not just a governess. He went on quickly.

"Fräulein won't mind. She belongs to a scientific nation, and knows that science is elevating."

"Yes," I cried, "elevating and thrilling! I hope Oliver will love science."

"How is that, Oliver," said his father, turning to the little boy who had already finished his milked toast and was looking rather sleepy. "Do you know what a quadruped is?"

No answer.

"You know what a bird is, don't you? It hops on two legs."

"Yes," said Oliver, still a little sullen, "it hops *away*."

"But a horse or a dog or a cat or Dumpy, if he were livelier, would run away on four legs, wouldn't he?"

"Oh, yes," Oliver replied, now almost wide awake.

"Well, that's why a cat or a dog or a horse is called a quadruped, because it runs away on four legs and not on two, like a bird or like a man. In a bird the front legs have become wings, and in us they have become arms and hands."

By this time Oliver's eyes had become round and he was quite serious and silent, already feeling, I am sure, the grandeur of science. But at that moment the ice-cream was brought, and a beautiful portion, complete in its caramel basket, was put before him, as before the rest of us; and the ice-cream, for the time being, became more interesting than science. Such lovely ices, too, with green and yellow and red leaves made of candied fruit, and spun sugar to rest in instead of cotton wool—for you know that really good fruit here comes packed in cotton wool, as if it were a doll or a jewel. And the buds were *confitures-à-surprise*, my dear, so that when the thin caramel shell burst in your mouth, it startled and electrified you by suddenly discharging its secret drop of the sweetest and strongest cordial! I haven't time—it is 1 a.m.!—to tell you of the mince-pies, always made for Thanksgiving; but ours were quite special little ones, one for each person, and served with rum flaming all round them, as in an English plum-pudding. We shall have plum-pudding of course for Christmas, and I am already enjoying the taste of it in anticipation, with its rich solid sugar sauce! But those unexpected drops of liqueur, what a pleasure! Not even Goethe when his soul cried, *Verweile doch* . . . But I can't possibly leave out the champagne which, alas! we sha'n't have for Christmas because the Doctor will then be far away, basking in the tropical sun. I think you once did taste *Sekt* at our Herr Bürgermeister's son's wedding; but this is French champagne, much more delicate and potent and transporting: a sip or two quite enough to lift you into the sphere of the Ideal, with all lovers and poets and mystics like Goethe and Dante and Omar Khayyám and Solomon—only of course it wasn't *Solomon*—in his passionate Song of Songs, with its depths of marvellous meanings. How miraculously the spirit is freed from the body and the whole negative, cruel, earthly side of things melts away, and the wonders of the Arabian Nights seem after all the most natural, innocent, glorious of realities!

But I am leaving you open-mouthed, Lieschen dear, waiting for the last course. It was nuts and dates and figs and raisins and pears and oranges and hot-house grapes. Of course I couldn't taste everything, but I never can let *dates* go by, because I think of the Bedouins in the deserts of Arabia, who eat almost nothing else; and it seems to me, as the thick luscious substance dissolves in my mouth, that I share that simple, intense, religious life of theirs, all endless journeys through the wide burning sands, and love under the full moon. I am going to say something dreadful, dearest sister, but I feel it, and though it be blasphemy one should always say what one feels. I can no longer cry with Goethe, *Verweile doch.* No: such loitering is unworthy of the German spirit! We must not cling to anything achieved, but stretch out our eager hands for ever to the Beyond. And I won't say, towards "Something Higher." I won't climb up any ladder set up for me beforehand, with rungs all numbered higher and higher, like degrees in the thermometer! What is that but a remnant of petrified metaphysics? The free, bold, pure German genius cannot be confined to such a single narrow path. It will forge its way out of Itself in any direction, in all directions, into the infinite, scorning all law save that which It imposes on Itself at each moment by living, molested by no facts, recognising no conditions, but creating always the next step by Its untrammelled sudden inspiration. Nature is a prison. As for me, give me Chaos!

Oh, I *must* stop. It is two in the morning. How sleepy and seedy I shall be to-morrow! Perhaps that last *too* beautiful green mint in cracked ice, with its exquisite little glass, cut like an emerald of a thousand facets, was too much for my sober judgment and I have been writing *Unsinn!* How rich is experience in this wonderful world of ours, even if experience for you and me is not always so overwhelming as it has been to-day for your ever loving and still *hopeful*

IRMA.

P.S. There is no one at present, but I am only twenty-two.

VI

The golden age of Dumpy, alas, could not last for ever. Oliver's legs grew longer; he began to love speed, and preferred his bicycle; and he was also a bit concerned about his personal dignity. He felt much too tall now for that low fat lazy little beast; it was like riding a toy elephant on wheels. The demon of self-consciousness had got into Oliver early, never to be exorcised. Dumpy was a nice old thing, but he couldn't be allowed to make his master ridiculous. One was responsible, in the first place, for oneself, and must always choose what was best, even at the cost of outgrowing one's old feelings and one's old friends. Thus without knowing it—although Fräulein may have dropped some hints to that effect—Oliver anticipated the maxims of Goethe, and sacrificed his heart to his self-development. Dumpy on his side, as if consenting to the sacrifice, opportunely went lame, and finally had to be shot; and Mrs. Alden, who never spoke of death, said it had been thought wiser for Dumpy not to remain with them.

In spite of the coldness and distance between Peter Alden and his wife, with deep distrust on her part and perfect indifference on his, they agreed in many matters of policy, and especially in regard to the education of Oliver. At first, during his early boyhood, he should be brought up at home, like a young prince, though without courtiers. In this way he could be thoroughly well-grounded in his studies— something impossible in a modern school—and could acquire the speech and manners of a gentleman. But later on he must be sent to school; not for the sake of his lessons, but for moral and social reasons. The social reason plainly could not be snobbery: there was no older family in America and few richer than the Aldens, and even the Bumsteads were leading people in their own estimation. On the contrary, social relations were necessary in order to obliterate as far as possible the sense and the appearance of this immense superiority. It was imperative that Oliver should learn to live and to think democratically; that he should discover what American life was, not by inspection from his own point of view, like a supercilious foreigner, but by participation in it during his boyhood, and without criticism. He must feel at home in his country. He must begin by sharing spontaneously the habits and enthusiasms of his generation; otherwise he would never be able to influence them for the better. According to his mother's maxims it was only in order to contribute to the national life—of course by elevating it—that Oliver existed at all. His father was less certain about the purposes of existence, either in Oliver or in mankind; but he agreed that anyone destined to live in America needed to acquire the protective colouring that would enable him to move confidently in that medium and escape destruction or at least unmitigated misery. Peter Alden himself, in spite of the humour which covered for him a multitude of sins, both in himself and in others, and in spite of having been thoroughly initiated in his youth into a particular native circle, had found himself nevertheless a waif in his own country as well as in the rest of the world. That particular circle had been too narrow and old-fashioned; and in slipping out of it, he had also missed the general movement of national events and national sentiment. Not, as he said to himself, with a sort of mocking modesty, that either he or his country had lost much by that divorce: but Oliver being also his mother's son, might be expected to have more stamina, greater gifts, a more aggressive conscience, and a thicker skin.

Someday, therefore, Oliver must be sent to school; but the day was put off as long as possible, for the sake of his studies. He was a remarkably good pupil, somewhat calm, as if he had heard all these things before, but evenly absorbent, and evenly retentive. Irma, all love and zeal, had no difficulty in emptying into him her store of knowledge in German and English literature, in history and even in the classics. When it came to the natural sciences and mathematics the little lady was hard pressed to keep a bit ahead of her ward and appear to know what she was expected to teach him; and indeed, after a time, all pretence was tacitly dropped, and he systematically took the lead, while she became simply a pace-maker and sympathetic comrade in his career of discovery.

Oliver soon found, as he afterward used to put it, that there was a sunny and a shady side to the road of knowledge. The sunny side was the study of nature, where all exploration was joyful, and free from evil passion and prejudice. The same was true of mathematics which, if not so sunny as geography or astronomy or natural history, at least was pure from human taint. You were honestly challenged by your problem, and could work your way honestly forward until you came to an honest solution or an honest difficulty. Only non-human subjects were fit for the human mind. They alone were open, friendly and rewarding. Unfortunately the human subjects had to be studied too: and here—in history, languages, literature, not to speak of religion—all was accidental and perverse. Perhaps story-telling, just for amusement, might be very well for the theatrical sort of people who liked it; although Oliver himself had never cared much for tales and poetry and things supposed to be funny: he had been less bored than most children when let alone, and less pleased when prodded. But to tell stories and pass them off for the truth—what an extraordinary outrage! The histories and theories which people had composed in their heads did not appeal to him as visions, as incitements to the imagination, which is the way in which they really appeal to the humanists who cultivate them: and not caring for them as fictions, it never crossed his mind to mistake them for truths. On the contrary, he instinctively hated them for trespassing on that ground; they were counterfeits; they were rendered malignant by the very fact that they had a subject-matter more or less real, which they dared to caricature and diminish and dress up in the motley of particular minds. Yet this subject-matter itself was a sorry affair: a chaos of barbarous and ignorant nations, struggling for a wretched existence and rendering existence doubly wretched for one another. The human world was so horrible to the human mind, that it could be made to look at all decent and interesting only by ignoring one half the facts, and putting a false front on the other half. Hence all that brood of fables. But this flattering office of poetry and elegance did not redeem them in Oliver's eyes: they were only "frills"; and all such beautifications belonged to the shady side of knowledge.

In his boyhood, though words and ideas were lacking to express it, this puritan disdain of human weakness and of human genius was at work silently within him. It caused him to do his languages and history in a perfunctory way, with a certain inward and growing estrangement. He remembered the facts in the books easily, and the meanings of words, and the rules of grammar; but his mastery of these matters was a little sardonic, as if he resented that such things should have to be remembered at all. He found escape from that absurdity not only in those other purer studies, showing the sunny side of the world, but above all in bodily exercise. This was destined to be his sovereign medicine and sheet-anchor throughout his short life. A fit body might not make a fit mind, might even induce a certain mental sleepiness; but at least it would keep the mind sane. In a world where so little was sure, there was comfort in feeling sure of your nerves, your muscles, and your digestion. Moreover, exercise in the open brought Oliver into a genuine communion with nature, such as he never found either in religion or in poetry: the confident active sympathy of man with things larger than himself, and with a universal reptilian intelligence which was not thought, but adaptation, unison, and momentum. That groping labour which had produced the trees, the rivers, the meadows, which was piling up and dissolving the clouds, seemed then to engage his inmost being in its meshes and to turn him for the moment into the gladdest, the most perfect, yet the most dependent of creatures. And he could accept joyfully this dependence and this fugitive strength, feeling at the same time the immense promise of a thousand other perfections sleeping in the womb of nature, into which the strong soul of this moment must presently return.

Nevertheless, this escape, this private wordless religion, soon bred its own conventions and became compulsory and imprisoning in its turn. To go for a single day without two hours of vigorous out-door exercise was now out of the question. That would have been as improper and shameful as to lie in bed all the morning out of laziness, or to go unwashed, or to wear soiled linen. It would have meant physical restlessness and discomfort indoors, and the most horrible sensual moodiness in the inner man. Yet in the nondescript changeful weather of New England it was only occasionally possible to play lawn tennis with Fräulein, and seldom tempting, in that seared suburban landscape, to take long walks like an old man merely for the sake of walking. Nor was it often steadily cold enough for much skating or tobogganing. A sandy golf-links indeed existed, but at some distance, and unattractive; and the country was too hilly for bicycling with patience and a sense of freedom.

What better, thought Dr. Alden, when all these difficulties were set before him by the combined eloquence of his family, what better than that Dumpy should have a successor? Wasn't Mr. Charley Deboyse with whom he sometimes quaffed drinks and exchanged stories at the Somerset Club, on the point of selling his polo-ponies, some of which, like their master, were no longer quite keen and limber enough for so brisk a sport? And wouldn't one of these ponies, well-trained, light-footed, but not too frisky, be just the thing for Oliver?

"Polo!" cried Mrs. Alden. "Oh!" and her tone expressed the extreme of pain and of disapproval. Polo was an extravagant, dangerous, foreign game, fit only for desperately idle rich people, trying to be fashionable. Besides, Mr. Charley Deboyse *drank*; and she wouldn't like Oliver to have a horse that had belonged to *him*, or had been a polo-pony. However, she did approve of what she called horseback riding; and it was true that Oliver wasn't to play polo himself, or drink, or ever see Mr. Charley Deboyse. In the end, the shock having passed, she consented broad-mindedly to waive her objections and her misgivings: only stipulating that polo should never be mentioned in connection with the new pony, and that it should not be Oliver's pony exclusively but simply an extra horse in the stable, which might be put into a light cart, as well as ridden. A pony-cart, she instantly perceived, would be a real convenience. It would relieve Patrick and leave him more time for *useful* work; because in good weather she might drive herself in to town in the cart instead of going in the heavy coupé or the pretentious victoria, both of which involved a coachman. Hating the presence of servants in general, she particularly suffered at the thought of coachmen, and of those dirty, idle, smoking, sauntering, and surely ribald, profane, and socialistic cab-drivers who spent their lives waiting and waiting in the cab-stands of cities. What could one expect of such men's morals whose very business was to do nothing most of the time? Without Patrick, it would be much nicer going shopping, or to the post-office; and by taking Irma she wouldn't even have to get out at the shops; and she would be breathing the wholesome morning air, and at the same time accomplishing so much that had to be done in such a great household as hers. That trip to town in the morning, which wouldn't come every day, wouldn't give nearly enough exercise to a well-fed horse, used to hard work: for she confessed that from the point of view of the ponies alone, polo might be a good thing. Oliver might therefore perfectly well take the pony out again in the afternoon for a short ride. But it was most important that the boy should not get into the habit of thinking that everything in this world was provided exclusively for him and for his pleasure. Selfishness and self-indulgence were such a danger for young people, especially for an only child, with the example of his father too, who lived so much aloof, and wasn't really so ill as never to be able to do *anything* for other people. She was thankful that, as a girl, she had had so much responsibility thrown upon her, in having to provide everything for her father and her young brothers: she might not otherwise have learned to be thoroughly public spirited and unselfish, and to find a rich life in the Service of Others. Oliver too, if possible, must be made to feel that, if he was given the opportunity to ride, it was not for his idle pleasure, or for show, but only for his health, so that he might be able later to carry on his life-work better, and to have a greater influence for good in the world.

Young Oliver accepted the new pony—which was a beautiful creature—with a momentary flush of pleasure, yet silently, as if he felt a certain increment of dignity and responsibility. He must prove that he was getting only what he deserved to possess. Everything kept challenging him, as it were, to walk on higher and higher stilts, and forcing him to make a success of a ticklish and, at bottom, a needless business. There was satisfaction of course, in doing the job handsomely, and he was not in the least afraid: he knew he could do it: he was proud of the pony and of himself mounted on it so airily, and he was almost grateful—vaguely, to circumstances, to God, hardly definitely to his father; but at the same time in a not unpleasant way he was sobered, he was deepened. There was a quiet melancholy in privilege. One must accept privilege, because it brought a chance of greater achievements: but happiness, pure joy, would have come rather in having no privilege and being lost in the moving crowd. When a flock of birds took the air in a great wheeling caravan, only the birds in the middle were living normally: the leader was not enviable. He might be asked why he chose that particular direction, or veered as he did, and why he startled and summoned and hypnotised the rest to follow. What answers could that bird give? There must be leaders, or there would be no grandeur in life; but there was something tragic, something ominous, in being chosen to lead. Could that leading bird be said to be living for others? Was he not rather imposing himself upon them, and thereby turning what might have been his free life into a responsible thing? Was it their fault if they made a guide of him and blindly followed wherever he seemed so impetuously bent on going? And if he misled them, weren't his native innocence and courage turned into guilt?

As for those others, for whose sake the strange burdens of existence were apparently to be borne, they were principally his mother, Fräulein, and the occasional apparition of Miss Letitia Lamb or his father in the offing. These eminent full-grown persons were all his mentors, elders, and official protectors: none of them were in need of his assistance; he wasn't doing his lessons or taking his exercise for their supposed benefit. They all seemed to think, on the contrary, that they were continually and unselfishly benefiting him, and living for his sake. It was later, and to the world in general, that he was expected to repay all these attentions. *Others* meant that whole quarrelsome kettle of human beings in the distance, and their unknown posterity. How was he, poor child, to discover what he ought to help those unborn multitudes to become? Was he to trust the prophetic sympathy of his mother and the Unitarian minister as to what the good of others would be? Would those others like it any better than he liked what his mother and the Unitarian minister said would be good for him? He felt in his growing bones that he was being oppressed, that there was something horribly unnecessary and unrighteous in the arrangements of this world. He was often told that he had been particularly favoured, and was doubly responsible. Very well: and how was he to discharge that responsibility? By endeavouring to lift Others to his own level, so that they might be as responsible and as unhappy as himself? All those preachments, coupled as he could feel with a profound helplessness in the preachers, or with a satisfied ignorance and desperate bluff, fell upon his ears like so much rain beating against the window-panes. One mustn't quarrel with the weather; one must be cheerful and go out and take one's exercise just the same: one must grow strong and tolerant and indomitable within oneself, and let the winds and the people bluster.

His true counsellors spoke to him without words. They were the woods through which he rode alone, letting his horse pick his way through the unkempt scrubby undergrowth, and amusing himself by dodging or whipping aside the twigs and the hanging branches. Not one tree here lived for Others: not one insect, not one crawling thing, questioned its native impulse to thrive. Wasn't the only good anyone could do in this world simply to keep himself as undefiled and determined and complete as possible, and to let Others too live as they liked? He wouldn't crush them, he wouldn't torture them, he would even help them out of a trap into which they might have fallen, if their distress was obvious, and he could befriend them without compromising his own integrity. He could succour; but he couldn't abet or instigate all this swarming blindness of existence. Once in the race, you had to take your chances, and nobody could make you run faster than your legs would carry you. Nor could everybody win. *He* would win, because he could: yet it was curious how little pleasure he found in the foretaste of victory. In the woods even the tallest trees, that had fought their way victoriously to the upper light and air, were cramped and distorted; and their meagre crowns were often half-withered and bald. Was he to be like that? No: he could get out of the woods, into the open. And as he actually came out again on to the main road, he would pat the strong curved neck of his pony, or the smooth flank; and he would catch an understanding answer to his congratulations in the lighter step of the beast, or in his quivering nostrils. How pleasant and how various were the allies which a truly clear and masterful will could find in the world, and marshal against one's inevitable enemies! To surrender to those enemies, or to compromise with them, was not only to tarnish one's own soul, but to create new and more intimate conflicts and hasten towards dissolution. Never mind enemies. Rider and horse could strengthen and gladden each other in their spontaneous common career, forgetting who was servant and who was master, disdaining enemies, and disdaining death.

And there were other amenities in his boyish life, and other silent communications. He had learned to ride: he must also learn to swim and to row. And who more fitted to initiate him into these midsummer sports than Mr. Denis Murphy, who kept that boat-house by the mill-pond? Murphy's great days were over, but he had had them, and for those in the know he remained a distinguished personage. Fifteen years earlier he had been sculling champion of the world. Such fame, though it may lead in the end to but a humble place in human society, never quite loses its glamour in the imagination of contemporary sportsmen: and the presence of that superannuated hero in the neighbourhood had not escaped Peter Alden. Whenever he came up from his yacht in the launch it was at Murphy's landing stage that he put in; and for years the Doctor and the boatman had exchanged prognostications about the weather, or on the prospects of elections: and many a little bill had been paid and many a good cigar given, to predispose Mr. Murphy in the rich man's favour. When the proposal finally was made, to take young Oliver out on the water, and give him a hint or two about rowing, no business, however important, was allowed to stand in the way: and Oliver soon had his boating and his bathing togs at the boat-house, and ultimately his own shell and oars. Many an afternoon in summer, during his teens, was spent under Mr. Murphy's protection: for it became a matter not merely of barely learning to row or to swim, but of expertness in these arts, and even a little practice in boxing was thrown into the bargain. Mr. Murphy was proud of his young pupil: and Oliver not only applied himself diligently to doing well—which for him was a matter of course—but he felt a sort of confidence in this simple man, such as people of his own class didn't inspire. Bodily skill was something unmistakable: the proofs of it were material, and so were the forces with which you had to count material and sure; and even your own conceit or shyness could be easily corrected by the event. You were classed by your performance, not by your opinion or by anybody else's. That was such a relief. At home all was a matter of discussing opinions, and feeling bitterly how superior your own opinion was. But Mr. Murphy seemed to have no opinions. If you asked him what he thought of this, or thought of that, he simply grinned, and changed the subject. But he could tell you how things were made, and how things were done, and why things happened—that is, within the boatman's sphere. He was the first *master* Oliver had known.

Often the man and the boy would make long excursions together, for the most part in silence. It was not only possible to take a dip from the landing-stage at the boat-house, but it was possible to row, or even to sail, up to the northern end of the Mill Pond, a great artificial widening of the river above Great Falls, produced by the mill-dams; and there, in the silvan seclusion and silence of a sheltered cove, a lesson in swimming had a special charm. Mr. Murphy was a native of Ireland, where he had spent his youth: he felt that his pupil was a young gentleman, sometimes even called him sir; and he instinctively abstained from irrelevant talk in the boy's presence. Perhaps he felt also the greenness and coolness and glassiness of the scene, as somehow haunted by higher powers, and sacred to youth. Oliver by that time had become an idyllic stripling, slender in body and tender in mind, quiet, attentive, and courageous; always careful to swim or to row correctly, as Mr. Murphy had explained scientifically that one should row or swim, even if the oars sometimes grew rather heavy and the water rather cold. Yet the arts learned so scrupulously seemed somehow sad arts: they scarcely penetrated to the dumb potentialities of Oliver's being, which remained unmoved, as if waiting for something wholly different to call them forth. And the quietness of the boy, beneath all his dutiful diligence and evident powers, induced silence in the good man also: as if Chiron, the

Centaur, in the presence of the young Achilles, had refrained from snorting. Afterwards Denis Murphy would say to his wife, "That young kid of Dr. Alden's is a deep one. He won't live to be old. The likes of him isn't made for this world. Pity he's being brought up a heathen."

VII

Meantime, on the completion of Oliver's fifteenth year, it had been agreed that he should go to school. In any other household equally fastidious the choice of a school might have been a terrible problem; but in this case the question solved itself without difficulty. There was only one school that Oliver *could* go to. For Mrs. Alden disapproved of all boarding-schools on principle: they removed boys at the most critical age from the sacred influences of home and mother, and they were hot-beds of snobbery, rowdiness, cruelty, and immorality. To make up for this real wickedness they dressed up those young ruffians on Sunday in white surplices and made them file two by two with joined hands into choir, and sing sentimental anthems; so that their only idea of something better than brutality might be to become little angels in a perpetual choral service in heaven. And what was the result? That those silly boys in after life were at best nonentities, copied the fashion-plates in tailors' windows, married rich women, and were null intellectually, null morally, and null politically.

"Hurray, hurray," Peter would murmur admiring the conviction with which his wife could turn into virtuous invectives that secret jealousy which she felt towards people more fashionable than herself. And he concurred in the issue. Boarding-schools being excluded, Oliver must be sent to the Great Falls High School, which was the only day school within reach. Certainly Peter felt some regret that his exceptional son should have to be educated in an obscure provincial establishment, among common boys, and under mediocre teachers: yet was any alternative really more attractive? Were not all schools provincial in spirit, and all schoolboys barbarians, and all schoolmasters mediocre? Or if there were exceptions might they not be found at Great Falls as well as elsewhere? In his own boyhood the influence of Mr. Mark Lowe had been a happy accident. The crucial turn in everything must be left to chance. Oliver was well grounded already; he was only going to school in order to learn to live among strangers, to play games, to have comrades, and to find his own level in a nondescript world. For this purpose—the only use of schools—any school would do. In any school Oliver might acquire knowledge of men and boys, and test and develop his character.

In this way Peter Alden, who laughed at his wife's unconscious hypocrisy, succeeded in deceiving himself a little about his own motives. He had abdicated all formal responsibility for Oliver's education, and let his wife bring the boy up as she chose. It had been a kind of sarcastic gallantry towards her superior intelligence and knowledge of life; and it had relieved him of the enormous difficulty of making up his own mind. Yet his conscience, at bottom, remained uneasy. Wouldn't something entirely different have been infinitely better?

In reality, as schools go, the High School at Great Falls, Connecticut, had much to recommend it. The building was new, clean, heated and ventilated automatically, according to the latest and most expensive contrivances. Prosperity in this corner of New England had not banished conservatism; the Demos aspired to be cultured and refined. There was an Art Museum, and the Public Library, though the gift of Carnegie, was handsomely supported by the city council. Yet all these great opportunities (as they were styled) for self-education went with a certain survival of restraint. This model schoolhouse, ultra-modern in every other respect, had two separate entrances and two school yards, for boys and for girls, on strictly opposite sides of the edifice; and a severe brick wall, running like a vast bulk-head through the whole height and breadth of it, separated the two sexes; nor was it rumoured that any Pyramus and Thisbe had ever pierced a hole in it for exchanging kisses. Moreover, there was a special classical division reserved for boys intending to go to college: and all the teachers in this division, as well as the Headmaster, were men: a lucky circumstance, as Peter thought, because Oliver, except for Denis Murphy, had lived too long under the exclusive influence of women. Refinement, sentiment, moral intensity were all very well, but they should not be made the fulcrum of your universe, or that universe would come toppling down on your head. The great, the trusty educator of mankind was matter: and matter, in ladies' minds, was entirely veiled in a mist of words. And not in ladies' minds only. Most schoolmasters were people who had failed in the world, or who feared to fail in it: they knew matter only by the terror which they felt of it: yet even that indirect acknowledgment was better than a bland innocence and an unchecked indulgence in fabulation. Oliver would feel, however lop-sided his new masters might be, that they had one foot on terra firma.

To sit in front of a yellow wooden desk, screwed to the floor, in a yellow wooden chair, screwed to the floor likewise and scientifically hollowed out to fit one's standardised person, was a new sensation, and not unpleasant; the fact that there were eight such chairs and eight such desks in a row, and five or six rows of them, all alike, was somehow reassuring. Nothing was likely to happen anywhere in this new world except that which happened regularly everywhere and to everybody. Alden being alphabetically the first name in the class list, Oliver was placed in a corner seat in the back row, between two large windows; and without turning round or showing any undue curiosity, he could see most of the boys' faces, with the full sunlight upon them. They looked to him at first like so many small editions of Mr. Denis Murphy, and he rather liked them for that: not as if they were real people, such as the people at home, but boys in some picture-book or tale of adventure: simple, rough, gleeful, and together producing a certain rumble and vibration of herded life, like horses in their stalls or pigeons in a dovecot. He soon found, when it came to standing about in the School yard during the recess, or playing tag— which seemed to him a very small boys' game—that he had nothing in particular to say to them, or they to him. Their brogue too was something like Mr. Murphy's, only shriller, uglier, and more aggressive. He soon learned their dialect and slang, but it always remained a foreign language to him, as did common American speech in general. He didn't hate it; sometimes it made him laugh; it all seemed to him like a turn on the variety stage, meant to be funny, and really droll, though it might become too constant and tiresome. His own natural speech was that of ladies and clergymen. His mother, Fräulein Schlote, and Miss Letitia Lamb each had her own accent and intonation; but they had much the same vocabulary and were all equally punctilious and self-conscious in their way of speaking. They were always asking how this or that word *ought* to be pronounced, or whether this or that phrase was *good English*. Fräulein's Anglo-German standards could not always be accepted, but they counted with Oliver and accustomed him, from childhood up, to certain polite and idiomatic British phrases, of which he felt the rich savour; and then there was the authority of his father, to whom the three women would appeal in their grammatical perplexities, because after all he was a Bostonian, had spent his life travelling, and knew so many *other* languages. Oliver, in spite of his tendency to believe that whatever was natural in himself was right, was rather disturbed and uncertain on this subject. He couldn't be content, in speech any more than in anything else, with what was wrong or inferior or second best: yet it was most puzzling to decide what the absolutely best was, and so hard, even then, to live up to it. Language, for him, didn't belong to the sunny side of life. It was one of those human troubles in which the curse of original sin, and of Babel, most surely appeared.

It would be too much to affirm that in his three years at school Oliver learned absolutely nothing. In some subjects, indeed, his accomplishments already went beyond the demands of his new teachers; but he was beginning Greek and French; and even in other matters the authors read or the methods of treatment were often new to him, and enlightening. Moreover, there was the schoolroom atmosphere of laziness, mischief, mockery, and howlers: it supplied a fresh and crude human setting for all this imposed learning. Above all, there was the personality of the teachers. The school mind seemed to regard them as a sort of policemen to be circumvented as much as possible, and jeered at: but to Oliver they looked rather like poor monsters embarrassed by their pachyderms, with perhaps a spark of natural boyish soul still smouldering within. Particularly was this the case with the sarcastic wizened little man who taught American history and literature in a high quavering voice, with a bitter incisive emphasis on one or two words in every sentence as if he were driving a long hard nail into the coffin of some detested fallacy. Cyrus Paul Whittle might have made his way as a preacher or politician in his native Vermont, had his opinions been less trenchant and unpopular; and even as a school-teacher his position would not have been secure, if the Headmaster and the City Council had heard all the asides and all the comments with which he peppered his instruction. His joy, as far as he dared, was to vilify all distinguished men. Franklin had written indecent verses: Washington—who had enormous hands and feet—had married Dame Martha for her money; Emerson served up Goethe's philosophy in ice-water. Not that Mr. Cyrus P. Whittle was without enthusiasm and a secret religious zeal. Not only was America the biggest thing on earth, but it was soon going to wipe out everything else: and in the delirious dazzling joy of that consummation, he forgot to ask what would happen afterwards. He gloried in the momentum of sheer process, in the mounting wave of events; but minds and their purposes were only the foam of the breaking crest;

and he took an ironical pleasure in showing how all that happened, and was credited to the efforts of great and good men, really happened against their will and expectation. The great and good men were in themselves no better or wiser than the failures: they merely happened to be on the winning side. They had done something that survived and counted, whereas the failures—and Cyrus Paul Whittle thought of himself—had done just as much, only it disappeared and didn't count. Nevertheless—and here the dry flame of Calvinistic illumination would light up the man's eyes for a moment—you were not to be discouraged. Providence did wonderful things through unworthy instruments. You might be fearless and shrewd and without an atom of deference for anybody on God's earth, and yet you might be full of faith, hope and charity.

These sentiments sank imperceptibly into Oliver's mind, without awakening his attention; they were not incongruous with his own temperament; and they merged also with that herd-instinct, that sense that you must swim with the stream and do what is expected of you, which now became dominant in him. It was not Living for Others; it was not Doing Good. Those were just words to cover the desire of busy-bodies to manage other people, and make the world over according to their own fancy. This was something natural, genuine, spontaneous, like sympathy with nature at large. It was that very sympathy concentrated and intensified within the human circle. It was living *with* others, letting others live in you, being carried along by their impulse, adopting their interests; and all this not because you found their ways right or reasonable or beautiful or congenial, but just because those ways, here and now, were the ways of life and the actions afoot; and there was no real choice open to you to live otherwise or to live better.

So with the same docility, the same pluck, and the same sadness with which he had done his lessons at home, and taken his exercise, he now began to do at school everything that the school spirit demanded: which first and foremost, in the autumn term, was to play football. Eleven boys, with some substitutes, were to be chosen out of a class of forty; and it was evident that Oliver must offer to play, being the tallest and, as it soon appeared, the strongest and quickest of the lot. But he was new to the game and had to endure at first the mortifications of a beginner. All was not pleasure in the first scrimmages, being pushed and hustled and crushed and sworn at: but Oliver was long-suffering, not afraid of pain, resolute, and attentive;

and his pride was concerned to seem hardier than he was, and not to mind bruises and dirt. He continued to hate these things, but he learned to endure them. The tactics of the game were soon mastered: the worst of it was the malodorous rough crowding and fighting. He had to force himself to "scrap"; those boxing lessons of Mr. Murphy's were a help in many an extremity; only he should have learned to wrestle as well as to spar; and also the art—impossible to Oliver—of opportunely breaking as well as invoking the rules. However, with a little practice, the air gradually cleared. Opportunities came of showing his special abilities. Soon, in spite of his weight, he was removed from the line, and placed at half and finally at full back, which remained his normal position so long as he played football. It was a vast relief to find himself in most of the action, and in all the intervals and breathing spaces, whenever the whistle sounded, well out in the open, alone, with a wide field of vision to watch and to traverse. Refreshed and masterful at that point of vantage, he could easily nerve himself to buck the line and fight hard at close quarters, when that was required; and when the ball came to him in a comparatively clear field, he was entirely in his element running and kicking. His long legs, his clear eye, a sort of self-possession which was almost indifference, served him to perfection in a long run, or in a drop-kick; and in these respects he established at once a local reputation. Indeed, before the end of his first season he was moved from his class team to the School Eleven, where he was the youngest boy: and this unprecedented honour established him at once as a school hero. Murmurs that might otherwise have gathered force, to the effect that he was a sissy or a snob or a coward, were entirely silenced: the more that in a first encounter with the rowdy gang—which he soon learned to distinguish from the decent and neutral elements—his unexpected quickness in the manly art had discouraged open hostility. His contemporaries continued to eye him askance, as a swell and a highbrow—the juster word *prig* was not in their dictionary; but they suspended their ill-will, and waited for developments. The leaders of the school, with whom he now associated, approved of him, and the teachers also: and as in his studies he was invariably at the head of his class, it became gradually clear that opposition was useless and that he was heir-apparent to all the honours of the school. In his last year he would have to be elected captain in football and field sports: only base-ball, which he didn't play, would remain open to his rivals. His looks and manners came to be generally admired: he was the hero of all the smaller boys in the school: and the whispering groups pocketed their jealousy and democratic intolerance and decided to back him up. There was something diffident and apologetic about him which, at close quarters, turned away wrath. He was fair and civil to everybody, had no favourites, no clique, and indeed seemed to make no friends. At times the curve of his mouth grew serious and almost bitter; and a certain listlessness appeared in his attitude when he was not engaged in making some express effort. All his lessons and sports seemed to be taken up as duties, and executed unswervingly, as if to get rid of them as quickly and thoroughly as possible. True, other tasks at once took their place; his life now had absolutely no leisure in it; but at least there was a silent moment of peace as each duty—each enemy—was despatched in turn.

Perhaps in that flight of birds which Oliver had watched and wondered at in other days, the leader was not really a bold spirit, trusting to his own initiative and hypnotising the flock to follow him in his deliberate gyrations. Perhaps the leader was the blindest, the most dependent of the swarm, pecked into taking wing before the others, and then pressed and chased and driven by a thousand hissing cries and fierce glances whipping him on. Perhaps those majestic sweeps of his, and those sudden drops and turns which seemed so joyously capricious, were really helpless effects, desperate escapes, in an induced somnambulism and a universal persecution. Well, this sort of servitude was envied by all the world: at least it was a crowned slavery, and not intolerable. Why not be gladly the creature of a universal will, and taste in oneself the quintessence of a general life? After all, there might be nothing to choose between seeming to command and seeming to obey. If others envied him, he secretly envied them; would have liked to be simple like them, spontaneous and unhampered. Against cheating, dirt, and foul language he maintained his prejudices, and did not hesitate to show them; but in other respects his ambition was to be like everybody else. Externals were burdens: the fewer and plainer the better. He had a gold watch, one of his father's presents, and was willing to carry it, because it kept good time and allowed him to be always punctual; but he discarded the gold chain, and tied the watch to the lapel of his coat with a black thong intended for a bootlace. He noticed that many of the boys wore no shirt but only a sweater, perhaps with a jacket over it. He would have loved to imitate them: collars were such a hindrance and cuffs such a bother. His negative temperament, his impatient young reason kept asking:

What's the use of *frills?* He couldn't very well appear suddenly at home without a shirt. Even a tie was imperative: yet what an absurdity that was! A strip of flimsy silk, gaudily coloured, throttling you all your life for no reason. He always dressed for dinner, in grey trousers with pumps and a black coat: and his clean starched shirt and his black tie seemed to him appropriate then, because there couldn't help being something stiff about a family dinner: it was a good deal like going to church. But when it was a question of doing something, and doing it well, why dress up inconveniently? He would make a shy beginning of reform, as far as he thought he could stick to it.

"But Oliver!" cried his mother one morning at breakfast, "where is your waistcoat?"

"Upstairs. Hanging in the closet."

"Why haven't you put it on?"

"Nobody at school wears a vest—they call it a vest—except the teachers. It's a nuisance."

"But it's not *respectable* to go about like that. Your father always wears a waistcoat, and so did your uncles when they were boys. In the heat of summer, I could understand it: but now, in October, you'll catch your death of cold."

"When it gets cold I'll wear a pull-over."

"Besides, you will need the pockets."

Oliver smiled. His mother had twice shifted her ground, from respectability to health, and from health to convenience. He felt that his case was won; but he couldn't resist the temptation to rub it in a little.

"I have four outside pockets in my jacket and three inside; three in my trousers; and six more in bad weather when I'm obliged to wear an overcoat. Sixteen pockets. Isn't that enough?"

Mrs. Alden was silent. Didn't she manage with a single pocket, or rather with none, but only a portable reticule, to be forgotten on every table and every chair? But Oliver was warned. He must not press his advantage. Asceticism offended the polite world, and wearing a sweater instead of a shirt, except in sporting hours, was a privilege allowed only to the poor.

VIII

"I can't make out," observed Mrs. Alden, as she and Fräulein Irma sat fanning themselves in the north porch, "what is the matter with Oliver. Not a word has he uttered all through lunch. He's so strong physically, why should he be so terribly bitter and languid? I'm afraid it's something inherited from his father: weakness of moral fibre and a tendency to melancholia. These two years at school have been so splendid for him, keeping his mind occupied, and giving him plenty of out-door exercise in their school games: and with always keeping at the head of his class and winning all those prizes, one would think he ought to be more cheerful and lively, and more like other boys of his age. When my brothers went to that same school—and it was much shabbier in those days, in the old wooden school-house—they were perfectly irrepressible. They would come home to snatch a meal, and rush off at once on all their silly schoolboy affairs. And in summer they would go camping in the woods: but Oliver absolutely refuses to go again to Mr. Brown's camp at Skeater's Pond: calls it *godforsaken*—what a word to use about his own minister's summer home, and Mr. Brown so liberal and hearty and broad-minded, nobody would take him for a clergyman at all! Yet instead of that happy wild life with other boys, Oliver insists on staying at home all summer and reading. I'm sure it may be very good for his mind, but is it wise? His uncles may have made more noise, and been less considerate, but at least they never moped. Oliver is so critical of everything, so dissatisfied and disdainful. One would think he had been crushed by some terrible disappointment. I suppose the doctors would say he was passing a climacteric—trying to become a young man. Yet the worst of that should have been over two or three years ago. Isn't he almost seventeen? What a loss for us all that my dear father couldn't have been spared a little longer. He would have helped so much in this matter. He had made a specialty of such cases for years, and was so wise, so charitable, so scientific. You don't know how splendidly he pulled Dr. Alden himself out of all his difficulties and completely cured him—at least as far as a man of that age could be cured at all."

"But who better," Irma cried full of innocent conviction, "who better to advise Oliver than his own father? If Dr. Alden only knew, wouldn't he come at once and tell us what had better be done?"

"It isn't as if Oliver were really ill," Mrs. Alden retorted. "It's only moodiness."

"I know he feels the heat terribly," Irma went on, "he is tired. Think how hard he has worked, besides his regular lessons, with all the effort and responsibility about athletics, because he felt it would be such a disappointment for the school if at the interscholastic games he didn't win the two hundred and forty yards dash, and the hurdles and——"

"How can you remember those silly words? It does all seem so childish!" and Mrs. Alden rocked herself in her chair, half amused, half impatient.

"But it's his life, Mrs. Alden. I try to follow his life, to share it, to understand what makes him happy or unhappy. And I know the trouble he took, training for all the sports in which he thought he had a fair chance of winning, although some of them were new to him, or he didn't like them particularly. And how wonderful that he should win in them, just as he had foreseen! Not a touch of conceit or even of pleasure in it all, just firmness. 'If I can do it,' he says to himself, 'I suppose I must.' It's no use trying to think of amusements for him: they don't amuse him. Only when we read something very very beautiful, a very high thought, he seems at last to come to life, as if that were what he had always been waiting to hear, and had never heard. Not poetry that is merely beautiful: he doesn't care for Schiller or Heine or for Shakespeare or Shelley. It mustn't be beauty of words or of enthusiasm: it must be pure truth, even if sometimes sad. I was reading Schopenhauer to him yesterday—you know Schopenhauer is a most wonderful idealist and lovely writer, only, alas, a confirmed pessimist and horrid about women—but of course in reading to Oliver I skip all those wicked Mephisto passages, which I have marked beforehand with a cross. Well, when I read how everything becomes beautiful and as it were enchanted when we suspend our Will and see the whole world merely as an Idea, Oliver stopped me, made me reread that paragraph, and wouldn't let me go on until he had repeated it himself three times in the eloquent German, and knew it perfectly by heart. He is starving for great thoughts, Mrs.

Alden, his soul can't live without great thoughts. We poor imperfect people, and all our muddled human affairs, are a great burden to him, a *foreign* world. Not that he is in the least arrogant or unkind, or dislikes humble people. On the contrary, it's people with pretensions that he can't endure. Didn't he want to ask Tom Piper, the apothecary's son, to lunch the other day, not at all because he cares particularly for the boy, but just out of kindness? And didn't you notice how flushed and disgusted he was, though he said nothing, when he found that it couldn't be, because the Pipers are shopkeepers? No: it's rather a trial to poor Oliver to be pursued by affection. I can see how I annoy him sometimes by being too emotional or, as he calls it, too German. And only just now, when Tom Piper came up to ask for Oliver and invite him to a picnic, and I said that Oliver was out, probably gone in his canoe to lie under the trees in the Upper Mill-Pond, I couldn't help adding quite frankly that Tom had better *not* ask Oliver to the picnic. Oliver was very tired, quite worn out by hard work and the heat, and it was better for him to have a complete rest, yet I knew that if asked he might feel that he ought to accept, so as not to seem sulky, or ill-natured, although it couldn't at present be really a pleasure or at all good for him. I could see that Tom Piper, who seems to be a nice modest lad, was terribly disappointed, having come up the long hill for nothing in this dreadful heat, pushing his bicycle; and it's evident that he adores Oliver; yet he thanked me in a hesitating way for telling him the truth and said that indeed he didn't want to disturb Oliver or to intrude, but had hoped they might go canoeing sometimes during the vacation, because in the School terms Oliver was always too busy to see much of any of the boys. It's a strange puzzle, because Oliver needs more friends, more sympathy, and yet the friends he makes and all their attentions seem to mean little to him, except more weight of obligation.—Perhaps some great change would set him right. What a pity that we can't consult Dr. Alden."

"It wouldn't be impossible to consult him," said Mrs. Alden, a little impressed by the earnestness with which the good Irma considered the matter. "He happens to be in Boston, kept there by delays in getting his yacht ready—brand new, and already in need of expensive repairs. His summer's trip has been spoilt: all because of that foolish insistence on building a new yacht when the *Hesperus* was quite good enough until last year: and why not now? Because he is being governed by designing wicked people: and it's no use warning him. He knows he is a victim, and he laughs at it! It amuses him to see all those idle men in the yacht making merry with his money, and he is almost grateful to them for letting him peep in and have some of the fun. Heaven knows if the new boat is at all seaworthy—they say it's a fancy ship and not like anyone else's—and likely to sink with them all one of these days in mid-ocean. But it's his folly: and if I asked him to come and see Oliver, and he found that the boy is merely out of sorts and overgrown and has nothing really to complain of, he might blame me for making a fuss and interfering with his liberty."

"But I have heard him so often praising you for *not* making a fuss and for *not* interfering!"

"Write to him yourself then, if you like—I have no objection—and tell him why we are worried, perhaps foolishly, by Oliver's condition. That won't oblige Dr. Alden to come or to do anything unless he chooses."

Peter Alden disliked writing letters. One had so often to invent the sentiments one was obliged to express: and those conventional beginnings and endings annoyed him, and made him feel like a fool. He answered, whenever possible, by telegraph: and the next day Irma received a long despatch, suggesting that she and Oliver should join him in Boston. A few days' cruise in Massachusetts Bay, while they tried the new engines, might do Oliver good.

IX

Dearest little Lieschen!

How surprised you must be to see your dear exiled sister dating her letter from *Boston*! Yes, I am freed! The poor lonely little bird has escaped from her gilded cage! I am alone in this world-city! ! ! How did it happen? Have I quarrelled with Frau Alden and am I an outcast beggar? Have I eloped with my young lover—alas, who should he be?—and am I secretly married? No: nothing so upsetting. The Herr Doktor has simply asked my Oliver to join him in his pleasure-yacht, and as Oliver—so his father and mother think—is too young to travel alone, I have come to Boston with my dear pupil. Of course nominally he isn't my pupil any longer, since for two years he has been going to school; but in fact we study and read together just as in the old happy days, especially during his vacations. At first the thought that he was to be sent to school was terrible, and I had to offer to leave and go back to Germany, or perhaps to Milwaukee or Chicago or some strange place, and try to become an ordinary German schoolteacher. But they said no: they needed me; and I wasn't to be Fräulein or a governess any more, but Irma and one of the family. How the tears ran down my cheeks, and how I *had* to kiss Frau Alden, and Oliver too, though I had never kissed either of them before, nor have I since. What? Never kissed your little Oliver even at first, when he was four years old? No: it was forbidden. In this country it is wrong to kiss your children! Yet you see they don't grow up quite heartless on that account; perhaps quite the contrary.

You have read in the papers about our terrible heat-wave. In New York people are sleeping half-naked on the roofs or in the parks, workmen are collapsing and children dying. Even at High Bluff the thin shade of the pines gave little shelter: the sand and the dust of pine-needles under foot radiated heat like an oven. Oliver could go swimming: but it isn't possible to keep one's head always under water: he said his eyes ached with the glare, and the dusty trip to the river and back more than cancelled any relief he might have got from the bath. Here in Boston too, it is oppressively warm; but yesterday there was a whiff of east wind, and we breathed again for a moment.

You may ask, why didn't Frau Alden come with her son herself? Ah, that is a strange mania of hers: leaving home, for her, is out of the question. How often I suggested, in the first years, that we might go for a few weeks to the seaside or in the winter to Washington or to New York. Oliver could still have had his lessons with me as usual in the morning; in the afternoon we could have seen the sights, and in the evening, after putting him to bed, we could have *gone to the Opera*! But no, Frau Alden wouldn't hear of it. The journey would be so fatiguing, the hotels so crowded and noisy, the strange hired beds so creepy and unpleasant, the food so messy, too rich, perhaps poisonous, and the other people so loud and vulgar. In summer the heat everywhere was as bad as at home, where we had greater comfort and more space, and Great Falls was really not far from the sea—the salt winds might blow up the river for many miles—and the Bumstead House was on such a high hill that really it wasn't worth while to go to the mountains. That is what she *says*: but I know that she *thinks* also that, at a fashionable watering-place, or in a great city, she mightn't seem very well dressed, and might be taken for my mother. For—would you believe it?—though she has so much money, she hates shopping! She gets on with one or two old frocks, always black or navy blue, that can be covered up almost completely, when she goes out, with a "handsome" tailor-made coat and furs, or a silk mantel in summer: and once she has on her pearl earrings and necklace with those fine lace ruffles that are now worn down the front with an open neck, she feels that she is well enough dressed to impress Great Falls, where everybody knows she is rich and above criticism. In the evening at home she always wears the same dove-coloured gown, with white lace, until it is in shreds, and then she has another made as much like the old one as possible. This Priscilla costume she says is right for the wife of an Alden: and it keeps her from having to think, like a foolish *Backfisch*, what she shall put on. Oliver is just like his mother in this respect. He never wants more than just enough clothes for use, and always the same things in the same colours. What a wicked malicious goddess Fortune is, that cruelly gives the money to the wrong people! If you and I were only rich, how happy we should be! And here are these very rich people—they don't know themselves *how* rich, because the Herr Doktor will never tell, and perhaps is a bit vague about it in his own mind—people who ought to have everything, and they have nothing! A handsome woman, little past fifty, who doesn't mind looking old, will never travel or go to a theatre or an evening party or deck herself out in splendid clothes, but wants simply to sit at home, quiet and stately, and to feel perfect! A Quaker queen, her husband once called her, and she was frightfully pleased. They both like retirement and monotony as if they were ninety. Is it because they feel if they tried to do anything else, they wouldn't do it very well? So they simply exchange a few stupid commonplaces at home over their roast chicken and bread pudding, and sit for an hour afterwards in the drawing-room pretending to read, looking every few minutes at the clock and suppressing a yawn, because Frau Alden doesn't think it *right* to go to bed before half past nine.

You ought, though, to see *my* evening house-dresses! One is skyblue and the other peach-colour. I cut and sewed them both myself on the sewing machine, and you can't imagine how sweet I look in them! The blue one has black velvet bows, and I wear a red rose with it, or some geraniums from our flower bed (we haven't a real garden, only grass and the pine-woods beyond) for the sake of the aesthetic colour-harmony. The peach-coloured dress is all trimmed with autumn leaves *appliqué*, which I cut out of remnants of rich brocade, left over from making a work-bag for Frau Alden's Christmas present; and the stitching all round each leaf, and the stems, are in real gold thread! It is much admired; and with this gown, when I can get them, I wear *white* flowers.

I still play my old Chopin pieces sometimes, or sing one of my old dear Schumann songs, but I haven't any time for practice. Lately, however, I have made a great discovery. Oliver has a beautiful tenor voice! I am giving him singing lessons; but he doesn't like singing, as he says, "to show off." Only once in church, where the congregation is supposed to join in singing the hymn, he let out his voice a little. I think it was because he liked the melody— the *Adeste Fideles*, but to such poor English words—and he could easily run up and down those scales in his full natural note, without either thinning out and squealing at the top or gasping and becoming voiceless at the bottom, as happens to most of us. People at once began to look round slyly, and then glance at one another with a benevolent smile, so that I could almost hear them thinking—"What a fine voice that young Oliver Alden has, and how enthusiastically he joins in the singing. Is he going to be a clergyman?" Because you know, except the paid quartet, nobody here more than hums the psalm-tunes. Naturally, as soon as Oliver noticed that he was attracting attention, he stopped, and has never sung in church since. Sometimes, when we are in the marble summerhouse at the very top of the Bluff, he will really sing something: but there we haven't a piano, and we can't make much progress. I am sending you his latest photograph, which doesn't do him justice, because there is a sweetness and manliness in his ways which can't be photographed, but you will see how distinguished he looks with his large clear eyes and pale hair, so tall and slender and unassuming. The young sons of the Grand Duke of Weimar, whom we once saw, you remember, at the railway station, looked a little like him.

But what am I writing about? I have such a garrulous mind, and you want to hear about my wonderful journey. Yet it doesn't matter if I have been reminiscing a bit, because I have the whole evening before me, and nothing to do, alone in this strange city! Why didn't it occur to them that I too might be too young to travel alone? I am scarcely yet thirty-four and people take me for twenty-five. From behind, they say I look eighteen. Yet they leave me unprotected, as if there was no danger, in a hotel full of men! But why, oh why, couldn't I have sailed with them in that splendid yacht, out in the great wild ocean? How happy and thrilled I should have been, *the only woman on board*! I hinted, but it was no use. Nobody wanted me.

Well, on arriving in Boston, Oliver and I went to the hotel on Beacon Hill, where the Herr Doktor always stays. He lived very near there when a boy, with a mysterious older brother who leads a hermit life there still, but whom the Doctor never sees. Yet in an uncanny way he loves to haunt the old places, turn the familiar corners, and go to the same long-established shops, though now the best hotels are in quite a different quarter. So when the Doctor and Oliver left and went to the yacht, I moved here, where the waiters are white—they were *black* at that other hotel, which takes away my appetite for a moment, though it soon comes back again. The Victoria is in the residential region, more suitable for a young lady travelling alone. And what have I seen? Oh, so many things: the Public Library, and the Ludovisi Throne, and Mrs. Gardner's Venetian palace; and I might have gone also to Faneuil Hall and the Old North Church and the Bunker Hill Monument; but it's so warm, and my time has all been taken up shopping. I haven't bought very much, but oh, the gorgeous things I have *looked at*! With these new loose fashions, home-made dresses will fit perfectly; but I have got a winter coat—half price on account of the heat—and *two* new hats, and some lovely linen. You will say where are all my savings going and what shall I live on when I am an old maid? But no: my savings are intact, because the Herr Doktor gave me a cheque for 200 dollars, and my travelling expenses will hardly be more than 50; so I have a little margin for pins! I have also been to the dentist because while the one at Great Falls does very well, he is old, and the one here is young and a German and nice-looking and doesn't hurt so much. But he is married. Unfortunately at this season there are no great artists playing at the theatres, and no good concerts: but of course I go every day to the cinema, and *gloat* on it. Love at such close quarters! It almost seems as if it were myself that is being kissed. Too much of this, I feel, might not be good for me; but Oliver is returning in a few days, and then all your dear sister's *Erlebnisse* will have become, alas, but an *Erinnerung*!

X

Cities, for Oliver, were not a part of nature. He could hardly feel, he could hardly admit even when it was pointed out to him, that cities are a second body for the human mind, a second organism, more rational, permanent and decorative than the animal organism of flesh and bone: a work of natural yet moral art, where the soul sets up all her trophies of action and instruments of pleasure. No: for him cities were congested spots, ugly, troublesome and sad. Boston, when he first passed through it, seemed to him nothing but Great Falls multiplied. True, he was not expected on this occasion to look at anything: and he became spontaneously attentive only when the cab dropped him and his father before a large wooden shed, labelled in great letters: *East Boston Ferry*. The covered pier was built out over the water on slimy piles, which looked rather rotten: and the green sea-water itself was stained in livid metallic colours and meandering curves by the refuse from local drains, or from tugs, coal-barges, and idle steamers. The ferry-boat arrived, creaking against the loose walls of piles that pressed it into position; the crowd pushed ashore over the draw-bridge, adjustable according to the height of the tide: and the embarking crowd pushed no less impatiently aboard. Presently the great steel lever, shaped like a cocked hat, that surmounted the ungainly craft, began to oscillate, beating like the heart of some monster in agony. The paddle-wheels began to slap the water with increasing fury, and the big raft-like ferry-boat, each rounded end indifferently bow and stern, carried them in precisely seven minutes across the channel to the deeper side of the harbour. The crowd, pushing hard once more, bore them by main force into an unpaved road, through which trains ran. Long rows of freight-cars stood in a siding, profusely painted, pasted, and inscribed with all sorts of labels. Smoke stacks of different heights and colours were visible above the sheds and shanties lining the road: masts also, here and there. There was a liquor-saloon at every corner and often a fruit-stand, with a little oven beside it, hissing steam and roasting peanuts. Presently they turned down a muddy lane; on one side invisible machinery was thumping loudly behind a brick wall; and at the end they emerged upon a wooden pier, which trembled, but didn't quite give way under their prudent tread. A gangway led them into what seemed a large excursion steamer under repair; and from there they slipped down on to another deck, which somewhat to Oliver's surprise, proved to be that of his father's new yacht, the *Black Swan*. In the confusion of sheds, hulks, piers, and overtopping steamers, her lines were hardly distinguishable to an unpractised eye. Moreover, his father had stopped to talk to a stranger: an affable young man, broad-shouldered and ruddy-faced, in a white-topped yachting cap cocked very much over one ear. He wore a double-breasted blue coat with brass buttons, most brightly polished, duck trousers freshly ironed, and spotless white shoes. Half a word on this or that seemed to suffice for his father and this florid young man to understand each other perfectly: they spoke in a low voice, briskly; the stranger had an air of smiling confidence as if to say: I have done thus and so, I knew it would be all right; and this assumption seemed to be confirmed at once by a little nod from the Doctor, signifying, Quite right; just what I wanted.

"Oliver, this is Mr. Darnley, our Captain. He tells me he is putting you in the Poop, which is our state apartment. Perhaps you'd like to see your quarters."

The Captain first touched his cap, and then proffered a broad and muscular hand, clean and well-shaped, but bearing evident signs of having done rough work. In that frank grasp, though it was gentle enough, Oliver's unprepared fingers felt a bit thin and hesitant. But how could a sea-captain look so very fresh and youthful and sportsmanlike? And when he said *How do you do?* how could his voice and air be so singularly engaging and unembarrassed? Ah, he was English. That fact might explain his being so different from all known people, and combining qualities which, according to Oliver's preconceptions, were incompatible. He seemed more of a gentleman than one's own friends, and more at one's service than one's own servants, so ornamental and yet so simple, perfectly boyish and perfectly manly. That he was English was evident in his speech, for though he used some Americanisms and consented to call things by their American names, yet some of his phrases were innocently British, and he spoke glibly, without joking or forced excitement, in a voice that was pure and low, with airy modulations. That a bluff sailor, talking business, a person who surely hadn't been to College like Miss Letitia Lamb and wouldn't insist that the early bird had come *earlily*, should yet utter commonplaces, and even swear, in such a cultivated way—that was the paradox.

The cabin boy was now taking their bags below, and Oliver followed his father down into the bowels of the *Black Swan*, like a young Jonah exploring the Whale. At first to the bewildered passenger the entrails of any marine monster are a puzzling labyrinth: descents precipitous, walls curved, passages devious, familiar furniture dwarfed, distorted, compressed for the uses of a life not normally human. Having no points of comparison in his previous experience, and no eye for peculiarities in naval architecture, Oliver hardly noticed the unusual disposition and ornaments of the cabin. "This is the Poop," said his father, opening a last stout narrow door. "It is our library and museum, and from these old-fashioned ports you may survey the sea in a semicircle. My yachting friends laugh at me for trying to build myself a junk or a frigate and say I shall be smashed to smithereens one of these days in my Poop by a following sea: but we have taken every precaution: resistance and buoyancy are exactly calculated: we are never in a hurry, and can always heave to: and I am not going to sacrifice my preferences to the tyranny of fashion. I like to feel here like some old admiral bringing home the spoils of the Indies. My spoils are only a few Chinese knick-knacks, collected in my younger days, and a few sour-sweet memories of adventure, nothing out of the ordinary: and I am not conveying them anywhere—certainly not carrying them home—but simply ruminating on them uselessly in my old age. It is unfortunate to have been born at a time when the force of human character was ebbing, while the tide of material activity and material knowledge was rising so high as to drown all moral independence. I have been a victim of my environment: but I have not surrendered to it. I have surrendered only to my own limitations. This Poop is my throne of retrospection: it shows me the wake of my ship. From here you may watch the receding water, not from a great height—I am no philosopher—but from a cockle-shell life-boat, sufficient to keep you for the moment afloat and dry. You rise and sink with the waves—I hope you won't mind the motion. When not too violent, I find it soothing and symbolical. The sea carries us like a nurse in her arms, not with the unsympathetic fixity of the dry land, which never yields in the least to our childish pressure. Here you feel the whole buoyancy of the vessel, the elastic strength with which she rides the sea. It was in ships of this size, or not much smaller, that the ancients sailed when they conceived the horses of Poseidon, prancing and plunging, yet carrying the seated god victoriously forward. You who are fond of riding ought to enjoy sailing."

With this, Peter Alden, whose eyes had been measuring abstractedly the stretch of water that already separated them from the shore, turned again to his son, whose presence he had almost forgotten. "You are expected to sleep on this couch. It is only a mat stretched on a frame and covered with a cushion which for coolness I should advise you to remove. A mat on the ground in the East is thought sufficient to sleep on, and this is softer, being suspended in mid-air. In the evening pillow-cases will be supplied for these pillows, and even sheets, if you absolutely insist upon them. I, for my part, have discarded Christian beds. I know that people nowadays put brass bedsteads into ships, to avoid the damp and vermin of the old-fashioned bunks; but those cumbersome standardised modern beds are neither nautical nor rational. They disfigure a cabin, which to my mind should be like a sort of hermitage, a workroom and oratory for the sailor's inner man. We are so much in the open at sea, conscious of vast distances around and above, and of inhuman forces, that we need to huddle and curl ourselves up in a private corner, to knit our poor humanity together again. You shouldn't feel in your cabin that you are in a grand hotel. As to beds, they belong to the peasant civilisation of Europe. Our barbarous ancestors were afraid of being cold, and their pride was to heap up as many mattresses as they could afford, filled with lumpy sheep's wool, and to sink into the middle of them, heaping on top of themselves any quantity of blankets, coverlets, and quilts, and a great feather balloon almost touching the dais suspended above; and then to draw close on all sides thick and magnificent bed-curtains, for protection from air, light, or indiscreet glances. Smothered in such a dark nest, your overfed half-drunken gentleman was invited to snore: and love in such a smelly breeding-hole was ignobly deprived of sight, which might have inspired love and touched it with laughter and wonder. They do these things better in the East. They make love when they feel love, and lie down to sleep when they are sleepy, and nature irresistibly closes the eyes. You will say that there are beds in Homer; but they were thrones, the thrones of matrimony: and I grant that even our northern farmer's beds acquired a certain dignity, when

kings and great ladies held court in them; as society people in our
time find them convenient in the morning for breakfasting and telephoning. But in these cases the bed returns to the character of a
divan, which is what I should like to substitute for it. Here is yours,
equally useful by day or night; and as at least we have learnt to wear
pyjamas and not to go to bed in our day underclothes, like our
malodorous elders, you have only to lie down and, if you are cold,
cover yourself with a rug, and sleep the sleep of nature. To-day we
have a smooth sea and light breezes. Nevertheless, when you unpack,
don't leave anything lying loose. Everything in lockers or drawers,
ship-shape and tight. Here is the bathroom. Perfectly modern, you
see. I have no prejudice against modern improvements when they
simplify life. We three have to share this bathroom; but as you take
only shower-baths, and don't have to shave, you won't have any
difficulty in arranging with Lord Jim for your turn. As for me, my
hours are so much later that I shan't interfere with your morning
ablutions, however prolonged. I am going to turn in until lunch-
time. You can go on deck and amuse yourself as you like. I see we
are making way, and shall soon be out of the harbour."

A slight tremor and rumble had indeed been sensible for some
time under foot, in proof that the new engines were performing their
office. Left alone, Oliver's first impulse was to look out of the window.
He felt cooped, magnificently spacious as his cage was supposed to
be. He could touch the ceiling with his hand. The two gilded Buddhas
in the corners smiled at him in a heathen fashion, as if they were at
home here and he wasn't. He needed to make sure that the familiar
natural world still spread around him, and to take his bearings in it.
And indeed through the open ports he could see a stretch of sparkling water, with the two spreading and fading lines of foam made
by their gentle passage. Beyond appeared the confused shipping and
huddled roofs of the harbour frontage; and in the distance, above a
bank of smoke shrouding the city, a single glittering speck shone
through the haze—the gilded dome of the State House. Who could
"Lord Jim" be? The young officer was Mr. Darnley. Could he be a
lord masquerading as a sailor? And why was his father suddenly so
different, so talkative, airing his views, and making long speeches as
if to himself? But what was the use of conjectures? He would unpack.
He would go on deck. He would see what was going on. All vibration
and whirring had now ceased, yet the ship continued to move. The
sunlight shifted its place rhythmically across the lacquer panels, the

deck was perceptibly tilted to starboard, and now much further off in that quarter a little wave broke every few seconds into white foam. They were under sail. They were really at sea.

On deck, to Oliver's eyes, the spectacle was overwhelming. Some untapped reservoir of emotion seemed suddenly to burst within him and flood his whole being. But why? A ship under full sail in halcyon weather, how often has it been praised and painted and photographed? Beautiful, certainly, but hackneyed, like the daisy and the rose and the lark and the nightingale, and all the other commonplaces of popular poetry. And Oliver cared little for poetry: to his adolescent mind raptures over the beautiful were simply silly. Had he never, perhaps, felt the beautiful until now? The spread of canvas, unexpectedly enormous, at first alarmed his instinct by its aerial incalculable boldness: if the gods suddenly blew a little harder what would become of all these vast gossamer wings? Yet at once the sense of security was restored and heightened into a sense of power, by the evident steadiness and friendliness of that harnessed force. The gods had made a covenant, a conditional covenant, with man, and promised, if he obeyed, to carry him on their shoulders. Everything trembled and everything held; each part was alive and self-propelling, yet all moved together slightly swaying and justly balanced in a firm advance. The wildness of a topsail or a flying jib was like the treble voices of choir boys in a glorious anthem; while the taut sheets and halyards, the yards and booms, were like manly baritones and basses, holding the ground note and sustaining the harmony. And the background to this choral beauty was hardly less wonderful. An archipelago of summer clouds floated lightly in the sky, and the long almost imperceptible swell of the Atlantic was ruffled pleasantly by a multitude of little sunlit waves. The islands, the lighthouse, slowly shifted their perspectives, and here and there a distant steamer, or a coasting schooner, her deck piled high with lumber, seemed to encourage them in their own idle voyage by testifying that there were havens and rewards for vagrance beyond the unbroken emptiness of the sea.

Oliver spent a long time in the bows, watching the sails and the water: he peeped wonderingly into the forecastle, the galley, the officers' quarters, the engine room, and even the hold. Here and there a knot of sailors, like a troop of stout monkeys, barefoot but spotlessly dressed in white, would make way for him, or seeing how young and green he was, would offer a word of explanation, before they pattered down a hatch or clambered up the rigging. It was only his own cabin, which had seemed merely luxurious, that he was disinclined to explore.

"Not bored, I hope," said his father, as Oliver finally came aft again.

"Bored! It's the grandest sight I have ever seen. If only Fräulein were here, how she would cry *wundervoll! wunderschön! herrlich!* and *grossartig!*"

"Look out. The sea when you like it too much swallows up all your intelligence, before gulping you down in person.—Well, it's almost time for lunch, and later Lord Jim—I mean the Captain—will take you in hand and teach you the names of everything. It's a chief part of seamanship, as of science, to know how things are called."

"But why do you call him Lord Jim if he's a plain Mr.?"

"It's a trick I've fallen into, a mere nickname. His Christian name is really Jim—James—but I glorify it into Lord Jim after the hero of Joseph Conrad's story. You've read it?"

"Oh, yes: but did Mr. Darnley ever leave his ship to sink with all the passengers, while he slipped away himself in the only boat?"

"Not that: but long ago he got a black mark against him of another sort—was dismissed from the British Navy when he was a midshipman—and he took to a wandering life, only going westward instead of eastward, and sank for a time rather below his station. He is a clergyman's son, like the Lord Jim in the novel, and a first-rate sailor."

"The only trouble with Lord Jim," said Oliver, who had given much thought to this point and discussed it at length with his mother and Irma, "was that he dropped off into a dream at critical moments— very bad for a man in authority—as if he had taken some drug. Does Mr. Darnley do that?"

Oliver did not particularly notice that his father looked up, as if surprised, and said rather hastily: "Just the opposite. This Lord Jim drops off into a dream, as you say, only on shore, in lax moments, when some chance acquaintance cracks up a gold mine, or a horse sure to win the Derby. At sea, and in a crisis, he is wonderfully alert, and sees at once what is happening or is likely to happen. He has the true military gift, and would have made an excellent fighter, if he could have stayed in the Navy."

"Then why do you call him Lord Jim at all? Has he been King in some savage island?"

"Only king in this boat. He lords it over me here; but I confess he does it very well, and to my advantage, just as your mother does at home. He saves me a lot of trouble and, I believe, a lot of expense. I should have had to give up the sea by this time, if I didn't have him to look after me. Besides, if two or three living persons should die without male issue, he might really be a lord some day, because on his father's side he comes of an aristocratic family; only I understand they are uncomfortably poor. Nothing to live on but a vicar's stipend."

At this moment the Captain himself appeared at the cabin hatchway, hatless and smiling: but he perceived that he was the subject of conversation and stopped short.

"Lunch!" cried Peter, as if reviving at the thought: and then, as he joined the Captain, he added: "Oliver was asking me whether you were the son of a duke or only of a marquis."

Lord Jim grinned broadly, and with an affectionate gesture made Oliver pass before him down the ladder, saying confidentially in his ear:

"I am only the son of a poor parson, but your father likes to have his little joke."

The business of sitting down at table and ordering drinks now covered up the slight awkwardness of the previous moment: but for Oliver the matter of food and drink and the novel arrangements of the cabin, and the officiousness of the steward all passed half-realised, as in a dream. What could have induced his father to invent something so absurd as that he, Oliver, should have asked such a question? Nothing indeed could be more remote from his sphere than knowing or caring whose younger sons might have the title of lord prefixed by courtesy to their Christian names. Why was his father so different here from what he was at home? At home, like the rest of the family, he was always scrupulously truthful; a little ironical, perhaps, at times, at being obliged to be so accurate, but never fibbing, or joking, or inventing impossible things, and mystifications of this whimsical sort. Nor did he ever expatiate at home on his personal feelings and opinions: you could only guess what they were by his quizzical way of describing his earlier adventures, or the course of public events. Yet that morning in the Poop he had been holding forth in a visionary fashion which Oliver didn't quite understand. Perhaps it was here that his father felt really at home, and showed his true colours. Here he seemed to be surrounded by deference and smiling affection;

here he could tell playful lies without fear of anyone calling him to book. But why this particular lie? Why insist so much on this odd fancy, this nickname for his captain? Wasn't it rather in bad taste, and likely to give offence? The Lord Jim of Conrad's story was a nice fellow; but the point of resemblance being that both young men were sailors in disgrace, wasn't it cruel continually to remind Mr. Darnley of this circumstance? Yet Mr. Darnley didn't seem to mind: liked it, apparently, as if being called Lord Jim really ennobled him or at least smartened him up. Or was he only pretending not to mind? Oliver, being sensitive and isolated, was a good observer, and he watched the young captain closely, more closely than ever in his life he had watched anyone before. This young man was most deferential in manner, as towards a superior military officer or a constitutional monarch; yet he seemed to be sure of his ground, and capable of becoming familiar and cheeky, like a prime minister who really held the reins of power. The Doctor for his part appeared to regard Mr. Darnley with a sort of affectionate pride of possession, as one might a big dog, whose fine aspect and vigorous antics are made doubly engaging by his quick obedience. And Jim Darnley seemed to accept this ambiguous position with an air of polite gratitude, even at the mockery of being called a lord when he wasn't a lord. Was he silly enough to be actually flattered and glad to carry on the farce? Or was he so much at home in humiliation that he didn't mind it, as when the big dog, after being detected in evil doing, feels he is forgiven, and comes fawning up with his tail between his legs, but the tip wagging? Might it all be an act of subtle kindness on his father's part, meant to compensate young Darnley as much as possible for his disgrace, and to rehabilitate him in his own eyes? Could it conceivably amount to saying: "You are really a first rate fellow, like the Lord Jim in the story, and we needn't pretend to forget the past. I accept it. Let us build openly on that basis." What was that past? Why had Jim Darnley been expelled from the Navy? Of course Oliver wasn't going to ask. Not only would the question be impertinent, but it might suggest that Oliver himself took a special interest in the matter, when he didn't and couldn't, because it was none of his business. No doubt some day, without asking, he would be told.

The conversation at lunch was chiefly about the new engines, and the cruise they were to take later; and when the very obsequious steward—also an Englishman: in fact everybody seemed to be English on board—had removed the cloth and served the coffee, the captain said he would fetch the blue-prints, and disappeared.

"You see what a capital captain I've got," Peter Alden observed, as he blew rings with the smoke of his pipe. "I found him by the merest chance in Vancouver, four or five years ago. That season when I went salmon fishing with Jack Flemming. He seemed a mere boy. He was then clerk or cashier at Shepherd's Hotel, which is the head-quarters for that sport; but I gathered at once by his talk that he was a sailor and a sort of young gentleman who had run away before the mast, like Dick Dana. Not two years before the mast, because he had good naval training, but on all sorts of odd jobs: and when the rush came to the Klondike he had been in command of a tug and of various other vessels, and had already a master's certificate, not only for steamboats, but for sailing vessels, both fore-and-aft and square-rigged. For the moment the Alaska trade had died down, and left him without a ship. It then occurred to me that I might try him as mate in the *Hesperus*—I was my own captain in those days—and he jumped at the chance: and ever since he has been my right-hand man, and a great comfort to me."

Talk was interrupted by the subject of it returning and spreading out three or four great sheets of blue paper with diagrams in white. They were not very intelligible to Oliver: but he noticed that as Lord Jim, pencil in hand, pointed out and explained the various details to the Doctor, he had hooked his other arm familiarly round the Doc-tor's shoulder. What impudence! A stranger taking liberties with Oliver's father before Oliver's eyes—liberties which Oliver himself would never dream of taking or, to be frank, would ever like to take. True, *he* had never had blue-prints to explain to his father, or any-thing in common with him except his meals. This outsider was be-having more like a son, and the old gentleman more like a father, than Oliver had ever seen anyone behave before. Was such familiarity odious? Or were the reserve and cramp odious which had always prevented such familiarity at home? Was this interloper offensive, or was Oliver himself cold, shrivelled, heartless, and unacquainted with the feelings of a son? However that might be, it was evident that his father led a double life, and had a double character. In his second, newly discovered capacity, he could cease to be silent, retiring, and perpetually ironical; he could unbosom himself; he could feel and accept affection; and he could grow eloquent and play with fantastic similitudes, for his own subtle amusement, like a sort of poet in life, to whom nothing was quite real.

How many problems in one brain, in one ship, in any smallest fragment of the world! They were sailing, under full canvas, before a very gentle breeze: for a while, in the summer haze, they were out of sight of land. Something of the leisurely spirit of a long voyage seemed to have descended upon them, when for days or months you are content to wait on the good will of the winds to hasten or to relax your progress. Here they were, calmly wafted from the invisible to the invisible, with no other ocular evidence of human existence or habitation than this one ship and her crew. At length something in the horizon, hardly distinguishable from a bank of cloud or a streak of shadow in the water, was pointed out to Oliver. Then a white light-house became visible, then the low-lying shore of Cape Cod, a few rocks among sand, and the lazy waves breaking upon them. Nature here seemed to breathe very slowly, and to have fallen asleep. The *Black Swan*, as if obeying the genius of the place, dropped her anchor, and furled her sails one after another: and a primeval torpor descended upon her, as if the sea-bird had reverted to the water-lizard, basking in suspended animation and existing—as perhaps all slumbering substance exists—merely by floating and waiting for nothing in particular. Yet something in particular will some day happen. Nothing is more treacherous than the peace of nature, when we fancy that the mountains were compacted to endure and to sleep for ever. Such material peace is a surface phenomenon, a mask for internal and incessant war. Matter is full of hidden springs and unexpressed affinities; some furtive influence here, some secret impulse there, will presently set in motion an insidious drift, destined to disrupt that equilibrium. A curious evolution will follow, or a sudden explosion.

XI

Since there was nothing doing and the flat shore was not very interesting, Oliver had stretched himself, with his hands behind his head, on a bench that partly surrounded what in a small yacht would have been the cockpit and in a great ship the quarter deck. In the *Black Swan* it was something betwixt and between: a part of the after-deck, between the Poop and the cabin skylight, over which when they were in port an awning could be spread, and even a rug with some wicker chairs and a table; for this boat was no racing toy, but a floating bungalow, or houseboat, yet not meant to lie half hidden under the willow branches of some inland back-water; rather to sail sturdily from sea to sea, and be a home for the hermit at the ends of the earth. In that recumbent position Oliver could study the intricate connections of the rigging, admire the enormous masts, booms, and spars, all tightly swathed like well-folded white umbrellas; and he could watch the uncertain but always graceful gyrations of the long club pennant floating from the mast-head. In him this mood and this posture were alike unprecedented. He felt lazy, placid, free from responsibility. Euphoria had seldom reached in him such conscious perfection. Evidently the change of air was having an effect.

The captain was walking about the deck, smoking. In one of his turns, as if by chance, he sauntered up to Oliver, stopped square in front of him, took the pipe out of his mouth, and said a little gravely:

"Your father is not feeling quite fit. He has turned in and won't leave his cabin this evening. He hopes you won't mind dining with me alone. That deuced hot weather ashore has upset him a bit: you know—his old dysentery. It will be nothing. He knows what to take for it: has had a jolly lot of experience doctoring himself. To-morrow what with the salt air and a good rest, he will be all right again."

Jim Darnley re-lighted his pipe and continued his walk; but after another turn or two he stopped before Oliver again.

"I say, how would you like a dip in the sea before dinner? More than an hour and a half till sunset."

Oliver sat up, but looked a little doubtful.

"You can swim, can't you?" Jim asked, with the slightest hint of a sneer, as if there was no knowing of how many things an American Mother's darling might be incapable.

"Oh, yes: but I'm afraid I haven't brought a bathing suit."

"Good Lord, you don't want a bathing suit here. This isn't one of your damned watering-places with a crowd of old maids parading along the front; and if there's anyone in the village with a spy-glass, that's their own affair. Just throw your things anywhere. The boy will look after them."

Oliver said nothing, but the problem for him was far from solved. Shyness, he knew, was a stupid irrational feeling, to be lived down. He had heard that other boys at school, in midsummer, sometimes sported naked in the lower river, behind the lumber sheds: but he had never joined them. His swimming had been only with Mr. Denis Murphy, an instinctively modest man, who even in dressing and undressing preserved all the scrupulous precautions of a monastic decency. Whatever the old oarsman may have seen and done in his salad days, he could conceive no other standard of propriety in the presence of his betters, especially of so young a boy put in his charge. At home, too, Oliver was accustomed to ignore and conceal every-thing indecorous: yet in theory, and when speaking of Greek statues, his mother and Fräulein always asserted that there was nothing im-proper in simple nakedness. And just as a boy would be a coward if, having had only hot baths at home, he was afraid of plunging into cold water, so he himself would be a coward if because in the past and at Great Falls (which was a frequented place) he and Mr. Murphy (who was a middle-aged man and fat) had worn one-piece suits when bathing, therefore he should be ashamed all his life of being seen stripped anywhere and by anybody. Besides, it was a maxim dear to his pride that to the pure all things are pure: you could do in a high-minded way the very things—like going to church or playing games—which some people do superstitiously or low-mindedly. Consequently, to feel any nervousness on this occasion would have been absurd, and he was going to be perfectly calm and unconcerned about the whole matter. Nevertheless his shoe-laces somehow got into a knot, and his gold collar-button fell and rolled into the water.

Meantime Lord Jim had called a sailor and given some orders; had touched the cabin bell; had himself unhooked a span of the deck rail, had undressed in an instant—for to Oliver's surprise he wore no underclothes—and was vigorously swinging his arms and expanding his chest, evidently in preparation for diving. What a chest, and what arms! While in his clothes he looked like any ordinary young man of medium height, only rather broad-shouldered, stripped he resembled, if not a professional strong man, at least a middle-weight prize-fighter in tip-top condition, with a deep line down the middle of his chest and back, and every muscle showing under the tight skin. By contrast, Oliver felt very slim, rather awkward, and a trifle unsteady on his long colt-like legs and bare feet, unused to the smooth hard contact of a sloping deck, strangely warm in the sun. Was he expected to dive too? The height seemed rather formidable. But at that moment the gallant tar, who in spite of his bluff manner and affectation of indifference, felt his responsibilities and was watching the lad out of the corner of his eye, relieved Oliver of all anxiety, by saying over his shoulder, in a civil voice:

"You'd better not dive from here if you aren't used to deep water: and mind, it's salt. Run down to the foot of the ladder, and jump in from there." With that he took a last long breath, and dived, describing a magnificent parabola and striking the water with a hard sound and a clean splash, like a porpoise. Oliver watching intently, lost his self-consciousness. In an instant he was at the bottom of the gangway, holding on to the ropes by which it was suspended, and waiting for Lord Jim to reappear.

A long time passed. Where was he? He couldn't have slipped under the yacht and come up on the other side, in order to fool Oliver? A shark? A cramp? A sunken rock that had stunned him? Oliver wanted to run up on deck, but what was the sense of that? He wanted to call, but he hadn't a voice to call with. The suspense was becoming agonising when at last, a long way off, the surface of the sea broke, a dripping round head, puffing and spluttering and snorting shook itself out of the spray; first one arm and then another began angrily beating the water. It was all right. There was Lord Jim, slowly forging his way back, hand over hand. Oliver was glad of a long moment in which to recover his equanimity. He mustn't seem to have been horribly frightened. He mustn't seem to know too little or to care too much. His dignity assured him that he wasn't really green or silly: it was Lord Jim who was an anomaly, a sort of conjuror to perplex anybody. Yet never in his life had Oliver felt such an awful stoppage, such a ghastly drag and emptiness within him. Was that what people called terror? A dip in the cold water would restore his nerve. He jumped in, when Lord Jim was only three yards off, and for the moment escaped observation.

A float, conveniently festooned with a rope that swimmers might take hold of, had been put overboard to be their resting-place between plunges. Although unsinkable, it was awash or submerged now on this side or now on that, when either of them, and especially Jim Darnley, offered to sit or to lie upon it. There was no need of talking; but Jim sometimes said a word or Oliver asked a question. How long could a man swim under water? And how far? Which sort of strokes are to be preferred? Is floating on one's back really good for much? Did Lord Jim ever mean to swim the Channel or the Hellespont, like Lord Byron? And Oliver then fancied he saw a resemblance between these two Leanders. Jim's hair was like Byron's, brown and curly and growing far down the middle of his forehead, which was high over the temples. Beginning to be bald! Oliver wanted to ask how old Jim was, and almost did; but it was a rooted habit in him to think of what he would say before he said it: which caused him almost always not to say anything, and to miss his chances in conversation. As the pleasure of sporting in the water wore off, however, Jim stayed longer on the raft, and became more communicative. Swimming, he said, wasn't a subject to talk about, like golf, unless you were a damned professional or the sporting editor of a pink newspaper. Swimming was merely a way of taking cool exercise; but it wasn't sufficient to keep a chap really fit. It produced a lot of blubber, as in the whale; and he did it only for pleasure, in very warm weather. To keep in good condition he had to pull weights every morning: a beastly nuisance, but what else would you have? It was worse to be fat and flabby. You didn't want to look and feel like a pig.

Oliver felt how true that was. Training, training, training. There was no help for it: not for the sake of winning in anything or breaking records, but just for your own sake.

Exercise, Jim went on, wouldn't save you from being a silly ass, if you were born one. But it might put a bit of ballast into you, if you carried too much sail aloft; and he tapped his forehead. "I've noticed," he added, "those ridiculous foreigners—French, Italians, and dagos generally—now they've taken up cycling and tennis and boxing and boy-scouts and all that sort of thing, well, they don't shout and gesticulate and make monkey-faces so much as they used to. I expect they're more sensible, too, about women. They used to be always leering and boasting, and telling tall stories about their own prowess; or else they were dumb, quivering, and haggard because they were in love. Now they are more decent, and if it wasn't for the language, you might take some of them for Englishmen. It makes any man saner to work off all those city-poisons out of his blood. Parliament was a decent place, when all the members were country gentlemen and sportsmen: but now—just look at it!" and he spread his arms out as if pushing away the whole despicable tribe, and dropped into the water.

The tide was turning. The line slackened which held the raft fast to the yacht, and they drifted in the slow swirls of the uncertain current a little to one quarter, so that the whole length of the boat came into better perspective. Oliver felt, without analysing, the beauty of her lines; she seemed to ride the water not smartly, like other yachts, but somehow lazily and luxuriously, as if her head (which was the Poop) were comfortably pillowed, while she kicked her foot nonchalantly yet aggressively into the air in a bowsprit wonderfully bold and long.

"She has a lovely figurehead," said Jim, "only we can't quite see it from here: a flying swan in black and silver, with a red beak. It was a Japanese design your father found somewhere and adapted: and he really designed the whole boat; he knows a lot about ship-building. But we had the devil of a time getting the builders here to understand his ideas."

"But why call her the *Black Swan* and not *Hesperus*? We thought at home that *Hesperus* was such a nice name. And how can a ship all white sails be a black swan?"

"Yes. Ladies *would* ask that question. Get your father to explain it. For one thing, though, a black swan has white wings when it flies, because the underside is white, like the inside of a nigger's hands. *Hesperus* was just a pretty name that didn't mean anything; and the boat was a commonplace yacht: might have been designed by any New York shipbuilder for so many dollars. She was like a rich alderman's house built by the borough architect and furnished by Maples. A good sea-boat enough, and fast: but racing is the last thing your father would meddle with: he hates all that row and all those people. I wonder that with his tastes he kept the *Hesperus* as long as he did—sixteen or seventeen years; yes, ever since you were born. Let me give you a tip: men between forty and fifty when they seem most flourishing and most important, are apt to be dead inside, dead as logs. They have succumbed to circumstances; they have given up everything they might have liked; they are caught like old Samson in the treadmill. Your father has never asserted himself enough: has a despairing way of being patient, when there's no need of being patient. Not worth the trouble, he thinks, to try for anything better. When I first joined the *Hesperus*, I saw he was always sighing for his *Old Junk*, because there he had had all this Chinese stuff of his, which was now rotting in storage; and there it might be rotting still, if I hadn't encouraged him to sell the old *Hesperus*—plenty of fools to buy her—and build himself a true blue-water ship after his own heart. For mind you, it wasn't merely to house his old curiosity shop; it was to please his sailor-mind. The *Hesperus* was a schooner, like all your regular racing yachts: very convenient for handling with a small crew and sailing close to the wind and making port in quick time, so as not to miss dinner and sleep ashore. But your father was dining and sleeping aboard in any case. He wasn't obliged to land a party of sea-sick ladies, who must get home before dark: a larger or smaller crew didn't matter to him, especially when I was there to look after them; and he had cruised for years in the Far East and the Mediterranean, in native boats with a great brown sail stretching across the mast that bore you before the wind like a sea-god: because there's no grandeur in a ship unless she's square-rigged. Your fore-and-aft boat can only be trim and slick or at best graceful. Here at least we have the fore-mast square-rigged. That great fore-sail and fore-topsail lifting her along—it makes all the difference. I'm sure your father was never happier. All last winter whilst the *Black Swan* was building and I was in New York looking after the details, his letters from Egypt read like a schoolboy's. 'Only make sure,' he would write, 'that she will float and sail grandly, like the Doge's barge when he went to marry the Adriatic, and I will see to it that she is even more mirabolous inside than out.' And now, if he wants to go to Egypt, or Athens, or Naples, he can go there in his own ship, more comfortably than in the old days, and easier in his mind. When he was a young man, you know, he was always worrying about what people might say, but now he doesn't give a damn. I, too, have had my dip in the Mediterranean. I was picking up a good bit of French and Italian, which I shall have to brush up. It was at Villefranche, in the *Thunderer*, that we had the big row, and my future was ruined."

Oliver shivered perceptibly, and sat up. The sun was about to set, red and flameless behind a bank of haze. "Shall we turn in?" said his new mentor. "Let's not swim back. We'll haul the float up to the ladder." And he began to tug at the rope that connected them with the *Black Swan*. Oliver thought he ought to help. Their raft was far too unsteady for standing on; even sitting or crawling on hands and knees it wasn't safe; and in hauling in their line they more than once tumbled over each other, and were pitched into the sea. Amid laughter and mock imprecations they scrambled on deck. Oliver's clothes had disappeared, but he saw a towel, a bath-robe and his own slippers laid out as if by magic on the bench. Why should he have shivered on such a sultry evening? And the shyness of an hour before seemed a ridiculous dream, the experience of some silly baby who had ceased to exist years ago.

XII

In all the freshness of clean linen and clear blood after his hard exercise, Oliver felt extraordinarily fit. Happy thought of Lord Jim's that they should dine in their pyjamas. The rule on board, he had said, was to dress for dinner, because it helped to keep up the ship's discipline and gave the Doctor's table all the air of the ward-room in a man-of-war. But that evening the Doctor wasn't dining: and for them to go to the other extreme and eat in their dressing-gowns if they damn chose—something the mate and engineer would blush to do—marked the same distinction in a different manner. As to dining in the open air, the Doctor always did so when in port, weather permitting. Indeed the table, Oliver observed, was set with full ceremony. A Chinese lantern in the centre, carved ebony and painted silk, cast a thousand coloured reflections on the glasses and silver. A bottle of champagne and one of soda-water tipped their noddles somewhat drunkenly in a silver cooler. Lord Jim, a cigarette pendent from his lip, was picturesque in his Oriental garments, and dominated everything, told Oliver where to sit, and with a glance now at the steward, now at the cabin-boy, kept the feast going in perfect tempo. Oliver didn't notice the food and he ate it all—as he didn't ordinarily eat strange dishes—without demur. His champagne glass had been filled for him before he could interpose a deprecating hand. He left the wine standing for a while, but later with the devilled chicken, he reflected that no better occasion was likely to present itself for tasting champagne for the first time. There was nothing *wrong* about it: the question was only whether he was old enough, and this evening, on the whole, he thought he was. He drank half a glass; it was immediately refilled by the steward, but to no purpose. No: he didn't like champagne. He *dis*liked it; it made him positively feel (like Pindar) that the best of things was water. All sensation in Oliver was, as it were, retarded; it hardly became conscious until it became moral. It spoke for the stomach, not for the palate. What he asked of things was that they should produce a happy unconsciousness of all instrumentalities, and set the mind free for its own flights. To be happy was to sing; not to be made to sing, or to sing by rote, or as an art, or for a purpose, but spontaneously, religiously, because something sang within you, and all else for the moment was remote and still. Things were truly beautiful, like a ship under full sail, only when they suggested the free movement of life and liberated it in yourself. But champagne evidently was just an artificial stimulus—how useless!—and a forced pleasure—how *un*pleasant!—only calculated to smother your reason in foolishness—how sickening! All this luxurious living of his father's and Lord Jim's, all this loitering and sipping of mere sensations, was a weary business, and rather wicked. As to food and drink, anything would do that didn't poison you, that wasn't a *drug*; but when he was playing football and hadn't time to go home for lunch, so that he could choose what to eat, his favourite fare consisted of three dishes, eaten perched on a high stool at the lunch-counter in the railway station: oyster stew, to warm his insides; beef sandwiches, to fortify him against the coming exertions; and a small bowl of custard, to remove all taste of gross food: the whole washed down with one or two glasses of cold milk, also productive of euphoria. He wanted nothing more choice; and the exotic arts of his father's cook were entirely wasted upon him.

Not so the boyish frankness of Lord Jim's conversation, which ran on in an artless matter-of-fact way over everything in heaven and earth, from the most public matters to the most private, as if he were simply thinking aloud, except that he would turn to Oliver now and then with a slight smile, as if to say, Isn't it so? Isn't that the way you would feel about it? Oliver knew what it was to be talked to anxiously or affectionately or in that cheerful cordial over-heated manner which at Great Falls was called being pleasant; but now he was being entertained in an entirely new fashion. The conversation didn't seem to be edited at all for his benefit. He was invited to overhear it, as in those bazaars where a sign by the open door reads: Admittance free. And it was easy to enter. Everything in the world seemed to be viewed by Lord Jim as a boy would view it, without mysterious reservations or inaccessible prejudices. The shady side of knowledge, the human side, seemed just as intelligible and natural to Lord Jim as the sunny side had always seemed to Oliver. Perhaps, when your eyes got used to artificial light, you might run and play about human affairs just as easily as about natural phenomena. Perhaps human affairs *were* natural phenomena, and the whole trouble came from trying to regard them otherwise. Never had Oliver heard anyone talk who had so much experience and of such strange worlds—the sea and the Klondike and the British Navy and Anglo-Catholicism; yet never had anyone talked so simply about it all, as if everything were a matter of course and equally approachable. Not that Lord Jim didn't laugh at people's ways and swear at them: he did so copiously and impartially, yet somehow humbly and without malice, as if he really had no right to expect that things should be different. Things might be absurd, they might be monstrous: but it was all like walking through the Zoo, and looking at the hippo and the cobra, the peacock and the giraffe. Rum creatures: but what were you to do about it? Just so the dignities and powers of human beings seemed to be simply their social hide, horns, and feathers; a grotesque equipment, a bit awkward for you, perhaps, if you were unarmed, yet a beastly burden for them also.

When, however, the madeira had followed the champagne and the whiskies and sodas had followed the madeira, and the steward and the cabin boy had ceased making irruption like comets into the solar system, the Captain's talk became more personal.

"Your governor was telling you, was he, that he calls me Lord Jim? You wonder why perhaps. Did he explain?"

"He said you had got into some trouble like Lord Jim in the book, only of another sort."

"But he didn't say what?"

"No."

"It's no secret. It filled columns and columns in *The Times*, not to speak of the penny papers. For days there wasn't a City gent in a first class carriage who didn't sit as solemn as an owl gloating on the scandal all the way up to London. There had been a full dress court martial. And what for? Because a few snotties had been overheard calling a spade a spade. Immorality in the British Navy! The old admiral and captains were pretty well scared. They reread the K.R. and the A.I. and even sent for the mess rules, to make quite sure of the law. They practised putting on a long face before the glass, as if they were going to read prayers, and if they had some recollection of young larks of their own, they severely closed down the hatches on that watertight compartment, and decided to look and feel like Queen Victoria, or at least like Prince Albert. How much better such a thing would be managed at Eton or Radley—which was my School for a year before I went to Dartmouth. Those old parsons and

schoolmasters, instead of making a public row, would have quietly
sent down any particularly bad boy, and frightened the rest with a
stiff sermon, rising with so much eloquence from those low practices
to heavenly thoughts, as to have turned the boys' budding emotions
from nastiness to religion, and very likely, in the end, would have
made little curates of the little beggars. But your naval and military
duffers, though they may go it pretty strong themselves upon occasion, when anything smelly comes up to them officially get into a blue
funk and don't know what to do except to look ferocious and apply
the full rigour of the law, lest anyone should think them lax in their
Christian principles. Their downright sailor minds jump at once to
extreme conclusions, as if there were nothing in human nature between white and black. Now the judges at our court-martial—those
who weren't fundamental asses—ought to have known very well that
most of us, at least, were innocent: innocent, I mean, of the assault
and battery which their pure minds immediately pictured. God knows
we had talked, talked too much, and used the most vulgar language:
and if we had initiated any little Naval Galahad into mysteries that
he hadn't investigated already on his own account, he ought to have
been thankful for it: because it's one of the curses of boyhood to be
scared white about unmentionable matters, and to think that what
happens to everybody is a horrible secret peculiar to oneself. But our
talk in the gunroom had gone too far, and we had got out of hand;
because the junior sub-l'e'tenant not much older than the rest of us,
wasn't a gentleman at all, but a blooming Bloomsbury radical who
thought himself deuced clever, and wanted freedom in the Navy;
and instead of shutting us up at the beginning, he laughed at our
low language and turned a blind eye on our tomfooleries; glad to
imbibe a few modern ideas more advanced, by Jove, than his own,
and proud to encourage free speech and liberty of conscience. Pretty
soon the Commander got wind of it. Now you see how it is. English
law is all a sham. It forbids you under horrible penalties to marry
your deceased wife's grandmother, and insists on letting you off for
talking, no matter how much harm may come of it. But in fact you
can't be let off, not if society is to hold together. A man who gives a
wrong twist to your mind, meddles with you just as truly as if he hit
you in the eye; the mark may be less painful, but it's more lasting.
Mind what I tell you: freedom of the press and Hyde Park oratory—
even if it goes on in Parliament—are going to be the ruin of England:
and when I say England, I mean America also and France, and the

whole damned show. It may take a little time yet, and we may not live to see it, because after all we British are a practical people. If we can't legally punish a man for what he has said, we find him guilty of what he hasn't done. It's tit for tat, and there's a sort of rough justice in it, though every step is a lie and the whole proceeding merely window-dressing. After raising such a first class scandal our court-martial couldn't back-water and say: All my mistake! They had to vindicate their watchful authority by imposing a severe sentence on somebody. So five of us midshipmen and the sub-l'e'tenant were dismissed the service. Some of the judges, I must allow, understood the case perfectly, and the verdict wasn't unanimous. And three or four years later, because the mother of one of the lads wouldn't put up with the disgrace, and was rich enough to keep the lawyers suing and appealing for revision, the case was actually recalled and judgment reversed. But I was out of the Navy and in the Yukon, and it was too late for *me*."

"If you were acquitted," Oliver cried with all the head-boy's keenness for precise logic and legality, "if you were acquitted, why weren't you taken back, and why didn't you go on in the Navy as if nothing had happened?"

"Because something *had* happened, and the only thing that really counts. I was a marked man. I was classed. Being acquitted is nothing in this world. Being accused is what makes all the difference. What another man may think or even know about you does you no harm, so long as your public standing is unchallenged and you pass for an ordinary person; but your best friend will drop you if he finds you are in bad odour. Besides, I was too old then, and used to being boss. It would have been hell for me in the gunroom with those youngsters and those silly rules—I should almost have been happier in the lower deck—and the superior officers would have looked at me askance, because I had too much experience and could criticise them. No, I was done for, as far as the Navy was concerned. I don't mind so much now, but at first it was horrible. Damned unfair, too, to my poor father who had made every sacrifice for me, and was cut to the quick. I hadn't the heart to go home, but wrote to say I was leaving the country. I went to sea in a Canadian liner, at first as a steward; and then picked up all sorts of jobs. My mother I did see privately. We met one night in the station at Didcot, where I was changing trains on my way North. There were no secrets between us. If I had been guilty of murder she would have stuck to me all the closer. She had an old grudge of her own against society, and her heart was with her young cub, no matter what he might do. She took disgrace good-humouredly, with a shrug that meant: 'The beasts! They're no better than you and me, but they put on airs because they're richer.' She was bred to poor people's hard life, who nose their way about like animals between the gaol and the workhouse, never knowing what will become of them to-morrow. Morality is immensely simplified from that point of view. It consists of cheating the hangman and getting your pint of beer."

Oliver was silent. He thought of Punch and Judy. Wasn't that their morality? There was more wind in all this talk of Lord Jim's than his own lungs could take in at a breath. The currents which this flood of words may have set flowing within him ran far too deep to come at once to the surface.

Having had his say, and being asked no questions, Jim gulped down the rest of his whisky-and-soda, put his pipe in his pocket and said he would take a turn below to see how the Doctor was getting on. If Jim was aware that he hadn't altogether cheated the hangman and still had, as it were the noose round his neck, at least he was drawing very superior beer, and plenty of it; and he couldn't help chuckling silently at how well, so far, he had got off. Here he was, under the influence of a balmy night and a good dinner, yielding to the pleasure of talking endlessly about himself, living over his picturesque past, and proving to the hilt that he was an injured man and a gentleman. And this without a single lie; for it wouldn't do to lie to these people. They hated lying worse than anything else. And here were fresh possibilities to consider: there might be shoals ahead, or there might be a safe anchorage. He mustn't let his ship gather too much headway in an uncharted channel. The Doctor's health was precarious, and at any moment this young Oliver might become owner: or he might take Jim's place in the Doctor's affections. It was one thing to be captain of a luxurious yacht and as good as adopted son to a millionaire; it would be quite another to find oneself without a job or a patron, or perhaps plain sailing-master in some racing boat, or second mate in a tramp steamer. Better that the old man should hold out a few years longer, until the boy got a thorough liking for the sea.

Oliver had entirely forgotten his father. Absence in this parent seemed as normal as presence was normal in his mother. Peter's habit of absconding and retiring to his own room, even when at home, made his eclipse on this occasion seem perfectly natural. Why should Jim trouble about it? Probably he didn't really, but simply wanted to stretch his legs. Oliver too got up. Yes, a lovely summer night: stars, harbour lights reflected in the sea, and the single calculated flash of the revolving light-house, more significant, Oliver considered, than all those natural marvels, with its witness to the determination of civilised man to live as little dangerously as possible. What a fool, after all, that Nietzsche was. Poetry and philosophy and sermons purposely went off at a tangent, purposely lied, in order to make an impression. The simple truth. What a liberation, what a relief! How easily a man might square his accounts with the universe if he had the courage to face it. "Lord Jim's mother"—and here Oliver's latent feelings began to grow articulate—"Lord Jim's mother stands up for her young cub against the world, while my mother—I never saw it so clearly before—always stands up for the world against her young cub. I don't like lies: and I don't like them in favour of morality, any more than against morality. They make morality false, they make it hypocrisy. It's not the frank fearless people like Lord Jim who are immoral, but the 'moral' people who are cowards and liars. I won't put up with their falsehoods. They shan't scare me any longer. First admit the truth, and then make the best of it. That's a man's work."

Oliver was so absorbed in his ethical meditation that it startled him suddenly to hear a voice at his elbow.

"Admiring the landscape?" said Jim. "It's less dismal by night than by day in this blasted Cape Cod. Your father's all right. You know these sleeping-draughts of his don't always work, and he might be restless without being quite awake or master of his movements. Then I have to talk to him soothingly, as you would to a baby, and try to cut off any bad dream that may be troubling him, because he can hear and mind well enough, as people do when hypnotised, and I can turn his thoughts to something pleasanter, as he's used to my voice, and make him do anything that's necessary: only he doesn't remember afterwards anything that happened in his trance. But to-day he is resting quietly. Got the mixture just right. The very thing for him after being so long ashore in this heat. Besides Boston always works the devil with his nerves. You see he wasn't a tough chap like me, to stand the blow he got when he was a lad. It pretty well staggered him, giving murder such a close shave, and having to quit. No wonder that a modest sensitive man like him should have been scotched for life."

The normal flow of Oliver's mind had been paralysed by the first part of this announcement, and it was only half consciously that he reacted to the second part.

"You mean," he said haltingly, "you mean because my grandfather was murdered in that horrible way?"

"That too. But after all the old gentleman having been chopped up was no more your father's fault than it was yours. That was ancient history. But killing a man yourself on a dark night in the College Chapel, even if by a sort of accident, might rather make you see ghosts afterwards."

"My father *killed* somebody?"

"Yes, of course. Haven't you heard of it? When he had to leave the University and travel abroad with a tutor? That was what kept him so many years wandering in the East, and uncomfortable whenever he came home again."

The paralysis in Oliver's mind began to yield to a sort of nightmare. He saw circles moving within circles, each one darker and deeper than the other, and who could tell how far the blackness and the hellish depth might descend? Yet this vortex was purely mental. He could see plainly and steadily through the turmoil of his thoughts the level shadows of the sea and sky, and the harbour lights, and the lighthouse lantern revolving punctually, to prove that nothing was changed in the order of nature. Fortunately the night concealed the pallor of his face; but he felt cold all over, and had to muster up all his training in courage and self-control to keep himself from trembling perceptibly. Gradually his reason recovered its scope, and he began to put these new facts together into some sort of perspective. And the focus of everything, the red hot evil to be faced and smothered first, was not the word murder which had been pronounced so airily. It was the other evil thing.

"Did you say," he asked with an effort, "that my father takes drugs?"

"Of course he does. Didn't you know that either? They must be blind at your place if they don't see it. All doctors dope themselves more or less, it's so easy for them. He takes a dose or a sleeping potion or an injection of sorts whenever he thinks he needs it. It's perfectly legitimate. He's a medical man. He experiments on himself scientifically, and what are you going to do about it?"

"But you say he falls into a stupor and is helpless in your hands as if he were dead drunk or hypnotised or worse. And you laugh at it."

Poor Oliver at home had the run of two doctors' libraries, one of them an alienist. There was little he didn't know verbally; yet what a surprise to see those hideous medical abstractions stalking through the real world! A great lunatic asylum was at his door, but he had never visited it.

"Laugh? Why not? Would you have me cry? In this world you have to take people as you find them. I allow sometimes it's a bit awkward for me, because he relies on me to tide things over and keep him from being bothered when he is under the weather and mustn't be disturbed. I do my best. I should be a pig if I didn't. By gad, if he was my own father he couldn't have treated me better or more handsomely than he has from the very beginning. He took a fancy to me, I suppose; and he liked to have somebody on board that could be a companion, and that he could trust to look after everything. For me it was the greatest stroke of luck in the world: to have a gentleman for employer, good pay, good food, good presents, and (what's more) confidence and a free hand to run the yacht as I choose. It's as if she were my own boat. I engage the crew, the steward, the cabin-boy—not the cook, because your father wouldn't give up his Indian curry for anything—and I chart out the course we shall take and more or less plan every detail. Of course, by this time, I know his tastes. And I save him a pretty penny, because he has no idea of money, doesn't care how it goes, and lets everybody cheat him. I am supposed to have something to hide, but I don't hide it. After our very first cruise off Vancouver, when he had seen me handle our little schooner in a gale and he offered to engage me, I made a clean breast of everything and showed him the copies of *The Times*, which I always had by me, with the *verbatim* reports of the court-martial. He glanced at the papers for a moment and then brushed them aside; I expect he had read the whole thing at the time of the trial, and remembered it well enough. 'I don't care a fig what you have done,' he said. 'The only question for me is what you will do; and at your age the one thing doesn't follow from the other. It's different with us old fellows. I'll wait till you do me an ill turn and then I'll begin to object to you.' Those were his very words. Kind, wasn't it, to a young chap struggling against a bad record? And it's wonderful, these four years, how well we have pulled together."

Oliver had not been listening, though his ear took in the words and recalled them afterwards. Now he was under the spell of a sort of horror, a blind need of escape where there was no issue.

Jim, in the silence, divined what was going on.

"I'm afraid," he said, "I've given you a bit of a shock. I'm sorry."

Oliver's pride repelled the suggestion of any failure of nerve on his part. He might be caught unawares, facts might be unexpected, but he would never be without courage to face them. Had not his ancestors for generations girded their loins for wrestling with the Lord, scorning delights, cleaving to righteousness, sure of the triumph of righteousness in and through themselves? Here was an occasion to prove his true mettle.

"I'm glad," he said rather brokenly, "I'm glad to have found this thing out. It's better to know the truth. Still, *you* needn't have told me about it. In you it was a breach of trust."

"Well, well," thought Jim, hardly restraining the impulse to whistle. "Was there ever such a young prig? We are as hoity toity as that, are we? Never mind: better humour the little Pharisee than quarrel with him. Very few things in this world are worth quarrelling about, and certainly not the moral tantrums of a boy of sixteen. Let him wear his blooming principles like mayflowers in his buttonhole, until they drop off."

Jim Darnley was one of those affectionate and fatalistic creatures who are not sensitive to justice and injustice. He could wince like a whipped dog, and come back to be petted. He was content to be scolded, if he wasn't disliked. The ruling powers of this world were like an impulsive mother who might make her child cry but didn't oblige him to let go her skirts or his faith in the kisses and sugarplums to come.

As for Oliver, he was angry—angry at having been stunned, angry with Jim for having struck the blow, angry with himself for having lived in such a fool's paradise and not having known these things before. Yet anger was itself a foolish feeling that he couldn't admit should overcome him: it must be only righteous indignation at something intrinsically wrong. Now what was wrong in this case, if anything, was his father's conduct; yet about this he might feel shame or even dismay, but not anger. No case whatever then for righteous indignation on his part, only for sorrow, for patience. No reason for blaming Jim, or blaming himself. Yet how intolerably wrong the whole thing was, the whole corrupt world from which there was no escape, and where such things happened!

"Would you like to go below and see for yourself how your father is? I don't think he expected you this evening to come and say good-night, but nothing would be more natural. He's not likely to wake up, and you'll see that there's nothing to worry about."

Yes, Oliver would like very much to do that. Any semblance of action seemed a relief; he could imagine he was bestirring himself somehow to set things right. And Lord Jim was so considerate, so affectionate, such a tower of strength to lean on, helping him down that unfamiliar cabin hatch in the dark, without a shadow of resentment at having been found fault with unjustly—unjustly, Oliver now repeated to himself with a certain strange satisfaction. And he couldn't help smiling at the idea that perhaps *that evening* his father didn't expect him to come to his bedside to say good-night, as if at home they ever went to one another's bedside. That was a place for professional nurses only, in case of necessity. The members of his family no more thought of entering one another's rooms than of opening one another's letters. Lord Jim had probably been brought up in one of those higgledy-piggledy households where nobody has anything of his own, but all wear one another's socks and ties, and sleep four in a room and two in a bed—horrid habit!—or even in some vast public dormitory, as in an infant asylum or a second-class hospital, or like cadets in a naval training ship: and here Oliver couldn't help smiling again. These invisible smiles, breaking out amid his tragic thoughts, had already half dissipated the cloud that hung over his spirits before they came to his father's cabin.

The light was low, but sufficient for eyes coming out of the dark, and the lustre was rendered omnipresent by multiple reflections from lacquered walls and porcelain objects. His father lay propped high, very lean and bronzed by habitual exposure to the sun and the sea-air; his bald head and thin hands looked dark and swarthy against the white pillow and the white night gown on which his long fingers were spread out symmetrically. His eyes, rather than in sleep, seemed closed by a voluntary drooping of the eyelids, as if in order that a deeper life might flow undisturbed; and there was a faint ambiguous smile on his lips, not unlike that of the two Buddhas whose golden shrines decorated the Poop. Oliver had expected trouble, and he found an image of peace. He had been nerving himself to tolerate, or if possible to repair, the ravages of vice, and he seemed to be rebuked somehow by a strange spirit of holiness, as if life could ultimately escape from perpetual dying and become supreme recollection.

Doubtless Peter Alden's comatose condition was a wretched parody of Nirvana, produced by black arts and destined to be ephemeral; and a judicious observer examining that spectacle by daylight would have found it whimsical and cheap. What was Peter but one of the hundred shrewd, rich, spare, defeated Americans of his generation, become a man of the world and left high and dry in it? Neither he nor his Buddhistic sanctum, with all the old junk in it, would have struck a connoisseur as more than eccentric and capricious—a faddish refuge for debility, a pleasure-dome decreed for burning incense-sticks, a polite imitation of an opium den: and an incense-stick had actually been burning that day in one of those china bowls, only the excellent artificial ventilation of the new yacht had already blown away the fumes and most of the odour. But young Oliver was no connoisseur, nor fit to become one; he noticed only what affected his moral life. Yet a man whose only knowledge of admirable works of art is drawn from photographs or translations, and who has no just idea of the originals in their inimitable native force, may find nevertheless in the presence of those counterfeits, a fresh fountain of insight and enthusiasm welling up in himself. So our budding transcendentalist was made inwardly aware, by his father's slumber, of a new possible dimension of moral life. *Dope*, Oliver said to himself, was the worst thing possible. *Dope* was the very denial of courage, of determination to face the facts, a betrayal of responsibility. *Dope* was a cowardly means of escape, of hiding one's head like the ostrich, and choosing not to know, or to act or to think. And yet, in close association with that miserable *dope*, appeared this strange serenity, this cool challenge to the world, this smiling and beautiful death in life, or life in accepted death. Here was an ancient, an immortal conviction, which the modern world chose foolishly to ignore: the inscrutable, invincible preference of the mind for the infinite. Could it be that life, as the world understands it, was the veritable *dope*, the hideous, beastly vicious intoxication? Was obedience to convention and custom and public opinion perhaps only an epidemic slavery, a cruel superstition; while to sit with closed eyes in a floating hermitage, as in a Noah's Ark in the Deluge, might be enlightenment and salvation?

"Hello," said Jim incongruously, "he has left his clothes all in a heap and forgotten to empty his pockets or ring for the boy. Must have felt devilish weak." With all the decision and authority of an old valet, Jim began to examine the Doctor's garments, to lay out watch, wallet, loose money, keys, and letters in their proper places upon the dressing or the writing table; and having done so, he proceeded to fold the clothes quickly and expertly, and to lay them out on the divan opposite that on which Peter Alden was reposing.

"Doctor," he said, laying his hand on the old gentleman's shoulder and speaking low, but close to his ear, "Oliver and I have come to see if you wanted anything before we turned in. Good night."

There was no answer but a vague responsive movement, a slight readjustment of posture, to prove that the words, at some depth of consciousness or unconsciousness had not passed unregistered. Jim ushered Oliver out of the door, and whispered a word as he closed it, himself remaining inside. There was one of the humbler offices of nurse to be performed, which are embarrassing for a third person to witness.

Good heavens, thought Oliver, here was his father being served, nursed, and looked after, his weaknesses accepted, his tastes consulted, his opinions honoured, his old age defended, and helped to flow pleasantly far from the world. This stranger who wasn't ashamed to be a servant, had the feelings and the privileges of a son, not as sons really were, but as they ought to be; whereas Oliver himself—but here was Jim again in person, turning on the lights for him in the Poop, telling him to ring for his early tea when he wanted it in the morning—as if Oliver had ever heard of early tea—and to order whatever he liked for his breakfast. Jim breakfasted in the officers' cabin with the mate and the engineer. One had to keep an eye on the crew, and be friendly with one's pals.

As he turned away, Oliver stopped him. "I oughtn't to have said that it was a breach of trust to tell me about Father. You thought I knew. Even if I didn't know it would have been only right for you to tell me. And I'm sorry too for what I said about his being helpless in your hands. It's not your fault; and I think he couldn't be in better hands than yours."

At the High School in Great Falls when two boys made up a quarrel the approved ceremony was for them to shake each other violently by the hand for several seconds, in evidence that all ill feeling was past. Oliver was conscious of having made a very handsome apology, was rather proud of himself for it, and put out his hand in the prescribed manner. But Jim not knowing the ways of the country, neglected to shake, and took Oliver's hand affectionately in both his own, held it for a moment, and said, "That's all right. I didn't give it a thought"; and then he proceeded to pat Oliver on the back, as if the good little boy and not the gallant tar himself, needed to be comforted. And Oliver, though his expectation and his pride were cheated, did somehow feel comforted. Pride began to seem insufficient and unnecessary. There was something else more genuine, more honest. This was the first time anyone had caressed him, since Fräulein twelve years before had stopped stroking his bare legs. It was the first time he had found anyone brushing away all laboured scruples and all false shams about the facts of life, and transferring everything simply to the plane of human nature. The world seemed larger, more habitable, more friendly to Oliver than ever before, and this at the very moment when the shady side of life, in his own family, began to uncover its painful depths. Ah, the depths in Oliver's own experience had always been painful. It was a relief to admit it, to see that probably it was so in everybody. Why pretend that one's relations must be particularly perfect? Why more perfect than other people? Why be obliged to pretend that one was perfect oneself? His mother wouldn't go with them to St. Barnabas, in spite of the nice music, because she said it was degrading to call ourselves miserable sinners. The words might be old-fashioned, but what if the thing was true? Wouldn't it clear the air to confess it?

All the ports were wide open. Oliver turned off the electric light, too garish for his mood. Perhaps he understood better now the meaning of those Buddhas in their gilded shrines: but he still hated their aspect, their loose fat bellies and squinting eyes. Better the soft dark night, and the wavelets patiently lapping the overhanging stern with a quick liquid sound. The vast breadth, the tireless monotony of nature were also soothing and liberating; they too, were enlightening; and they were a saner influence than human religion under which to lie down and sleep, because they didn't substitute one dream for another. They were not drugs.

XIII

In spite of his strange bed, if bed it could be called, and the bright sunshine and the vibration of the engine started in the early hours, Oliver slept later that morning than ever morning had suffered him to sleep before. It was as if in his unconsciousness—for he didn't remember to have dreamt—a muted voice had kept whispering within him: *Sleep on; no hurry; no school; no family breakfast; nobody waiting. Rest, rest, rest. You are free.* And as if obedient to this new gift of animal liberty, he had defensively hidden his face in the hollow of his arm, like a beggar asleep at noon in a public square. The first fruits of his tragic discoveries and of his deeper readiness to live had been a sudden capacity for indolence. He felt more at home in this world, as this world became wider, more unkempt, and more indifferent.

On deck Lord Jim, already sextant in hand, was standing near the man at the wheel. The ship was rolling slightly and very slowly in the long placid swell; no land was in sight, for they were making a loop into the open sea for a ten hours' run to test the new engines, the dead calm being most favourable. Lord Jim wore a self-contained preoccupied air very different from that of the day before. It was his watch. In his white cap and buttoned jacket, he stood square on both feet, his arms akimbo and his eye scanning the horizon. But he was officially affable.

"Not bored by the sea yet? It's a dull life, after a bit, even if you love sailing. Your father likes the water, because at least it isn't the land. Reading—with a little choice eating and drinking, and laughing at me for being such an ignorant bloke—is what he amuses himself with on a long cruise. You'd find it deadly, a young chap like you, all alone."

"But you are young yourself," Oliver answered, and whether this meant that Jim too should be bored, or that he would prevent Oliver from being so, in any case it was a compliment, and Jim smiled broadly. He loved compliments, and he loved being young.

"You know, I'm almost seven-and-twenty. Don't look it, do I?"

All ages above twenty then seemed to Oliver beyond the pale of youth: and twenty-seven was a vaguely remote term, suggesting marriage, long moustaches, and "being in business"—images unpleasing to Oliver's mind, which he couldn't associate with Lord Jim. Ten years older than himself! He had no idea, he said, that so young a fellow could be as old as that. And what did Jim do at sea to keep from being bored?

"But I *am* bored. All sailors are: not for having nothing to do, but fed up doing the same damned things all day and all night all the year round. Not one moment safe and free for yourself. Always one dirty little job after another, cursing the weather, cursing the food, cursing the officers, if you're a flatfoot, or cursing the crew, if you're the captain, or cursing the captain, if you're one of the other officers, and generally cursing yourself, if you're an honest Christian. Seafaring is a poor man's job, and a dull job. The danger, when it blows, is not exciting; only doubles your work, and makes it dirtier. Nobody would go to sea, if it wasn't fated. But here's the water, always tempting you; and men being fools, somebody will always be putting out to puke and to drown in it. After the puking and before the drowning, it's a deuced hard way of earning your living. And the thing that keeps you at it, when you've time to think and aren't too sleepy and too weary even to dream, is the idea of reaching port and going ashore."

"But what has a sailor to do ashore? I should think you'd be more bored there than ever."

"There's one thing ashore, my boy, which there's not at sea, at least not for most of us, and that's women. If you reach your home port, there stands your wife or your sweetheart waiting for you—if she's had the patience to wait; and if it isn't your home port, there's always a temporary sweetheart or a temporary wife to take pity on your blooming person and on your blooming money, aching to bestow themselves on the deary darling. Then when your wife or your sweetheart, temporary or permanent, has clean emptied your pockets and your manly spirit, and you're left besotted without a penny and without a wish, you go to sea again, and begin to dream of your next pay-day, your next port, and your next gorgeous fortnight of wedded bliss."

"If that's all sailors live for," Oliver observed somewhat bitterly, "I don't see why you don't all stay on land. Sooner or later you could find some day-labourer's job, and go home to your wife or sweetheart every day of the year."

Jim, when he felt the least beginnings of hostility, had a smiling obsequious way of turning away wrath and if possible ingratiating himself anew in the world's favour. "Quite so," he said, "that's just what most of your sad dogs say to themselves, and never go to sea at all. But once you're a sailor, it becomes a habit. You know the ropes; you know the life and where to look for a berth, when you're without one; you've signed on before, it's easy to sign on again. So most of us jog along through life between blinkers, nothing to the left or the right, and nothing in front but what you've done before. Perhaps, too, there is another reason. You dream of the women, when you're not near them; but when you've got them, and they've got you, after a while you are jolly glad to be rid of them. You're jolly glad of a month or a year of plain hard living, all your duties prescribed, all your work commanded, everything provided, a round of breezy solitary hardships, and a bit of tobacco in between."

Oliver's fresh-blown marine enthusiasm was rather dashed by these melancholy professional views. "You're tired of the sea," he said. "You don't really like it."

"I don't mind it. I'm used to it. I'm earning my living. I'm doing myself well, and I'm putting by something against a rainy day. One day I'll go home—one day very soon, perhaps—and begin life afresh."

Something about Jim's way of saying this made Oliver ask:

"You think my father won't live long?"

"No, to say the truth, I don't expect he will. He doesn't care to live long."

"You mean that he will kill himself?"

"No, not now, I hope not. But he might drop at any time. All his arrangements are made as if he was to die to-morrow."

"Good morning," said the future dead man, rising like Lazarus out of the cabin hatch, shuffling a little in his gait, smiling through his smoked goggles, and evidently inhaling the warm sea-air with a deep pleasure.

"Oliver," he said, stretching himself languidly in the long wicker chair which the cabin boy unfolded for him, "you see we are providing you with perfect weather. Neptune wants to make a favourable impression; but don't trust him. He has a nasty temper, and can sulk like a savage. Has Lord Jim told you that we are making for Salem?

No? It's a place for you to see, the home of some of our ancestors, and there are relations of ours still living there. It was the first place, as a boy, where I went boating; and I also have a sentimental attachment to it on account of the clipper-ships that used to sail from there. I should have liked the *Black Swan* to have been a full-rigged three-masted vessel; but it was impracticable. Too large a crew needed, and the right men not to be found. Don't nurse any illusions about what Salem may be nowadays. It's a sad town, uglier than Great Falls, with less modern life in it."

"If you could have had your clipper-ship, would you still have called her the *Black Swan*?"

"Dear me, dear me, I never thought of that question. Perhaps not. Too many parts, too many ropes, sails too small in relation to the total force. *Arachne*, perhaps, or *Galatea*: thin-threaded and propelled by doves. But I chose *Black Swan* for deeper reasons: old hobbies of mine. What are they? Perhaps rather confused by this time, rather remote. You know I like Orientals, and their way of using words is far subtler than ours. There's no poetry in identifying things that look alike. But the most opposite things may become miraculously equivalent, if they arouse the same invisible quality of emotion. Even the sound and rhythm of words, in a sensitive language, have some congruity with the nature of the things signified. So, to my feeling, the words *Black Swan* make a good name for a ship merely as a matter of euphony: they are incisive at the bow, and gentle and spreading at the stern. It is not imitation, yet I seem to hear the forward push through the ruffled water. But these words are already the name of a bird: and that puts your taste on trial a second time. And I like the simile involved, because the swan is a lazy broad-bottomed sort of bird, that floats and doesn't race, yet on occasion can stretch its long hard neck like an arrow, and fly surprisingly. Then, as to the *black* swan in particular, it is exotic and comparatively rare, and used to be thought impossible. That's a little hint to the philosophers. Besides, black in itself has a function and beauty more recondite than white has, and deeper. It is the ultimate background of space and of consciousness, satisfying intrinsically, and by contrast a source of precision and liveliness in other colours. It tires less, it protects more, and wise old swans prefer it."

Oliver joined his father in laughing a little at this, but he was not convinced.

"Didn't you have reasons of that kind for calling the old yacht *Hesperus*?"

"Yes, I had at the time, but they were personal. It was a symbol for my state of mind then. *Hesperus*, for other people or for myself now, would be merely a pretty name, like *Sea Gull* or *Wild Duck* or *Albatross* or *Ocean Wave*, or, who knows? *Sally* or *Mamie* or *Susie*."

Peter drawled these last alternatives dreamily, as if amusement in him had yielded to a vague helplessness. His thoughts drifted back to the time of his marriage, to the home-coming from all his defeated experiments. Hadn't he imagined at that time that a sort of evening star might still charm the twilight of his life? The yacht was to be the focus of those memories and of this quietude, and the name *Hesperus* would signify them to his mind—pleasantly, because the evening, he hoped, would be more satisfying than the morning. And in fact, though his evening star had not been particularly brilliant, these last sixteen years had passed in comparative peace. Now somehow that equilibrium seemed to be disturbed. He was turning again to the east. Could there still be a morning star for him there? Oliver, perhaps. Would it be possible to rescue this beautiful diligent boy from being simply his mother's son, and win him over, to fulfil some of the hopes that had cheated his father? Might he come in time—and not too late—to understand himself and the world and the age in which he lived; above all to understand America, and throw his understanding into arresting words or, better still, into contagious actions?

"Oliver, I hope this winter—has Lord Jim told you?—to revisit the Mediterranean. This boat was planned expressly with that idea. You know that my pleasure is to coast along as if I were an explorer, putting in for the night, whenever possible, into some little harbour. Those high coasts and those little old ports with their stone quays make a better setting for such wanderings than our Atlantic shores. Many of those towns were great and busy in antiquity, and the whole history of Christendom is embedded in their walls. There are ruins, but there are also palace hotels. Some day, perhaps, you will come with us, and examine those things for yourself at leisure: because books and tours are not enough. You must let your mind be saturated with the genius of those places, with their ancient *numina*. Not for the sake of historical knowledge—you needn't be a professor unless you like—but because there is no sounder or more vivid way of understanding human affairs, especially wars and religions. In conceiving the past you see the present as you ought to see it. The ignorant are always dupes of what they think they know."

"I have been looking at your books in the Poop," said Oliver. "Are those all you have on board?"

"No. Those are only our stand-bys, books that bear rereading. We have others—precious or rare ones—put away, and the current books we pass on to the officers' cabin, and Lord knows what becomes of them."

"Why haven't you any American books?"

"Haven't we?" Peter murmured, apparently surprised. "Didn't we have *Moby Dick* in the *Hesperus*?"

"Yes," Jim replied, "and there's also Walt Whitman."

"But Mother says nobody reads Walt Whitman except foreigners. I thought he was English."

Oliver wondered at the loud laughter that greeted this confession. He might have made a mistake, but why so much merriment?

"But he's the great, the best, the only American poet," Jim burst out, "the only one truly American. Do you mean that you've never read him?"

"Oliver has been brought up on the classics, and Walt Whitman isn't yet counted among them, at least not in our family. No reason why Oliver shouldn't read those effusions, but I don't think he will like them. I don't read them myself: so that, as far as we three are concerned, Oliver's mother is quite right. Only the Englishman reads Walt Whitman."

"But you *have* read him, only you choose to disparage all great poetry."

"I confess I don't care for poetry that is long-winded and over-bearing, poetry that fumes and preaches. The poetry of Western nations is chiefly rhetoric—eloquence in metre. So Shakespeare in the long speeches, though not in the songs, nor always in the sonnets. I think it is useless to try to beautify things in general, and that is what all speechifying poets do. Walt Whitman no less than the others. When a rhetorician composes long poems about God or Satan or the Universe or Agricultural Labours or Love or Liberty or Revolution, I don't say he may not propound important truths, although I doubt it, nor that his moral sentiments may not seem edifying to people of his own sect; but I say he is not a poet. He carries a load. His Pegasus is a pack-ass with wings attached that flap in time as he plods along. Consecutive and progressive eloquence is all very well; and a political flambeau may pass from hand to hand and start a universal conflagration. But poetry is something secret and pure, some magical perception lighting up the mind for a moment, like reflections in the water, playful and fugitive. Your true poet catches the charm of something or anything, dropping the thing itself. His feeling is rapturous, mocking, musical, sad; above all it is involuntary."

Jim had disappeared to work out his observations. Didn't he know by heart what the Doctor was going to say? But he returned for a moment and emphatically laid the *Leaves of Grass* on Oliver's knee. "There you are. Read a bit and judge for yourself."

There was a book-mark in the volume, which opened of itself at a passage heavily scored in the margin. *I could turn and live with the animals, they are so placid. . . . They do not weep for their sins. They do not make me sick discussing their duty to God.*

Dope, thought Oliver, himself a little somnolent in the noonday heat and the soft air, *dope* in another form. A lazy refusal to look backward, or to look ahead. A hatred of reason, a hatred of sacrifice. The lilies of the field. Work wasn't worth while. Work wasn't necessary. Why should his father object to this sort of *dope*? And he read aloud a part of the passage.

"Don't you like that?"

"I like the first three words: *I could turn.* Deeply felt, they would mean conversion, repentance. They might have been spoken by Buddha or by John the Baptist."

"But you don't like the rest?"

"I should have liked it well enough if he had said he could turn and *no longer* live with the animals, they are so restless and merciless and ferocious, possessed with a mania for munching grass and gnawing bones and nosing one another, when they don't make me sick saying they are God's chosen people, doing God's work. But Walt Whitman is as superficial as Rousseau. He doesn't see that human conventions are products of nature, that morality and religion and science express or protect animal passions: and that he couldn't possibly be more like an animal than by living like other men. His rebellion is no conversion, no deliverance. He pretends to turn—for it is largely affectation—only from the more refined devices of mankind to a ruder and more stupid existence. He is like Marie Antoinette playing the shepherdess."

It seemed to Oliver that being away from home wonderfully loosened his father's tongue; also that his sleeping-draughts didn't seem to cloud his intellect. His views might be wrong, but evidently he knew his own mind and had his wits about him in criticising other people. For the moment, however, there was a lull, and his eloquent parent behind his dark goggles seemed to have gone to sleep. Oliver read on for a page or two. His attention kept wandering. He turned to *Drum Taps*; but there too everything made merely a rumble in his head. He let the book close, and his eyelids closed after it. Yet in a sort of dark music-box within him, words continued to form themselves into phrases. "Call us animals: what difference does it make? Some animals are decent, like my horse Charley, called Charley because he used to belong to Mr. Charley Deboyse, who was *not* decent. Some animals are beastly, like toads and monkeys and Yep the gardener's cur. Walt Whitman seems inclined to slobber over everybody, whether decent or not. Is that why Lord Jim likes him? I must ask him."

XIV

They had dropped anchor for the night in a deserted inlet behind the harbour of Salem, protected from the encroachments of petty commerce and suburban "homes" by bare rocks on one side and a salt marsh on the other. In the midst there was an ample channel, well known to Peter Alden. It was a safe anchorage, cheerful and secluded, which the flowing tide divided into broad sparkling belts of sea-blue and sea-grey. In this marine desert, in the absence of more classic tritons and dolphins, the two young men were again swimming round their little raft, when an impertinent cat boat appeared doubling the point, and beating resolutely up the channel. A thin old man was at the tiller; and as he luffed and brought his boat alongside, he could be seen leering in their direction, with the caustic smile of your true Yankee who knows-it-all and has scant respect for the unnecessary follies of other people. "Boys will be boys," he seemed to be saying. "P'raps they think they enjoy it; but I guess it's nigh on to forty year since a drop of water has touched *this* belly."

Without the useless ceremony of hailing or of asking permission, he made fast to the ladder and boarded the *Black Swan* as if climbing into his own roost, while in his abandoned boat the loose boom dangled to leeward in harmless insecurity; the sail flapped idly, an occasional tremor running across it, as when an old cart horse, left confidently by the wayside with the reins flung over his neck, spasmodically but patiently shakes the flies from his flanks. It was ten o'clock in the morning. The July sun was glaring with naked ferocity; the salt breeze seemed to pickle their skin after the sun had scorched it. Oliver like the prudent youth he was, had supplied himself with a white canvas hat, which being his only article of dress gave him the look of a very youthful and slender Hermes. But Lord Jim, in spite of possessing something like the tightly curled natural helmet of the god began to feel the heat uncomfortably in the temples and the nape of the neck. "Let's go aboard and see what the rum old chap is after. We'll make a match of it: once round the float and then home.

Take as wide a sweep as you like and I'll keep outside. Not that way, this way," he added, waving his hand in a circle, "from left to right, like the sun and the college wine."

"That's only so because we're north of the equator," Oliver observed fresh from his school geography. "If we were south of it, the sun would go from right to left."

"Gad, we're clever. Newton minor may go to the head of the class." Jim laughed, but there was a side to Oliver that he didn't fancy. He had intended to race in earnest, having given a generous handicap; but now he took his time, dawdled and splashed about, and let the boy win by an enormous margin. You couldn't expect these young Americans to feel as you do. For them everything was tart and numerical. Better let them have their sport by themselves.

They were drying and girding themselves on deck, when the Doctor approached, a letter in his hand.

"Here is Cousin Caleb Wetherbee who has spied us from his tower—he has a telescope—and sends to invite us to dinner this evening, and to spend the night. 'You,' says the the note, 'and my friend the captain and that interloper who I suppose is your young hopeful?' Shall I accept for everybody?"

"Righto," said Jim, "except that I can't stay the night. Must be on board in the morning."

At home Oliver never asked questions about people or family history: his mother said those things wouldn't interest him; and it was quite true that until now they never did. But here all was changed. The most indiscreet subjects might be canvassed and the most interesting information obtained. He had known Lord Jim for only two days and there was absolutely no secret between them. His father too had become strangely communicative. Who, then, was Cousin Caleb Wetherbee?

"He is in some ways the most remarkable member of our family; on my side, I mean, and I daresay your mother has never seen him and wouldn't like him if she had. He is a hunchback, and a cripple, an enthusiast who has gone over to Rome and built a Benedictine Monastery at Salem in his old family orchard. The apple trees that I used to climb as a boy, with woeful results to my digestion, are now in the middle of a cloister: and I must say they look much more decorative and venerable; while I know by experience that the monks' home-made cider and apple pies are palatable and harmless. But Caleb Wetherbee's own aspect at first is rather horrible; it may take you a little time to overcome the repulsion. He will give us an excellent dinner, a fish dinner, because to-day is Friday: but that is a welcome challenge to an expert host, especially at this season when there are no oysters. To-morrow, if you will stay on, we shall probably be invited to the mid-day meal in the refectory and you will have a chance of seeing mediaeval manners, and even dishes, surviving and adapted to our age and country. Caleb Wetherbee is a learned man; is writing a history of religion in America—including the Spanish part—and it will be beautifully different from Prescott and even from Parkman. He has soaring metaphysical views, a mystical enthusiasm which he manages to combine with his ardent Americanism—because he is a warm patriot in his odd prophetic way."

That afternoon, with the pleasure natural to man—who is a land animal—of feeling terra firma under their feet, they walked the mile or two that separated the landing-place from the old Wetherbee mansion. This they could see a long way off, crowning a slight eminence above the sea. Before the square wooden house, painted white and yellow, with green blinds, stood a screen of great elms, their rude ribs far too gigantic for the scanty transparent foliage that hung from them in fringes. The cornice, the carved door, the porch with its slender columns, had a certain frail elegance, as of a Puritan dame daring at last to powder her thin straight hair, and to put on a little rouge. Was not virtue the best gentility? Was she not at heart, and in all her traditions, as much a lady as any duchess? The rest of the old Wetherbee place had been enclosed by its present owner in a brick wall, over which the low roofs of his monastic buildings peeped modestly among the apple-trees; except for a high campanile rising over the whole, with its open arches growing more and more airy with each superposed storey, after the Romanesque fashion. The bells occupied the lower apertures: but the topmost loggia, where the great bell would have been if it had been required, Mr. Wetherbee had reserved for his private work-shop and observatory, availing himself of the privileges of a founder; and here in fine weather, up a small lift installed for the purpose, he would come with great bundles of books and papers; here he would sit down to compose his history, or to draw inspiration for composing it. It seemed to him that from that perch he could descry the rocks and forests of the new world reaching out to the north east towards Iceland and Norway and the stormy Hebrides, like arms begging to welcome the men of the dark North, strong-handed and stubborn-hearted; while from the mouth of the Mediterranean, over wider and sunnier seas, he could see the painted sails of Columbus bearing westward in a little compass the whole heritage of Rome and Byzantium, of Islam and Spain—religion civilised by learning and passion civilised by policy. These were his moments of intuition. When it came to setting the facts down on paper the abundance of reports and the meagreness of them were alike discouraging. The mind became a blank, the body ached, and the work had to be left for to-morrow. *Mañana*, the great American shibboleth; and it was this word that Caleb Wetherbee had chosen for the motto of his future book and for the symbol of his faith.

Being the youngest and new to the house, Oliver was able to remain in the background, while his father and Jim said how-do-you-do to their host and indulged in the usual commonplaces. He had a moment in which to look about and swallow his first surprise. Cousin Caleb was a monster, perched like a parrot on a high chair, in which he wheeled himself restlessly about, among a confusion of books, atlases, maps, and papers heaped upon tables and chairs, and often on the floor. He fingered everything and removed everything, and in spite of flurry and hesitation and self-interruptions, he seemed to know where everything was. His grotesque pasty features looked larger than human, and his head preternaturally broad, with its sad pop eyes and dishevelled hair; and he seemed fiercely ready to defend his poor body with those long monkey-like arms and bent legs, like some wounded colossal spider. His enormous loose mouth was somewhat out of control and his speech spasmodically vehement or gentle, without much reference to the matter of it; as if the bellows within him blew suddenly of itself, and then refused to blow, when with a vehement effort he was compelled to tear up his words by the roots from the depths of his suffering body. Yet the sense of what he said, in its gentleness, contrasted strangely with the violence of his manner. Under excitement, when he was enforcing his favourite opinions, his whole contorted frame would tremble distressingly; before he could compose himself a few bubbles of foam would rise to his lips and threaten to ooze out; and from time to time, as he became aware of them, he would wipe them away with a handkerchief held painfully in his very long and unsteady fingers.

"Ah, so this is your Oliver, this is that green sprout of a Benjamin that you have been hiding from us for these sixteen years in the recesses of Connecticut. Oliver, if you have a good head, as I am told you have, come to live in Boston. I say 'come' because, for all the sacred ties, old and new, that hold me here in Salem, I don't give up my little house on Beacon Hill. Your father knows that every Sunday evening during the winter months the table is laid for six in Mount Vernon Place. All my friends are bidden: first come first served. *The five that first arrive may stay: the rest must come another day.* That makes a kind of doggerel which is the motto of my establishment. When you are at Harvard—of course you will go to Harvard—you must be one of my *habitués.* Don't be afraid of finding nothing but old people and invalids; it is mainly the very young that are not afraid of me. For the old I am a back number, and they can't abandon their comfortable firesides to visit a monster and hear uncomfortable truths. Yes, come to Boston. There—at least among our old-fashioned families—you may almost escape the scramble outside, the low boasts, the ugly language, the aggressive commonness of modern life, and its idiotic pleasures; you may smilingly disregard the press and the pulpit and the professors, not opposing them, since they are parts of the extant system and may be useful, but passing them by in your own mind, and preferring to be simple, and to take them and yourself for no more than you are. That's what you may see your father doing, and well-bred people all the world over: for it's only people who don't know the world who are fooled by the world. Poor prodigal world, let us not insult it: let us pray for it. But meantime, we must remain ourselves, as Emerson remained himself, only not on those stilts of his, not with that self-worship; because the world was no more made to serve us by illustrating our philosophy than we were made to serve the world by licking its boots. Now in Boston and at Harvard, for an intellectual man willing to stand alone, the opportunities are unparalleled. He finds quietness, he finds books, he finds music, he finds sympathy; he may even find, in many a suppressed soul, a sincere openness and readiness for the light. It was in good old honest sharp-witted Boston that light came to me, and I was converted; not to the faith of Boston itself, but to the very opposite: and what could be more to the credit of Boston than the facilities it offers for such a jump? Therefore I say, young man, if under your smooth blank egg-shell of polite humanity you have a soul in you, go and hatch it in Boston. And the benefit won't be entirely on your side. Boston and Harvard have need nowadays of new blood, of fresh spiritual courage. They are becoming too much like the rest of the country, choked with big business, forced fads, and merely useful knowledge. Our fearless souls of other days have left no heirs. We need to break away again—were we not always come-outers?—from intellectual professionalism, from the slough of wholesale standardised opinion, from the dulcet mendacity of the pulpits, from the sheepish, ignorant, monotonous, epidemic mind of our political rulers, well-meaning and decent as a whole, but oh, how helpless! At Harvard some do break away, in feeling if not in doctrine. There is Charley Copeland and Barrett Wendell and William James: sentimentalists no doubt—yet what else can good men be without the Faith, and seeing only the wrong side of the tapestry? America is the greatest of opportunities and the worst of influences: our effort must be to resist the influence and improve the opportunity.

"You look shocked and a bit offended: why do I say that America is the worst of influences? Because it imposes vices which regard themselves as virtues, from which therefore there is no repentance at hand. It imposes optimism, imposes worldliness, imposes mediocrity. But our mediocrity, with our resources, is a disgrace, our worldliness a sin, our optimism a lie. That is why I have built this monastery. I am supposed to be a student of history; but I study the past only to discern in it the beginnings of the future, the good seed apparently choked by the tares, yet destined to survive them. This is a dark age for the spirit, an age of secret preparation. We mustn't expect our people to understand their own predicament for decades, perhaps for centuries. God will take his own time. But we are not a people abandoned by God, at least not yet: we are his chosen people, though still under the Old Dispensation. Consider the dutifulness with which we trudge, the ardour with which we pursue any aim once set officially before us. Consider our trust in education. Consider our brave, incorruptible, devoted women. Consider our American Catholic clergy, bred in the atmosphere of material progress, so virtuous, so active, so successful, so like the very Apostles—before the coming of the Holy Ghost. What an enormous effort and accomplishment, materially considered, as yet without moral benefit—on the contrary, with a ghastly vacuity, vulgarity, and hopelessness for a result. Would God have allowed such a tragedy if it were not to prove a lesson in wisdom? Is our tower of Babel—our science, our comforts, our machinery—to collapse in dishonour, and to be remembered, if at all, only as a vast blunder? I cannot think so. It is an unintended preparation; and all the materialism that now distracts us from salvation will later be consecrated to salvation, like those Egyptian obelisks in

Rome which the Popes have set up afresh on pedestals inscribed to the true God, and have crowned with the cross and with the star of Bethlehem.

"Let me prophesy something which you, Oliver, may live to see, though probably not the rest of us: all this headlong prosperity and activity will one day—perhaps very soon—collapse at a word, like the walls of Jericho; nor is any great blast necessary, mere time and mutation and inner loosening will do, by which dust is forever returning to the dust. Against that day of trouble and light I have established my monastery: a fortress to resist all heathen influences, an outpost to seize all spiritual opportunities: a few monks—not more than thirty—gathered from all American nationalities. My Abbot is a French Canadian educated in Rome, and we have several Mexicans and Cubans. When the Archbishop requires them, they help unobtrusively in parish or mission work; but essentially their duty, for the present, is to keep true learning alive and perform the liturgy in its perfection and completeness. They are willing to study and to pray unobserved, keeping the lamp burning until the coming of the Bridegroom. A sanctuary for recollection, a nursery for repentance, a nest-egg for the Holy Ghost."

"I am glad," said Peter to his son, "that you are hearing your Cousin Caleb unbosoming himself. You may not understand or accept his views, but at least you will learn not to believe the Germans when they tell you that there is only one living or respectable philosophy in the world at a time. All philosophies are open to us always. The next generation may very likely turn its back on what we call progress, and revert to some settled tradition, either that which your Cousin Caleb follows, or some other. You missionaries," he added, addressing his host, "are always pure-minded and heroic, while in opposition, but if you had your way, you would soon grow fat and worldly in authority: not to speak of the intellectual illusions, as they seem to me, which you would make inveterate. Let the world, I say, have its fun. Let it cook in its own broth; and let those whose nerves are tougher than yours and mine enjoy the bustle of unregenerate America, and make the whole world whizz faster and faster with one identical deafening infernal roar. What an experience for mankind, and what a subject afterwards for the moralist!"

"As to intellectual illusions, Peter," the old cripple retorted, a little nettled, "don't talk about them with a superior air, as if you had avoided them yourself. There are only two radical alternatives open to human faith. Both are hypotheses. To accept either is to run a risk, to lay a wager; but the gamble is forced upon us by life itself. To live is to bet, because the conduct of life pledges all our poor assets, and pledges our soul, to the one side or the other. You may choose the broad and obvious path of heathen philosophy, fancifully decorated, if you like, by some heathen religion. That is the only path open to the unregenerate natural mind, until repentance has given it pause and revelation direction. You will find yourself in an immeasurable physical or logical or psychological universe—your analysis of its substance and movement really makes little difference, for in any case your soul, with everything you love, will be a pure incident, long prepared and soon transcended. Your life will be a tragic or a comic episode in a universal hurly-burly of atoms or laws or energies or illusions. I don't say you may not find such a life bearable or even entertaining; all the animals take to it with gusto, and why shouldn't man, if he is nothing but a talking, laughing, machine-making animal? But there is an alternative, which is to believe in the human heart, to believe in the supernatural, and to refuse to follow the great heathen procession except perfunctorily and provisionally. Those who deliberately choose this alternative cannot be taxed, for that reason, with intellectual illusion. We can formulate just as well as the heathen, or perhaps better, the results of cold observation, and the views with which the unaided intellect must be content: but we appeal to a higher court. We impose on all natural facts and on all natural desires a supernatural interpretation. A miracle, we say, has occurred, both in the manger of Bethlehem and in our own souls; and we have understood that astronomy and biology and profane history may show the universe to be manifestly heartless, yet in reality it may be the work of a divine heart of which our heart is a distorted image; and every event in it may have been expressly designed as a stimulus or occasion or punishment for the thoughts of the heart. Now this supernatural faith often breaks out incoherently and remains silent, or is crudely and haltingly expressed in contradiction to natural beliefs which it has not the power to discard. But there is one and only one thorough, consistent, realistic, encyclopaedic expression of faith in the human heart. It is Catholic dogma: the dogma that God has become man, actually and historically and for ever, with all that is involved in that mystery. Any revisions and reforms of Catholic faith are backslidings into heathenism; they deny, in some measure, the supremacy of the human heart, and of the miraculous: and in that measure they lead back, covertly but inevitably, to the heathen highway of a feigned conformity and a real despair. And while I admit that heathen philosophers may judge a supernatural reinstatement of the human heart to be a pathetic fallacy, yet the believer in a divine heart is not without many a confirmation of his faith by his own experience and by the fruits which this faith has always borne among the faithful."

Having preached his sermon with gusts of involuntary vehemence, through which here and there a latent sweetness seemed to crop up, like flowers among rocks, the old wretch felt that he must change the subject.

"I needn't ask," he said, "if you have had a prosperous trip. I saw you boldly entering Crow's Creek, and admired the way in which your great *Black Swan*, with her new-fangled engines, can defy calms and winds and tides, and manœuvre like a duck in a village pond. An old sea dog and a young sea dog together can manage anything. Do you remember the day when we first gave Crow Creek its name? We observed something black before us in mid-channel. 'The black flag of a sunken pirate,' I suggested, having the stronger imagination. But you, having better eyes, said it was a crow wading. You profit today by that experience, and keep to the outer basin. Not many ships touch at Salem nowadays. No clippers flying before the trade winds to China in ninety days. That was like all our American achievements, a fine feat, something it took a hard keen type of man to perform: but our victory was too rapid; it proved shallow and short-lived. What did we take to China and Manila? Ice. Ice to be melted in a day. And what did we bring home over a whole hemisphere of blue water? Tea, crockery, hemp. Your Spaniards, with all their slowness and trammels, had been sailors to better purpose. Certainly their gold melted in their hands more quickly than ice; but it made a brave show for a moment; and in exchange they had brought to the New World the best heritage of the Old, they had opened to the farthest and humblest nations the way to truth and salvation—Ah, here I am again on my hobby-horse, and you will laugh at the mania of an old cripple.—But how is my cousin Oliver being brought up? Unitarian?"

"Really," said Peter laughing, "I don't know. I doubt if any particular religion is being pumped into him."

"We have a pew in the Unitarian Church, but we don't go there much, because Mother usually wants to rest in the morning; and Fräulein and I, when we're alone, like to go to St. Barnabas', because

it's nicer. There's a boy-choir instead of the quartet at the other place;
but Mother thinks the Unitarian minister has sounder views about
history."

"Naturally, naturally," Caleb growled. "He probably has the latest
view on every subject. You know what the French King said about
Massillon: 'If he had spoken a little about religion, he would have
spoken a little about everything.'"

"Oliver has had a German governess who is a priestess of the
Goethe cult. What does she call it? Realistic idealism, romantic classicism, or pantheistic individualism?"

"She calls it simply philosophy," Oliver replied, feeling that his
father was frivolous and his Papist cousin hopelessly prejudiced. "She
says that philosophy is always outgrowing its own systems, and that
Goethe had outgrown all the philosophies up to his day, but that we
haven't yet outgrown his, because it sums up all our science."

"Don't let the Germans cheat you, my boy," Cousin Caleb began,
horribly grinning. "They are greater bluffers at philosophy than any
smart Yankee ever was at the game of poker. Their manipulations
of history are always different and always scandalous. It is all a play
of wilful arbitrary perspectives, hiding what you please, and joining
what you please. Nothing else is required for them to pose as the
latest leaders in the march of thought. Blow, blow, thou Zeitgeist;
thou art not so unkind as the truth would be to these self-advertising
prophets. Yet they are good teachers, Oliver, because they have the
true workman's respect for his tools: they put you through the mill;
there is as much humility in the grist of their brew as there is pride
and impudence in the froth of it. Learn to burrow with them; learn
to love your work; but come often out of that Nibelungen smithy
into the sun. The passions of those quarrelsome tinkers are ridiculous, and their ultimate conclusions are worthless.

"Goethe at least was not a professor, though he talked a little like
one at times. He was a great man; could be a lyric singer at one
moment and a primitive naturalist at the next, poring over prismatic
colours and volcanic stones like an innocent savage. But he also knew
the world and was very learned; and he lived in a somewhat manageable society, where his personal initiative told, and he could become the Napoleon of letters. But what a diabolical guide for the
soul! Worse than Voltaire, worse than Rousseau, more fundamentally
immoral, more insidiously dissolute and invertebrate. I said he knew
the world: but he worshipped the world—worshipped nature and

life and society and convention or whatever else we call the world—which proves that, at bottom, he *didn't* know the world. He was taken in by it; he sold his soul to it, like his blackguard of a Faust. He was convinced that there was nothing else to do; that to sell your soul to the world was salvation; and he put religion on the stage like a ballet, to crown irreligion, and give it a final blessing with the trombones at full blast, and the angels singing hallelujah. Could a mind be fundamentally more vulgar? Worse than Walt Whitman slapping his hairy breast in the Brooklyn Ferry and saying, What a good man am I! Goethe, instead, having married his cook and got his title of nobility, lounges in his Western-Easterly Divan and affably offers you, in a golden snuff-box, the dust of worldly wisdom and the ashes of his soul."

Oliver laughed, laughed with a flush of excitement and merriment that quite transformed him, as if his old head on young shoulders had suddenly opened fresh communications with the vascular system. "Oh, if only Fräulein could hear that! How she would stare! She wouldn't understand one word of it."

"But *you* understand," Cousin Caleb cried triumphantly, glaring at Oliver with the globular eyes of an ogre. "I can see that *you* understand."

"Yes, I think I understand. Goethe was what you call a heathen. He said we must renounce, but he didn't. He gulped the whole thing down."

"Except the best things, Oliver. He renounced *them*. He had no taste for *them*, and no room."

"But I don't see how you can think him worse than Walt Whitman. In Walt Whitman, as far as I can see, there's only rigmarole. But in Goethe there is the Rathskeller in Leipsic and Faust's study and Mephisto and Gretchen and Mignon and Götz von Berlichingen and Egmont."

"Admirable, capital, true!" the old monster exclaimed with enthusiasm. "Our young Daniel knows what he likes. Goethe belonged to the great line of pictorial artists: Shakespeare, Raphael, Rubens, down to Dickens and Victor Hugo. Romantic illustration, picture-books, creations. Goethe created Mephistopheles, he painted Gretchen; but his love-lorn ladies and gentlemen and his philosophy were only for his own time. Faust himself, without Mephistopheles, would be a ninny; and therefore the great mind of Goethe decided that all good would be insipid without evil, and that the world is moved not by love of God but by love of woman. Was there ever a coxcomb on so grand a scale?"

There was a general laugh in which Caleb Wetherbee himself joined. But Oliver was too deeply stirred for laughter.

"Cousin Caleb," he said, leaning over towards the old wizard who no longer seemed a repulsive stranger, "then you agree that Faust was never really saved at all? It's what I keep telling Fräulein. He had sold his soul to the devil in dead earnest, and he never repented. That *Himmelfahrt* at the end shouldn't have been put in: it's just a frill; and Goethe was inconsistent."

"What? At your age you've seen through that trick, which has taken in the wise and the learned? Yet it's clear enough, and I don't think Goethe meant to deceive. He supposed that nobody would be so stupid as not to understand. Of course there was nothing but life in this world. What better salvation could you hope for? What worse damnation could you fear? Of course it was right to sell your soul to the devil, as it had been right for Adam and Eve to eat the apple, because otherwise there wouldn't have been any pagan Greeks or any romantic Germans or any Wolfgang von Goethe. Life wouldn't be worth living, you see, if it weren't reckless and sinful."

"Then," Oliver persisted, still flushed with excitement, "then the *Prologue in Heaven*, too, would be nothing but a bad joke. Fräulein says there's the deepest wisdom in it, and the secret of life, but I say it's Old King Cole poking the devil in the ribs and telling him to keep the ball rolling."

"Who is this boy of yours, Peter," Cousin Caleb cried, "who is this boy of yours that sits here disputing among the doctors and putting us all to shame?"

"But I'm more than twelve years old," Oliver observed demurely. "I'm almost seventeen." And he wondered why the old men laughed. The gospels to him were a German story-book, and he felt sincerely modest.

His father, still smiling, had taken up the conversation in a changed tone.

"When Professor Norton says that Goethe was not a gentleman, I suppose we must all agree with him. But what does that matter? Very soon nobody will know what a gentleman was, unless he reads up the gentleman-concept in some German book of *Kulturgeschichte*. But as to Goethe being a heathen, you can't say, Caleb, that he despised the human heart, can you?"

"Despised it? No: he cultivated it, as my monks do their peaches against a sunny brick wall. He watched each prize heart ripen, and admired its velvety texture and colours richly fused. He was a connoisseur in hearts. But he didn't trust the heart, not even his own heart in his warmest love-affairs. He never probed the heart for its ultimate, its eternal object of love, in order to worship that object at all costs. Certainly he was no gentleman. He could never say yes to the heart, and he could never say no to the world."

Jim Darnley had risen to say good night, and without a word Oliver rose too and came up behind him to shake hands with their host.

"What," cried the latter, "must you go too? You know it's come on to rain and you will have a chilly trip in the launch. It may even be a bit rough going round the point."

"Don't you want to stay and see the monks and the monastery?" Peter added, a little disappointed at this reluctance in his son—how well he knew it in all his acquaintance!—to come to close quarters with anything morally new or alien. Must Oliver too be a stay-at-home intellectually? Must he be spiritually a coward?

"I don't mind the rain. I like it," Oliver replied covering his shyness as well as he could with polite smiles. "Thank you very much, but I think I'd rather go back with Lord Jim."

"He wants to see if I can't run the launch against the rocks, or lose my way in the night. It would be such a lark."

The old gentlemen didn't insist. There was something blushingly decisive about Oliver's look, something uncompromising and ready for revolt, under the effort to be civil. When the door had closed behind the young men, the two elders looked at each other. "I am afraid," said Peter apologetically, "these boys nowadays are keen on nothing but sporting sensations. I told Oliver about your model monastery; but the thing is too remote from his experience to have any interest for him."

"Isn't this his first escapade from home? He's fascinated by boats and by the sea—you ought to sympathise with that passion—and he is happier in your young captain's society than in ours. You don't blame him, do you? It's the heart leading. The heart ought to lead. Some day, when he's older, you must bring him again, and things will be different. What a privilege as we grow old, to have a son like this—our battered old bodies starting afresh, all our mistakes not yet made, all our vices not yet acquired! Ten years, twenty years hence, what will the world have made of him? No, Peter: don't think that I altogether envy you for being a father. I live in the future too, thinking of those who will come after us in this teeming America, not—fortunately for them—the heirs of my body, but in some measure, I am sure, the vindicators of my mind. We were always a circumcised people, consecrated to great expectations. Expectations of what? Nobody knows: yet I believe God has revealed to me something of the direction of his providence. I thank him for my deformity, because without it I should probably have been carried headlong—what strength have I of my own?—by the running tide of our prosperity and triviality, and never should have conceived that we in America are not addressed to vanity, to some gorgeous universal domination of our name or manners, but that without knowing it we are addressed to repentance, to a new life of humility and charity. And I seem to see plainly that your wonderful boy may be one of the first to hear the call, one of the first to forsake their nets by the sea of Galilee."

XV

Meantime the child of prophecy was bundled up with Jim Darnley in the narrow *carry-all* supplied by Caleb Wetherbee, and imperfectly defended from the slanting rain by strips of gutta-percha buttoned to the thin poles supporting the top. How tactfully Lord Jim had managed to dispel the awkwardness of that leave-taking! Oliver mightn't quite long to be cast on the rocks or lost at sea—though really, with Jim, it wouldn't have been so bad; but he did want to get out into the open air, and feel the night wind in his lungs. And Jim, by his banter, had amused the old men and made them forget to be overbearing, as old people like to be, and to brow-beat you for your own good. What a relief to escape from the fustiness of that old house, where not one horse-hair walnut chair, not one Victorian engraving, seemed to have been moved for forty years. Yes, and to escape from that sense of a prison in the background, a labyrinth of linked superstitions from which, if you were once caught in it, there might be no escape. Oliver seemed to detect a sort of hospital smell hanging about the place, an empty uninhabited white look of suspended animation. Or was it only those high-falutin morbid discussions, that odious intensity about theories?

At any rate, how reassuring to lean here against an honest unpretending comrade and feel the weight and firmness of that friendly body, like a wall of strength. How perfectly, too, Lord Jim had behaved that evening, looking so particularly smart and handsome in his dinner-jacket, with his high complexion and thick hair—such an image of youth and soundness and simplicity, where all else was crazy or horrible or helplessly supercilious. Never had Jim tried to slip in a word, to show that he was no less intelligent than the others, if not more so. He had simply listened, passed the drinks and cigarettes, laughed at the right moments and appeared to be vastly interested even when Oliver himself was being catechised. And this modest silence of Jim's had been far from causing him to seem dull or awkward or out of his element; on the contrary, he had made the success of the party by giving everybody a sense of pleasantness and sanity in the background. Jim mightn't set up to be a highbrow; but he could talk like the intellectuals when he chose, and with a saving twinkle in his eye which was quite beyond them. Uncle Harry, though a professor of Applied Christianity, and Uncle Jack, though editor of the *Boston Butterfly and Busy Bee*, were howling barbarians in comparison, hayseeds and country bumpkins, always joking about what they knew and sneering at what they didn't know. Yet Lord Jim hardly seemed to realise how clever and terse he was, and seemed to take his remarkable intelligence as a matter of course, as if everybody by nature moved on that level. It was simply odd and amusing to him if anybody fell below it.

Phew! No more problems for the present. How splendid now to dash through the boiling black water, raising great sheets of foam, doused often by the spray and letting the gusts of rain beat playfully on your great oilskin coat, provided with so much foresight by your thoughtful friend. How absorbing to share his alert look-out, measuring the distance to this or that light, and deciphering this or that uncertain shadow. How jolly to feel the instant effect of his hand on the wheel, or his finger vigorously punching the buttons and levers of that furious little engine, whizzing and bounding through the storm. And afterwards in the *Black Swan*, reached much more quickly and unerringly than one would have expected, what comfort to feel safe at home, everything ship-shape, nothing on one's mind problematical or controversial or embittered or hopeless, but just free sleep and free talk and a round of plain jobs and plain pleasures, in sympathy with the things turning up and the weather blowing.

It blew for the next day or two rather dismally, and induced Peter Alden to remain at his cousin's ashore, until sunshine and a fair breeze should promise them another pleasant excursion under sail. For Oliver, on board, the east wind was a marvellous tonic; even the smile and the loose paunch of those gilded Buddhas in his cabin seemed to lose their malignity. The grotesque and the luxurious were disinfected by his own keenness of mind: that whole outlandish world became a pleasantly negligible background, like a Persian carpet. He opened the gilt wire doors of the lockers in which the books were packed; some on shelves in the ordinary way, others—the larger and more precious ones—lying on their side one over another, after the fashion of the East. They were splendid editions, often interleaved with additional illustrations, curious, rare, or romantic, evidently in many cases originals: the *Arabian Nights* and Shakespeare, *Don Quixote* and Dr. Johnson, Fielding, Sterne, Swift and Dickens. There were French books in sets: Montaigne, Saint-Simon, Casanova, Balzac and Taine; and there was also the Bible in thin volumes, English or German, with the most advanced commentaries. Oliver looked them over as one walks through a museum, passively, stimulated for a moment only, even by the most piquant illustrations, and soon fatigued. Lord Jim, he thought, had exactly the right way with licentious things; he wasn't shocked, he might laugh heartily, but at the next moment his mind was on something else. Certainly Oliver didn't want to read any of those old-fashioned long-winded works: they were all so unnecessary, so disreputably human, so content with the shady, humorous, fantastic side of life. Out of sight in another locker he found something more to his mind: old books of exploration and adventure, Captain Cook and Doughty and Livingstone and Sir Samuel Baker. The human element there was in close enough contact with nature not to seem silly, and there was at least a little geography and a little sea-faring to ventilate the literature.

He also made the acquaintance of the mate and the engineer, modest rather silent persons who treated him as a superior and not as a boy; and he gradually became reconciled to deferential speech and manners in the steward and the cabin boy. Wasn't it really simpler and less wasteful to ask people in the morning what they required, and then to write out the menu in pencil on a little china stand, so that you needn't eat what you didn't want? How different the way of serving, too, from that of old Annie at home, who with an air of authority, rather impatient and disapproving, would slap down your plate before you, already overcrowded with sauce, vegetables, and potatoes, as if she said, "There! That's what there is for you to eat. Eat it." Here everything was passed to you apologetically, you were thanked for taking notice, and your smallest wish divined or remembered, as if it were a shame that the service wasn't solid gold and all the viands ambrosia, as a proper young gentleman, like you, Sir, would naturally expect. After all, considering the matter quite impartially, Oliver decided that it was good for you to be set up on a pedestal and put on your good behaviour. You had to live up to the fine sentiments assigned to you, and you ended by acquiring them. Gross things, like feeding, became seemly and amiable. You no longer gulped down your grub moodily, like a beast, and pretended not to give a damn. You were challenged to refine your perceptions and to purify your motives. You became a gentleman.

Books, in this atmosphere fell into the background, and became accessories. No wonder his father liked only satirical books, and books beautifully bound and illustrated. Books had no authority for him. They were ornaments, like mirrors, reflecting things at second hand. The best of books had to be *written*: it was something artificial, intentional, rhetorical, simply by being a book. In reading it, before you judged it to be a good book, you had to compare it with the real world, or with your real thoughts. Why not stick to these directly, and save all that trouble and confusion? There was plenty of instruction in things, and real life was romantic enough. What story could be more interesting than Oliver's own experience, lounging in this cosy cabin, after the cloth had been removed, and talking till after midnight about everything under heaven with a perfectly sane commonplace man, a free sailor, a *young* man, in spite of his long experience, who reasoned better than any book, having read very few of them, and was utterly free from commitments and compromises and affectations and axes to grind and religious manias?

"You don't think, do you, that there's anything in what Cousin Caleb Wetherbee says? Why should anyone want to patch up some horrible old creed that broke down long ago?"

"The reason is plain enough," answered the oracle of horse sense and manly ignorance, laying aside his pipe and mixing himself a second whisky-and-soda. "Haven't you noticed, when he talks to you, he looks as if he would like to make love? Poor chap, he can't make love, not to any purpose; and he takes to his religion as a substitute. He couldn't be just a Caliban, could he? Wasn't strong or wicked or well enough to revenge himself by hating and cursing. Had to beautify himself somehow, and transform himself into a lovely bridegroom. Couldn't be done except by a religion that should turn him into a saint."

"Couldn't he be a saint and love nature and love humanity, as Emerson did, without being converted?"

"Oh, well, you know what I mean. An old barebones like Emerson doesn't *love*; he isn't a *saint*. He's simply a distinguished-looking old cleric with a sweet smile and a white tie: he's just honourable and bland and as cold as ice. Old Wetherbee couldn't be so self-satisfied. He couldn't smile and smile and wait for the end of the show. If he was to keep afloat he needed a life-preserver—some good sound tough illusion to buoy him up. Otherwise there would have been nothing left for him but to duck under."

"Don't you think he ought to have killed himself? What's the use of living like that?"

"Of course it would have saved him a lot of trouble: but when people are deformed or ill or old or mad they are more viciously wound up to live than ever. You can't expect them to kill themselves because we find them unpleasant. Only the most sensitive of your blooming Japs would do that. Old Wetherbee is fighting for his life. Won't let go his bone, will clench it with all his teeth until death, and expect the resurrection."

"How horrible!"

"He has a better time of it than some people. Suppose his back aches, or some critic makes hash of his opinions: he has only to turn on the big reflector. The scene is transformed, and where everything was hellish darkness and confusion, here is the whole glittering *corps de ballet*, row behind row: Heaven! Just as the prophets and doctors said it was going to be."

"Cheap, isn't it? How can people like to deceive themselves?"

"They don't do it on purpose. Religion takes hold on them just as drink and women take hold on the rest of us. There's the advantage of being a sailor. The sea was never a Christian and never will be. Your religions can spring up only on dry land, very dry land, all rocks and pits and sand deserts and burning sun, except for an occasional terrific thunder-storm from nowhere. That's what that blasted Palestine is like—I've seen it—and that infernal blighted Arabia. People discover God only where he has cursed them. If poor old Wetherbee weren't humped as he is, he wouldn't think as he does. You can't see straight if you are crooked, and it's only your deuced lucky chaps that can get on without illusions. Your father, for instance; and I'm not sure that he's much the happier for it. My own father too, although he's a parson, gets on without them, and being poor it's all the more remarkable. But then he's no hunchback: a well set-up old Englishman or Scot—I don't know which—and a philosopher by nature who honestly doesn't care a fig for money or position. Besides, he knows the secret of theology and of Christian piety and is at home in the English liturgy: lovely, sweet channel through which to pour out your feelings, not personal enough to be blushy and not committing you to a single damned dogma: because nobody nowadays is expected to take the Bible seriously or the catechism or the thirty-nine articles. But I tell you, it's a rare thing for a man to strip himself clean like that of every rag of false comfort. It makes the deuce of a hard life."

"Goethe didn't have a hard life, yet I don't believe he had any illusions."

"He was one of your lucky dogs, wasn't he? Still had a glad eye for the gals at seventy-two," and Jim yawned, and proceeded sleepily to knock the ashes out of his pipe. "Don't know much about him: once heard *Faust* with your father at the Paris opera. Jolly show." He glanced at the clock over the sideboard, got up, and straightened himself. "I say, let's have a look on deck before turning in."

They had a look, and Jim seemed to perceive various points of interest on board and over the water. At any rate he walked away forward and got into an interminable conversation with the sailor on watch. Oliver could see nothing but darkness and wetness. The thick soft air was pleasant enough; and he filled his lungs and exhaled completely—a little Yoga-like exercise which his father had recommended. What could be friendlier than this invisible, indefinite, all-permeating ether, that perhaps fed the stars and certainly fed the spirit within you? Here Goethe had been in the right, in spite of Cousin Caleb; he had breathed in the ether freely, and had breathed it out again warmed; breathed it out completely, fearlessly, joyously. He had obeyed every vital impulse; had shaken off every chain not forged by nature in putting us together, every bond not itself a fibre in our vital organism. Life as it came seemed to him divine—not happy, happiness was not the test—but such life as you were primed to live and couldn't be yourself without living. Goethe was at home in nature and at home in himself: that was why Cousin Caleb hated him. Certainly nature had treated Cousin Caleb cruelly, as far as his body was concerned; yet she had given him a good mind. Couldn't he be content with that? How beautiful it might have been: a pure disinterested mind in a crooked misshapen body, like a light still burning clear in a crushed lamp, because the oil of it was sweet. Oliver wouldn't have minded the physical deformity, could have got used to it, pitied and even loved it, if only the poor wretch had not insisted on turning the universe upside down in order to explain his own misery. He wanted the whole world to be sick, in order that he might pretend to be well. As if in the health of the world his own sickness were more than a fleabite! What was the use of having a mind at all, if not to recognise this disproportion, and live, as far as your spirit can, in sympathy with the health of the universe? But people were cowards. They were so frightened at the truth that they shut their eyes and kept saying their prayers, as if the truth could be changed because they didn't see it. When cowardice was so foolish, couldn't anybody be simple and brave? "Yes," thought Oliver, "one person at least: *I* can."

XVI

When Fräulein Schlote and Oliver returned to Great Falls from their outing, which had been prolonged for two weeks, they both looked surprisingly transformed, she in her new marked-down costumes and hats from Mesdames Smith and O'Leary's, and he with his wilted spirits revived, a positive flush of warm blood under his tan, a new playfulness and firmness in his speech, and a neck that grew noticeably straighter out of his shoulders. It would no longer be necessary for his mother to be always telling him to sit up; and this intelligent lady with such evidence of improved health under her eyes might almost have been inclined to admit that she had overestimated the perils of this flight from home, had not various small signs of demoralisation begun to appear in Oliver, like the first smudges of black cloud in a windy horizon.

"Oliver!" she was compelled to cry on the very first day at luncheon, "you are eating with your left hand! You know how I disapprove of it, and Letty Lamb feels most strongly about it. To eat with the left hand and still hold the knife in the right is almost as bad as actually sticking the knife into your mouth. It's what you'll be doing at the next moment."

"Letty Lamb *would* say so," Oliver observed with a benevolent smile, causing his mother and Irma to look up astonished. They had not heard Jim Darnley remark that ladies *would* ask why the *Black Swan* didn't have black sails. "Of course," Oliver continued, "I do look as if I meant to shovel in the food hand over hand, like sailors hauling in the main sheet." Having finished eating and laid down both knife and fork neatly parallel on his plate, the question ceased to be practical and could be treated with impartiality. "We had a discussion on this point on board," he went on with the air of having lived at sea all his life, "and Pa said that among the Mohammedans it wasn't only bad manners to eat with the left hand, but was a religious misdemeanour, because the Prophet (may his name be exalted!) had never done so; but the thing wasn't altogether a superstition because the ancients had always eaten lying down and propped up on the left elbow; so that the left forearm and hand were not free and couldn't be raised and brandished gracefully. Only your right hand could hover over the big pot of stew, like a bird, and fish out the chosen bit exquisitely with three fingers. Anything else would have been dirty. Even this took lots of training. In order to turn the morsel and keep it from dripping, each finger had to work separately yet in time, like so many animated chopsticks. But Pa thought that for us, sitting up and armed with a knife and fork, it was absurd not to use the left hand when convenient—as absurd as if you were sitting at the piano and had to drop the treble in a hurry at every bar in order to play the bass also with your right hand." And Oliver, after reporting all this in the tone of an amused witness, proceeded to consume his apple pie slowly and deliberately—it wasn't very good—in the forbidden manner. Fräulein silently but visibly chuckled and Mrs. Alden visibly but silently fumed. The ceremony of dropping your knife, poising it insecurely on the rim of your plate, and changing your fork to the right hand before consuming the least mouthful had always annoyed the good German lady. It seemed such a needless postponement of one of the pleasures of a rich, full, and crowded life.

Mrs. Alden felt that it was useless to repeat what she had said a thousand times, that the Doctor was a scoffer and defended on purpose everything old-fashioned and outlandish, and that she was sure that *to-day*, in *America*, the *best* people never ate with the left hand. On this occasion she confined her protest to her emphatic example: but the majority went against her. At dinner that evening Fräulein ventured quietly to go over to the enemy, and to do as Oliver did. It was an open rebellion. Not only had Oliver long since established his right to soft shirts in the morning and to no waistcoats and to a bootlace in lieu of a watch-chain, but now he had declared his independence in the vital question of table-manners and had caused Fräulein to relapse into her original German piggishness. Oliver meantime was smiling inwardly—so confident had he grown of his strength—at the unmentionable fact that he was actually wearing no underclothes. This indecent lightening of the weight of life, conscientiously decreed and justified in the boy's journal on hygienic and moral grounds, remained long undiscovered. Mrs. Alden, years before, had generously deputed to Fräulein all supervision of the family linen.

Like other boys on their travels Oliver had carried a Kodak to the yacht, and his first care on returning home was to have his films developed and to exhibit the snapshots he had taken of the *Black Swan,* the crew, the various scenes visible on shore, and also his time-exposures of the Poop, and of his father's oriental cabin. Mrs. Alden looked at everything perfunctorily, with a sigh at the waste of time and money involved in such caprices; but nothing could exceed the keenness and enthusiasm with which Fräulein pored over the photographs.

"And who is this fine young man," she asked, "in the white trousers? It might almost be a junior officer in the German Imperial War Navy."

"Lord Jim," Oliver replied laconically. The more he took Jim as a matter of course, the more advanced and extensive he felt his own experience to be.

"Lord Jim?" said his mother waking up. "Who is Lord Jim?" She was not accustomed to dissimulation, and her tone of exaggerated coldness and indifference showed that she knew perfectly well who Lord Jim was.

"He's the Captain. His name among mortals is Mr. James Darnley, but the immortals—that's Pa and I—call him Lord Jim."

Fräulein rejoiced to see how classically well-educated, how literary, her pupil was daring to show himself. He had sometimes seemed to lack a feeling for style. Now at last he was proving the results of her labours. She was sure that Goethe himself, when a boy in his wonderful Frankfort home, might have talked in that Homeric style; and even if his worthy mother (like Frau Alden on this occasion) hadn't caught the reference, his well-read father at least would surely have done so: or even if the allusion had escaped everybody, it would have betrayed the busy humorous play of fancy in the mind of the young genius himself; and after all, what was really more important to genius than the play of its own mind?

Mrs. Alden took no notice of genius or style: she felt too deeply the importance of social propriety and of moral influence. "I don't like," she said, "to see you imitate your father in giving foolish nicknames to his dependents, and being over-familiar with them. It is not dignified."

"Oh, I don't call him Lord Jim to his face, although he wouldn't mind if I did. I call him Jim."

"How can you, when he is so much older, and not in our own circle? And it's not as if he were *frankly* a servant."

"He's a clergyman's son, socially just as good as we are, and wonderfully young for his age. Don't I call Fred Brown *Fred*, though he's more than twenty-six, and I don't know him, or want to know him, half as well as I do Lord Jim, after eating and bathing and talking with him nearly all day for a fortnight?"

"That's quite another matter. Fred Brown is your own minister's son, and has gone to your school. You couldn't very well call him Mr. Brown without confusion. But the captain of your father's yacht isn't a suitable friend for you, apart from his age. He is a foreign adventurer. You wouldn't call Mr. Denis Murphy *Denis*, even if you did go swimming with him."

The abysmal difference between the two cases made Oliver speechless. Why try to explain? Mr. Murphy had been a hired man, an old man, doing his work silently and respectfully. Jim was a splendid comrade, an ideal elder brother, a first and only friend. Two young men alone in the wilds, sharing the same adventures, eating, working, and sleeping in company find life reduced to what both can share. Deeper or ulterior differences between them are submerged in this physical unison; and this unison, especially when experienced for the first time, lends a marvellous excitement to the merest trifles, and makes the simplest confidences seem precious and rare. What a pleasure to blurt out the obvious, which before one had never observed, or to name the unnameable, and throw off the incubus of polite reticence! For the first time Oliver had forgotten to watch and to study himself, and his diary had overflowed with descriptions of another person—his words, his ways, his probable feelings—all this written in a finer hand than usual, with notes and additions, and scrupulous corrections. Even the touches of commonness or cynicism which he couldn't help feeling in Jim, didn't altogether displease our young puritan: they prevented him from finding his new friend affected, supercilious, or too English, and they were a relief from the eternal proprieties and hypocrisies of home. They were even a pleasant contrast to his father's exotic tastes and languid aestheticism. So much so, that after a few days Oliver had complained to Jim of his quarters in the Poop. That sixteenth century Admiral's cabin, with all those carvings and paintings, all those lockers and chests holding mysterious treasures, made him uncomfortable. He couldn't sleep pleasantly in a Chinese curiosity shop. He would like something plainer.

"Come and sleep on the lounge in my cabin," Jim had replied. "You'll find that plain enough, if you don't mind *me*." And to be sure, the captain's cabin, large and well aired, rather resembled a modern clinic—walls and ceiling white and immaculate, and all the furniture, as far as possible, nickel and glass. The only meretricious ornament was a wire rack for photographs stuck all over with Christmas cards, heads of lads in naval uniform, female beauties more or less professional, some with affectionate dedications and also illuminated postcards of Mount Vesuvius, the beach at Brighton, and the Brooklyn Bridge at night. There was an old invitation, somewhat soiled, to a public dance, and some tinsel from a Christmas tree. In quite another corner, over the writing-table, was a framed etching of an old village church overshadowed by thick trees, and an enlarged photo of a little girl, showing Jim's features very much purified, within an aureole of fluffy blond hair. Those were Jim's trophies of battle, and these were his family gods: his young sister and the church at Iffley where his father was Vicar.

To this sanctum of a commonplace young man Oliver had quite contentedly transferred his own nest. A couch after all, with sheets and a blanket, made a more comfortable bed than the mat in the Poop; and in this cabin at least there was no mocking suggestion of things occult or superior to himself. He disliked to feel, and to be compelled to acknowledge, the existence of anything not to be dominated, and not relevant to his own life. Such things, his ego declared, had no right to be: and yet there they were! In Jim's quarters Oliver had been spared this metaphysical humiliation. Nothing surrounded him that was not approachable, nothing that at bottom was not inferior. Spiritual pride and fleshly comfort had combined to pacify him, to convince him that all was well. The sound of Jim moving about or whistling and humming in the bathroom had been pleasant to him, and sometimes the two had had long talks in the dark, from bunk to bunk, concerning all the secrets of earth and heaven. Was it now conscience through his mother's voice, or was it blind injustice, that would cut him off for ever from his one all-important providential friend, who not only had opened to him the real world of men and of hard fact, but was his father's mainstay, indispensable to his peace and comfort?

Yet to say these things to his mother would only make matters worse. Every word uttered in Jim's favour would confirm her in her hostility. Oliver was accustomed to letting her air her unreason unmolested. Silence committed him to nothing. It was sweeter and juster than recrimination. It cleared a wider prospect in his own mind. It didn't pledge him, as headstrong argument might, to stick to his own opinion, perhaps formed hastily and needing revision. Yet now in Oliver's silence there was not the least grain of concession. He was evidently keeping all his powder dry. He turned to Fräulein with another photograph: there was Jim again, talking with Pa.

Irma liked her almost German sea-hero even better in this photograph than in the other, and her poor heart ached that she should have been prevented from seeing this nautical paragon, and perhaps . . . Not that she didn't admire army officers also; yet there seemed to be a special poetry about the infinite sea.

The next day at lunch she was so greatly agitated that she forgot to taste the cup of clam broth that stood, in danger of getting cold, on the blue plate before her.

"The Herr Doktor," she panted, lapsing into German in her excitement, "has sent, oh, such a wonderful surprising telegram! Oliver is to go for six weeks more to the yacht, and so as not to interrupt his studies, I too—just think of it, gnädige Frau—I too am to go with him. That kind, handsome, unselfish young Captain is actually willing, for poor dear *Me*, to move out of his private stateroom and sleep in the officers' cabin. How wonderful, how heavenly, how unexpected!"

Poor dear *Me* already saw herself married to the gallant navigator and spending the rest of her days being wafted with a checker-board sail among palm trees and coral islands, like Cleopatra in her barge, singing the barcarolle from the *Tales of Hoffmann*. Or rather—for true idealism, she knew, must be realistic—she saw him Captain of a great Cunarder and herself the mother of a whole brood of young sailors, waving to him on his fortnightly return to their happy seaside home.

Mrs. Alden's pale puffy face had been growing darker, a positive greenish yellow, and her back stiffer. "Irma what are you talking about? You don't suppose that Oliver would wish to leave home for the whole summer, and expose his health to all the dangers and discomforts of cruising about in desolate places, where those foolish old men go—just for a change—and call themselves sportsmen? If he should be ill, where would he find a doctor?"

"But there's Doctor Alden himself," Irma murmured, astonished, and feeling that something had gone terribly wrong.

"And what sort of lessons could you give him, deadly seasick as you would both be all the time?"

"I think," said Oliver quietly, "that we are both willing to risk it, aren't we, Irma? We may be seasick at first, but we'll get over it, and become good sailors for all the rest of our lives. It's well worth it."

"Oliver!" cried his mother severely, "you don't mean to say that you're actually thinking of accepting this proposal?"

"Why not?" and in spite of his intention to be calm, Oliver's voice trembled a little.

"Because, for one thing, I absolutely forbid it. But you ought to understand my reasons, and I am sure you do, in your heart of hearts. It is all nonsense about your health and the hot weather. The fresh sea winds blow up our great broad river, and on this high hill, apart from a few warm days such as there are everywhere, our summer couldn't be more healthy and pleasant. If you *really* needed a change and sea-bathing, any *honest impartial* doctor would recommend Nantasket Beach or Cape Cod or Rockaway Point, and you could go there for August perhaps, with Irma, and I should make no objection, although personally I always think in these summer trips there's more bother than benefit. No. Health and a change of air are a mere pretext. Would you, both of you, be so terribly excited if you were really going for a cure? What's all this flurry about? Those two weeks in the yacht—prolonged, Oliver, contrary to your promise, and there the contempt for all principle begins to appear already—those two weeks have positively turned your head. You've caught a new tone, a strange dislike for everything at home. It's not the sea or the yacht or the starry heavens; it's not your poor father's conversation, who never says very much, and never made any impression on you before. It is, I know it is, the influence of that disreputable young captain—much too young to be a captain, and much too disreputable to be a friend. I know a thing or two about him, although I've always refused to meet him. Your father is so hopelessly weak that I never could prevail against the disastrous ascendancy this stranger has acquired over him: made him sell the old yacht which had been perfectly good enough for fifteen years, and build this new one—utterly fantastic and very expensive. That man means to make your father leave this country altogether and live only in foreign ports, where the young rascal can amuse himself in his own fashion. And now to stand by and see *you* corrupted, an unsuspecting decent boy, and alienated from everything that is serious and right—I won't allow it. My life's work sha'n't be undone by an infatuation of yours— an infatuation you will be thoroughly ashamed of yourself when you get over it—and it won't last; that's the one comfort about it. But meantime your education might be spoiled, your mind poisoned, and I've taken such pains with it, consulting with your uncle Harry, who is a specialist in education, and helped so far—I gladly admit it—by Irma, although now she seems to be encouraging you to take the wrong course. It was a mistake to let you go to the yacht at all. I felt it in my bones, but I allowed myself to be persuaded, for fear of seeming prejudiced and unreasonable. I won't make that mistake again. It is my duty to save you, if possible; if my life-work hasn't been all in vain and you are not lost already, if you haven't been always secretly deceiving me—you are so silent—and haven't been always thoroughly false at heart to every high principle and to me and to this house and everything we stand for."

Mrs. Alden's high bosom heaved, she almost sobbed, her eyelids twitched and contracted over her pale eyes, and the thin line of her lips became convulsed and at moments uncontrollable; but she was tearless, and having exhausted her fund of words she worked off her remaining emotion by tightly grasping the arms of her chair.

Never had Oliver seen his mother struggling in such a way with passion. The spectacle, in one habitually so passive and cold, was distressing. Irma, aghast, began to whimper disjointedly, saying that the Herr Doktor must know what was best. He wouldn't expose his son—a perfect son—to evil influences. There must be some dreadful mistake somewhere.

Meantime Oliver had left the table and gone to stand in the open window, vacantly intent on surveying the trees, the sky, the grass on which the circular sprinklers were spreading a mist of necessary moisture. He was determined to be calm and just, and couldn't bear the spectacle of his mother breaking down. Not that he pitied her or warmed to her in the least: on the contrary, he was afraid of hating her too much, of being repelled by her weakness as well as indignant at her injustice. Eloquent retorts and refutations of all she said came trooping into his mind. If Lord Jim had been condemned by a court martial—which was certainly all his mother knew against him—the sentence had been afterwards revoked and he had been exonerated. If he was rather young to be a captain, that was so much to his credit; and he was not only perfectly competent as a skipper but also as an engineer, and had abundant experience of command at sea. And if he wasn't very well read or accustomed to ladies' society, he certainly had the address and manners of a gentleman, much more so than uncle Harry, who had learned all he knew of education out of books and lectures. Besides, wasn't he, Oliver, old enough to know different kinds of people? Had he no character of his own, that he was to become the image of anybody he saw? Being just to people different from oneself, or even liking them, didn't mean that one was going to imitate them. Lord Jim was a first rate fellow of one sort, and had fought an uphill fight to make his way in the world. How absurd to suppose that Oliver would go out of his way to copy him!

Full of this eloquence he turned again towards the middle of the room. In doing so he caught the reflection of his own figure in the long glass of the open French window. He had his hands thrust deep into the side pockets of his jacket: a pose utterly new to him, which he didn't know he had assumed. It was copied from Jim Darnley. No: he might as well not attempt to deny the obvious. His mother had penetrated to the root of the matter. Undoubtedly nobody could help being influenced, at least unconsciously, by the people he was happy with and loved. Yes, you needn't blurt out the truth, when it touched your private feelings, but you must recognise it and build upon it. Better avoid all recrimination and stick to the practical issue. He sat down again before his plate and proceeded to consume the preserved peaches and cream which he had left untasted and didn't like.

"If you feel so strongly about it, Mother," he said at last, "the only thing for us to do is to write to Pa and give all your objections and see what he decides."

"What *he* decides!" Mrs. Alden echoed scornfully, recovering all her magisterial assurance. "I suppose he *invites* you, he doesn't *summon* you. All you have to do is to refuse."

"No, I can't refuse without giving the true reason," Oliver retorted with the whole integrity of his nature in his clear voice. "He is just as sure that it's good for me to be in the yacht as you are that it's bad; and after all he is as much my father as you are my mother."

"Yes, indeed," Fräulein interposed eagerly, "and besides he is a doctor of medicine, and it's he that pays for absolutely everything."

Oliver wished that Irma hadn't added this last observation. No doubt it was pertinent. Even that house, which his mother regarded as her sole property, was hers only because her husband had rescued and restored it and made her a splendid present of it when it was about to be desecrated or destroyed. Yet it wasn't magnanimous to rub in these humble truths at such a moment, when the debate was supposed to move on a higher moral plane, where nothing was to be considered except the ultimate benefit of Oliver himself.

"Father," the boy went on, disregarding the interruption, "thinks that my book-learning is excellent for a boy of my age, but that I haven't been thrown enough into the society of young men, only of the boys at school, who may be very good boys, but he says they have nothing in them but the raw materials of humanity, and are so much behind me in everything that being with them can only tend to make me conceited. He says that I've drawn all my ideas and prejudices from ladies and clergymen; and ladies, he thinks, if ever they get a glimpse of the world as it really is, don't dare to set the truth down in black and white. It is too shocking to their feelings. As for the clergymen, he thinks they are simply the ladies' oracles, putting their delusions into words for them, and painting the universe all pink and blue for them to be comfy in. For this reason Pa is glad that I cottoned at once to Lord Jim—*cottoned* is the word he used—it was such a healthy influence for me, and so timely: because there never was anybody like Lord Jim for dashing off everything in bold black and white, regardless of all prejudice, and yet without any claims to being bookish or clever. And I was quite old enough, Pa said, to get a little intellectual airing and to discover that the particular philosophy I had been brought up in was only a convention, like all philosophies, and probably a convention that was wearing thin, and would be a handicap to me if I didn't outgrow it."

"Just what I thought, just what I felt was going on behind my back," Mrs. Alden burst out, gathering afresh her rhetorical impetus. "An ambush, a stratagem, planned to undo all that I have done for you during these long years, and to turn you into a good-for-nothing carping critic, an idler, and a bad American. It's an outrage. A father planning the corruption of his own child, and gloating on it beforehand! Of course if you leave the decision to him he will take you away. I can't prevent it, because—though it's a hideous injustice—the father is still the legal guardian of his children, and not the mother. That's a remnant of mediaeval barbarism. And he will avail himself without scruple of that odious law. Cowardly people, when they are forced at last to fight in the open, are doubly cruel. I can expect no mercy. But if I can't save you, at least I can clear my own conscience and decline to have anything more to do with your perdition. Tell your father this: He may be richer than I, as Irma says; but this house, at least, is mine, and if he takes you away from me now, he must keep you for good. I won't ever receive either of you again into my own sacred home."

There was a long silence, broken only by the vain attempts of Fräulein Irma to stifle her sobs. "What?" she murmured at last. "Is Oliver never to come back? And what is to become of poor me? Must I return again to Germany?"

Mrs. Alden never had loved Irma, and at this moment positively hated her for her tears and her stupid reverence for the male sex and for masculine tyranny. But, like Oliver, his mother was constitutionally inclined to resist impulse and to take long views. In the midst of this family storm she was looking coldly ahead and she saw before her a desolate future; a very uncomfortable and bothersome future, too, if she should no longer possess the faithful Fräulein to keep house for her, sit with her of an evening, read to her, and do her hair, which was getting thin and needed to be carefully spread and secretly supplemented. After all, the eventual absence of Oliver had always been foreseen, and wouldn't be much less tolerable than the absence of his father, or that of her own father and brothers. Men were by nature detachable, like false hair: but the absence of Fräulein, after all these years, would create an unpleasant vacuum in the future establishment. The image of this establishment, as it loomed before Mrs. Alden in her tragic excitement, was far from unpleasing. She felt like the priestess of some temple of Minerva, indignantly driving from her precincts the strangers who had profaned it: and in heroically banishing her husband and son it didn't once cross her mind that she had nothing of her own to live on. She knew Dr. Alden too well to imagine that, under any provocation whatever, he would cut off her supplies. The more purified and inaccessible her temple became, the greater was the obligation of the public, rebuked and excluded, to support it handsomely. There would therefore be peace with plenty in her sanctuary, as well as a conspicuous purity: and the picture of her old age to be spent in that sacred guardianship encouraged her in her heroic resolve. But she required an acolyte. There was always Letitia Lamb to fall back upon:

and yet Letitia was growing old; she was delicate; she had some troublesome hobbies and a little money of her own. Just because she was an older and closer friend than Irma, she would be harder to get along with; she wouldn't make so serviceable—Mrs. Alden meant to say so *sympathetic*—a companion as Irma. No: this excellent Fräulein mustn't be allowed to depart.

"I don't say anything about *you*, Irma. We can arrange about you afterwards. This sudden craze for sailing in the yacht in *your* case isn't wickedness; only childish love of excitement. You have always seconded my efforts about Oliver's education. You have tried to do right. In any case *he* couldn't remain with us after next winter, as he is going to college: but that has never meant that *you* were to leave us. You can always remain here with me. I wish you to think of this house always as home."

"Ah, dear Mrs. Alden," Irma cried, joyful in the midst of her tears, and threatening to embrace and kiss her generous, her magnanimous protector. But she was prevented in time. This was no moment for weak feminine effusions.

"Very well," Oliver said firmly, as he got up and prepared to leave the room. "I will write at once to Father, and tell him what you say."

XVII

DEAREST LIESCHEN,

After my great thrilling letter of last night you will be thirsting to hear the sequel: perhaps to-day's letter will arrive with yesterday's. I hope so; you would be spared days of false hopes and false alarms for your little exiled sister. What I have suffered! We thought at least we should have a day or two to recover from the hateful scene of yesterday; but this afternoon comes a long long telegram from the Herr Doktor, making everything ten times worse. I never cried so much in my life, not even on that sad September day when I left home and abandoned you all, heartless wretch that I am, in order to live with rich strangers in this queer foreign land. The worst of it is that I must shut myself up here, in my own room, to have a good cry, because the family detest every natural expression of feeling. It is terrible. Half the pleasure of crying is missed if there's nobody by to pity and comfort you. Here, after crying my eyes out, I feel almost as much bottled up as before. I can never forget my troubles, because I must remember never to speak of them. No wonder so many people go mad in these old puritan families. I sometimes have a horrible thought. Perhaps my good sweet Oliver himself, when he comes to be forty or fifty, will break down! And it almost seems as if to-day something had happened to prepare the way for that dreadful end. The terrible responsibility of deciding his own future, the future of his family, even the future of poor Me, has suddenly been laid upon him at the age of sixteen! Why, you will ask, and how was it possible? My dear, it is all done out of kindness, with the idea of not abusing authority, and being liberal and highly considerate. But it is all a hideous self-deception, a cover for moral weakness. These people who leave you free are really cowards, undecided on every important question, and without true faith in anything. After all Frau Alden is right. The Herr Doktor has a lamentably feeble character. He means to be kind, and is generous with his money, but he abdicates his rights and avoids his duties. He makes *il gran rifiuto*, which is treason to life! She, at least, with all her selfishness and bigotry, is staunchly human. You know where she stands, and you can count on her. Here is the good Herr Doktor's wicked telegram to his son. I know it by heart.

QUESTION NOW MUCH ENLARGED STOP HOW WOULD YOU LIKE TO DROP SCHOOL AND SPEND NEXT WINTER ABROAD STOP TUTOR MIGHT PREPARE YOU FOR UNIVERSITY NO NEED STICKING TO WILLIAMS

COLLEGE YOU MIGHT GO TO HARVARD OXFORD HEIDELBERG OR
WHEREVER YOU WISHED STOP EXPATRIATION DANGEROUS BUT DAN-
GER ALSO OF DRY ROT AT HOME STOP TWO MOST CREDITABLE LIVING
AMERICANS JOHN SARGENT AND HENRY JAMES BOTH EXPATRIATES
STOP I DON'T WANT TO TEAR YOU AWAY AGAINST YOUR WILL NOR
TO LET YOU BE COERCED INTO MISSING THIS CHANCE IF IT TEMPTS
YOU STOP MAKE YOUR OWN CHOICE NO HURRY COULD JOIN US
HALIFAX OR QUEBEC SIGNED FATHER

Such a long telegram—it must have cost several dollars—and no word
about poor Me! Frau Alden, too, totally ignored! Whatever happened, I saw
myself cheated of that wonderful sea-trip, those interesting *dangerous experiences and possibilities*, even of a chance to be cured of sea-sickness! I saw
myself condemned to sit here till I grow old, perhaps deprived of my dear
pupil. Yet how could I wish him to stay? No Oxford, no Heidelberg—
although as to Heidelberg, the castle, so wantonly ruined, may look beautiful
in the pictures, but I prefer Bonn. The noble Rhine flows by, and our Kaiser
Himself was sent to Bonn, so it *must* be the best place. In any case, what a
splendid adventure for Oliver! His *Lehrjahre*, his *Wanderjahre*, full of poetic,
romantic, many-coloured interest! His fine mind becoming truly cultivated,
gelehrt, humanistic, scientific, universal, like that of our great Goethe! No, I
could not selfishly wish him to reject his father's proposal. My greatest
satisfaction must always be found in his happiness.

I had myself taken the despatch from the telegraph-boy, because there is
25 cents extra to pay for coming up the hill, so that all telegrams are brought
to me first, as I pay for everything (of course putting it down in my housekeeper's book) and I ran breathless with it to Oliver. "A telegram for you.
Probably from the Herr Doktor. Oh, do let's see what it says." But he took
it quietly and read it to himself; he read it twice without a word to me, and
thrust it into his pocket. "I'll show it to you afterwards, when I've thought it
over. Can't now. I'm going paddling for a bit first." And off he went headlong,
down the wooden steps which the Herr Doktor has had made on the steep
side of the Bluff, so that Oliver may not have to go such a long way round
to school. I wasn't angry, because I knew, when he turned away so hastily,
and with his throat so dry that he could hardly speak, that he was in great
trouble. How well I know that feeling! The need of being alone, the need
of seeing ourselves and our decisions on the background of our whole lives,
past and future, and of universal, indifferent, all-healing Nature! So I waited
as patiently as I could, and, Lieschen dear, I prayed! Yes, I prayed; because
although it is a mystery how it can be reasonable to pray or how prayers can
ever be answered, yet prayer is the only means in perplexity of raising our
thoughts to God, and preparing ourselves to bow to his will. And presently
Oliver returned, looking calm but rather tired—the weather is so frightfully

hot—and threw himself into one of our long low wicker chairs in the school-room balcony. "There's the telegram," he said. "See what you think of it."

"Oh, Oliver," I cried when I had read and thoroughly understood it, "what a tremendous decision for you to make! What is it going to be?"

"I don't know yet. I must tell Mother first, and listen to what she has to say. But I've thought the matter over carefully, every side of the question, and I am quite clear already on some points. In the first place, I don't want at all to go to Harvard or Oxford or Heidelberg. Williams is good enough for me; just an honest college among the mountains where a lot of decent fellows go from all parts of the country. I hate crowding into some big fashionable college calling itself a university where all is frills and snobbish-ness and shams. You can study the best science and history in books, wherever you are; and if I want to hear any famous professor, I can go and hear him afterwards, when I am a graduate. So *that* part of Pa's plan is put aside at once. On the other hand I don't care a fig for all Mother's objections to Lord Jim and the yacht and the influence of Pa's ideas. She is prejudiced, she is simply wrong; and when people are in the wrong, it would be wrong to pay the least attention to them. There's no such danger for me as Mother talks about. Even if I wanted to be like Pa or like Lord Jim, I simply couldn't: and besides, I don't want to be like them. But I enjoy being with them. It's a splendid life and I learn a lot, just because the point of view is so different, and Lord Jim is an Englishman and has been a common working man and has seen the rough side of life, and yet is a gentleman and awfully nice to me. I do want terribly to go back to the yacht, but only as Pa suggested at first, as far as Quebec, and return by rail. That's what I should like to do: and that's the second point clear in my mind.

"But now Mother interferes and says that if I do that I can never come home again. That would mean that I must quit school at once, and miss my last year. But I'm Captain of the football team, and the boys count on me for winning the great games this year with the Hartford High and the Providence Academy, because Mr. Coit's school this year doesn't count: and I should be backing out and leaving the whole school in the lurch. I'm not sure that I have a right to do that, just for my own pleasure. There's one doubtful point: and another doubtful point is, supposing I were willing to drop the School, whether I'd like studying with a tutor. Who do you suppose he'd be? If Lord Jim knew Greek and Latin, I'd jump at the chance; but my tutor would probably be more like Mr. Trill"—Have I told you, Lieschen dear, that the Rev. Algernon Trill of St. Barnabas comes to give Oliver extra Greek lessons?—"He might be some long-haired chap in goggles, raising a dirty fore-finger, fussing over details, and not letting me study in my own way. It wouldn't matter very much, because I daresay I could pass the Williams entrance examination now, without working next year at all: but do I want to float about a whole year in foreign parts, without my old books, without football or field sports, or any exercise at all—because in winter Lord Jim and I couldn't very well go swimming?"

I assured him that at Nice or Cannes or even in Greece or Egypt, he would find plenty of tennis and golf tournaments to play in, and that on board he could always do gymnastics or learn a sailor's work—could become a naval man, like the young Captain. It was useless for me to remind him that he would be making excursions ashore too—seeing Athens and Rome and Baal-bek and the Pyramids: all this left him cold. It was only by mentioning natural beauties—the Bay of Naples, the blue grotto at Capri, the Greek islands, the Dolomites, Mount Rosa and the Jungfrau, that I could arouse any semblance of interest. My dear pupil after all is an American; to him the past is foreign and dead. He is a boy, and the football matches at school seem more vital to him than the history of mankind.

There is something else too, dearest Lieschen, very strange about him, which I never quite understood until to-day. You would have expected him to have been angry and exasperated with his father, as I was, for throwing this terrible responsibility upon him, when it's a father's business to use his experience and determine what education is best for his children. But not at all. Oliver, though agitated, was deeply pleased and proud, and rose to the occasion like a born commander. You see, it is their sex. They love to feel strong and make decisions and run risks: yes, they love to bet and gamble, to seduce women without remembering the consequences, and fight wars without necessity and without any particular purpose. It is nature blindly arming her instruments to their individual ruin. We women too like to have our own way, but under cover of some authority, God, or a husband, or at least public opinion. It would frighten us to stand alone, but your true man loves it. Men are so much more romantic than women who, if we must confess the truth, are born domestic animals, whereas men don't become tame until they have lost their youth, or have missed it. I saw this plainly to-day in Oliver. After dinner—he sees his mother only at meals—when we passed into the parlour, he gave his mother the telegram, saying he hadn't wanted to show it to her while Annie was in the room. Think of the coolness of that! As if he couldn't have taken it to his mother earlier. But he loved having it hidden in his pocket, and everybody unconscious of hanging on his will. And now he positively made a show of being considerate, of wishing to preserve family secrets from the servants, and of coming dutifully to consult his mother, when he had secretly decided not to pay the least attention to her views. That is what men are by nature. Tyrants!

Frau Alden at once understood it. She offered no resistance. She was ice. She read the telegram without a quiver, as if it had been the evening paper, threw it disdainfully on the table, settled herself in her corner as usual, took up the large flat book—*The Illustrated Life of Washington*—which she pretends to be reading, (the book-mark has been a whole week between the same two pages)—laid it open on her lap, clasped her hands over it, and finally, as nobody spoke, looked up at her son and said softly:

"What are you going to do?"

"I haven't decided. I want to think it over to-night. I'll let you know in the morning." He picked up the telegram with an air which I couldn't help thinking a little boastful, as if he were winning a trick, or snatching the ball, in a hard game, from his opponent. He pocketed it almost defiantly, as if it was his charter of independence, as indeed it is. Yet my heart ached also for Frau Alden. How cruel of him to march off like that, without asking for her advice, so plainly saying that henceforth in his life she counted for nothing! Yet this cruelty was only the other side of his integrity, of his severity with himself. His decision must be taken alone, alone with God: and it wasn't to be an easy decision. It wasn't to be reached at once, in the interests of his own pleasure.

You know that my room is on one side of the schoolroom and his on the other, with doors connecting: and several times during the night I heard him come into the schoolroom and turn on the light on his desk. I could see the thin line of light under my door, and hear him occasionally move his chair, or walk about, or go out on the balcony—there was a full moon—and stay there, as it seemed, for hours. Finally—for I couldn't snatch more than scattered moments of sleep—I heard him come softly to my door and slip a piece of paper in under it. Then he went out into the passage, down the stairs and up again. I could guess now what he went to do: to slip a note under his mother's door also: and to leave on the hall table the long thick letter he had been writing to his father, for me to stamp and post in the morning. It was morning already; and when I had waited a while, to make sure that he had finally gone to bed, I got up barefoot and silently picked up that piece of paper. The dawn by this time was quite clear, and I read these words, written in his round boyish hand, but with the lines spreading irregularly and running down hill, which he doesn't usually do: "Have decided to stay. Don't expect me at breakfast. Haven't been to bed all night and want to sleep. Please ask Mrs. Mullins to keep my milk and two raw eggs on the ice for me till I come down. Ⓐ" This last scrawl is the monogram which he always uses for a signature—boys are so full of whims about their names and initials. Do you think psychology could explain that?—I have told Oliver that his monogram (as you can't tell which letter comes first) is the Alpha and Omega of our Saviour: but he pays no attention and goes on using it.

Well, here was everything settled! Nothing more to happen. Yet I couldn't sleep. It seemed as if peace could never really return to this house. I got up again and took my bath and did my hair, although it was frightfully early, not yet five o'clock; and I began this letter to you. What a comfort in all these changes and uncertainties to know that you, Lieschen dear, are still at home and ready, I trust, to receive your poor little sister! And who knows? Before long I may be really coming back, and we shall spend our old age sitting in the crooked old *Rathhausgasse*, gossiping all day together.

P.S. Something wonderful has happened. You will say it was nerves and lack of sleep, but I have had a psychic experience, a positive *vision* when I was wide awake. I had finished this letter and was going down to breakfast, it being nearly eight o'clock and we always strictly punctual, when in passing on tip-toe through the schoolroom I noticed that Oliver had left his door ajar, for he suffers so much from heat that he has had a long hook affixed which holds it a little open, to let the draught blow through on these oppressive nights; and I couldn't help stopping to peep in, and see if all seemed quiet. Suddenly on the opposite wall, perfectly clear and distinct, although the light coming in patches through the blinds and curtains was subdued and uncertain, I saw a life-like picture of *Christ on the Cross*! I knew perfectly well the picture wasn't there. Religious pictures are the last thing Frau Alden or Oliver would tolerate in their rooms. If they had a picture at all, other than family photographs, it would be *A Scottish Shepherd and His Dog*, or a *View of the Yosemite Valley*. I looked again, hard; I tried to see if there wasn't some optical illusion, if those lines and colours, as in a picture-puzzle, couldn't fall into a totally different composition. But no: though the head was bent and the face in shadow, nothing could be plainer than the one arm, thin and long, but muscular, nailed to a golden cross, and the thorax sharply outlined, every rib showing, and the body below sucked in painfully, slender and hollow like a greyhound's. I could distinctly see the fingers curled stiffly inwards towards the palm, and even the nail that pierced it. It was not the Christ, so classical and well-combed and rosy, of our modern religious art, but one of those uncouth mediaeval images, haggard lean stiff and out of proportion, which you see in wayside Calvaries in the Tyrol or in Bavaria, so gaunt, so pitiful, so truly religious and deeply German. Suddenly, I noticed the frame. It was the frame of Oliver's looking-glass, tilted forwards over his dressing-table. Yes, what I was seeing was only a reflection, a reflection of Oliver himself. His bed, with its headpiece against the same wall as the door, was being mirrored in the glass opposite. He lay propped high in it, with one arm thrown straight out and resting on the broad brass bar above his head—which made the golden cross of my vision. And what I thought was the nail was only a blister, caused by the oar, because his hands so soft and smooth outside, are callous and lacerated inside with rowing. He had thrown off the jacket of his pyjamas, as well as the bedclothes and was naked down to the hips: not naked as we ordinary home-bodies look when we are *undressed*, all one dead pasty colour like a sugar-loaf or a Victorian statue, or those white gloves—for weddings!—blown out with air, which you and I used to gaze at in the shop windows in Göttingen, and never had money enough to buy. No: this slender body was all bronzed and sunburnt, in different tones like some old, old ivory crucifix, once perhaps white, but now mellowed and stained with all the varied patina of accident and time. To think that it was supposed to be sport, to be pleasure, that cut all these lines and stretched all these thin sinews in a mere boy, as much as asceticism ever could in any old cadaverous hermit! However, I could breathe freely at last. Everything was explained naturally. And yet though you may call it *Aberglaube*, I feel that all we say to explain such an experience rationalistically can't destroy its mystical reality. Here I had had my vision, due if you like to my predisposition, possibly to that silly monogram working in my dazed stupid sleepy head. Very well: but something had predisposed me in that direction. What? Certainly not my wishes or my natural turn of thought. You know how I loathe any girl who is superstitious or *dévote*. Then why didn't I recognise Oliver at once? Why did my mind interpose that absurd illusion? Ah, I was predisposed by watching my dear pupil all these long, long years, by feeling so intensely the movement of his mind, by seeing—as he can't see himself—how his nature is always being smothered by his circumstances, and how it will be smothered more and more the older he grows. It is hideous, a misguided sacrifice, a conscientious suicide. Christ at least died to be glorified, to vindicate his knowledge that he was the Son of God. But my poor Oliver—I think now I was quite wrong in fearing that some day he might go mad. He has too much self-command, too much sweet reasonableness for that. But will he ever have the spiritual clearness, the spiritual courage to be himself? And if not, being suppressed and hopeless and morally confused, will he have the physical stamina to live on? Could he, like so many good people in this merciless world, survive his true self, and go on living after becoming a sort of person that he hated to be? My vision answers that question for me. My oracle says: No! He would die young and unhappy. And this obscure modern martyrdom would be sadder in its way than that of Golgotha. It would not save any world. It would not even save any soul.

XVIII

Mrs. Alden had defied the enemy and had come off victorious, but she had been thoroughly frightened and was little inclined to risk a second encounter. Her apparent victory enabled her to retreat with dignity and abdicate magnanimously the authority which she had hopelessly lost. Oliver had chosen to stay, but he was a changed being. His boy-life under her wing had come to an end. So had his apprenticeship under the faithful Irma. Home was not home for him any longer: it was a railway station where he must wait a year for the next train. That very habit of superior judgment and disapproval which his mother's example had always encouraged was now turned against herself. He had passed over to the enemy taking with him his arsenal of puritan virtues—his integrity, his courage, his scorn of pleasure, his material resourcefulness, together with a secret and almost malicious sense of alliance with the Unseen. The young sheep's dog by chance had smelt blood, and the ancient wolf-nature had awakened within him. He might still trot busily round the flock, and do no positive mischief; but he would move henceforth with a new alacrity, with head and tail up, as if to give visible warning that his service, like the shepherd's own, was that of a master.

This state of affairs could hardly conduce to happiness in the family circle. Mother and son avoided an open rupture by never referring to their differences; there was an unavowed tension in the air, and meals were silent and sad. Yet, after all, the two had always been reserved by instinct, and had led separate lives. Luckily Fräulein Schlote was on the best of terms with both parties; if her heart was wholly with Oliver her interests and her womanly sympathies allied her with his mother. It was she who conveyed to each the mind of the other, trying to explain away all that might seem unkind. Mrs. Alden was gently led to understand that Oliver could no longer yield to her authority against his own judgment. His father had given him a free hand, and his independence, being a fact, might as well be conceded as a right also. Especially as he was going to use this independence in doing essentially what his mother wished. He would complete his last year at the local school, and he would go to the country college where her brother was a professor. To Oliver, on the other hand, Irma conveyed a semi-official assurance that, if he carried out that plan, his mother would never again oppose any of his movements or friendships.

Accordingly all went smoothly when a second long telegram arrived from Peter saying that it was perhaps as well that Oliver voted for safety first. No great harm in one more year at school. When all-important football and momentous hurdles had been disposed of, Oliver might join them in England for the summer. Would he and Irma like a trip now to Niagara and the Yellowstone Park? Cheque followed.

Yes, they thought they would like such a trip very much, and thanked him for the thousand dollars. Letitia Lamb would keep Mrs. Alden company during their absence. And everybody concerned, though a little sore and disappointed, tried to appear satisfied. Niagara Falls and the Yellowstone Park were duly visited and admired. The comic incidents of the journey were laughed at and recalled again and again. This hotel was pronounced excellent, that other disgusting, this excursion tiresome, and that scene entrancing; and Irma reported every detail in gushing letters to her darling sister at Göttingen. Life, she said, in spite of those underlying great disappointments which gave such depths to one's character, remained always rich and full, and the world marvellous. But Oliver, though he went through it all good-naturedly, was not altogether comforted. Nature lost her friendliness when you were herded into her presence in the wrong mood, and commanded to admire; after all it was not the exceptional spectacles, the wonders that made nature one's great companion, but the steady flow, the inevitable equilibrium of her sustaining life. And the impudent hand and vulgar voice, compelling you to look at this and to praise that, simply intercepted the influence which beautiful things might have exercised over a free mind. And so very few things were really beautiful, so very few left you happier and more refreshed. Perhaps his mother was right. Better not travel, if you wished to admire the world; if you wished to think highly of your fellow men, better not hug them too close. He could feel the disappointment, the bitterness, in his father's kindness; the mixture of contempt and consideration with which he allowed his son to choose the duller, the safer, the meaner course. Ah, it hadn't been for his own pleasure or happiness or hope of a brilliant future that Oliver had chosen it; only because he felt bound, pledged, entangled by the roots, as it were, in his present duties, and *couldn't* choose otherwise. It had been a disheartening sacrifice. Why couldn't his father pity and love him for it, instead of despising him?

A curious film of unreality and worthlessness now seemed spread over his daily life. Even school work, when he took it up again, occupied him only north-north-west. When the wind was southerly there was a strange void in his bosom. He understood now the old notion that the soul had had previous lives, and was not really at home in this world. The routine of the day seemed a fiction to which he condescended, as if he were playing in private theatricals. The characters were assumed, and not very well done; yet, you must pretend to be in dead earnest, till you actually forgot that you were not. But for him a trap door had opened into the cellarage of this world's stage, which other people seemed so strangely ready to tread all their life long as if it were the bedrock of nature. Yet every step you took on those shaky boards revealed some old folly, some ramshackle contrivance which once may have produced conviction in children watching a Christmas pantomime—children who long since had died of old age. And in the opposite quarter, aloft amid those torn hangings and dingy backdrops, a ray of sunlight had pierced. It had gilded a beam of atoms in the thick dust he had been unconsciously breathing: it had disenchanted the paste board castles and daubed forests of his artificial world. But it was not romance that was shattered; it was slavery, drudgery, superstition. That vital air outside, that freedom, that simpleness, that natural light—how much more romantic they were than any moral melodrama invented by the frightened dreams of mankind! That was why some people thought so much of Goethe and others of Walt Whitman; these poets seemed to liberate them from moral cramp; but pedantry and preaching and yawping were unnecessary for that purpose. It was enough to go to sea.

In his home life, football more than anything else restored his conventional tone and dispelled this mystic alienation. It was a curiously homœopathic remedy; avowedly a game, a great passion about nothing, a severe duty frivolously imposed. There was a kind of desperate joke in plunging into this sport, and suffering for it. It called out all the young animal instinct for play, for fighting, for rivalry. It had the saving grace of being hard physical exercise, of purging, rinsing, exhausting the inner man. It banished to the dim background all the complexity of human affairs, and restored the dull pleasure, the mute confidence, of merely living and being carried round with the spinning earth in an open-eyed sleep. There was a sort of stupid satisfaction in having done something, no matter what: but wasn't there anything better that one might do keenly, clear-mindedly, with one's whole soul?

That the prophet of this change of heart was Jim Darnley, that it was Jim that Oliver missed, that it was Jim's bluff philosophy that he dreamt of adopting or infusing into his own, Oliver never confessed to himself plainly, or wrote down in his diary. He deliberately assumed that the trip in the *Black Swan* had been a holiday incident, something finished and done for; better put away all thought of it, and attend to business. Nevertheless, when a remote possibility appeared of seeing Jim again, if only for one day, no tropical dawn could have been swifter than that which suddenly flooded Oliver's sky. All sense of doubleness, of unreality, silently vanished: instantly he found himself telegraphing and writing and planning—yes and even prevaricating—with a singleness of purpose which excluded self-consciousness. He changed so sharply that he didn't know he had changed. His determination left no stone unturned, and carried everything before it. Yes, said the reply to his telegram, Jim was at the Manhattan Hotel and would still be there on November 19th. Yes, said the reply to his letter, the Yale management were happy to let Mr. Alden have one more complimentary ticket to the Princeton game, for the three dollars enclosed; and hoped he would turn up early at New Haven in the autumn and try for the Freshman squad. Good athletes, they added, always had a fine time at Yale, and found financial and other facilities for prosecuting their studies. An unofficial adviser would meet him on arrival and show him the Coop and the Y.M.C.A., useful to join at once, and would make him feel at home right from the start.

How splendid, thought Oliver, forgetting altogether the inhumanity of his joy, that the mate of the *Black Swan* should suddenly have died at sea, and the engineer should have left at Bermuda, so that Lord Jim had to come back to New York, to engage other officers! And how lucky that this should have happened just when Oliver, too, was going to New York, with the coach and the manager of his school eleven, to see the Yale-Princeton game! And how completely—though Oliver himself didn't notice the fact—all interest in that game for its own sake had subsided, and all curiosity about tactics and signals and mass play had yielded to the single vivid anticipation of Jim Darnley sitting there beside him! Nor was that anticipation disappointed. Hardly had Oliver and his school friends found their places, when a ruddy face, surmounted by a fresh bowler hat, worn at a sporting angle, was seen bobbing through the dense crowd, looking with good-natured uncertainty for the seat indicated on the bright blue ticket in the young gentleman's hand. How affable he looked, how big and brawny, and how beautifully dressed—too well dressed, Oliver would have thought, had he not known that Jim was a sailor. His shore clothes would naturally be spotless and a little festive, and he might be excused for looking—wasn't it partly in Oliver's honour?—as if he had just stepped out, entirely renovated, from the barber's and the tailor's and the habberdasher's. Besides, he really wasn't too well dressed *for him*, and his own person entirely eclipsed the splendour of his accoutrements. Powerfully built, yet slender in the waist and conspicuously masculine, with those clear blue eyes under those bold eyebrows, he was incredibly cheery, smiling, gracious, and inquisitive. The other two youths from Great Falls were impressed almost to speechlessness, and after a few clumsy civilities abandoned the stranger altogether to Oliver, as being too high class for their purposes. Indeed, it was always a comfort to be rid of older people, and an Englishman was as remote a being to them as a giraffe at the Zoo. For Oliver on the contrary all the sluices seemed to be suddenly opened and he found himself carried buoyantly along in the mid-stream of Jim's affectionate confidences. It *had* been a bit awkward having the mate die like that—quite unaccountably. He had been rather out of sorts and faultfinding; perhaps he had helped himself to some of the Doctor's medicines, and made a mistake about them. Anyhow, he wasn't a great loss. In fact Jim had had his eye for some time on a better man, a really decent sort, well-spoken and willing, who was out of a job. But the trouble was the engineer, who was also the second mate, leaving at the same time. Oliver should have seen the burial at sea. The Doctor wouldn't read the prayers; said it was the Captain's business, and a parson's son ought to know how to intone them. "And so I do," Jim went on. "Wasn't I a choir-boy once, like a chirping sparrow? But not on such an occasion. It would have seemed like mockery. I spelled out the prayers gruffly, as if I didn't know them by heart, and missed the sense in places, like your true honest sea-captain with a lump in his throat. Your father had promised to give the responses, but his voice could hardly be heard; and it was only the engineer who snapped them out, as if he had been denouncing somebody: and he gave notice that day, and asked to be paid off at Bermuda. Moody owls, some of these sailors are; you never know what yarns they may be spinning in their thick heads; and they hardly know themselves, only suddenly they'll flare up and do something foolish."

Ferocious cheering, now on their side of the field now on the other, made conversation difficult. But in the lulls Jim wished the rules of the American game to be explained; he proffered his impressions on the scene and on the playing as so many little ignorant absurdities of his own, for Oliver to correct; and he listened to Oliver's explanations and comments as being authoritative, and most, most clear and interesting. Jim had evidently had a good lunch and was looking forward to a good dinner. He found the cold wind exhilarating, and the hard narrow seat amusingly primitive. There was not nearly enough room for his broad shoulders in the slice of space democratically allotted to each spectator, by a management intent on gate-receipts and a record crowd; but this uncomfortable tightness helped everybody to keep warm, obliged Jim's arm snugly to encircle the young Oliver, and made conversation possible even in the din of the football songs and the organised cheering.

Jim Darnley was one of those rare Englishmen who can be honestly happy in the United States. Once his ear hardened to the language and to the other sounds, he could adapt himself heartily to the American way of enjoying oneself. There were certainly plenty of good things to enjoy, if you made rich friends and had money in your pocket; and as to the good things that were absent, Jim was too sensible and too positive to waste his time thinking about them. If ever he felt homesick about anything, it was for the English country or the British Navy: and these remote regrets were a rather pleasing sentimental indulgence adding to his self-respect, and giving him a nice background without spoiling his present pleasures. He admired money, success, power, and sport, all of which he found in America conspicuously blazoned; and having no occasion to identify himself with the new world, he was perfectly content, so long as it treated him well, that it should be whatever it chose to be. For him it was a passenger steamer in which, by chance, he was booked; he didn't expect the discipline or splendour of a flag-ship, or the small quiet comforts of home. Suffice it that the steamer was big and fast, the

weather favourable, and the passengers accommodating. America for
him was all like this American football match. He wasn't enquiring
how the thing might be justified. There it was, larger than life,
without begging your leave. Whether Yale or Princeton won didn't
concern him; no more whether eventually Yankeedom went to the
dogs or pocketed the universe. He had laid no wager on the issue;
and if some other people had bet high and cared enormously, that
was their affair. An odd sight, these two compact masses of humanity
on opposite sides of a field, whose aspect could change instantly from
that of Rome after Cannae to that of twenty thousand demons frantic
with joy.

"Why do they care so much?" Jim whispered confidentially in
Oliver's ear—not that he was interested at all in the explanation, if
explanation there was, but simply by way of expressing the odd
feeling of coolness and amusement that isolated them both and
brought them together in the midst of that pandemonium. For by
chance, in this case, Oliver too was absolved from the social obligation
of caring for that for which everybody cared. Neither his school nor
his future college was involved in this contest. He could watch the
hectic strategy of those players and the frenzy of that public almost
with the same indifference as Jim. Yet not quite, since he felt secretly
guilty for being indifferent. He was an interloper on those Yale
benches. It might have been clever of him to fool the management
and let them think they could coax him to go to Yale when he was
determined to go to Williams. They were hoist with their own petard;
yet his conscience was not altogether happy about it. Moreover, he
knew that if it had been his own school or college playing, he would
have been carried away with the rest, and Jim would have thought
him as inexplicably mad as he thought this howling rabble.

"Odd, isn't it?" Jim went on, not receiving any reply. "I suppose
people aren't ashamed of doing or feeling anything, no matter what,
if only they can do it together. And sometimes two people are
enough."

Certainly two were enough, in that instance, to establish a private
current of sympathy, and heighten the sense of union in contrast to
the outer world. Not only in that swaying grandstand did Jim prove
the most appreciative, jovial and affectionate of guests, but he had
taken the trouble—wasn't it wonderfully kind and friendly of him?—
to get tickets for the play in the evening: not for the grand musical
review, *She's a Lulu*, to which Oliver's school friends were going, but

for Forbes-Robertson in *Hamlet*. And what was still better, because it played up so gallantly to Oliver's lead and to his unspoken wishes, Jim had actually changed his room at the Manhattan, for one next to Oliver's, so that after all the confusing sights and emotions of that day, the two friends might talk everything over at leisure, and renew those night-long discussions of theirs in the *Black Swan* which the lash of domestic tyranny had so harshly interrupted.

Jim, for his part, was rather satisfied with his own conduct. To take young Oliver to see *Hamlet*—what could be more pat? What could make a better impression on the Doctor, or even at High Bluff, if the family ever heard of it? And what could mark this red-letter day more indelibly on Oliver's mind—who had hardly ever been in a theatre and had never seen Shakespeare on the stage? And with that profound impression, the image of Jim himself would be for ever associated. The thing was well worth the money, even if the tickets came rather high. Besides, for his own sake, Jim was not sorry to recover on occasion the pose of a man of the world. When he had money in his pocket, during the first days of each month—but that day, unfortunately, was already the 19th—he liked nothing better than to swagger into the stalls of a fashionable theatre, or even— what cost nothing—into those of a cathedral choir. He knew how to behave in both places; and though he might be slightly bored, he was repaid by a sense of reunion with the moral bulwarks of England and of the world.

These higher proprieties were more pleasantly discharged, when the calls of the inner man had been pacified: and before that long high-brow performance of *Hamlet* and after those three hours in the nipping autumnal air, it wouldn't be amiss to have a little dinner at the old *Café Martin*, where the Doctor had often taken him, and where the bill might be hung up. In those days the place preserved its red plush benches, marble-top tables, and vast mirrors in which the glass chandeliers cast their multiplied reflections, with that of the Second Empire: very like, Jim was pleased to think, the *Café Royal* in Regent Quadrant. A certain old-fashioned dignity was here combined with informality. This was everybody's club, a continental institution; and it ought to reconcile Oliver's democratic conscience in advance to the particularly good cooking and the choice but solid viands about to be offered him. He might even be persuaded to taste the excellent pommard destined to warm the cockles of Jim's own heart. There would also be something pleasing and flattering in being recognised by the old French *maître d'hôtel*, who would remember exactly the kind of *filets mignons, sauce béarnaise*, which the distinguished mariner especially relished. Yes, and Monsieur Jules would be impressed enormously—why are we so fond of impressing servants?—with the new phenomenon of Oliver, such a tall, serious, aristocratic-looking youth, under the captain's wing. Indeed, all the waiters looked at them with curiosity as, glowing with health in their nice evening clothes, they made their way to the table already reserved for them: and on being informed of Oliver's identity, Monsieur Jules overflowed with respectful smiles and little congratulatory bows, and begged to be allowed to present his compliments to the young gentleman on being the son of *monsieur le père de monsieur*. The reflected glory of several millions fell quite visibly upon Jim himself, upon the table, the waiters, and the entire reanimated restaurant. All concerned—except Oliver himself—felt that they had risen a peg in the world, and that the world was somehow more beautiful than it had seemed a moment before. Needless to say, the *filets mignons* were done *au point*, and the cobwebby bottle of pommard lying cleanly swathed within its straw cradle was officiously tipped with extreme precautions, to keep the captain's glass always full. Though the dinner could be charged to the Doctor's account, it was impossible under these circumstances not to give a generous tip to Monsieur Jules, and something to the *sommelier*, and to the other waiter. In this world, Jim reflected, you must pay even for being admired.

What better theme than *Hamlet* for orchestration by young emotions, when the world still surprises us for being so wrong and transports us by being so beautiful? *Hamlet* provokes speculation, and without speculation, without wonder raising afresh the most baffling ultimate questions, the fervid confabulations of youth would not be complete. Philosophy is a romantic field into which chivalrous young souls must canter out bravely, to challenge the sinister shadows of failure and death. The sublimity of the issue establishes a sort of sporting fellowship even among opposite minds, and the green battlefield draws them together more than their contrary colours can avail to separate them. Oliver had read *Hamlet* carefully in the schoolroom and had learned from Fräulein Schlote all that Goethe in *Wilhelm Meister* has to say about the play and the hero. Jim hadn't read Shakespeare at all, but he had seen *Hamlet* played once before at the Old Vic, and knew what he thought of it. It was, he confided to Oliver, by way of excuse for what he was about to hear, a rum old play, full of bombast and absurdities, but with a lot of topping lines in it that everybody had heard quoted. They were just the sort of thing that a clever chap like the hero might get off, but he was rather a muff at love and at politics, saw a ghost, and pretended to be mad in order to hide the fact that he was a quitter.

Oliver eagerly refuted these ignorant heresies, yet couldn't help chuckling at them. They gave him an occasion to maul their ridiculous author, and call him a fleshly brute without one glimmer of poetry in his soul. Hamlet, Oliver explained, was perfectly brave and firm when once sure of being right; but he had a tremendous intellect, tremendously pure and superior to all cut-and-dried opinions of ordinary people and even of science. This was what rendered him unfit for the everyday world. He couldn't play his part whole-heartedly in human society, because he saw how one-sided and wicked were all the principles that governed it. The spirit in him, Goethe had said, burst through vulgar conventions as a young growing oak would burst through a little fancy flower-pot, if you had planted it there. One reason why Hamlet feigned to be mad was that he was aching to publish many a truth which it might have been rude to mention if he had seemed to be sane. When he tells Ophelia to go to a nunnery, it is his true mind that is breaking through. In this scene Oliver thought that Forbes-Robertson had made a mistake. He had looked knowingly over his shoulder, to where the King and Polonius were hiding behind the arras, as much as to say that now he would put an antic disposition on expressly to deceive them. But why choose this moment, and precisely the antics that would break Ophelia's heart? Had Hamlet no insight and no tenderness? Surely, in Ophelia's presence, he didn't give a fig for those two old sneaking blackguards. He was thinking of Ophelia exclusively, and he spoke as he did, not because he didn't love her, but just because he loved and idealised her so much that he hated the idea of having her crushed and vulgarised in such a horrible mess as he now saw the world to be. At the cost of his own happiness, if he survived at all, he wished to save her from all the awful things that may happen to a woman when she marries and has children. He wanted to save her from everything coarsening, from everything degrading. Rather than that, he was willing to seem cruel to her now and to let her think him a heartless beast or a madman.

"Perhaps," said Jim with a paternal smile, "*perhaps* you know what you are talking about. It's mysticism. My old Pater drops into it sometimes in his sermons. When people fail in the world—and Hamlet had been cheated out of the crown and hadn't the pluck to resent it—they always say the world isn't a fit place to live in. But it's all bally rot about Ophelia. Hamlet had to jilt Ophelia in the play, so that she might go mad and scatter flowers and drown herself in the village pond, and make a lovely popular melodrama. Of course Hamlet wouldn't have behaved like that, if you stop and think; but you mustn't stop and think. You must be impressed. The talk about a nasty world and living pure in a nunnery was just the cant of those days. Every pulpit rang with it; as if one of your intellectual cads nowadays, after seducing a girl, said, 'So sorry, my dear. Can't marry. Believe in eugenics, and the doctors say I'm consumptive.' It's just window-dressing to keep himself in countenance while he sneaks away. If you took it seriously, you ought to go yourself into old Wetherbee's tame monastery, and never marry."

"Nonsense," cried Oliver a little ruffled. His smouldering Protestantism had been blown upon, and there was an indignant spark. He knew it was his duty to marry some day, as it was his duty to go to college and to play football and to choose a profession. Fortunately the duty of marrying didn't come round at a fixed date like the other duties, and he needn't think of it yet for years and years. But what an insult to suppose that he would flinch from it when the time came! "Of course," he went on aloud, blushing a little because unaccountably he remembered the first time he had undressed in Jim's presence, on the deck of the *Black Swan*, and how silly he had been about it, "of course I shall get married some day. The world has to be kept going, like a ship in mid-ocean. It would be cowardly for a sailor to jump overboard, after having signed on for the whole voyage, just because he was sick of it, like that engineer of yours. Why on earth did he quit? Of course, a man might die, like the mate—what did you say the mate died of?—or he might feel utterly unfit, like Hamlet, morally paralysed and overwhelmed, and might confess he was beaten. But *I* don't mean to be beaten. *I* don't see my grandfather's ghost, although he *was* murdered; and when I'm engaged, *I* shan't go and say to the dear thing: 'Get thee to a nunnery—because everything is so sad and I have tuberculosis.'"

Jim seemed momentarily vexed at something. It had been so hot in the theatre. They must stop and have a drink. Oliver, on the contrary, sipping his plain soda, felt strangely happy. At the dawn of experience the promise of happiness is happiness enough. Yet empty happiness, like a plain soda, might prove a trifle insipid in the end, and one of the first impulses of suddenly happy people is to form eager and elaborate plans for the future. The winter, Oliver knew, would soon be over, school finished, the football championship secured, and a new record established in the high hurdles. Then he could join his father and Jim again for the long holidays. With his father he would visit those English cathedrals that meant so much to Letitia Lamb: and with Jim he would go to the music halls, to Ascot, and to the Eton and Harrow match at Lord's: above all, they would explore Oxford, and spend a week-end with Jim's parents at the Vicarage at Iffley. "It's a lovely nook," Jim had declared, "with a lock and a mill—only I hear the mill is burned down—and the most beautiful tall trees, and a winding river with quiet back-waters, where we can go swimming if it's not too cold, and broad green fields with a lot of cows in them—if you like cows—and a ring of low hills in the distance to close in the landscape. There is plenty of boating and canoeing and sculling; we can float down to Abingdon in a punt; and on the way I'll show you Radley—St. Peter's College—where I went to school for a year before joining the Navy. You shall see what English life is like, so simple and pleasant, and English houses, so nestling and separate and cool, each with its jolly garden, where you may bowl or play tennis or sit and have your tea, and such a bright fireside in the evening, and such peace. There are nowhere such fields and meadows and animals as in England, nowhere else such horses or dogs or sheep. Only the donkeys are smaller there than anywhere else—I mean those on four legs—and yet you never saw such sturdy little beasts. And you will discover for yourself what a mutton chop can be, or a cold leg of lamb, or a joint of beef or of mutton, or green peas, or apple tart and cream: and as for the English climate, people may say what they will about it, if they have been brought up in cotton wool and can't stand a drop of rain, as if they were lumps of sugar, and must shiver at the sight of a bit of mist hanging over the river, or driving over the downs: but for all that, it's the mildest, softest, freshest, most invigorating climate in the world."

Poor Jim! He had to be forgiven, Oliver felt, for these sentimental prejudices. They were his protestations of loyalty to himself, in the teeth of his hard luck. Naturally a new country like America must be *really* superior to every other. Hadn't it been established in the full light of experience and reason, all the rubbish of ages cleared away, all the superfluous fat of old human nature worked off and reduced to clean hard muscle? Such a country stood on an unrivalled eminence and could afford to help and appreciate all other nations, instead of hating and fighting them, as they hated and fought one another. A good American needn't fear to face the hard facts at home, or the queer complicated facts abroad. Yes, Oliver meant to travel: not as his father had travelled, in the spirit of a dilettante and an exile, but in order honestly to learn the state of the world, and to understand his own country better and work for it more intelligently.

"Surely," he thought, as he tucked himself into his cold fresh bed in the early hours, "I haven't broken training. The rules say you must be in bed on Saturdays by midnight: they don't say anything about not talking afterwards." He took the half-dozen long breaths recommended by his father. Nice that this room was free from smoke, with the window open at top and bottom as wide as a guillotine window admits of being opened. Nice to have defeated the boasts of the tyrant radiator, guaranteed to keep the temperature at 68 degrees Fahrenheit, in spite of all that nature or man might do to prevent it. Oliver hated above all else fustiness, sultriness, and smells. Even after the most agreeable company there was a relief in solitude and silence. He still had several hours free for sleep before his boisterous friends on the other side should come to rout him out. Fortunately, that darkly dawning day was a Sunday. They would have a very late, very heavy breakfast, just in time to load themselves with the Sunday papers—in order to read all about the match they had just seen— and to catch the one slow fetid country train that would take the rest of the day to jolt them home. These images of the morrow were deeply present to Oliver's inner mind, as his nest grew warm and sleep began to overtake him. No fear that he shouldn't wake at the appointed hour, even if his obstreperous comrades and the preconcerted telephone bell didn't violently arouse him. The coils of duty in his moral alarm-clock were tightly wound, and the inward bell would ring infallibly. With that unremitting tension of virtue, or of possible sin, always in the background, it was safe to let pleasant visions float across the surface of consciousness. How splendid Lord Jim had been all that day, so bold, so easy, so frank, so affectionate, so disinterested, and at bottom so terribly intelligent! Certainly Oliver would go to England in the summer. Certainly he would stay with Lord Jim at that gabled stone parsonage, under those great luxuriant old trees. Certainly he would love Jim's metaphysical old Pater and his comfortable old Mater and his lovely fluffy-haired little sister, Rose.

PART III

FIRST PILGRIMAGE

I

Peter Alden felt at home in London. Not that he knew the town well—not to speak of the Metropolis—or had lived long there; but within the bounds of St. James's and the Parks he could lead the life of his choice. Here everything was arranged for his comfort and pleasure. Existence lost its acerbity, and all the conventions seemed designed to oil and to make silent the machinery of fate. The world, as it were, had been strained through a sieve: only the decent, the concordant elements had filtered through, with only the approved flavours; and the incidents of one's normal day seemed to gain in flattering depth what they lost in variety. They were just the incidents which, if free, your inner man would have provoked. The bachelor's London of his youth—which still lingered on within these precincts— had been thoroughly safe, thoroughly settled, thoroughly equipped with the requirements of manly comfort and propriety, meant to be demanded with lordliness and used with discretion. Here was the government of gentlemen by gentlemen and for gentlemen. Here the gentleman in Peter felt strangely at home.

He liked the ladies also without exactly loving them. They seldom intruded into Saint James's, but sometimes he was asked for a week-end to the country and could admire them in their simplicity and fineness. Not all were Dianas: not all wore their beauty and their jewels with a divine serenity, almost without words, and by a divine affinity formed a right judgment on every subject. Not always did the brooks ripple in their voice, or the blue sky shine in their incurious eyes; nor did their aristocratic nostrils always quiver or their bodies leap in the ardour of the chase. Some of them made up for being less perfect by being more aggressively good: well-washed hard pedestrians, sensibly dressed, and honest as boiled potatoes without salt: parsons' wives or dons' wives or spinsters and widows boarding genteelly at Brighton or Richmond or Bath. These were the very places where Peter himself, in order not to spend Sunday in London, would stay for a day or two at the best hotel, and drink whiskey-and-sodas with some retired major or colonel whom he had once known in the East. Sometimes the more blear-eyed of these pensioned heroes would leer at a passing female of quite another sort: some obvious scout of the *demi-monde*, or perhaps some distinguished veiled actress, looking like an elegy on lost youth; or perhaps they introduced him to some lady of a more ambiguous and characteristic sort—the advanced woman who combined freedom in morals with a loud competence on every public question, and perhaps wrote novels—not good novels. The only good novels he knew of written by a woman, were those of a lover of gardens, with an amused understanding of mankind and a just affection for whatever in them might be flowerlike and human: but Peter was an incorrigible Epicurean in his judgments though a rather troubled one in his heart; and nothing seemed to him more odious in this world than the people bent on reforming it. The truly sweet fruits of existence were to be picked by the way: they were amusement, kindness, and beauty. But reformers blindly pursued something else, which if realised would probably be worthless; and meantime they screamed with a fanatical hatred of everything human.

In comparison with emancipated women the old-fashioned domestic galaxy of wives and daughters, sisters and tender aunts, seemed to him ministering angels; and England contained, he knew, many devoted myriads of them living in obscurity. But they lay beyond his rather limited orbit: he was like a planet constrained by his own inertia and the forces of gravity to circle in the same round; and free will, if he had it, was a useless faculty, since nothing appeared beyond his path that could tempt him to leave it.

Twenty years earlier, in the 1880's, he had resided for several seasons in London, and had been made foreign or honorary member of two or three clubs. Americans in those days had not yet been accepted wholesale, with a secret grimace of resignation, in view of their wealth or of the national interest. As Americans they were not at all wanted; but as individuals, when any of them once got a footing, they might be embraced with a sublime indifference to what might be their position in their own country. You ignored, you even forgot, that they were Americans at all; and they in their turn, while things went swimmingly, forgot that they were not Englishmen. A certain testy old general, in regard to Peter, would never admit the contrary. "They pretend," he would splutter, "that this Alden chap is an American. Impossible. He doesn't look like an American, he doesn't talk like an American, he doesn't dress like an American, and he takes such *sound views*. Alden is not an American."

This sort of welcome, if alluring in some ways, yet had secret disadvantages. Short of completely transforming himself—which Peter's old ingrained reflexes and conscience forbade—he was compelled to sail perpetually under false colours, and to suppress alien feelings which he could not eradicate. The acceptance he might find in England, no matter how simple and hearty, must always remain incidental; no radical bond held him to anything there. A sense of moral solitude haunted him in the most familiar places and the most agreeable society—doubly so now that his older friends, like that incredulous general, had disappeared. Even Peter's old lodgings had ceased to exist; and the other side of Jermyn Street, from which he no longer could see the trees and the church tower, seemed in itself a place of banishment. At the club things were less changed: even the other members, though they had new faces, preserved the excellent old manners, and politely ignored him, respecting his favourite corner and never seeming to look for the illustrated paper he was reading or the desk at which he was writing. The food, too, was the same, if less lavish; and the servants showed the old training, with but little more haste. In the Parks where, weather permitting, he rambled the whole afternoon, there was a positive increment of beauty: lovelier flowers, thicker trees, cleaner waters, peopled by ducks and swans more learnedly selected and bred. Only the riders and horses, the carriages and footmen, betrayed the gradual eclipse of aristocracy.

Musing on these things and going these rounds, Peter awaited contentedly the arrival of his son and Fräulein Irma, not without dreading it a little. But he had taken preventive measures of self-defence. Oliver would go to spend his first English Sunday with Lord Jim at Iffley: that was what the boy most desired. And as to Fräulein, she would be despatched at the same time to revisit her old school at Southwold in Suffolk, whence she could proceed conveniently to her native Göttingen: the through ticket, by the Hook of Holland being supplied for her beforehand by the generous forethought of her patron. When eventually Oliver returned from Oxford and Lord Jim had shown him London—they would manage that in two or three days—it would be time for father and son to undertake their projected excursion through the English country, in order to satisfy the anxiety of the home circle, where Letitia Lamb had declared that the

most interesting and elevating thing one could do in England was to
make a tour of the Cathedral towns; and also, Mrs. Alden had added,
to visit the Highlands in order to see Tintern Abbey and the Lake
of Killarney. She herself when a girl had seen the Lake of Killarney—
probably idealised—in one of Boucicault's plays, and certainly *there*
it had seemed very beautiful. And as to Tintern Abbey, hadn't a
professor of Chicago University sent a questionnaire to all the teachers of English in the United States, and hadn't they decided, by a
large majority, that Wordsworth's lines on Tintern Abbey were the
best poetry ever written in any language? The influence of these
famous scenes, which belonged to the past of America as much as of
Europe, might help to balance any evil tendencies to be found in the
characters of foreigners.

Peter, for his part, would gladly have washed his hands of the
whole business. Wrong, certainly, and unfair to the youngster, to
spoil him for living in his own country. But what if living in his own
country spoilt him for living with himself? His money—since this
inexplicable money was as much the son's as it had ever been the
father's—his money would eat him up. It would suppress and exter-
minate his natural fineness. It would bury him deeper in the universal
avalanche. It would render him anxious and perturbed in his own
conscience, and odious to the poor or to the less rich. "Really," said
Peter to himself with profound amusement, "I was lucky to slip out
of it as I did. Saved by committing murder. I have been useless, but
at least I haven't hurt anybody intentionally, and may perhaps have
done a little good here and there in a sneaking sort of way. I haven't
hated, I haven't feared, and I've preserved my intellectual liberty.
This boy is too virtuous. He won't lie to in a gale, and he'll be wrecked.
All ships must be wrecked at last, or broken up into junk in some
shabby port—which is less glorious. Let the lad at least enjoy this
summer holiday, and keep the memory of a patch of blue sky. Curious
how little satisfaction there is in having even the most exemplary
offspring. Oliver by the mere problem of his future and by the very
look in his eyes seems reproachfully to inquire why he was ever
brought into this world. It might have been better if I had never
married. It would have been easier to do the right thing by society
at large, writing a book of travels, or one on ships in the sixteenth
century, or collecting works of art and bequeathing them to the
Boston Museum. But for a son, for an actual living soul, how should
one ever know what is best?"

II

There was only one Sunday train not leaving too early for morning heads still buzzing with the music of *Rigoletto* and dazed with confused images of supper at the Savoy: a slow train wending its gentle way through Buckinghamshire by High Wycombe and the Chiltern Hills. They were alone in their first class carriage, and Jim had composed himself to sleep on the cushions opposite, while through the neat little frame of the open window the bright landscape formed for Oliver's dreamy eyes a fugue of green and tender harmonies, full of shifting light and shade, sheep, cows, hedges, ditches, and rural silence. In Oxford there was not a hansom to be found at the ugly station or its ugly surroundings: and the one ancient cabby with his ancient horse and fly refused to drive them so far into the country as Iffley. Jim, in a tone of vexation at not being permitted to be lavish, grumbled that there was nothing to do but to take the tram. They would change at Carfax and, their bags luckily being light, they could walk from Iffley Turn to the Vicarage. It couldn't be helped; and without confessing it he was not unpleasantly aware that this arrangement would save him at least ten shillings: for, although the railway tickets could be charged to the Doctor's account as travelling expenses, in his own place he must insist on playing the host. Besides, as he observed to Oliver, the top of a 'bus is better than the inside of a hansom for getting a first glimpse of the town. They would pass the Broad and the best part of the High, and Jim could point out six or seven colleges, Saint Mary's and Magdalen tower to his respectful but rather undiscerning young friend, who when expected to admire something particularly beautiful, asked how old it was, or how the name of it was spelled.

When at last, somewhat hot and belated, they reached the Vicarage, the family, according to the frowzy kitchen maid, were at Vespers in the church. "Come on," said Jim, "let's go too and hear the old man preach. He's always very short, and he'll be jolly pleased."

The Vicar saw them at once, as he looked up and repeated the words: "Here endeth the second lesson." The suspense in which a clerical intonation leaves that phrase seemed for a moment to pass into his whole being. They had entered noiselessly through the little north door, left open at that summer season, and a beam of the evening sun had entered with them, gilding their two blond heads, Jim's tenaciously curling and wiry, turning to chestnut, and Oliver's naturally pale and lank, but at that moment dishevelled by the journey and intricately catching the golden light.

The Vicar, a spare tall man with sunken blue eyes under his heavy eyebrows grown grizzled and bushy, waited for the young men to sit down, which they did on two little chairs in front of the font, where the sunlight fell full upon them. He waited also, as it seemed, for something within him to take shape and come to the surface; until folding his hands afresh over the open book—rough large hands, for he was his own gardener—he began very gently, as if communing within himself.

"In this lesson we have read the words: *An Angel of the Lord*. Let us consider for a moment what these angels may be. I will not dwell on the opinions of the Fathers concerning their nature. Those are learned and devout speculations worthy of all reverence; but what anything may be in its own nature, whether we speak of angels or men or material things, is a point known with certainty only to God. To us an angel is essentially a messenger, as the Greek word indeed imports; and it is the angel's message that is the veritable angel to us. I think, my dear friends, that all things are angels. You must not imagine that every angel is a gracious and smiling child, playfully diving through the light, or shedding it from his wings; there are angels that bear a sword, and there are fallen angels that bring temptation. We may discern messengers of the Lord in these also, not directly, as if the thought they bring or the action to which they prompt us were divinely commended, but indirectly, in that they come to us by God's leave and in some respect at least are commissioned, through warning or suffering or labour or sacrifice, to lead us back to Him. There is nothing in this world, believe me, that may not be a mediator to God for those who seek Him sincerely, and an oracle of God to those who have ears for His voice. That sorrow may be a sacrament of reconciliation, you all know by experience; but there are other austere angels, perhaps hardly less unwelcome in aspect, yet no less rich in grace. For example, there is the Truth. The Truth is a terrible thing. It is much darker, much sadder, much more ignoble, much more inhuman and ironical than most of us are willing to admit, or even able to suspect. In what Christian family, in what young man or woman apparently shielded from every evil, would not the Truth unveil some unlovely mystery? We are all miserable sinners. We are all unhappy at heart. And the Truth of natural fact also, the truth of science, what a stumbling-block it is. How anxiously, how insecurely, the Church strives to protect the treasure of her faith from that merciless flood. Yet all Truth is an angel of the Lord, even a part of the divine being: for Saint Augustine tells us that God is not merely good but is goodness itself, not true, but the Truth. Yet we think in our levity that the Truth may be dangerous and that it might disprove the existence of God. Oh, the unbelief of us believers! If the Truth be not verily, in some respect, what our prejudices suppose, or what our selfish passions would require it to be, how should salvation and religion hang on maintaining that prejudice or rendering that fatal passion inveterate? Lift up your hearts, rather, and cleanse the inside of the cup. Presume not to dictate to God what God shall be, or what He shall do. Run forth to Him as a child to his father, mould your wishes to His eternal decrees, accept the place and the nature He has assigned to you, and your ignominy will become your glory, and even in the midst of this earthly life and its wretchedness, you will be living among His angels. Summer and winter, youth and age, riches and poverty, will be His messengers, abiding only for a moment, yet revealing to you in that moment the very texture and pattern of eternity. And death is the last, the greatest, the most broad-winged angel of all. He comes unbidden and mistrusted; yet to those who have inwardly renounced the world, he brings peace and healing and spiritual union with celestial things: whilst he slays with the sword of wrath and of calamitous ruin those who have not renounced it."

That was all, or all that Oliver could retain: for at times the very intensity of his attention, held by what he had just heard, made him deaf to the sequel; and the scene too was absorbing, and somehow hypnotic in the concentration of its depth and colouring: that narrow, solid, monumental little church; those dozen or two modest and scattered worshippers apparently intent each on his own devotions; the Vicar's clear refined voice, with its liturgical modulations; the open door, the sunlit churchyard outside, silent but for some bird in the thick trees, come to join, as it were, in the service; and Jim by his side, Jim in church, and somehow not out of place there.

The service over, Mr. Darnley let his modest choir of two men and four boys precede him to the vestry—a mere cupboard where the parish register was kept and the surplices were hung; and having divested himself of his, he turned rather shyly to Oliver.

"Ah, yes. This is you. So glad. So glad you came to Vespers."

Out of the pulpit, the Vicar was quite another man. All the calm eloquence, all the ease and inspiration were gone from his speech. He seemed like a raw, bony, rather rude schoolmaster who said only the most conventional things in the most conventional see-saw. There was also a short square woman in black, loitering near them. Oliver at first supposed her to be some poor parishioner, or perhaps the caretaker, but she turned out to be Mrs. Darnley. Nobody minded her. Jim, who had shaken hands with his father, seemed not to notice her. But there, too, was Rose, with unmistakably the same hair as in the photograph: a tall, serene child, who attached herself at once to Jim without question and looked confidently at Oliver, as if she regarded him also as part of her domain.

"Come and see your room first," she said, taking him by the hand, "and I'll show you the garden afterwards. We should have given you the blue room, because it's the nicest: but we thought you'd rather be next to Jim, as you are his best friend, so we've put you in the gable room; but we've brought up some things from the blue room, to smarten it up, and I've put flowers for you in all the vases."

On reaching the gable room, the little hostess let go his hand, stopped, called back the dog that preceded them, smiled, and discreetly shut the door on the young gentleman. He heard her light step, tripping down the stairs, and a moment later he could see her in the garden below, chasing her dog.

"I say, you did sing that hymn like a lark: happened to be one you knew, I suppose," Jim observed as they went downstairs. "And you noticed what the Old Man did? Changed his sermon altogether on the spur of the moment, when he saw us come in. I told you he'd be pleased. The angels were you and me—nice angels!—and he had to ask the man at the organ to change the hymn to suit."

"It was a beautiful sermon: so inspired."

"The Old Man is always like that when he's alone, when he lets himself go. At home, of course, it can't be, because there's Mother. Even Rose is in his way, because Rose isn't religious: a little pagan, a little housewife, a little garden fairy, who looks after him, but doesn't believe a word he says; laughs at him. She'll laugh at you, if she hears you talk philosophy. She thinks grown-up people are just harmless idiots, like the birds twittering. But the Old Man can't come down gracefully out of his element; feels dreadfully out of it in this world, doesn't honestly belong here at all. He's honest only in church: the opposite to all other parsons I ever knew."

In the garden—which Rose forgot she was to show him—Oliver felt a little lost. Rose and Jim and the dog played and talked together as if he wasn't there: perhaps he was expected to join them, but he didn't exactly know what they were about. However, the Vicar came out of his study and called him. "You have seen the inside of our church: let me show you our West door. This is the bit the tourists photograph. You see, it is a monument of a rude age, not very ancient yet morally altogether remote, when minds were dark and narrow, and life full of danger and hardship, even for the rich. Those were little dirty men who fought in armour, wilful, custom-bound, and short-lived, like seamen in the northern seas, which indeed some of them had been; and their clergy was a band of young converts, or indoctrinated boys, imperfectly grounded in the spirit of the faith, and carrying their barbaric notions of honour and of lordship into the Church. They had lost, or had never learned, the noble arts. See how they worked. Those mouldings, that crude round window, are like the designs of children or savages: woven or hacked decorations, as in basket-work or stitched garments."

"Yes," Oliver interjected, "something like the basket patterns of our Indians."

"Quite so; and when they had their way they painted and gilded it all in red and blue and green and bright brown: very dazzling and violent it must have looked. As we see it here weathered and washed out and gnawed by time, the crudity of it may pass for austerity and force. Time often flatters the past by half erasing it. This architecture was not meant to be austere, it was meant to be rich; but the materials at hand were rough and the artist inexperienced."

"It's certainly very decorative," said Oliver, but detected in himself the tone of Letitia Lamb, and wished he hadn't said anything.

"Earnest, honest work," the Vicar went on, "and their construction was superior to their ornament. It went back to the Romans. See those central arches and all this older part of the walls: they are magnificent. And the best part of it is the spirit; that those simple men should have worked so devotedly, with such technical zeal, for the glory of God and the salvation of souls; so that their work has served its original purpose uninterruptedly down to our day, and we still may join those incomprehensible barbarians in their faith and prayer, when all else in their lives is grown obsolete and terrible. I wonder if the great things you do in America are dedicated in that way to eternal interests, and whether in a thousand years your sky-scrapers will stand to serve the same purpose which they serve to-day."

"The sky-scrapers aren't meant to last, but we build colleges also."

"Colleges are hardly the same thing: they are ambiguous institu-tions. You will see the colleges here in Oxford. In part they are ancient, and as many people think, far too old-fashioned in their customs and learning: yet they would horrify their founders. That is because they are not dedicated simply to God and to the soul of man, but rather serve professional thrift and competitive vanity. I suppose you have been taught—and it is our Lord's doctrine—that to serve our neighbour and to love him is to serve and to love God. But that is only when you love and foster in your neighbour his participation in divine life, his approach to some sort of perfection. If you love him for his weakness, because he succumbs to you, or serve him in his folly, you are devoting yourself to the service of his vices; you are his worst enemy, as well as God's: and you hate his soul and destroy it."

"Do you think we all have souls, sir? Jim says he hasn't any, but only life."

Mr. Darnley laughed.

"Has Jim been repeating that, and trying to confuse you? It's one of my little jokes. Of course all men, even animals and plants, have souls. Life itself is a triumph of the soul. But there are instrumen-talities requisite to bring down from heaven the particular happiness of which each soul is capable. Some souls fail in vivifying the body: matter is too much for them, and they die young or of some disease. Others are lost in the world. Poor Jim! I tell him he has no soul, because he feels no need of spiritual things, and seems not to suffer for missing them: but his soul at least performs her bodily functions gloriously. The vocations of souls are different. Some can be happy and beautiful in the body, others in the world, others only in the spirit. Yet in a man the perfection of merely bodily life or of worldly arts is somehow tragic. That was the tragedy of the Greeks. That is what I tremble for in Jim. I love him dearly, coming to me, as he did, out of my most grievous entanglements; and his troubles have been a greater tribulation to me than my own ever were. His virtue is bodily, his charm is bodily, his happiness is, and always will be, bodily. And in singly exercising his natural gifts—and what more can we ask of a free soul justly?—he must offend the world, and he must neglect the spirit. Nobody can unite all the virtues. Our Lord himself could not be a soldier, nor an athlete, nor a lover of women, nor a husband, nor a father: and those are the principal virtues of the natural man. We must choose what we will sacrifice. The point is to choose with true self-knowledge. You, my friend, if I am not mistaken, are an ἀνὴρ πνευματικός, a spiritual man by nature: I am not sure how far, without loss of anything better, you might be an athlete or a soldier or a lover of women. Now you are a boy, everything seems possible; but everything is not possible together. Something tells me you have the higher calling. I could see it during the sermon. When I quoted some spiritual saying of St. Augustine's, or of some other master, you looked up; there was light in your eye; you understood. Not that any of us is likely to reproduce a thought just as it once arose in another man's heart. How should we do that? Or, if we did, how should we know we had done it? But we may swim in the same sea; we may understand the prophets as we do the poets, each time differently, each time plunging in some direction a little further into the divine harmonies of things, and welding their sacred bonds. You can understand, and you can sing. That is a gift: you have a beautiful voice, yet with something in it that perhaps may be rebellious to training. You may never be able to sing what you don't feel; you may never be an artist. Yes, my dear Oliver, you are an ἀνὴρ πνευματικός. It is a great privilege, a tragic privilege. For just as the merely natural man ends tragically, because the spirit in him is strangled, so the spiritual man lives tragically, because his flesh and his pride and his hopes have withered early under the hot rays of revelation. Even the Church is no ultimate home for the spirit. We churchmen must accept one another's inspirations. We must pray together. Thereby our enthusiasm may gain in volume, it may burn more fiercely, but by an unspiritual contagion. Religion ceases to be a radical conversion, a thorough cleansing of the heart. It becomes a local heritage, a public passion, a last human illusion for the spirit to shed."

A cracked little bell tinkled angrily from the parsonage. The Vicar sighed.

"There. We are being called to supper." And as they moved across the lawn he murmured, not querulously but as if meditating on an eternal truth: "You will see that the goods of this world have not been showered upon me."

In the dining-room Jim was talking with his mother, whilst Rose was fetching the dog's food in a white plate, not allowing him to touch it until she had neatly and squarely set it down on a tiled corner of the floor.

"What are we having to-day, Mother? A little roast pig?" Jim asked with a broad smile.

"Always nagging," muttered Mrs. Darnley, secretly mollified by feeling her son's arm round her waist, "always grumbling and dissatisfied, as if I grudged you the best of everything. And if rich people don't like what we have to offer them, as is our little all, let 'em stay at home and sate themselves off their gold service. We have what we always have, plenty of bread and cheese and a nice fresh head of lettuce, and knowing what young people are, because I was once young myself, there's what was left of that smoked beef; and little as will be left of it, I warrant, when they're done with it."

"We might have had a steak or something," the Vicar murmured, as if reproaching himself for his want of foresight.

"You might have had a whole joint of mutton, if you'd only said so, and given me the money for it. You're not asking me to drive the cow to the butcher's, and let him cut a steak for you? And where should all the milk come from that Rose has to drink?"

The smoked beef and lettuce seemed to Oliver excellent, and the bread and cheese substantial enough, especially as he was allowed by Rose to have some of her milk, instead of the copious pints of beer that Mrs. Darnley supplied for the gentlemen, and poured out for herself.

After this feast Jim announced that, since it was Sunday, Pater would read aloud to Rose something nice out of the Apocrypha whilst Mater dozed. Oliver and he had been cooped up all day in a railway carriage and were going for a walk. In view of this Rose came up to her brother to kiss him good-night, and turning to Oliver stopped for a moment and then kissed him too. "I'll bring you your tea in the morning," she said, "when I bring Jim's." Oliver muttered, "Oh, thank you," but not to take the trouble. "It's no trouble, I like it. I *always* fetch Father's tea, because he takes his so early, but now it's the holidays and I don't go to school, I may fetch Jim's too, no matter how late, and yours."

Poor Oliver hated to have to explain that he took no tea, nor anything at all, in his room in the morning; but how could he help saying it when it was the truth?

Rose murmured, "Oh!" a little perplexed and disappointed; and as the young men disappeared through the garden gate, she wondered why God had made some people so queer and stupid.

III

As soon as they were clear of the toll-house at the mill, and had got their full stride in the fields beyond the lock, Jim looked about him with the cautious secretly triumphant air of a player sure of winning the rubber.

"Plenty of light yet," he observed sagaciously. "Only two miles there."

"Two miles where?"

"To supper."

"But we've just had supper."

"Not a bit of it. Shouldn't I have made a jolly row if that were all we were to get! I kept my mouth shut—and there wasn't much to put into it—because I was going to bring you to supper at Sandford. The place will be closed of course, but that doesn't matter. The landlady is a friend of mine, and she's expecting us."

A brisk walk is not favourable to conversation, and the two friends only now and then exchanged a few words. But their minds were not idle; and though the thoughts running through the two were unlike in swiftness and colour, they were aware somehow of flowing in unison, like a lake-stream and a mountain-stream meeting, but not yet merging, in a single river. The loveliness of the vast evening seemed to overarch and temper them both. What a strange sense of safety, of jollity, of endless potentiality came over Oliver in having this warm-blooded creature at his side. How far in the distance, how meagre and alien, his old life at home seemed in comparison: very like the trivial voices of a boatful of trippers, belated in the twilight, that reached him across the water. And how wonderful too, in quite a different direction, the Vicar showing this inexplicable interest in a mere boy, and this insight, such as not even the good Irma was capable of: this learned religious elderly man treating him as an equal, as a mind, as an independent immortal spirit, into whom to pour his best thoughts. How beautiful were austerity and poverty and obscurity. What a revelation that there might be in the world places and persons untouched by the world, lives in which only nature, only religion, only friendship were real.

Whatever Jim's thoughts may have meantime turned upon, they must have been no less buoyant. He was all alacrity, and when they reached Sandford Lock, he ran ahead over the footbridge and disappeared, Oliver hardly knew through which door; for there were several, all apparently locked, in the ivy-covered wall of the King's Arms Inn. Daylight had almost faded, and the moon was not yet risen. A last boat of holiday-makers was drifting down stream beyond the open lock-gates; and the deep pit of the lock remained empty, its black slimy walls still dripping and sending up a breath of dampness, a trickling sound, and sundry acrid vegetable odours. Otherwise the place was silent and deserted, and Oliver flushed with walking, felt a slight shudder. Presently Jim called him to come round by the back door. It was after closing hours and the bar and coffee-room must remain sealed, on this Sunday night, in sepulchral silence.

They traversed a vague billiard-room, where the tables, on which other furniture was stacked and covered with ghostly sheets, loomed like ships in dry dock. Beyond, through a dark passage, they turned sharply into the glare of a small sitting-room. A lozenge of shining table-cloth seemed to fill most of the space; and over it dangled an enormous flimsy red lamp-shade, fringed with moth-eaten tassels, some of which, in twos and threes, were missing altogether. In a corner stood a disembowelled arm-chair, covered with a dirty tidy. Jim drove away the large white cat that was dozing there, and invited Oliver to sit down. Through the open door evidences reached him of a kitchen beyond, with the voices and aprons of two or three women moving about in it. Jim was everywhere, fetching bottles from the bar, and whispering to the kitchen maids, who tittered, or answered back in mock anger; then he would return to Oliver, setting down his prizes on the table with an air of mischief and exultation.

"Here you are. Minnie—that's Mrs. Bowler the landlady—is making some devilled eggs. She's a great hand at it; and there'll be a veal and ham pie with hot peas and potatoes, and then a gooseberry tart with custard, because the Sunday trippers have gobbled up all the cream with their strawberries. Piggish of them, wasn't it? But you won't mind. You're fed up in America with strawberries and ice-cream. And what will you have to drink? Not a whisky-and-soda? Not beer? I know, some shandy-gaff. You don't know what that is, but you'll see."

"Will the young gentleman have it bitter or moild?" asked Mrs. Bowler, who had now come in. She was a pretty woman, not much over thirty, tall and self-possessed. She seldom smiled, not from forgetfulness of her feminine vocation, but because she felt sure of her old friends and could stand on her dignity with strangers. She ruled over the private bar like a grand lady over her salon; while her husband or the maid served in the tap-room. But when the hour came for closing, that good man, who believed in doing to yourself as you did to others, was allowed to come into the bar and go to sleep on the lounge, where at that moment he was already snoring.

As Oliver wasn't sure what moild might be, he said "Bitter, please." Jim instantly approved, averring that shandy-gaff should be mixed with bitter, else it was too sweet.

Mrs. Bowler presently brought the amber beverage foaming in a glass mug, certainly pleasing to the eye, whatever it might prove to the palate; and as she closed the door behind her and sat down with her guests, a pleasant silence as if of old familiarity and mutual confidence fell upon the little party.

"So you are the master's son," the lady began, turning a pair of large inexpressive eyes upon Oliver, and slightly nodding her head, as if in far-reaching meditation. She was leaving the enjoyment of her savoury dish entirely to the young men, and sat a little apart, with her hands in her lap. "And an only child, I believe. Now you have all come home to England, I expect you won't want to go away again, will you? I hope Jim brought you over comfortably?"

When a feeling and a fact were present to Oliver at the same moment, his instinct was to describe the fact and leave the feeling unexpressed. It seemed the safer, simpler, less selfish procedure; and the consequence was that as he grew older his conversation became drier. On this occasion he felt how incredibly insular it was to suppose that England meant home for everybody. But he couldn't find words to say so politely. Better correct only Mrs. Bowler's misapprehension regarding the whereabouts of the yacht.

"We didn't come to England in the *Black Swan*. She's in the Mediterranean. I came in the *Kaiser Wilhelm*, and Jim and my father overland from Marseilles."

Now those large inexpressive eyes were turned steadily upon Jim. Why should he have lied to her? Why should he have let his fancy wander among bare possibilities, and babble of fine things that perhaps were never to be? Jim in fact seemed to have got rather red, but perhaps it was only the devilled eggs which were hot and highly spiced, or the whisky-and-soda, which was probably rather strong and throaty.

"Then nothing is settled yet, and you're going to sea again."

"Of course you're going to sea again. What would my father do without you?"

"No knowing what may not happen in a twelvemonth. We may all be dead." And Jim in uttering this oracle, appeared to press Mrs. Bowler's foot under the table.

"No knowing indeed," she sighed, taking the hint. "Even the youngest of us. But it's unearthly how some old people keep it up, without a sound organ in their bodies, as if they enjoyed mocking the doctor and keeping the sexton spade in hand, waiting by their open grave." Mrs. Bowler shuddered, and glanced in the direction of the bar, where her second husband was reposing. It happened to be also the direction of the churchyard where, a little further off, her first husband also reposed.

Conversation was now diverted obscurely to things and persons unknown to Oliver, and he had time to observe the little den they were sitting in. A velveteen curtain was drawn across the window and a vast velveteen lambrequin hung over the chimney piece, on which stood numerous vases and china figurines, various photographs in frames, two large sea-shells, and a weasel in a glass case. The walls were covered thick and high with sporting prints, some silhouettes of ancient dandies in high neckcloths and a curly lock of hair, and of ladies in feathered hats; also enlarged crayon drawings of defunct relatives, the men looking like cross-eyed Macedonian bandits, and the women like anaemic martyrs, also cross-eyed. In the centre, over the mantelpiece, hung a motto in black-letter, worked in worsteds, and reading: "God bless our Home."

Suddenly after a pause, Oliver heard Jim asking,

"How's Bobby?"

"Asleep upstairs."

"I'm going up to have a look at him."

Mrs. Bowler glanced at Oliver, as if considering what was to be done with *him*.

"Oliver won't mind," said Jim, standing up very straight, and pushing his chair in under the table, as if the seance here was finished and not to be renewed. "You can amuse yourself looking at these curios, or if it's got a bit close here, go and look at the lock by moonlight. It's quite romantic. Only don't fall in. It's the deepest lock in the Thames, and you might drown in it."

Up the stairs he leapt three steps at a time, and Mrs. Bowler followed meditatively, holding a candle.

The interest in those village nicknacks being already exhausted, there was nothing left but to explore the lock. Inn-yard and garden were deserted and somewhat spectral in the moonlight to his unaccustomed eye; but he found his way round to the river. The mill-stream was gliding swiftly under the arch of the paper-works, just below the inn, which looked large and forbidding like a fortress. Bales of rags or paper were heaped on the dock; and from beneath it the water rushed out into a great whirlpool. A long glittering reach of river opened out beyond, closed in the vague distance by the black trees of Nuneham Park and the black boathouse of Radley. It was a strange discomforting scene, with a damp chill in the air, like being at sea on land. Twice Oliver went back to the inn. No sign of life. At last he stretched himself in that lopsided old arm-chair, and closed his eyes. The door was open, and the light blazing under the red lamp-shade. There Jim would find him when he had done seeing Bobby.

Perhaps five minutes more elapsed, perhaps half an hour, before Jim's cheery voice roused him from his doze.

"Come on. We're late. Bobby woke up, and I couldn't leave before he went to sleep again, else there'd been a row. Mrs. Bowler asks me to say good-night for her. She'll have lunch ready for us to-morrow— I say, I've forgotten my watch," and Jim disappeared again up the dark flight of steps—now only two at a time. His voice and Mrs. Bowler's could be heard alternating at the head of the stairs, smoth-ered and brief, as if exchanging a few last words. At last the inn door closed behind the two young men, and was instantly bolted from within. The lady must have followed close behind them in the dark.

Once free of the bridge formed by the lock-gates, they got into their stride and cut across the fields where the towpath followed the loops of the river. Presently, as they slowed down to open and shut one of the gates, Jim stopped.

"After all you have seen and heard, I might as well let you into the secret. Minnie is my wife—not legally, because there's old Bowler; but she was my first flame and practically it's as if we were married. And Bobby's my son."

Luckily Oliver still had his hand on the closed gate and could steady himself. Jim's words were in his ear, but he was not thinking of them, nor of Mrs. Bowler or Bobby. No images. Only a sickening blank, as on that first afternoon in the yacht, when Jim had dived and seemed never to come up again. Yet there was a strange difference. Now Oliver was not waiting. There was nothing to look for, no future. Only the cold fact, like a grave stone, that Jim had gone under for good.

They had resumed their walk, and the dead man's voice continued speaking.

"You mustn't tell your father. He mightn't like it. Oddly enough—you can't imagine why—I think it might hurt his feelings. Old people never think of you except as you were when they first noticed you; they don't admit that you can change. Your father knows well enough I am no Galahad, and never was. He doesn't mind if now and then I spend a night ashore and keep mum about it. You can't talk to an elderly man about your love affairs; it wouldn't be proper. Besides, he likes to think that all this nonsense is of no importance to me really, but like a sort of dream, and that he holds the first place in my life. You see, he's grown rather fond of me: depends on the silly rot I talk to keep him in good humour. In fact, he took a fancy to me from the first. I was very young, and looked younger, yet I was a handy chap and could do my job smartly and seemed to enjoy life like a young porpoise or a little pagan tin god. That's what he used to tell me. And he wouldn't like to think that I had become something different, was a sort of family man, with a child four years old; and it would be even worse if I were regularly married."

Oliver as he listened began to understand better why he had felt such a shock a moment before. The shock was past. Everything seemed now natural, clear, desolately clear. Just what would have been expected by anyone who wasn't a fool.

"Of course I won't tell my father, and there couldn't be any harm in telling *me*."

"Good Lord," cried Jim, surprised at Oliver's tone, "you don't mean that you are too young to know? You can't say I'm leading you astray, giving you a bad example. I'm showing you the horrors of vice, the thorns in the rose of love, as ugly as fish-hooks and as long as harpoons."

"Then you don't care for Mrs. Bowler?"

"Care for her? She's an old friend, a good sort. I like her well enough. But think of my hard luck. My lines thrown here in Sandford Lock, a woman older than me, a poor woman, twice married, with all the old rakes of the county buzzing round her, and Bobby, who might be well enough in himself, impossible to call my own, or know what will become of him. It's a sad business. Old Bowler doesn't count, never counted. She says she has nothing to do with him, is true to her sailor lover, summer and winter. But that's a lie: she's a regular man-hunter, in her quiet way. She got hold of me when I was a mere lad, home on leave from the training-ship. It was my first affair. That was in the days of her original husband, who was the landlord and proprietor, and had married her for love—a jealous brute, always prowling about, and the opposite of poor Bowler in everything, except love of drink. He came to a sad end—not so sad, because he left her the place and now she has the licence in her own name. Drowned one fine summer night, very like this, nobody knew how, except that he was probably dead drunk already when he fell into the lock. Then, after a decent interval, she took on Bowler to cover appearances and have a man about the place; besides he had a tidy sum in the bank to recommend him. As for me, I've only turned up here at rare intervals, and with so many other men floating about, nobody suspects me particularly, except that Mater knows, and Bobby is getting to look so damned like me, that it's a bit awkward. But Minnie's a good girl, and fond of me—didn't she give us a nice supper?—and Bobby is perfectly legitimate, legally, only I'm ashamed to have given him Bowler for an official parent; it's a horrid fate for the poor kid. Sometimes I feel like pitching the old sot into the lock after his predecessor, marrying Minnie, and becoming lawful land-lord of the King's Arms. Not half bad, eh? Jolly job for one's old age."

"You might as well have married her when her first husband died," said Oliver bitterly. "You would have saved yourself the trouble of having to murder Bowler. Hard luck, I suppose. You weren't here. You were at sea."

"Not at all. I was here, very much here. But I was a blooming cadet on leave, expecting to be an admiral. A future admiral, at seventeen, can't marry a woman who keeps a public house. It isn't done. But now I should be rather in my element; also straightening things out for Bobby as my father did for me."

Oliver was silent.

"I'm telling you all my secrets," the other went on, "and those of my people. I suppose I may trust you."

"Oh, yes. You may trust me." And Oliver smiled to think how much safer, how infinitely safer, those unpleasant secrets would be in his heart than on Jim's loose tongue. Yet what but this vice of blabbing, this shamelessness, this indiscretion, had made Jim such a boon from the beginning, such a comfort, yes, and such an anchor of safety? Worst of all was to be deceived, to live in a fool's paradise, and not to dare look the truth in the face.

"Well, my poor Mater, you have seen what she is. She was a farmer's daughter in Islip; and when my father was a Bachelor at Keble, reading for Holy Orders, he used to walk a lot alone, with a Greek text in his pocket, about the woods at Wood Eaton; and one day there he came upon her by chance, also alone, and somehow, before they knew it, the irreparable had happened. They met again occasionally; and my father fervently considered, as you may imagine, what God and the angels would do in his place, and promised to marry her as soon as he had a living. But then I threatened to turn up at once. The wedding had to be hastened, and poor Pater had to confess everything to his superiors and got a bad name for life, and a wife that other clergymen's ladies wouldn't visit. It has been a beastly handicap. At first he had to go away to the North and teach in a board school; and it was ten years before he could take orders or get a decent living. Not that he would ever have become a bishop, even if he had married a duke's daughter; he's too religious; but by this time he might have been a dean somewhere, or head of a College. Floored by a humble marriage and the tell-tale date of my birth. Clerical gossip never could drop it: though officially I'm perfectly all right"—and here Jim parodied the tone of a parson reciting the funeral service—"I was sown illegitimate, but I was reaped legitimate. Could actually succeed to the damned family title if it came round to us; yet something of a bar sinister has always lain across my path. Never quite myself except with my mother, like your true bastard. We both feel that the world's against us. And that hideous sacrifice of Pater's, behaving as the angels would, quite wasted after all; because I was disgraced in a much worse way afterwards on my own account. No use kicking against the pricks. Better in the end Bobby should think he's Bowler's son. Then Minnie needn't talk like a wicked wife wishing her old husband would finish dying."

"Oh, I thought she meant my father."

"Your father? How should she mean your father?"

"Because she seemed to expect that you would be giving up the sea and settling in England. That would be when my father dies and the yacht is yours and you can sell her and have a little capital to start with."

Jim stopped short in his walk and faced his friend squarely. "Now by all that's holy, if you don't like me having the *Black Swan*, I'll sell her back to you for one dollar as the Doctor sold her to me. What am I to do with her—a constant ruinous expense even when she's not in commission, and nobody to buy her? I'd much rather the Doctor had made a will, leaving me a cash present, or a tidy little annuity. But he wouldn't: said he was pledged, and couldn't bequeath anything out of the family. Could only give me the yacht now and the collections in her—*they* will be easier to dispose of—and meantime bound me with a lease, renewable at his pleasure, simply for the amount of my salary; and he pays all the expenses, so that in effect everything works out just as it did before, so long as he lives. But for God's sake, Oliver, don't think I'm plotting to rob you of your money. I have something of my own in the bank, and am still young enough to make my way in the world. If luck went against me, I could always get a job as a working-man, I know what that means; or I could take a good long dive into the sea, and never come up again."

"Why go on like that, Jim? If my father left you half his money, or all of it, I should be delighted. I daresay he'd like to, only he can't—he doesn't dare—on account of Mother and other people. He told me about giving you the *Black Swan* because he has a feeling that he won't live long, and he couldn't leave you a legacy. He had made a will when he was married, and promised his wife not to alter it without her knowledge—of course leaving everything to her; and he hates making a will or making a row. But he has telegraphed to Boston for that will and has burned it up. The yacht is already yours, and I shall have two-thirds of his fortune when I am of age, instead of merely the allowance my mother might have given me. Not that I want it. I'm to be a clergyman or professor or something of that sort: I shall have much too much money. But he wants me to be independent: and one reason, I'm sure, is because he sees that I—that we are friends, and he knows I would look after you, if you were ever in trouble. And of course I will, no matter what happens."

Suddenly Jim took Oliver in his arms, with a great bear's hug, and positively kissed him. "You're an absolute angel, and no mistake. Pater saw it this afternoon, when he preached that sermon. He has second sight. The Doctor has always been a trump, and you go him one better."

IV

When they arrived at the parsonage there was still a light in the Vicar's study and the Vicar himself came to open the door. "You are late. It's past midnight. But don't make any excuses. I'm not going to bed yet, and you've been philosophising in the moonlight. Young friends are like lovers, except that they don't talk about love—a single and tiresome subject—but about everything under heaven, as if the world were just discovered and waiting to be conquered. Quite right. Your young dog must turn round and round and thoroughly tread down the spot where he's going to curl up. And how the old mind loves its comfortable old dog-basket! Good night. Sleep as late as you like in the morning. You see we have no breakfast—I mean no breakfast hour."

Jim led the way upstairs and into his room, talking and expecting Oliver to follow. But Oliver stopped at the door and said good night.

"Come in while I undress, and you can put out the light for me when I'm done. Can't reach it from this damned bed."

"Not to-night. I'm turning in."

"Not vexed? No ill-feeling?"

"No. Only sleepy. But please don't ever take me with you again when you are going after women."

Long and softly Jim whistled—expressly not loud enough to be heard across the thin partition. His fists were quick enough in self-defence, but when attacked intangibly his impulse was to cringe, to be artful and conciliatory. Loving flattery as he did, and living by favour, he hated to give offence. "What's wrong now?" he asked himself judicially as he turned off his own light and crept into bed. "We didn't go to Sandford after women but after food. It happens that food requires cooks, cooks require a mistress, the mistress requires love, and young men require pleasure. A chain of natural causes and no contrivance of mine. Probably it was Minnie's fault for eyeing him like that, under her eyelashes. No man's too young for her, no man's too old. She measures them with a glance. No, old gal, no use ogling and angling. Slippery young trout, you'll never land him. Then perhaps we kept him waiting too long: but with Minnie in that mood, how could I help it? I expect he smelt a rat, felt left out in the cold; yes, by Jove, he was envious. Old Adam waking up at last, my boy, and setting up the deuce of a howl? Congratulations. But by gad, you'll have to find your own way to the temple of Wenus. I'm no pander or court chamberlain to be arranging secret interviews for his Royal Highness. No need of warning me to keep off. Your virtuous chap may be lovely at home or singing in College Chapel; but the devil take me if in real sport I want a pal who's a coward. I know the sort. Your muff doesn't want to hunt in pairs; afraid you'll find out that he's bagged nothing. Nosing round a bit of old cheese for years, and never nibbling, until at last by chance, when he's thirty-seven years old, he makes a dab at it, and the trap snaps down and his neck's broken. That's what happened to the Doctor, and the son will be like the father—only worse, because he was born tired. Think what the Doctor might have done for me, if he'd not been married—" and Jim yawned, stretched himself luxuriously, and allowed his half-formed visions of what might have been to turn into dreams.

On the other side of the partition more troubled reflections were turning into dreams of less comfortable augury. Oliver was glad there was no door between the two rooms: he needed to be quite safely alone. The moonlight was enough to undress in; and the unfamiliar, inhuman aspect of everything, as in a cubist picture, seemed to relieve him of the horrid incubus of facts, and allow him to mock them, as it were, from a distance. Why should his heart ache at these absurd conjunctions of events, when his body was well, and nothing threatened his future? Hadn't he always felt that the human side of the universe was its evil side, that only the great non-human world—the stars, the sea, and the woods—could be truly self-justified and friendly to the mind? Ah, if he could only learn to look at human things inhumanly, mightn't they, too, become intelligible and inoffensive? This moonlight was a good medium, an unearthly medium, through which to view the earth. As he leaned, half undressed, out of his little dormer window—what a frail leaded casement it had, how old and ill-fitting and diminutive!—he could see the great masses of trees casting their black shadow over half the church tower—a square, low, battlemented tower that had stood for centuries on this riverside knoll, severe amid so much rural softness, warlike and emphatic amid the pleasant nullities of peace. He remembered that old line out of which Browning had made a poem: *Childe Roland to the dark tower came.* Wasn't there another knight called Oliver? What had become of him? Hadn't he died young? Perhaps that Sir Oliver too had been a spiritual man by nature, and unfit for this world, who could sing only what he felt and had no art in him. How soon the Vicar's words had been confirmed about Jim: altogether a bodily man, a fleshly man, caring only for food and women, money and a snug berth; not caring really for his own father, nor for Oliver's father, though affectionate enough externally—because Jim was affectionate—yet counting on the Doctor to die soon, so as to pocket his legacy; not caring even for the sea nor for the beautiful *Black Swan*, except as an asset; longing to sell her and never hear of her again, and go in for some dubious underhand speculation ashore. "He doesn't care," said Oliver to himself, gathering head in his unspoken eloquence, "for that horrible woman either; finds her a convenience, because she's a good cook, has a little money and needn't be paid; and she loves him in a loyal motherly way, as well as also in the other way desperately; and she needn't ever be made his legal wife, but will always be content with the crumbs of his affection—no, not crumbs, but dust and ashes. He *does* care perhaps a little for his mother and Rose and Bobby—because they're not yet in his way: they're his pals, in a sense, just as Mrs. Bowler is: but I'm not his pal. It never crosses his mind to care at all for *me*. I'm only somebody to talk to, a mirror to see himself reflected in to his advantage, a little brighter and better polished than the cabin boy, or the sailor on the watch, though perhaps not quite so appreciative, not quite so accommodating, as the new mate. Oh, he's delighted with me of course, and takes a lot of trouble to please me, as he does my father. What could be better than a sentimental rich friend to pour one's griefs into, one sure to hold his tongue and to supply money *ad libitum*? And what does it matter whether this invaluable friend is young or old, clever or ridiculous? Oh, I shall never lose Jim as a handy-man, as a hanger-on—Mother was right about him there after all—but *as a friend*? Can he ever be a *friend*? He's inclined to be honest and useful and faithful; he enjoys commanding the yacht brilliantly and being a good fellow. But that's only his professional duty—like being on duty in the navy—or his nights off with a convenient chum who will pay for the drinks. All the time, in his heart, he's thinking of something else. He's thinking of Minnie and Bobby. Yes, like a true Englishman he's thinking of home—'God bless our Home'! It may not be this Mrs. Bowler, it may not be this Bobby, but I can see him years hence, grown rather portly and bloated, walking to church on a Sunday morning with his wife and his little boy. And I can see myself pointing to him and saying 'There goes Mr. James Darnley. He was once Captain of my father's yacht, and I still send him a cheque at Christmas, as one does to some poor relation that one never sees. But Lord Jim died long ago.'"

When at last Oliver's head dropped on his pillow, his train of thought was not interrupted. It merely lapsed into a different key, became more rambling and uncontrolled, carrying more completely with it the helpless acquiescence of his whole mind. In a word, he stopped thinking and began dreaming. Tightly controlled and inhibited as he was in his waking hours by all sorts of critical judgments and moral anxieties, he had by nature an intuitive mind, unprejudiced, pure, and pervious to every ray. In sleep his fancy could become dramatic, proving how deep the seeds of his impressions had sunk, and in what a fertile soil.

So after the experiences of that evening, when his eyes closed, he again saw the light burning in the Vicar's window, and finding himself alone outside, furtively and in great trouble he crept up and knocked. He wondered why he wore this little black coat, much too short for him in the sleeves, and with only one button left to keep it together in front, when he had nothing on under it. It was strange he should be all in black, when his mother disapproved of mourning. And he sat in the study on the edge of a chair, dangling his black hat between his knees, and finding great difficulty in explaining that his father had died, and left everything to Jim, and would Mr. Darnley kindly take him for a choir boy, and let him write down his beautiful sermons in shorthand, because he had learned, as an extra, to write shorthand at school. But Mr. Darnley said he was so sorry, Oliver might have a good hand, but he would never do for the Church or for reporting sermons, because he could only write what he felt, and he might leave out an iota and the Vicar would be burned at the stake.

So, feeling very sad, Oliver walked by the river, and when he came to the King's Arms, it was a ramshackle little tavern, with only one room in the first storey, quite wind-blown in the midst of a black heath on the stage at Covent Garden. It was pitch dark, and there was tremendous thunder and lightning. Now he understood why he was dressed in black: he was playing the part of the unhappy lady disguised as a boy who knocks at the tavern door in the midst of the storm. So he knocked; and Mrs. Bowler, who was Maddalena, let him in most kindly, and took him to the bar. "Poor young gentleman," she murmured, "you are shivering all over. Let me give you a drop of something to warm your dear young heart. You can't sit down on the lounge, because it's occupied, but you may rest your head here on the cool zinc of the bar, and then it won't matter in the least how much you cry, because the tears will all drain off nicely through these little holes in the middle." And indeed the lounge was occupied, like the tables in the billiard-room, by something long and bulky wrapped up in a sheet; but Oliver wouldn't lay his head down on the zinc because it was covered with filthy smudges, like the lines of foam that a wave leaves on the beach when it recedes and gurgles; and he was made sick by the smell of stale beer. Besides, there was a wet shilling on top and how could he rest his head on a wet shilling?

"Good gracious," cried Mrs. Bowler, "who on earth left that shilling there?" And Jim, who was dressed up for the part of Sparafucile, said it must have been the Duke who came to make love to her. He had left it for a tip. "A tip to the landlady! What an insult!" Mrs. Bowler went on, "but we mayn't drop it into the cash-box, because Bowler has made up the accounts for the day, and it's after hours and the police would be down on us." So she pocketed the shilling and wiped the counter with her apron, and now Oliver had where to lay his head. He felt exactly as once when he had taken laughing-gas at the dentist's and could hear every word that was spoken, although the others said he was unconscious.

"They are both doped," said Mrs. Bowler, "and you can do it now. Take him and throw him into the lock as you did my first husband." But Jim scowled and blushed very red, and muttered: "I never threw him in. We had a scuffle on the towpath and he fell in because he was drunk." "Yes," she retorted, "and because you pushed him; and of course you couldn't jump in after him and save his life, because everybody knows you can't swim. But you might at least have thrown him the life-preserver that's hanging there useless for years, waiting for such an occasion; but you scooted across the fields as fast as you could run, hoping that nobody had seen you that night in Sandford. You might as well throw this other old chap in after him now. What ever else are we to do with the body?"

The lights went out and Jim, staggering, carried the great heavy sack to the edge of the Sandford Lock; but Oliver knew that it wasn't his father's body in the sack, but some one else, still alive. Now his father in person came out of the inn like Lazarus from the grave, in his black goggles and a white surplice, holding a prayer book in his hand. And behind him, whispering in his ear, stood a little man with black hair, partly bald, looking terribly displeased and threatening. And the Doctor asked where the dead man was that they had come to bury at sea. "Down at the bottom already," said the little angry man, who Oliver now knew was the engineer. "The Cap'n tipped him overboard in a devil of a hurry, with lead in his pockets." Then Oliver's father threw off the surplice and tossed the prayer-book into the water. "So much the better," he said. "Now I can go and sleep a little longer."

Mrs. Bowler and Jim were hiding in the wings and whispering, "We've made a mistake." Then Jim came forward stealthily and opened the sack, uncovered the face, and waited for the lightning. And when the flash came, it was Oliver. "Never mind," said Mrs. Bowler kindly. "What does it matter after all if we've bagged the son instead of the father? We've got the yacht anyhow." But Jim threw up his arms in despair with a great shout, only instead of saying "*La Maledizione*" he said, "Lost Oliver's money." "Don't be a fool," Mrs. Bowler cried, shaking him by the arm. "You silly ass, don't you know this is all an opera? Oliver isn't really poisoned. I put some bitter in his shandy-gaff because you said if it weren't mixed with bitter it would be too sweet. He's perfectly all right really, and will come to presently in order to sing that last lovely duet."

"Sing that duet?" said Jim scornfully. "It's a woman's part, and this is only a super, any pale-faced guttersnipe picked up in the street for sixpence, to be carried in the bag, because your prima donna objects to it and isn't usually as light as a feather. Anyhow in England and America, the Doctor says, that duet isn't sung, because after *La Donna è Mobile* the audience are all putting on their cloaks and anxious to get out and find their carriages."

Oliver struggled hard to lift his head and to beg them not to say these dreadful things, because he could hear them. But he was somehow prevented from stirring or uttering a syllable.

Now Bobby came running up in tears, holding the *Black Swan* upside down in his hand and blubbering that it was no good, he couldn't sail his boat in the lock; the place was full of dead men floating in sacks. "Nonsense," said Jim; "how could you see they were dead men if they were in sacks, and on this dark night too, without any moon? They must be bales that have fallen from the dock at the paper-mill, and have floated into the lock."

"Yes," Mrs. Bowler added very distinctly, "especially as heavy bales are sure to float up-stream." But Jim didn't hear this, as he was walking away very fast, saying a yacht was an expensive toy and he would never have given it to Bobby if he had been able to sell it and put the money in a gold-mine. Then Mrs. Bowler, more kindly than ever, came up to Oliver, took him by the hand, and asked him into her back-parlour. "When I saw that it was you, Mr. Oliver, in the bag, I was horrified. Such a trim young gentleman, and so generous and kind; indeed it was a shame. How could I make such a mistake? I had meant it to be only the Doctor; and to say the truth, if it had been Jim himself my heart wouldn't have been broken. He isn't as he once was when a sailor-lad of your age. It was only human to have a tender spot for him then, as I should have for you now, if you weren't so proud and so serious. May be you ain't used to women. It's natural in a young gentleman of your years to be a bit shy, and I'm sure it's becoming. But it can't last for ever, can it now?" And with that she kissed him. But he liked her kiss even less than he had liked Jim's. It was a false kiss, longer and nastier and harder to shake off. Jim at least had been spontaneous, had been carried away by honest joy, had hugged only Oliver's money, and pledged with a brotherly kiss the promise of never being disowned, but being helped out of any hole he might get into. But Mrs. Bowler's was the kiss of the serpent, pretending to love him, coiling herself about him in order to steal his money after sucking his blood. It was odious, it was loathsome, it was intolerable: and Oliver awoke. His eyes, after a moment, saw clearly where he was; he recognised the gable room to which Rose had led him. No storm, no melodrama, only bright moonlight shining in silently through the little dormer window. Yet the emotions of his dream persisted. All that mad tragedy was still going on behind the scenes; and perhaps in real life, as in the theatre, what went on behind the scenes was truer than the public spectacle.

V

The sun had climbed half way up to the zenith when Oliver looked out the next morning from his little leaded window. Rose was playing with her dog in the garden, and on the rustic bench directly under him the Vicar and Mrs. Darnley were sitting in front of a small breakfast-table. "Don't keep this tea standing any longer," said the Vicar's voice. "It will be poison. Make some fresh for the boys when they come down."

"We can't be serving two breakfasts and two luncheons and two dinners every day, because the fine gentlemen keep late hours," Mrs. Darnley's voice retorted. They spoke in low tones, but the wall served as a whispering gallery in the perfect silence of the garden-close. "Soon," the lady continued, "they'll be requiring separate breakfasts in their rooms, served on a silver salver, with hot-house fruit and a breast of cold pheasant in a bath of jelly. If they relish their bit of kidney floating in cold grease, or cooked to a cinder, they are welcome to it at any hour: contrariwise they must be satisfied with honest bread and butter, like the rest of the family. What rich men in yachts may feast upon, I don't know, but to be seasick on, I daresay salt herring is beyond compare, and the cause of some people coming so extraordinary thirsty ashore, as well as hungry."

Brought back by these sounds to the real world, and refreshed by a cold tub, Oliver was soon in the garden. "No thank you, Mrs. Darnley; I haven't a great appetite. Anything will do: a glass of milk if I may have it. We had a second grand supper last night in Sandford—a little surprise Jim had up his sleeve."

"More than one surprise, I expect," said the good lady, dropping her querulous tone for one of dull despondency. She liked Oliver for being abstemious, and almost forgave him for being rich. She sat down on the bench beside him as he was having his milk, uncovered the marmalade for him to help himself with his bread and butter, smoothed her black apron, and sighed.

"I hope you don't think ill of me, Mr. Oliver, for a shrewish tongue. A hard life sours an old woman, and the world was always against me."

"It's a shame you should have so many small worries," Oliver replied, feeling an unexplained sympathy with the old lady, "and I hope I'm not putting you to too much trouble. But you can't have any great troubles with the Vicar near you, and Jim and Rose. I should think the proudest lady might envy you your family."

"Ah, the little troubles, Mr. Oliver, they ruin a woman's life. It's the devil, I do believe, as sends us the toothache and the east wind and the tax on beer. As for your grand sorrows, they are a parcel of our common humanity, like funerals; and the Lord designs them for our good, to wean our hearts from this sad world. There's where the Vicar can comfort me, where I don't need comforting; and it's almost a pleasure to grieve, all hung in weeds, like a weeping willow. But the price of eggs, Mr. Oliver, the price of eggs!"

"I suppose it's because I've always had plenty of everything, but I should say: Why buy eggs? There's rice and potatoes. My father and Jim care about food; but I never know what I'm eating, certainly not when I'm with them. It's enough to listen to their talk, and with Jim it's enough to look at him. You should see him in command of the *Black Swan* in a stiff breeze. You'd be proud of him."

Oliver had made an effort to revert from his momentary feelings to general truths, and had hoped to please the old lady. He was disappointed in the result. Mrs. Darnley looked preoccupied and asked sadly:

"How much do you know about him?"

"I know a lot. I think he's told me everything. At least he's told me the worst."

"He's not leading you into evil courses?"

"Oh, no. He says he's warning me. But his ways aren't evil ways for him, because the Vicar says he's a bodily man, and has the bodily virtues. But for me all that side of life isn't very attractive. It's melancholy, if there's nothing more." As Mrs. Darnley seemed to receive this explanation quite coldly, Oliver tried a different line and added, "My father thinks the world of him. He said to me once that Jim had been the joy of his life."

"Once, eh?" she replied, continuing to look quite grave. "Not so much now?" Then, coming a little closer, and putting her dusty and rather ill-smelling head close to Oliver's, she whispered:

"Is your father leaving him any money?"

While considering what to reply, Oliver noticed that the hair over her temples was thin and faded, and quite different from the frowzy brown front, like Queen Alexandra's, which she wore on top.

"No: I don't think he's leaving Jim any money, exactly: yet Jim hasn't been forgotten. I can't explain just the arrangements that my father has made, because it's a family secret."

"But has he anything to gain by your father's death?"

"No. I should say he had everything to lose."

"Indeed he has, and it's what I tell him. But he was born under an evil star, Mr. Oliver, an evil star. Who of us would be in trouble, if we knew our own good?"

And Mrs. Darnley sighed a sigh of relief—relief at having seen the worst, and generalised it, and expressed it in words of wisdom. Philosophy thus honoured and dismissed, she turned again to Oliver.

"Now it does seem to me as you're looking a bit pale. I'm going to fry you a rasher of bacon, just a sliver. It won't be two minutes. We mustn't let your young blood run white on cold doughy bread-and-butter and blue milk. Such a sweet young gentleman too!" And she bustled into the kitchen.

Oliver ran after her to prevent her. He couldn't eat anything more. He only needed the fresh air; and there was Jim rattling down the stairs, and saying it was time to start on their excursion.

Jim punted, and Oliver with Rose at his side lay on the cushions facing him, while Topsy, her dog, squatting at the extreme bow sniffed the breeze, watched the water flow mysteriously under him, and seemed to lead the way and part the air like a figurehead. It was a pleasure to watch the firmness and precision of Jim's punting: not the least splash or superfluous effort, but always the timely sagacious thrust and easy recovery, though at times, in order to take full advantage of the current, he was obliged to plunge the pole almost up to his hand in the water, and to straighten himself quickly, like a steel spring uncoiled, for the next stroke. Very soon, helped by the stream, they had passed the railway bridge and the island, and were grazing against the garden bank at the King's Arms.

Oliver would never have recognised in this smiling spot the squalid scene of the night before, confused as that scene now was by the images of his dream. Here was a vivid lawn with rustic chairs and tables under a spreading tree, a garden-wall covered with roses, little arbours cut in the shrubbery and a hum of bees in the air. The inn too was transformed: a thick screen of ivy covered it, gaily broken by window-awnings, striped red and white; a flagstaff with a great ensign lazily flapping; a little toll bridge by the boat rollers; and lock-gates musically dripping and holding out their long antennae for the children to mount upon, as upon hobby-horses, or to help push, when the culminating moment came for opening or closing them. Certainly, when the lock was emptied, it looked rather deep, and its sides dank and slimy, and those wet chains were cold to the touch; but when the lower gates opened and the rift of light between them grew wider, a bright vast pool spread out beyond, branching into back-waters, and leading on to a broad straight reach of the river, flanked on one side by wooded slopes, and bordered on the other by the most beautiful meadows, through which a green path slightly meandered between great patches of buttercups and daisies. Larks were singing in the sky, and the very thumping of the paper-mill, now in operation, seemed to give forth a reassuring and jovial note, as if nature looked kindly on honest human industry, and could adopt it and interfuse it with her own labours. "No," thought Oliver, "there is nothing sinister here. It is only I that take things hard. I am shocked at human nature. I have been trained to disguise everything, to conceal everything, to find it intolerable that the truth should be what it can't help being. Why is human conscience so exacting, so impertinent? In nature, if things were let alone they would be perfect. No doubt they can't help interfering with one another and making a dreadful mess of it. But how lovely each natural thing would be, if it could only be true to itself!"

Jim had gone into the inn to order the luncheon—which it was agreed Oliver should pay for—and have it served in one of the little arbours. Oliver was making the punt fast to the bank, when he heard Rose expostulating: "Oh, Bobby, whatever is the matter? Your pinafore is wrong side out." And she was proceeding to remove and to readjust that protective upper garment upon the sturdy figure of a little boy, to whom pinafores were evidently a matter of lordly indifference, but who was alternately interested in an apple he held half-eaten in his hand, and in Topsy, a strange being that frightened him a little but attracted him very much. This conflict of interests soon had a sad end. The apple in the struggles with the pinafore rolled in the dog's direction, and Topsy picked it up, thinking it an offering of friendship; but finding it like so many offerings of friendship, not at all to his taste, he ran and dropped it under the hedge, in the black mud. Bobby, thus losing at one blow both his objects in life, began to cry, and having begun, and not knowing what else to do, went on crying louder and louder. A basket of fruit—very superior fruit—had been placed in the middle of the arbour table. Oliver seized a beautiful red and green apple and ran with it to Bobby. The howling dropped in pitch and in intensity, but there were still sobs and flowing tears. In fact, the new apple was too large for Bobby's hand, and he couldn't hold it safely. When he was taken on Oliver's knee, to be further comforted, it was observed that one of his legs was badly bruised and bleeding. Oliver was one of those boys who have full pockets: the depths of his loose clothes always enveloped a quantity of letters, cards, pencils, pens, string, knives, and photographs. From this store a fat pocket book was now extracted, which contained in miniature a surgeon's complete apparatus. Oliver had indeed been the doctor as well as captain of his football team, and nothing was more familiar to him than bruises and bandages. Bobby's wounds were accordingly instantly washed and disinfected and covered with a neat square of lint, crossed scientifically by pink strips of adhesive plaster: and the child, who had been vaguely suffering from an accumulation of forgotten griefs, felt a general relief, and seemed inclined to quietness. His flushed cheek was now laid against Oliver's flannel shirt, while his small hand still pressed the globe of the new apple, to insure possession, as of a mother's breast.

This domestic idyl caught Jim's eye on his reappearance. "Hello, has Bobby been making himself a nuisance? Come on. Things will be getting cold." And he asked the maid to take Bobby away.

"I don't want to go away," said Bobby sullenly, clinging to Oliver's coat. "I like you better than Madge and Mummie." A second tragedy might have ensued, but for Rose, who called Topsy and sent an orange rolling across the lawn for him and Bobby to run after. When the orange had got nice and soft, she said, Bobby might suck it.

Jim counted on showing Oliver his old school at Radley, and they strolled through the fields to St. Peter's College. There were old housemasters and matrons and college servants to be visited, and old familiar spots to be found curiously smaller than they used to be, and less significant. And a moment was to be spent in the chapel where Jim—who was not insensible to religion—had had his first mystic experiences; but the place now looked to him bare, commonplace, and crude. Meantime Rose and Oliver had ample leisure to sit on a stile and watch some of the boys playing cricket. These made a pretty picture, moving about the green field in their white flannels; but Oliver didn't altogether understand the tactics of the game, and the explanations which his companion offered only complicated the mystery. Soon their desultory talk turned to other matters.

"What a nice child that Bobby is," Oliver observed. "Do you see him often?"

"Only at the children's Church feasts at Littlemore. We all go there because at Christmas there's such a lovely tree, and a play on the Nativity, and nicer presents than at Iffley or Sandford. Of course Lady Gwendolen gives them."

"You don't ever see Bobby's mother?"

"Oh, no, indeed."

"Why not? Don't people like her?"

"She's the landlady at the inn."

"And aren't there any nice landladies?"

Rose was silent. Her young mind was categorical. When it came to argument or to generalities it stopped short. She didn't look for reasons or believe in them. Things simply were like that. If other people reasoned, she didn't mind. That was itself one of the dull facts that required no explanation and admitted none. She found she got on just as well without reasoning.

"But you like Bobby himself?"

"I might like him."

"How is that?"

"If I took him home and kept him clean, with his pinafore not inside out, nor his leg bleeding, I might like him then."

"I see," Oliver pursued becoming really interested. "His surroundings are bad but you think he has the makings of a nice boy."

"Yes. He is like Jim."

Oliver wondered what this might mean, and how her mind worked. It seemed birdlike in the precision of its instincts and the little jumps it gave this way and that. Yet the soul of this young girl seemed rather bovine in its perfect placidity. She expressed her most personal feelings as if she were reporting that to-day was Monday or that the horse had four legs.

"Do you mean he looks like Jim?"

"He doesn't look like Jim, because he's only four, and Jim is an old man."

Oliver laughed. "But Jim is a *young* man. If you call him old what would you call your father?"

She smiled a little, as if to acknowledge a hit, but added, quite unshaken in her opinion: "My father doesn't count."

"Well then, if Jim is an old man, whom would you call a young man?"

"*You* are a young man."

He laughed again, and felt an impulse to kiss her, but unfortunately he seldom followed his first impulses, and in thinking it over he let the occasion slip. Yet as questions didn't seem to embarrass her, he went on with his catechising.

"Why then is Bobby like Jim, if he doesn't look like him?"

"Because he isn't always nice. Sometimes he is, sometimes not."

"I see. A moral resemblance. But I'm sorry to hear you say that Jim isn't always nice. Surely, he's always nice to *you*."

"Oh, well. Perhaps he's always nice to me. But he isn't always nice really."

"How can you distinguish?"

"Of course I can. Topsy's always nice to me, does as I say, but he isn't a nice dog really. He's a mongrel."

"Dear me, I thought you loved Topsy. You're always playing with him."

"I like him better than nothing, but I ought to have a really nice dog, like Lion at Iffley Court. Topsy wags his tail at me, but he's ugly."

"I don't see, if somebody is always nice to you, like Jim, how you can find out that he's not altogether nice in himself."

"Anybody can see that."

"Of course nobody's perfect, if that's what you mean."

"Oh, yes. Some people are really nice always, nice inside."

"Your father, perhaps?"

"Yes, and you."

"Dear me. I'm afraid you're making a great mistake."

"I'm not making a mistake. You are good inside, just as Father is. You would like to be nice to everybody. But you don't know how." And she added, correcting herself, "Except to Bobby. You *do* know how to be nice to Bobby."

Oliver now was doubly sorry he hadn't kissed her, but this was hardly the moment in which to retrieve that error.

"Perhaps you're right, if it's only that I mean well."

"No. That's not all. Mother means well, and she's good to me. But she's all wrong really."

"What a dreadful thing to say! This is a worse mistake than the other. Your mother isn't all wrong."

"Yes. She ought to be all different, like Lady Gwendolen. Father is really better than Mother, although he can't make a decent cup of tea, and he's really better than Jim, although he can't put on his tie straight, and I have to do it for him."

"So you know how to do things nicely, just as Jim does."

"Yes."

"And are you all good or all bad really, or mixed like him?"

"I'm not mixed. Still, I'm not all good nor all bad. I'm nothing."

"You mean that you are indifferent, that you don't care?"

"Yes."

"And if you tied my tie for me and taught me how to do everything, wouldn't that help me out of simply meaning well, and wouldn't it help you to care for something and to be really good, as your father is?"

"Perhaps. But I don't believe I can change."

"Say that you and I were married. How would that do?"

"I don't know."

"Would you *like* to marry me?"

"Oh, yes."

"All right. It's agreed. We're going to be married as soon as I am an old man and you are a young woman. And as we're engaged I think I may kiss you."

"Of course."

"And now let's run and tell Jim we are going to be married. How pleased he will be."

"He won't be pleased. He won't believe it, and Father and Mother won't believe it. You'd better not tell anybody, because you don't believe it yourself."

Oliver laughed and kissed her again. It was much easier to keep the kissing up than to make a beginning. He said this would be a lovely secret, and if it seemed almost too good, and they couldn't quite believe it now, they would prove it some day and be happy ever after.

VI

On the way back to Iffley Oliver took his first lesson in punting, standing at the bow; he was soon proficient enough to take charge alone at the stern, and manage the steering as well as the shoving. His body was a sensitive instrument and his mind traced readily all the analogies of physical motion. The mechanical novelties of the case were soon mastered; but it was much later, if ever, that he began to feel the charm of this placid form of locomotion, or of floating idleness. A punt is a clumsy craft, yet curiously sensitive and lightly gliding—a gondola become foursquare, broadly based and homelike, with some rudiments of a houseboat. Houseboats and punts and gondolas could never be congenial to Oliver's temperament; they seemed dead ships, dismasted, inert, fit only for backwaters; he missed in them that adventurous force, that steady defiance of the elements, which made the glory of sailing and boating. Nevertheless this new exercise, like all bodily action, restored peace and balance to his mind. Thought is never sure of its contacts with reality; action must intervene to render the rhetoric of thought harmless and its emotions sane. As Oliver punted, he felt the distress and suspicions of the previous night receding like a tempest. A sort of luxurious convalescence mounted through his veins, and he recovered the smile of intelligence. Certainly those discoveries retained their sinister suggestion—more sinister and unsavoury the further they were probed. But what of it? The darker and more entangled the world turned out to be, the freer and clearer the spirit became that was able to dominate it. And could all the mysteries and miseries of the universe take the freshness away from that air, those fields, the song of those larks, or those loves of children? Oliver remembered his first night in the *Black Swan*, when this same Jim Darnley had revealed to him other sinister secrets; and strangely enough, after the first shock, far from upsetting him, that intelligence had relieved him of a terrible incubus. He had awakened from a false and ghastly calm, had begun to live intelligently, with a sense of power and with sound self-knowledge. So it might be again now.

Those dull grey clouds that had always cloaked his sky, in gathering now more thickly and becoming blacker, would prove their mutability. Between them he could already see patches of the blue beyond. Before he had learned the truth about his father, he had never cared for him, but on learning it, unpleasant as that truth was, he had begun to care; instead of feeling ashamed, he had felt awakened, stimulated, initiated, and called to exert his own will. Yes, and on that same night, by his tone of complete comradeship, by his utterly frank and unabashed confessions, what a blessed revolution Jim had provoked in him, laying the foundations for such sympathy and friendship as he had never known before, and at the same time illuminating and pacifying his poor childish ignorant conscience. Now Jim had confessed or half confessed other things, rather shady, rather steep things, which Oliver had hated to hear; and perhaps the worst remained unconfessed, and would come in the future. Well, these fresh discoveries might make him suffer, as he suffered already at the shabby side of his friend's character; as he had suffered at that dubious supper—had Jim paid for it, or Mrs. Bowler?—and at being basely kept waiting for such a purpose. Jim, who in so many ways behaved almost like a servant—getting tickets, looking after luggage, posting letters, calling cabs, and relieving him and his father of petty cares—had acted on that occasion like a man hoodwinking a boy. It was ignominious; and, yet far from being alienated, the virtuous and proud Oliver was only the more painfully attached, the more inextricably bound. He would be dreadfully sorry if his misguided friend got into some mess from which there was no issue; but that was no reason for giving him up; on the contrary. If people could know everything, absolutely everything, about one another, would they love one another more or less? More, Oliver thought; and that was why life was so uncomfortable and hateful in a world where everybody was hiding his conduct and his true feelings from everybody else. Mr. Darnley, being a clergyman, might put it on the ground that nobody loves us more than God does, who yet knows absolutely all our faults. This didn't mean that our faults were not faults; or that God doesn't punish them, and send us to hell for them—which of course was only a figurative way of saying that they brought hell with them into our lives. If we knew everything about one another we should probably be very much sadder, very much more terrified and desolated; we should see how little the people who loved us understood us, and how much the people we loved despised us. Yet we should be reconciled even to all this wasted affection and this hostility at cross purposes. We should love and forgive everybody as we love and forgive ourselves; because we should then understand the irresistible bent of all sorts of creatures, even when this bent was fatal to them or to ourselves.

Thus our young moralist tried to soothe his wounded conscience with the balm of pantheism, and to gild the shady side of human life in the sunshine of nature. Yet his conscience at that very moment was taking a cruel revenge. Jim could not be disowned, though he were a millstone round one's neck. He must be helped, tolerated, forgiven to the bitter end; and in this way that ardent friendship, which had seemed an escape from moral slavery, a door open to infinite happiness, had itself become yet another commitment, yet another anxious and sorrowful duty. Where was that infinite liberty now? Where was that young fearless experienced masterful guide? Vanished: proved to have been illusions.

"Odd," said Peter Alden to himself, "that the boys should have tired so soon of Oxford. I know it's the long vacation. The place is full of foreigners and trippers and forlorn pedagogues, male and especially female, who assemble and meet together to peer into the darkness of each other's minds. Yet I thought Jim, with money in his pocket, would enjoy swaggering about the Mitre Hotel, coaching to Woodstock, punting in the Cher, rowing in the Isis, and cultivating his higher self by sitting, on rainy afternoons, in the choir of the cathedral, when the anthem swells and the shades of evening mitigate the modern glass. But no. He was all impatience to return to Marseilles and inspect the yacht, safely docked as she is and safely looked after. I daresay it's the zest of his new proprietorship. He fears rats will get into the hold if he's not there to stamp on the deck and peep into the cabin. Poor dear Jim. I have always liked him for his weaknesses—they were such a bond—as much as for his virtues, and he has plenty of both. . . . I see how Oliver might be bored in Oxford. He can't reach the inside of anything from the outside. Magdalen tower or Peckwater Quad or the garden front of St. John's means no more to him than a picture postcard. He took to the yacht at once, because he sailed in her; he took to Lord Jim because Jim unbosomed himself and irresistibly captured sympathy for all his little troubles and pleasures. Oliver needs to penetrate first into the inner life of a thing, by a moral participation; and then perhaps the outer form may acquire a meaning for him. In Oxford in term-time, living within a college, he might begin to understand. Jim is no guide to those delicate affections; he hasn't a cultivated mind; knows nothing of devout learning or collegiate manners; admires only the barges and the blazers and the Bullingdon Club. I might have gone down to Oxford myself, and tried to give the boy some hints: but after all, is it so important that he should understand? Is it even worth while and for his ultimate good? Perhaps the kindest provision of nature, when she abolishes something—and she is always silently abolishing everything—is to abolish the memory of it at the same time, or very soon afterwards. Otherwise life would be nothing but what it is for my brother Nathaniel, a succession of funerals. Look at England. England is always dying gently, cheerfully, the executioner succeeding to the government. Catholic England—the England that was a part of Europe—died at the Reformation. Romantic England died with the Stuarts. Commercial, naval, Protestant England died the other day with Queen Victoria. Yet something survives—something inferior but for the moment capable of existing. We may now have another England that is a part of America. Why drag the weight of those vain affections? Let the dead bury their dead."

These sentiments made Peter the more melancholy the more he convinced himself that they were rational; and his impulse as he revolved them, with young Oliver on his hands in London, was to do the opposite to what they suggested, to be languidly irrational, and to make a last attempt to let his son feel the charm of England—of the England that was about to disappear. Would he look up some old friend and ask to be asked to some great house in the country? That would be too much trouble; he wouldn't himself enjoy the visit, and he might even not get the invitation. Cathedrals and Scotland and places open to visitors would be as ineffective as Oxford had proved. Oliver was too exacting for a tourist. Yet if colleges were empty early in July, schools were still going full tilt. Wasn't Harold Van de Weyer's little boy, Mario, now at Eton? Happy thought. They could go down for the day without giving up their lodgings in Jermyn Street, and Oliver would experience the sensation of having a foreign cousin and peeping into an English public school.

A self-possessed young gentleman, still a little chubby and only just fledged into a tailcoat, was waiting for them, a day or two later, at the station in Windsor. He stood observant but perfectly calm, as if there were infinite time for everything to come round as it chose. If his American relations turned up, well, there they were, and one must do the honours; if they didn't turn up, what of it? His top hat, slightly ruffled, was tilted at a comfortably rakish angle rather on the back of his head, his hands deep in his trousers pockets, his fresh lips pleasantly parted, and his sensitive nose high in the air. He surveyed the movement on the platform as if it didn't exist, and there were nothing there but a carpet spread for the scene in which he was about to take part. Accident might play whatever card it chose, he was there to trump it. If the clarion of doom had suddenly sounded, he wouldn't have blinked, but quietly drawn his hands out of his pockets, removed his hat, and said: "Hello. Here's the Day of Judgment, so often announced, really come round at last. It's likely to be an uncommonly big show. How perfectly ripping. And what a delicious sell for those little bounders who were so busy reforming the world, just when it was going to be blown to atoms. Here's the good Lord coming in a cloud and saying: 'Don't trouble. I've decided to close down the whole establishment, and I'm going to pay you off your exact wages.' Wouldn't they be sick! Not me: I haven't ever done anything in particular but run about like a pet animal, wagging my tail and sniffing at corners; and it's of no importance to anybody whether I turn out to be a beastly little goat or a lovely little lamb."

If less momentous, the event actually set down for that showery day, was not less gallantly challenged; and without a moment's hesitation the right travellers were recognised and accosted as they alighted. Swiftly, but without flurry, the youthful figure advanced, a short body on long legs, slightly raised his hat and said with an inquisitive smile, "Uncle Peter?" and then, putting on his hat again and smiling more broadly added, "And Oliver. I'm Vanny—I mean, Mario: it's so silly having two names and two languages. How do you do? Your train's a bit late, else I might have missed you. Had some trouble in getting leave for the afternoon: Grand uncle from America: virtual guardian: highly distinguished, et cetera. Awfully kind of you to ask me to lunch. The White Hart is just at the corner. If you like we might have lunch first and see everything afterwards; and then, if you don't mind an early tea, I hope you will come and have it in my room. It's rather a hole, but Mr. Rawdon-Smith, my housemaster, says he's sorry but he has a meeting in his study at five, and can't ask you to tea himself. He'll try to look in earlier and make your acquaintance, and tell you what a good boy I am. I am really, you know, considering my origin. You see I'm half Italian and half American, and I ought to be half a Neapolitan beggar-boy on a doorstep picking fleas from his rags, and half a cowboy spitting tobacco: and I tell Mr. Rawdon-Smith he can't expect me to be as good as if I were a pure Nordic and true blue Briton. But then why was I booked for Eton at all? I'm blest if I know."

The boy was so exquisitely dressed, so merry, so unconcerned about everything, so innocently sparkling that to Oliver he hardly seemed human at all: more like some Chinese figurine, all ivory and silk, that should suddenly have come to life, begun to dance, to quote the poets, and to laugh at everything in this ridiculous real world.

"Sending you to Eton," Peter replied, "was your father's doing. His heart was set on it; you should be brought up like an English gentleman. He made your mother promise, in spite of religion, and your grandmother in spite of expense; and he mobilised his whole English acquaintance to render the thing possible. And it wasn't easy. Naturally they don't want outsiders."

"That's half the fun of it," Mario chirped with a just perceptible smile. "It's lovely seeing them wince. I read up my history-lesson in some French book and then tell the Master that what our book says is only the British view, and disproved. It annoys him a bit. And they're horribly nervous because I'm a Catholic, though I don't breathe a word about it. They prefer Jews. You see they can't *turn* Jews: but they know that if only they opened their eyes, they'd have to become Catholics—I mean, those of them who are believers at all."

"Yes," Peter chuckled, "and then where would the English gentleman be? Gone up the spout like the Cavaliers. Your English gentleman must be deeply reverent and must never profane his religion by fussing about it. Yet it's no idle possession. It insures him against ever liking the things he doesn't like."

"As if he didn't like spinach," Mario interjected, bubbling over with quiet laughter.

"Quite so; and the spinach in this case is the pope.—But how do you get on with your studies."

"Oh, Latin's nothing, only old Italian—if they would pronounce it decently—and putting verses together is like a puzzle, rather entertaining; and of course, I don't need to do French. But Greek is a bore, also mathematics, and I'm rotten at it. The other day I said σίδερος was a star. That was a crisp one: they thought I was ragging and I was swished for it. After all what counts here is sports. Of course, I'm a wet-bob. It's more painful than cricket, when you're pulling a race; but it's jollier most of the time, not so idiotic. You're not particularly playing against anybody. You're enjoying yourself: and there's always something lovely in moving through the water."

"That's what Oliver and I think. He likes nothing better than sculling, when he's free; but he has been playing football for the sake of his school. Last year he was their Captain."

"Oh, really," the young Etonian murmured, looking at his transatlantic cousin with new eyes. "Of course he *would* be, but how splendid.—We have to play footer too in the winter half—that's in the autumn. Nasty work: just a muddy scramble for most of us, like little boys at a private school; but it's soon past—the year at Eton has three halves, besides holidays—and I try to forget about it. In the Lent half one isn't so prodded; there's running and fives. Fives I don't half mind—almost court tennis, isn't it?—and this year when I drew Engleford for a partner, who is a friend of mine and wonderful at it, I took such enormous pains that I just didn't make him lose the cup. Of course, I should love riding and fencing; may do a little fencing next year; but beagling here is beyond me—takes a lot of oof. Still, I ride and fence in the holidays when I'm *chez ma mère* in Paris."

All this was addressed ostensibly to Uncle Peter, who listened and smiled benevolently; it rippled out with an accent and idioms new to Oliver, which seemed to him a sort of beautiful bird-language. He could not understand how a boy not nearly his own age, in fact almost two years younger, could keep up this flow of conversation with an elderly relative, so equably and spontaneously, with this quiet slight smile of polite deference. The boys he knew never addressed their elders except to ask for something, or mutter a complaint. They were capable only of gabbling and fooling among themselves, inciting or jeering at one another; and if by a rare chance they were walking with their parents, they didn't lead the way in this fashion or move sympathetically in company, but trudged along silently, bent on their own thoughts, as if they were dogs in leash. The gaiety, the merriment of this mellifluous youth, laughing at his own troubles and at all the world, were quite beyond human nature, as Oliver had experienced it: something like a young prince in the *Arabian Nights*, counting as many years as the full moon days, and breathing his irrepressible sentiments in the words of poets: or like the *Cherubino* of Mademoiselle Favart at the opera, panting with suppressed life beneath a demure exterior. Yet nothing could be more manly, and even rakish, than this voluble stripling. If instead of his topper and tails and immaculately fresh white tie, he had worn lace ruffles and a cascade of blond curls, the armour of perfect courage could not have glistened more visibly on his breast, or the sword-hilt in his hand. If the boy seemed to Oliver fantastic and over-elaborate, he also seemed somehow alarming and strangely formidable. The bonbon might be charged with dynamite.

Although Vanny had not addressed a word to his cousin directly, he had not ignored him. Out of the corner of his eye, or in an occasional glance, he was observing his points. Mario knew he was producing an effect and liked to produce it. He was defiantly vain, not with the common vanity of looks and clothes, which he took for granted, but with the excitement of power. A duel had commenced. Each of the boys, in his own temperature, was feeling the presence and the mind of the other. Oliver, who all this time hadn't put in a word, felt passive and dull and somehow out in the cold. How could his father and this young manikin keep up such a stream of talk, a sort of verbal court tennis, as if they had known each other all their lives, and were of the same age? And why was Oliver himself made to feel inferior, when his pride assured him that this inferiority touched only trifles and false accomplishments, which were really faults? In every matter of consequence his own ways were superior and right. He remembered his mother once saying what a mistake the Van de Weyers were making in bringing up that young Mario like a foreigner. He would never be fit for anything either at home or abroad. Yet at the same time Oliver asked himself: "I wonder what *I* shall be fit for? Here is this penniless orphan apparently riding the very crest of the waves, while I toss about heavily like an old hulk in the trough." Yet Oliver had every advantage on his side: age, money, athletic prowess, solid education, tried character, the will to do right. Yes, perhaps if he could see himself in a truthful mirror, he might even appear to be handsomer, taller, stronger, with a franker and sweeter smile. But what was the use? Here this slip of a Mario came down upon him like a ray of sunlight, like one of those beautifully dressed Gabriels in the old masters, a young page from a heavenly court, upborne on his rainbow wings and scarcely touching the ground, as he gallantly bent one knee, and delivered his diplomatic message with exquisite elegance and a mere suspicion of mischief in his eye: or like some Bacchus leaping from his chariot in pursuit of Ariadne, amid satyrs and leopards fawning at his heels, as if he had borrowed the magic arts of Orpheus to charm them; whereas Oliver himself stood pale and tongue-tied, stolid and correct like an academic Saint Sebastian, a dull model of the studio, bound hand and foot and unaccountably become a target for a thousand arrows.

Vanny meantime was mentally taking notes: "Remarkably good-looking. Big but sensitive. For an American quite civilised. Silent, probably intelligent. I think he'll do."

VII

At luncheon Vanny made himself useful interpreting the wants of his hosts to the waiter, suggesting lemon squashes for himself and Oliver, yet not refusing a glass or two of his uncle's sparkling hock. He conveyed much miscellaneous information about the School, the Court, and the Castle, and listened appreciatively to his uncle's jokes, murmuring, "How stupid of me," when the point had to be explained to him. He managed to make even this obtuseness agreeable, laying it to the misfortune of never having lived in God's own country; and it was a double pleasure to Peter to be called upon sometimes to explain his wit, and be suffered to relish again all the hidden twists of it. Indeed the absurdity of things is woven into them so inexhaustibly, that we never tire of the drollery we have once really perceived. Toward the end, however, Peter grew silent, and coughed repeatedly; finally he went out for a moment and returned looking rather pale. It was a cool showery day, with floods of sunshine slanting here and there through the rolling masses of cloud. He had caught a chill he said; and would have a fire lighted in a private room and stay quiet, while Mario showed his cousin the sights.

The boys strode out into Castle Hill, and the cicerone at once began his explanations.

"This is Henry the Third's tower, and genuine, but the big round tower is a sham, all hollow inside and without a roof. Built by George the Third to improve the prospect of the Castle from the Copper Horse, as he was to sit there and gaze upon it till doomsday."

This badinage fell flat and it was now Vanny's turn to explain his playful allusions. Besides, one tower was evidently very like another in Oliver's eyes. Vanny tactfully desisted from further architectural comments and led his cousin directly into the Park.

"Of course you don't know what the Copper Horse is; how should you? Queen Victoria didn't. 'What is that?' she inquired once, when somebody happened to mention it. 'The statue Mum, at the end of the Long Walk.' 'Not at all. That is not a copper horse. That is the statue of my Grandfather.' There you can see it now: that grey speck on the horizon between the trees. As it's King George the Third, and he's prancing there in effigy and viewing his own hollow work with hauteur and apparent satisfaction, I say he built the tower on purpose to be an object of posthumous contemplation by himself from his monument. Silly ass, you'll say—myself, I mean, not George the Third. And so I am; but I have to amuse myself somehow."

"You don't like your School?"

"Eton is Eton. We don't have to consider particularly whether we like it or not. I suppose it's better than other schools. It's certainly better than the Æsculapians I went to at Brussels when I was a small boy. We were such sneaks there, walking out two by two in uniform, and we had such nasty tricks, you can't imagine. Of course Eton is a populous school. One can be lost in it. All depends on the House you're in. A lower boy is apt to have a horrid life of it, if he's a sensitive chap, and can't swim with the tide. I didn't mind. It was all so ridiculous. You get some hard knocks, but it's glorious, sometimes, in other ways. I was lucky in my fagmaster. Had to look alive, and go half the time without my breakfast. But I was protected. He was a frightful blood, and I learned what's what. And this Half, when I'm in Fifth Form, the way is clear. You may be shoved into a corner and forgotten, but you may do very much as you please. M'Tutor, too, is priceless. A bit sullen, because I'm rotten in Greek, except that I've learned all Sappho and Anacreon by heart for him; but he loves my Latin verses—I get them out of old Italian books. Sometimes my quantities are false—that's horrible for the poor man—but otherwise he says they have the cachet of the Renaissance; and we cap Latin verses to one another like an eclogue. It's great sport. But you mustn't judge Eton by me. I'm a sort of pariah here, and I have to make it up to myself by laughing at them. Of course, I'm ridiculous too; but isn't everybody ridiculous? The difference is that some people see they are ridiculous and some don't. They're rather disturbed about me here, and are considering the propriety of writing to my mother that I'd better pursue my studies elsewhere."

"But why?"

"I am an evil influence. I explain to the boys what love really is, and though it interests the boys tremendously, it shocks Mr. Rawdon-Smith, who is a bachelor."

Oliver looked at Mario rather steadily and said: "And *what is love really?*"

Suddenly the youngster was abashed. For the first time he felt younger than his cousin. He felt cheap. But the Æsculapians at least had taught him how one may always recover one's moral balance by confession, by self-knowledge, by changing into the key of humility; and he broke out: "I'm sorry. I was talking rot."

Oliver could see that he had blushed very red, and that his eyelashes trembled. But the surprising thing was that instead of being alienated, or feeling rebuffed, he presently seized Oliver's arm, and pulled him away from the direction of the Castle entrance, towards which they had turned back.

"I say, you don't really want to see St. George's Chapel or the State Apartments, do you? If you don't, there's no reason why you should. We can walk to the Copper Horse instead, if you'd rather."

"I suppose I ought to see all those things," said Oliver, reverting from his impulsive to his scrupulous conscience, "but I do need a little exercise, and I do like trees better than buildings."

"All Americans do, only they won't say so. It's natural, because at home you live in the forest primeval—I mean, when you're not shooting up an express elevator to the thirty-ninth storey."

In saying this, Vanny clung tighter to Oliver's arm, to make it clear that if he laughed at Americans in general, because he laughed at everything, he would have liked Oliver to laugh at everything with him.

"I sometimes wish we did live in the real country, instead of at Great Falls. There seems to be more country life in England, even here close to London, than in America. All this may be artificial, but how green and spacious it is, and how quiet! I suppose when things are so quiet they must be comparatively dead."

"Some of these old trees are, anyhow—the whole place is going to pot, like our playing fields. You've come just in time to catch a glimpse of them before the end. I suppose everything old is bound to die sooner or later, yet sometimes things with a long past have all the more kick in them. At least it's so with unpaid bills."

As they walked on talking, Oliver began to feel a speculative distance, a veil of pastness, separating his inner man from his own words. His words were uttered only by his body. They were an echo of his mother, of Irma, of Letitia Lamb. Whenever he spoke, they seemed to him to be speaking in him, while a new self, or rather an eternal self newly awakened, seemed to be listening. What? Were these trees dead? Even those half hollowed out, like Egyptian sarcophagi, were still thick and green and prolific in their gaunt branches. Were these deer dead, watching him with gleaming eyes? Were these children dead, so fresh and smart and soft-spoken, driving by in their pony-cart, as in a basket of flowers? Or was Mario dead, comparatively dead? Why, there was more life in his little finger than in Oliver's whole body. He was all sparks of fire, all shifts of quick feeling and brilliant light. How dull in comparison, how soggy, tired, sleepy, vague, heavy, ignorant, and uncouth, Oliver felt himself to be!

Peter Alden, after resting and warming himself for two hours, dreaded the walk down Castle Hill and the whole length of the High Street; yet he disliked to disappoint his nephew and to have made this whole excursion, officially, for nothing. He would slyly fortify himself with a little medicine, and drive down in a fly. Vanny apologised for his room being rather in a mess. Indeed, a round tub, still wet, was standing against the wall by a mock wardrobe, absurdly narrow and tall, which was evidently the bed. A blazer and cap and an old pair of gloves had to be removed from the old arm-chair to accommodate the elderly visitor. The boys squatted on a pile of books. He was lucky with his books, Vanny explained, because having nothing to do with lessons, and being generally in French or Italian, nobody bagged them. He didn't need to hide anything but his cribs and his dictionaries.

"Not a very cheerful prospect," Peter remarked, peering through the open top of the window up what seemed a sort of well, surmounted by nondescript chimney-pots and attic windows.

"Beastly hole," Vanny admitted, "but then as it's dark all day, one never looks out of the window,—What's the odds?"

The tea-things, however, when set down on a wooden box covered with a table-cloth, proved to be irreproachable. There was a small silver service, brilliantly clean, and charmingly reflecting the dancing lights of the two candles. The china was pretty, if not costly, and there was a festive cake and a plateful of small sandwiches. Oliver, at home, was master of a spacious bedroom and sunny sleeping-porch, a complete bathroom, and a study walled round with bookshelves— there was nobody to steal the books—and furnished with writing tables and Persian rugs and deep leather chairs; and he still used as a gymnasium the vast work-and-play room of his childhood under the house rafters. Yet with all this space and luxury, he never could have had anyone to tea, or received visitors elsewhere than in the common parlour downstairs; and as for having anything served in his rooms, if he had wanted so much as a glass of water, he would have had to go down to the dining-room and help himself to it out of the monumental ice-water urn, always standing there coated with vapour and freezing to the touch. This dingy little room, by comparison, seemed to him princely. Here were feasts, here was freedom, openness, laughter, lordliness, simplicity. There were no closets, and no skeletons in them. Guests were welcomed without fuss and without shame and entertained nobly, with whatever you had to give them.

Presently Mr. Rawdon-Smith put in an appearance: a tall large-boned man—he had been a Varsity oar at Cambridge—with thick close cropped grey hair, a tightly drawn mouth, and one shoulder much higher than the other. His white tie was askew, and threatening to come undone, and his hands very large and red, were dirty in places. He said Hm! to the visitors, shook hands limply, without looking at them, and made room for himself on the narrow window-seat, with a sweep of the arm, which this time sent the blazer, the cap, and the old gloves to the floor. Then he protruded his nose over the tea things and said:

"I hope you have some plain bread and butter. I can't eat your indigestible shop cake, or your sticky sandwiches—Three lumps please, or four perhaps. They look rather small.—And you, Sir, I understand, are Vanny's guardian?"

"Oh no," Peter replied placidly, expressing by a tone of amiable frankness that secret amusement which he was feeling at the bad manners of this fashionable pedagogue. Why was it, that under priests and pedants, who themselves often had no breeding or knowledge of the world, the rising generation seemed to acquire a maximum of those very qualities? Was it because the boys had to practise deference and dissimulation towards persons whom they despised? Or was it because, beneath the most outrageous professional crotchets, they discovered the presence of firm traditions and beautiful pieties? Or was it rather that boys, under an irrelevant clerical tyranny, might manage to educate one another, and even some of the masters, establishing exact sporting standards for their free lives, and learning to pursue only a few chosen beautiful things, and to endure and despise all else that might ensue? Surely this last was the predominant principle at Eton. The young barbarians were at play not only in the playing fields, but (through the unwitting connivance of their masters) in School and Chapel also; for what was all this lovely faded religion and lovely faded learning, but play of imagination? To sport and to play: to trust, maintain, and refine the inspirations of the heart—what else was the principle of honour, of that aristocratic liberty, fidelity, and courage which made the gentleman?

All this simmered in Peter's brain, while his lips continued politely to address Mr. Rawdon-Smith. "Mario's natural and legal guardian is of course his mother; but his grandmother who is my sister, has undertaken to pay for his education. His grandmother wishes to know how he is doing at Eton, and it is in her behalf that I come to see him, as well as for my pleasure."

"Then strictly," said Mr. Rawdon-Smith, finishing his first cup of tea and asking for the second, "strictly you are not Vanny's guardian at all."

"No."

"And am I to understand that his grandmother, who appears to exercise decisive authority over him, is your sister?"

"Yes."

"Then strictly," Mr. Rawdon-Smith went on, pursing his lips and turning to Mario, who was showing Oliver the *burry*, or hanging cupboard, in which he kept his tea-things and other treasures, "strictly this gentleman, whom you described to me as your uncle and guardian, is not your guardian, and is not even your uncle."

"No, sir; but I said *practically*; and he is my grand-uncle, which is grander."

"A decidedly more distant relationship. But I daresay in America what with divorce and dispersion over inaccessible territories, your family relations become rather complicated and impossible to trace, and you are lucky if even *practically*, as you call it, you have any uncles or parents at all. You could never tell us exactly what your connection is with Colonel Van de Weyer; but at least your name was familiar to us and distinguished. It gave us reason to have great hopes of you; and in fact you seemed quite like an English boy: certainly not like an American child. My sisters and I," the Housemaster continued, turning again to Peter, "are fond of Vanny. We are fond of all our boys. But we receive many applications from well-known families who wish to send their boys to this House; and we should naturally give our own people the preference. Not that the Headmaster or I have any prejudices. We believe in a sane mind in a sound body. Of course we expect all our boys to be gentlemen; although the Collegers, who are on our original charitable Foundation, need not be all strictly gentlemen by birth. I was a Colleger myself, and esteem it an honour. We are happy to think that manly spirit, pure religion, and free government were not meant by Providence exclusively for Englishmen. We are glad to see them spread more and more widely as the world advances. But how should this be possible, if we allowed these healthful influences to be contaminated at their source?"

"I quite understand," Peter replied. "Many people in the United States feel just as you do. And in regard to Mario, his family have often considered, if he is ultimately to live in America, whether it wouldn't be wiser and more prudent that he should finish his education there. Nevertheless, in deference to his father's last wishes, we should dislike to take him away, especially if he prefers to continue here, and you are willing to keep him."

"Of course I'd rather stay here," Mario interposed, "so that I may see my mother in the holidays. If I can't stay here, I want to go and live with her. It isn't impossible to study in Paris. I might go to the *École des Beaux-Arts*. I don't believe I shall ever live in America, and if Groton were such a good place, you would have sent Oliver there."

Poor Peter winced. Not that he nursed any illusions about Groton, or had ever wished to send Oliver there. But he smiled to think how ineffectual that wish would have been, if he had entertained it.

"Grotton? You mean *Gro-ton?*" repeated Mr. Rawdon-Smith inquiringly. "I seem to have heard of such a School. Near Canada, I believe."

"You may have heard of the Rev. Mr. Peabody, the Rector. He was once at Cambridge, I should think about your own time."

"No. Never heard of such a person.—Stop a moment. Wasn't there an American named *Peaboddy* who founded some charity in London? Very likely he also had the idea of introducing Public Schools into his own country. Capital idea, but was it feasible? Are his Public Schools at all like ours?"

"We've always had a public school in every village," Oliver declared a little ruffled. "We didn't need Mr. *Peab'dy* to introduce them."

"How is that? You must mean free schools, board schools, provided schools. We don't call that sort of thing a Public School. A Public School is a foundation where the scholarships are given to the best boys on examination." And Mr. Rawdon-Smith proceeded to explain further the character of Public Schools in general and the pre-eminence of Eton in particular, while Vanny interspersed more or less humorous illustrations. "You see," said the Housemaster warming to his subject and thinking that this tall American youth, if crude in speech, was rather attentive and intelligent, "we have a feeling that Eton and Winchester are in a class apart, spiritually nobler than all other schools. Yet there is a difference between the two, within this finer category. Winchester is more remote, more self-centred. They even preserve in Latin the pre-Reformation sound of the letter A. Their boys are more apt to take orders, or enter some so-called learned profession; whilst Eton, nearer London and under the shadow of Windsor Castle, is a sort of University in itself and rather a nurse of soldiers, statesmen, and men of the world."

"Wasn't Lionel Johnson, sir, a Wyckhamite," said Vanny, smiling sweetly and with apparent innocence. "M'Tutor thinks him the best of contemporary poets."

"A most unfortunate preference, most unfortunate, and quite un-justified when we have Kipling and Stephen Phillips and Sir William Watson, happily free from all vague Celtic verbiage and superstition. Yes, and I was forgetting the Poet Laureate, who is an old Etonian."

Mr. Rawdon-Smith was not a poet himself. He had never read Robert Bridges.

Vanny's eyes twinkled. "M'Tutor says, too, that the reason why Eton and Winchester are inimitable, is because Henry the Sixth and William of Wyckham were saints, and now up in heaven they keep praying for all us boys and I suppose for the masters too except that of course the masters don't need it, though Mr. Mildmay didn't say so; so that not one of us who have been at Eton or Winchester will ever be finally damned, even if we turn atheists and commit suicide; because M'Tutor says there's plenty of time for grace to work between the moment you pull the trigger and the moment of death; and I expect when a poor chap, just because he's been jilted by his best girl, throws himself into the Thames, at the first gulp of salt water and sewage he jolly well wishes he hadn't. But, you see, when your Harrow or Rugby bounders are going to blazes, there are no saints in heaven to care a damn—I'm sorry—to make intercession."

"Stuff and nonsense," cried the Housemaster, annoyed at such unseemly familiarity with religious things, as if another world actually existed. "Mr. Mildmay is laughing at you. These clever young men like to be fantastic. You mustn't suppose they believe all they say."

"He admits that this about Saint Henry the Sixth and Saint William of Wyckham is only a pious opinion and not yet a dogma of the universal church. But he says that the early councils did nothing but turn pious opinions into Catholic doctrines; and when next there is a truly Œcumenical Council his most beautiful ideas may actually become articles of faith."

"Dangerous levity," Mr. Rawdon-Smith grunted, "most dangerous levity. The Headmaster wouldn't like it at all. Mr. Mildmay is a learned young man, exceptionally learned in Low Latin and Late Greek; but he lacks experience. He will soon see the uselessness of bewildering his pupils with these Byzantine fancies. Bastard theology: and, what is worse, very bad taste, very bad taste."

With this, Mr. Rawdon-Smith, looking for some sign of agreement and confirmation of his sound principles, turned towards Peter, who had been keeping a rigorous silence. But Peter was sitting limp in his arm-chair, his head gently drooping over one shoulder and his eyes closed. The Master and the two boys glanced at one another, each afraid of moving first; but after a moment Mr. Rawdon-Smith's dictatorial promptness reasserted itself.

"What? Gone to sleep, man, when I am talking to you? We can't have that, we can't have that." And the infuriated schoolmaster was about to shake poor Peter out of his placid but uncivil slumber, when he unexpectedly came up against something hard, and rather hurt himself. It was Oliver's arm, interposed sharply. "Don't touch him," Oliver cried in a muffled voice, as if by a sick bed. "He's not well. I know what to do." Suddenly he had felt, as it were, the telepathic spirit of Jim Darnley—whom he hadn't thought of all that day—entering into him and giving him assurance. Jim would have managed perfectly in such a case. Surely Oliver himself wasn't less capable of doing so.

"Go and see if the cab is still at the door," he said to Mario. "My father caught a chill this morning," he explained to Mr. Rawdon-Smith, who had retreated to the window, fuming but at a loss how to attack these interlopers, who were not exactly his pupils or dependents. "He has probably taken some medicine—some sedative—and it's overcome him."

Yes, the fly was waiting below. There were only a few steps to descend. Oliver determined to get at once out of that house. He would then consider at leisure, in the free air, what he ought to do next. He laid his hand on his father's shoulder, as he had seen Jim do, and spoke softly but very distinctly in his ear. "It is time for us to go. See if you can't stand up." And Peter, without more than half opening his eyes, helped by his son, rose slowly to his feet, and shuffling, but without great difficulty, allowed himself to be led out. Even getting him into the fly proved easier than might have been expected. Mario mounted the vehicle first, and gave his somnambulous uncle a helping hand from the inside, while Oliver supported and pushed him in from below. Mr. Rawdon-Smith scowled at them from his house door; and as he turned on his heel, felt the hot vapours of his wrath a little lifted. At least the old drunkard had been packed off, before any of the other masters arrived for their meeting.

VIII

With his father safely ensconced in one corner of the carriage, Oliver breathed freely, and, as if giving the signal for the next move in the football field, knew what he would do, without analysing his reasons.

"First, let us drive to a doctor's. Do you know a good one?"

Mario, half frightened, half amused and keen for adventure, was sitting, round-eyed, on the front seat.

"Oh, yes. A lovely one, not one of those regular horse-doctors they have for the boys." And he gave the cabman an address in Castle Hill. "I go to him, when I've had a cold, on account of my mother. He sends her a report in French, and reassures her. His practice is rather amongst Windsor families, and the young officers of the garrison, when they need a specialist. He's youngish himself—modern, you know, and scientific."

Mr. Morrison-Ely—they didn't call him Dr.—was in his office and came out hatless to see what was the matter. His manner was at once officious and cocksure—very un-English, Oliver thought—and though he was not bad looking his thick features and black curly hair also seemed rather foreign. Mario had had time to drop a hint about his American uncle being inclined to narcotics, and not minding expense.

"What has he taken?" Mr. Morrison-Ely inquired, at the same time attempting to smell Peter's breath. "Morphine? Opium? Put him to bed and let him sleep it off. Where are you stopping? London? No: better not attempt travelling for a day or two. *The White Hart?* Righto. You couldn't do better. I'll step in with you and see that he's made comfortable.—A nurse? Hardly necessary, but still, if you prefer. Our young friend will be freer to amuse himself.—What? Little Mildred? You still remember her, do you?—Yes, I know she's disengaged. Nothing easier. In ten minutes she'll be here."

With Mr. Morrison-Ely so ready to help, and all the porters at the hotel, Peter was triumphantly borne upstairs, like the Pope at a great festival, only without a tiara; his head, in fact, hung and nodded rather distressfully. A spacious apartment was available, the same to which Peter had retired earlier; the fire still smouldered pleasantly on that chilly afternoon, there was an ample lounge for the prospective nurse, a bathroom adjoining and a smaller bedroom for Oliver. When Peter was undressed and propped professionally in the monumental bedstead, Mr. Morrison-Ely duly tapped his chest, listened to his heart, and registered his blood-pressure. Nothing serious for the moment. Heart rather erratic, lungs weak, low general condition. Curious how some men live to be sixty without ever having learned to exhale.—He would call to-morrow morning, and make a fresh examination.

Exhaling being one of Peter's hobbies, Oliver suspected there might be some flightiness and slap-dash about this medical busybody: yet the man seemed to prescribe nothing dangerous, and agreed at once, as if it had been his own idea, when told that mineral water and boiled arrow-root were Peter's choice when convalescing. "My father," Oliver added, "is a physician himself. When he recovers full consciousness he will know what treatment to follow."

Little Mildred having arrived, already armed with the doctor's instructions, and having put off her bonnet and cape, and laid her small handbag in a corner of the bathroom, where she could make her toilet in private, she was further initiated by the two boys, speaking alternately, into the requirements and idiosyncrasies of her patient. Oliver was made a little uncomfortable at first by a bold way Mario had of standing close to her and looking straight into her eyes. It couldn't be flirting, because when people meant to flirt or to make love Oliver knew how they laughed and joked and hid and looked bashful; whereas Mario with this young person, who seemed a nice well-spoken brave little thing, was gravity itself. Yet somehow, if it hadn't been for this strange seriousness—was it preserved perhaps, out of respect for his father's illness?—Oliver would almost have thought that Mario was up to something. No matter. Fancying things, and wondering about other people and their affairs was too silly, and a degrading waste of time. The important thing was to consider what he himself must do next.

They had no luggage. Did they have enough money? Oliver never carried more than a small sum in his own pocket: he liked to feel personally poor. What had his father brought? Again the image of Jim Darnley, this time going through the Doctor's pockets and laying out everything in order, became an *idée force*: as if hypnotised by it,

Oliver began with his father's mackintosh, which was nearest at hand, and pulled out gloves, scarf, handkerchief, and guide-book from the capacious pockets.

"I'll do that for you, sir; you needn't trouble," little Mildred said, coming up with a friendly placid air that pleased Oliver and gave him a sense of security, as if in crossing over a plank he had found a handrail to steady him.

"Thank you, if you don't mind. But I was looking for my father's pocket-book, because I'm afraid we haven't enough money."

"That will be in this coat," she replied, holding out Peter's jacket with the inside towards Oliver. And to be sure, from the inside pockets emerged a passport, a cheque-book, a thick wallet, and some long business envelopes with American stamps and return addresses printed in the corner.

"Oh yes," said Oliver, unfolding the inmost recesses of the wallet. Within, unmistakable pieces of crisp white paper, printed floridly in black, lay flat and immaculate. "There seem to be a lot of banknotes."

"And they are tenners," Mario exclaimed, with a relish and a quick eye denied to the virtuous Oliver. Yet it was the virtuous and groping Oliver that deliberately slipped the whole treasure trove into his own pocket.

The old man's keys, also, having been fished out of his trousers, his young heir felt himself in command of all the forces in the field. "Now," he said, apparently addressing his two interlocutors, but in his mind addressing the whole universe, "now I must go back to London for our things." They might be telegraphed for, Mario suggested; there was probably a valet at the Jermyn Street place who could pack them and bring them. No: Oliver couldn't trust strange servants. Well, then, there were shops at Eton. Why not go and get everything needed for the night, and avoid that tiresome trip up to London? But such a thought struck Oliver as impossibly wild and scatter-brained. What? Reduplicate all your belongings, and find yourself loaded with a whole new set of useless articles? But he didn't say this. Something warned him that it might have sounded small-minded and stingy. How could these aristocratic young paupers be such spendthrifts? They revelled in waste. What pleasure-domes wouldn't they build if they had the money? But money wasn't a sort of magic spell to cast about you and to make the world dance for your pleasure. Money was a trust, a responsibility. You mustn't think you had it just to save you trouble and fatigue. On the contrary,

Money kept you running and working and planning and struggling, until you dropped. That was what a poor little gilded moth like Mario couldn't understand. So, swallowing all these reflections in one gulp—for Oliver was as quick in intuition as he was deliberate in action and speech—he said: "My father would miss his old slippers and his old razors in the morning. I think I'd better go to London, pay the bill and see to everything myself. There's nothing for me to do here. Nurse will watch, and send for the doctor if necessary."

The decision in Oliver's manner and his air of optimism were so evidently forced: there was such an underlying distress and bewilderment in his eyes, as he picked up his hat, and said haltingly, almost with a gasp, "In any case I shall be back this evening; I suppose there are trains"; that Mario ran up to him, caught him once more by the arm, and said: "I should like awfully to go with you."

"Why shouldn't you? Come on."

"I haven't any money."

"What does that matter?"

"But my leave is for Windsor only, not for London. I have to be back for Second Absence."

"I'm sorry. Couldn't you get fresh leave?"

"There's no time. I'd go without it, if it wasn't for the station guard. They won't let me through in this rig."

At this moment Peter's hat, lying with his mackintosh and gloves upon the sofa, caught Vanny's eye. It was a soft Homburg hat of the latest fashion, rather light grey, with a black ribbon. Peter Alden had never abandoned a certain variegated style of dress, a trifle youthful and a trifle bohemian. It was a link with his salad days. As he prinked before the glass he felt he was invisibly putting his thumb to his nose at the Juggernaut car of old age and respectability. He smiled reminiscently at his own gently comic parody of elderly fashion and elegance: things he had despised when young, preferring solitude and remote corners of the earth; but now they wore somehow an air of friendly propriety; and as the elegance and fashion in question were faded, and entirely his own, they involved no sacrifice on his part of comfort or freedom. As Vanny observed that evidently new hat, that light brown mackintosh and those white gloves, an idea struck him. He seized the hat and tried it on. It was a perfect fit. He seized the mackintosh. This was certainly far too ample for him in the skirts, but Peter being rather narrow-shouldered, and Vanny, for a boy, just the opposite, the garment was quite right round the neck and in the length of sleeves. By boldly tightening the belt it could be made to flare in the skirt, most suitably for a ballet. But a white tie was impossible. Would Oliver let him borrow his father's black one with the red dots. And even the old gentleman's grey coat and waistcoat would be better than tails. Tails were not worn in decent society—not without a topper. Never mind the loose fit. It had come on to rain. The mackintosh would cover a multitude of creases. And Vanny tilted the hat over one eye, deftly giving it a fancy shape, and began to dance silently before the glass, in a fit of suppressed merriment. "Ain't I a nut," he whispered. "Ain't I a perfect Johnny? Young theatrical gent come to wink at Windsor Castle." And holding his uncle's stick, which had a gold nob, by the middle, he twirled it round his fingers, and gave an extra twist to his slouch hat. "Now I have it. You'll do the American and I'll do the South American. Between us we'll be the whole new world." He waltzed his cousin three times round the little room, rushed him downstairs, out by a side door, and down the steep lane leading to the railway station. It didn't matter if he was observed, provided he was not stopped. Haste was explicable: an up train was on the point of leaving. The two bits of return-ticket in Oliver's hand gave an added touch of genuineness to the two trippers, and the guard was too much preoccupied bidding them "Urry-up, sir," to harbour any suspicions. Half reproachful, half good-natured, he bundled them into an empty carriage, and received Vanny's last sixpence for having actually held up the train for as many seconds. Meantime Oliver fumbled for the pocket where he kept his change; and being in doubt whether he ought to repay his cousin or let the sixpence pass as of no consequence, he cut the knot by saying:

"Would you mind taking my change and paying for everything? I get so mixed up with these shillings and pence and florins and half-crowns."

Vanny was only too delighted: not only that he liked having money to spend, even as proxy, but that after all what he had come for was to help Oliver, to smoothe things out for him in his trouble. Still flushed and panting a little with the flurry of his escapade, he settled down beside his cousin in one corner of the empty carriage, forgot his borrowed clothes, forgot the unusual weight of silver in his pocket, and wondered why only accidental worthless people like himself had a good time in this world, while the great and good like Oliver were unhappy.

IX

Not many days remained before the end of the Summer Half, and the genial Mr. Morrison-Ely proposed to move Peter, whose heart wasn't at all behaving as it should, to quieter and more comfortable quarters. A particular friend of his, a French Master at Eton, was willing to make an exception and to sub-let his rooms for the holidays. They were stocked with a collection of the most curious and interesting books, which couldn't have been entrusted to anyone save to another bibliophile like Dr. Alden. They would be invaluable for whiling away the long days, until the patient should be well enough to travel. The cooking was simple and excellent, and as there was no other lodger the landlady would be entirely at their service. Little Mildred, of course, would be retained, so that nothing need be changed in the attendance on the old gentleman; while Oliver would be free to scour the country by train, on foot, on horseback, or on a bicycle, as his fancy might dictate; or he could run up to London for an occasional change of scene and ideas.

With apologies to the spirit of Letitia Lamb, the cathedral tour was indefinitely postponed. Yet for Oliver's education nothing was lost. Eton, even with Mario gone, or rather by his ghostly presence in the void of his absence, proved an inexhaustible lesson-book. Oliver began by exploring the place in the wake of the ordinary tourists, but by repeated visits and half-crowns he soon won the affection and loosed the tongue of the official guide. Special doors and special secrets were unlocked for his benefit; and the names and uses and dignities of every spot and every object were revealed to him. Yet the pleasantest moment came when he was left alone in Upper School, or in the Ante-chapel, and could browse among the monuments and inscriptions, and re-people that emptiness with its retinue of shades. He read books about Eton. And as the gossip of the place, and the singularities of life in it, grew familiar to his thoughts, his eyes also were gradually opened to the charm or quaintness of the picture. He began to distinguish styles and periods of architecture—not *kunst-historisch*, after the manner of Fräulein Irma and Miss Letitia Lamb—

but by a human instinct, as one distinguishes people and things of different moral quality. He began to form his taste. A monastic rigour, an air of devout poverty and hardship, still seemed to him to hang about the College. In the Chapel, the sublime skeleton of mediaeval faith could be seen stalking in stone, and through the garish modern foreground prayer might still pass in the night, or in the blast of the organ. He felt a Tudor courtliness about the School Yard, a domestic warmth in its red brick, a curious romance in its pinnacles and turrets. Within, in certain portraits of the eighteenth century he could recognise the stamp of a martial boldness and elegance, while commercialism, compromise, and worry marked those of the nineteenth. The twentieth—what little there was yet of it—betrayed a frightened retreat before democracy, and the dominance of athletics. What the dominance of democracy and athletics could mean, Oliver knew by experience. It was a double tyranny which he took for granted without protest, like that of sunshine and rain. Only certain picturesque qualifications of it here arrested his attention, certain remnants of spontaneous, foolish, traditional sport. These boys might be driven but they were driven by other boys. They were not yet public athletes. Had he himself ever been a boy? Had he ever *played* at all? Had he ever contrived the least bit of mischief?

It was too late to begin now. In spite of wealth and ancestry, he had been condemned to be a common boy, a *tug* like the charity scholars in this College. Never mind. Austerity, meagreness, commonness in early circumstances gave a certain elevation to one's views of the world. Later the vanities might become familiar, they would always remain foreign and disconcerting. That was a safeguard. Better not to be able to like his father's gilded Buddhas or privately printed books. And yet, the aggrieved stranger to that artificial world certainly missed something. Wasn't it more mature to take it all jovially, as Jim did, or lightly, like Mario, who danced through the whole show as if it were a lovely ballet or a grand opera? If the *beau monde* could dazzle, there must be some brightness in it, something that it was a natural joy for the eye to look upon. There would be no sweetness in love, no loveliness in music, unless the depths of one's being rose to the call and came to life, perhaps for the first time, in creating that illusion.

Thus a new sensibility appeared in Oliver's mind. His memory remained that of the head boy in his class, eager for "facts" and for the "correct" answer to every question. As yet, he didn't trouble to ask whether the question itself happened to be correct or at all necessary. Nevertheless, across the miscellany of prosaic information a certain breath of understanding began to blow. Images fell into groups and invited the imagination to piece them out. The facts, the occasions, the causes were merely curious: to attempt to trace them was an endless, dark, deceptive task. But whatever they may have been, these facts had flowered into ideas, into harmonies. The book of experience had become for Oliver a book of poetry; and as he read the words he heard the music to those words.

"Still reading about Eton?" Peter observed, noticing the illustrated jacket of a sort of gift book that Oliver held in his hand. "The charm of the place seems to appeal to you more than I should have expected."

"There may be a charm about it, for some people and at a distance"—the pathos of distance filled Oliver with scorn—"but really, when you come down to particulars, life at Eton seems to be rather shabby and horrible. Why do people put up with it? I can't understand all these little boys—rich little boys—submitting to be fagged and tormented and whipped into playing football in the mud, whether the poor little wretches are fit for it or not. And all these big foppish boys letting down their trousers meekly, to be 'smacked' by their captains or 'swished' by their masters! If it were at Squeers's School in *Nicholas Nickleby* I might understand it—just intimidation and tyranny and sheer brutality practised on helpless orphans by some sneaking blackguard setting up for a schoolmaster. But in the most aristocratic school in the world and under Anglican parsons"— and Oliver thought that if some Anglican parsons were beasts like Mr. Rawdon-Smith, others were saints like Mr. Darnley—"how is it possible? Then all this fantastic etiquette about caps and colours and blazers and waistcoats and stick-up collars and wearing pumps in the street and walking on only one side of it—how is it kept up? Yet the greatest puzzle is that with all this cruelty and silliness life in the place seems to everybody a great privilege—even to Mario who rather laughs at it—and is loved so passionately by the very people who have suffered from it: because the reformers who hate English Public Schools are usually freaks who never went to them."

"Dear me, what a lot of questions you raise that probably nobody can answer," Peter murmured, not really perplexed, but dreading to stir up the deposit of ideas floating, half inanimate, like submarine animals, at the bottom of his mind. The glassy sleepy surface of it, the routine of trifles and commonplaces, sufficed for his daily thoughts. Yet he was pleased to see his son so wide awake intellectually. These were precisely the matters that had occupied Peter in his own youth, during his prolonged travels; and his experience of human affairs had not failed to take some shape in his mind summed up in a few catch-words and maxims, round which his half-benevolent, half-contemptuous philosophy gravitated. He would make a little effort to be serious, seeing how serious this youngster was. He would try to brush up his old first principles, or rather his last conclusions, to meet the questionings of so innocent a beginner.

"England," he said, "is an easy enough country to live in, but very hard to understand. It never has understood itself: it exists by a living compromise between incompatible tendencies. We in America are simpler; we have jettisoned three quarters of the English ballast; we have kept little but the positivistic, commercial, colonising strain which was dominant in our ancestors. But they—apart from a few Southerners—were drawn from an extreme party in England: and what you find here at Eton is precisely the other strain in the English medley. No wonder it surprises, perhaps annoys, you. Yet it is the great Christian, the great classic tradition. It is the vision of Jacob's ladder."

Here was one of Peter's catch-words, one of his old shibboleths, which had come up of itself, perhaps for the first time in years. The sound of it, the echoes of it, as he uttered the words, acted like a fuse. A whole train of ideas, of episodes, of juvenile discussions was, as it were, ignited and made to live in his mind. He felt rejuvenated. He readjusted himself on the sofa on which he was lying, and warmed to the argument.

"Jacob's ladder, you will say, what do I mean by that? Let me try to tell you. Do you remember Cousin Caleb Wetherbee and his opinion about Goethe? Yes, and you seemed then to understand Cousin Caleb's reasons, although you naturally continued to think Goethe a great, wise, and good man, even if a heathen and not a gentleman. Well, Jacob's ladder is the fabulous moral order imposed on the universe by the imagination of Cousin Caleb and Plato and conservative Anglican gentlemen; but the heathen imagination in Goethe and Emerson and you and me, and in your liberal British intellectuals and philosophers, has outgrown that image. Instead, either we impose no moral order on the universe at all—which I think would be safer—or else a moral order such as we expected to find in our own lives when we were young and romantic. I suppose, as a matter of fact, there is an obscure natural order in the universe, controlling morality as it controls health: an order which we don't need to impose, because we are all obeying it willy-nilly. But this half-deciphered natural order leaves us, morally, in all our natural heathen darkness and liberty: and we are probably little inclined to devote ourselves to ascending and descending the particular Jacob's ladder imagined by Platonists and Catholics and Conservative English Gentlemen.

"But what on earth, you will say, has this antiquated Jacob's ladder to do with fagging and fancy waistcoats? It has everything to do with them; because if the moral universe really had but a single scale and a single order, then each lower creature would justly look up to those above him, would back out respectfully to let his betters pass, and would aspire, if possible, to resemble them; or if this was too much to hope for, at least he would feel a borrowed glow in loving and serving them. There is your fag justified. And the higher species naturally have ornaments which to them are a matter of course, like his tail to a peacock; but for a trembling inferior creature, like the crow, it wouldn't be much use to wish to emulate that gorgeousness, at least not in this life; yet it is edifying for him to know that there are such glories in the universe; and as for the dutiful pea-hen, who is far from shabby herself, it is a delight and a wonder to contemplate in her lord and master a splendour she is not destined to wear. There you have your coloured waistcoats."

Peter laughed his long, chuckling, almost inaudible laugh, and Oliver laughed a little too, by force of physical contagion, but without much relish for his father's humour.

"I don't yet see," he said coldly, "how your Jacob's ladder would justify flogging, or oppression and compulsion generally. Did the little angels have to kick one another in order to keep moving? And then, nowadays, we don't believe in Jacob's ladder, at least *I* don't; and why should I think a Pop or a Captain of the Boats necessarily better, for instance, than Mario, who at Eton is a nobody?"

"Ah, thank you," cried Peter, more in the swing than ever. "You remind me of essential points that I was leaving out. This matter is so complicated that one can't keep all the threads of it well in hand. Why have we free Americans a certain sneaking tendency to be snobs? Proud romantic heathens that we are, like Nietzsche, or like Walt Whitman, why do we feel an unavowed inclination to worship the archangel in a light blue cap—or a pink one, if he is elderly—standing at the top of Jacob's ladder? Because, my dear Oliver, our heathenism is still green and bashful. We are imperfectly weaned from feudalism and Christianity. Our pride in freedom is a mere affectation: we put it on in order to stifle our deeper conscience which still believes in Jacob's ladder. For if there were really only a single right path and a single right goal for all of us, if we were all innately addressed to the same virtues and the same truths, then evidently discipline would be necessary to keep us in the narrow way and raise us to the summit. A repressive regimen, half Spartan, half monastic, would then not really repress, but exalt us and save us from vulgarity and dishonour. And as to suffering, if you have suppressed or abused your true nature, suffering sooner or later is inevitable, and it must continue so long as the vice lasts. The suffering may be a means of mortifying and outgrowing your sins; and in any case it will be a proof and an unwilling confession of them. On this theory then, there is no cruelty in inflicting a timely punishment, and no disgrace in undergoing it. Penance becomes requisite for all of us, and salvation possible. Humility and glory go hand in hand and are justified together. Discipline is rational and martyrdom is crowned.

"So the old soul of Eton believed; and tradition here still represents sound thrashings and gruelling races as rungs in Jacob's ladder. To have passed through these troubles seems to clarify a boy's character and make it calmer. He has been initiated into the mysteries, and he feels—I daresay by an illusion—that the result can't be worthless when he has paid such a price for it. And is he wholly wrong? Isn't there really less dross about him—less wind and humbug and helplessness—than about most of us?"

All this seemed to Oliver rather in the air. Why dwell on the consequences of a false hypothesis? Or was the hypothesis possibly true? And he broke in, rather impatiently:

"But do you believe in Jacob's ladder yourself?"

"Believe?" Peter answered, as if bewildered. "Dear me, I don't believe in anything nowadays, if I can help it. Didn't I say that Jacob's ladder was a myth? It's a picture of what the universe would be if the moral nature of man had made it. I suppose in the universe at large the moral nature of man is a minor affair, like the moral nature of the ant or the mosquito. But our moral nature is everything *to us*; to us the universe itself is of no consequence apart from the life we are able to live in it. Jacob's ladder is a picture of the degrees which this moral life of ours might attain, in so far as we can imagine them.

It is a poetic image. Those who mistake it for an account of the universe or of history or of destiny seem to me simply mad; but like all good poetry, such an image marks the pitch to which moral culture has risen at some moment. To the morally cultivated, Jacob's ladder shines distinct and clear: it becomes vague and broken to the morally barbarous.

"Therefore I say, *Floreat Etona*! I say it feebly, because I am feeble and scattered. Circumstances never allowed me to gather much sap, to assert myself vigorously in any direction. But I am not envious. I like others to be beautiful and strong. If I am old, if I am tired, I will not for that reason ungenerously call down upon the universe the principle of blight. *Sonent voces omnium liliorum florem.* Let everything flourish that is capable of flourishing. Let everything bloom that has within it the seed of a flower."

"Isn't the flower of the lily one thing and the flower of the dandelion another?" Oliver interposed with a certain scornful fervour, thinking of Eton and of the High School at Great Falls, Connecticut. "Would you cultivate both equally? Or if there isn't room for both, would you let them fight it out, backing both sides at once? Or would you wait for the finish, and then say you had always been backing the winner?"

Without answering this question, Peter dreamily abandoned himself to the full tide of his thoughts. "Ah, those lilies, those lilies," he murmured, "not the lilies of the field, but rather—in the escutcheon of Eton—not counting the golden *fleur-de-lys* which is merely regal—those three lilies *proper* on *sable*, symbols of childhood and of saintly souls! How dear Harold Van de Weyer, your friend's father, loved those lilies! You know he was daft on heraldry, mad over the decorative, ornate, swaggering side of it. *Mirabolous* was his highest term of praise. But the splurge must not be empty: it must all be the foam of a salt sea wave, the rhetoric of a profound passion. Heraldry was just that: behind the calligraphy stood war, lifelong allegiance, hereditary grandeur. This elegance would have been foppish, if not backed by so much gallantry and power. Harold himself had no endowment, no mastery of any artistic medium. Yet never was there anybody more genuinely appreciative and discriminating. His taste was delicate, his judgment adamant. Nothing mixed, nothing vulgar, would go down with him, no matter how dominant it might be or universally admired. So he entirely skipped the sickly aestheticism of our own younger days, also their gross pride; entirely skipped Ruskin and Swinburne and Browning. By instinct he held fast to the baroque, to the heraldic, to brave simplicity and free sportiveness—to the art of the gentleman. It was the same in music. He skipped Wagner, and worshipped his wife. You know that Mario's mother is a born genius, with a contralto voice which, if she had been a vulgar singer, might have shaken the heavens and uprooted the earth; but in her the depth is not intentional. She is calm as a goddess and docile as a slave; and the greatest wonder in her singing is the rising sweetness and joy of it, the quite spontaneous *fioriture colorature, sfumature* that break out in it as if they were the trills of a caged canary. Here again, in another medium, as Harold felt, were lilies on a sable ground, traceries and filigree, fine-spun silver and gold, glittering on the velvet robe of a Mater Dolorosa, like so many constellations in the abyss of night and of nothingness."

Peter made a little pause, somewhat surprised at his own eloquence; and then he added, in his usual tone of humorous apology:

"In the East, you know, art is like that—overwhelmed but calli-graphic. I suppose I like it because I am short-winded myself. It confirms an old feeling of mine about poetry—I mean poetry in the deeper sense in which it merges with love and with religion. Poetry, I say, is like spray blown by some wind from a heaving sea, or like sparks blown from a smouldering fire: a cry which the violence of circumstances wrings from some poor fellow. This cry or spark or spray is flimsy in itself and playful, yet there's tragedy behind it. Enchantment paints these fantastic heraldries on the shield of loyalty, or perhaps of despair."

Peter had had his say. He glanced at the window: it was dark and shaking a little in the autumn wind. He glanced at the fire: it was burning pleasantly. He settled his head on the cushions, closed his eyes, and composed himself for a little nap until dinner.

Oliver could not be so easily comforted, and he needed comfort. He could find no peace unless he justified his natural sympathies theoretically and turned them into moral maxims. If they couldn't bear the light of day, the test of being made explicit in words, he wouldn't allow them to govern him in the dark. He had broken once for all with his home prejudices. He had vowed himself to universal sympathy, understanding, and justice. To set up Jacob's ladder again would be to restore the moral servitude from which his conscience had so proudly broken loose; it would be to wall in the infinite and try to live again in a little earthly paradise between four little rivers.

The universe wasn't that sort of garden, nor was the human soul that sort of vegetable. Life, for the spirit, was no walk in a paved city, with policemen at every crossing: it was an ocean voyage, a first and only voyage of discovery, in which you must choose your own course. He could no more believe in Jacob's ladder than could his father. Both had drunk too deep of the sea, the one by experience and the other by intuition. The old Calvinists, Oliver felt, hadn't been puritan enough: you were not pure at all, unless it was for the love of purity: but with them it had all been a mean calculation of superstition and thrift and vengeance—vengeance against everybody who was happier and better than themselves. They had flattered themselves that at least the Lord, if no one else, particularly loved them: that God had sent down Moses and Christ expressly to warn them of dangers ahead, so that they might run in time out of the burning house, and take all the front seats in the new theatre. And they didn't dare call their real souls their own; wanted to smother them; wanted to find out, in some underhand way, what was the will of God, so as to conform to it, and be always on the winning side. But God had laughed at them and fooled them. There was really no knowing which way the universe would drift. Your hard-boiled moralists were idolaters, worshipping their own fancies, and hypnotised by their own words. They had perched at a certain height on the tree of knowledge, had stuck fast at a certain point up the greased pole of virtue. They could climb no further; and from there they had turned and pecked ferociously at everybody below them and screeched ferociously at everybody above, invoking their hard dry reason to discredit all that was beyond their own meagre and cruel morality. But this reason of theirs was just *their* reason, their effort to entrench themselves in their limitations. Not only was such a thing useless and in the end impossible, but perhaps in the moral world there was no single pole, no single tree on which heights and depths could be measured, like record tides. Perhaps the ways of knowledge were incommensurable, like different languages or different arts, one way of knowledge mathematical, another historical, another psychological, another poetical; and perhaps the kinds of virtue were divergent too, and incomparable. The lion and the eagle were ideal in their way: so were the gazelle and the lark in theirs. Who should say which was better? Better in what sense, according to what standard? In one mood you might say: Better be like Jim Darnley, fleshly, since you are living in the flesh, hard enough, coarse enough, loose enough to feel at home in the crowd. In another mood you may say: No: better be like Mario, refined by nature, clear as a crystal, merry without claims, brave without armour, like the lilies of the field or the lilies of Eton. Or in yet another mood, why not think it better to be as Oliver himself was, burdened but strong, groping but faithful, desolate but proud? It was a foolish debate: free and infinite spirit, in a free and infinite world could never stop short at any point and say: This is truly right, this is perfect, this is supreme. Perhaps the whole pilgrimage of spirit was the only goal of spirit, the only home of truth.

But what was he saying? A goal? A home of truth? Was there anything here but chaos and a welter of impulses, a truth composed of illusions, a home all perpetual unrest? If the spirit of life was really free and infinite, what difference could there be between freedom and madness? The whole adventure of existence became no less horrible than enticing; you had to close your eyes, to stifle your reason, in order to take sides somehow and continue to live. But the one thing Oliver could not do was to stifle his reason and close his eyes. How, then, should he go on living?

At eighteen these moral tempests thunder terribly in the distance, they make a mighty pother in the upper regions of the head: but nature somehow is not unhinged. The digestion remains good, the skin fresh, the eye clear; your heart continues to beat gloriously for no reason, and your legs run away with you at a great pace over hill and dale. That very sense of freedom and infinity which threatens your self-esteem is itself a symptom of your youthful energy. Nature has canalised a part of her freedom—if we may call it freedom—into your particular organism: and so long as health prevails,—a very determinate and specific health—your free soul dances and your empty mind expands to embrace infinity.

But by an entanglement in thought, and by a hereditary prejudice, young Oliver's romantic sympathies were perturbed. He demanded some absolute and special sanction for his natural preferences: as if any other sanction were needed for love, or were possible, except love itself. Love, without that impossible absolute rightness, seemed to him a bewitchment. All life, unless you share it, is evidently a bewitchment, a groundless circling and circling about some arbitrary perfection, some arbitrary dream of happiness, which there is no antecedent reason for pursuing and no great likelihood of attaining. Not having the key to this secret—the open secret of natural life—

his reflection came to a stand. The puzzle was too much for his wits, and useless thinking became a torment. He shook himself together, tossed the hair from his forehead, and ran out into the night air, across the wet fields. Hadn't Hume, too, with less excuse, turned in the end from philosophy to backgammon?

X

It was the month of August, yet rather autumnal, with lowering clouds and rain and a briefer twilight inviting the pedestrian indoors to all the freshness and dryness of open windows and an open fire. Autumnal too was the mood in which Peter Alden would sit there by his well-shaded lamp in the pleasant interval between tea and dinner, reading some savoury old author and learning again to look at this poor world with humour and at its passions without passion. The future, for him, held nothing urgent or alarming: he was not afraid of winter or of death, and for the moment neither pressed unpleasantly upon him. The grisly prospect in that direction, with its broad peace, rather liberated his attention and allowed him to turn with the greater intellectual gaiety to the carnival of facts and ideas filling the world.

As for Oliver, pensive too but preoccupied, as youth must be with itself, the approaching winter brought the picture of home, if he might call home a place he had never seen: but at least he would be again in his native country, amid ways and people that he could take for granted. Everything at college would be superficially new to him, yet deeply familiar and unfathomably dull. He knew beforehand how he would plod. Football, class-rooms, text-books, essays to be ready at precise dates, half-anxious, half-drowsy hours passed blinking at his work. He knew the palpitating uneasy feeling of the days before an approaching examination or approaching vacation or approaching game. As to people, comrades or professors, there would be plenty of them and they would be well enough. No occasion to trouble about them beforehand, one way or the other. While his feet worked this academic treadmill, he knew what springs would be watering his secret mind. They would not rise in those arid regions. There, everything would be dry, brittle, obvious, wooden, and deadly new. His inner life would flow from remote fountains, from unshed tears of his own. No, it wasn't sentimentality: it was pent-up life, pent-up indignation. Why should everything be wrong when, so easily, everything might be right? Why did the world stick so stupidly in its old ruts? The core of his being was alive and plastic. He felt responsive to distant possibilities, and without neglecting to exercise such organs as he actually possessed and alone could use, he was aware of other more delicate and richer ways of living possible to others, as if the ox were aware of the gazelle, or winter had some premonition of summer. In future this knowledge would subtly qualify his home thoughts and his home actions and render them more gracious. He must deepen his roots in his native soil, draw up as much sap from it as possible; then his mind and his purse—for Oliver was frank with himself about the power of money—would be the better able to spread themselves justly and to some purpose over the rest of the world.

Suddenly, in the midst of this quietness and these meditations, a domestic bombshell exploded. A cablegram from Mrs. Alden commanded Oliver to bring his father home at once. Otherwise she would sail for England herself and take charge of everything.

Peter, aghast, looked at his son reproachfully. What could the boy have written to his mother? Why had he written at all? That was a sad mistake. Now all their peace, all their pleasant desultory talks would be at an end, all this happy saturation with pleasing images and harmless thoughts—What a fatality! And there was no escape. Unfortunately he wasn't well enough to flee in the opposite direction to that from which his wife threatened to approach. He couldn't even go to London; otherwise he would drive to the India Docks, and take ship for India or China. If he died at sea, at least he would die in peace, and would offer the sharks a parting banquet, even if not a very succulent one; and at least he wouldn't be buried in the Bumstead family lot at Great Falls, Connecticut. In any case he couldn't endure the kind attentions to which his wife would subject him. They would kill him; and why suffer a cruel death, when a peaceful death was easily possible?

These reflections were not audible, yet by his father's evident consternation Oliver could guess what they were. He stammered an explanation, almost an apology. He wrote a letter—a short letter—every Sunday to his mother. He had promised to do so. It wouldn't have been honest to conceal the fact that his father had been taken ill at Eton, and that they were stranded there. The post-mark alone would have betrayed the fact, if he had attempted to conceal it.

"Tut, tut," Peter growled. "You might have posted one letter at Maidenhead, and the next at Staines, and the next at Richmond. Our only address is care of the bankers. I don't like to be routed out against my will."

Never had Peter found fault with his son before; and Oliver thought these reproaches utterly unjust. He had behaved quite properly, in the only possible way, and his father was fretful because he was ill. Indeed, his irritation seemed to be passing away of itself, for he was smiling.

"Well, we're in a fix," the poor man added in a resigned tone. "Let's see if we can get out of it. Take a telegraph blank and a pencil, and let us compose a diplomatic despatch." And slowly, with a quizzical smile playing about the corners of his mouth, he began to dictate: *Father better. Leaving as soon as possible for South of France with good nurse. I sail for home September first. Don't undertake voyage yourself. Utterly useless.* "We will amplify one sentence," observed Peter judiciously, after perusing the proposed telegram with caution. "We will say, *'Please* don't undertake *long* voyage yourself'. That will sound more as if you had sent the telegram and not I."

Those two polite considerate words were not enough to deceive the practised eye of Mrs. Alden. She saw that it was the Doctor's effort to keep her away. He was probably not better, except that he might have had worse moments. When the first of September came, he would be worse again, and keep Oliver from sailing. The poor boy's feelings would be worked upon. He would be told not to abandon his dying father. And this dying father would live on, drag him to Marseilles, carry him away in that ill-fated yacht, cause him to miss his college year, and subject him to the evil influence of that wicked young Captain. Hadn't she employed a detective agency to look up the man's past and his present, and hadn't they discovered the most appalling facts, though nothing that she hadn't already known by instinct? It was a wicked plot to destroy whatever conscience and sense of decency might still remain in this weak, this sentimental boy. She would take the next steamer for Liverpool and defeat that conspiracy. She would sail from Boston, because the Boston boats would surely be safer: and the Cunard Line was of course the only right one—Letitia Lamb always travelled by it. Her reply to Oliver's cablegram was brief: "*Sail Saturday Lucania.*" It was truer, she was happy to think, than the long one she had received, less expensive, and more expressive of a strong, upright, determined, unselfish character.

On receiving this reply, Peter's feeling was not one of anger, nor even of defeat. Poor Harriet, how she was punishing herself for her folly! It made no great difference to him. If he wasn't well enough to escape before her arrival, he would send her a polite message, saying that under the circumstances it would be wiser for them not to meet. There would be nothing in such a course to surprise her. In her grandmother's house, before her mother was married, hadn't all the family lived in their respective rooms, never exchanging a word or having a meal in common? She wasn't coming on his account, but to snatch young Isaac from the sacrifice: she represented the voice of the Lord arresting the hand of this unnatural father. In refusing to see her, he would only be making explicit the estrangement which, at heart, had always existed between them. Yet why should she expose herself to a needless rebuff which he would be sorry to inflict upon her? Was it too late to dissuade her from coming?

"Oliver," he said aloud, "I am sorry that your mother should put herself to all this trouble for nothing. You know how unhappy she will be away from home, and how little used she is to travelling. Every slight impediment or misunderstanding will upset her. And she will be making the journey alone. Irma is in Germany, and Letitia Lamb will have to be left to watch over the precious house. Then your mother will suffer from sea-sickness and hate all the food everywhere that may not be exactly as it is at home. Yet what can we do? I see only one means of stopping her. I believe there are German ships touching at Southampton in the middle of the week. If you took one of them and, when already on board, telegraphed that you would be in New York in six or seven days, surely she couldn't help seeing the folly of coming to fetch you when you would be crossing her path in the middle of the Atlantic. Do look up the sailings in *The Times*—that is, if you are willing to be packed off in such a hurry. Of course I should be sorry to have you go. But I understand you are determined to do so in any case before long: and these few days with the row impending, will have been spoilt for us. By leaving at once you might be relieving your anxious mother of her fears, and saving her endless worry; and by letting you go I might be returning good for evil—rather an achievement in so weak and selfish and un-Christian a person as myself,—What do you say?"

"No, I don't want to run away like that. I think Mother is misguided. Why should we change our plans because she chooses to make a fuss? I've come to England for my vacation and I mean to spend it here. Besides, I don't like leaving you alone. I have written to Jim that he must be here before September first, to look after you. When he's here, I shall feel free to leave, although I hate to do so."

"You have written to Jim? And you are going home although you hate to do so?" Peter, surprised, amused, and impressed, looked at his son as if seeing him in a new light, as if some familiar object, supposed to be inanimate, had suddenly begun to dance. Then, laughing quietly to himself, he went on: "I wonder if Jim will turn up. What a scene! Imagine your mother arriving in high dudgeon, to find Lord Jim standing by my deathbed and filially closing my eyes. *Impayable*, if only I could still be winking one eye and not too far gone to enjoy the comedy. But aren't you rather lordly with our Lord Jim? He's not our servant. He's on his holiday, gone to Marseilles bent on business or pleasure of his own. He may snap his fingers at your summons."

"Oh no, he won't.—Besides, I don't see why it's so dreadful that Mother should take this ocean trip if she wants to. Many old ladies do it for pleasure. If she has a bad time she has only herself to thank for it. Why doesn't she trust my word?"

"Certainly this boy," thought Peter, "is atavistic. He has skipped his parents and drawn his character from his remote ancestors. He's like a two-edged sword, as merciless in one direction as in the other." And he continued aloud: "Haven't you given your mother some reason to fear that you might have changed your mind? Perhaps in those little Sunday letters of yours you have mentioned your visit to Iffley, and how much you liked the church, and the sermon and the Vicar, and the Vicar's comical old wife, and his lovely little daughter— what's her name? Violet?"

"Rose."

"Better have been called Violet. Rose is a little vulgar.—And perhaps in another letter you mentioned Mario, and what a wonderful boy you thought he was, and how you two youngsters had sworn eternal friendship, and how it broke your heart not to be able to see him again, perhaps for years. Possibly you added that nevertheless you were perfectly happy here, sculling in your skiff, and wandering over the empty College and School and Chapel and fields, and reading all about the strange complicated picturesque life that people led there. And if you only said a quarter of all this, your mother would easily supply at least ten more quarters out of her imagination. She has probably concluded that you have been seduced. I confess I had almost expected that you would be. Last year, when you decided to follow your mother's plans and go to Williams College, you hadn't seen any of these interesting things or interesting people. Now your position has become paradoxical. You admit you love all these things, and yet you abandon them, while you cling to your old resolution, although you hate it. Your mother hasn't realised what a puritan you are."

These words pleased Oliver immensely. They were not a compliment. To be complimented was to be told what other people valued, not what you really were. Here at last was a recognition of his true nature. What a relief, what an encouragement, to be enlightened and confirmed in his self-possession, in his integrity! And the young philosopher smiled his sweetest, his most beautiful smile, a smile that revealed an incorruptible innocence and strength within, shining in utter kindness and openness upon all other things. Of course his father's way of talking was hopelessly playful and ironical, exaggerating everything and turning it into farce. Of course Oliver wasn't *abandoning* the new things he cared for, in the sense of ceasing to care for them; and he didn't *hate* the old things at home. They were his foundation, his support; and he wasn't going to kick away the stool he stood on, and hang himself. Certainly it wasn't flattery to be called a puritan; in most people's mouths it was the opposite. Yet puritan he was conscious of being, and determined to remain, if this meant being self-directed and inflexibly himself. He could not conceive repentance or a change of heart. One might throw off a foreign incubus, or develop a latent faculty; but it was impossible to change one's origin and the circumstances that had made one the sort of being one was. It would be silly to wish to do so. There was plenty of time and space in the universe for those other kinds of people; here and now and in his body there was only room for himself. Yet from his own station, in his own heart as nature had endowed and limited it, there might arise, as it were, a vapour of spiritual freedom, a many-coloured sympathy, a sincere joy in all other sorts of perfection. If puritanism meant stupidity, ignorance or hatred of the beautiful, then it was wrong to be a puritan, and he wasn't one, or at least didn't wish to be.

Meantime Peter too was lost in a brown study.

"Why are you sure that Lord Jim will interrupt his holiday and come and play nurse-in-chief to this invalid? He has nothing more to expect: he knows I've burnt my will, and won't make another."

"Because it's not you he's counting on now, it's me. Besides money isn't the only point. He's full of enthusiasm about the way you have treated him, and he really cares for you—more than for me."

"But haven't you told me that his mother, who is in his secrets, mysteriously warned you, and advised us to make it for his interests that I should live to be a hundred? Don't you think, if he were looking after me, he might make some mistake in the medicines, as he did, apparently, in the case of that poor mate of ours?"

Peter leaned forward and rearranged the coals in the fire as if to give time for his insinuations to sink into Oliver's innocent mind. But Oliver's mind was less innocent in this regard than his father imagined. The distress of his dream after that evening in Sandford returned to him. Could that dream have been clairvoyant? And how could his father speak so pleasantly of Jim, and with such evident affection, while hinting that the dear fellow was capable of poisoning his friends and even his greatest benefactor?

"Please don't think," Peter resumed, "because I indulge these cynical suspicions, that I am disappointed in Jim or accusing him of abusing my confidence. At my age one has little confidence in anybody. Then Jim is such a child, so transparent, so outspoken, that he has put all the threads of his plot into my hands without knowing it. Perhaps he has let you discover something too. There is somebody—some Eastern potentate—ready to buy the *Black Swan*, of course not for a tenth of her value, but for what seems to Jim a mint of money to thrust into his pocket, and quite enough to break the bank at Monte Carlo. As he might never find another bidder—*Black Swans* are a rare taste—he is anxious to sell; perhaps he has already initialled the contract. That's what he went to Marseilles for, and what keeps him there. But the poor chap can't get the money until he delivers the goods, and my life-lease—or my lease of life—interferes. I have inadvertently led him into temptation. You mustn't show your dog a biscuit and when he has jumped once or twice, not give it to him, but walk off with it in your pocket. You spoil his education, and he may snap at you. Now I had done something for Jim's education. I had introduced him to a great many things and a great many ideas that he would never have heard of otherwise. I have taught him how to live well, how to judge and observe people. I mustn't spoil my own work now. He must have his biscuit at once. I am going to write to him—I should already have written—that I shall never again be well enough for cruising, that I abandon my lease, and that he may sell the *Black Swan* at the first opportunity."

"What?" cried Oliver, dismayed as if a blow had been struck at his own happiness. "Give up the *Black Swan?* Give up the sea altogether? Not have Lord Jim any longer in your service, to keep you company, to amuse you, to cheer you up?"

"I am going to retain little Mildred. She will take care of me. She's the sort of companion I need now."

There followed one of those curious moments when two people are conscious of having the same unspoken thought. Didn't Peter Alden have a son? Wasn't this son old enough to assist him, intelligent enough to understand him, free, and at hand? Why couldn't Oliver step up and say: "*I* will stand by you. *I* won't abandon you in your last illness, when you are alone, threatened by the very man you have loved and befriended most. Damn Williams College. Isn't your society, isn't my experience in living with you, better than any university? Don't you pour into me all sorts of curious well-digested knowledge, fit to make me twice the man I should ever become playing football and hearing my uncle Professor Harry B. Bumstead lecture through his nose on Applied Christianity? What's the use of adding one more standardised unit to a hundred million standardised units? If I could be turned into something a bit different and a bit better, wouldn't it be a blessing all round?"

But no. Oliver couldn't say these words. They stuck in his throat. And Peter divined this incapacity in his son, felt this element in him of petrified conscience, of moral cramp, this dutiful impediment to breaking away, and reshaping his duty in a truer harmony with his moral nature. The poor boy felt obliged to strangle himself, to force his spirit into the customary grooves. There he sat hanging his head, without courage to do what his heart prompted.

Peter, too, was conscience-bound. His delicacy forbade him to re-open a subject that had cost Oliver, a year before, so severe a struggle. But that scruple was unnecessary. The boy might now have a clearer notion of what he was giving up, or postponing; but on the other hand, the choice this time wasn't agonising. Either way, it involved no sacrifice and promised no happiness. How vividly he could see the smoke rising from Mount Vesuvius in the coloured postcard in Jim's cabin; and it now seemed cheaper than the smoke of a cigarette. He could also paint in his mind's eye, after other photographs, the round-headed wooded hills about Williamstown, Massachusetts, or the snow-covered paths crossing the College Campus: everything frosty and brittle, everything crude. Yet how reassuring was that peaceful American scene! There might be no depth, no inside to anything, only a homely, hurried, mechanical life; but that conventional routine was what his heart needed, a sort of protection for it against itself, a means of banking the fires and living sanely meantime among indifferent things. What a relief to be innocently, foolishly, perpetually busy! He must get back, he must get home.

"The thing is hopeless," Peter concluded, aware of his son's decision, though not perhaps of his deepest motives. "This model boy has no ginger in him, no fire. You show him the most lovely things, the most pungent facts, and he takes notes, and goes home to do his chores. Looking after me would only be doing chores of another sort. He will never live in the mind. Light will never quicken him, transport him, become his true life. Jim, with his grosser nature, is more satisfactory. He knows how to laugh. Of course he must be pampered, and enticed away from the inferior things that entice him. The art of government is to render the interests of the governed identical with your own. Then, if your subjects are intelligent, as Jim is, you needn't fear assassination. Having taken this precaution, I might find life with him still worth living. It might still turn, like champagne, into gaiety.—Ah, if only my old organism could hold out, I might still enjoy existence for a few years, in spite of the mistakes I have made. I might take a sunny villa at Nice or Cannes. I might keep my Indian cook, and this little Mildred to nurse me. She would make a capital housekeeper as well. I should be warm. I should look out over the sea. I should be at peace with everybody. We could have a room ready for Jim to occupy whenever he was out of funds, which would be most of the year. Oliver too might visit us in his holidays, open his grey eyes wide as an owl's, and perceive everything except the humour of anything. But it's too late. I am falling to pieces. Better omit that idyllic epilogue, and bring down the curtain where the action ends. The action might seem to be rather my wife's: she comes to give me a beating. But I can meet that assault in the spirit of old comedy, and get the laugh on my side. I can collapse before she strikes, and let her beat the air. More decent, too, to come to an end suddenly, opportunely, in a clean little heap of ashes, like the one-horse shay. My disappearance now will liberate everybody: Jim can have his money, Oliver can salve his conscience,

Harriet can have her way. The last action of my life will be the kindest—kindest to others and kindest to myself."

When Oliver had left the room, Peter made a little effort, crawled to the writing-table, and took out a small case of medicines from one of the drawers. He had often considered what would be the best combination for the purpose in hand. He hadn't been able, he thought with a discreet smile, to experiment like Cleopatra on her slaves, in order to see which expired with the greatest appearance of luxurious contentment: but he had experimented within limits on himself; and in his present feeble condition, no great increase in the dose would be required. Did he have enough of the right ingredients? Yes, apparently, just enough. It wouldn't be necessary to replenish his stock by writing to his old London chemist, who had supplied the medicine chest for the *Black Swan*. Nor need the obsequious Mr. Morrison-Ely be bribed to wink at the business. Just enough! Like Socrates when he drank the hemlock, Peter would have to omit on this occasion the libation due to the gods. That patron of medicine-men, Asclepius the Saviour, familiar with serpents, would have to go without the thank-offering prescribed for an easy death; but surely so humane a deity would accept instead the gratitude of a heart which he was about to liberate from long weariness and uncertain palpitation. All was ready. Papers, bank account, even clothes would be found in perfect order. There was nothing more to do but quietly to go to sleep and never to wake up again.

XI

"Well, I never!" cried Mrs. Alden, dazed, fatigued, frightened, and angry, as she sank into a comfortable arm-chair in the "bridal deck suite" which she and Oliver were to occupy in the *Lusitania*. "Nothing but difficulties, everything wrong! At least, the worst is over at last—except this voyage." And she glanced suspiciously at the square patch of blue sky visible through the cabin window, for fear it might be clouding over. "I hope you are right and that this ship is better than the *Lucania*, which Letitia Lamb said was so steady. Steady? Oh my!"

"At least the *Lusitania* is faster: five days," Oliver observed, with that air of quiet authority habitual with him now when talking to his mother. "The Boston boats are all old tubs."

"I never should have thought I could go through it all without breaking down. It upsets me even to think of it. Of course I am not one of those weak women who are always bemoaning their troubles. It's so useless and wasteful to live over the horrid past. I simply dismiss it, and put it out of my mind, so as to be free and clear-headed for each bright new day. But just consider what I have had to suffer—all on account of your poor father's weakness and self-indulgence, and your own stubbornness—insisting on coming abroad, when there was no need. First of all, think of being compelled to leave the house empty—well, of course in the end Letty Lamb decided to stay and look after it, in case of burglars or fire or the servants making a caravansary of it, or worse, for their rowdy friends; and this when it was plainly Letty's duty—and I must say for her that I think it would have been her pleasure also—to come with me and relieve me of a part, if possible, of my heavy responsibilities. But no: she was obliged to see me start to face these dreadful trials alone, your father not in his right mind, and you an inexperienced boy in a strange country. And all because that selfish Irma had left me, in order to go and sentimentalise over her old home where she couldn't be of any use, except to astonish her German relations with all the great things she had seen in America. Really, it is incredible how selfish people are, when they hear every Sunday that one should live for the service of others, and it never occurs to them to apply the sermon to themselves. She must have a holiday just when you, too, were going away, and were being misled—it's too awful to think by whom!—into staying in the wrong places with the wrong people. And as to Irma, I can't think on getting this sad news—and she was one of the persons I telegraphed to first—why she didn't come at once to join me, and help me a little, at least about trifles, when she owes me *everything*; but in her exaggerated letter, full of so many things in praise of your father which were not strictly true—though I know she is carried away by her emotions, never having been trained to suppress them, and really believes half what she says—she gave an excuse about not wishing to offend some poor cousins she had promised to visit, and said that after spending a single day with them she would take the first steamer directly for New York and arrive probably before us, so that everything in the house may be running as usual when I get home, and I needn't feel there has been any catastrophe, except that you are at college and the Doctor *in heaven*—she *is* so old-fashioned and sentimental!"

Here Mrs. Alden drew a deep breath, glanced again at the window to make sure that no black clouds were gathering, grasped the arms of her chair, and looking directly and witheringly at Oliver, continued her oration.

"Then to think of that horrid accident, missing all your letters and telegrams! How should I have suspected that a nice hotel, recommended by Letitia Lamb, could suddenly have been closed, and pulled down, and not a trace of it left, so that the policeman hadn't even heard of it? Letty had said—you know how discriminating and wise she is—'The Thackeray Hotel for me, because it faces the British Museum and there I feel closer to Phidias and it isn't expensive. But for you, Harriet dear, Long's Hotel in Bond Street, because Phidias for you isn't so important, and as you are *not* going to Paris, you might—without having to climb into one of those poky dangerous hansom cabs, scurrying so close round corners,—you *might* like to buy some comfortable warm wrap or some new hat or gloves; and of course Bond Street is the place; or the Burlington Arcade when it rains, which is close by.' So I wrote that I knew you couldn't leave your father and come to Liverpool to meet me, he was so low; but you might come to London—not to the railway station where we might miss each other in the crowd and oughtn't to display our

private feelings in public, and besides I should be too busy, having
to pick out my own things and count them, since I knew they didn't
give baggage-checks in this queer old-fashioned little country; but
you were to join me at Long's Hotel as soon as you heard I had
arrived, and tell me where your father was—because I couldn't believe that you would have kept him all this time uncared for in a
country boarding-house; and I meant, the very first thing, to go and
see our Ambassador and ask him if there wasn't an *American* nursing
home in London, or if not, what native one he could recommend, so
as to have your father conveyed there at once in a decent ambulance.
Well, imagine my dismay that Bond Street—I mean Long's Hotel
there—didn't exist, and all my letters and telegrams lost! My old
cabman who had white hair and a red nose and carried all my things
heaped on the roof of his dingy little coupé, which they called a four-
wheeler, seemed at first to have heard of Long's Hotel: but the
policeman I called—for I couldn't understand a word the old cabby
said—had never heard of the place, until another policeman came
up and said, 'Yes, mum; there used to be an hotel called Long's Hotel
hereabouts in the old days, but it was pulled down years ago,'—which
I thought rather rude of him, as if I had seemed an old woman; and
he half grinned at me, too, as if I could be expected to know everything they chose to do in London when I didn't live there. And what
was I to do? Go to that other inexpensive second-class hotel near
Phidias and the British Museum? It might be *dirty*. So, in despair I
cried 'Drive me to the station'—'Which station?'—'The Station for
Eton!' because then I felt in my bones that everything was bound to
be at its worst, and that you would be there: or at least they would
tell me where you had gone. What a nightmare, if I should have
come all the way from America, and then not be able to find you!
But the cabman and the two policemen, and a little crowd that had
gathered, all looked stupid. There was no station for Eton. Where
was Eton? *Which* Eton? Then a very nice-looking young man coming
out of a shop and seeing my trouble, though an Englishman, was
really rather kind and obliging, and said the station for Eton was
Paddington; and he couldn't have smiled and smiled more pleasantly
if he had been an American. Then at the ticket office when I said
'Eton,' the man inquired 'Windsor or Slough?' I repeated '*Eton*,'
wondering why they had a deaf man selling tickets. And he said there
was no train for Windsor for more than an hour, and that I should
arrive sooner by Slough. I thought he said slow, meaning a slow train;

and being by that time resigned to anything I decided to take the slow one. Getting there sooner by going slowly I thought was probably an English maxim."

"Latin," Oliver corrected, who was nothing if not a scholar.

"I daresay it's Latin too; anyhow, they gave me a ticket marked S-l-o-u-g-h, and I didn't know how to pronounce it, in order to ask at each station whether we had arrived at it or not. However, they said Slah-o, to rhyme with cow; and when I saw the place—and it turned out to be the very first station—I thought it really candid of them to have called it Slough after the Slough of Despond; although if they had called Slow, to rhyme with low, or even Sluff, it wouldn't have been inappropriate—such a mean little station, and mean little houses, and such a drizzle, all in a bog. What a place for you to have kept your poor father to pine away in!"

Oliver disdained to defend himself. He knew what his mother's rhetoric was—an enthusiastic vice, an irresistible need of misrepresenting the facts, as she couldn't help knowing they were, in order to render them conformable to her imaginative impulse. If she had been a poet or a saint this faculty might have produced magnificent fictions; but she was only a self-assertive woman, living in a humdrum world; and it was on the vulgar level that her fancy worked, doing a perpetual injustice to her real understanding. Oliver, though living secretly on a higher plane, was accuracy itself in regard to facts; and like a patient but despairing schoolmaster, he noted, and sometimes corrected, his mother's fables. Slough, he observed, on this occasion, was said to be a particularly healthy place. He had just read in *The Times* that it had a low infant mortality, few deaths from child-birth, and no slums.

"*Child-birth*, indeed," thought Mrs. Alden. "How dares he? Never would he have mentioned such a thing to me a year ago: and now it slips out as innocently and without apology as if he had said *sparrow*. He has been contaminated: those corrupt men have debased his mind and spoilt his manners. But his father at least was timid; he might have *wished* to be coarse, but he didn't dare. He had never heard an indelicate word in Beacon Street. Oliver is braver; there he takes after me; and when a brave man loses his principles, there's no knowing where he will end. That is an awful thought."

Yet this awful thought, for the moment, remained unuttered. Harriet was secretly afraid of starting disputes with her son: sometimes by his proofs and more often by his silence, he caused in her a horrid sensation of having been in the wrong. Besides, the impetus of her memories now carried her past this marginal fault-finding, and she picked up another of Oliver's words which had less dangerous associations.

"No slums!" she cried in a tone of withering indignation not uncommon in her. "I saw nothing else. If that marsh is a healthy place for England, what must the rest be? Such a slow, one-horse hack, too, and such a long drive between soggy foggy fields—why did they build their school, I wonder, so far from the station? Or why don't they move it to a better place on some hill? Well, I hadn't got over my sense of burning injustice at everything, when we reach the little house, all choked with ivy and hollyhocks and window-boxes, where you were living; and there I find you, sitting before a desk covered with piles of papers and the drawers half pulled out. 'Where is your father?' And you, looking so pale and troubled, saying, 'Didn't you get my telegrams? He died five days ago.' Imagine my poor dazed feelings. The telegrams lost because there was no Long's Hotel any longer! Of course, at bottom, this sad news was no great shock. I was expecting the worst; especially since I suffered so much on board and realised how awful it was to be away from home. But dead *five days*! To think that I shouldn't have been allowed even to be present at the funeral! And how horrible that now the body should have to be *disinterred*, when perhaps it was too late for embalming, and there were so many formalities and difficulties in having it conveyed to America! Naturally, I had always expected to bury him in our Bumstead lot at High Bluff, since now his home was there and he had become one of our family: and I shouldn't have objected on principle to cremation. It's mere superstition to imagine that what happens to the body can make any difference to the spirit: and cremation is *cleaner*. But, perhaps—the thought is too ghastly—it was too late even for that. Anyhow when we went to the Embassy to make arrangements, after being kept waiting, as if our business had been of no special importance, I never saw the Ambassador at all, but only some over-dressed young secretary who hardly let me explain the circumstances and ask whether it wouldn't be better to telegraph directly to Washington—because I *know* Theodore Roosevelt, although there was such a crowd at the Reunion of the Daughters of the Revolution that perhaps he mightn't remember me distinctly—when the secretary said they didn't deal with that kind of business, but that I must go to the consul-general, in quite another part of the city. At least, he gave me a card with the address of the Consulate printed in large letters, and ushered me politely out of the door, though he seemed to be rather pressed for time. And then at the Consul's where we had to wait again nearly half an hour, the fat horrid bald man was positively rude, interrupted me twice while I was speaking, to attend to somebody else who broke in upon us—as if my affairs were not strictly private and most painful—and the moment he had at last gathered what our trouble was (as he called it) he rang the bell, and at once—without ever getting up from his desk-chair twirling on a pivot—when a middle-aged person in glasses appeared, he said, 'This is Miss Riddle who is in charge of our Deceased Citizens Shipping Department. Miss Riddle will explain everything,' and actually motioned me away without rising, so that you had to open the door for me yourself. What manners! And I thought Miss Riddle in her own office rather looked at me askance, because I wasn't in formal black, although of course not in loud colours, so that I had to explain that I disapproved of mourning because it was wrong to fondle and foster one's sorrow, instead of turning hopefully to one's next duty. She seemed to have heard that before; and she gave more attention, I thought, to the few words you spoke than to all I had been saying. That was because she was a woman—although so far from young and you a mere boy. They ought to have *men* to deal with these matters, and I am sure a man would have shown more real sympathy with my feelings. However, she so strongly advised me to do as you said, and leave the body where it was, that I consented to go and see the grave. And I must say that the little churchyard—we had a ray of sunshine that day at last—did seem a quiet poetic spot, and its being abroad perhaps might be symbolic. Your father was such a traveller, and so little attached to his own country. The Curate too was very civil. I could see the interest he took in you; and when he opened the little Church-door for us and remained outside himself, with such a respectful religious air, as not wishing to interfere with the sacredness of our feelings—although of course we only walked round and looked at the little place, and weren't going to kneel down or pray, as if that were any use—I almost think that out in the churchyard, as he stood bare-headed with his hands clasped behind his back, he was silently praying for us.—Well, I have let you have your own way; and now that your father is gone, it is only natural that you should think of him lovingly and try to do everything as he would have wished."

With this, Mrs. Alden looked for the third time at the sky, not now so blue as before, and thought she felt some rising and falling of the ship; and she was afraid she had better lie down and rest a little before lunch, she had had such a trying morning.

XII

Indeed, when lunch-time came, Mrs. Alden still felt too *tired* to go down to the crowded dining-room. The reaction, she said, of suddenly having nothing to do after so many wearing days of worry and exertion, had made her feel how much she had over-taxed her strength and how much she needed *perfect quiet*. The stewardess had brought her a cup of beef tea, and it was really more than she wanted for the present. Oh, no, he needn't hurry away. It was only her nerves and her digestion: her *mind* wasn't tired at all. And here was a letter she didn't quite like to throw away without letting him see it. It was certainly *meant* for him to see. She had found it unopened among his father's business papers—doubtless it had slipped by chance between larger sheets and had been overlooked. And she handed him an envelope lined with coloured tissue-paper. The stamp was French and the post-mark Paris. He knew the hand-writing, big and upright and rather like print, a little unsteady and laborious, with some boyish decorations. There were several sheets. Absorbed at once, he sat down on the window-seat to read.

> 5, RUE DE SAINT SIMON,
>
> PARIS, *August 2.*
>
> DEAR UNCLE PETER,
>
> Mamma and I both hope by this time you are very much better. She is not very well herself, else she would write separately to tell you how grateful we both are for the wonderfully kind things you have done for me. Mr. Rawdon-Smith, directly he got your letter with the cheque for the South African War Memorial, became very nice to me indeed, and went at once to see the Head and the Provost, and they are frightfully pleased not only with the money—*ça va sans dire*—but with what you said about Eton and British officers. They said they had never known an American who understood England so well, and I get the benefit of it because it is all arranged that I am to return at least for one more Half, and to have a better room.
>
> I never had such a pleasant surprise in my short life as when I got those two bills *receipted*, as if by a miracle. I had so often seen them before, with a yawning blank where 'received with thanks' ought to be. It was really most

kind of you to pay them, perhaps it was Oliver's idea, but how good of you to be willing to do it! It lifts a weight off my mind, and when I turn over a new leaf in the winter Half—because I really mean to—I shall find the page quite clear. That helps a lot. Thank you a thousand times.

What a pity that you were taken ill, just when I hoped so much that you and Oliver might come to Paris. He said he had to see the English cathedrals, but I knew that was nonsense, and that it was Paris he needed to see to complete his education. It would have been lovely to see him *épaté* before the tomb of Napoleon, although he might have tried to conceal his feelings and might have pretended that there was a monument twice as big at Great Falls and twice as ugly. But he would have had to admire the *Tour Eiffel*, because that might have been built in America, only it wasn't.

I hope all this is only put off, and that you will soon be here on your way to Switzerland. I hated to say good-bye at Charing Cross, when Oliver came to see me off and gave me that lovely present. Perhaps you don't know of it, because it was a gold wrist-watch of his own which he had never worn because he says he has a prejudice against them. I haven't, and Mamma too thinks this one is beautiful.

I am so happy you came to Eton. After all that has happened it seems as if I had known you and Oliver all my life.

Your affectionate and most grateful nephew

MARIO.

P.S. I hope Oliver has kept up having tea, and can now take *two* cups. In time he will want three, and when he is an old man, *four without sugar*.

As Oliver read this letter, the presence of his mother before him, the very ship they were in, his father's death, the college life he was about to begin all faded from his mind. His expression was transfigured; his thoughts were evidently wandering amidst imaginary scenes and enchanted memories. For a long moment after finishing, he was still under the spell, and when he looked up and saw where he was, his countenance fell suddenly. He felt as if a breath of chill damp air were blowing from some underground place. All hopes, all pleasant vistas, all secret comfort had vanished. Nothing remained before him but patience, grit, work, and silence.

His mother, who observed the change, was mortally offended. She reacted at once against the new tendency in her to acquiesce in her son's wishes and secretly to respect him. Her life-long hostility and exasperation, because he was a separate being, not merely her offspring and an extension of herself, now burst out with the greater fury.

"Why did you give those extravagant presents to this little boy? I can see he is horribly knowing and glib for his age, as foreign children are. His mother is a professional actress, or was going to be one; and how do you expect an Italian opera singer to bring up her one little curly-headed ape of a child? Like a poodle and like a scamp. Why did you wheedle your sick father into paying the boy's debts, and encouraging him in his spendthrift habits, when you know he is penniless and ought to be learning the strictest economy? No doubt he wheedled you first. I daresay he amused and flattered you, probably begged and begged like those ragged urchins in European cities, asking for a penny and turning a somersault. For the pleasure of watching his tricks—and being taken in by them—you allowed your poor father to stay in that awful swamp and to perish there."

Oliver folded the letter, inserted it in its envelope and put it in his pocket, mechanically buttoning his coat over it. He was accustomed to unjust and absurd tirades from his mother. Not only was he ready to let them pass unanswered, when answering them would have been too easy, but he took pains to notice and retain certain points, often important ones, in which she might be right. It was a hideous misrepresentation of the facts to say that he had kept his father at Eton for Mario's sake. They stayed at Windsor because they were caught there: and after ten days the School had broken up and Mario had left for Paris. Then and not before, at the doctor's suggestion, they had moved to Eton from Castle Hill (which wasn't exactly a swamp) and had settled down in perfect peace and comfort, until she threatened to invade them. Yet when she said that he had allowed his father to perish, that blind shot, by a sort of *ricochet*, hit the very centre of Oliver's conscience. The previous year he had overcome a temptation; he had resisted the immense lure of the sea, of the yacht, of Lord Jim; and he still congratulated himself on that decision. But now, when what might seem the same choice had been offered to him again, and he had stuck to his guns, the case was really entirely different, even reversed; for now there had been no temptation, no lure; only a cool option between two paths, neither of them very attractive. The harder course now would really have been to change his plans and defy his mother: to shake off his provincial harness, get out of his groove, and plunge into the whirlpool of the great world since he was blest with ample facilities for swimming. But his nerve had failed him; and now his puritan scruples led him to fear that in taking the easier course he might have taken the wrong one.

Had he done the sporting thing, would his father have killed himself? Wouldn't he rather have revived? Mightn't father and son have started out, as gleeful as two truant boys, for Naples or Greece or Egypt? So, if in reality Oliver had allowed his father to perish, it was not as his mother accused him of doing, but precisely by proving incapable of casting off her influence and snapping his fingers at her world.

All this lay unexpressed in Oliver's consciousness and for the moment inexpressible. He was constitutionally little inclined to find fault with himself: he sometimes felt his limitations and was galled by them; but he was acutely conscious of his integrity and couldn't blame himself if, in trying to do right, he sometimes made a mistake. It was too late, in any case, to correct the past; and he turned pragmatically to another matter that concerned the future.

"As to helping Mario Van de Weyer," he began calmly, as if discussing some minor household arrangement, with no wound in his heart, "it was Father who asked me to find out if Vanny hadn't any little debts that we might pay for him. It never would have occurred to me that a school-boy could run up bills at the shops, or have other debts. But Vanny said he had only two, one a tailor's and another at what he called a sock-shop; and when he told me what this sock bill amounted to I couldn't believe it. However nice his socks might be, they couldn't have come to such a sum in his short life. And you should have seen him laugh. A sock-shop at Eton, said he, isn't a habberdasher's but a pastry-cook's: and then everything was explained because there is always a temptation to have a bun, especially when your fag-master hasn't allowed you time for breakfast, or another boy has gobbled it up. You see, owing this money was no sign of great wickedness and dissipation; and Father thought the family ought to be more generous with Vanny's mother. She is only getting the same allowance that her husband had had when an art-student in Paris, and though Aunt Caroline paid Vanny's school bills, he didn't have pocket money enough considering the place he was sent to and the other boys' standard of living: which was a shame, because being stinted might embitter him and defeat the object his father had at heart in insisting he should go to Eton. But it hasn't embittered him at all; on the contrary it has made him twice as humorous and disinterested. Still, Father said he intended in future to send them something—a thousand dollars—every year at Christmas; and now, of course, we shall have to do so."

"Shall we? Not *we*, in any case. There are plenty of deserving poor to provide for, without squandering vast sums on foreign flatterers and parasites. If the will turns up, as this letter did—and I haven't had time or wits to look through the documents properly—they won't get a cent. But suppose the worst: that the will was really burnt or stolen, no matter by whom; your friends will still have to wait three years for their Christmas present. For three years, being your guardian, I shall be able to protect your interests. And three years is a long time for beggars to hold out an empty hand. In a few months they will have tired of writing you nice letters. They will have forgotten you and, let us hope, you will have forgotten them. Such people live fast. Every six months they find a new set of friends and protectors."

"I daresay," Oliver replied with a half-smile, conscious of his hidden batteries, "and I shouldn't have said *we*. Of course the thousand dollars a year will be charged to me only. But my friends won't have to wait. They'll receive their present this Christmas."

"How will you get the money?"

"Borrow it."

Mrs. Alden made a movement as if she were going to lift her hands to heaven and remain open-mouthed. But she arrested the impulse in time. To strike an attitude, though natural, was wrong. Outwardly she merely winced and remained speechless; but her fancy was vividly picturing her son, at eighteen, in the hands of money-lenders, a criminal—because it was illegal for minors to contract debts—and recklessly dissipating his fortune before he came into it. Her very silence, her frightened eyes, and her contracted muscles told Oliver well enough what she was thinking.

"I shan't have to go to the Jews. Father foresaw everything. He knew you wouldn't sympathise with all the objects I might want money for. That's why he burned his will. He wished me to be free to choose my own course and my own friends. I don't want all this money for myself. It's merely a trust. And here at once is a perfect occasion for doing a true kindness, because Father said the poor rich are often much harder up than the rich poor; and if you refused to authorise me to draw this money, he told me expressly what to do. I was to ask Cousin Caleb Wetherbee to advance it. He is likely to be appointed executor, because Uncle Nathaniel is too old. In any case, Cousin Caleb was willing—Father had already consulted him—and he mentioned one or two other friends of his to whom I might go. And don't think I shall be ruined. I shall be saving large sums every year, and so will you, because Father was much richer than we supposed: and when I am of age, I am to pay everything back with interest at six per cent, compounded half-yearly; but Cousin Caleb will refuse the interest, because he is a disciple of Aristotle and Thomas Aquinas, and disapproves of usury; and when he refuses it, I am to give it to him in the form of a present for his monastery—religious picture copied from some old master, or something of that sort. So you see everything has been arranged beforehand, and you might as well avoid complications and let me have those thousand dollars at Christmas."

Such a cool concerted attack admitted of no answer; all Mrs. Alden's positions seemed to have been carried by storm. Yet she was not left without resource. People who don't live in the light of reason, who won't observe, but think on by blind brain-work, can always avoid correcting themselves or admitting defeat. When stopped short by a contrary fact, or clearly refuted, they merely abandon one automatic train of thought, and pick up another. For a lady particularly, these by-paths abound. She may always change the subject. If she is young she may become suddenly gay, or playful, or tender. If she is mature she may roundly impose her own conclusion by sheer personal ascendency; or she may grow sarcastic and contemptuous; or she may not feel well.

"Oh, no," moaned Mrs. Alden, "I really can't discuss this absurd matter now. My mind isn't working. My head aches. Please ring for the stewardess, and see if you can't open that window a little wider. More fresh air might do me good."

Presently the window had to be half closed again, because there was too much draught. She was afraid their cabins after all were on the wrong side of the ship. How could she know it beforehand, if they didn't have the decency to say so? The stupid stewardess couldn't suggest anything better than to go and sit on deck. It was a lovely afternoon, and the coast of Cornwall in sight. Two chairs had been reserved for them on the other side, just outside the door, in the most sheltered corner in the whole ship. Yes, Mrs. Alden decided to try it. Would she be warm enough? Which chair would be better? In the right hand one she would get more sun; but no, on the whole, she thought she should feel the draught less in the other. Oliver tucked her feet in between two rugs, one beneath upwards and one above downwards. He tied to the back of her chair that little red pillow from her own sofa at home. She sent him back to the cabin for her salts, with a quaver in her voice and an air of hopelessness as if she had said, "I am sorry to trouble you—I never trouble anybody—but how should I have forgotten anything so important— I never forget anything—except for this great sorrow brought upon me by you?" He always showed to his mother all those obsequious attentions which according to his code of manners were due to every lady. He was never less polite because she was his mother, and never more devoted. It was not a personal matter. He was simply doing his Duty to Others. This duty now seemed to involve that he should sit next to her, at least for a few minutes, and listen to what she had to say. For now that the interruption had served its purpose, she seemed disposed to open hostilities in a different sector.

"Really," she began, as if about to relate something curious and interesting, "I had quite forgotten that expensive wrist-watch which Mr. Wetherbee sent you last year. What an odd thing for him to do, and how uncalled for! No wonder you were shy about wearing such an article of jewelry, something so unsuitable for a schoolboy. Now another schoolboy has got it who won't be troubled by shyness. I daresay he has his hair perfumed and in a permanent wave. Letitia says all the young Italians do, they are so effeminate. But it's almost worse in an orphan child."

Effeminate! Oliver couldn't help laughing at an idea so exquisitely contrary to the fact. Yet he knew what his mother meant, and he said aloud: "At first sight he did offend me a little: he seemed conceited and flighty and rather dandified. But he isn't a child: slight but strong and almost as tall as I am; and he already has to shave, which I don't, though I'm a year and a half older. What seems swagger in him at first is really only courage—you never saw such perfect courage and gaiety and elegance. It's partly, I suppose, the manner of the place; yet he's not like other Eton boys. He worships his mother, and gets his whole deeper side from her and from the clever people she knows in Paris. Frightful amount of knowledge of the world: but he laughs at it all so merrily that it doesn't seem out of place. I never heard anyone say so many witty amusing things, as if he couldn't help himself. They are not jokes. They are just fancies running over. Then—what you wouldn't have expected—when that dreadful moment came and father fell into a lethargy in the middle of the tea-party and before that brute of a housemaster, Vanny behaved splendidly, as if such things of course would happen any day, and helped me to lead father out and get a carriage, and a doctor and a nurse, all in an instant, and without one thought for himself or his housemaster or Eton or what anybody might say or think of us. Imagine what it meant for me, alone in a strange place with father unconscious, to find such a friend who knew all the ropes and was so devoted and so active and so affectionate."

"Yes, an affectionate friend you had never set eyes on before that very day."

"I know: that makes it all the more wonderful. True, we were cousins."

"You think blood did it? I'm afraid it was money. He kept you there to pay his debts, and to give a large sum, which might have been put to good uses at home, for a perfectly useless and hideous War Memorial, simply in order to influence those snobbish people to keep him and treat him as if he were the son of a millionaire. Then, for the sake of going to London with him and giving him those absurd trinkets, you abandoned your sick father, who might have died in your absence."

"Oh, no. Father was almost well by that time, slept and dozed most of the time, and had the nurse with him. The boys leave very early in the morning. I was back for lunch, and we drove out that afternoon as usual."

"Why go to London at all—such a horrid journey—just to see the child off? What ceremony!"

"I hate to talk about all this, Mother. It won't interest you. But you force me. Why can't you trust to my feelings being right and let me go my own way? Well, he had come to London with me once before, on the day Father was taken ill, just to help me, and cheer me up, and not let me go alone. He had relieved me of half the worry— almost turned it into fun—catching trains and taking cabs, and getting things packed, and scurrying back again."

"But you paid for everything."

"Of course I paid for everything—except the kindness. You can't pay for kindness. And what do you suppose was going to happen to him, and he knew would happen, in consequence? He was *thrashed* for coming to help me, *birched*, *swished*, or whatever they call it: actually thrashed because it was against their ridiculous rules, or rather—for the rule itself might be right enough—because they are too stupid and wooden-headed and domineering to see when a rule *ought* to be broken. He was thrashed—think of it! Suppose *I* had ever been thrashed! And he knew he would be thrashed, and yet did it for my sake with all the cheerfulness of a summer morning. And when I found it out by chance, because one of his friends mentioned it and said it was a d—— a *great* shame—of course he hadn't breathed a word of the matter—when I told him how terribly, how horribly I felt about it, he merely laughed and said they were always being *swished* for one thing or another, that it wasn't an indignity, as I supposed, any more than getting caught in the rain or having a tooth stopped. Schoolmasters were only like rain falling or dentists boring a hole into you. They were unpleasant but unimportant. Nobody really minded what they did or said, not even they themselves in their own hearts. They were just parrots in gowns or surplices, and drew their real morale from the boys, or from their own boyhood. The pupils were usually a better sort or more up to date than the tutors, and had their own code of honour, which alone mattered. The Head, who did the *swishing*, was a great swell and merely acted on the reports he received; and he didn't *swish* very hard. It was more like a solemn religious penance—or would have been but for the part exposed to view. And even that odious Mr. Rawdon-Smith, his housemaster, who was the person really to blame, Vanny said was merely opinionated—all teachers had to be—and when in difficulties he got flurried and overbearing, partly because he had too many things to think of, and his house wasn't in very good odour. It was a hard life the old codger had to lead, like a tug-of-war, always pulling and never getting any for'arder. He said too—but I won't tell you that—or, rather, yes I will tell you—he said being thrashed was like women having children. The first time it was awful, because you were scared, as the strokes kept on coming; but afterwards, although perhaps it hurt just as much, you weren't scared any more; you knew it would be all right soon, and you were ready to have it happen again and again any number of times."

Oliver did not suspect it, but this was a home thrust. His mother had taken every precaution after his birth never to have another child; and as she publicly approved of large families, especially when of pure native stock, she let it be understood that her less fortunate lot was due to her husband being so much older than herself—he was eight years older—and having such a broken constitution. Superior as she thought herself, she was far from suspecting that the foundation of morality and intelligence had been sapped in her, and in her tribe. She had lost the blind physical courage normal in all animals and necessary to keep the world going. What she noticed on this occasion was that Oliver had referred to *childbirth* again, supplying this time the proof positive of what of course she had guessed: that he was quoting and echoing the gross language of his foreign friends.

"I quite agree," she observed, "that these mediaeval schools are cruel, and degrading to the character. Their best pupils hunt foxes and go into the army: and I have heard of Englishmen who are not ashamed of having been in prison. All schools, I am afraid, coarsen the moral fibre; and that is why I was sorry to have to send you even to the Great Falls High School, although it is of the best and least contaminating, and you had me and Fräulein at home to counteract any evil influences that might reach you there. What can be more demoralising than to live under rules which you allow yourself to break, and are proud of breaking? How can you avoid cheating, lying sneaking and mockery under such a system? That is what this sad young Mario is learning only too well. You see how cunningly he set out to amuse and flatter your poor father and you, and to show himself effusive and affectionate, at first sight, all for the sake of money. To be sure, his mother has set the example. Those people *marry* for money"—Mrs. Alden's theory was that she herself had not married for money, but on principle, because a married life was so much higher, more normal and more unselfish. "And if people marry for money," she went on, "why shouldn't they make themselves agreeable to their distant relations with the same object? Do you suppose a flighty spoilt child could *love* a sick old man like your father? Do you think he took a fancy to you suddenly and for no reason, as you did to him? He's not such a fool. What is there in you that he could care for? He wants your money—and he is getting it."

Oliver was white with rage. But as rage was not a sentiment which he supposed himself capable of, or could allow himself to express in words, he merely got up from his deck-chair—which in itself had annoyed him, being too recumbent for his taste—thrust his hands deep in his pockets, and made his way between the life-boats and other encumbrances on deck, to where, with his back to the ship, he might see nothing before him but the sky and the water. They looked dull at that moment, and leaden; yet they were beyond the vileness, the littleness, the gnawing selfishness of mankind. Merely by looking at them it was possible to enlarge one's spirit and heal these self-inflicted wounds.

Mrs. Alden felt the gulf, the impassable gulf, widening and widening between herself and her son. She didn't wish to bridge it: not only was that impossible, but there was a certain strange pleasure in the tragedy of it. She had nothing to retract. She had been right in everything.

Presently Oliver returned, and without saying a word, picked up the books and rug from his chair, evidently with no intention of sitting down again. "I see," said Mrs. Alden, "that I am making you unhappy and filling you with hatred of your own mother. But it was my duty to warn you. You don't want to live in a fool's paradise—which wouldn't be a paradise long. You wish to face the facts—don't you?—even if at first they seem unpleasant. And when you are used to them, you will be glad you faced them, and thank me for having pointed them out."

"Oh, yes, I wish to face the facts, and I am facing them," he said turning full on his mother with a hardness which he felt was not anger but merely superior insight into those facts, which he understood better than she, and from more sides. "I must do what I think right, but I shan't forget your warning, and *you needn't repeat it.*—I'll come back in an hour to see if you want anything."

In his own cabin, as he thrust *Tom Brown at Rugby* into the pocket of his great-coat, and put on a knitted jacket against the cold wind blowing, the reverberation of those parting words of his, *"you needn't repeat it"* pleased him enormously. Just because they were defiant, just because they were insolent, he was glad he had uttered them. This was no wanton insolence, but a fair warning on his own part. He would rather be exploited by his friends than mortgaged to his enemies. His allegiance in any case must be to his own conscience, to his own reason. On that basis he was not in the least afraid of the future—fool's paradise or virtuous hell, or whatever you might call it.

XIII

The windward side of the deck was too windy for reading, the lee side too crowded. He couldn't desert his mother in order to install himself a little further down the same row of cackling old ladies drinking beef-tea and chattering young girls munching apples and biscuits. He wished to feel he was in a ship at sea, not in an overcrowded boarding-house. Exploring and dissatisfied, he found his way to the after-deck, where the second-class passengers fore-gathered. An occasional interloper from the first cabin was not frowned upon, though the second cabin people were strictly forbid-den to trespass amidships. The normal order of nature here reas-serted itself against the accident of progress. Higher beings might sink, because they enveloped and contained the faculties of the lower: but lower beings might not rise, because the higher faculties were beyond them. Oliver liked to feel that he contained and enveloped within himself all the lower faculties of man, although since he was manifestly called to exercise the higher, he might not find time or occasion to exercise the others. Yet it would be pleasant and whole-some to exercise them when possible. He liked, or imagined he might like, sometimes to recover and enact the primitive clansman or the solitary hunter or even the mere animal or vegetable within his human nature: yes, it might be an extraordinary relief, an ultimate home-coming, if one could lose oneself and be absorbed again in the mere weight and potentiality of matter. Existence was a complication, a commitment, a pose. Of course, to play the game you must follow the rules: but why this game, or these rules? And why play at all? There seemed to be two selves or two natures within him; one, pure spirit, that might play any game and lodge in any animal; the other, this particular human, American, twentieth century male person called Oliver Alden. He was perfectly content to be this person and play this part. If by some magic he could elude the creative circum-stances that had made him himself, he would find his spirit caught in another set of circumstances, and talking through another mask: and what would be the advantage of that? The point was not to be oneself too blindly, without winking one eye. After all, one's real self was universal spirit. Travelling second class (or in England third class) was a slight shift in the universal direction. There was something warming cheerful and human about it. He remembered what his father had said, when asked if he thought Jim Darnley a gentleman. "When Jim is in the company of gentlemen he can behave like one. When he is with common people, I daresay he becomes one of *them*. He likes common people just as I do." "Stop a moment," Oliver had put in. "When you are with common people you are more the gentleman than ever. You are very kind, very simple, very friendly; and it is they that become civil and refined for the moment, and not you that become common. But isn't it the other way with Jim?"

Peter had laughed his inaudible laugh and agreed that perhaps the gentleman, in the old chivalrous sense, was vowed to his order, and incapable of not being a gentleman under any circumstances. There were things he was pledged not to do and not to allow. Neither he, nor anyone in his presence, must ever be cowardly, cruel, mean, ungrateful, foul, or disloyal. So that the gentleman though always respected, was often disliked. He wasn't the most accommodating of companions, and those who were not gentlemen were happier when he was out of the way.

Oliver also remembered that other speech of his father's about the lilies in the Eton arms; and he felt that now he understood it better.

He had reached the extreme stern, whence he could watch the seething wake of the vessel receding like the rapids of a river. There were no deck chairs so far aft, and he sat on a bench surrounding a low deck house covered with a tarpaulin. The place was abandoned by people thinking they chose better places, and probably choosing worse. Here, at least, was the wonderful happiness of solitude. Oliver re-read Mario's letter. There was a subtle satisfaction in hiding in the open, and feeling what a deep secret might lie hidden in things perfectly innocent and published to the world. You might lead a double life without duplicity; indeed, you must, if you had any inner life at all; for about the important things you always had to be silent. Here in the safety of the second class no emissary of his mother's would dream of disturbing him and deafening him with useless disputes. He was happy in the mere sensation of voyaging, bearing inexpressible possibilities locked up somewhere within him, together with strength and courage somehow to reduce them to acts. It mattered comparatively little what the particular adventures might be;

the spirit of the action and the manner of it would transfigure anything. The point was to be a gentleman, to be vowed to defend and exalt the beautiful in all things, to be the champion of tenderness, of honesty, of liberty. Mario—for the name and the image of his cousin had not lapsed from his mind—Mario must not be lost. It was he, Oliver, that would preserve him. He would plant himself like a bare stout stick beside that sprouting rose-bush, as in the Vicar's garden at Iffley he had seen the gaunt bare branches of a judas-tree supporting a crimson rambler already in full leaf. Really those dry sticks too were secretly alive: soon every brown twig would bud and the purple flowers, modest and short-lived like the flush of dawn, would spring as if by miracle from the wood, and the dark green leaves would follow after and make a spreading shade. So the two striplings would grow up together, upright and firm, covered with a profusion of roses, and so intermingled that no one could tell whose was the strength and whose were the graces.—How jolly here at sea were those grey distances hiding no danger not to be gladly faced, no on-coming wave not exhilarating and easily breasted! How pleasantly ironical this moral calm in the midst of motion, this pause full of acceleration, this security in forging full steam ahead into the invisible! The spirit felt at home beforehand in the unknown future, as it did in the forgotten past. Like the sea, it was greater than any islands or continents of fact that might nestle within it. It was an inviolate witness of all mutations, a poet turning all human tragedies into music, all human folly into laughter. Yes, the spirit was inhumanly happy in the very miseries of the world, and not puzzled or oppressed by all the world's contradictions, because the very life of the spirit was the painful joy of conceiving, of solving, or of enduring them. Why clamour about things, as if they ought to be easier? Why protest against ill fortune and death, as if one ought to have been especially favoured and immortal? "I find myself here," said Oliver to himself, almost audibly, "from here I must start. No matter how the weather may turn, I must see the end of this voyage."

Restored by his philosophy and by the freshening wind, he turned up the collar of his great-coat, wrapped round his feet the rug he had prudently brought with him, pulled *Tom Brown at Rugby* out of his pocket, and settled down to read. But he did not open the book: instead, he turned the guns of deliberate reflection upon his mother's position. She was no fool. She had laid her finger more than once on the tender places of his soul. He felt in his bones how true it was that money was important to the Van de Weyers. There might well be no better way to their hearts than gifts and the prospect of gifts. Yet they had hearts, and if you took that way, you found they had them. Of course, if he had been a poor cousin, instead of a rich one, Vanny would never have written that nice letter of thanks, because there would have been no occasion; and the cousins couldn't have made those little trips on half holidays, or had those little treats, or bought those little things, or planned those great things—those endless explorations geographical and moral—because they wouldn't have had the wherewithal, or as Vanny put it in his comic Latin, *cum quibus*. And very likely they would never have met again, or kept up a correspondence, as now they would. But all that was a matter of worldly fortune. There was something else, which his mother chose to ignore; there were persons. "That day in Windsor Park," said Oliver to himself, "when he felt I didn't like the tone he was taking, why did his eyelashes drop, and his lip tremble, when he said, 'I'm sorry. I was talking rot.' Because I was rich? Suppose I had been the poorest of poor relations, but still myself, would it have happened differently? No: it would have happened exactly the same. It was one conscience bending before another, one mind trembling before another mind. And in the train did he always sit close to me instead of opposite, because I am rich? He wants to see things as I see them, when I see them, in the same light, from the same angle, so that there may be one object for two minds, one feeling in two persons. Everything then becomes a new bond of union. And when I talked, did he listen in that absorbed way, and find something to cap my thought, and to decorate it, to make it a thousand times more just and witty, because I am rich? He *does* like me for myself; he *does* want to understand me; he *is* ready to condemn anything in himself that I might think wrong. When we are together he is happy, just as I am happy. I daresay he doesn't think much about me when I am out of sight; but he likes me when I am there. Because Mother never loved me, she won't allow that anybody else can. Yet some people do. Not Lord Jim, I know, though he likes to be chummy. Not Father, really, though he was interested in my future. They both thought me poor stuff. I overheard them one day talking about it. My grandfather had been a terror, a ferocious Calvinist, amassing a fortune by grinding the faces of the poor, and consigning them afterwards to hellfire. There's where our money comes from. He was worth murdering, but nobody will mind me enough to murder me. Father himself was all the other way, limp, kind, lavish, and humorous; yet he had force enough to choose his own way, to explore the world sceptically, and not to be roped in or annexed by anybody, not even by Mother. But they think I'm just negative, just passive, turned out like printed wallpaper, the third sloppy wash in the family teapot. That I should be the head boy at school, and row and play football, seems to them childish: it means nothing in their world, a fault if anything, because it is so prim and conventional. But it means something to Mario. *He* knows the difference between a good athlete and a minus quantity. And he loves that physical force, that trained courage. It may not be directed upon anything important, but it's there; and I have more of it than he, or than most of his friends. He says he's fed up with the ways of the young men he knows. The English are all right but mindless, just a nice pack of hounds; and the French and Italians are cheap stuff, smelling of cigarettes and eau-de-Cologne, drinking and swearing and gambling and buzzing round the women and cavorting on stallions. Being with me, he says, is like going from the city to the country—and he says that to laugh at me, because I'm provincial. But I know he means it also in the other sense, that it's like getting away from mud and noise and darkness into the green fields and the mountains.

"Besides, Mario is not the only one. There's Irma. I'm her Siegfried. And Tom Piper, I'm his hero too. And Cousin Caleb Wetherbee, who gave me the gold watch, and thinks God has chosen me to be a second Messiah. Yes, and a lot of other people who hardly know me: Mr. Darnley, and the Curate at St. Giles and Rose and even Bobby. I'm not a cipher for them, or just somebody who is rich. Yet all these people, in one way or another are poor unfortunates. They like me because, being young and tall and all that, I pay attention to them and treat them kindly and make them feel that, for a wonder, somebody likes *them*. And money counts immensely with them too: not that they expect any material benefit for themselves, but that they like to put on their Sunday clothes, as it were, and feel in touch with a better world. Snobbery, but only in the better sense: love of a nicer prospect than one's back yard. Now the grand thing about Vanny is that it isn't my outside that he cares for, as if nobody at all young or pleasant or well-connected ever came in his way. It's my inside. He himself is ever so much handsomer, more brilliant, accomplished, and fashionable than I could ever dream of being, and so are a lot of his friends; he doesn't need me to amuse him or excite him or flatter him. And I shouldn't wonder if he had already had a complete love-affair or two with some chamber-maid or some grand lady, in spite of his ridiculous youth. I'm sure he has. Perhaps with little Mildred. Oh, it's not he that needs comforting, but I. He feels it, and wants to comfort me; and he does it by trusting me, by asking for my opinion in everything and building on it as if it were gospel truth. And this with so much confidence, with so much pleasure, as if he had never understood things so well or been so happy before. He counts on me; and in that light having money becomes a comfort too, instead of an awful nuisance. He needs steadying; is a bit dizzy with his butterfly existence and his uncertain future; and as the cows on a hot day like to get under the trees, he likes to get under my shadow. When he takes me by the arm, as he is always doing, it's not at all to mark a sort of clannishness, like a fraternity pin, as it is with the swells at Eton; it's rather as if he said: 'I don't care where we go, but I want to go with you.' It's love. And if Mother says no one can love me for myself, it's a lie."

Having reached this comforting conclusion, and beginning to feel rather cold, Oliver got up, put the unread *Tom Brown at Rugby* back into his coat pocket, filled his lungs to their depths with salt air, felt he had his sea legs on, and struck himself approvingly a great blow on the chest, by chance over the very place where he had put his cousin's letter.

He was about to turn away, after a farewell look at the rushing stream that marked the speed of the vessel, when suddenly he felt a heavy warm hand clapped on his shoulder. The surprise somehow was not pleasant. "Lucky at least," he thought, "that coming up so stealthily from behind, he didn't lay both his big hands over my eyes and say, *Guess who!* He might be capable of it."

"How's this? Moping? Startled you a bit, did I? You don't like to have an old friend barging into you like this, without first sending up his card. Sorry. Promise never to do so again.—A pretty friend you are, not to let a chap know when you're in trouble. If Minnie hadn't seen the Doctor's death in the paper and wired at once, God knows when I should have heard of it. At Iffley they never know anything. Had only just time to catch this boat, scrambled aboard when the last gangway was half in the air. And I haven't been in bed for two nights."

Oliver wondered what Jim Darnley could be doing here, so unexpectedly and so officiously. Why had he taken this ship? Why was he going to America at all? It seemed, although it was but six weeks since they had separated, that he looked coarser, shorter, thicker, redder in the face. At least it was evident that he hadn't shaved that morning, and the old purple-and-red striped muffler tucked in under his jacket half concealed a not very clean collar. That jacket itself, thick and weather stained, with the leather binding at the wrists and pockets worn shiny with hard use, was surely a relic of days long past, when Lord Jim had worked in a tug-boat on the coast of Alaska. Did putting it on now symbolise a return to hard times and tough morals? And this gallant young tar, only a year ago so smart and smiling, so youthful and luxurious,—looking almost like an officer in the Imperial German War Navy—what a disillusion poor Fräulein would suffer if she could see him now!

"You see how it is," and he glanced apologetically at his own person, as if conscious that he was not being admired, "I hadn't meant to look you up to-day—was going to send you a little note to-morrow telling you that I was on board—but seeing you musing here all alone, I couldn't help saying howdy, could I? Don't think I boarded the *Lusitania* by accident. I knew you were on board: saw the advanced passenger list at the Cunard Office: very first names on the top of the first class: *Mrs. Peter Alden, Mr. Oliver Alden.* And having urgent business in New York, I thought: Here's a chance. I could have a long quiet talk with you on neutral ground, here in mid-Atlantic before you are locked up at home in that country college."— and Jim scanned the sea with all his seaman's coolness and discernment as if the fact that it was roughening interested him professionally. "Of course, as to your father, I needn't express my sympathy. It's as bad—really twice as bad—for me as for you. The Doctor was everything to me—everything. And I wasn't expecting the end quite yet. If I had known—I shouldn't be in such a hole. But what's the use of whining? We must keep a look-out for'ard and not aft—as we are doing here." And Jim laughed in his old pleasant clear-headed way, as much as to say: "I bear no grudge against fortune; I take everything as it comes; I don't set up any pretensions or standards or special requirements; but when a plum comes my way, I'm damned if I don't snatch it."

Meantime Oliver had in mind to explain that he hadn't telegraphed at once to Marseilles, because, with his mother in charge, it would have been worse than useless for Jim to put in an appearance. But instead of this, quite without his consent, a rather impertinent question came to his lips.

"You're in the second cabin?"

"Rather: and nice and cheap it is too. I'm getting my passage for nothing. Came aboard without a ticket; but the Bursar is an old friend of mine and he's made it all right. There happens to be a big cabin—a double one—given up at the last moment and fully paid for. I'm berthed in it all alone like an Admiral. Mind you, I'm working my way across: helping the Bursar prepare his papers for the damned Custom house." Some innuendo in the tone of these words caused Oliver to remark: "But you're not overworked."

"No," Jim replied dryly. It didn't mortify him to feel that he was giving himself away. On the contrary, he liked being understood so readily. Yet the ground was a bit dangerous, and both remained silent, watching the seething wake, now grown shorter and somewhat serpentine in the rising sea. As if troubles were brewing, the leaden waves came on faster and darker, and more obviously staged one behind and above the other; while the whole broad stern of the ship was pitching ponderously and floundering now to port and now to starboard. Beneath, the waves churned up by the screws slapped one another furiously and hissed like a nest of aroused serpents.

It was decidedly time to go and look after one's mother.

XIV

The next morning there was still a stiff breeze and a heavy sea, but the sun was shining brightly between scudding clouds, white though laden here and there on their lower edges with shreds of the departing storm. There were rainbows northwards above the breaking waves, each time the spray flew: the upper decks were clean and clear. Oliver had had a good English breakfast, almost alone in the big saloon; and he decidedly felt that a sea voyage was something glorious. His mother had spoken to him, somewhat brokenly through her closed cabin door. She thought it would be wiser for her, for a day or two, not to go on deck at all; it was really too cold and comfortless and agitating; and she needed a *complete rest*, so as to be *quite fresh* for all the hard work and important decisions that would now fall upon her at home. Would he please tell the stewardess again to be sure and bring that arrowroot really hot and milky, because not only Letitia Lamb but even Emily Fixsome—who wasn't at all a good sailor—recommended it highly for convalescents; and would he *please* lock his own door—it was awful to hear it banging—and not leave it merely hooked, because then it *rattled*.—Yes, that was absolutely all she wanted that morning.

Thus liberated, hatless, with the wind blowing his sandy hair merrily in every direction, Oliver stalked along the hurricane deck, then deserted and drying in the sunshine. His heart was buoyant, as if he had been Alexander ready for the conquest of the world; and yet, what was there to do? Drinking in the sea-wind, after five minutes, seemed insufficient. Should he look up Lord Jim in the second cabin? He couldn't help laughing, though not with unmixed pleasure: the irony of that mock title struck him with a new force. Why should Jim be on board at all? It would have been so much better to have been left alone, with this wonderful ocean around one. There was four times as much water as land on the globe: it would be enough if one fourth of our time and of our hearts were given to human affairs and the other three quarters to—what? Nature, truth, God, call it what you will: that larger inhuman something that surrounded humanity, sustained it, and made it ridiculous. Second class! Our whole human world was horribly second class: no need of drawing snobbish distinctions within it. And Oliver laughed aloud at the absurdity of classes and at his mother's delusion, thinking that the Bumsteads and the Aldens and all their unhappy constrained ways were absolutely first class, when in fact they were only *one* class, with its wretchedly meagre, forced, insecure, second class standard of firstness. No: Lord Jim mustn't be disowned for going second class. Perhaps that was precisely his good side. The top and the bottom seemed equally natural to him, and equally contemptible. He seemed perfectly natural and perfectly contemptible to himself. And from a certain height, at a certain distance, wasn't that right? Wasn't it what Jim's father taught in his inspired sermons *de contemptu mundi*? Ah, what a perfect creature Jim might have been, were there only sea and no land, only ships and no ports, only men and no women! Your young Triton was helpless against land poisons; the most vulgar seaport debauchery could infect and destroy him. Here was Lord Jim, after a month of London or Marseilles or Monte Carlo, woefully down at heel, coarsened, degraded, slovenly, unwashed, grown miserly if not dishonest, just when he had come into a lot of money—how many thousands must the yacht be worth, with everything in it?—and reeking of low cunning when he might for once have been generous and straightforward. But Jim could dive deep and swim a long time under water and come up again as fresh and jolly as ever. These were not new degradations for him; it was not for the first time that he had now been flirting with crime. All this vice was in the bastard's background, it was his native soil. The wonder was, what he had managed to raise upon this sad foundation: how much capacity and good humour and liberty of mind he had developed notwithstanding, pushing his way through a rough world like a stout porpoise or a little puffing tug, enormously powerful for its size, and splendidly asserting its right of way.

The trouble was that after all man was a land animal. He could live at sea only on land provisions; and into the midst of an infinite ocean he was bound to lug his tight little cask of land-water, or he would die of thirst. The sad human side of things was their near side: we could rise to the happy impersonal spheres of nature and truth only if we had first prudently organised our bodies and our societies, so as to have eyes to see and telescopes to help them. That was why the life of your pure adventurer, of your utterly free mind, was so tragic: it was uprooted, it was a cut flower: and Oliver hated cut-flowers and didn't wish to be uprooted. Yet, it was sad, too, it was ignominious, to be held down by one's roots, to be planted for ever in one accidental spot: and he couldn't help envying and admiring the flying mind, the defiant heart, not held back by the fear of death from the joy of living. Might it not be that we were all in reality upon a pilgrimage: that what the rebels abandoned was not our true home; that those who thought themselves deeply rooted were only deeply entangled; and that the ultimate advantage of gathering sap and feeding on the world was to have strength to renounce it nobly?

All this philosophy, which I have phrased for him, lay inarticulate in Oliver's mind: definite and certain was only the resolve that Lord Jim should not be abandoned. Since for some unknown reason he was on board, it would be cowardly to avoid him. And foolish, too; because, pleasant or unpleasant, there was always matter in his talk; yes, and magnetism in his person. If Oliver's father had been here wouldn't he have gone at once to the second cabin and had a drink with Jim and a long chat? And Jim's own father, that saintly learned man, wouldn't he positively have preferred the second cabin or even the steerage, and the society of his not too virtuous son, to all the dull ponderosity or gilded silliness of people in the cabins-*de-luxe*?

Impelled by these high sentiments, Oliver passed the barrier into the after deck. A few of the hardier passengers, wrapped in rugs and wearing knit woollen foolscaps, or shawls over their heads, were ranged like Egyptian coffins in the lee of the deck-house. He circled the whole stern, but Jim wasn't there. Strange that a sailor shouldn't love this splendid weather and should sit by preference in some malodorous close cabin. He must be pulled out, aired, ventilated, reminded of his genuine pleasures and of his young friend, his *superior* young friend—for Oliver had learned from Schopenhauer that groundless modesty was a fault—his one remaining link with decency: because the Vicar's influence over his son was like that of the starry heavens, at once too sublime and too constant to make any difference.

Accordingly the young Apostle braced himself to seek his lost sheep in the second-class smoking-room; and he had to brace himself actually, in order to force open the stiff little door, and step over the high brass frame that formed the threshhold. There, to be sure, sat Lord Jim playing cards, with a whisky-and-soda—though it wasn't ten in the morning—at his elbow, in what seemed rather rowdy company: some young, others fat and middle-aged and evidently of the Jewish persuasion, but all looking more or less sallow, bloated, and dishevelled in their nondescript clothes. Winy puffs of smoke came from their loose mouths, and stale stinking threads of it rose from the ashtrays, to meet and fuse in the upper air of the cabin and form layers of yellow cloud, hanging lazily there, dubiously lighted by some ray of sunshine struggling through the barred sky-lights; until, caught in the draught, those murky fleeces suddenly mended their pace, and scurried out through the ventilators, like sheep over a hedge. But Jim himself in the centre seemed unaccountably different, not only from the rest of the picture, but from himself of yesterday. He looked ten years younger—positively twenty, though in that case certainly a champion boxer or football player. Not only was he beautifully shaved, shorn, and ruddy this morning, but radiant as a village bridegroom in an immaculate white silk shirt and sky-blue knitted silk tie, and newly pressed light grey clothes, with the softest of many coloured woollies in lieu of a waistcoat. His air was that of a professional sport or, as perhaps Vanny would have said, a regular nut. Oliver hated fine clothes for himself, but had now learned to tolerate them in his English friends, whose function in part was to be decorative; and this suddenly recovered bloom in Jim's person actually delighted him. "Just see," he said to himself, "what a good influence I have over him! He has worked hard for two or three hours in the gymnasium, or had a Turkish bath, or perhaps both, and has dressed himself up in his best new clothes—although *that* wasn't necessary—simply to prove to me that he is still his old self, and second class only occasionally, voluntarily, and out of bravado, because he's beyond such distinctions."

That the transformation had occurred for Oliver's benefit was quite true. Jim—in spite of the cold reception he had met with the day before—was sure that the boy would turn up that morning. That coldness, Jim thought, was merely an effect of surprise and momentary displeasure: the very opposite of indifference. That unpleasant impression could be easily effaced. Jim would show at once that he was a young war-horse that might have been harnessed by mistake to a coal-cart, yoked, galled, bespattered for a while, yet not ashamed to have done that job lustily too, and by no means broken down or cowed or gelded. And when his expectation was fulfilled, and Oliver appeared, evidently in search for him, a gleam passed over his eyes, eyes that looked wonderfully clear and blue—matching his tie—in the midst of that tanned visage and under those heavy eyebrows. He pretended to take no notice, and went on playing his hand; yet it would not have escaped a subtle observer that he had straightened himself in his chair, and was playing more quickly, as if the end were in sight, and with a more concentrated attention. His whole person declared: I knew you would come, I was expecting you, wait a bit, I will be with you in a moment. And indeed, with his last trick (which he won) he gulped down the rest of his whisky-and-soda, rose, and asked a washed-out youth who had been looking over his shoulder to take his place at the table. Then, with an assurance and momentum peculiar to his movements, he swept Oliver out of the room. "Beastly hole, this. We don't want to stay here. Come and see what a tiptop cabin I've got."

"But it's so beautiful on deck," Oliver murmured, hanging back. Yet he allowed himself to be pushed by main force through another door and down a labyrinth of narrow passages. At each turn or at each flight of stairs, there was a mock tussle, Oliver bearing, as in a football scrimmage, with his whole weight against the onset, or dodging and escaping as if he himself held the ball. It was like a gambol of schoolboys or of puppies: though taller by two or three inches, Oliver felt like a stripling matched against a man's strength; and something feminine in him found pleasure in prolonging a resistance which he knew would be overborne. The big dog might throw him but wouldn't bite him. There was an essence of laughing victory in defying a greater physical force which he knew to be morally at his mercy.

"Here you are," Jim cried, out of breath, as at last he drove Oliver through a cabin door, and bolted it behind them. "Isn't it a lovely stateroom? Meant for three, and I have it all to myself. Quieter, too, I daresay, than your bridal suite, with the wind howling by and the women cackling. Turn in here whenever you want to be alone. You'll find the lounge under the port-holes perfect for reading."

Large as it was the cabin seemed to Oliver close and fusty. All the appointments were cheap, and a bit shabby: and the wash of the sea, swift, leaden, and livid, swept every fifteen seconds over the port-holes and horribly darkened the den, while the whole ship rolled ponderously and everything trembled. He was no lover of luxury, but he hated confinement. The merest suggestion of being smothered, of being drowned, was agony to him. And why had Jim bolted the door? To keep it from banging like the one above that disturbed his mother?

"Let's go out on deck." He spoke with so dry a throat and looked so troubled and serious, that whatever high jinks his friend might have been ready for were definitely cut short.

"Feeling the motion a bit, my young land-lubber? All right: but now you know the place, if you ever feel lonely in your palatial apartments, you can always come here, day or night, to read or to sleep."

Oliver shook his head.

"Don't like the smell of the second cabin, eh? Well, if you prefer, I could jolly well slip into your quarters, at night I mean, and we could keep a watch or two together, as in the old days."

Oliver shook his head again. They were on deck by this time and he had recovered his equanimity.

"Of course I'd love to see you, there or here—what difference does the place make? But it can't be while we're on board, not this trip, because my mother wouldn't like it. Luckily your name isn't in the passenger list, and she doesn't dream you're on board. If she knew it, she'd be in a terrible state. I don't think I'd better come often and join you even here on deck. Someone would be sure to see us from the palm lounge which looks aft, and it would get round to my mother. I know she has no right to object. It's understood that I may choose my own friends. But she and I don't agree very well as it is, and we had better avoid a fresh row. I'm sorry: but it's nasty doing anything that one has to hide."

"Some people think hiding adds to the fun," Jim answered, grinning broadly. Oliver had never noticed before how large his teeth were, and how uneven. He had fangs like a tiger. It might be jolly for a while to play with the wild beast's cub, so soft and cat-like; but what if one day it suddenly snarled and scratched? There seemed to be a terrible unmasking involved in ceasing to be young. Playing for fun became gambling for money; even laughter began to hide an evil intention. A middle-aged man in the press of life couldn't afford to have friends any longer. His so-called friends were only such of his enemies as he might hope to use or to govern. Peter had once made an observation of this sort; and he had added something his son now remembered and began to understand: that a man willing to be friendless might yet be kind. Friendship was a pagan ideal, the boyish sentiment of comrades in discovery. The tenderness of maturity and disillusion had another colour: it was charity. Jim could recover at moments a false bloom of youth, and with it the full flush and recklessness of friendship: the thing wasn't feigned, yet it was treacherous. The man had really outgrown that phase and would shrink back at once within the hard shell of his calculated interests, real or imaginary.

These wise suspicions were overlaid as usual in Oliver's mind by the flood of his sympathy with outer nature.

"How glorious it is here," he said, seizing his friend by the arm and drawing him to the rail. "I can't see how anybody like you, who has once been a sailor, can ever live happy on shore. They say the sea is monotonous, but look at it! It's more shifting, more living than the land, and yet more constant. Always the old crescendos and diminuendos, the same squalls and calms, the same blues and greys; but you never know when they blow or where; and you must always be on the watch and are never tired of watching."

"Do you know, young man, that you are talking damned poetry? The plain prose of it is, how a man may earn his living. That's the question with me now. I'm threatened with ruin. The Bey of Tunis— your father must have told you about it—wanted to buy the *Black Swan*. We were a long time at Tunis last winter: your father said it was the most unspoiled of old places. Wind got round that he spoke Arabic: he was invited to the palace: and the Bey's sons returned the visit on board. We gave them a magnificent luncheon and a trip under full sail. They were enthusiastic; they wheedled their old father; and discreet inquiries followed whether the yacht could be purchased. I told them the exact truth, that she was leased to your father with the privilege of renewal indefinitely, but that perhaps he mightn't care to keep her much longer; and there were some negotiations about the possible price. The old nabob is probably used to squeezing everybody dry, and wanted her for almost nothing; but I might have sold her to him now, to save the horrible expense mounting up every month, when she must be berthed, watched, scraped, overhauled, taxes paid and insurance, and oneself fed and clothed meantime on nothing. I telegraphed from Marseilles; and the answer was: *'Yacht no longer desired.'* Luckily, there is someone else in the offing. The very day Minnie wired I got a cablegram: *'If Black Swan for sale with collections communicate with Charles Deboyse, Somerset Club, Boston.'* That's what I'm going to America for. But there's a fly in the ointment. I don't know how much old Deboyse cares about the collections, or knows about them. They are no longer complete."

Jim made a long pause, to light his pipe, producing a box of fusees and waiting to strike a light with all the leisurely precautions and the quick action necessary in war or in a fresh wind. The first puff drawn, and the precious fire properly hooded with his hand, he resumed his confidences.

"Now that is what I wanted to talk to you about—the books and the collections. Naturally, my first thought is to carry out your father's wishes. He didn't want you to have *all* those books, or *all* those curios. They were hardly the sort of thing you would care for. That was one reason why he gave me the yacht instead of a present in cash or a legacy: he didn't want you or his executors to meddle with his private treasures. I was just the sort of confidential chap who could dispose of them quietly and to my own advantage. And in this respect that rum old Bey of Tunis would have been just the person: he didn't want any books or any antiques, genuine or faked: even the Buddhas were heathen idols that it would have shocked him to behold. So that, by selling the *Black Swan* to him, I could still have kept the books and the bric-a-brac to sell separately. There's a chap in London, rather a friend of mine, the very devil of a sharp Jew, who palms off old masters on the American millionaires: and he likes to have a few genuine objects in his shop, to set the tone: and he's offering me a thousand pounds for the Chinese collection alone, because Chinese art is now the fashion. But you don't care about fashion, do you? All you want is some memento of your father; and I meant to keep the standard works for you: Dickens and *Don Quixote*, and so on, with all the rare illustrations: at a pinch you might swallow the *Arabian Nights* also, to show to your friends in private; and now you are going to the university you might make your rooms simply lovely with some of the Indian stuffs and the Buddhas from the Poop, to remind you of the *Black Swan*; so that when the young ladies come to tea, they would have something to talk about. 'Oh, Mr. Alden, where *did* you get these lovely things?' And with a bored air, knocking the ashes off your gold cigarette with your little finger, you would reply, 'Ah, that's nothing. Trifles my ancestors picked up centuries ago in the Far East.'"

Jim had squeaked the young ladies' rapture with rather a droll imitation of the American accent; but Oliver could only smile a little sadly. He didn't want mementoes of anything; he remembered only too well. He didn't want gilded Buddhas or Indian silks or American girls to tea. Yet the caricature Jim had drawn, so contrary to his own instincts, reminded him somehow of Vanny. Vanny might really be happy surrounded by beautiful things. When *he* went to the university he might quite properly have artistic rooms, like those Oliver had seen in Peckwater Quad at Oxford, belonging to an Irish poet called Lord Basil Kilcoole.

"At Williams I shouldn't like anything showy in my college room. I should feel like a fool. But later I might like some of Father's books— or even the Buddhas." He hesitated. The prospect left him cold. He felt vaguely that beautiful things are just as much a burden as ugly ones. "Besides," he added, "all this truck is legally yours. I couldn't take anything without paying for it, and I haven't the money."

"Haven't the money? But you'll have millions in just three years. Old Charley Deboyse is a good sort. He was often with us in the *Hesperus*. I'll explain the matter; and if he buys the whole lot I'm sure he'll set aside for you anything you might fancy; especially as it would be precisely what he doesn't fancy himself. The devil of it is that I've sold one or two choice statuettes already. Had to. You never heard of such a damnable run of bad luck as I struck this time at Monte Carlo."

Getting no manifestations of sympathy on this calamity, he smoked awhile in silence, then changed the subject.

"Besides, there's another reason for settling this yacht business. You know I have already done a bit of acting for the Cinema—two years ago in New York when the *Black Swan* was building; jolly tar jumping into the water—real water—to save damsel in distress—real damsel; and though swimming rather than love-making got me the job, I could do the hugging and kissing rather well too; and I think I shouldn't be half bad at the kind-hearted burglar business and the forger business and the kidnapping business and the night-club business, when the young villain—that's me—dopes the wicked duke and carries off a million pounds in bank notes which the vile aristocrat had put in his pocket in order to seduce the heroine. I'm sure I could do it all to the life, showing at the same time that I was a jolly good fellow at heart, only unfortunate like your namesake Oliver Twist, and that the lovely innocent heroine and my pious old mother couldn't help loving me. There's some use in having seen a bit of the underworld when one was young. Of course I play under an assumed name—I'm Jack Lister—and Cynthia Nevil isn't the girl's real name either: she was Bella Iggins at home. We mean to do only two or three films in the States, hot ones, just to turn an honest penny during our honeymoon, while things are settling down and I get my money. Then we'll take a riverside cottage at Surbiton or somewhere, and live happy ever after. A chap at last needs to get married. It's the comfortable thing in the end. You have everything provided for you under one roof, and you lie placidly at anchor like the old *Victory* at Portsmouth, glad not to be dancing aimlessly any longer over the wild blue waves. As for Cynthia, or Bella, she's the sweetest, bravest, cleverest, most hardworking girl that ever was, so pretty that you'd never tire of looking at her, and so sensible that you feel safe for the rest of your life."

"You're sure she will suit you better than Mrs. Bowler?"

Oliver had never heard such a stream of bad language as this question provoked. It was not directed precisely at Oliver himself; rather against things in general and the unoffending Mrs. Bowler in particular. Yet some spatterings of the mud seemed to reach him, and he instinctively drew back to avoid the bombardment. To a man really in love, his words might have seemed offensive: but what nonsense for Jim to be really in love! He was a baby with women. He cuddled up to his Cynthia-Bella as he cuddled up to his Minnie Bowler: they were nice motherly bosoms on which to rest. The Surbiton cottage was just a silly dream, like becoming landlord of the King's Arms at Sandford. He wouldn't ever marry; or if he did, in six months he would be divorced. And he would curse Cynthia then as he cursed Minnie now.

As Jim's anger cooled his impulse to fawn came again to the fore. He hated to be disliked, was convinced that at bottom there was nothing to dislike about him. It was all a mistake: and he need but explain himself and be quite frank in order to be restored to universal favour. Where did this young prig get all this cynicism and severity? Sheer ignorance, pure prejudice. Had probably been brought up to think all actresses immoral and no marriage conceivably happy unless the bride was a chaste orange-blossom. Jim relighted his pipe, and let his good nature come again to the surface.

"I expect," he said smiling, "with your vast experience you are cured of love. You know it can't last. Your father used to say that love at best lasted two years, because in a normal state of society a first child would have been born by that time and the foundations laid for the second. After that the man was a *pater familias*, and needn't be a lover because he was a proprietor. That's all very well; but it sounds a bit theoretical when a chap is actually in love. Every man thinks his own case an exception: and he's right, because each case is really different."

Oliver couldn't help being conciliated and warming again towards so warm a creature, so solid, so honest, and so clever. But a gong was sounding for the second cabin luncheon, and he remembered his mother. He murmured an ambiguous good-bye, about coming to read sometimes at the extreme stern if the weather was fine. Jim answered only with a nod of acquiescence; and allowed the boy to walk away alone and somewhat embarrassed, as if ashamed of being in the first class and having to abandon so engaging a friend for being in the second class, perhaps in more senses than one. And this friend wasn't in the least ashamed of his second-classness; on the contrary, rather regarded it as a coign of vantage, from which all other classes could be judged at their true worth (which was always ambiguous) and could be occasionally visited, as one's fortunes varied, leaving one's true self perfectly free, neutral, and classless. Content to stand where he stood, Jim Darnley wasn't going to accompany his rich friend forward, to the barrier of the first cabin, where it would have been necessary to halt ignominiously. He would stand pat here, and wait for Oliver to come back. And his eyes followed the youthful retreating figure with an occasional sly glance, half contemptuous and half benevolent.

XV

During the rest of the voyage they were seldom together. Some days were stormy, and when the weather cleared, it was not always feasible for Oliver to leave his mother and the friends she had made on board. When he dared, he took two or three books under his arm and said he had found a quieter spot for reading, carefully omitting to add that this quiet spot was just over the screws, where there was an incessant churning sound, a pronounced vibration, and a good deal of pitching. Even when he reached this windy retreat, Jim didn't always turn up. Evidently he had other preoccupations besides merely keeping a look-out for his first-cabin friend. But Oliver, if a trifle saddened in his solitude, was rather relieved by it. He hadn't come by appointment; he had come freely, in order to read; and he would open his book and make himself comfortable in his chosen corner. But he didn't turn many pages. "Jim is lying low to-day," he would say in his thoughts. "Perhaps he hasn't shaved this morning, or is wearing old clothes. He thinks I don't like to see him shabby; and I don't. But he doesn't understand me. It's not that being down at heel, even if it were real and permanent, would frighten me away. If he were honestly poor, what possible difference would that make to *me*? Should I be ashamed of being seen with him because he wasn't well-dressed, as if I were a snob? What I am afraid of is that he may dress up too much, and be flashy and lavish and luxurious. *That* makes me uncomfortable, as his gambling does, and his running after women; and yet I know it's all a part of him. He wouldn't be himself if he wasn't free and reckless and non-moral, and wasn't so quite consciously and defiantly. You can't have Falstaff and have him thin. He thinks I'm lonely, and need him to keep up my spirits. But I'm not lonely. I like to be alone. I bring two or three books and hardly read them: there is so much anywhere in Nature to see, so much to think about. And because he finds a sort of comfort and jollity in drink and sensuality and rowdiness generally, he thinks I might do so too. But I couldn't. I hate pleasure. I hate what is called having a good time. I hate stimulants. I hate 'dope.' It's all a cheat. While the pleasure lasts it's nothing but a sort of flurry, more than half trouble. When it's over, there's just emptiness. You only blot out from your mind for a moment all that you really care for, loosening your hold, and making a fool of yourself. Jim would say that by holding back from the hurly-burly, and always remembering the things I really care for, always keeping to the three lilies in the Eton arms, I remain unhappy, I remain desolate. But if the world is desolate, why make believe that it is gay and beautiful? I'd rather be desolate than drunk: and that's the alternative.

"Perhaps Jim is making another mistake and fearing that, if I stop seeing him often or going about with him, I might forget him and turn him down later, though I have promised not to. He doesn't see that it wasn't merely a verbal promise, a business engagement which anybody might cancel and take back. It was a trust left me by my father; and more than that, it was a question of being true to myself, to all that Jim has meant to me. What might I have become without him? A cypher, a ninny, a hypocrite, a molly-coddle, thinking I knew everything because I got high marks at school, and that I was a man of the world because I belonged to some college fraternity. I couldn't rub him out of my life if I tried; and I am not trying. There's no danger for me in that quarter: the evil temptation comes from the other side. He won't corrupt me as Mother thinks: it's she that might frighten me away from my duty. Because I have a duty to him, yes, and to his family, just as I have a duty to Vanny: not merely giving them money, if they need it, but perhaps helping them in other ways. Think how Jim gets together and straightens himself out the moment he sees me—I mean, the moment he sees someone who accepts him, who makes it worth his while to be decent. He gets a whiff of the lilies, and he says to himself, 'By Jove, what a sweet scent, what a lovely flower!' Yes. And remember. Sweetness and loveliness don't grow out of nothing. They grow out of flesh and blood, out of the mud and the sunshine; and if I rejected Jim as he is, I could never become what I wish to be."

Meantime in the second cabin, as if he felt the light of these reflections focussed intensely upon his person, young Darnley too was ill at ease.

When he had lost at bridge more than he liked to lose, relying as he did on always winning something handsome in the long run; or when the vapours of drink and tobacco had actually got too thick for him, and he went for a walk on deck and a breath of sea air, sometimes his thoughts would revert to Oliver. "What can one make of such a chap? Is he vexed with me? Is he worried about me? Ever since that night at Sandford he seems to bear me a grudge. Why should my doings make him unhappy if he isn't fond of me? And if he's fond of me, why be so bitter and offish and contemptuous? I verily believe he's jealous—jealous of Minnie and jealous of Bella; as if I shouldn't place a young friend like him high above all the women in the world, if only he dared call his soul his own and had the courage of his feelings. Not that I care a fig on my own account. I'm not pining for love. I've simply tried to be decent, to be friendly, partly on his father's account; and when I saw him following me about like a dog, and hanging on my words and aping my ways, I took the thing as a matter of course, steering as safely as I could between father and son. The Doctor wished to have his home-bred boy cheered up and thawed out a little: but the plan succeeded rather too well; and the old man couldn't help feeling it a bit, if his son seemed to be cutting him out with me, and I seemed to be cutting him out with his son. That night when Oliver insisted on coming away with me from old Wetherbee's in spite of wind and rain, the Doctor wasn't pleased. He stayed on shore for three days: partly out of magnanimity, to leave us free to enjoy ourselves as we liked, but partly, I could see, sulking and piqued, because his son wasn't more in sympathy with his own tastes. Afterwards too, when Oliver turned him down about leaving home and coming with us to the Mediterranean, what did the old man say? That sometimes we do the right thing for the wrong reason. He meant that the boy had been a fool, yet that on the whole for our own comfort, it was better to be rid of him. A youngster of that age, always at table, or coiled up quietly in some corner, kept us from feeling at our ease: it was almost as if there had been ladies in the party. But now with the Doctor out of the picture for good, we two young chaps have nobody else to consider. Nobody's feelings to hurt now. Nobody else's business what we do or don't do. Why doesn't he play up, when I give him every encouragement? He can't be afraid of me—not after all that's happened. More likely afraid of himself: thinks he oughtn't to care. But if you're a little smitten with a friend, what harm can there be in showing it? Was there ever anything more innocent? Poor lad! Caught before birth in a trap, born in captivity, like the young lions at the Zoo. One of your tied-up, muscle-bound, hood-winked fools, smothering his little spark of hot life in a heap of household ashes. But it's not Oliver only—he's not very original—it's the whole bally lot. There's the oddest crinkle about these respectable Americans. His father was like that too, not originally, perhaps, but ever since I knew him. And haven't I seen the virtuous rich husband in Paris, from Boston or from Seattle, desperately determined to see life at last, now or never, do or die? His dear sweet little old wife is tired with shopping and has gone up early to bed. He looks at his watch. Only nine o'clock. Lovely opportunity. Confidentially, he inquires of the hotel-porter whether he recommends the *Folies Bergères* or the *Moulin Rouge*, and afterwards which secret night-clubs in Montmartre are the most,—well, most characteristic. He carefully puts down the names in his notebook— in pencil, to be easily rubbed out later. Ultimately, when he has seen all that he supposes to be the naughtiest things going, he boldly sets up two beauties to lobster and champagne, tries to translate his American jokes for them into atrocious French, while they hide their yawns and powder their noses, anatomising at the same time the women at the other tables. Then, when it comes to going home, he politely shows the two sirens into a cab, genially slips a crisp banknote into their hand, takes off his hat, waves it, and shouts hilariously: 'So long, my dears, bye-bye, glad to have met you, see you another day. *My wife is waiting for me at our hotel.*' Wise man, I daresay: but why cultivate the acquaintance of certain people at all, unless you mean to go the whole hog? As for sipping champagne and talking about the weather, you might as well do it with the King and Queen in the State banqueting room, and bow your way out again without paying a penny.

"I laugh at the poor mincing ham-strung ridiculous cowards for stopping at the preliminaries, at great expense to their purse and, damn me, to their dignity. Yet the truth is they don't miss much. What is love-making but a recurring decimal, always identical in form and always diminishing in value? True; yet it's a part of life, and it's no use trying to live on principles contrary to nature. You must go in for existence blindly, before you know what will come of it: when you've found out, it's time to quit. Nevertheless your knowing child, your wary philosopher, who dips one toe in the water and draws back, saying it's too cold and bitter and dangerous, at least saves himself from drowning, and possibly he even gives some of the rest of us a helping hand. Think of the Doctor. What a topping patron! I couldn't have had better luck if I'd struck a gold mine. The son will never be like that. He's unhappy at having money and afraid of

spending it; but at least he's a safe bank, an assurance against accidents. When Cynthia and I are married—at Iffley: idyllic scene, white
dresses, simple tea on the velvet lawn—I'll ask him to be my best
man. He will excuse himself: unavoidably prevented by a football
final or a prize essay or an appointment at the dentist's. But he'll
send me a wedding present to make you blink; and he'll stand god-
father by proxy to the first baby, or to a whole string of babies,
without in the least ousting Bobby; because Bobby has already made
a place for himself in Oliver's heart, and the little bastard won't be
forgotten. No: and there's Rose, too. What a devilish lucky notion of
his that he'll wait till she's eighteen and marry her! Where did he get
that tip? It never had occurred to me: yet why not? And he's the sort
of chap to stick to it, unless some designing motherly widow bags
him first. But they'll never fetch him through the senses. He doesn't
like women as women; that sort of stickiness makes him sick: he's
afraid of it; he loathes it. A poet without words: you must get him
through his fancy, through his fine sentiments; and to a poet's fancy
what can your stiff marguerite say, so flaunting and foreign, or your
New York rose on a wire, compared with our English daisy? Nothing.
They are weeds, rubbish, in comparison, and he won't pluck them—
or rather, he won't let them pluck him. Useful thing, continence.
Jolly thing, tenderness. One is never happier than when other people
are good."

PART IV

IN THE HOME ORBIT

I

For two years Oliver had not seen the sea or anything beyond it. A sort of ritual rhythm, a sense for distinct moral seasons, had established itself in his mind; and this period had been consciously one of maturation, of quiet routine, of patient study. The surface of his thoughts had been fully occupied with college life; even the holidays spent at home or in the mountains with Irma, had been devoted to the same round of systematic reading, unremitting physical exercise, and social duties. He had grown still a little taller and a good deal broader—a more austere and deeply chiselled likeness of his big mother. His features had acquired a certain firmness and repose, a certain dulness, obscuring the delicate transparent quality they had had in boyhood. He seemed a perfectly conventional, model young man; yet under this commonplace mask, a secret drama was always being played in his mind, and a suspended allegiance to absent things made his daily routine somewhat perfunctory. At a certain depth he continued to live always in the light of another world, where only such things moved as had touched his heart.

Now, in the second September after his father's death, accident brought a part of that hidden life to the surface. Mario Van de Weyer, on his way to Harvard College, was landing in New York; by chance at the very time when Oliver was obliged to be there for an intercollegiate committee meeting, to revise the schedule of football games for that season. How lucky, he thought, that without needing to mention it at home, he could meet his young cousin, this strange American who had never been in America, at the moment when he set foot for the first time on his official fatherland. Lucky to be able to see the boy at once, give him the right start, break the ice for him—if you could speak of ice when the thermometer marked 90 degrees in the shade—and not let him form a disagreeable first impression of the ways of the country. All was knowing how to manage. Oliver's presence would help to smoothe over the rough places; so would Oliver's purse.

In regard to money Oliver was already proving himself a good manager and economist, like his father. Neither the father nor the son was ever a man of business. Both were indifferent about money; Peter thought of it humorously and luxuriously, Oliver ascetically and sadly: to both the accident of riches seemed absurd and unmerited. Yet both died richer than they were born. Generous as they were, the fingers of their left hand instinctively counted what those of their right hand scattered. Oliver had managed to secure a handsome allowance; he had established the practice of asking his guardians to pay separately all his subscriptions to public or academic objects; for he said his contributions should be in harmony with his real income, not with his allowance; and he had repeatedly extorted special grants—always for admirable purposes—by the threat of borrowing the money if it were refused him. By living very simply himself, and avoiding all small expenses, he had saved a considerable sum: so that apart from his trustees he could already exercise his private generosity secretly and at his own discretion. Being rich, under this aspect of having power, was very sweet to him. He might actually do some good. The power of wealth had the same unchallengeable reality as athletic proficiency. If you could run a hundred yards in ten seconds, you could, whether people thought it foolishness or not: and if you could give or spend a hundred dollars here and a hundred dollars there, without trouble, you could: and that was a wonderful lengthening of your arm for action. So now, he anticipated clearly that the presence of Mario in America would prove an expensive pleasure; and the thought delighted him. He would be doubling the range of his personality without contaminating it; broadening his field of action and influence to the uttermost reaches of his cousin's life—and these might stretch rather far. He would be enabling another person—and what a charming person!—to live charmed and remain charming.

So happy was Oliver in this assumed office of elder brother and providential guardian, that he almost hoped some difficulty might arise, so that he might get Vanny out of it with flying colours; and he was seriously considering whether in the circumstances and presuming that this impecunious boy couldn't be bringing in anything dutiable, it would be wrong to offer the custom-house inspector five dollars to finish his examination quickly. He had engaged for Mario the room next to his own at the Manhattan Hotel, where he always stayed. Oliver's nature was already so well-knit, so self-determined, that it was self-repeating, like that of an old man: all his days, all his plans, all his friendships tended to run through the same phases. He had also secured a seat in the Pullman car direct to Newport the next morning: the lad, who knew nothing of American ways, must be personally conducted to the right train and despatched safely to the welcoming bosom of his grandmother's family.

So it happened that day that, without being a reporter, Oliver found himself wearing a reporter's badge pinned to the inside of his coat, and starting *sub rosa* in the press tug to meet the steamship *La Lorraine* at the Narrows. Jim Darnley—who was often in New York, though never nowadays at the Manhattan Hotel—had arranged it. His address was at a Marine Agency near the Battery and nobody knew where he lodged. The faithful Oliver, when passing through New York, always remembered him. They had dined together the previous evening at the *Café Martin*. Jim, though growing a little bald, was more youthful in spirit than ever, and full of projects and utopias for land and sea; and he no sooner heard of the young cousin arriving by *La Lorraine* than he suggested the genial thing to do.

"The French boat," he said, "won't be at the Narrows much before noon. The Press Superintendent is a friend of mine: I'll get you a press-ticket to go out on the tug to meet her. There will be a crowd of reporters, on account of Gorgorini and half the opera company being on board. You can sail with your cousin up the harbour, and point out to him the Statue of Liberty and the sky-scrapers, in case he shouldn't notice them. No trouble about getting you a reporter's badge and a pass. Aren't you an editor of sorts of your college paper? Precisely, and you will be reporting the arrival of the Metropolitan Opera Troupe, and interviewing Madame Gorgorini. If you're new to the business and don't care to tackle her, it's not in the least necessary. You can interview your distinguished cousin instead. I've done some reporting in my day, and I can give you a tip. She would be sure to say that coming back to dear America was like returning to her sweet old home; and you would add that she never looked younger. Meet me to-morrow at 9.30 at the door of the City Hall, and I'll introduce you to Mr. Moik Hennessy, the inspector. No jollier boss in all Tammany."

Oliver winced, but agreed. He often found himself carried along by the ways of a world that wounded him in every fibre. To keep out of the scrimmage, when you were once in the game, would be a form of self-betrayal; you couldn't be true to yourself if you backed out of your own undertakings. So he led his football squad with a cold heart. It mattered little what your task was; the great thing was the inner liberty and security to be preserved in doing it. He could afford to bend to the blast. There was a kind of contemptuous friendliness in doing so, and it saved time. If you bent, you were less likely to snap or to be uprooted; and you could revert to the perpendicular, and grow again straight upwards, when the wind died down. With this mental reservation you might acquiesce in the catch-word methods of political eloquence, in the tricks of sport, in the avalanche of big business; and merely by smiling, you could neutralise all the indecent assaults on the mind committed by scientific advertising and professional humbug.

Jim was rather a trial, always officious, always doing slightly the wrong thing in slightly the wrong way, always afraid he might be forgotten if he didn't send you a Christmas card or foolish cutting out of some newspaper; always reminding you that now in a year— no, in exactly thirteen months—you would come into your money. Yet, through this coarse medium, how many contacts became possible from which otherwise your own glass shell would have completely insulated you! Not only contacts with the rough or the gay world, which it was well to know something about, but contacts with the very things you loved best, with the sea, with Iffley, and now curiously enough, with the long-lost Mario. How much pleasanter, after two years' separation, to go out to meet him at sea, instead of waiting helpless at the pier, waving and shouting and smiling, in the intense discomfort and heat of the place, while the long file of passengers, insecure in their footing, and overloaded with bags and bandboxes, golf-sticks and rugs, stumbled down the steep gangway! How splendid, to be able to talk quietly for an hour, and find their old selves beneath their new faces! And what a surprise for Mario to be met on board by his stay-at-home cousin, and landed in triumph where he expected to arrive alone and unwelcomed, and ruffled by the thousand little difficulties and mistakes inevitable to a stranger!

Besides, it was a pleasure to have escaped from the sultriness of the city. Here no doubt the sun was even more dazzling and burning, reflected like a great chandelier from endless dancing mirrors in the water; yet the sting of salt vapour in the air had some freshness in it, and the tug, panting like a bull-dog, created by its onset the semblance of a sea breeze, while making a violent fuss about it. And there, looking rather like a tramp steamer, the black hull of *La*

Lorraine presently loomed, stopping her engines and consenting to be boarded. Up the side Oliver climbed by a rope ladder, following the more impetuous professional reporters; he jumped the rail, and found himself on the dingy main deck, abandoned to his resources. Rapidly he circled the upper decks, searching amongst the groups of passengers with an eye keenly pre-determined to recognise its appointed object. No Mario. He inquired of an apparently friendly steward, and was conducted to Mario's cabin. No Mario there. Lounge and smoking-room could easily be swept at a glance, having been emptied by the happy excitement of reaching port. Never mind. The boy would be sure to turn up on deck in a few minutes. Then one of the reporters who had been in the tug, seeing Oliver obviously waiting and on the look-out for somebody, pointed with his thumb in the direction of a noisy group of foreigners and said confidentially: "There she is." At that moment, above all those cries of competitive conversation, rose a piercing but rather tuneful and theatrical scream. A diminutive Pekinese pup could be seen held out over the water at the end of a slender brown arm evidently rather vigorous; and in the sunshine, on the wrist of that arm, Oliver recognised Cousin Caleb Wetherbee's gold watch. It was Mario, with his back turned, and hedged in by a tight circle of laughing, shouting, and gesticulating foreigners. Presently the arm was withdrawn, without having dropped the puppy: and instantly there was another clear sound, a resounding slap, followed by a fresh outburst of laughter, this time somehow less hearty, and unpleasantly cut short; and as if by a common impulse the group of noisy people opened out, and was quickly thinned. Mario himself, now wholly visible, turned about. For a moment he faced Oliver vacantly, then flew at him with open arms. "Oliver, Oliver, Oliver!—No"—cried Mario, "you're not changed at all; only bigger, bigger and stronger. Come at once and be introduced to Madame Gorgorini."

But hadn't they been quarrelling? Wasn't Mario pressing a handkerchief against a very red cheek and ear? Oh, well, that didn't matter. It wasn't a quarrel: just the opposite. She had merely been scared about her Pekinese dog. Mario had sworn to drop the little beast in the sea, and drown it, unless she confessed that she didn't love it as much as she loved him. She had confessed it, had got her ridiculous toy-dog back, had covered it with kisses, and had boxed Mario's ears for having given her such a fright. But the confession held good. She owed him not only more kisses than she had wasted on that hellish little imp, but full compensation for that slap in the face. By Jove, it had been a stinging one! She knew she must pay up handsomely for smacking him, and very soon, too. Perhaps that was why she smacked so hard!

A slight smile parted Mario's lips as he said this, half sensual, half bitter, and a light passed over his eyes, full of secret memories and expectations. He seemed to Oliver a new person. He hadn't grown at all into the English model, but away from it. In fact, during these two years he had spent only one "Half" at Eton and the rest of the time with his mother in Paris, in Florence, at Italian watering-places. The boy Vanny had disappeared, only the ageless and inscrutable Mario remained. He still looked the sporting youth, but not in the homely, hard-working, sailor fashion of the Anglo-Saxon; he seemed exotic, only half human, a faun or amiable demon, very delicate in his strength, strangely agile and supple, as if of another race, and incalculably capricious. He was bronzed all over like a statue, and the waving ends of his brown hair had been bleached here and there in the sun and looked like pale traces of gilding in some ancient image. Could this be Oliver's cousin? Could it be his school friend? Yet one thing seemed absolutely unchanged: the affection of this strange hyacinthine creature for himself. Not the least hesitation on his part in recognising, embracing, clinging to Oliver in the old way; not the least shyness or doubt, or suspicion of any interval elapsed, in making him feel that he was enormously loved and trusted, and must allow himself to be carried bodily along in the swift current of his cousin's interests.

So now Oliver was lugged by main force before a plump blooming lady, delicately painted and delicately dressed, holding herself well, calm, but with life and sensitiveness tingling in every fibre, pouting a little now and then at the uselessness of what other people said, and flashing occasionally a pair of tremendous black eyes; yet for the rest rather languid and passive. She didn't offer him her hand but bowed and smiled slightly, saying something—he wasn't sure whether in French or in Italian or perhaps in a mixture of both—as if at once saluting and upbraiding the *giovanotto americano*, the *méchant cousin*, who was going to take Mario away. The whole circle—for there were several persons standing by, the lady being one of those human creatures who cannot endure to be alone for one instant—the whole circle continued to jabber unintelligibly to Oliver, and with extraordinary speed, all throwing out simultaneously little short phrases, and nobody apparently listening to anybody else. Oliver realised for the first time that the primary use of conversation is to satisfy the impulse to talk. General conversation bored him because he was naturally silent.

They were now at the dock and everybody in a flurry. Not so Madame Gorgorini. She allowed herself to be served and let her maid count her parcels for her. But they must say good-bye. This time she graciously held out to Oliver a soft affectionate hand: you would never have suspected how hard it could slap: and as a sort of *finale* came a fuller, more lingering flash of those black eyes, quite submerging him in their sweeping illumination, like twin light-houses revolving in unison. Yet that overwhelming glance was all kindness, and the coquetry of it was almost drowned in motherly resignation.

"I forgive you," she seemed to be saying, "I accept you. I see you are a nice boy and you love him just as I do, only for his own good. You may take him away now for a few hours. See that he doesn't get into any mischief, and send him back loving me more than ever. I am not unreasonable, I am not jealous, but I confess I have a woman's heart, a mother's heart, and I can't be cruel."

Thus generously liberated for the day by the reigning sultana, Mario had to go and say *au revoir* to her Grand Vizier or Impresario, and to all the other ladies of the troupe; also to the Captain and the Second Officer and the Doctor of the Ship, and to fee his steward. "Let's be the first to land," he whispered to Oliver, and climbed half up the rail where the gangway was being made fast. "Great moment. About to touch my native land for the first time. I suppose I ought to kiss it, but I won't." And he laughed at the slimy planks, the heaped-up cases, and the scattered rubbish that covered the pier.

"But where's your luggage?" Oliver asked, always provident and concerned for realities.

"Haven't any. I mean, it's all being looked after for me by the manager."

"And the custom-house?"

"Everything will pass with the company's stuff. He has my keys, in case of trouble."

"But does he know where to send it? I've got a room for you at the Manhattan Hotel."

"Oh, really? How nice of you, how like you! And it will be convenient for the day—to wash up and all that. But for the night I'm booked at the Brevoort House, where Gorgorini goes. She would never forgive me if I didn't turn up."

Oliver began to feel useless, a feeling he particularly disliked. He had expected something so different. Where was his poor little cousin Vanny, whom he was to guide, protect, befriend, and usher gently into a bewildering new world? This tender novice seemed to know all the ropes. To occupy two different rooms at once in two different hotels and sleep in neither of them was apparently quite usual with him: the sort of thing that naturally happens. Quite natural, too, that other people should pay for them. Moreover, he seemed little impressed, so far, by the wonders of the landscape. He had given only cursory semi-professional glances at the shipping and the docks: he had laughed at the Statue of Liberty and said, "How Third Republic!" Even the sky-scrapers had seemed a matter of course and just like the pictures. Evidently his interest—for he was keen enough—lay in other quarters, in people, in their ways, in his own vital temperature. He seemed to find it delightful, landing in this way perfectly free and without impedimenta, like the herald Mercury alighting by chance in New York; but this Mercury had no hat. It was packed, he explained, when Oliver somewhat anxiously inquired after it; for somebody had given him such a lovely hat-box with a place for everything, that there was no need of carrying a hat on one's head at all: besides, it was too warm for hats. Even Oliver, always so correct, was carrying his in his hand; and how did he come to sport such a lively ribbon, white and purple stripes? Ah, of course: they were his college colours. He was a blue—and white and purple were only a higher form of blue as evolved at Williams. But hatlessness was not the worst of it; even in those pre-war days some of the very young went about hatless. The worst of it was that Mario wore no tie, and his flimsy shirt was all unbuttoned and thrown open in front, so that when he laughed you could see his chicken-bone! That was a Continental liberty unheard of in America; certainly you couldn't lunch at Sherry's or at Delmonico's or even at the *Café Martin* in that rig: and Oliver began to perceive that liberty is something aristocratic, and that in a pure democracy you must always do, and always think, what other people like. Mario wasn't aware of it yet: he didn't seem to mind attracting attention; perhaps he positively liked it, as some dreadful women did. Perhaps he wouldn't mind even being laughed at. He would say he was contributing to the gaiety of nations, and would vastly enjoy laughing at himself.

Somewhat bewildered by these moral problems and feeling somehow forlorn, Oliver took refuge in his practical competence. Having
no luggage, they needn't take the expensive hack which he had
expected to charter, but could reach the decent part of New York by
the elevated. On the way, Mario couldn't help noticing that he was
embarrassing his excellent cousin. As they came down the stairs into
Broadway, some street-boys even hooted at them. "I say, I seem to
be disgracing you. Would it help if I got a tie?" And Mario pointed
to a shop-window, lighted like a modern stage, in which ties, socks,
and handkerchiefs, all of one colour, were displayed with ostentatious
simplicity. "Come and choose one for me really *comme-il-faut.*"

Oliver was relieved, grateful, delighted. Nothing flatters us more
than to be consulted by a connoisseur on his own specialty. He looked
for the nicest tie in the shop: and his eye was caught by a long sky-
blue knitted-silk one: it seemed the most festive, the most attractive,
somehow the one *right* tie. That it happened to be the dearest was
not an objection, when once Mario understood that he was getting it
as a present. Blushing with pleasure he adjusted it before the glass,
knotting it loosely, as a knit tie requires, pulling his shirt straight,
and smartly buttoning his thin blue jacket by its one brass button at
the waist. "I say," he cried, delighted with the effect and still more
with the presents, for the tie had involved a gold safety-pin to keep
it in place. "Rather like changing ties in the train on the way to Lords
for the Harrow Cricket Match, isn't it? How jolly!" He had no doubt
that the choice of that colour was meant to remind him of his late
transit through Eton, always glorious in retrospect. His mood in
response became decidedly that of the school-boy going home for
the holidays, meaning to behave nicely and make a good impression
on his loving and generous relations. Gorgorini on this occasion was
the equivalent of school complications not to be mentioned at home;
she should be completely suppressed for the time being.

Oliver, on his side, felt that the sky had cleared. He had re-estab-
lished his ascendancy, and that in a double way, as a good Puritan
should, partly through the ascendancy of his conscience, and partly
through the ascendancy of his purse; and this twin sovereignty would
be reasserted whenever the cousins were together, no matter what
Mario might be up to when out of sight. He had now been rendered
perfectly presentable, even if still a little conspicuous: but after all it
wasn't the lad's fault if his appearance was so striking. Oliver was also

pleased with his own good taste in choosing that particular tie: it couldn't be better. He had completely forgotten one very like it, deftly knitted at Iffley by the clean and delicate fingers of little Rose: the blue tie Jim Darnley had once sported in his honour in the second-class smoking-room of the *Lusitania*.

II

Until the novelty wore off, letters came almost daily to Oliver recounting his cousin's adventures.

Why didn't anybody tell me, he wrote, that America is the most enormously amusing place in the world? I shouldn't have wasted these long nineteen years away from my legal country. Cloudcuckooland and Lilliput and Barataria are nothing to it. Laughter and *blague* all the time. No wonder that Pinkie—that's the schoolgirl I met in the train—says she has to iron out the corners of her mouth whenever she gets home, they ache so with laughing. How did I "meet" Pinkie? Nothing simpler. Had caught her eye once or twice when I was talking with your uncle. Went out to the platform to say goodbye to him at New Haven. Coming back, tripped over her umbrella, which happened to be sticking out into the aisle. "Beg pardon, so sorry, my fault, hope I didn't break it." "Oh, no; and it wouldn't much matter if you did, because it's broken already," and she laughed merrily, as if a broken umbrella simplified life. Seat next to hers vacant. Pleasant chat. Two hours. But she was going on to Boston, and at Providence I had to say goodbye and get into my Newport car—not nearly so jolly, because I was perched in a revolving chair, equidistant from everybody: and equidistance is death to all interesting society. She gave me her card, Miss Pinkie Brock, Spruce Avenue, Allston, and I'm to take her to the cinema next Saturday night. So there, I have one charming friend already in cultured Boston.

Your uncle Jack Bumstead—what a lucky chance that we should find him taking the same train. All the way to New Haven he told me a string of funny stories—not so much funny in themselves, as spiced with an amusing irony of his own. There was a far dim twinkle in his eyes—such tired eyes— as if he wasn't amused at his jokes but rather at the absurdity of having to laugh at them. I suppose professional wits are like that when they get old and sick of being *pagliacci* and stuffed with straw. Hopeless and disappointed at bottom, probably an early broken heart never properly repaired. When the man passes our house in Paris crying: *Réparateur de faïence et de porcelaine*, my mother, who is very practical but has romantic ideas in reserve, says: "*Oh, la, la!* You can no more mend broken crockery than a broken heart." But in America everybody seems to pretend that crockery and hearts are never broken, and that there's nothing to do but to make jokes. "What!" said Uncle Jack—for it's agreed that I'm to call him Uncle Jack too—"Not stopping to see New Haven? Never even heard of New Haven, Connecticut? Tut, tut. We must change all that. Most famous place on earth. World-wide supremacy. Holds three acknowledged unchallenged unchallengeable world-records, each calculated to keep New Haven scintillating on the gilded pinnacle of Fame's steeple like a weather-cock in the rays of the rising sun—not that a newspaper man like me ever sees the sun rise; but that's poetry, and everybody can make poetry out of what he hasn't seen. What are the three things for which New Haven is world-famous? The oldest woman, the biggest mosquito, and the greatest insane asylum on earth."

I thought I might not have heard of the mosquito or the old woman, but wasn't the great asylum at Great Falls?

"Poo! Those are only common certified lunatics shut up against their will. The crazy men at New Haven rush there by instinct, pretend to like it, couldn't be happy anywhere else. And they don't *call* their place an insane asylum. They *call* it Yale College."

When I heard this I said at once: "I see you're a Harvard man," and your uncle was enthusiastic, clapped me on the back; said I was the young duck taking to the water, hadn't been in the country twenty-four hours and knew it down to the ground. They must get an amendment passed to the Constitution so that, in spite of having been accidentally born abroad, I might be elected President of the United States. And it was then that he asked me to call him Uncle Jack and to write for his comic weekly paper. "Yes," he said, "I *am* a Harvard man, and not ashamed to whisper it to you in private, since you have discovered it; but don't let it go any further. It might injure me in business, if they knew I was a highbrow in disguise. Why do I say Yale people are mad? What would you say of a man who built himself a house without windows lest he should be observed sitting in it saying Zugum-Zugum and drinking ginger ale? And what if all his friends thought doing so the highest prize in life, and cried hush, hush if anybody mentioned it? Mad, stark mad: but you mustn't suppose for that reason that Harvard men are sane. After all, everything is comparative."

I asked him why, then, you hadn't gone to Harvard, and why some people thought Williams even better.

"Nobody thinks Williams better," he said, "except my fool brother, who was sent there in the old days for cheapness. The cheapness stuck to him; and when my father saw him turned into a muscular theologue, he was sorry he hadn't sold the gravestones of his ancestors and sent Harry to Harvard."

In another letter Mario wrote:

What a shame that you should never have seen Grandma or Edith or little Maud. I can't understand it. Wasn't your father almost brought up by Grandma? And she's such a dear, and so naughty! Perhaps that's why you were bundled away, so as not to be contaminated by her worldly notions.

But you'd like Edith. She's not only very beautiful but terribly intelligent and well-informed and religious and wonderfully dressed in a style that is rather her own, and yet fashionable: *le dernier cri* simplified, *stylisé*, and made slightly nunlike and ritualistic. She's not too old, like Conchita—I mean Madame Gorgorini—who of course is a *femme faite* and perhaps rather disturbed you; but I like a woman who disturbs me. On the other hand, Edith's not too young or a silly chit of a girl like Pinkie. Pinkie wouldn't suit you at all. With Edith you couldn't find any fault whatever. She is ideal. Perfectly natural, too; puts you at your ease at once and understands you thoroughly; and so wise, so kind, so perceptive. She has been giving me lessons in manners. Apparently I made a *gaffe* in excusing myself for not coming at once to stay with you at Great Falls. She says I wasn't expected, that your mother never has people to stay; that even among people who move more in general society, it isn't here as in England where you wire to a friend asking if you may come to-morrow for the night, or next week for a few days and stay for the races. That isn't done here. Even rich men hardly have such elastic establishments, or enough servants. You must wait to be asked; and you won't be asked often, except to dinner and evening parties. So I'm being re-educated: but when I said I couldn't come to Great Falls you did ask me to come to Williamstown. I am invited there: and I mean to come on my first long holiday. Don't be surprised if you see me arriving in a cloud of dust and thunder and lightning. I am to have a motor-car. The girls here have a little one, a torpedo, and they're astonished how fast I can make it go. They won't take it to New York, because there, of course, they need a covered carriage; so that when they leave Newport for the winter, I am to have it. Uncle James said nowadays it was almost expected that a boy at Harvard should have a "bubble": and that I might keep the torpedo, because it really wasn't suitable any longer for young ladies as old as his girls, even in the country. Isn't it luck? So, if I haven't broken my neck, I will soon give you a lesson in driving.

Finally came a series of letters from Harvard, scraps of letters getting shorter and shorter, and degenerating into postcards.

Claverley Hall isn't the shadow of a college: sort of railway hotel: brick apartment house in a muddy road, with a lot of little flats, like a bee-hive. Standard student's furniture, made by the thousand, yellow wood and green leatherette. Yet Uncle James thinks it the best place in Cambridge, where one is rather expected to have one's rooms. No food, if you please. Must go out even for breakfast. Have it standing up at a counter, with my coat collar turned up to my ears, because it's damp and cold here already. Coffee, cornflakes and cream, sometimes a baked apple. Occasionally, when I'm very late, between half past ten and eleven, I find one of the professors having exactly the same thing before his morning lecture. Spoke to me to-day; had seen me once at Windsor years ago, and was a friend of my father's. Small world. But the great thing to do at Cambridge is to go into Boston. Have lots of friends there already. Ladies charming: they have read everything; nice clothes, good food. Men dull, cordial, and harmless. Am getting so many invitations to lunch and to dinner that I don't mind having no food at home. . . .

My next door neighbour is a nice chap called Boscovitz. Knows French and has a lot of books. They say his father was a Jew and a jeweller, but has been doubly converted into a country gentleman. Still people can't forget the facts, and young Boscovitz isn't liked here: has to console himself with his books and with riding. . . .

Have been out riding with Boscovitz, I on a hired hack. Met his lovely sisters, three of them, and went to their house to tea. Dazzled, completely dazzled. Conservatories, tapestries, beautiful furniture. Mother a Polish countess, girls wonderful, and each completely different. Papa away. Perfection. . . .

Have now got a regular hired horse. Wrote to Uncle James about it. He says perhaps it's hardly expected that a Freshman should ride. Yet, as I don't play football, perhaps for the moment—*Bref*: horse sanctioned. . . .

Sorry, but can't get to Williamstown. Have to drop a billet doux every morning in a box here. Not addressed to a lady but to Professor Barrett Wendell. It is called a Daily Theme. Must be at least one page of specially ruled and prepared paper, and not more than two pages. Automatically teaches you to write good English. Indispensable training for the tabloid press, and for controlling the future thought of humanity. Besides Edith is coming to Boston for a fortnight, and I must dance attendance. . . .

How splendid! Williams to play Harvard here next Saturday! Of course you will be with them. Will meet you on arrival and make plans. You must stay at least over Sunday. We might lunch with Edith and dine with old Mr. Wetherbee. When he discovered that I was a friend of yours, he became enthusiastic. Thinks the world of you and your father. What a pity you can't leave your rustic seat and come to Harvard where—besides doing Daily Themes—you might have a glorious time.

III

"Look, Oliver, who's come to see you—your cousin Edith."
For twenty-four hours our friend had been lying with his left leg in plaster, suffering a good deal of pain, and—what he minded more—feeling rather feverish and sick from the after-effects of the anaesthetics they had given him, first in the football field, when they laid him on the stretcher, and afterwards here at the hospital, when they had set the fracture. But there were compensations, and that day he had not been unhappy. "No more football for me this year," he had been repeating to himself. "No more football ever." He felt a great peace. One duty at least was finished and done for, one old enemy vanquished, and vanquished gloriously.

But here was Vanny again—Vanny had been with him all the previous evening and all this morning—and here was Edith, that Edith whom Vanny was always talking about. He looked at her, as an invalid may, with rather helpless round eyes. He was a child again for the moment, not expected to go through the civilities or raise his head from the pillow. He saw a tall young woman, perhaps twenty-five, and rather commanding. Her pale face was half buried in furs. Pinned to the large flat muff that hung by a cord from her neck, he noticed a bunch of crimson roses.

Meantime she was speaking in a clear quick voice. "Yes, Mario and I have come, only for a moment. The nurse says you had some fever last night—naturally, with a broken leg. You must be kept quiet. But you look very well"—and her intelligent eyes rested on him with a searching look that expressed at once medical discernment, civil attention, and affectionate concern. "Very well indeed," she repeated smiling, "and entirely different from your pictures in those dreadful papers." As she spoke she kicked aside, with the tapering end of her shoe, a disordered heap of Sunday newspapers, which littered the floor, each displaying enormous headlines and enormous views of the football match of the day before. "Let's put this rubbish away. It's a disgrace to civilisation." In a moment, assisted by Mario, she had gathered up and folded those innumerable sheets and piled them up neatly in a corner.

"No wonder he doesn't look like this sheeny," Mario was saying. "It's not his photo at all. It's a man called Otto Altstein who played last year for Columbia. They hadn't one of this O. A. in stock, so they put in the other man for having the same initials."

"It may have been an honest mistake," Oliver interposed in a spirit of conciliation. "Altstein pronounced in English, is very like Alden. And they couldn't find one of me in football togs, because there isn't any."

The young lady noticed that he spoke in a quiet low voice with a slight smile, as if his thoughts rested on something distant, something that rendered the visible foreground incidental and a trifle absurd. He was no ordinary person. He had a mind.

"And how are you feeling?" she asked turning to him afresh. "Quite comfortable? At least you have a lovely view, and I suppose they take good care of you."

"Oh yes. It was very kind of them to bring me here instead of to the ordinary hospital. Mr. Stillman—you know he has just given this Infirmary to Harvard—Mr. Stillman happened to be on the side-lines when I was hurt. He insisted on having me brought here, though I have no right to it, as I'm not a Harvard man—not yet." Again a certain quiet light came into his eyes, as if reflected from a great distance.

"They were thoroughly ashamed of themselves," Mario broke in, "and jolly well ought to be. It was an outrage. They smashed your leg on purpose, the blackguards. Everybody saw it, everybody knows it, but of course it can't be said above a whisper."

"Such a thing's not planned," said Oliver. "It happens. It's in the spirit of the game. And knowing that it's in the spirit of the game makes part of the sport. Football brings out the fighting instinct, and you do things you wouldn't do in cold blood. I myself could never warm up to it. That's why I was never a very good player."

"Not a good player," Mario cried, half indignant, half admiring. "Listen to that! Not a very good player when you've just made the most wonderful touchdown ever seen on Soldiers Field—everybody says so—and won your match all alone against a big college."

"The touchdown was rather a fluke."

"Nonsense. Not a fluke in the least. Didn't you run through the whole Harvard team, dodging a man here, knocking down another there, shaking off a third who had actually tackled you, until you had a clear field, and could wheel round and plant the ball just behind the goal posts? Was there ever anything more quick and clever and deliberate? You had seen your chance, you had set your teeth, and off you flew. And didn't the crowd realise it, that nothing could stop you, that you had all the trumps in your hand, that the whole run was made the moment you started? Perfect judgment, perfect tactics, and such speed! And when you came back to kick the goal, was there the least doubt that you would do it easily? You never were more yourself than in those five minutes. A fluke, indeed! Didn't the Harvard people expect that you'd score again, if ever you fairly got the ball under your arm? That's why they pounced upon you so wickedly in the next scrimmage, and broke your leg. There's always some blackguard in a side, as in politics; the rowdies take the lead and carry the party with them. They work themselves up about nothing, they don't know why, until they can't stop themselves."

"That's life," Oliver said, remembering his father. "But I don't say kicking the goal was a fluke. I can kick place-goals regularly when I'm feeling fit, unless there's a high wind, and there wasn't much wind yesterday. You're wrong, though, about expecting me to score a touchdown like that again. The thing is too complicated. I might be just as ready, but you could never repeat just that combination of circumstances. That's why I say it was partly a fluke. The thing did itself. It simply carried me along with it. I felt light on my feet, and let myself go. I didn't do it. I just knew it was happening, and had to happen."

"Had to happen, you mean, because *you* had the ball."

"Naturally each man counts for what's in him. But football was never in me really. I've been forced into it."

"Surely," said Edith, "it must be a great experience to make a run like that, so exciting even for the rest of us."

"You were there?"

"Mario insisted," and she looked about somewhat uneasily, as if caught in a trap. "I can't say I like the game as a whole. It's so brutal. There's something secret and too intense about it, something vicious."

"Yes," said Oliver under his breath, admiring her insight. "Those great providential moments come so seldom, when everything runs itself and goes right. Usually every move is forced and planned and fussed over and pushed into you against the grain. A horrid tyranny.

And all for what? Just to win, as if it made any difference who won—and to fill the Sunday papers."

"Then why do you play at all, if you don't like it and don't think it does any good? You men are such cowards. You don't dare call your souls your own."

"I couldn't refuse to play for my school. I couldn't refuse to play for Williams. They needed me. It would have seemed selfish and effeminate. But now it's finished. I'm laid up for the season; and next year I shall be here at Harvard, not playing at all, but just studying."

Edith, saying "How much nicer that will be," now made those scarce perceptible movements—glancing at the door, adjusting her furs, beaming on her host—which betray an impulse to say goodbye. "We mustn't tire you. It was such a shame to be cousins and not to know each other. Next year, when I come to stay with my aunt Mrs. Brimmer, Mario must bring you to see us. To-morrow we'll bring you some flowers. Perhaps for a day or two you'd better not have books. Meantime I'll leave you these. They'll keep until to-morrow." As she spoke, she snatched the crimson roses from her muff—all but one—and arranged them deftly in a glass which, in the twinkling of an eye, she had taken from the table and filled with water.

"See how women admire brutality, however they may speak of it," Mario observed, raising his eyes to the ceiling. "Here you are visiting a strange young man in his bedroom, and overwhelming him with delicate attentions, only because he's made a ridiculous touchdown."

"Visiting the sick is nothing special. We Little Sisters of Saint Elizabeth visit the hospitals regularly, and the prisons. And we all notice that it's precisely the rough young men that seem to appreciate our motives best, and are most grateful and deferential. The women, especially the old women, sometimes mock at us; but we have to accept that too, as a part of our discipline in charity. You know," she added, turning to Oliver, "I'm a trained nurse with a diploma as good as this good woman who is nursing you."

"I wish then you could take her place. She means well, but she's so fat and unwieldy that she fills up this whole little room, and almost smothers me."

The great white bulk of this excellent woman appeared in the doorway, as if to confirm the description. The doctor had forbidden callers to stay more than ten minutes.

"Good-bye, then, until to-morrow, and good night." So saying, Edith, as if to prove her professional expertness, pulled the bed-clothes quite straight and smooth, with a little lingering affectionate pressure in doing so against Oliver's ribs.

"I'll send Jimmy the barber in the morning to shear you," Mario said in his turn, "and even to shave you, if you like to think you require it." He laughed at the suspicion of yellow down round the corners of Oliver's mouth, and the sides of his chin. "At any rate, you needn't any longer look like a Hottentot. It's disgusting," and he passed his fingers through his cousin's great shock of hair, such as football players developed in those days as a protection against broken heads. But the gesture which began or pretended to begin in mockery ended in affection.

The bed on which Oliver lay propped up on several pillows was placed with its whole length against a broad window or row of windows, almost a wall of glass. Beyond a bend of the River Charles, visible just below, the grey mass of the Stadium, the scene of yesterday's battle, rose above the ground mists covering the marshes, while the smoke of two or three factory chimneys made the sky lurid in that quarter. On the other side was the leafless purple wood of Mount Auburn; and in the midst a wintry sunset spread its crimson and coppery bands and touches of fire. The hour, the silence after so much talk, the opiate still at work to keep out the pain always knocking at the door, and the sense of complete relief from anxiety, all combined to throw him into a placid reverie, a dream with the eyes open, in which things past and future, jumbled together like figures in a faded tapestry, dim images of spirited scenes, flowed by in procession.

"Roses," a voice within him was saying, "crimson roses. The petals are getting a little purplish at the edges. Some have already fallen on the table. These are the roses he gave her yesterday when he dragged her to the Stadium, so that she might learn to think me a hero. I defeated Harvard, something of no consequence to them, an accident, merely a practice game. Williams never defeated Harvard before, probably never will again. Now their emblem, a bit wilted, has been brought round to me as an offering, as a prize. They are receiving me handsomely, I shall be where I belong. Because I am coming to Harvard, and then crimson will be my own colour. Or will my crimson, too, be rather purple at the edges? Shall I ever be really a Harvard man, or only a Williams man who has abandoned Williams? Shall I always have to turn away from what surrounds me in order to look for my true place? Must home for me always be in the distance? How should I ever rest, if there is something better? When I see and adopt the better thing, don't I make it mine, don't I prove that it was always mine by divine right? Why should it still seem half foreign and unsatisfying? If I undertook to move in the same world with Mario and Edith—aren't we cousins, and haven't I every worldly advantage?—shouldn't I somehow fail? Wouldn't they always laugh at me a little, as not really one of themselves, but only a country cousin to whom they meant to be kind?

"When they talk together in their little asides, murmuring some quick phrase, they seem to be speaking a foreign language, as if I were a stranger or a child, not intended to understand or not capable of understanding. Between the two, there is a sort of telegraphy, a private code, the same objects strike them simultaneously, and they see the same amusing or absurd side of everything. They twitter like lovers, and they might seem to be laughing at me, as at everyone else: but it's not so really. For a moment I am sure she preferred me to him, felt I was stronger, more to be trusted, more to be pitied. . . . Yes, and Mario, too. He says he's in love with her, but in sober fact, he cares more for me, much more. With her he's all deference, all attention, all devotion: follows her suggestions, cultivates her friends, seems to adopt her views, plays the moonstruck page to her ideal queen: all of which won't prevent him from matching marbles with the other pages, and romping with the ladies' maids. The whole thing is play-acting. But when he turns to me, he's in earnest. Then the froth only serves to hide and to laugh away his true feelings, and to pretend they don't exist.

"Was it merely because I've been hurt, was it because I'm lying here helpless as a baby, that they both fondled me like that, Edith no less than Mario? Did it mean nothing, or did it mean a lot? It meant a lot. Perhaps not to them—they are so full of flighty affections—but it means a lot to me. It means that here at last are my natural friends, people of my kind, the sort I always ought to have lived with. Not Mother, not Father, not Irma, not Jim, but Mario and Edith. With them I am at home at last. Yes, in spite of all differences, across all the barriers.

"What would barriers and differences matter, if only in myself I had a world to belong to, and knew where I stood? Everything would work together then, and find its place. Haven't I another Rose at

Iffley, a white rose, a tight hard little bud of a rose? She will never be too heavily scented, as are these crimson roses. She will not open in a New York greenhouse, but in a cool English garden, under gentle rain, in the tender wild light of cloud-castles built by the sun upon the sea.

"Cloud-castles! Perhaps that's all that anything can be. Mr. Darnley lives in a cloud-castle of his own, very lofty no doubt and very logical, far more lofty and logical than the Church he is supposed to belong to; yet his little daughter is too clever to believe in that cloud-castle of her poor dreaming father's, and laughs at the idea of living in the air. The little materialist is sure she lives on earth, and is proud of not being visionary. But what if the earth were another cloud-castle? Why quarrel about dwelling places that the wind piles up and disperses? How is the spirit within me compromised—the pure spirit, the observer—if it be mother or father, sweetheart or friend that smiles or frowns on me for the moment? All these images are shifty and misty and treacherous. What endures is only this spirit, this perpetual witness, wondering at those apparitions, enjoying one, suffering at another, and questioning them all. If I keep this spirit free, if I keep it pure, let roses be red or white as they will, let there be no end of wars of the roses; let me wear the rose of Lancaster or the rose of York; neither will taint my soul or dye it of a party colour. Did I turn purple because I wore purple in the football field, or should I turn crimson if I wore crimson some other day? Let them dress me up in whatever gaudy blazers they choose, let them nickname me as they like: I can always strip my spirit naked in the night, and my true self will be always nameless."

IV

The little primitive motor trembled a good deal and was noisy. Sometimes Mario had to crawl under it on his back, to get the chain clear or oil the bearings. Nevertheless it carried him and Oliver (as soon as he could get about on crutches) all over town and country. It was a wonder how fast and smartly Mario could make it go, turning and squirming, avoiding ruts and holes and stony places in the ill-kept roads; all, too, not only without serious accident, but preserving his nice hands, if not always immaculate, at least always unscathed and presentable. Merely a question of gloves, he said: plenty of good old loose cast-off pairs. If cats in gloves couldn't catch mice, gentle-men in gloves could perfectly well handle machines, if only they used their wits also, and applied just the right pressure in just the right direction at just the right place. Oliver, who rather prided himself on his mechanical accomplishments, was surprised and a little humbled by so much handiness and dexterity in his ornamental cousin. How could this young fop, this professional lady-killer, be so practical; and why did things, no less than women, yield at once to his touch and dance to his piping as if, inaudibly to vulgar ears, some magic flute were compelling them? By contrast, Oliver (quite apart from his bandaged leg) felt heavy and clumsy in mind and in body, older but less experienced. Instead of introducing his foreign cousin to Amer-ica, he was allowing the newcomer to explain America to him, taking him to new places, showing him new people, and becoming a link between Oliver himself and many a homely thing disregarded before. On the surface, Mario was all laughter, appreciation, enjoyment; he found all the food good and all the girls pretty; and the sayings of the country "characters" seemed to amuse him vastly and never to be forgotten. Yet behind this joyousness there appeared a strange detachment; perhaps it was the detachment that made the joyousness possible. Oliver, who somehow felt responsible for everything or at least linked to everything by natural bonds, couldn't see anything agreeable in chowder or in shop-girls or in tobacco-chewing keepers of livery-stables: nor did the cordiality of the genteel world give him any particular pleasure. But Mario saw everything in comic relief against the background of his own foreign experience; and the novelty, far from annoying him or spoiling his fun, turned everything for him into an irresponsible carnival. Sometimes Oliver thought he laughed too much, or at things that were perfectly serious, as if nothing in America could be anything but an intentional farce. At other times Mario made him envious: he seemed to have in himself some secret ballast, something solid in reserve, enabling him to play the fool safely to the top of his bent.

They drove to Groton. In a day or two spent at Newport, Mario had had time to meet one of the masters and several of the boys; and he had since come across many old Grotonians at Harvard. They had all urged him to visit their school. They all allowed it hadn't yet quite the same glamour as Eton—they all called it *glamour*—but they were sure he would be interested in seeing the improvements they had made, while preserving all the real and rational advantages of an English public school. Mario wasn't interested in comparing one system of education with another, but Oliver was, especially when the Eton that had so much excited his imagination was one of the terms of comparison. Yet only Mario, as an Eton boy and a Van de Weyer, had been asked or was welcome. He had not been expected to bring a friend, a Williams friend, whom Groton had scarcely heard of. So that all the attentions and explanations were directed to Mario, who didn't listen, but simply liked hob-nobbing with agreeable people; while Oliver, who was all attention and intelligence, was given the cold shoulder.

While they were eating at the inn—for they hadn't been asked to dinner—they reviewed their impressions.

"Do you think this place is really better than Eton," Oliver asked. Mario laughed.

"Isn't it odd? That seems to be always in their minds, and when they are not boasting they're apologising. Why do they care?"

"Naturally they care. These Church boarding schools have all been founded on the English model, and the question is, how far they have kept all the good points and corrected all the bad."

"What rot. They haven't adopted the English climate, have they? They haven't imported English boys, or even English masters? They haven't got the English countryside and country houses nor the English Church. They haven't got the British army or the British Empire. What's the use of being jealous? You can't measure different things by the same standards. You've heard how they talk—the masters, I mean, and the masters' wives. It's all just as I knew it at Eton, they say, only see how much nicer! Better baths, better ventilation, more suitable class rooms—Upper School is so ill-suited for its purpose! No cruel absurd wall-game, no fagging, no vices, and above all a simpler purer religion kept even more unmentionably in reserve for great mystic moments. Everything superior.—"

"Except the result," Oliver added, who didn't like Groton boys. "Tap an Eton mind, and you find the Odes of Horace. Tap a Groton mind, and you find the last number of an illustrated magazine."

"Oh, well, you're making comparisons again. Groton boys are awfully decent—nicely groomed to run in harness. It's only a few sentimental asses that are ashamed of being what they've got to be, and try to bray as gently as a sucking dove. As if the only thing nowadays weren't to bray with gusto, to kick up your heels in your own paddock, and not to put on a surplice for afternoon tea."

To feed Oliver's idealism they stopped on their way back at Concord. They looked at the little bronze Minute Man by the bridge, with his Emersonian inscription; they looked at the mouldering Old Manse; they looked at the dreadful little house in which Emerson lived, and at his cold little sitting-room; and then they looked at each other. Could such great things leave such mean traces? Could such recent things be already so distant from a young man's mind? Mario whistled, and thought about luncheon and about getting home by the best road; but to Oliver unseen things loomed all the larger and nearer in that visible desolation. The meagre woods, the sluggish river, the frail monuments were eloquent in their pathetic inadequacy, as if the spirit that had blown here had disdained to stop and to become material, and had spread and transformed itself to infinity into unexpected things. He liked Concord in its external humility and inward pride, so much like his own. This place had at least one spiritual advantage over Groton: it was sad.

When the wounded hero returned to his alma mater he was not greeted with effusion. Almost it seemed as if a chill had descended on the Lambda Pi Fraternity house, where he lived; his friends there resented a little that after vanquishing the enemy he should have passed so completely into their camp, remained so long away, and required no attentions. The College at large, too, seemed to bear him a grudge for winning a merely personal victory, as it were *hors concours*, and allowing himself to be hurt in a skirmish, leaving them without their best player in the final battles with their proper rivals. Oliver felt the thinner air, the moral vacuum, forming around him, and he didn't mind it. He was absorbed in his books, and more than his Fraternity or his athletic friends, he began to cultivate a certain Coffee Club in which a few local wits or free spirits met after dinner. There were two or three young instructors in the company; they were harmless; they were not geniuses; but each of them had some special knowledge or some intellectual hobby; and in that academic Noah's Ark each had his head out of some window, sniffing at the weather outside. It was to them that Oliver introduced Mario, when the latter in midwinter came to pay him a few days' visit. But Mario didn't much notice those young professors; they were just beaks. It was at the Lambda Pi that he at once found his centre, and spent all his time. Oliver, carried in tow by his cousin, was drawn again into the talk, the feasts, and the pranks that he had for some time cast off as childish. Within those two or three days the *Pi Lambs*, as they were called, got up a feast and a theatrical show. Mario arranged the fable and played the principal part of Pierrot, introducing his little repertory of songs, some English, some French, some Italian; he was enthusiastically elected an honorary member of the Fraternity, and in his speech of thanks, after promising to found a Chapter of the Lambda Pi at Harvard, he knew how to make facetious references, in the approved local style yet with a touch of foreign wit, to the events of the day and the little characteristics of the members. "As to my worthy cousin," he observed, "Brother Oliver Alden, you mustn't be surprised if you see him nowadays walking about abstracted and Hamlet-like, with his mouth open and his tie loose. He is not in love; he hasn't seen a ghost: but he is secretly engaged in composing his thesis for a Ph.D.—fortunately in the German language—on the secret significance of Longfellow's poetry. It will be a revolutionary work and epoch-making. People will say Before Alden and After Alden as we say B.C. and A.D. He has already half-reconstructed the lost document Q from which that rogue Longfellow drew his best-sellers. It was a mediaeval collection of Milesian tales of a— well—most unpleasant character. The originals of Evangeline and Priscilla—though Oliver's ancestress—were no better than white slaves. All up-lift will be gone from the cry, Excelsior. It will no longer re-echo in any Christian home. Hotels called by that name will be avoided by self-respecting financiers. Banished, too, will be those household words:

She stirs, she moves, she seems to feel
The thrill of life along her keel;

and the sands of time, flowing faster than ever through the hour-glass of progress, will erase the footprints of Hiawatha and of the good man Friday."

Oliver smiled tolerantly at all this fooling; he even joined in the songs when they were such as the College Glee Club—of which he was a leading member—might sing in public. Sometimes during a quiet evening or at the Coffee Club, he would be asked to repeat his own favourite arias, which he performed with a lovely voice and tremendous suppressed enthusiasm, astonishing Mario, who had never been allowed to discover this gift of his cousin's.

"Why on earth didn't you tell me you could sing like that," he exclaimed after the first revelation. "It is wonderful, and my mother would kiss and hug you if she could hear it. But why do you choose such romantic things, such foreign things, that have nothing to do with what you can possibly have felt? Nothing but *Do you ken John Peel* and *Bring the Bowl which you Boast* and *Gentlemen Rankers*. What have you to do with gentlemen rankers or cavaliers or fox-hunting? Purely English things, and old-fashioned at that!"

"And, there's the Eton Boating Song," someone suggested. "Sing that, Olley. It's your best."

"I won't sing that," said Oliver, blushing, "before a real Etonian who may be sick of it. Let him sing it himself."

There was a general demand for Mario to perform. He had a light voice, and a variety-show manner of half speaking half singing: but he rattled off his own accompaniment at the piano without looking at the keys, and winked on occasion at the audience; whereas Oliver had to be accompanied, and stood up straight and abstracted, as if in the presence of Allah.

"I'll sing the first two verses," Mario replied, slipping on to the piano-stool, "but the rest is bally rot—sickly Old Etonian sentimentality. Now all join in the chorus." And when he came to the lines:

Skirting past the rushes,
Ruffling o'er the weeds,
Where the lock-stream gushes,
Where the cygnet feeds,

he stopped for a moment, took a puff of the cigarette that he had left on the edge of the piano, and said in an aside:

"Yes. That's it. There's the charm of Eton," and then he launched the chorus:

We will see how the wine-glass flushes
At supper on Boveney Meads.

These diversions, heartily as he entered into them, were far from absorbing all Mario's energies. He discovered at Lenox a Professor and Mrs. Simpkins, old friends of his father's, who were spending the winter in the country for economy. They had two charming daughters. Miss Eugenia Simpkins was perfection. Beautiful, gentle, and wise. There was nothing superior that she didn't love—Bach, Mozart, and Beethoven, Giotto and Botticelli, Blake and Turner. There was nothing inferior at which she didn't shudder. She played the violin, and being much older than little Madeline, she assisted her father in completing her young sister's education; so that Miss Madeline Simpkins was perfection too, only of a rounder sort. It almost seemed that she might have been amused, if she had dared. A suspicion of fun quivered under her eyelashes and in the corners of her mouth. Mario said she was a peach; and he was sure Oliver would admire Miss Eugenia. They were asked to luncheon on a Sunday. The house was religiously quiet; not one speck of dust; flowers everywhere, discreetly placed; charming old-fashioned manners; one glass of sherry; a stroll in the garden; a little music in the picture gallery, where there was a drawing by Mantegna. Professor Simpkins said he had once attempted to teach history at Harvard, but had found at once that history was impossible to teach. So was every other subject. People must teach themselves or remain ignorant, and the latter was what the majority preferred. Mrs. Simpkins sighed, and said it was too true; and all the governments were drifting straight towards a wicked war. Miss Eugenia could not deny it; it was most sad; and yet somehow the arts seemed to have flourished sometimes in the midst of war, and even of crime. The age of Dante had been deeply troubled. Miss Madeline said nothing, but looked very sweet, and smiled in the most friendly way at both the young men when they took their departure.

"Isn't it a lovely family? Cultured up to the eyes," said Mario, as he turned from the Simpkins' drive into the public road and gave the little motor its full speed.

"I shouldn't mind the culture," Oliver observed, "if it wasn't so bottled up. They're frozen stiff in a thermos-flask, and if you uncorked it they would melt away."

"Madeline isn't frozen stiff. She might melt, but she wouldn't melt away."

"The older one is really handsomer. You can see she is a nice person, and she says intelligent things. Madeline looks as if she wanted to be kissed."

"She does want to be kissed, and it's a shame not to do it. If you only gave me five minutes—"

"You wouldn't want to marry that sort of girl."

"Who talks of marriage? I can't marry them all. But I like them all—or most of them.—I say, Oliver, were you brought up on the bottle or did you have a wet-nurse?"

Oliver laughed at the idea of a wet-nurse. Fancy Miss Tirkettle in that capacity! Nobody had a wet-nurse in America. Of course he was brought up on the bottle.

"I thought so," Mario exclaimed triumphantly. "You don't know what a woman is. You are not comfortable with women. It's all because you never loved your mother and she never loved you. That makes all the difference. My mother suckled me at her own breast. She would have given up the stage, given up music, given up everything rather than not do it, or let anybody else touch me. I seem still to remember it. But suppose I couldn't remember it; the habit would be there, the impulse, the confidence, the love of softness, the sense of power. Even when I was a little boy every woman to me meant Woman. A room full of them was vastly exciting, like an orchestra. You would have laughed to see me perform before the lot of ladies, Italian or French, that used to come on Tuesday afternoons to the rue de Saint Simon, to make vestments for poor parishes; and when the *goûter* was brought in—green mint and cakes—I was allowed in too. You mightn't suspect it, to hear me now, but I once had a lovely voice, very high and very flexible: and as my mother is a *mezza*, almost a contralto, we could sing together the most exquisite duets—*Quis est homo* and the letter scene from *Le Nozze di Figaro*; or I would stand on a great square stool that seemed to me like a real stage at the Opera, and sing away all alone. Don't imagine me a little Lord Fauntleroy in a black plush suit and a lace collar and red silk stockings. I had only a dark blue cotton blouse, buttoned behind, such as poor boys wear, with a leather strap for a belt, and bare legs: and when I was singing I would pull the belt down on my left side, where the sword was supposed to be, as if I were resting my hand on the hilt; while I pressed my chest with the other hand, or pointed sublimely to the ceiling at the long final high note. My mother always taught me my songs, how to breathe, how to phrase, how to pronounce, how to put in just enough expression and not too much; because good music has the emotion that is appropriate already in it, and it's a sin to drown that musical emotion with gross unmusical bawling and screaming. That's why almost all singers nowadays are so un-musical—so crude and so violent. They won't let the music sing through them, but must substitute barbaric yawps of their own. Natu-rally, a child is only like a flute: you can't make him tear a passion to tatters; and I used to do the most difficult things quite innocently— *Caro nome* and even the Queen of Night—with an immense success, which I didn't quite understand. But when I finished I would go the rounds, kissing all the ladies, my mother first, of course, and also again at the end. Most of the ladies would kiss me back, some *du bout des lèvres*, as they kiss one another, but some of them quite hard; others no kiss at all, only a little pressure of the hand. One day I overheard one of them saying to another in a stage whisper, '*Un bel maschio.*' '*Sicuro!*' I put in proudly, a bit offended that the point should need emphasising at all; and those that understood Italian laughed a great deal. Somehow I appreciated even then, when I was nine or ten, what it all meant, this being a male amongst females. I felt a great glow: something that made me open my nostrils and breathe deep. My mother understood my excitement. I think she liked to see it. Yet it all ended in tragedy. Perhaps everything, if it doesn't break off in the middle, has to end in tragedy. One holiday, when I came back from School in England, my mother looked at me once or twice strangely, and then burst into tears. Why? Because my voice had changed. She said I should never be able to sing properly again: the most wonderful sopranos were never any good afterwards. But I know that wasn't the only reason—not the chief reason—why she cried. If my voice had changed and I was turned into a man, the falling-in-love business, the running-after-women business was sure to begin presently. It wouldn't be a farce any more, as among those Tuesday afternoon females who were all old. It would begin in dead earnest. In fact, it had already begun: and though she didn't know it, she guessed it. That was why she cried."

"It must be hard for mothers," said Oliver trying to be objective. "They must hate to think that their sons may not always be as pure as they used to be."

"Nonsense. They don't like us to go gallivanting with other women, because they're jealous. They don't want their baby-boy to love any-one else, and they don't want anyone else to love their baby-boy. It's instinct: but my mother had no reason to be jealous in my case. They can't cut her out—not any of them, nor all of them together. She's wonderful. So reasonable, so tender, so resigned, so devoted. And so determined, too, so magnificent when she stands up to her full height and outshines everybody. She's still young, hardly forty: and what do you suppose she did, as soon as she felt that on going out into the world I might begin to forget her or even be ashamed of her? She took up the challenge, began to practise her music again, began to sing in public, first at the *Sacré Cœur*, then at charity concerts, finally at the Italian Embassy, and in private houses, professionally, for a high fee: and when on an anniversary of Rossini they gave a special performance of *La Cenerentola* she sang the title rôle and created a *furore*. She said she did it to pass the time and to have a little extra pocket money, and she did get better clothes: but I knew the clothes and the singing and the perpetual practice—for you've got to work in order to sing—were all for my sake, so that I should still be proud of her, and see her shine, and adore her.

"Well, on that very day when she found my voice changed, in order to cheer her up, I asked her to try me and see if I couldn't do some man's song. It seemed that my voice, what there was of it, was going to be a baritone, and I could already hum in my boots, if not sing. So we sat down together at the piano, on that same large square stool which I stood on in the palmy days of my childhood: and I put one arm round her waist while with the other hand I turned the pages. And what do you suppose she had chosen for my first man's lesson, and began to play for me softly, and then to sing the words, until I had learned it? *Deh, vieni alla finestra*, the serenade from *Don Gio-vanni*—a love song for her little cockerel, but not a real love song, not serious: something to palm off out of bravado and in disguise on my valet's best girl! Do you catch that? My real love was to be still for my mother; all the rest was to be nothing but nonsense, a licen-tious dream, or a romp in a carnival. Because you know in that song there is really a lot of passion, but without illusion, Mephistophelian. What tact, eh, what insight? Prophetic, wasn't it? Well, after I had learned the air and the words, and had sung it once or twice *sotto voce*, we tried it in earnest: and when I had come to the end triumphantly, she finished off that mocking accompaniment so merrily, with such an exaggerated *scherzo*, that we both laughed out loud, and kissed each other, and she said: 'You will always love your poor old mother better than any of those other women, won't you?' And I said, 'Always.'

"'You will never let any of them separate us?'

"'Never.'

"And so it's always been and always will be."

Mario made a pause, which Oliver didn't break. They exchanged some casual words about the road and the weather: but both felt that the subject wasn't exhausted, that the scene remained set and the stage empty.

Then Mario began again. "You must come to Paris next summer and let my mother teach you to sing. She'd love to. She would understand you. Of course, you'll say you can sing as it is. You have a great voice—if I only had a voice like that!—and you make nice sounds, sing like a choir-boy, no—that isn't fair—like King David himself enforcing his views. But that's not knowing the art, it's not transporting yourself out of yourself. Can't do it, eh? Are a philosophical egoist by nature? Well, my mother would get you out of that hole. Not by argument, my boy: by sympathy. What is it to be transported out of oneself? The very same thing, at least in music, as to get down deep deep into oneself, down to all one might have been and might have felt, if all these confounded accidents hadn't prevented. You must be transported, you must play a part: there's no art without making believe, without illusion. But you can fetch all that out of the very depths of yourself. There needn't be anything insincere or foreign about it. On the contrary, it's just freedom. All you must do is to shake off your crust, your artificial shell, because it *is* artificial, and is merely cramping and tormenting you into being what other people expect or what circumstances require. Art takes you beyond all that, as if you were mad, or a poet, or in love. You are inspired: and then, if you sing, everybody that hears you is transported with you. That's when the whole house goes wild and shouts and claps, as if you had let loose a thousand devils, or angels, inside each of those poor johnnies in the gallery. And you have. Or you would, if you would only come and let my mother teach you to sing."

Oliver smiled. He was quietly pleased to see how much feeling, how much depth, there could be in a creature like Mario, apparently so flighty. But for himself he saw no new opening: on the contrary, he felt how inevitable and right his own practice was.

"Why then," he protested, "do you laugh at me for liking old English songs that have nothing to do with my life at home? Singing isn't talking or doing business. It's more like praying, or as you say, like letting out the inner man that circumstances have suppressed. You live then at a different tempo, in another world. There you find everything developing and coming round perfectly, instead of stumbling along in the dark and never getting anywhere. I like poetical and idealised and formal things just because *they exist*, because they have wholeness, so that you can trace them and retrace them; you can sing them again and again. When I repeat them, I have done something, I have lived through something great. I am no longer merely a section of the common sewer through which anything may flow. But I don't want to play a part, or sing in an opera, or be applauded. Music is too much a part of myself; and Mr. Darnley says I can sing only what I feel: so that your mother would find me no good."

The subject dropped; but Oliver that evening writing his diary, carried his reflections a step further. Was it right to be transported out of oneself at all? Wasn't it just shirking, a mere escape and delusion? Wasn't it what had created all false religions? And when the spell of that sort of dream had faded and you looked about you in the grey of the morning, or in the grey of old age, wasn't it what led you to suicide? If men had no imagination they could feel no discouragement. Perhaps all this religion and philosophy and poetry and art were a disease to be killed off presently by natural selection.

V

In spite of these forebodings Oliver never flinched in his determination to pursue higher things. If natural selection at present was unfavourable to those higher things and threatened to extinguish them, that was hard luck and saddening; yet what difference could it make in the loyalties of a spiritual man, an ἀνὴρ πνευματικός, such as Mr. Darnley said that Oliver was? The higher things remained always the higher; their eclipse was something local and temporary; they might still be approached or even attained in happier days by others, if not by oneself; and meantime they continued to be the goals of life by the ineradicable bent of human nature, in spite of all human confusion and blindness. From above they over-arched and united the aspirations of all souls capable of self-knowledge, and made them friends to one another in the spirit. Since he was young and rich and materially safe, Oliver found this sort of moral suspense decidedly bearable: there was even a certain acrid pride in fighting a rearguard action, and defending the right in the darkest hour of its fortunes. When he sang *Here's a Health to King Charles*—which he did gloriously—he felt that what the cavaliers had been in the seventeenth century it was the puritans' turn to be in the twentieth: the martyrs of a poetic and chivalrous cause. Not, in this case, a lost cause: since truth and reason were not historical accidents, like the House of Stuart, but could never die out or forfeit their divine right. There was accordingly something leisurely, something quietly ironical, in Oliver's assurance of being on the right side; also something domestic. His mind was distrustful of far-reaching radicalisms or utopias; it was content with a firm sense of direction guiding it steadily in its home orbit.

The broken leg had been a signal for a change of heart: not at all a pathological conversion involving repentance, but a placid transformation, sloughing off one set of organs to put forth another set. He must continue to take hard healthy exercise, and for that purpose he, like Mario, got himself a horse; but he would turn his back on all competitive, official, organised athletics. He must continue to

study; but all this College routine of courses and examinations and
degrees must be wound up and bundled out of sight as fast as
possible. Yet legally: Oliver's sense of propriety required him to finish
what he had once begun, and not to be scatter-brained. Williams
College would give him his degree for three years' work; he had
amply justified that concession; and he would ask to receive that
degree a year after his departure, when the rest of his class received
it, so that he might not seem to have deserted either his college or
his comrades. At Harvard he would begin a new life, like a poor,
unknown, solitary student. During September, when the place was
deserted and Mario still in Europe, he made a special pilgrimage to
Cambridge to look for suitable quarters: no Fraternity House, no
fashionable dormitory, not even any lodging house where romping
undergraduates would always be breaking in, howling at this, borrowing that, and creating pandemonium. For an interloper like himself, the college office would hardly have a room available. "No," said
the clerk in a drawling, contemptuous tone. "We weren't *keeping* it
for you; but we *have* got one vacant room in Divinity Hall, on the
ground floor. You can have *that*, if you want it."

"Divinity Hall," to Oliver's ears had a pleasing sound. It might be
just the right place. Guided by the map, he found his way to an
unpaved side road, leading nowhere, but shaded by spreading trees.
There was green grass; and on one side a rather squatty old brick
building, with large square windows. The vacant room, too, was low
and square, and rather spacious: but with no bedroom, no bathroom,
no heating, no running water: only an iron grate in the fireplace,
and a cheap paper peeling off the walls. Would this do? What would
his mother think, if she saw it? But she wouldn't see it. He remembered how warm and pleasant a coal fire had been at Eton, and how
a kettle could always be kept simmering beside it. He could have the
walls scraped and glazed like Jim's cabin in the yacht; he could get a
bed that, by day, would be a sofa, and a screen to cut off the washing
things in a corner. The one electric bulb hanging from the ceiling on
a wire, might be replaced by a shaded lamp, white inside, green
outside, suspended over an ample writing table. He could bathe after
his exercise at the boathouse or the gymnasium: besides, the janitor
said that there were showerbaths in the passage. Yes, the room would
do beautifully, so retired, so modest, so safe from all intrusion. Close
to Divinity Hall was a new library, a perfect place in which to find all
the German philosophers too voluminous to have at home, all the

learned reviews, all the dictionaries, and an atmosphere of whole-souled, devoted study. He would live in Divinity Hall.

He was giving a last look out of the window, towards Norton's Woods and Shady Hill, when he heard the janitor saying:

"Ralph Waldo's name isn't there. Guess he hadn't a diamond to scratch it with."

On one of the window panes there were indeed some names and dates and initials scratched rather illegibly by former occupants.

"Ralph Waldo?"

"Yeah, Ralph Waldo Emerson. They say he lived in this room. It weren't in my day. *I* don't swear to it."

Strange, Oliver thought, that he should have chosen Emerson's room without knowing it. Irma and his mother, except that it was wrong to be superstitious, would think it a special Providence. All protests against the meanness or discomfort of his lodging could now be silenced with a word. "What was good enough for Emerson is good enough for me."

To this paradise of plain living and high thinking, Oliver hastened even before the required date. His shell had been sent before him and installed in the boathouse. On his first afternoon in Cambridge he paddled out early, to explore the upper river. It had then been freshly "improved", its banks piled up into little dykes, correctly curving, with paths laid out in new yellow gravel, and rows of infant trees in curl papers. So taught the way it should go, the sluggish Charles wound its way seaward from what promised to be the coun-try, or at least a suburban park. Oliver, watching the circles which his oars made as they placidly dipped in and out of the water, passed his old friends of the year before: the Stadium, gaunt and deserted at the other side of Soldiers Field, and the Stillman Infirmary, its red and white somewhat less glaring, its young trees somewhat more leafy; and he recognised the broad window against which his bed had stood. Pleasant now to be without pain, unconfined, with the full use of his limbs and of his faculties, free, yet fully occupied, alone, yet loved. Pleasant to be exploring a new river, a new town, a new university, new ideas, and new ways of living; yet not as a tramp, without a settled mind and resources of his own, but benevolently, observantly, with discriminating eyes; like Faust walking out on a Sunday evening amongst the good burghers of Frankfort, and won-dering why that little devil of a poodle ran so between his legs. But Faust was not really young. Mephistopheles had cheated him and made him young only in appearance. He remained at heart an old reprobate, with a bitter taste in the mouth, and a diseased intellect, forcing him artificially to live hard and to try to know and experience everything. Had he been really young and a gentleman and had he gone sculling—much better for clearing the brain than making love to a waitress—he needn't have felt obliged to turn up his nose at the *Gemütlichkeit* of the Rathskeller, or at that delightful song about the flea going to the tailor's. One wasn't always in the mood for merriment; Oliver himself seldom was; but that wasn't anything to be proud of; it was a limitation. Not everybody could be like Mario, innocently enjoying all sorts of frolic and ribaldry, without turning a hair and without being defiled; because he touched these things as he did the grease of his car, with gloves on, which he could pull off and throw into the gutter. But to feel superior for hating simple things was to be a prig; it was to revenge oneself on the world, to one's own cost, for not knowing how to live in it.

With these thoughts floating like light clouds through the upper air of his mind, Oliver was solidly conscious of the concerted rhythms of his back and legs, of his hands and oars. He was rowing beautifully on the home stretch, thoroughly warmed and limbered up, yet not exhausted, and defying the sundry strains and sores of a final spurt, filled as he was with the joy of bringing the thing off handsomely, just for the pride and pleasure of doing so. He would have shot past the boathouse—there was only one in those days—had he not suddenly held the blades firm in the ruffled water, and come to a dead stop just at the float. It was a finish like those which in other days were the pride of superior coachmen, who sweeping in at a smart trot would bring their high-stepping horses bang up to the master's door.

As old Silas, the boathouse man, helped him in with his shell, Oliver noticed two tall men in flannels, at the other end of the landing stage. One was apparently an undergraduate and the other a man of thirty or more; and as they continued their earnest and apparently endless conversation, they both seemed to be eyeing him askance, and wondering who he was. Ten minutes later, when he came down dressed, and congratulating himself that it would soon be time for dinner, there they still were, deep in the same urgent discussion; but now the younger man broke away, and deliberately accosted him.

"I beg your pardon," he said in a level voice as if asking the way of a policeman, yet with a humorous apologetic smile at his own curiosity, "but is this Mr. Alden?"

"Yes."

"Not Alden of Williams who—who made the touchdown?"

"Yes. I've finished there, and come to Harvard for my Senior year."

"But we didn't know anyone ever *rowed* at Williams. Never heard it was a fresh-water college."

"It's not. I've rowed only at home, when I was at School, and in the vacations."

"But how's that? Dr. Wilcox and I—this is Dr. Wilcox, our head coach"—and Oliver was now obliged to shake hands with the older man who, he observed, had a jaw and a red moustache like Mr. Theodore Roosevelt, and an iron fist like the Kaiser—"Dr. Wilcox and I were watching you just now and admiring your sculling."

Oliver laughed. On account of his touchdown people found it incredible that he should do anything else. Must he explain that he wasn't just a football player?

"I was taught sculling by Denis Murphy, the old champion. He keeps a boathouse now at Great Falls, Connecticut, where I live."

On hearing Denis Murphy's name Dr. Wilcox became uproarious, shouting that of course that explained everything. "Nothing like being coached by the right man," he cried, clapping himself on the chest and nudging his friend, with an exaggerated air of self-satisfaction. "Mr. Remington—Mr. Remington is our captain of the crew this year"—and as this was a sort of return introduction of the person who had introduced him, perhaps Oliver and Remington ought to have shaken hands at this point; but by a tacit agreement they left that out. "Mr. Remington and I ought to have recognised Denis Murphy's methods at sight; but your form is a bit different, something personal, and of course you haven't his weight. Your style is smoother, less jerky, without any loss of drive"—and Dr. Wilcox was going to repeat all his formulas for making a perfect oarsman in six weeks, when he suddenly looked at his watch, cried, "The deuce!" said he was damned if he hadn't an engagement at six o'clock; it was six o'clock already; happy to have met you; the deuce again, he had forgotten his bag; ran upstairs to get it; hoped to meet you again; hadn't time to go round by Harvard Square; must run all the way through Allston to catch the Brighton Avenue electric; good-bye; and so long.

When finally the energetic doctor got away, already very hot, with his long tie flying and his loose flannels flapping against his hurrying legs, Remington looked at Oliver, Oliver looked at Remington, and they both smiled a little. They were glad Dr. Wilcox was gone. They were not sorry to find themselves together.

The part of Cambridge where the boathouse stood was then half waste land and half slum: rubbish heaps and negro shanties with an occasional lamp-post askew: a sort of squatters landscape or museum of back-garden architecture long since vanished from there, but now visible in the outskirts of Paris. A single muddy street led to Harvard Square and the Yard: so that, inevitably, on his first day at his new college, Oliver found himself walking through the town with the Captain of the Varsity Crew. He had no mean idea of his own quality and position: nevertheless, to be suddenly perched in this way on the topmost rung of the ladder did rather take his breath away, and he was silent. Remington, on the contrary, kept up a flow of casual talk, as if vaguely chuckling and grumbling to himself about things in general.

"Strange how dead everything is here, only two days before college opens. Not a soul in Cambridge. Old Silas said you had brought your own shell with you, and meant to go out every day on the river, till it froze up. Nice shell, that of yours. We were looking at it while you were upstairs. I've always thought Skinners the best boat-builders, but our inner circle is rather pledged to the other firm. As to rowing here out of season, I don't see how you're going to manage it. The river may not freeze at all; but nobody rows here in winter and the boathouse is closed. We get the running squad going and practice on the machines.—Don't like machines, eh?—Of course, sculling as you do for pleasure, and all by yourself, you can very well afford to dangle about enjoying the fresh air and admiring the sunset: but we've *got to train. We're not in the crew to have a good time, but to win the Yale race.*"

Remington had said these emphatic phrases in a different tone from the rest of his lazy talk, more strident and more vulgar. He had become positively snappy. Evidently those maxims were not coined in his own mint; they bore the stamp of official athleticism and distorted his pleasant temperament. He happened to be a big young man with no bent in particular; they told him he might "make the crew," and that in that case it was his duty to try for it; and if he proved to be the best man available, it was his duty to be Captain and give all his heart and soul to the work. He wasn't altogether sure about his heart and soul; but what else could he do? He was in for it. Oliver understood his new friend's predicament at once; he had had experience of it in his own person. An instinct told him that Remington would be mightily pleased, at bottom, to hear his official cant contradicted.

"Win the Yale race? Do you think you're likely to win it in that way? I daresay you'll win, because the Yale men have the same machines and the same sort of coaches. They're driven too, only perhaps they're driven a bit harder. But isn't the whole system wrong? Training is all very well to gain strength and to correct little tricks that a man may fall into. Training prevents waste. But the thing itself, the real rowing, must come from inside. You can't begin from the outside and tell a man how to row or swim or sing or write poetry. And I don't believe it's less so pulling in an eight than in single sculling. On the contrary, then there's all the more danger of not getting together. If a man walking alone chooses to ramble and look back, there's no harm done except that he loses momentum and feels rather like a fool; but if he gets out of step marching in column, the whole show is broken up. You must keep contact from a centre; everyone must feel as the others feel, and must make them feel as he does. Otherwise there's no life in the boat. That's what military music is for, and church music also. You might feed up a pack of giants and coach them at the machines till they went like clock-work; they'd be useless when they got afloat, unless a sort of electric current ran through them all, and turned them into one water-insect with eight legs. Don't you feel as if the outriggers and the oars were parts of your body, and you went leaping along on them like a sort of grass-hopper? But where's the electric current to come from in an eight? From the poor little cox? Probably he hasn't enough electricity in him to keep him from shivering in his own skin, let alone igniting eight big hulking beefy fellows all duller than himself. You'll say, of course, from the captain: but how is he to do it, by talking? It ought to come from the stroke, if only he were sure of himself and had magic enough in him to control the others. The vital centre has got to be in one place, not drifting about vaguely and dropping into eight or nine separate places. And it's likely to do so, because each man is really complete, with a vital centre of his own, and must be kept under a tremendously powerful spell, else he becomes independent. Your jockey can manage so easily, because the vital centre is naturally in him, and his mount is only a mare or a gelding. Your gelding might be as fast, mechanically, as you will; he would never stick to it in a race, without a rider who wasn't a gelding. Now your stroke shouldn't be just one of eight horses, trying to run abreast; he must be the jockey too, straddling the whole lot; and he's got to have enough vital force in him to mesmerize all the others, and keep them going from his own centre."

Remington smiled incredulously. He liked Oliver, but he couldn't take stock in ideas, much less in outlandish mystical ideas about a plain matter like rowing. "Mesmerized, is it? I knew about swinging together, but I never knew we had to be mesmerized to do it. I've pulled in two four-mile races, the first time I was sick at the end, but I didn't once notice that I'd been mesmerized. It's true," he added, with the chuckle of a happy cynic giving his own case away, "it's true we've never won."

They both laughed. This sort of quizzing and nonsense rippling the surface of the mind gave Oliver a masterful feeling of quiet depths beneath, which rendered those verbal puzzles ridiculous and joyous. Remington excited this sort of laughter in him more than anybody he had known. It was laughter like his father's: perhaps it had been people like Remington that his father had known and laughed with in his youth.

"You'll say, every man has his own vital centre," Oliver went on. "How are you going to get at it, so as to mesmerize him? I don't know how, but it happens. Call it animal sympathy, or herd-instinct, or contagion: it's as when you slip on the ice because someone else has slipped in front of you, or when you know what another man is going to say. Or it's like a flight of birds wheeling together in the air and keeping in perfect formation. The movement is elastic and naturally finds its balance. They haven't practised on the machines, and it's all done without a cox or a stroke or a captain."

"And, thank God, without a head coach." Remington had no misgivings about their mutual understanding, and was betraying his secrets on first acquaintance, without any sense of indiscretion.

They had reached Mt. Auburn Street. "You don't live in Claverley by any chance, do you?" Remington asked, stopping before the sandstone steps at the door.

"No. I wonder if you know my cousin Mario Van de Weyer. *He* lives here."

"No. I don't know him." The tone of this retort was so sharp, it expressed such an immense distance and such a fixed determination to keep that distance immense, that a chill fell suddenly between them. But it passed away no less suddenly when Oliver added:

"I live in Divinity."

"Not possible? Isn't that somewhere beyond Memorial? Never heard of anybody living there." That remote region had one clear meaning to Remington's mind; it meant poverty. How could a man who had his own shell and such a grand air—for in spite of his simplicity, Oliver had it—live in the obscurity and banishment of Divinity Hall? Anyhow, that idea completely erased all associations with Mario Van de Weyer and his objectionable ways.

"I know it's rather out of the way and old-fashioned," Oliver explained. "That's why I was able to get a room there. I wanted to be alone and quiet. I've come to Harvard to do philosophy."

"They haven't roped you in yet for the football squad?"

"They'll never do that. I've sworn off football for good. Nothing but a little sculling, and golf later, perhaps, just for fresh air and exercise—to clear the brain."

"And to relieve the vital centre," Remington grunted, offering his hand. "Will you come to the boathouse to-morrow at three, and go out with me in a pair-oar? Be on time, so that we may get away safely. I warn you, if he sees us starting, Dr. Wilcox *will cox*."

VI

Divinity Hall did not protect Oliver from busybodies. On the contrary, the emissaries of various athletic bodies seemed to be positively encouraged by finding him in such seclusion and apparent poverty. Opposite Divinity, behind the trees, rose a vast factory-like, red-brick edifice, then half finished, the Chemical Laboratory; and in its shadow the old Theological School seemed absolutely derelict and overpowered. Was not enterprise everywhere crowding out reflection? What could a needy athlete have come to Harvard for, except to play? He must have been bribed: public opinion took that for granted. No doubt there were rules against such migrations. The days were over when the doctrine of *laissez-faire* had been orthodoxy at Harvard, and a career had been open to experts even in sport. But the rules as yet were elastic and local; exceptions could always be made; you could always prove, in a particular case, that there was no vestige of professionalism. When Oliver protested that he was at Harvard merely to study, the words had a familiar ring. Of course, study was what he had come for; but if they couldn't put him into the Varsity squad at once, it was his duty to try for his class team: wasn't he a regular member of the Senior class? Refusals for a while served only to prolong the discussion, or bring visits from even more influential personages; and nothing would ever have cooled the ardour of those recruiting agents, had it not begun to be bruited about that Oliver Alden was rich, very rich. In that case, he was surely eccentric, living as he did: and an eccentric rich man might perhaps mean what he said. Peace began to return to Oliver's retreat, peace in a sort of vacuum: he was ignored as systematically as he had been pursued. He was set down as belonging to that odious category of outsiders who hung loosely on the fringes of college life: odd persons going about alone, or in little knots, looking intellectual, or looking dissipated. They were likely to be Jews or radicals or to take drugs; to be musical, theatrical, or religious; sallow, or bloated, or imperfectly washed; either too shabby or too well dressed. The tribe of these undesirables was always numerous at Harvard. Nothing was ever to be got out of them for the public good—not even money.

Undisturbed, Oliver could now sit in his free hours in the most remote and sunniest corner of the reading-room, in that clean new Divinity Library, scarcely recalled to the consciousness of human society by an occasional footfall in the distance. There, many books were within reach of his hand, not to speak of the countless others procurable from the vague recesses of the stack. What a sense of competence and freedom to be able to read German easily, and what a look of surprise and delight came into his professors' eyes when he mentioned that circumstance! He was already half way up the ladder when he began to climb. Yes, and he could read Greek too, without too much trouble. He had spent the previous summer in the Vicarage at Iffley, where Mr. Darnley had coached him on parts of Homer and Plato and the New Testament, and had persuaded him to begin his study of philosophy at the beginning with Thales and Heraclitus. So now he had the text of the pre-Socratics open before him, with his dictionary and translations and commentaries; together with a large fresh note-book actually blackened with a page and a half of notes. He was going to attack the whole thing humanistically, as Mr. Darnley recommended, without any anxiety about ultimate conclusions. He would come out of the wood somewhere, when he least expected it; or if he didn't, at least he would have gone on a great journey. That everything was made of water, or that life was nothing but the restlessness of fire somehow dispersed and half-smothered in its own ashes—those were notions not unmeaning or uncongenial to him as he paddled alone along the grey shimmering stretches of the river, under the grey clouds; while the autumn mists shrouded the distance and made the whole human world seem more like some old incredible report than like a present reality. Alone: because after the first day's spin in the pair-oar, the holidays being over, it had been impossible for Remington to join him: how should a captain of the Varsity crew have time for boating?

This solitude, half pleasant, half melancholy, was not to last long. The second half-page of the note-book was still blank when one rainy afternoon he heard the three well-known notes of a motor-horn sounding *Hei, Siegfried* outside his window. It was Mario, in the new superb car that Oliver had given him, only a three-seater, but already powerful and long like a locomotive, and surprisingly silent. That little chime was their signal. Mario had selected it, the first three notes of the bird's song in the Wagnerian wood; because he said (agreeing with Fräulein Irma) that Oliver was like Siegfried; while the little bird that came to wake him up from his boy-dreams, and teach him a thing or two about life was Mario himself. He had come from Newport by road at the last legal moment: the next morning he would have to report his choice of courses for the year, and as yet he had no idea what those precious courses would be, Oliver must help him to decide. But first they must go to Claverley and unpack. So Zeller and the pre-Socratics were put aside, the half-page in the note-book remained blank. Obediently Oliver mounted the running board in the rain, since the other two seats in the motor were heaped with luggage. Just like Mario to rout him out on the way, covered with dust and mud, instead of going to his own place first, and making everything shipshape, as Oliver would have done, and looking up his friends afterwards. As if the only object of his trip had been to see his cousin, and not to begin his term at the University! "Damned nuisance, all these belongings," he muttered. "Wish I could live without luggage. But what are you going to do? You can't wear the same shirt every day, can you? Then people keep giving you such lovely presents—dressing cases and golf-clubs and all that sort of thing— which you can't throw away; and they do pile up."

Talking of presents reminded him of Oliver and the new car; and he launched into a eulogy of all its virtues, wondering at the average speed he had been able to keep up that day, in spite of the weather and the state of the roads. But they had reached Claverley, and as he threw open the windows of his ugly little rooms, he blew out his breath audibly, as if to reject the ambient infection. "Beastly hole! Don't think all this ghastly furniture is mine. It's the janitor's. I merely take it on for so much a year, and don't have the bother of owning anything. Possessions are such a bore. In this way, I could quit in five minutes without leaving a trace. At least they've cleaned the place up nicely. Hello! Look at this. There's actually fresh white paper in the drawers; none of your old newspapers, but stiff new blotting-paper, almost like cardboard. It's that blessed Pat Milligan; his doing. The goodies adore him, because he's an Irishman and a Catholic. He got them to scrub the whole place, just because I had written that I might be late, and hated the idea of finding everything littered with last year's rubbish. But he must have provided the paper himself. The poor innocent man took me at my word, and made a symbol of it!"

"Is Pat Milligan the janitor?" As Oliver said this the coldness of his own tone surprised him. He felt that he understood better why Remington had said so pointedly, "No: I *don't* know Mario Van de Weyer."

A momentary flash of offence came into Mario's eyes, only to yield at once to a peal of laughter.

"The janitor! Pat Milligan is the most distinguished person in Cambridge—really the only distinguished person. He's a poet, a pauper, and a saint. But if you wish to know what people *think* he is, he's merely an instructor in English and proctor here in Claverley. More important, he's my best friend—I mean of those I had here last year. You'll see him. He's wonderful to look at: pale with a lot of red hair, cerulean eyes, and a mouth that can breathe hot anger. Shelley, if Shelley had been a Christian. He writes the most beautiful poetry, most of which he won't show to anybody, except sometimes a few lines to me. When you talk with him, don't cast any aspersions on Ireland or on religion, or he'll flush red and make you blush redder.—Now I've got to go and thank him. Do make yourself useful and go on unpacking while I run up to see if he's in his room."

Why should people be admired for being emotional and deluded? Oliver felt that on the whole he didn't care for poets. And it wasn't religion, in any sober or manly sense, to run amok over some passionate fancy of your own, and be ready to torture yourself and other people rather than admit that it was all froth. True religion must recognise the power actually at work in the world and study its workings honestly. And if the truth didn't supply a very succulent feast or cooked just to your palate, why not be a little less gluttonous, a little less fastidious, and swallow what you've got to swallow?

Patrick Ignatius Milligan, Ph.D., was out: not unintelligibly, since it was past seven o'clock and he was presumably at dinner. But where should *they* dine? "*I*," said Oliver, firmly, feeling that his own personality must have its innings, "*I* feed at Memorial Hall."

"Good Lord," his cousin cried, "you can't *feed* there. You merely starve on the musty smell of carrots and stale soup. There's always the same thing for dinner: one thin slice of ribs of beef, a sickly pink with a great white nerve running through the middle, and floating in grease and water; some washed-out peas in a soap-dish apart, and one chocolate eclair that's been tempting the street boys for a fortnight in a confectioner's window. I know, because I've dined there more than once with Pat Milligan at the instructor's table in the tower, that ought to be better served than the rest, but isn't because they only pay the same price. Memorial is all right for him, because he's vowed to fasting and other penances. One boiled potato, all pimpled and pitted as if the dandelions were ready to sprout on it, will keep an Irish poet alive for a week. Ireland is a very watery country at best; not much sap in it, nor granite. He says himself it wasn't created like the rest of the earth, but that once the green waves climbed up a little too near to heaven, and couldn't slip down again: and that was Ireland. Besides, he can't afford to eat, because he sends half his wretched little salary home to his people and gives the other half here to the official poor. But you! A magnificent Nordic of your sort must be fed magnificently. You can't keep your first class engines going without shovelling in good beef and good mutton every few hours, and good drinks too, if your spirits are ever to warm up and you're actually to feel or to think anything. Else you just flop, like the old Saurians that tried to live on grass, but couldn't find grass enough in the whole world for a good breakfast. There's a first rate table at Mrs. Haunch's. Charley Street eats there, and they'll be delighted to have you. Too expensive for me: besides I don't need to eat anywhere—not that I fast, like Pat Milligan—but that I wait to be invited, or pick up a bite anywhere, or go to the North End to the *Napoli*. To-day, the Hollytree will do nicely for both of us. Only eggs on toast, steak and baked potatoes, and apple pie, but all excellent, hot, fresh from the grill which you can hear sizzling; nothing but coffee to drink, but you don't mind, and we can have a liqueur at the club afterwards."

"What club?" Oliver inquired, a bit alarmed at being appropriated in this airy manner and pulled out of that studious solitude in which he had planned to live.

"The *Lambda Pi*, of course, which Stephen Boscovitz and I started last year. You belong to the Fraternity already and you're to be admitted to our Chapter at our next meeting. The place is rather bare and primitive as yet, with only the steward to do all the work; we can't very well eat there unless we cook our own eggs.—So, come along."

Oliver found himself pulled into the street by main force. After all, why should he resist? Hadn't he come to Harvard simply because Mario was there? Had it been really for the sake of philosophy mightn't he have preferred Oxford or Berlin or Marburg? Queer little nook that *Hollytree Inn* into which he was bundled, down in the basement of that queer little Dutch doll's house, islanded in the middle of that muddy road. He believed he wasn't luxurious or squeamish; but his instinct recoiled for a moment before that pine table covered with oilcloth, that pewter fork, that black knife, the kitchen plate somewhat chipped and discoloured. He found it a little difficult to begin, and to reassure himself he sipped the tall glass of milk that stood before him: that, at least, was cold and pure. A good appetite did the rest, together with the irresistible example of Mario, so absolutely at home in the place, exchanging amenities with the old shuffling proprietor, cook and waiter—three functions in one person—and seeming to relish the feast far more than if it had been spread before him at *Voisin's* where he would have had to look *blasé* and hardly to notice the viands. And if Mario with his varied experience and lordly manners and beautiful clothes and hands so extraordinarily agile and sensitive, could like eating in this hole, how absurd for poor Oliver to be critical! He ought to like it too. Yes, he would try to like it.

Presently, across that greyish white oilcloth, they began to debate the urgent question what courses Mario should select. "I have it," he said suddenly. "You've chosen your courses: I'll simply choose the same, and then each of us needn't do more than half the work. You can go to the lectures and tell me what the professor says, and I will tell you what to think of it.—I had that damned *Elective Pamphlet* somewhere—286 courses to choose from, I believe—but I've lost it."

Another copy of this noble document was produced from Oliver's pocket, with several pages nicked at the corner, places scored, and marginal notes. "Prof. talks through his nose in a see-saw,"—"Instructor very young and easy-going. Sits on the desk and lets the class do the talking."—"Russian Jew. English not intelligible."—"This lad tries to be funny."—"Lectures like a gramophone and quotes statistics."—"Too old. Coughs and spits in a bandanna handkerchief. Rambles and reads extracts out of his own works."—Oliver had been doing what at Harvard is called "sampling courses" and in Germany *hospitieren*: dropping into all sorts of class-rooms to compare their attractions, as if they had been rival cinemas.

"What have you picked out?"

"First, Indian Philosophy. Professor Woods."

"Not half bad. Might be rather *chouette*. What's the hour?"

"Mondays, Wednesdays and Fridays, at 9 o'clock."

"Nine o'clock? At nine o'clock I'm still in Nirvana."

"There's the College bell to wake you."

"How should it wake me if I don't hear it, and how should I hear it if I'm asleep?"

"Well, here's something more important. Professor Royce, Metaphysics. Tuesday, Thursday and Saturday, at 12 o'clock."

"Can't be. At twelve o'clock I'm out riding. It's when the Boscovitz girls take the morning air in the Brookline Parkway.—What is metaphysics?"

"Who are the Boscovitz girls?"

"You know perfectly well. Haven't I written you about them? They are themselves, which is as much as to say *exquises* charming and like nobody else."

"And you know perfectly well what metaphysics is—at least you know it as well as anybody does. That was metaphysics you were talking just now about the College bell, that nothing can happen unless one is aware of it. That's called idealism; and it's wrong."

"If it's wrong, why do you want to study with Royce? Isn't he an idealist?"

"He's the best man going, and I don't have to agree with everything I hear."

"If he's their best man I might as well hear him too. I can go to the lectures in bad weather—and there's a lot of it—or when the Boscovitz girls say they're not going out. And sometimes I get back by twelve o'clock. Do you suppose it would upset Royce's logic if I appeared in my stock and riding-breeches? No? Then I'll put down metaphysics at 12 o'clock, as a merely provisional hypothesis. What else are you taking?"

"Plato in English: *Republic*, *Phaedrus*, and *Symposium*. First half-year only.—Light and airy. Shouldn't take it except that I'm reading up the subject and the lectures will serve to keep up my interest. Just the thing for you."

"Who's the professor?"

"Santayana."

"Good Lord, I can see all I want of him outside. I'll take you to tea in his rooms. If you ask him what classes you'd better join in philosophy, as he can't very well say, 'Join all mine, and don't join any others,' he will tell you that it doesn't very much matter; because in any system of philosophy you can find something important—to avoid: and you're much less likely to fall into the snare if you've seen it spread out plainly before your eyes than if you were wandering about unsuspectingly with your nose in the clouds. Besides he has expressly warned me off his own lectures; he says it would be highly dangerous for me to become more civilised than I am."

"Then you can't take Phil. 4, which I was going to recommend because it comes in the afternoon, when we rude brutal fellows are bent on taking exercise. Ethics: intensely civilising: just the thing to turn your rough diamond into a soft velvety worm or a purring kitten. I'm not taking it myself. I've come here to read books and to learn facts—at least historical facts—not to cultivate sentiment. If the facts are before a man, he will know well enough how to feel about them. If you come to him with a religion, or a system of ethics, and tell him what he *ought* to feel before he really feels anything, you merely make a sham and a hypocrite of him. That's the way I was brought up, and it's criminal. You've got to spew the whole thing out and begin afresh on the basis of reality."

"Agreed. We'll put it down that both of us are far beyond ethics. But what else can you recommend? I've got one course, and I need four."

"Sorry, but I can't help you. As it happens all my lectures come in the morning. Lucky, because it leaves me free to go out on the river."

"Why shouldn't you row in the morning, or get a horse and come riding with me instead? I'm becoming suspicious. Haven't you some Boscovitz girls of your own, only they air themselves after lunch instead of before? Perhaps that course in ethics isn't so bad after all: everybody else seems to like it. I'm going to try it. You've been abusing it only because you wanted to deceive your conscience and invent reasons for being idle all the afternoon. And you don't know what you're missing: because I'm sure that your afternoon friend—isn't it Remington?—can't hold a candle to the three nymphs I sport with in the fresh dewy morning. No longer three, unfortunately. This year they'll be only two; the eldest is already married to a Graf Otto von Kuchenschloss or von Gipfelstein or von something else and is gone to live with him in his gingerbread castle in Bavaria; but she isn't giving up any of her old friends, she says, and I'm to go and stay with them at Lindenhöhe, if that's what the place is called, whether her husband, who is fat and bald, likes it or not. You can't think what a good friend she is—so entirely able to take a man's point of view, and yet laughing at you all the time, and keeping her dignity. 'Here comes the basilisk,' she would say when she saw me riding towards them: for it would have been rude not to join them when we happened to be riding in the same place at the same hour. They are slender blondes, with pretty eyes turned up a little at the corners, Chinese fashion, especially Griselda, who is only sixteen and as mischievous and strong as a schoolboy, only of course cleverer, being a girl, and with a lot of good sense and firm piety behind her larking, although she pretends there's not. You ought to see how exquisitely she turns up her little snub nose and says 'Rats!' so that it's lucky we are on separate horses at least a foot apart, else I should have to kiss her.

"Their father is still in business, not in a jeweller's shop, of course, but as an expert in gems, and they say he makes a lot of money. Goes to New York every fortnight to appraise anything special that may have turned up, and every summer to London, Paris, and Vienna, to buy up any rarity that's in the market. But his passion is for flowers, and he has the most wonderful conservatories; every possible climate under glass with electric sunshine when required. The walls and doors and balustrades and fountains are all in keeping with the plants, here Chinese, there Japanese, there Persian, French, or Italian; sometimes with genuine old garden gods and grottoes. And old Boscovitz, with all his Shylock shrewdness and eye for a bargain, has a sort of Biblical poetry in him; shows you about as oily and obsequious as if he were going to sell you something for ten times its value; whereas it's the other way and he loves you for loving his things and treating him with affectionate respect, as a great personage, which indeed he is in his way. Sometimes he picks me a little bunch of the rarest and loveliest flowers for a buttonhole; and it's amusing, when he has chosen his best flower and his best leaf—for the leaves are often the most marvellous part of it—how he wants to stick the thing into my coat with his own hands, like a village lass flirting with her yokel; only his fingers are so thick and clumsy that he can't manage it, and pricks himself with the pin, and I have to come to the rescue, and say, 'Oh, Mr. Boscovitz, how awfully kind of you, but let me do it. I don't need a pin; there's a little loop here below the buttonhole on purpose to hold the stems down; English tailors are so provident.' And in a jiffy the flower is in its place; or if there are several and more than you want to wear—because he is ridiculously lavish—I take half or three-quarters of it and in the twinkling of an eye I've stuck it into old Bosco's own buttonhole, before he knows what I'm about; and he's terribly pleased, but shy; because he's very simple in his person, a bit ashamed of himself, perhaps, and would never think of wearing a flower. But I tell him he ought always to wear one, because the flowers must all wish to say thank you, and to make him festive and happy, as he has made them. And as for Mrs. Boscovitz, or the Countess, as he always calls her, she sits by the fire like a pale ghost or a sacred image, while the family flit in and out, or sit for a moment beside her and tell her the news. She doesn't speak any language properly, but a mixture of everything, with a French sauce: calls her husband Boscovitz a little regretfully, as if apologising for having married him, but she was starving, and he was such a kind man, and she thought that in America no one had any prejudices about race or religion, and there were no social distinctions; and she sighs when she tells me so and adds, *Quelle erreur!* Then she wipes her eyes to think that Olga has left her, to live so far away; and complains of Griselda for being such a tom-boy: but what is a mother to do in these days. '*Ah, cette enfant,*' she murmurs helplessly, '*c'est une polichinelle.*' She even confides in me that her daughters have no real delicacy, and will wear any sort of plain linen. 'It eez shocking, *il faut des dentelles.*' We have heart to heart talks, the Countess and I. I tell her about my mother, and the duets I used to sing with her when I was a soprano, the same lovely things, as it happens, that the Countess used to sing in Poland with her music teacher, before her father was executed and everything confiscated: and she used to play her own accompaniment on the harp. 'Ah,' she says, 'ask your dear mother to come and make us a visit. I will have the harp tuned, and we will sing those old duets together, we two old women, very softly, when there's nobody to make fun of us, and we shall be so happy.' At this point Griselda bursts into the room and pulls me out of my chair. 'There you are at it again, making Mamma sentimental. It's so bad for her. Come and let me beat you at a set of tennis. I'm dying for exercise.' And she does beat me—sometimes. But there's another game, more exciting than tennis, to which she's always challenging me; and if she expects to beat me at that, she'll have the surprise of her life."

There was a pause, long enough for Oliver to feel distinctly that he would never like the Boscovitzes and would never like Pat Milligan. They had a bad influence on Mario: made him fantastic and made him wicked.

"Now," the wicked one went on, "you know more about the Boscovitz family than you could gather from all the gossips of Boston in a week. But please don't think that the old man, because he's a little soft and emotional, is a fool at bottom. Soft-hearted, but hard-headed. He had to be christened in order to marry the Countess; but he only changed his name from Israel to Isidore, so as to keep the same initial, and not to disturb his business signature. As to religion, he's all suavity and sympathy with everybody, but naughty in his own mind. 'Don't repeat this to the Countess,' he said one day with a wink, 'I was never enthusiastic about being a Jew, but the first drop of baptismal water washed me of all desire to be a Christian. One religion is as good as another when good people practise it and believe they believe it. It's a play they like to act; they compose a part for themselves in it much more important than the rôle that falls to them in real life. It's a great safety valve; it reconciles them with existence. As for me, I find religion enough in the love of beautiful things. Jewels and flowers seem to me different forms of the same beauty: jewels are flowers petrified and become luminous: while flowers are jewels become sensitive and frail, swaying in the wind, and dying young. And there's a third form of beauty, combining the other two, and that's a good woman; because a good woman is like a flower in her body and like a jewel in her mind. Keep to good women, my boy, and you'll be all right.'"

"I suppose he wants you to marry Griselda."

"I might do worse. But what's the use of talking? I'm not going to marry for ten years, if ever. Where should I live, what should I do? If old Bosco wanted me to take root in an office in Boston and bloom for life in his conservatory, I wouldn't do it for all the flowers and all the jewels and all the women in the world."

"Why not?"

"I want to be a Knight of Malta."

"What nonsense you do talk. And all those extravagant things you pretend people say to you I'm sure aren't real. They're made up."

"Not made up, but we've got to change the truth a little in order to remember it.—I say, it's time for bed. Let me have that Elective Pamphlet. When all is quiet in the middle of the night, between one dream and another, I will collect my thoughts and see if among these 286 fountains of wisdom I can find two more at which a gentleman may drink with decency."

VII

In remote corners of that formidable programme, certain "advanced courses" were announced "primarily for graduates": narrow mountain paths up which learning might be traced to its sources, always in the green earth; because at its springs science becomes again as fresh and humorous as sensation, and history as exciting as sight-seeing or gossip. An old letter, an old manuscript, an old print attracted Mario; the insignificant details of it were so significant. To unearth them had all the flavour of an indiscretion. He chose a half-course on Villon and the troubadours, one on Saracen art in Spain, and one on the military history of Europe in the seventeenth century. These classes of three or four members would meet in a room in the library, or in the professor's study. When a youth so obviously gilded, so unmistakable a prince charming, presented himself for admission, those worthy gentlemen looked at him with some surprise over their spectacles: but five minutes of his conversation reassured them. His flow of language in several languages, his quickness, his offhand acquaintance with popes, kings, and artists, convinced them that here was an exceptional young man, a connoisseur by temperament, already at home amongst rare things. He was soon the glow-worm in that learned twilight; and when the other opaque worms had departed, the professor would sometimes detain him, to explain the ramifications of some historic scandal, or to show him the coats-of-arms and the portraits in some imposing quarto, with their Latin epigrams; child's play to Vanny, though he was tactful enough to let his mentor spell them out, and parse them laboriously, as if they were difficult enigmas. On his way to these little gatherings he might be seen trudging through the deserted Yard of a late autumn afternoon, with a great green leather pouch under his arm, such as nobody else carried: worn and baggy, but still decorated with a magnificent silver monogram and crest, which served as a clasp. This faded heirloom had accompanied his father on his first sketching tours, when "dear Harold" felt he was to be a second Turner, taking the Alps and the clouds by storm. Later, when architecture and heraldry were in the ascendant, the great portfolio and its embryo Turners were a resource for the little Mario on a rainy afternoon; he was encouraged by his fond father to finish the sketches, and put in pirate schooners and royal frigates into the Swiss lakes. Empty now, those great leather pockets served for conveying books and papers from one college lecture-room to another; and the old associations seemed to make the new studies more entertaining and less pretentious. It was with a buoyant stride and flushed cheek that he would hug the old pouch and run to his lectures. The odds and ends of learning stuck pleasantly in his mind, like the adventures of a Gil Blas or a Casanova; it was the little events, the glimpses of old life, like the cadences of old poetry, that had the savour of truth. Perhaps there were no great events: a great event was a name for our ignorance of the little events which composed it. Summary views were necessary to the rhetoric of politics; they were gross masks made for the public eye, or made by it; but the humble truth of things was woven into their finer texture; it lay in the forgotten passions and forgotten accidents that really determined every turn of events.

Meantime, in that room in Divinity Hall which had once cradled the sleep of Emerson, Oliver, evening after evening, would sit at his desk, within the bright circle of light cast by the one lamp hanging from the ceiling. Papers and books were spread before him, as if for hard work: but often he would lean back, motionless, his gaze vaguely lost in the environing shadow, and his mind employed in steadying the pivoted chair which supported his person—supposed to be the *right* chair to go with a desk—and keeping it from screwing to the right or screwing to the left, or bobbing insecurely forward and back. The gyrations of that seat seemed a symbol for the state of his mind: a dozen irrelevant vistas opening and fading before it, and none leading anywhere or worth exploring. The athlete's after-dinner torpor possessed him: he might be the first to rise from table at Mrs. Haunch's; he had had to eat a good dinner after his hard exercise in the wintry air; for now that sculling was impracticable, he had begun to run with the hare and hounds, or, at Remington's invitation, with the crew squad. Besides all this philosophy belonged to the shady side of the world: it was all a chaos of talk, of argument, of opinion. Babel: everyone quite sure, and nobody really knowing what he was talking about. But as you had to take exercise for your health, even if it made you sleepy, so you had to study philosophy, so as not to be too ignorant and not to make up your mind unintelligently about ultimate things; or at least to justify you in not making your mind up at all.

Yet there were moments when the intensity of Oliver's inner life broke through to the surface. His ideas then ceased to be straggling and clumsy and merely refractory, and came out in strong words. After all, his education had been excellent; he was at home on the higher levels of feeling and knowledge, and had hardly been contaminated at all by the cheap sentiment and catch-words of the day. Beyond that, he possessed by nature an incorruptible spirit, hating compromises and vagueness, and not afraid to be cruel in the interests of truth.

It was during these days, in a moment of intellectual euphoria, that he composed the "thesis" on Plato which was the occasion of my great interest in him, and indirectly the first cause of this book. He had been reading the *Phaedrus* and the *Symposium*, and had dutifully made a correct, if rather meagre, summary of their doctrine; but personal comments were asked for; and it was here that, for once, he let himself go. It was not the spirit of Plato, nor of Emerson, his predecessor in that student's chamber, that now descended on Oliver: it was his own spirit that inspired him.

Plato, he wrote, may have been a great philosopher, but he knew nothing about love. He talks only about desire. It is true that desire and love may be sometimes felt for the same person; a man may occasionally desire his wife, and also may love her unselfishly. But he may desire some other tempting woman without loving her; and he may feel love without desire for his children and his friends.

Love is therefore entirely different from desire, and unselfish. It may lead a man to give up his life for others, both by living for them and by dying for them. He may be content to be ignored by those he loves, and be satisfied in knowing that they are noble and happy.

The sorrow which love may bring is also unselfish; not an itch for pleasure or society, but moral distress at seeing those most dearly loved suffer undeserved misfortunes or turn out unworthy.

Plato tries to show how desire may be for all sorts of superior things, beginning and ending with the beautiful. Yet these superior passions remain always desires, to be satisfied by possession, in a kind of orgasm. I believe that later Platonists, who were Christians, have even carried this into religion and talked about the ineffable and blinding bliss of union with God. This idea, if God be a superhuman spiritual being, seems absurd as well as blasphemous.

420   The Last Puritan

A beastly consequence of Plato's confusing love with desire is that he allows desire to pollute friendship. In friendship there may be love, perhaps the highest and most intense love, but there is not a bit of desire; or if desire ever creeps in, it is by the intrusion of mere sensuality, which has nothing to do with friendship and is at once driven out by friendship, when friendship becomes clear and strong.

On the other hand Plato is frank and clear-headed when he says that *being in love* is a kind of madness. Fortunately this madness is short-lived, like that of the March hare.

He is right also in pointing out that desire may be refined and turned toward noble objects. Intellectual pleasures may come to be preferred to creature comforts, and music or the beauty of nature to almost everything else.

When it comes to the Absolute Idea of the Beautiful, if this means perfection for every creature after its own kind, I can see that a desire for this would really be identical with love. It would not be a selfish desire ending in a swoon of pleasure. We can never feel in our own persons the ecstatic bliss of being a perfect porpoise or a perfect eagle. But reason in us may correct our human prejudices, and may convince us that other forms of life are as desirable for other creatures as our own form of life is for us. If this is what we are to understand by Platonic love, I think it is a high insight; but I wish Plato had made it clear that unselfish love can drive out desire at every turn in life and not merely at the summit of philosophy.

In the middle of this last word *philosophy*, as it stood in the manuscript, a long break had evidently occurred. The ink at the end was thinner, the slant of the letters different and more awkward. Oliver was indeed in the act of writing that word with all the gathered impetus of conviction and all the joy of finishing a long task, when "*Hei! Siegfried*" sounded on the motor horn outside his window, and his pen remained suspended in mid-air. What could Mario possibly be after at this time of night, during this first snow-flurry of the winter? But here he was himself, bursting into the room, throwing hat and gloves on the table, and dropping, wrapped in his great fur coat, into the one arm-chair.

"You must come at once with me to Boston and bring the car back. Am going to New York by the midnight train, and sailing for home to-morrow morning. Leaving college—leaving college for good. Have to, for two reasons, two decisive reasons; but I'll tell you everything in order on the way. Come on. No time to lose."

Oliver, with perfect steadiness, with perfect patience, looked at his watch. There was plenty of time, an hour, where fifteen minutes would be enough. But Mario was nervous, pale, not with his usual wits about him. Had he taken his ticket? Also his passage? Yes, everything had been arranged. Mario had been rushing about Boston all that early evening, telephoning, saying good-bye. And where was his luggage? Only this portmanteau and these small bags? Yes, Stephen Boscovitz and Charley Street would send the rest to Paris after him, and some of his books. He had been distributing most of them to the fellows at the club. Oliver could have the motor, and also his room; the rent was paid in advance; it would be so much more convenient and comfortable than Divinity Hall. All the way to Boston, what with the speed of the open car, the driving snow and the sharp cold, they could exchange only a few phrases about these trifles. Not till they were in the train, seated in Mario's compartment, with half an hour to spare until midnight, did Oliver turn on his friend and ask:

"Now, what has happened?"

"You know that Mrs. Cyril Trumpington, with two girls of her Company, was coming this afternoon to see Harvard, I mean, to see the glass flowers and the Stadium, and to take tea in my room. Pat Milligan, Steve, and Charley helped to do the honours. As they were leaving Mrs. Trumpington got into her own closed car with a man she had brought with her and one of the girls who said it was too cold for an open motor, while the pretty one, Aïda de Lancey, came in my car with me. We hadn't got to the bridge when she became very agitated. 'Oh, Mr. Van de Weyer, please let's go back, I've lost my purse. I must have dropped it in your rooms.' So we turned round, and shouted as we passed to Mrs. Trumpington, who was behind us, why we had to go back. Aïda all the way kept fidgeting and fretting. How could she have dropped it, why hadn't she missed it at once. How frightfully stupid of her. I couldn't fancy how much it meant to her. Only a tiny chain-mail one in silver, but such a treasure, from her very dearest, nearest friend in the world. She was trembling all over, and leaning hard against me; cold, I suppose, and almost hysterical. When we reached Claverley, I turned on all the lights and began to search about the floor, and the litter of chairs and tables: we had brought in a lot of Stephen Boscovitz's things for the occasion. No purse anywhere. It must have fallen in the bedroom, where the ladies' cloaks had been left. We went to look. She was standing close to me—you know how small that bedroom is—touching me, trembling. Suddenly a little cry, half scream, half sob. 'Look,' she said, stretching out her arm full length. There, tight in her hand, she had been holding the little purse all the time. Had she known it from the first, or was she so crazy that she hadn't known it? Never mind. It makes no difference now. By that time, I had her in my arms, and we had fallen on the bed together.

"What of it, eh? Such things happen sometimes. But the devil of it was that we were caught. First I heard steps and voices in the hall, then a loud knock, then a key turning in the door, and the sound of several people bundling in. There was Pat Milligan's voice saying, 'I knew he was out. He went to escort those ladies home.' Then the janitor's voice, grumbling: 'Ain't that his automobile standing outside? And he's left every light on full blast; even in the bedroom.' And then a shrill jeering muckerish voice—it was the telegraph boy— 'He ain't out. He's in there. Guess he ain't alone either.' By that time I had pulled myself together a bit, stood in the bedroom door and turned off the light inside; but that fool of a girl, instead of keeping quiet, began to speak, and we were lost. Besides, I think they had all caught a glimpse of her—enough to know it was a woman. Still screening her as well as I could, I sent the janitor away. I would explain everything to Mr. Milligan. The messenger boy wouldn't go, and grinned knowingly. He wanted a dime. I gave him a dime. Then I turned to poor Pat Milligan, who was white as a sheet. 'I'm terribly sorry. This has been an accident. Absolutely unpremeditated. You know that ladies were here to tea. I had permission. After leaving, one of them missed her purse. We came back here to look for it; the rest just happened—I don't know how it happened. I'll come up to your room later this evening and hear what you have to say. Now, please let me take her home quietly.' He didn't breathe a word, and went out very slowly. I'm not sure that he didn't cross himself at the door. I had the hardest job of my life trying to comfort him afterwards. It ought to have been easy, because then I'd made up my mind to quit anyhow. He might report me—he had to report me, of course; but it wouldn't do me the least harm; they might expel me, if you can expel a person who has already left. And as to betraying his little friend, and ruining my reputation, he needn't feel any qualms, or any conflict of duties. My reputation in that sort of way was ruined already—think how Remington and his set detest me; and he wouldn't be betraying me, because I would then and there, at his own desk, write a letter to the Dean reporting the facts exactly as they happened, and saying I was leaving Cambridge that very night. But the dear man was wounded in his religious feelings. He had actually seen something improper, had spied upon a licentious episode, had found his pet pupil in the arms of an actress, had grave reason to fear for my soul; and besides it was depressing to have me vanish in the middle of my Sophomore year, when after all I made the one dash of colour in his drab existence. Poor Pat Milligan. The whole thing is twice as hard for him as for me.

"Well, when we were alone again, I begged her to be a sensible girl, to stop crying, and consider that no harm had been done really. It was only a step to the car, and quite dark in the street. Nobody had seen her so as to recognise her except Pat, perhaps, who was a gentleman and would hold his tongue. Besides, even for him, who she was would be only an inference, because it couldn't have been the other girl who was a nonentity. She washed her face, looked in the glass and put on some fresh powder. Once in the open, she recovered her spirits, and was quiet and calm. After all, it wasn't her first scrape. As for me, I assured her, she needn't worry. If I had to leave College, I shouldn't be sorry: glad, really, on the whole. In fact, everything would have been lovely, if only those loud beasts hadn't broken in upon us like that. A telegram! As if a telegram couldn't wait!

"'They said it was a cablegram,' she murmured, a little anxious. She had now adopted me for a life-long friend, as they always do.

"I had a horrid presentiment; actually gave the car a jolt; but I'm always getting cablegrams, and Aïda had to be disposed of first. At the hotel we had an affectionate parting, till to-morrow, all happy promises, and no serious regrets.

"Then, by the light over the hotel door, I read the telegram."

Mario stopped a moment; then, without looking at Oliver, grasped his arm so hard that it hurt, and said under his breath:

"My mother is dying. I hope to arrive in time. That's my other reason for leaving, and leaving at once."

Oliver didn't know what to say. He felt horribly helpless. He looked again at his watch. It was one minute before twelve. They went out on the platform, and as he stood on the step, shaking hands, the train already in motion, he remembered his trump card.

"Have you enough money?"

"Yes, but I borrowed all the cash Steve and Charley had in their pockets. You might pay them up. And you might go to the bank to-morrow morning and guarantee my cheques, in case I've overdrawn my account."

Yes, Oliver would be glad to do that, glad to be able to do anything.

The train was gathering speed, and the darkness absolved them from attempting to express or to disguise their emotions as they waved good-bye.

VIII

At the garage Oliver rang several times before he could wake up the man supposed to be the watchman, who swore at him, asked who in hell he was, and what in hell he had to do with Mr. Marius Van de Weyer's auto: Marius being a third and most correct form assumed by Vanny's name in the Harvard catalogue. Even when the garage door was opened, and the car safely backed into the dark interior, the man was too stupefied with sleepiness or drink to understand that henceforth the car was to be Oliver's: but never mind. That could be explained later to the boss of the establishment. The thing to do now was to warm up by running the quarter mile up hill to Divinity Hall through the first snowstorm of the year.

The thesis on true love lay derelict on the table under the full glare of the circular lamp. Odd that he hadn't turned it off as usual. What had gone out of itself was the fire: he ought to have raked it and banked it up before leaving. The hour was scandalous for an athlete, and a tenant of Divinity Hall. Nevertheless, in gathering up the scattered sheets of his thesis—scattered by Mario's hat when he had flung it down on the table—Oliver stopped to add the missing letters to the word philosophy, completing the first half which meant love with the second half which meant wisdom. He opened the window as usual; musty cold was worse than the most biting air; he threw his travelling rug over his bed for extra protection, and determined to have a good night's rest. The best way to meet a sudden shock was to go on as if you hadn't felt it. He closed his eyes, assumed the posture habitual to him in sleep, and as the bed got warmed persuaded himself that he wasn't at all upset. He would go to his lectures in the morning as usual, hand in that thesis on time, and run with the crew squad afterwards. That was now become a sort of engagement. Hadn't they tried him at stroke this week in the tank, and hadn't the experiment astonished everybody, first that an outsider, who perhaps wasn't eligible at all, should be put in that place, and then that he should have done so extremely well? It didn't astonish *him*, he knew the reason and so did Remington; and so long as there was any chance of helping his friend to win the race he couldn't decently excuse himself. And yet what a prospect of slavery, of hardship, of responsibility, of strain, probably of disappointment! Why do it? It was always the same trap, the same circle of compulsions. You *must* take exercise; and if you are wanted for a team or a crew, you *must* serve; and in order to serve properly, you *must* surrender the greater part of your time, energy, and interest: you must level yourself down for the moment to the virtues of a professional football player or oarsman. But this would be the last time. If only it could serve the purpose and help to win the Yale race; but would it? Would they put him in at stroke? Would they have the strength of mind to keep him there?

This work with the crew made it really convenient to move to Claverley. Mario's room was just under Remington's. They would be able to signal to each other by tapping on the floor or ceiling. Too bad to leave Divinity Hall, so excellent for reading and for writing theses. Yet even here you could be interrupted. And there was a sort of constant interruption in keeping the fire going: if you forgot it, how cold the place got: too cold to work, or even to sleep. No hot water either, no bath, no separate bedroom. At Claverley he would be sleeping in the very bed where that afternoon—But he dismissed the thought. It was a superstition to give a moral identity to material things. It was like worshipping fetishes and saints' bones. What nonsense, too, to suppose that this was a better room because Emerson once occupied it. It was a beastly hole: impossibly far from everywhere, and impossibly cold.

He debated for a while in his mind whether it would be better to get up, put on a sweater and throw his great coat over the foot of the bed, or to stick it out, cold as he was; but this latter prompting he thought wasn't really stoical; it was a mere shrinking of the flesh from being momentarily colder. It was irrational. He got up. Back in bed in an instant, better protected, he felt distinctly more comfortable. Also more lucid, and less intent on going to sleep. The pictures before his mind ceased to be narrowly confined and urgent, as they are in dreams, and became more speculative and far-reaching.

His three years at Williams had been dull, except for that one touchdown, but they had been satisfactory on the whole. Was his Harvard life proving a success? He had come to Harvard in order to be near Mario and to look after him; also in order to escape athletics and solve the problem of the universe. And what had he found?

That the problem of the universe was never in a worse mess than in the minds of the Harvard philosophers, take them together or take them singly: and that he was going to muddle that problem a little more by taking on the most ambitious and severe of athletic jobs: to stroke a 'varsity eight. As for Mario, the boy couldn't have been more affectionate or more amusing when, at odd moments, they were together: but as to being looked after, you might as well try to look after a comet: he had careered about in his own eccentric orbit just as if you didn't exist, and now had flown away altogether. And that wasn't the worst of it. In his apparent flightiness, in his womanizing, he was lordliness and serenity itself. He didn't need your advice, he didn't respect your philosophy. He loved you, perhaps, a little, because he was warm-hearted, and you had been kind to him: yet in his heart he dared to despise you, yes, and to pity you. First you make him a present of a magnificent auto, such as you would have thought much too fine for yourself, if you had wanted an auto at all: then you come to Harvard, hoping to moderate his speed in that auto and out of it: and now within three months, before your quiet influence has had time to tell, he upsets himself in the gutter, slinks away in disgrace, incidentally requires you to do night work for him which a paid chauffeur would grumble at; you are cursed for it by another underling; and you find that luxurious motor foisted on you against your will, when you had drawn up a severe plan of study from which all motoring was excluded. Someone might say: Why not sell the motor, if you don't want it? But he couldn't very well do that.

At this point in his meditations Oliver shifted his position in bed, and forgot to pursue his train of thought directly. In fact, his economic conscience recoiled from the waste of selling a new car for the price of an old one; on the other hand his genteel conscience recoiled from expressing that fact baldly; and his total consciousness skipped over the difficulty, and took a new tack. The car would certainly be convenient at times; he might take Remington all over Boston and Brookline on Sundays; he might go home in it for the vacation. What a treat for Irma to be taken so swiftly and comfortably to all sorts of places she had never seen. He would have preferred a plainer car for himself; but after all, if you must have a thing it was better to have it of the best quality. Later, when he went to Germany, and lived among simple, earnest, truth-loving people, full of unselfish enthusiasm for the things of the mind, his serious studies would really begin. They were impossible here, with so many other duties.

"After all," he murmured half audibly, more wide awake than ever, "life isn't what it's cracked up to be. It's just a trap. You're caught in it, and can't get out. Unless, that is, you're quick and clever like Mario, cheat the hangman, and slip your young head out of the noose, just as the noose was going to tighten. He hasn't any resources, he hasn't any plans, yet how clearly he always knows what he wants to do, and how swiftly he does it! To-day his whole prospect in life changed in five minutes, and he remained absolutely the same, absolutely his own master, deciding everything himself, and not dragged hither and thither like me by all sorts of side issues. And not master of himself alone, dominating that little actress of his, coolly leaving her for Charley Street to console to-morrow, when he goes to explain that Mario is off to Paris: of course commanding me; no doubt commanding his grandmother, and never returning to America except to convince her, perhaps, to increase his allowance. Very neat, very pretty: he might have nothing and he has everything: and I might have everything, and I have nothing. I am caught, and he is free.

"Yet that's not the sort of freedom for me: mine must be of another kind. When my leg was broken and I lay in the Stillman Infirmary, and Mario and Edith came every day to see me, and brought me flowers and books and entertained me with all sorts of talk and with imitations of those absurd people who are called society—then I was free; then I was stronger than Mario and stronger than Edith. While they twittered round my bed, I was quietly laughing at them. Because it was they that were caught in the trap then, running in a flurry from engagement to engagement, from polite lie to polite lie, afraid of being late, concerned about their clothes, hating the officious persons buzzing round them, liking others, perhaps, from whom they were cut off. But I was lifted out of all that because I was laid low, free because I was bound, master over events because I was helpless. My ordinary life had been suddenly arrested, and the spirit in me had escaped at a tangent, into a sort of heaven. Then I could accept their attentions as Mario accepts my money, almost without thanks, as if he were doing me a favour and giving me a function in life. And the joke of it is that he is perfectly right, as I was perfectly right. Coming to see me, having me to think about, was at that moment the happiest part of their day; just as now without Mario to think about and to pull out of his difficulties, I shall be twice as unhappy. Unhappy? Am I unhappy? Yes, at bottom in a dumb sort of way, as perhaps everybody is. It's a matter of course. I shall be too busy to think of it: and if you never think you are unhappy, are you unhappy at all?"

He wondered: and as if taking the hint nature suspended that wonder till it became vacancy, and at last he fell asleep.

IX

His fast motor carried Oliver rather further than he had expected: to the door of his aunt Caroline's old-fashioned house in Gramercy Park. Edith had written what was called a cordial and cousinly letter. Grandmama, she said, wished her to ask Oliver to come to them for Christmas, or if he was celebrating that feast at home, to come as soon after that day as possible, and stay for the rest of his holidays. They had been counting on poor Mario too. It was so sad about his mother. No wonder he was upset, and felt he couldn't return to Harvard, where the boys are so *frivolous*, but wanted to begin a fresh, serious, manly life on his own account. They would all miss him so much; but of course desired what would prove best for him in the end. They knew all that Oliver had done for him so generously and nobly, and they felt it was a real bond, apart from their relationship. So that all of them, including Maud, who was looking over her shoulder, hoped he would *always* make that house his home, or his hotel, whenever he came to New York. He would be perfectly free to go where he chose, and see his other friends; but there would always be a place for him at table. The upper floors of that house were half-empty, so that if it should happen that they couldn't give him their best spare room, he would always find one that would do for a young man of austere habits, such as Mario said he was.

"Of course you have accepted," Mrs. Alden observed in an unusual tone of approval, when her son showed her this letter. "It's time you should begin to make *decent* friends. Your aunt Caroline is not a high-minded woman; has never cared for anything except fashion and gossip. She neglected her duty to your poor father, when he was a boy, and more an adopted son of hers than a younger brother. Later, she merely made fun of him in his troubles, and let him go his own way; not because she disliked his real faults, but because he wasn't wicked enough, and didn't abandon his duty to me altogether. I verily believe she would have been delighted if he had abandoned me and run away in his yacht openly with some notorious woman. It would have given her something to laugh at. But she's so old now that I daresay she's harmless. You are not so stupid as not to see that when she scoffs at good things and good people, it's because she doesn't understand them. Her grand-daughters have been brought up better. Their mother was a sensible woman. Edith is certainly an exceptional girl, really gifted, though perhaps she lets her idealism carry her too far in some directions. That High Churchiness of hers, for instance, and this exaggerated interest in her Italian cousin, who seems to have taken her in, as he has you. But he'll throw his mask off as soon as his grandmother dies and he gets her money, and then you won't hear from him again, either of you. Really at the last meeting of the Daughters of the Revolution she made a wonderful speech—the only young girl to speak at all. She looked so beautiful and calm, as if inspired, and so refined at the same time and ladylike that I was proud to be able to tell everybody that she was my niece."

"What did she say?" Oliver asked innocently.

"Oh, I couldn't repeat it exactly. I don't remember the words, but the spirit of it was what we all liked so much, and that she should be so self-possessed at her age, and show such a command of language. I'm glad that it's she that has invited you, and will introduce you to her friends. It's time you should know ladies, high-minded women, and not only ignorant boys or rough young men. I do hope you will learn to choose your friends wisely. That is a great test of character. Sometimes a boy may be inveigled into bad company at the beginning through ignorance or force of circumstances, but if he recoils in time, it may be a useful lesson."

So admonished and almost blessed, Oliver had been dismissed by his unselfish mother and given *carte blanche* for sentimental adventures: a fact that somehow supported and encouraged him in his vague feeling that now he was stepping into a sort of sacred grove, like Orestes in Goethe's *Iphigenia in Aulis,* and that the priestess of these healthful shades would be Edith. She might be rather mixed up in curious old superstitions and stubborn prejudices, but she was essentially superior to them, essentially humane. She would know how to walk resolutely through those mists, and lead him back with her into the sunshine. She was to be his matriarchal inspirer, and he was to be her young hero and lover.

The traffic of New York rather disturbed these poetic images, and they had faded altogether before he brought his motor hesitatingly to a stand-still in Gramercy Park, in front of what seemed a likely house, numbers and door-plates being illegible in the darkness. A man in livery and gaiters ran presently out of the area, and reassured him. Yes, this was Mrs. Erasmus Van de Weyer's. His things would be carried in immediately, and his auto taken round to the garage. He needn't trouble. The habits of self-help ingrained in an American collegian would have made Oliver almost prefer to carry in his own bags, and stall his motor himself. He felt again as on his first day in his father's yacht; but he remembered how soon he had learned to accept the obsequious attentions and constant presence of all those underlings, who at first had rather annoyed him. After all, this was his father's family, almost his home; it was absurd, it was a little humiliating, to feel like a stranger in it. He must accept these fashionable externals as a matter of course, and not behave like a green-horn.

He was half-way up the front steps, when the door opened of itself, and a demure and most superior housemaid in immaculate cap and apron actually curtsied as she let him in; and she took possession of his hat and coat with a little smile and bustle of realised expectation. Without further prompting she threw open an adjoining door, announcing in a clear voice: "Mr. Alden, Sir."

A tall gentleman rose slowly from the depths of a leather chair, turned on Oliver with an air of premeditated welcome, put forth a formal hand, and made a little speech.

"Ah, yes, yes. We were expecting you. Your aunt Caroline has asked me to welcome you in her name. She never comes down except for dinner. This evening she wishes to dine with you alone, in order to talk over family matters. Afterwards the girls would like you to join them at the Opera. Here is your ticket. You will find them in our box with their aunt, Miss Stuyvesant, with whom they are dining. I myself have a public engagement. We didn't know on what day you would come, and this is a busy season. The maid will show you to your room. In these hard times we have given up our men-servants. Your aunt dines at half past seven. She expects people to be punctual; but if you are ready earlier, come down to the drawing-room, where you will find her. Don't be surprised if she shows some little emotion: she was very fond of your father. He was about your age when he lived with us; I was a very small boy then, but I can still remember him. The girls will explain to you the further mysteries of this household, and will see that you are made comfortable. We are all very glad you could come to us, and hope you will feel entirely at home. Here is your latch-key."

During this speech, which was delivered standing before the fire, Oliver had time to observe his distinguished cousin. Mr. James Van de Weyer was correctness itself. Nobody was ever more scrupulously washed, shaved, and shorn. You could see that he had had blond hair, of which very little remained, faded and turned half grey; and there were still blotches of bright colour in his fair complexion. He wore spats and a fold of piqué edging the opening of his waistcoat and framing in his voluminous dark tie and pearl pin. As an echo of the gay days of Beau Brummel and the lavishness of wearing one waistcoat over another, this fashion was a sad failure; yet it suggested that the wearer moved in the highest circles and was a diplomat if not a banker. Mr. James Van de Weyer conformed to it for that reason. In morals he believed in good taste, and in matters of taste he obeyed all the commandments. He considered at every turn what was expected of him; and he felt he was appealing to ultimate standards when he said: It is generally believed, or It is coming to be held more and more widely, or It is thought in Wall Street. On this occasion he had been a little embarrassed. It was unfortunate that Oliver, who was said in Wall Street to have inherited a handsome fortune, should have come to the house for the first time rather as a representative and friend of Mario's, who had so sadly disappointed the expectations of his family. At first Mr. James Van de Weyer had liked Mario, and pronounced him a charming young man of excellent manners; and although it was not in the pecuniary interests of his own daughters, he had not opposed his mother's project of adopting her grandson, and leaving him half her money. But he had soon begun to observe that Mario had grave faults; he was irrepressible and inclined to mockery; and at Harvard he hadn't done, in any way, what was expected of him. He hadn't distinguished himself in any sport; he hadn't been asked to join any well-known club, when a Van de Weyer was expected to make at least the A.D.; and now he had run away without a degree, mixed up in some silly imbroglio, and not caring to come back and attempt to retrieve himself. Still the boy had brilliant parts; he might some day amount to something; better not talk about him at all until one knew what to expect.

A generalisation at once established itself in Oliver's mind as he followed that well-spoken, attentive, intelligent housemaid up three long flights of stairs. In this family it was the women who were nice. It was they who would understand him and sympathise with his feelings. He wasn't sure about that chauffeur in gaiters who had taken possession of his car. Would he drive it wrong and then curse it? Would he meddle with it unnecessarily and clean it properly? And how stiff and formal Cousin James had been, not once mentioning Mario, whereas this mere housemaid had the decency, the friendship to say at once: "This is Mr. Mario's room that you are to have, sir. This is his mother's picture on the table, just as he left it. We thought you might like to see it." And though she didn't materially wipe a tear, you felt that her sympathies were enlisted on Mario's side because he loved his mother, and on Oliver's side because he was Mario's friend. With Edith for a presiding genius, and even the maid so perfect, he was sure that Maud and his aunt Caroline would also be just right: different, of course, but just as it would be immensely pleasant and encouraging that they should be.

The photograph on the table wasn't a recent one, such as Mario had had at Cambridge, but represented the great Maddalena in her younger days, and in a theatrical costume. Oliver didn't like it. The resemblance to Mario seemed a caricature; those bold features, handsome in a man, were too marked, too gross, for a woman. The whole spacious room seemed a sort of family museum. It was filled with furniture and ornaments evidently discarded by the march of fashion: sentimental engravings in gilt frames; faded oval photographs of ladies in hoop-skirts and corkscrew curls; water-colours by feminine hands; chairs belonging to old drawing-room sets; heavy chests of drawers with marble tops; and a monumental bed, with a perplexing wealth of quilts, pillow-shams, eiderdowns, and silk hangings. The objects upon the long marble washstand were enormous, edged with gold and green bands, and decorated with gilded sea shells. Fortunately it was not necessary to disturb them. There was a small bathroom with modern fittings adjoining, where Oliver very expeditiously made his toilet.

The stairs down which he presently came debouched suddenly on the landing of a grand staircase, running only to the first floor, and opening through two arches into a long narrow hall or gallery furnished like a ball room with nothing but pink damask seats under mirrors, and dimly lighted by a few electric candles with pink shades. No aunt Caroline there, only a grand piano at one end. Perhaps it was a music room. As he turned to look elsewhere his new pumps made a slight tapping sound on the parquet floor, and at once he heard a deep but very clear and individual feminine voice saying sharply:

"Don't dawdle out there, whoever you are. Come in and let me see you."

The voice came from the other end of the room, where he now noticed a screen in front of a wide door; through the top part a larger room was visible, and the flicker of an open fire playing on the ceiling. Weathering the screen he descried by the farther corner of the fireplace first a frilled white muslin cap like a pagoda, and then beneath it the ample form of his venerable aunt, black lace mittens on her hands, and a black watered-silk train spread majestically over the carpet. She looked fixedly at him for a moment, then slapped her lorgnette down hard on the newspaper she had been reading, placed both objects together on a little table by her side, and without rising stretched her two arms with outspread fingers dramatically towards him. It was impossible to hesitate. She demanded to be embraced.

"So this is Oliver, this is the little Oliver they've been keeping from me all these years, till he's not little Oliver any more, but this big strapping handsome Oliver, that Edith and Mario admire so much. I hope you deserve it; but you're not much like your poor dear father. Darling Peter, the world never did him justice. He was such a sweet quiet baby, always smiling, when I used to carry him about and play I was his Mama. He needed to be loved; and when everybody turned against him, for no reason, for no fault of his own, he was too modest to defend himself, simply drew back, allowed himself to be suppressed, and married Harriet. Oh, I know Harriet is a fine woman. I mustn't say anything against her, because she's your mother; and they say you are like her; but that's not true. You'll never be fat. You're distinctly an Alden. I begin to see it: the long legs, the shape of the head, the refinement. You're like your uncle Nathaniel; what Nathaniel might have been if he wasn't a fool.—But tell me, did you know your poor father well? Were you old enough to understand him?"

"I was eighteen at the time of his death. We had been alone together most of that summer. He told me a great many things then: his ideas, the things he cared for. I think I understand what his troubles had been, in every way."

Aunt Caroline leaned over and pressed Oliver's hand.

"Your father was happy at the last. He was happy about you. He wrote to me about it. I want to talk with you a great deal to-day, because on the other days we have people to dinner, and I see nobody at any other hour. Not that I dine; only a dish of gruel; but they are bringing you some cutlets or something, on a tray, and I will talk to you while you sit here by the fire and eat. And first about this affair of Mario's. What sort of woman was it? Are there likely to be any unpleasant consequences? No promise of marriage? No divorce?"

"There can't be any such things, can there, when a man isn't of age? Mario is a child in these matters. He makes love like a bird. Besides—I don't know how much he told you—in this case it was the lady's doing entirely. He wasn't to blame, except for not resisting, if you blame him for that."

"We don't ask him to be a Joseph, nor a Saint Joseph. Who was she?"

"A little actress who plays minor parts with Mrs. Cyril Trumpington. Unmarried, but not inexperienced."

"*Respiro*. Do you know her name?"

"Aïda de Lancey."

"*Basta*. Not a word more. No details. That tells me all I care to know. Such things only concern me because I have adopted Mario. I sold my carriage and horses—I had the only decent carriage remaining in New York—in order to be able to support him. I can't drive in the Park any more, unless James lends me his ridiculous vehicle, which is so low I can scarcely crawl into it. And what's the pleasure of driving in a closed carriage and so fast that you neither see nor are seen? He has that machine to go to his office in; and the traffic is so dense nowadays that it takes him half an hour, and he reads the morning paper all the way! They are destroying the dignity of life: but never mind. It's your affair; you young people will have to stew in your own broth. I shall be out of it, and for the moment, I am content. I sit here and remember the good old times. There was something glorious in driving out, well dressed, in your open landau, with a smart high-stepping pair, a coachman and groom high on the box, and a little frilled parasol to keep the sun from your nose. But don't think I mope because the past is gone. I shouldn't enjoy it now; not among these new people. That's the advantage of having reached the second period of old age. In the fifties and sixties, you may regret having to give things up; you may make an occasional desperate effort to be still young; but in the seventies and eighties you're only too happy not to have to bother. Nature would be kind enough to us, if we quietly consented to be natural; she would strip us of our desires before she denied us our satisfactions. And there

are always satisfactions left, if you choose the right ones. What a joy
Mario has been to me! The moment I saw him my mind was made
up. What a charming boy: as gentle as my dear, dear Harold, with
some of his little tender ways; yet stronger than his father, more
definite, more beautiful: that terrible pagan Italian stamina mixed in
and stiffening our northern flabbiness. I tremble at it. I adore it.
What a ray of light in this household, where I haven't a man left
except poor James, and not a child except poor Maud. Your Cousin
James is displeased with him for wishing to remain in Europe, and
not finishing his Harvard course. Poor James has the superstition of
college clubs and college classes and college degrees. Did you ever
know anything so silly? What a waste of young ardour to be so
agonised about games and about absurd secret societies like Masonic
lodges! Not that I think your studies, if boys at college ever studied,
would do you much more good. What could Mario turn to here when
he left the University? Painting like his father, or heraldry? But then
like dear Harold he would run away to Paris again, or to Venice, or
to whatever place was the fashion for dilettanti. He might as well stay
there, and do the thing more thoroughly, beginning young, like a
real apprentice. He can always return here when he likes, and with
some prestige to keep him in countenance. The sad thing is, that
now with his mother's death he feels reckless, wants to do something
desperate, join the foreign legion, or plunge into this new fad of
flying, and break his neck at it. I know, in the old days, a brilliant
boy like that would have gone into the army, and there are always
wars somewhere in which to be killed. Mothers had that trial to
endure; and I suppose it's no worse now with motors and aeroplanes
and submarines, and whatever else those scientific busybodies may
find to invent. We blame these dangerous innovations and those fatal
wars, both equally needless, equally murderous. We talk as if without
such scourges we should be safe. But we are never safe. Didn't my
dear Harold perish in the lap of peace, full of the joy of living, in
innocent raptures over everything beautiful and rare? And afterwards James's boy, when he was beginning to give such promise,
snatched from us by an accident. It was that blow that made Edith
turn to religion, because her young brother had been everything to
her. She had been wrapped up in him. But I don't care to deceive
myself. At my age it's not worth while. Those imaginary comforts
only spread the wretchedness out thin, turn you into a poor simpering, self-deceiving hypocrite, and spoil the few honest pleasures you

might still have enjoyed. The great sacrifice is imposed on us in any case. We are all bereft. Even if death seems to spare us, time itself slowly kills everything we love. Our children grow up and escape us; they become not ours. Better be brave, my dear Oliver: better be generous and say to this terrible fate that weaves our lives so sadly together: Do what you will. Take my treasures away singly, or take them all at once. You will have taken my heart with them. This empty hulk is not me, that remains stranded here."

Aunt Caroline had been growing emotional and at the last produced a lace handkerchief and made two little dabs with it at her eyes. "There," she cried, straightening herself up impatiently, "I have been inflicting tragedy upon you, and making a fool of myself. Give me your hands and help to pull me out of this sofa. I must get to bed and sleep off my tantrums. One, two, three. Up you go."

Once on her feet, she took his arm, leaning on it heavily, with a cane in her other hand, and began to hobble towards the door. Though she moved slowly, there was force in her stiff old frame. She pulled Oliver back, she pulled him round, and curbed him to her own heavy paces. Her weight, her imperiousness, the sweep of her silk train dragging behind them, impressed Oliver with a sense of grandeur altogether new to him, yet decidedly congenial. He straightened himself instinctively. He marched willingly at that slow pace. He was proud of the old lady beside him. He was at last where he belonged.

Half way down the music room Aunt Caroline halted, and let go his arm.

"I hear you are a sort of hero, in games of course, but also in other things. I'm not sure I know what a hero is, or that I like heroes. I never heard of a hero in our family. Poor Erasmus, *mio sposo*, wasn't a hero; no more was dear Harold, nor is James, whom you saw downstairs this evening. Your poor dear father too; you know how far from being a hero *he* was. I almost think you had better give up heroism, and be like the rest of us. It must come from your mother's side." She shook her head emphatically as she spoke, leaving it doubtful whether what shook it was a nervous affection or force of conviction or mere waggery. Something monstrous about her made him say:

"Don't you think there is something heroic about Cousin Caleb Wetherbee?"

"Caleb Wetherbee," she retorted sharply, "is deformed. He is not normal in his mind: deformed people never are. You may call it heroism, if you wish to be kind: but it's really desperation. That's what I don't like about heroes. They don't know what to do, so they stand on their heads, and expect to be admired for it. There are always people to applaud mountebanks. Don't be a clown, Oliver, be a gentleman in your thoughts. Don't rant. Don't befuddle yourself by telling enormous lies, and then believing them."

She seized his arm again and crawled a few steps further. Then she stopped once more and said in a lower voice:

"Tell me, did your father kill himself, or was it an accident?"

"I think he was perfectly willing to die. Everything was in order. That night he particularly wished to sleep soundly, and he took the risk of never waking up."

"Just as I imagined. He saw that you could choose your own course sensibly, that you were emancipated from your mother. After that, he felt no more responsibility, no further need of living. And why live when you're not needed, and when it's no pleasure?"

She sighed, thought of the various cares and duties that, as she liked to fancy, still claimed her in this absurd world. She took a short step backward, raised her lorgnette, and affectionately perused Oliver from head to foot. Why shouldn't he be a good match for poor Maud, who wasn't at all pretty?

"Is it true, as they say, that your father left ten million dollars?"

"Oh, no. Not half that: a good deal less than half."

"But even so, you already have two or three millions in your own right?"

"Isn't it dreadful?" Oliver murmured. "It seems so arbitrary that I should have it, and it's so hard to know what I ought to do with it. At present I spend only a small part, and the money simply accumulates and doubles the responsibility." These words, as soon as he had uttered them, sounded wrong in his own ears. Why on earth did he air his scruples like that, and talk like a prig? As if to erase the horrid impression, he added aloud: "How much better Mario would manage, if he were in my place."

"Mario has as much now as is good for him: but later, I don't doubt he would know how to be rich. It's an art or a tradition. Don't think you've done your duty if you distribute your money in pennies, one for every beggar, and leave the world as flat and desolate as if there were no wealth in it at all. The use of riches isn't to disperse riches, but to cultivate the art of living, to produce beautiful houses, beautiful manners, beautiful speech, beautiful charities. You individually can't raise the lowest level of human life, but you may raise the highest level."

Oliver felt he loved his Aunt Caroline. What a splendid old woman, how spirited, how wise! And as they reached the end of the passage, and the door of her room, he kissed her goodnight. He felt remarkably satisfied, and confirmed in his expectations. This was the right family for him. And the right thing for him to do would be to marry Edith. It would be easier then to know how to spend his income. She would regulate all his social duties, and he would be free in his mind to think, to study, to take the right side intelligently in all higher matters. How ideal that life of theirs would be! Seldom, if ever, had the future seemed to him so rosy. It is true that those cutlets on a tray had been only a part of a nice little dinner, eaten with relish after a whole day's fast driving in the cold wind. He had even made an exception, not to seem fussy, and had drunk a part of the half bottle of champagne. But there were older and deeper sources for this new glow of happiness. Here were people—and wise, shrewd, unprejudiced people—who loved Mario and believed in him; who agreed with Oliver also about his father; who, if they had known the circumstances, would have agreed with him about Jim Darnley too, and about the Vicar; agreed even about Rose, because that was only a children's fairy tale, and not a serious engagement. In a word, he felt now how rightly he had felt always, and how rightly he had acted. Could there be a better omen for the future than that the past should be thoroughly sound, no wrong steps taken, no occasion missed? Aunt Caroline had been a benevolent sibyl—she looked like the sibyls of Michael Angelo—giving him a favourable oracle, and he issued from her grotto full of valour and high hopes.

X

When he reached the theatre the performance had long begun, and in the semi-darkness of the box he stood a moment embarrassed, not quite recognising anybody and wondering what he was expected to do. But from one of those shadowy figures, the nearest and the most vaporous, a long white arm at once extended towards him, and a pleasant ungloved hand pulled him down into a vacant chair.

"We mustn't talk," said Edith's voice in a whisper. "This is almost like church. We knew you had arrived safely. Papa telephoned. This is my aunt Miss Stuyvesant, and Maud."

Beginning to see better in the twilight, and reassured, Oliver shook hands discreetly with the two other ladies.

"Too bad you have missed the Rhinemaidens," Miss Stuyvesant murmured. She looked rather like a female parson, dressed in black up to her chin, with a faded complexion and a bitter sweet smile. But when you looked closer you noticed that her partly grey hair was very elaborately dressed, that her black cuirass was of the most delicate lace, with a low gown under it, and that round her neck was a curious necklace of semi-precious stones—in fact a rosary—with a small enamelled crucifix pinned gracefully over her heart. This lady helped to explain Edith's form of piety: but how was she herself to be explained? Oliver rather expected religious dames to disapprove of the theatre, as well as of amulets, totems, and idolatry in general: but here was a form of ostentatious devotion that carried the cross to the first tier of the Opera.

"Never mind the Rhinemaidens," a third very different laughing voice rippled out mockingly. "They'll flop about again next week in the *Götterdämmerung*. And perhaps Rhinemaidens are an old story to you. Didn't you have one for a governess?"

"How did you know that?"

"A little bird. *Hei! Siegfried!*"

"Hush," said Edith, "we mustn't talk. They are looking round at us in the next box."

This Maud seemed rather bird-like herself, pert and restless. She had a receding chin and lively popping great eyes, with a lot of frizzled hair such as Mario called *la beauté des laides*. Not at all like Rose Darnley's really beautiful hair, spread in broad masses, and not crimped artificially. Oliver was afraid he wouldn't like Maud.

All this, however, floated in the margin of the picture. The focus was Edith. Her voice, her manner, the dominating sense of her presence and influence were what they had always been. She put you at your ease. Her good sense, her tact, her sympathy produced a feeling of safety, that euphoria which to Oliver was happiness. Yet you felt you were moving on a lighter plane than your own, more refined, more resolutely excluding everything inferior, and yet more comprehensive in outlook, surer in the knowledge of the world. Unlike the ladies of Great Falls, she was perfectly unaffected—at least she affected nothing but being perfectly natural. She had no "company manners." Now that he knew his aunt Caroline he could see this matter in a new light. The naturalness, the pluck, the frankness were genuine in the grandmother; and the granddaughter was well-bred enough to have learned to be, or at least to seem, equally spontaneous. Yet there was a difference. Aunt Caroline would have sworn at you, if she had felt like swearing, without considering whether it was Christian or lady-like; but Edith, feeling instantly that it was neither, would have restrained herself. This after all was the higher form of virtue, even if less amusing. Yet that evening, with her personality unchanged, Edith's aspect was entirely novel. He had never seen her before except in street clothes. Now she seemed a vision of loveliness unadorned. Without being in the least immodest she looked like Venus just risen from the foam of the sea. A cloak all swansdown or white fur or white feathers was thrown back over the arms of her chair. In this nest, gracefully poised, she sat for the most part motionless, every line of her figure as clear-cut as in a statue, and tinted only with the slightest flush of life. Her heavy brown hair, *à la Cléo de Mérode*, was looped in classic waves round her delicate head, her neck, long and slender, descended towards a bosom surprisingly visible, yet in its purity evidently beyond reproach. She wore a few large jewels in the form of clasps or bands or brooches holding together her flimsy garment, and she carried a mother of pearl opera-glass on a long stem, as if she were carrying a lily. Sometimes, too, she opened a large white feather fan, not to fan herself— that was not done any longer—but to screen her eyes and cut off the crowded house, so that she might lose herself more completely in the music and poetry of the drama. Her complexion, her form, her movements seemed altogether transfigured into something dream-like and higher than human.

There were no *entr'actes* in the *Rheingold* and it was not until the end of the performance that the lights were turned on and people could move and see each other and really say how-do-you-do. Miss Stuyvesant now looked older, and decidedly wrinkled; Maud looked rather nicer, really lively and youthful, with a clear natural complexion, beautiful teeth, and a frank smile; and as to Edith, she lost nothing in the bright light; on the contrary, as Oliver helped her with her cloak, proximity only confirmed the reality of her charms and made them almost embarrassing. But why shouldn't a woman be wonderful and adorable? Wasn't that her function? Better take the bull by the horns.

"I had no idea," he said calmly, "that you were so beautiful."

She glanced at him a moment to make sure in what spirit he spoke. No: he was not impertinent, not jocular, not flirtatious. He had made a simple observation of fact. Oliver's admiration might be profound, but it was philosophical. There was nothing aggressive about it. She smiled affably, tossed her head slightly, and preceded him into the lobby.

These first impressions seemed to him easily absorbed and mastered. He was adapting himself quickly to the circumstances of Edith's life. Operas, evening gowns, and ritualistic aunts could be accepted as matters of course. He rather liked them. They came in nicely as a sort of perpetual mild joke to fill in the blank spaces of life. Edith in turn would soon begin to adapt herself to his mind, to his intentions, until the understanding between them was perfect. He would take her for a long drive the next afternoon, and they would have a heart to heart talk.

In the morning when he came down as if to a family breakfast, he found that this ghastly institution didn't exist in that household; but since he was up and dressed the admirable parlourmaid suggested having something in the coffee-room which was also a sort of little conservatory; and there, perfectly happy, he absorbed his scrambled eggs and the morning paper under the glorious rays of the sun. Should he improve this lovely day to take a stroll, perhaps toward the Battery, and enquire at the Marine Agency whether Jim Darnley was in New York? Not a bad idea: and he was picking up his hat and gloves in the hall and disdaining an overcoat, when tripping down the stair like a small avalanche, came Maud, wreathed in her morning smile.

"What? You too, up so early? You see, I can't get over that horrid feeling that it's time for school. Can you? Besides, I'm terribly busy. I have to keep house and do the shopping for the whole family. Grandma doesn't stir, and Edith is busy about higher things; and we should all starve and go in rags if it wasn't for poor me.—But you weren't going out alone in New York, were you? You'll get lost."

"I'd rather go with you, if you'll let me. Or wait a moment. I'll go and get my car and take you wherever you were going. It will save lots of time." He was glad of this chance to offer to drive with Maud. He couldn't ask her to come later with Edith, it would have spoiled the party; and besides the back seat was hardly suitable for a girl, a mere hole to step into and catch the dust.

"What! Go shopping with a beau? You would be dreadfully in the way. So would the auto. They won't let autos stand in front of shop doors, and think how agitated I should be, conscious of you parked round the corner, waiting, waiting, waiting. However, we'll do something else. If you want a long walk, I'll go to the farthest shop first, it's in 59th Street, and you can leave me there and take a turn in the Park, or run into the Metropolitan Museum and complete your education."

When they were in Fifth Avenue, with the wintry sun pleasantly warming their backs, she began afresh as if innocently thinking aloud and finding everything irresistibly amusing.

"What could Grandma have had to talk to you about yesterday for hours, making you miss those Rhinemaidens that dear Aunt Miriam thinks you would have liked so much? The ravisher, of course. He has become the great problem of life for all of us. Hasn't he for you? And Grandma wanted to worm the truth out of you, in case he hadn't told her the whole story. You wouldn't betray a friend, would you? But don't look frightened. You can't have betrayed him; he had already confessed everything. We try to keep it from Edith, to spare her feelings. She thinks it was only on his mother's account that he left college. Why doesn't he come back, then, now that his mother is dead? It's a mystery; but of course Edith knows that if we look deep enough everything is a mystery. We must have faith. And she feels that it might be better for his real welfare, if he studied now for a while in Oxford, under that admirable old tutor of his, who writes

Latin hymns. At Harvard they are so irreligious. But I know the real reason. I heard him tell Grandma, that morning when he was sailing, and he came at half past seven to say good-bye. Wasn't it touching? Don't think I listened at the door. I'm not a bit curious. But my room happens to be directly over Grandma's, and there's a flue or something that connects through the chimney; and as she's a little deaf and you have to speak clearly, I hear every word spoken, even if it doesn't interest me at all. But that morning it was as good as a play. In comes Bridget to draw the curtains and bring a cup of hot milk. 'Woman,' cries Grandma, 'look at that clock. How dare you wake me up half an hour early, and spoil my beauty-sleep?'

"'I hope you'll excuse me, Ma'am, but Mr. Mario is downstairs. He says he's sailing this morning for Europe, and has something important to say to you.' 'Bring me my washing things,' says Grandma sharply; for she washes her face and hands cat-fashion every morning in bed, and puts on a fresh cap, and a decent peignoir; and then with the fire blazing and the sun pouring in, she holds her morning reception and reads her letters. And she wouldn't let Mario in until all the ceremonies were performed, and she had made herself look as nice as possible. She's always been a terrible coquette, Grandma, and the Ravisher isn't a stray grandson for her at all, a crowing baby, but just one last lovely young man. And he plays up wonderfully—I must admit it—and flirts with her as he does with every woman, young or old, except me, because I don't let him. Well, in comes Mario.

"'What's the matter?'

"'My mother. . . . Read this', and I couldn't hear the rest very well, his voice wasn't clear, and I'm sure they were kissing and hugging. Very improper, wasn't it; but they have such warm hearts. And when they had relieved their feelings on that sad subject, he began with the other story—half made up, I daresay—about not being able to return to college. Honest, though, to go into that, when he might have concealed it. I must say this for the Ravisher, he doesn't sail under false colours. And he wouldn't tell the girl's name, or anything about her, except that the whole thing had been an accident. Well by that time he had to be off, or he might miss his steamer. I happened to be in the hall when he came through. He left two letters, one for Pa and one for Edith—none for me, of course—yet I behaved like an angel, said I was so sorry about his mother, hoped he might find her recovering and would come back to us soon. And I didn't detain him at all—I hate to be a nuisance—but waved at his cab from the door like a darling sister. Don't you think I have an amiable unselfish character? It's so much easier for me really to be kind than to be spiteful. You should have seen us that evening at dinner. Pa and Edith had been all day digesting their two letters, and were herocially calm. Not at all what we expected of Mario, Pa remarked funereally. Sad disappointment. Uncle Harold's marriage had not been well-advised. You could never know what would happen, if you introduced foreigners into the family. Wild oats were all very well, but a young man shouldn't do anything to compromise his career or create a scandal. However, for his part, Pa would continue to do what he could for his nephew and to hope for the best.

"'But how is it the poor boy's fault if his mother is dying?' Edith protested, quite flushed. I think she had been crying. 'Would you have him indifferent? Would you have him let his wonderful mother die alone, three thousand miles from her only child? Suppose he misses a year at Harvard, or goes instead to Oxford. What does that matter? It may all be for his good. Think how young he is, only twenty, and how all this may strengthen him and sober him.'

"Pa hemmed and hawed, and Grandma had a little more claret than usual; and I didn't say a word. Wasn't it heroic of us? Just to keep dear Edith unspotted from the world."

This was too much for Oliver. He fell back a little, almost halted, and compelled his voluble cousin to look at him. "What do you mean? Doesn't Edith know that Mario is always having little affairs? Of course she knows it. And why make a mystery of this incident, which was hardly his doing, when it explains why he must leave Harvard for good?"

"Edith knows that perhaps, before he knew *her*, when he was living with his theatrical mother in those Mediterranean countries where the Church is so paganised, and when he was too young to resist temptation, he may have been led astray by shameless designing women. But now all that is past. He has lived under her influence. She has become his *Beatri-ce*: we all pronounce it like that, now, in Italian. She is leading him into higher spheres; it would be too dreadful to suggest that, when she is out of sight, he might still be at his old tricks. Such a thought she banishes as unworthy. It would betray so little faith in him and in herself. None of your little bedroom episodes, please, on the way up the *Paradiso*. Perhaps as yet he's only in the *Purgatorio*; but even there, what a relapse! I'm afraid she might have a horrible temptation to despair; to believe we are already in that other place where people *senza speme vivono in desio.*—Dear me, what a lot of Italian we do talk nowadays!"

"Yes. Your grandmother too sprinkles Italian on everything."

"She has brushed up all that young ladies learned in her day with their music, when they warbled operatic arias. It's pathetic. We've all had a new birth, especially Edith, and I've discovered no end of things myself, simply looking on, as it were, from the wings; because I don't count at all in this show. I'm just a super."

"Edith wouldn't think of marrying him, would she? For his part, I'm afraid—"

"She has too much sense. She likes to believe that she's making a great sacrifice; but as you were going to say, the grapes are green. She keeps her head perfectly. One's appointed work in the world after all is so rewarding. And there's one's health and strength to preserve, so that one may give one's best. Edith finds Delsarte exercises most helpful. She lies flat on the floor for twenty minutes, and she can do with half an hour's less sleep, without feeling or looking tired. There's ten minutes a day gained for her social work. Turkish baths and face-massage are also a help: so much better than taking aspirins when you're nervous, or other more dangerous drugs. Then you must think of your clothes, because it gives other people so much pleasure to see you well dressed, especially if you are beautiful to begin with. Edith feels that being beautiful is such an added responsibility. A plain girl like me needn't take so much trouble. She hasn't much to spoil or much to display. But if you're beautiful like Edith, you're bound not to hide your light under a bushel."

"She doesn't hide it, does she?" he said laughing. "At least, not in the evening."

"What? Has the good boy from the country observed that? I hope we don't shock you. Edith feels that it's necessary to be in the van, even in things that might seem of no consequence, like fashion and elegance. It adds to the prestige of a good Churchwoman if she is also a leader in society: otherwise people might think her piety was simply a consolation. But if she shines in the world, her unworldliness is above suspicion. Besides, personal prestige adds so much to one's influence; and the influence one has in higher circles spreads so much farther. Your work among the poor or the dying ends with each particular wound you bind up; but your work among the rich and young and influential is multiplied through them, and in the end reaches the poor in many more places. If Edith could only attract *you*, for instance, into the Church, how much more good that would do in the whole world than if she converted some poor drivelling old woman!"

"She wants to convert me, does she? Is she so scheming and jesuitical?"

"She says you have a noble character and great opportunities. But she works among the poor also. There's the Sisterhood of Saint Elizabeth, for visiting hospitals and prisons, and there's the new mission church at Staten Island, and the young clergyman there, who is so spiritual and may become a light in the Church. And yet, no. It's no use pretending. We may drown our sorrows, but there can be no real happiness in this world."

"And you, Maud, are you sure there is? What would it be like? Where do you expect to find it?"

"I? Why trouble about me? I don't count—But here's my shop. Good-bye, till lunch. Don't forget. At half past one."

XI

The motor that afternoon had scarcely swept out of Gramercy Park, and joined the procession of vehicles in Broadway, when Edith began what was evidently to be a long and confidential conversation. Her manner said: "I couldn't speak frankly before Maud: we must make the best of this occasion. I know I can count on your sympathy and understanding." She felt how gracious it was on her part to show such confidence in her young cousin, and to acknowledge a sort of parity between him and her, which of course there couldn't be: but she wished to be gracious, and tactful, and encouraging. Oliver would be a valuable ally. Whenever there was a crowded crossing or a van to pass, or any circumstance that required Oliver's whole attention, she would stop talking, would watch the manœuvre intelligently, without impatience or nervousness, and then, when the way was clear again, she would resume her talk, not as if she had been rudely interrupted, but as if the little interlude had been interesting and refreshing and she could continue now with a new impetus. Much as she indulged her imagination, she was sane enough to admit the continual intrusion of the real world into her daydreams, and even to relish it. Whenever Oliver said anything in reply, Edith not only listened and agreed, but at once developed the suggestion, showed how entirely she perceived the justice of it, and how it was really a part of what she had been meaning to say. Nor was her friendliness merely intellectual. If a corner rapidly turned or a sharp curve took her by surprise and threw her for a moment against him, sitting in his place as firm as a rock, she didn't seem to resent the accident. She didn't excuse herself or recover her equilibrium too hurriedly, as if frightened. On the contrary, she smiled frankly at her inexperience, and admired the skill and strength of her young companion. In those early days of motoring it seemed marvellous to go so easily, and intoxicating to go so fast. She was putting her life in this boy's hands: reasonably, no doubt, because he was competent and careful: yet this deliberate trust, overlying the sense of danger, produced a happy excitement very near to self-surrender. She remembered reading in the newspapers of countesses eloping with their chauffeurs. She understood that impulse. Oliver with his hand on the wheel and his eye on the road ahead possessed a physical pre-potency which he lacked altogether in his social capacity, as a country cousin. Ordinarily he might seem colourless and negative, at least in comparison with Mario or with her old admirer, Mr. Flusher Borland, who always beamed as if he had just had a cocktail and was about to make love. Here, in the open air, and in command, Oliver's very simpleness and reticence became impressive; beneath the quiet good boy there was evidently the potentially rough, masterful male. In his own mind at that very moment, though Edith had no means of perceiving it, he was half-consciously impersonating Jim Darnley, steering the launch out of Salem harbour on a rough night: and he was also impersonating himself in his capacity of football player, choosing the signal, and rushing the ball. The athlete and the me-chanic think democratically, and their tone is necessarily that of the common man; yet in that crude trial of power there is occasion for distinction and even for hero-worship. Oliver prized the physical man within himself precisely because in spiritual matters he felt so inse-cure, so desolate, so much alone. Mightn't he be safer, if not happier, if he could escape his privileges and be one of the common crowd? And his pride told him that he could hold his own there perfectly, and be easily first in the physical arts, where eminence is not mea-sured by fantastic opinion. To this artisan pride within him that human orchid, that social paragon, as he thought her, now sitting by his side, was nothing but a passenger, a female like any other to be looked after and kept in order; precious, no doubt, but precious as cargo. His own powers, his own intelligence, his own satisfactions then seemed to stretch into great distances, into the heart of nature, far beyond her social intuitions. He would always return to her willingly enough, with deference, with a sort of worship; yet in all his devotion there would be a mental reservation, and he would remain inwardly independent, essentially superior.

"What a contrast," she began, "this automobile is to that poor puffing shaking little thing of ours, that Mario had last year. It was so generous of you to get this one for him, when you cared to have none for yourself.—Yes, it is true that one likes to see him surrounded by beautiful things. He seems in his element among them. He isn't weighed down or corrupted by luxury, as some of our rich friends are, but dances away with it as merrily as possible.—Oh, exactly: he can give up luxury without being troubled or lowered at all in his own key.—As you say, it's his southern blood: but perhaps there's something less material about it, a disposition to see things in a spiritual light, something that may develop in him later. Now, he is so young! He would frighten me sometimes, driving, he seemed so reckless.—I know, he has a sure eye, and his hand is very quick. We shouldn't have expected him to have so much mechanical skill, with his father and mother both artists.—Really, I never thought of that. If one were an artist in everything, the professional arts *might* seem unnecessary or even clownish.—Oh! In heaven there are no Sundays? Did Mario say that? I am afraid he may have meant it frivolously. Yet I suppose it *is* nobler and more aristocratic not to be a mere artist. Tell me honestly what you think. You know Mario so well. Would it really be best for him not to live in this country? He's inclined to think so now, though at first he seemed to be delighted with everything, and to become absolutely one of us.—Oh, you think older men don't trust him, dislike his independence, wouldn't advance him in business? Certainly my father is disappointed, complains that Mario refuses to do what is expected of him, and wastes his time. But you don't think so? It would be so terrible if he were lost to us. I couldn't bear it. I don't mean merely that he should live abroad; that would be sad for us; he was such a ray of light; but after all, if it were for his good, we might make the sacrifice; and no doubt he would often visit us, and we him. But if he were wasted altogether, if he lost his youth, his fineness, without achieving anything, without becoming nobler and stronger—what a tragedy that would be! You have no idea how much he means to us, how much he means to me. I had been dearly attached to my brother Reggy, two or three years younger than me, whom we lost when he was eighteen. That was a terrible blow to me: it changed my whole life: made me see the reality of things, and our need of God; and when Mario came I felt he was a sort of messenger from Reggy—very different in every way except in being of the same age; and you know how devoted we became to each other. And now comes this sudden separation before we could see clearly what the future might offer him, and this sudden decision on his part, just when his mother is gone and he might belong to us altogether, to stay abroad, and make his own way among strangers. It seems to be only you that hold him, the one link left, because as to leaving me, or needing me, he hasn't the least qualm, not the least consciousness of loss or of wrong-doing."

They were in the ferry-boat crossing to Staten Island, in a silence broken only by the thumping of the engine. Oliver was relieved of his occupation as driver, and could talk more consecutively.

"Hasn't Mario written you of our plan for next year? He's coming with me round the world. We shall be at sea most of the time, because I want to go round South America, to get a glimpse of all sorts of countries, while I read up about them at intervals. He will have time to settle his own mind, and make plans for the future. If he goes to Oxford, it won't be until afterwards, and it wouldn't be too late. Now I have something to propose to you. Don't be surprised, and don't answer at once. Do you like the sea?"

"I like it well enough. Why ask?"

"You're not likely to be seasick?"

"Not particularly."

"Then I propose that you come with us."

"How do you mean? With Aunt Miriam perhaps, or with Maud?"

"Not at all. If they were on board, you would always be pairing off with Mario, and Maud or your Aunt Miriam would be left to me. You are to come alone."

"How extraordinary. What would my father say? Is it expected that an unmarried girl should go with two young men round the world?"

"But you needn't be unmarried. You could marry one of us."

"I like that. Marry one of you, no matter which? Are you proposing? And are you commissioned to propose for Mario at the same time? Couldn't he speak for himself?"

"He knows it would be a waste of time. I'm not commissioned. It's not necessary. Of course you could marry him—you could marry anybody—if you really wished it. But you're not such a fool. You know if you married Mario you would be terribly unhappy."

Edith drew herself up. She felt that her defences were being penetrated, that a bomb had fallen in her very citadel. She was not alarmed, because she felt impregnable, but she was irritated and took up the strain of tragedy.

"What have I done that my inmost feelings seem to be public property? You all talk about them among yourselves, and only to misrepresent them. There are so many things called love, and only one word for them all. Mustn't love, when it is real, be always different from what it ever was before? It may be true, in one sense, that I love Mario, yes, that we love each other: but it never crossed my mind to marry him. He is a child, a very much younger brother, a sort of spiritual son. What ignominy to make him marry me, to deprive him of his freedom before he is old enough to use it; to reduce him, as Grandmamma says, to a lady's poodle, performing politely before my friends like his Scotch terrier when he says, *Fais le beau!* Everybody would smile, thinking of the difference in our ages—six years the wrong way—and expect him to be unfaithful, to neglect me if he couldn't abandon me, or to loathe me if he couldn't neglect me. But that wouldn't be the worst of it. The worst would be that I should see him deteriorate from day to day at my side, the Society husband of a fading elderly wife, his ardour gone, his spontaneity stifled, still handsome, perhaps, but lifeless, still young but without a future, growing fat and dull, driven to eating and drinking too much in order to drown his discomfiture. Oh no, I will never marry him. Whatever affection and concern I may have for him will prevent me.—As for you, I never thought of you at all one way or the other, except as a friend of his."

The falseness of this last assertion was patent to Oliver, as well as the motive behind it. It was perhaps the only kind of lie that he imposed on his own conscience: to assert he was indifferent when only his senses were stirred. His senses, he pretended, were not himself. And in a lady, this hypocrisy was even more requisite. There were matters in which a woman—like a puritan—could not be honest. She must be stealthy, she must protect her modesty and feminine reserve, she must not reveal the ambush from which she may be found operating in the future. The more scornfully Edith might protest that she never thought of Oliver except as a friend of Mario's, the greater Oliver's ascendency over her was proved to be: so great that she was afraid of it and needed to disown it. The snub, therefore, wasn't a snub but an encouragement.

Pocketing this assurance and conscious of his real strength, he ignored that question for the moment. "I don't think the difference in age," he said, "would create difficulties. Think how Mario loved his mother; and he would look up to you and love you at sixty just as much or more than at twenty-five. But his love for you wouldn't prevent him from caring for other women in another way. He puts you on a pedestal apart from all others; but the others exist for him; a lot of them have excited and amused him at intervals, and a lot of them always will. I suppose it is his Southern temperament. He feels no inner reason why he should control himself, why he should suffer unnecessarily, or why they should suffer: because they care for him much more than he cares for them. You would have to put up with that; and I suppose, even if you wished to, your religious principles would prevent. And religion would be another sore point, because you could never convert him, unless perhaps you were first converted yourself and became a regular Roman Catholic. You may say there's very little difference, but for him the difference is total and complete. Your sort he says isn't religion at all, but a worldly precaution against religion, a homœopathic dose to keep religion from ever getting dangerous. So that you would never have his respect intellectually; and he would laugh at you when you felt you were most serious.

"With me, everything is the other way. The person I respect most, intellectually and morally, is the Vicar of Iffley, and he is an Anglican. And there's not the least danger for him of ever going over to Rome; because he too, though not at all for Mario's reasons, thinks the difference is radical. Originally, he says, Christianity was partly poetry and partly delusion. The Roman Church clings to both parts equally; Protestantism has kept the delusion and destroyed the poetry; and only the Anglican traditon is capable of preserving the poetry, while sweeping the delusion away. Now, the poetry of Christianity doesn't mean much to me as yet, because I wasn't brought up in it; but I admire and envy you and Mr. Darnley and all pious people for being able to feel it, provided it doesn't lead you to turn the truth upside down, as people do who think they are inspired, and mistake their poetry for literal fact. As to carrying on with other women, because my wife was three or four years older than I, that, to me, is a repulsive idea, and absurd. How should such a thing be possible, or at all tempting, where there is affection and confidence and true love? I can't understand such an impulse, except in people like Mario, to whom love means sensuality. It doesn't mean that to me. Besides, you will never be old, you will never change, and I have never been young and shan't change much either. I won't say I'm good enough for you, but I'm quite old enough; and at any rate I have never given my body or my soul to any other woman, and never would."

They had reached the church door, and she laid her hand lightly on his arm as if to say, "Let us drop this subject for the moment: I have so many things, such deep and tender things, to say to you about it." The youngest slip of a girl couldn't have jumped from the car with more agility or more grace than she displayed on this occasion; and with a latch-key of her own, inserted in the little round

Yale lock, she opened the door and led the way briskly into the church. Disdaining the stiff little pews she sank on her knees before the communion rail and buried her face in her voluminous muff. She approved of vocal prayer; and while her lips murmured a certain number of *Our Fathers* and *Doxologies*—the *Hail Mary* not being yet quite accepted in her circle—she was able to sift her impressions and let the line she would follow become clear in her mind.

Meantime, cap in hand, bulking large in his great leather motoring-coat, lined with fur, Oliver stood, strangely calm, surveying the place. He had just been making a proposal of marriage which he fully expected to see accepted in the end. If he was ready to risk it, and marry Edith, why on earth shouldn't Edith be willing to marry him? His whole future was thus being decided: yet he was never cooler. Is this, he was thinking, part of the poetry of Christianity? And as his eye took in the details he couldn't help smiling. How Mario, how Jim would have hated the place! It was an example of the cheap brick Gothic inspired by Ruskin; the walls were a terra-cotta red, the brown beams brightly varnished, the ceiling blue with tinsel stars. The yellow wooden altar showed the words, Holy, Holy, Holy, carved in Gothic letters; a bright brass cross and little pair of candlesticks stood upon it while, above, a crimson curtain, awaiting the stained glass to come, failed to produce a dim religious light; for through the other windows, too large for that brilliant latitude, the last rays of the sun were mercilessly flooding the place. A barn would have been less ugly. Evidently this was no place of worship raised by the poor to God, but one officially supplied by the rich for the poor who didn't want it. Everything was painfully machine-made and garish, except some dry chrysanthemums drooping on the altar. These Edith, having finished her devotions, snatched away quickly, and substituted some nice holly which she had brought for the purpose. Her business with the caretaker was soon despatched: indeed Oliver wondered what need there had been for this expedition, apparently so urgent. However, they were now side by side again in the car, with the hood raised for protection against the evening air, and with the headlights on. It was a cosy nook; and Edith could speak almost with as much trustfulness and depth of feeling as in a real confessional.

"Oliver," she began, "what you were saying just now affected me very much. I have been praying for you. Your way of feeling about love and marriage is so much finer than that of most young men, so much holier. I understand now why Mario is so devoted to you, and looks up to you so enthusiastically; because he does; he positively worships you. I shall always feel very much nearer to you after to-day. But let's not talk of marrying: it would be so precipitate, so ill-advised. That you should have thought of such a thing at all rather surprises me, when really we hardly know each other, and our interests in many ways are so different. And you are much too young: I won't say too young for me, if you are gallant enough to overlook that objection; but you are too young absolutely, you don't as yet need to marry. Your feelings seem to be in one way very deep and well-reasoned: but have you ever been *in love?* We don't, we can't as yet care enough for each other. And love is something so terrible. It promises such marvellous happiness, and it may bring such horrible sorrow."

"I daresay I'm not *in love*," he said rather scornfully, "if that means turning a kind of lunatic for the time being. But as to caring, as to feeling that you belong to me, as it were, by nature, and that I belong to you, I had that feeling in a sort of dream on the very first day I saw you, at the Stillman Infirmary. You have no idea how much it meant to me to see you at that moment; and when you came again and again, the thought was confirmed that you were to be my guide and defence, making clear for me all those social matters that I am stupid about, and helping me to do my duty in the world. It was not an illusion, it was a perception from the first that you were the most perfect woman I had ever seen, and the most perfect lady. Yes: and it wasn't absurdly conceited or arrogant in me to imagine that you would find your best life, too, in living with me, and devoting yourself to me. I am perfectly sure you would. And don't say that marriage is a very close relation, and that you don't like me well enough. You *do* like me well enough."

He had put his arm round her and drawn her up close, with a gentle but quite irresistible strength, and now he proceeded to kiss her. It wasn't easy, or very satisfying, as little but her nose peeped out between her hat and her fur boa; but he managed it after a fashion. The action, however, was far from advancing his wooing. Not that Edith resented the liberty or attempted to deny the allegation that she liked him well enough. He tempted her, he almost overcame her in his crude capacity of awkward lover, of casual male, almost dumbly begging and asserting his primeval privilege. Oliver's extreme youth, combined with strength and nobleness, ceased to be a disadvantage. A sort of dream-impulse ran through her mind to play Venus to this puritan Adonis. But the temptation was momentary. Her critical faculty, her social standards, at once reasserted themselves. Even in what a moment before she had called praying for him, she had felt his inferiority. He didn't know how to make love. He was thinking only of himself, planning a future, and asking her to marry him without so much as pretending to love her as a bride demands and deserves to be loved. His clumsy advances were not courtship: they were almost insults.

The need of driving the motor quickly and carefully out of the ferry boat, where it had been standing still, cut short Oliver's attentions, and allowed her time to think. She decided to be crushing.

"Really," she said, "you behave very strangely, and you seem to plan marrying just as you plan going round the world. It is an idea that pleases you. I happen to be one of the people at hand; and you want to go ahead without at all considering my feelings or Mario's or even your own. It's childish."

"I see," he replied slowly, measuring his words as if he were dealing them out over a counter, or writing them down in a college essay. "You think I'm a booby, a fool, an infant in goggles, solemnly proposing to marry you in order to let you fall more conveniently into the arms of your real lover, who happens to be my best friend. We should be playing a disgusting farce—the *Sorrows of Werther* with the sorrow left out. I daresay it was childish of me, but I didn't see the thing in that light. I was taking for granted that you had given Mario up. If you've really given him up, if you make no claims, if you expect nothing from him but care only for his own good, then it doesn't matter how much you love him or how much you are together; because then your love would be unselfish, and he wouldn't be an obstacle between us but a bond."

Edith hadn't expected such a home thrust. She felt she had really got into the confessional, and found a spiritual director rather more austere and mystical than she liked. This country lad evidently had plenty of experience, if not of love, at least of something very like love and perhaps better. She was afraid of him; and his severity and bitterness inspired respect. Respect and fear might turn to love. She also by chance thought of his money. He wouldn't be a contemptible husband. In fact, he was a great catch. And yet, no, it mustn't be thought of. There would be no real sympathy. She would be continually mortified, continually humbled. The whole card-castle of her life, beginning with her religion, would fall to the ground. That Vicar of

Iffley must be a very dangerous theologian. She must prove that true faith and Christian humility were on her side.

"My dear Oliver," she said in a tone of perfect serenity and impartial perception of the truth, "you are a rare being. You see into one's heart, and you have a spiritual discernment which is wonderful at your age. It has really been a terrible sacrifice for me to give Mario up—I don't mean not marrying him, for as I told you I never thought of that—but to give up seeing him, guiding his interests in the right direction; terrible to let him drift away again into an aimless foreign life full of temptations and evil influences. Still, he must be his own master, and we must pray that all may come round for the best in the end. Now suppose that I cared for you, too, a little: not so much as for Mario, of course, because I don't know you so well and we haven't so much in common; but suppose I liked you and admired you very much, as I really do. Don't you see that it would be my duty to give you up, just as I have given up Mario? Much more plainly my duty; because all the same objections hold, that you are too young and haven't seen enough of the world and need to develop very much more before you can choose a wife wisely: and then you don't need me, as Mario does, you are quite strong enough and sober enough and constant enough in yourself. Yes, perhaps I should be only interfering with your true vocation."

"Very well. I quite understand. I hardly expected you to say yes at once." He didn't speak again until they reached Gramercy Park, when with his hand on the door, before letting her out of the cage, he added firmly: "Remember that I have had a premonition, a sort of vision of what has to happen. I shan't change. When you know me better and have got used to the idea, perhaps you will decide to prove me a true prophet."

She disliked this hint of physical force, backed by some divine fatality. For a moment she wondered if it was possible that she should be snared, drawn by some uncanny power into quicksands from which she couldn't escape. But an hour later, when she came down to dinner, and saw the good Oliver standing there in his evening clothes, sleek and mild and freshly washed, the dangerous chauffeur, the rough swain, had entirely vanished. He no longer seemed a bit common but altogether commonplace, an insipid youth like every other insipid youth, the son of his mother, the nephew of his uncle the professor of applied Christianity, and of his other uncle the editor of the *New England Roadster* and of the *Boston Butterfly and Busy Bee*, those vulgar weeklies read by farmers' wives and commercial travellers. She blushed at her weakness of that afternoon, and she inwardly took back and covered up the concessions she had made. They must be regarded as not having occurred, or must be set down to mere banter and cousinly kindness. As a lover the boy was ridiculous, at once oldish and green. As a husband the man would be insupportable, a biting critic, a frigid tyrant, methodically making love.

XII

Oliver had no inkling of the sentence that had been passed against him. He was not impatient. He would wait placidly until the summer for a final answer; and he could see no reason why it should not be favourable. Wasn't Edith as approachable as ever? Wasn't the physical affinity between them undeniable and undisguised? Didn't he on several occasions snatch a kiss; and though she said Don't, and went on talking about other things, wasn't it certain that she was not displeased? And whenever the family were together, wasn't it to him that she looked for understanding, next to him that she sat, and with him that she would instinctively take sides, and afterwards, if they could be alone, carry on a prolonged discussion? Where there is intellectual sympathy, and also physical attraction, what more, he asked himself, could anyone want? He wanted nothing more. His own mind was perfectly simple and free, innocent of all worldly or religious entanglements; and self-consciousness in him, as in so many philosophers, intercepted intuition. Had he not been preoccupied with himself, with his own future and his own feelings, he would have detected at once the secret of Edith's friendliness, that it was half fleshly weakness, half social affectation; and that her whole deliberate ambition wedded her to something else, remote from him altogether. If he detected in her some artificial poses, he thought them harmless and rather becoming. They were the right antidote to his own starkness. Her religion was simply her overloaded way of feeling and talking. He was glad that Edith could indulge in these fancies, just as he was glad she wore such very low gowns and such artistic quasi-mediaeval jewels. They made her delightfully different from his mother and from the good Irma. They pushed him in a direction, away from his puritanism, in which he wished to be carried but hadn't the means of moving by his own initiative. They were the tints and convolutions of this lady-orchid. Something precious seemed essential to a beautiful woman, something slightly mysterious and slightly absurd. He was confirmed by this in his masculine poise, in his sense of holding the reins, and of being right in holding them.

He felt himself already the husband, the master, the affectionate father. It was just a bird of this plumage that he wished to attract and to tame.

He returned to Gramercy Park at Easter full of the same feelings, and meaning to force the issue. The time to start on his *Wanderjahre* was approaching. Edith must decide whether she would accompany him or not.

The Spring was not socially so busy a season as Christmas and the family would more often be found sitting, of a sunny afternoon, in Aunt Caroline's room, to which Oliver too was admitted now as a member of the home circle. Nor was this the only point in which he had learned the ways of the house. When Maud, on the first morning or two, peeped into the coffee room, she found no Oliver there. The maid explained that Mr. Alden now had breakfast in his room, and stayed there writing or reading until late in the morning. Maud accordingly continued to do her shopping alone.

It was Edith only who was still always away. If she turned up at lunch at all, she immediately had to run off again to some other engagement. When Oliver complained of this to his aunt, the old lady shook her head.

"Gadding, gadding, always gadding. Young women nowadays have quicksilver in their veins. They marry too late, and have to invent some sort of bachelor life to fill in the interval. At Edith's age, I had had three children. All these new public interests that girls take up are worse than vices. Their minds are so occupied with business that they can't fall in love; and then, when they tire of charities and politics and church work and going to lectures—and they tire of all that, as they wouldn't of cards—it's too late for a simple flirtation and a good-natured, sensible, commonplace marriage. They think they deserve at least a man of fashion who is also an ambassador and a Sir Galahad; and they end by putting up with some sallow artist or social reformer who most likely isn't a gentleman. Then visiting so many young scoundrels in hospitals and prisons has a disturbing effect on their minds, although they aren't aware of it. It awakens their senses; it excites and coarsens their feelings; it tears away every veil. Mixing that morbid excitement with religion, what a mess that makes of charity! Charity in my day meant putting your name down in public subscriptions, and dropping something into the plate in church; and it meant helping your old servants when in trouble, and finding decent situations for their children. It never meant becoming a trained nurse or a Little Sister of St. Elizabeth. I'm glad, Maud, that you at least haven't joined that pack of crazy females. The work isn't proper for a lady."

Maud looked up from the magazine she pretended to be reading and said with mock gravity:

"You forget that St. Elizabeth was a queen. It can't be wrong to do as she did."

"Why do you call Queen Elizabeth a saint?" Oliver inquired. "Wasn't she rather the opposite?"

A peal of laughter came from Maud, partly natural, partly rippling artificially. "Dear Oliver, you *are* a treasure. Almost as priceless as poor Pa. Not Queen Elizabeth of England, my dear, but Queen Elizabeth of Hungary. We can claim her, because she belongs before that sad schism, when a corrupt Italian Papacy broke away from the Holy See."

"How's that?" snapped Mrs. Van de Weyer. "You're talking nonsense."

"I mean from the Holy See of *Canterbury*."

"Maud! Don't jeer at your poor sister's illusions. After all they comfort her."

Aunt Caroline nevertheless laughed as heartily as her granddaughter; and Oliver thought they were both rather too much given to mockery. In an old woman it might pass for the cynicism of experience, but in a young girl like Maud it was odious. He had intended to ask her to go for a drive, but seeing that the day was particularly mild, he asked Aunt Caroline instead.

"No, no. It's too difficult for me to get in and out. Take Maud."

Maud threw down her magazine impatiently, and went to look at herself in the glass. "Don't compel the poor boy to invite me against his will," she said. "Anyhow, I can't go. I'm engaged." Having finished patting her curls with a satisfied air, Maud came and sat on the edge of her grandmother's sofa, and took the old lady's hand. "Grandma," she said softly, "you know that Senator Lunt of Montana is in New York. May I ask him to dinner this evening? Without him we should be only nine and one man short. Yes, yes, it's a family dinner. That's just why I want to ask him. He could be introduced to all of us at once, and have done with it. Of course he's no relation—not yet." Here Maud laid her cheek against her grandmother's and became a little agitated—"but he will be before long because I'm going to marry him."

Mrs. Van de Weyer looked at her granddaughter severely for a moment and then kissed her.

"Maud, what have you been up to? How long has this been going on? Have you told your father?"

"Not yet. It's only been going on since this morning—that is, officially. Last night he sat next to me at the Reids' and made love furiously all the time, only he was too shy actually to pop the question. But this morning he called me up on the telephone.—This is you? Yes. Good morning, How-do-you-do? You were so beautiful last night, etc. Then suddenly, he stops short.—Are you standing up or sitting down? Because I have a lot of things to say, and I don't want to keep you standing.—No, I'm not standing. And I'm not sitting down. I'm in bed.—He could hear me laugh, and I could almost hear the dear man blush. His first wife never mentioned *beds*. But he recovered quickly. He enjoys being shocked, it's all so new to him and so different. I could hear his voice—you know how slow and rich his voice is, because he's a Southerner really, though now he lives in Montana—saying 'First rate. Stay there and let me talk to you.' I let him talk and said that this was so sudden but if he telephoned again at three o'clock I might have made up my mind, and might tell him whether my grandmother wished him to come and dine with us this evening and be introduced to the whole family."

"Senator Lunt, ma'am," the maid announced, "is at the telephone and asks to speak to Miss Maud."

"There," cried the young lady, skipping away. "And it's only a quarter to three!"

Dinner that evening was put off for half an hour, to give time for the lovers to seal their contract in the morning room, while upstairs the event was discussed by the assembled family. Oliver, silent as usual, stood beside Edith, who herself hardly spoke. He noticed that she was dressed in solemn black, severe but scanty, and calculated to bring out her marble charms by the most tragic contrast. She didn't say that the Western Senator was not good enough for Maud, because that would be exaggerating Maud's merits: and she couldn't say that he was too good for her, because that would have been giving him too much importance.

"They say," Aunt Caroline observed, "that he is going to be President some day. *Meno male.* Think how it would sound: *The President of the United States and Mrs.*—What's the rest of his name?"

"Roscoe C. Lunt," said Uncle James.

"But what does the C. stand for? We can't allow initials."

"You remember, Mother, that Grant was Ulysses S. Grant, and that the S. stood for nothing, except just for itself."

"Grant was a horrible person. Senator Lunt has traditions; and the only Roscoe I ever heard of was Roscoe Conkling. That's it. *The President of the United States and Mrs. Roscoe Conkling Lunt.* I suppose we should get used to it."

"I'm afraid it's not expected that he should ever really be President. Montana is not an important state. He might possibly, some day, be Vice-President. He is the youngest of the Senators and much admired for his eloquence."

"Vice-President would do nicely. The President might be assassinated; and then, probably we should have Maud at the White House for a second term. I'm sure she'd do it much better than most Presidents' wives. She has more initiative, she was born a lady, and she wasn't born a fool. Besides she would be younger."

"And more modern," Uncle James added with an expression of concern. "What if she didn't do what was expected of her?"

There was a little flurry behind the screen at the drawing-room door, and in came the young lady leading her captured statesman by the hand. Oliver had never seen her look so radiant; she was in her best ball gown, all white and silver and rosebuds; and her laughing and mocking manner helped now to carry off an embarrassing moment. Her wits were sailing clear, above all the absurdities and awkwardnesses of her own little drama; and as they shook hands all round, when she came to Oliver, there seemed to be a flash of anger, almost a suggestion of tears in her eyes, in spite of her evident happiness and jubilation: as if she were saying, Please observe that the people who care for me are more important than those who don't.

Edith and Oliver were left that evening rather out in the cold, and as if marooned in their own unreality: while Oliver, who had seldom come across persons of consequence in business or in public life, listened to the Senator's conversation, carried on almost exclusively with Aunt Caroline. He talked of Montana, the climate, the vastness, the possibilities; modestly spoke of his property as "our business," and of himself as "we," including all his subordinates; but it transpired that he had the greatest cattle ranch in the world, that he loved that great enterprise and the country life it involved, and that his political work in Washington and his social relations there were rather a concession he made to duty and to the world, while his heart remained in Montana: and it was to Montana rather than to Washington that he wished to transport Maud, to be the civilised Eve of that rude paradise. It appeared, too, what was the secret source of that eloquence, not bombastic and old-fashioned yet poetical, for which he was noted. It was Homer. He had come when a young man across Bryant's translation of the *Iliad*; and he had been so impressed that he learned Greek in order to read the original: and the *Iliad* was for him, as for Alexander the Great, the one *vade mecum*. "I think," he said, "we can afford to skip everything since Homer: the interlude was all very well but means nothing to us now. But Homer is the foundation, just as real for us to-day as it ever was: genuine men in the genuine world."

Oliver, sitting on the other side of his aunt, didn't miss a word; even asked a question or two, to bring the Senator out, and set everything down carefully that night in his diary. Senator Lunt, he wrote, was a splendid man, still young, but a master of affairs, free from every prejudice, full of every generous feeling. Why couldn't Oliver himself be like that? Why couldn't he have lived in a ranch? Why couldn't he have skipped everything since Homer?

That, Edith pointed out when they discussed it afterwards, would mean skipping Christianity. Senator Lunt was a pagan. If he had any real kindliness, he got it from his Christian bringing up, and not from Homer. In Homer, as far as she had gathered, men were like cattle, bellowing and being slaughtered: and perhaps Senator Lunt liked the *Iliad* so much because it reminded him of his ranch.

Oliver took up this taunt with an enthusiasm that disconcerted her. "That's it," he cried, "Homer is merciless, covers up nothing, adds nothing, simply tells you the awful truth. Yet he walks on the sunny side of the world: it's tragedy in the sunlight, despair at high noon, death in the bloom of youth. And you feel that the sun will keep on shining just the same and that the next morning will be just as beautiful and just as cruel. Do you suppose Senator Lunt doesn't realise what his great ranch is for? To supply train-load after train-load of bullocks for the Chicago stock-yards. It's a long way off: he doesn't see the blood, he doesn't smell it, as Irma and I did when we went to the ghastly place; but he knows the horror is there, and has to be. And I'm sure that must be one of the reasons why he swears by Homer. Homer accepted things as they have to be, felt the beauty of them, and didn't indulge in any hocus-pocus to explain the horror

away, and incidentally to miss the whole truth and beauty of nature.
He saw everything by daylight; and so did Goethe, and so does
Senator Lunt. And don't think this is contrary to the truth of Christianity, to the *moral* truth of it, apart from legend and mythology.
Only, of course, Christianity walks in the shade, walks in the night,
sees everything from the point of view of the soul, and not as it really
happens and has to happen. You may say the point of view of the
soul is the ultimate one, and the one that matters. That's why Christianity is interesting, and philosophy and all the other religions: they
are true to the soul, perhaps, and reveal our moral nature. But they
don't show us this moral nature in its true setting as Homer does: so
that Senator Lunt can skip everything since Homer and yet have a
correct map of the world before him, with each thing where it belongs. That's so splendid for a man of action, so healthy, so much
better than grubbing and puzzling and playing with notions in one's
own head, as my poor father did, and as I do."

Edith was not pleased with these confused sentiments of Oliver's,
as she thought them to be, or with her sister's engagement. It was
distressing that the highest interests should be overlooked so blindly
by people who had every opportunity offered them, in their own
households, of learning better; it was sad that earnest young minds
like Oliver's should be misled by so many winds of doctrine. It might
be almost better for the boy to go into active life, into some bank,
perhaps: and then when older he might turn again to religious questionings with a better disposition, and a clearer need of supernatural
faith. She asked her father if he couldn't make a place for Oliver in
his office; and her father smiled on the idea. A young man with
Oliver's fortune was rather expected to be a banker; especially when
his property was miscellaneous, and his father had not been at the
head of any important business. Fresh blood and fresh millions would
come in rather well; the family bank was becoming somnolent and
old-fashioned: it was being forgotten, overshadowed by people like
the Morgans, always in the newspapers. Yes, a place might be found
for Oliver in the Van de Weyers' banking house.

On the day before his departure Edith kindly cancelled all her
engagements and arranged to devote her whole afternoon to her
young cousin. They would take a long drive. Oh, no, not again to
Staten Island. She was no longer a member of the committee in
charge of that little old mission church. How ugly that chapel had
been, after all, in spite of all she could do to create a religious atmos-

phere! The Reverend Edgar Thornton, although so young had been called away to a regular parish, where his great gifts as a preacher and guide wouldn't be so cruelly wasted: and a superannuated country clergyman, of the old Low Church school, had been put in the place, who frowned on everything devotional. The weather was so summerlike, why shouldn't they drive to Westchester and have tea with her Aunt Miriam, who had already moved out of town?

Conversation in the motor naturally turned on Maud's engagement. "If you admire Senator Lunt so much, I wonder you wish to travel about idly, and to puzzle over all those philosophical theories, quite arbitrary and unintelligible they seem to me, instead of beginning life at once in the real world. I am sure my father would be glad to take you into his office. And if you really cared for my friendship as much as you say you do, you wouldn't want to go off to the ends of the earth, instead of settling down soberly here in New York, where we could see each other constantly."

For some moments Oliver did not speak. He felt a great wave of desolation passing over him, an abyss separating him not only from Edith but from everybody and from everything. How could this most intelligent, most perceptive of women, fail so utterly to understand him? How could she seem so sympathetic and be so unkind? How could she pretend to be so religious and spiritual, and prove so incapable of the least devotion, and the least sacrifice? Finally, he slowed down his motor, and said deliberately:

"We should see each other constantly if we were married. I asked you to marry me, not to annex me. I wanted you to share my life: I didn't propose to adopt your way of living. You would be a wonderful help, a wonderful source of happiness. Why shouldn't you be happy too? What would you be missing that is worth having? You don't love anyone else better, not even Mario. I have known that from the first. But I see now that you don't believe in me. It doesn't occur to you that I might be worth helping, worth making happy. You don't see that I am struggling with a terrible problem, that I am trying to save my soul. And you don't care. You don't love me."

It was now Edith's turn to be silent. Her quick intuition prevented her from saying what first came to her mind, that saving his soul was precisely what she did care for. She felt the radical difference between what saving one's soul meant to her and what it meant to him. He was too deep for her; he was strange, heathen, obscure, and disturbing. She also rejected a second impulse, the impulse to hit back, to call him insolent, a mere boy making himself the centre of the universe and asking her to play the Martha to him if not actually the Mary Magdalene; to become a sort of domestic nun hanging on his words and obeying his precepts—the sort of slave that Calvin or John Knox or his favourite Goethe might have liked for a wife, to deaden the itch of sense in them, and to stew their dinner. No: the flame of spirit burned in him too clear to be mocked, and too sadly. She would take him at his own valuation, and turn the tables on him by her supreme kindness and sympathy.

Opportunely she remembered the beautiful sermon young Mr. Thornton had preached only the previous Sunday about the salvation of the heathen. He had spoken so charitably, so generously, removing any distress you might feel about those who seemed not to be Christians, and yet showing what a great privilege it was to belong to the true Church. Really, it seemed providential that those thoughts should be so exactly applicable to Oliver.

"Please don't say that I don't care for you," she began in her kindest and sweetest manner. "I care for you very much, and more the more I see of you. But you are quite right in thinking that I don't love you enough, I don't know you well enough, to be ready to give up my own life and lose myself entirely in yours. You hardly know yet what your life is to be, and you are asking too much. Later perhaps, you may deserve that absolute devotion from some other woman. Perhaps it's only because you are so young that you have turned to me at all or thought I could help you, being a little older and having more experience of the world. But, really, do you need guidance in such great matters from a woman, from a wife? In a Christian marriage the wife helps the husband in carrying out the duties of their station, she gives him hints, she restrains him when he might be hasty, but she doesn't assume the guidance of his spiritual life. Especially not for a person like you, who has so much depth: grace will come to you directly. All you need, in order to be sure that your inspirations come from God, is the advice of some very wise man, versed in the experience of the Saints. Yet essentially we have to live alone. In different degrees we are all put to that test. And I almost think you are one of those rare persons called to a solitary life in a special sense. Are you sure you need marry at all? Perhaps you don't even need the Church; because God has other children that are not of this fold. In antiquity and in heathen nations there have been heroic souls; and so in the modern world there may be some not yet called to the visible Church, but needing to live first, as it were, in the wilderness. It seems very sad; it is very mysterious; but possibly if any one of us believers, with the best intentions, tried to guide you, you might be driven away from God, rather than towards him; because God has always revealed himself in nature and history and in the conscience before he revealed himself more clearly and lovingly and miraculously through Christ in the Church. The right path for you now may be a rugged and lonely one; yet we may find in the end, perhaps in another life, that our different ways have brought us together."

This charitable sermon left Oliver cold. Somehow Edith, the Edith that had smoothed his bed-clothes at the Infirmary, and left him her crimson roses, the Edith that so many times since had seemed a goddess bending down to him so very, very near, the beautiful divine Edith had strangely evaporated. He had never asked her for ideas, for intellectual guidance. He had asked her for herself. She said he didn't need marriage. Not materially, perhaps. Materially he could get on without it. But he needed *love*. Evidently she didn't know what love was, or she hadn't any to give.

Aunt Miriam received them with that air of satisfied expectation which seems to say: I knew you were coming, and here you are. How much nicer than if we had met unprepared! Oliver hadn't seen Miss Stuyvesant since that first night at the opera. She seemed to be still wearing the same black lace dress, except that now it wasn't transparent, and the same ecclesiastical necklace with the little enamelled crucifix pinned over her heart.

"My dear," she gasped when they were comfortably seated and tea had been brought in, "I'm so glad you've come early, because before Mr. Thornton arrives I want to tell you what a *marvellous* success he is having in the parish. Even the poor like him, and he has visited all the summer residents, even those who are still in New York, and obtained such handsome subscriptions that the whole mortgage is practically paid off. In only three months incumbency, it is wonderful. But he has such magnetism; he seems to spread light and balm wherever he goes. Yet there's nothing like gush or sentimentality about him: on the contrary, great learning and lofty thoughts. The new class in Sacred History is crowded every Friday evening, and he has a leaflet printed for each day with a summary, most beautifully expressed. I keep mine, so as to have them bound at the end of the season. They will make a charming little book. Then of course, I needn't tell you, he has such a commanding presence and such a pure refined mouth. I'm sure, before long he will be made a Bishop. Besides——"

At this point the bell was heard ringing, and Miss Stuyvesant, with a knowing smile, looked at the chair and the tea-cup prepared for the young Rector, as if in pleasing anticipation she saw him already seated between herself and her niece.

Oliver, at the first glimpse of Mr. Edgar Thornton, recognised the type at once: perfect manliness consciously reconciled with supreme consecration. He had seen the like in England; only that Mr. Thornton was more hearty and affable in manner, and almost jovial, as behoved an American in the society of charming ladies. It was especially important for a young clergyman not to seem sanctimonious. Until the hostess brought up the subject, he carefully avoided talking shop. He only spoke of the swift sea-gulls he had been watching as he walked along the windy shore, and of the lovely early crocuses just cropping up through the grass: one he had observed in a shady corner bravely pushing its upward way through a patch of snow; and he told a story about the comical old woman who thought that the widow's mite meant that she might marry again. In fine, the tea-party couldn't have gone off more pleasantly; yet Oliver had hardly opened his lips, and as they got up to go, Mr. Thornton, wishing to be cordial, turned to him and inquired if he wasn't rowing in the Harvard Varsity crew.

"I'm at the training table," Oliver replied dryly, "but I'm not in the boat. I am a substitute."

XIII

Redtop, the Harvard training quarters at New London, was so near Great Falls, that on Sunday Oliver was able to motor to see his mother and Irma. He was glad of this chance to be dutiful and loyal to his past, when he was preparing to start on a long journey, perhaps not to return home for years, perhaps never to find home with its old aspect again, and its old inmates. And these Sunday visits, inspired by tenderness, were facilitated in a way he had hardly expected. A change had come over his mother during the last four years. She had become frankly old, passive, and a little vague. The sting to her vanity, in not having been her husband's sole heir, had yielded to time; she was much richer than before; she could delegate to the faithful Irma all her domestic and social cares; and she was proud to think of her tall son being rich and important on his own account, a sort of visible deputy in the great world to the self which she obscurely felt ought to have been hers. When he turned up, she was always the same, quiet, smiling, and rather silent. Only now and then a glint of her old masterfulness would appear, and fade quickly into resignation. She never questioned him about his doings or his plans. She felt that at bottom she would disapprove of them, but why trouble when she was helpless? She never upbraided him for being away so long, or going away so quickly. A day seemed to please her as much as a week, and she received him with the same placidity after an interval of seven months as after a fortnight.

"Mother," he said on the last Sunday in June, "I can only stay to-day for a moment. But would it trouble you too much next week if I brought Jack Remington, the captain of our crew, to spend Sunday?"

Mrs. Alden recoiled from the thought of a stranger sleeping in the house. Of course she had a spare room; yet she had never liked the idea of having her spare room occupied. If it had ever been occupied, she would have had a spare room no longer. Nor was that the worst of it. In the first years after her marriage, when some visiting lecturer or doctor had been actually invited to spend the night, and had momentarily deprived her spare room of its spareness, she had felt an unpleasant sensation whenever she passed that closed door. All the doors in that house, warmed as it was scientifically and equally in its entirety, were habitually wide open. A closed chamber door meant that sleep, or the mysteries of the toilet, were interrupting that life in common and in the public eye, which was alone healthy in the home or in the world. Not that those open doors signified any intimacy between the inmates: on the contrary, they were left open, as one might leave money lying on a table, or a letter in its open envelope. The threshold was a moral barrier stronger than any bolt; and nobody was thought capable of being so much as tempted to pry into another's privacy. Therefore a wooden door actually shut in your face, with a stranger behind it, could not help awakening sinister suggestions. Wickedness and disruption might be planted and plotting there in the dark, to spread their poison afterwards through the whole household. Conscious of an invisible presence, Mrs. Alden couldn't help glancing round corners, and hurrying stealthily through the hall. Her conventional social mind said: "I mustn't disturb that person," but her instinctive and dreaming mind said: "What if that person should burst out and pounce upon me?" It was decidedly pleasanter and more reassuring that the door of the spare room should remain open and the room empty.

These feelings of his mother's were well known to Oliver, and he added at once: "You wouldn't have to give Jack Remington the spare room. Irma says her old room in the school wing is quite ready; only a question of putting sheets on the bed and towels on the rack; and he will be entirely out of your way. He won't smoke or be noisy. On the contrary, he's likely to be feeling sore and despondent after the race. If he went back to Boston every acquaintance he came across would make him feel ashamed of himself, as if he'd done something disgraceful. There would be an awkward silence, or else the horrible creature would slap him on the back and shout: 'Never mind, old boy, we'll beat them next time.' As he is captain, he's nominally responsible, but I know it hasn't been his fault. They haven't let him have his way; and with me he can unbosom himself and lay the blame where it belongs. You know we are sailing together from New York on the Tuesday: we shall be here only two nights, and Jack won't have to face the Boston crowd again at all."

Mrs. Alden didn't reply directly. She turned instead to Irma.

"Why is Oliver always so pessimistic? Doesn't Harvard usually win the race? Why not hope for the best?"

"I *hope* for the best, inevitably, but I don't expect it. Besides are we sure that ultimately it's always for the best that Harvard should win? Perhaps in heaven they may bet on Yale."

Both ladies wondered whether this wasn't a blasphemous thing to say, but Irma on the whole supposed it was witty. Anyhow, as she brushed Mrs. Alden's hair that evening she pointed out what splendid friends Oliver had now—the Captain of the Harvard crew!—and how considerate and kind he was to others. Mrs. Alden sighed, and hoped this was true; but there seemed to be little joy to anybody in all this splendour and kindness; and there was more real comfort in laying one's head on a clean soft pillow, closing one's eyes, and not having to puzzle for the moment about kindness or splendour or the difference, if any, between wit and blasphemy.

The next Sunday after luncheon Remington was sprawling in a long wicker chair under the great porch, dropping one illustrated magazine and picking up another. Indolence and depression and sultry weather made the hours drag: Oliver seemed to be a long time packing and writing letters. Lazily—for what earthly difference could anything make?—he observed a thin young man pushing a bicycle up the long sandy avenue. Suddenly the intruder stopped as if surprised, and then came on hesitatingly up the path under the great wooden columns. Evidently he hadn't expected to see a big black-haired stranger so much at his ease in this place.

"Could you tell me, is Oliver Alden at home?" the bicycle man asked timidly.

"Yes. He's upstairs. If you ring probably they'll answer."

The timid young man rang and was admitted, while Remington picked up a third magazine. Presently he heard Oliver's voice and step in the hall, the carpets being removed for the summer. There was a mixture of pleasant surprise and of apology in his tone.

"But Tom Piper! Where have you been hiding all this time? And how did you know I was here? I wanted to write to you, but you know what these last days are. No time for anything you'd really like to do."

"You see," the other voice answered despondently, "I've been working hard too. The first year at the Medical School. They rather pile it on. My father said he'd seen you driving up Main Street yesterday, so I thought I'd look you up. But you have friends with you. Perhaps I'd better come another day."

"You can't come another day, because we're leaving to-morrow. There's only Remington—you know him, by sight at least. Come with us and have a round of golf."

Tom Piper didn't know Remington even by sight, and had never played golf, but he found himself being introduced to the black-haired young man, and told to climb into the back seat in the pointed stern of the motor-car. Nothing to do but to obey: yet he felt that his pleasure was being spoilt, and that he was spoiling the others' pleasure. Not that there would have been much pleasure to spoil. The fog of defeat had not yet lifted. Remington stalked away to drive balls about, almost at random, while Oliver attempted to give Tom a first lesson in putting. But it was too warm for golf; a long drive would be more refreshing; and they got again into the motor where Tom, if not greatly entertained, at least was in nobody's way. Yet he was on Oliver's mind who was made doubly sensitive by his own troubles to the disappointment of his old school friend. Tom mustn't be allowed to go away like that, snubbed, rejected, gladly forgotten. He must stay to dinner, schooldays must be recalled, the future discussed, some sign given of constant friendship.

Poor Mrs. Alden trembled again at the thought of a third young man at the table. Would there be food enough? Fortunately that day they were not limited, as usually on Sunday, to cold slices of the roast beef served hot at the midday meal. An exception had been made, a regular dinner had been prepared for the evening, and a roast chicken ordered, with sausages. On second thoughts, Mrs. Alden had discussed with Irma whether one chicken would be enough. "Do have two chickens, Irma dear, and then we needn't have the sausages: perhaps the young men of to-day may not like sausages." But now that Tom Piper was added to the guests, her hostess's conscience smote her anew. She no longer excluded Tom Piper on the ground that he was the apothecary's son. It was enough now that he was Oliver's friend; and besides, wasn't he going to be a doctor like her own father and her own husband? But still, in Tom Piper's case, she felt there was a fundamental fitness in sausages. At once she anticipated the pleasure, the sense of justness, with which she would place two large sausages on Tom's plate, together with a leg, not a wing, of chicken. She would be bounteous in hospitality, but dignified and discriminating in friendship: just as Oliver too, for all his unworldliness, was nice to Tom Piper out of pure kindness, without much joy to himself. "Run, Irma, please," she commanded, when the intrusion of Tom Piper had had time to sink fully into her consciousness, "run and ask Mrs. Mullins to have sausages to-night after all, plenty of sausages, in spite of there being *two* chickens. Tell her *three young men* are expected to dinner."

After so copious a feast, without wine, everybody felt more drowsy and dull than ever. Remington said he had letters to write, and disappeared. Oliver too had a letter to finish, a very important letter. Would Tom wait a few minutes and take it to post in the town before midnight? Irma, to fill the aching void, asked Tom if he liked music. Did he like Chopin? She was out of practice, but she would play him a nocturne, if he would forgive her fingers being stiff. But they were really so stiff, that she came presently to sit near him. So he was studying medicine? What a noble calling. What did he think would be the best occupation for Oliver? Not business: it would be a shame to waste such a fine mind, perhaps such a great genius, on business. Yet somehow Oliver didn't seem to be a poet. She wondered that he wasn't a poet. A philosopher perhaps. Yet a *professor* of philosophy, a professor in some college—that seemed too confined, too commonplace a life, for such a bold spirit. And for the same reason Oliver could hardly be a clergyman. He was too profound, too original in his mind to breathe freely in any church. Indeed it was very hard to say what he ought to do: he was well advised in studying and travelling first for a few years, before choosing a career. Fortunately, in his case there was no need of haste: and she cast a sympathetic glance on poor Tom Piper, as of one impecunious soul to another, half congratulating the lucky rich, and half upbraiding them.

A few minutes later Tom was putting a large envelope, abundantly stamped, into the side pocket of his coat, saying good-bye mechanically to the adored friend of his boyhood, and mounting his bicycle. The atmosphere of misery was so thick in his mind that he could distinguish no objects within it to be so wretched about. "It's down hill now all the way," said a voice within him. He could "coast" down the whole long road to the town. It had been hot work, and not for the first time, pushing his bicycle up all that distance. Perhaps he would never come up to High Bluff again—unless some day he was carried up to the cemetery, or to the asylum. It might be just as well, being dead or being mad. Oliver himself wasn't happy. Remington wasn't happy. Having been captain of the crew was a curse to him.

The only people who seemed to enjoy themselves were the cheap chaps, like Josh Burr who ran the soda fountain and was such a terror with the girls. Of course, Josh Burr was a mucker; but perhaps Remington would think Tom Piper a mucker too. Oliver had tried to be kind, the German Governess had tried to be kind, even old fat Mrs. Alden had tried to be kind at moments when she remembered. But it was no use swimming against the stream, the stream of circumstances. Better give it all up. Better spend your life going from house to house dosing people with aspirin—the best thing a doctor could do—until you took your last dose of aspirin yourself.

At the railroad crossing he had to interrupt his despair to wait for a long slow freight-train shunting and puffing and keeping the gates down for an unconscionable time. Two girls and a man on bicycles came up noisily and jumped off near him.

"Say, young feller," one of the girls observed, sidling up to him, "where did you git that hat?"

"He ain't got a hat, you silly," the other girl tittered, "can't you see?"

Tom mechanically pulled his cap out of his pocket, put it on, and moved his bicycle away a bit.

"No," said the first girl, "but I can see he's got a grouch."

The man, who was none other than Josh Burr, now came up and engaged Tom in conversation. There were facilities for two couples, which were difficulties for a party of three. The gates were now up. Tom had better ride with them through the wood.

"Come on," shouted the lady who had taken the lead. "It's awful cooling."

When Tom and his companion, an hour later, came out on the road again, silently leading their bicycles, he remembered the time it might be and the letter to be posted before midnight. He felt in his side pocket. No letter there. "You go on with the others," he said to his new friend. "I've dropped something. I must go back and look for it."

Painfully, with the help of his bicycle light he retraced his steps through the wood. Hopeless to find a letter at night through all that underbrush and rubbish and leavings of picnic-parties. Then a thought struck him, and he bicycled back at top speed to the level crossing. There, to be sure, quite visible and undisturbed, near the spot where he had pulled his cap out of his pocket, lay Oliver's letter, or rather half of it, for one half had sunk into the black water of the ditch running beside the railway. He picked it up by the good end. It was soaked, limp, blackened with cinders, heavy with the filthy water that had got inside. Impossible to put it in the letter-box. He pressed the water out, dried it as best he could with his handkerchief, examined it under the corner lamp-post. The address was hardly legible: the envelope was half ungummed. Besides, it was now past midnight. Useless to post it, even if that were possible. Should he push his bicycle once more up the hill, rout out Oliver, explain what had happened? But how explain the hour? If he had simply dropped the letter the loss would have appeared long before midnight. Read it and perhaps telegraph the gist of it in the morning to the person concerned? If it was a thing to telegraph, Oliver would have done so himself. No. It was all over with Oliver. All over with pushing his bicycle up that hill. He might as well throw up the sponge, burn his boats, burn the letter, and swear he had posted it. And he might as well read it first, find out how he had been trapped, trace the absurd meshes he had been caught in. He carefully unsealed the rest of the envelope and took out the letter. It was wet and soiled in places, but still legible.

Dear Edith, that you should have telegraphed, that you should have been troubled at the thought that I might be unhappy, gives me a last glimmer of hope. If you are sorry for me about a trifle like this, when I was not even rowing in the boat and expected defeat, surely you must be sorry for me about what really matters. Perhaps you think I've just got a childish notion into my head, and that I'm unhappy about you, just as I might be unhappy about a boatrace; that after a few days the smart will be healed, that it is a matter of no consequence whatever. The smart can be terribly sharp notwithstanding. Why should we care for anything, even for life, except that we find ourselves actually caring without any reason? Our hearts are set on particular things, and we can't help suffering if we miss them. I am hideously disappointed that you shouldn't believe in me, that you should prefer other sorts of people and other ways of feeling. Why do you prefer them? Simply because they are more conventional, easier to play with, less courageous? Can't you see that it is all unreal, or do you see it, and don't you mind the unreality? You will say that I am bitter, that I am unjust, simply because you have turned me down. They said so about the crew, that I was disgruntled and pessimistic simply because I wasn't put in at stroke. Yet I was right about the facts, and I had never wanted to be stroke or in the crew at all for my own pleasure—sculling alone is what I really like—but only for Jack Remington's sake, because I was perfectly sure that with him at seven and me at stroke, we should have carried the other men with us as if by magic, and the boat wouldn't have touched the water. I feel sure I am right also about you and me. The race is lost as things stand, lost for both of us, because alone I should be desolate, not knowing what I was living for, and you alone would dope yourself with pious fictions. Together we might be reconciled to the truth, happy in it; and think what strength that would give us! But you must first believe in me and trust me. I am good for nothing except at stroke. I must take the lead. You may say you can guide yourself, or be guided by people with more authority than I have. Of course I have no authority, but I have sincerity, and what is authority but the sincerity of someone else who lived long ago? There's no real authority except the authority of *things*. We run up against things, we must work with things, we must study things if ever we hope to change them: but apart from the authority of things, we are free, and there is no authority but our own reason. You would trust me, I know, if you trusted yourself. But you don't dare. Perhaps nobody trusts me except Mario. Perhaps he is the only person I shall ever be able to help. He is fearless, he knows what he wants, and I can help him to get it. He's coming round the world with me, he would come with me wherever I wished, not from subservience, but because he knows that I have nothing at heart except that he should prosper, that he should be altogether and splendidly himself, in a word, because I *love* him. If you could love me you would come too. Can't you? *It's not too late.* Telegraph to the Manhattan Hotel or to the *Kaiser Wilhelm*, and stop me. We could take the next steamer together. ⊕

P.S. Think how beautiful to be married privately without an engagement announced months beforehand or invitations or presents, or bridesmaids or newspaper reporters or rice thrown at us or champagne at lunch! To be married without falsehoods, without fuss, married before God!

Second P.S. Your friend Mr. Edgar Thornton might marry us in that prettier new church of his, freed from the mortgage. I shouldn't mind the Chartres east window because I needn't look at it; but he must give his boy-choir a holiday. I don't like processions of strangers celebrating my inmost feelings.

Tom Piper didn't know who "Edith" might be, but on reading the letter carefully a second time, he decided that he hated her. Out of his own hard luck, out of his degradation and helplessness there rose a kind of vindictive joy. He was glad he had dropped the letter in the mud. He was glad he had disgracefully forgotten it, dishonourably opened it and read it, and was about to destroy it. He would be doubly glad if, at such a price, he had saved Oliver. If the devil had arranged it all, the devil was a good fellow. That odious "Edith" would never get this letter. She would never telegraph. Oliver would never marry her, and it would be he, poor insignificant Tom Piper, who would have prevented it. Thank God, or thank the devil. Meantime, with the soiled and sodden letter in his hand, Tom felt like a murderer doubting how to get rid of the corpse. Not a scrap of that letter must be left to tell the tale. He gathered all the sheets and the envelope, wrapped them in his handkerchief, and thrust them into his trouser's pocket, where they couldn't fall out. At home, in his own bedroom, he would burn every shred of them in the stove; even the burned paper and ashes should be made to disappear. Anonymously he would be ruling over Oliver's whole life, though he might never see Oliver again.

At the Manhattan Hotel, the next Tuesday morning, and at the Bursar's Office in the steamer, there was no telegram from Edith. It wasn't an unmixed disappointment. There was a sad peace in it. He had done his utmost, he had done all he could honestly do. Now he was at sea again; and how much better that emptiness represented the true condition of a living spirit than did the constraints and compulsions and falsehoods of human society! Here were winds and currents to reckon with, here were hard necessities in shipbuilding, here was a sharp watch to be kept on board, and a strict discipline: yet the sea was not laid out in streets, there were no houses and lamp-posts and hedges: you might choose your course. Yes, and the most merciful thing was that you left no permanent furrow, and that the sea was as smooth and clear for the next man as it had been for you.

Later however, when he received his letters, one large square lavender coloured envelope at once attracted his eye. There was no mistaking it, nor the pale green wax with which it was magnificently sealed, nor the beautiful up-and-down hand, like a procession of giraffes. This couldn't be an answer to his letter. The two must have crossed. What a test for her words, read in the light of her actions! But he was in no hurry to read. They were at sea, there was no going back now, and he was bitterly, cruelly glad of it. One of those oldish methodical tricks which he had already fallen into was to arrange his pile of letters, like a hand at cards, before opening any of them. Those plainly important, or expected from his known friends, went to the bottom, to be read last and relished at leisure with a free mind; while that minor curse of modern life, advertisements, remained floating on the surface, to be skimmed off, as quickly as conscience allowed, into the waste-paper basket. That morning bills were in the ascendant, and these he habitually put in his pocket, to be inspected officially, with his cheque-book open before him. Next to the last was a note from Irma, praising Jack Remington, saying a good word for Tom Piper, admiring Mrs. Alden's calmness and courage on seeing her only son going away from her into this wide dangerous confused world, and finally wishing Oliver a good voyage and many great deep noble experiences. "Yes," he thought, "we will begin with these experiences at once, and see how great, deep and noble they turn out to be." He broke that thin heraldic seal, so spread out and brittle, with a certain relish. He felt hardly any excitement, only a sort of philosophic curiosity, ready for anything, not hoping for much, and smiling beforehand at human frailty and at his own predicament. What could have induced her to write this long letter, when it was clear that her mind hadn't changed? Was it mere coquetry, to keep him dangling a little longer? If so, she was wasting her beautiful note-paper and her beautiful hand-writing, because his last word had been said. As he unfolded the letter a slight but exquisite scent of violets detached itself from the sheets and transported him to the night at the opera when he had helped her on with her cloak and had first thought her so beautiful. Had she this perfume then? He had no distinct memory of it, but somehow this scent was hers, the scent of her body, perhaps, by some odd symbolism, the scent of her mind. But now for her explicit words. He would try how *they* smelt.

Dear Oliver,

There is a piece of news I must break to you sooner or later and I do it now so that you may start *quite free* on your travels, and not feel you are dragging an anchor or are tied in any way to any of us *poor weak women* at home. I hope you will forgive me for having hesitated a little, and perhaps encouraged you to think of me in the way you did. It was not the best side of us that attracted us to each other. On our best side we are really too different for complete sympathy. What you imagined was love for me was only what you would have felt at your age for any *good* woman that you saw familiarly and that took a great interest in you, as of course I did and always shall. I was drawn to you from the first by our common affection for Mario. I could see what a splendid influence you had on him, and how much he cared for you, and I couldn't help seeing you more or less through his eyes, although of course everybody feels that you have a noble character and are greatly gifted as well. You seemed to me already a stronger and rarer being than any of those older men, someone of whom I might more naturally have been expected to marry. Now I see that it would have been impulsive and *selfish* in me to have yielded to this sentiment, something *merely romantic*, when you were so young and had your life still to shape, and would surely find someone else later very much more suitable, who could identify herself with you in every way and make the happiness of your whole life. This would have been impossible for me, because I am so much older, with my tastes formed, and especially with religious feelings which are different from yours. Your way of thinking is very noble and deep, but as yet without faith, though I believe in the end you will see how necessary faith is and that you really always had it without recognising what it meant, that it meant *Christ*. However, you must live your life first, and I write to set you free from any sort of promise to myself, and to ask you never to think of me in that way again. You may not be altogether surprised to hear that I am engaged to the Reverend Edgar Thornton, whom you saw once at my aunt Miriam's. He is like you in being very different from all my old society friends in New York, but we have the same views on the most important subjects, and he thinks I shall be able to help him in the *very great* work that is opening out before him.

This was the piece of news I had to give you. Please don't mention it to anyone, as we have not yet had time to write to all our other friends, but Mario will have heard of it when you see him. I hope your journey together will be all you could wish, and that you both will always believe in the *unchanged affection* of your old friend and cousin.

EDITH.

PART V

LAST PILGRIMAGE

I

The journey round the world had taught Oliver little except how inevitably centred and miserably caged he was in himself: not merely psychologically, in his mind and person, but socially and morally in his home world. Go where he might, to Egypt, to India, to China, to South America, the foreground had always been an Anglo-American ship's company or an Anglo-American hotel. The dragomans and touts everywhere had squeaked some sort of degraded English; the first news every day had been from the London or New York Stock Exchange; and the home newspapers had reported the stale catastrophes of weeks before with a ghastly crudity. There was no private space any longer in the world, and no freedom: every chink and cranny was choked with the same vulgarity.

During those voyages Oliver had read up the geography and history of the countries they visited; but it had been Mario that had played the cicerone and introduced his cousin to the actual people and places. He had prevented Oliver from keeping out of adventures altogether or from taking them too seriously. Mario was still a child in his delight at any strange fact; he was very much a man in his experienced way of discounting that fact and looking beyond it. Impostors seldom deceived him. Sight-seeing, often so vapid and tiresome to Oliver, never failed to amuse Mario: he always found something incidental, besides what you went to see, that was worth looking at. To him the little episodes painted in the corners were often the best of the picture: they revealed the true tastes of the artist and the unspoken parts of life. What mastery, what lordliness there was in this independent way of observing unintended things and liking imperfect people! Wasn't Mario far less dispersed, far less distracted at heart, than Oliver himself? In every adventure, before every fact or theory, this decorative young man seemed to remain imperturbable; never repelled or scared, even by the ugliest faces or passions of the underworld; never lured beyond his intention, or shaken in his own tastes and judgments. Courteous and affable as he might be in appreciating everything foreign, he never asked himself, as Oliver did, whether those foreign manners or languages or religions mightn't be better than his own. Such a firm mind was like some royal park where an old tree here and there might once have been struck by lightning, and where many a harvest of dead leaves must have been swept up from the straight paths and spotless lawns; yet not a scar or a weed appears, everything is ready for the master's pleasure, and at any moment the fountains will play, the music sound, and the long windows open to let the good company stroll in and out with the familiar civilities.

So after his variegated experiences Mario had been confirmed in his native ways. He had reverted joyfully to every detail of his life in the rue de Saint Simon, where his mother's little apartment preserved as nearly as possible its old aspect, with the same *bonne-à-tout-faire* and with many of his old acquaintances. With equal ease and pleasure he had picked up the threads of his English connection. It had been decided that he should go to Oxford; and his old Eton tutor, now a Canon of Christ Church, had opened the doors to him of that stately college. There he had soon become inseparable from his Eton friend Lord Engleford and a high sporting circle: that Bullingdon Club which had seemed to Jim Darnley—not so absurdly after all—to be the cream of Oxford. Vanny now wore a white and blue ribbon in his straw hat, as Oliver had once worn a white and purple one, but with how much less constraint, with how much more gaiety, as if it were a flower in his buttonhole. "My hatband," thought Oliver, "was only a label on my luggage, which luggage was myself." Wouldn't it have been really better to live like Mario, not socially labelled, not insured or predestinated, but irresponsibly, even licentiously, within the limits of kindness and honour? Wouldn't it have been better, if only it had been possible?

But no: Oliver was sure it couldn't have been better. There might be something enviable in Mario's capacity to enjoy life on so many levels and to identify himself with people of so many descriptions. It might be enviable to be interested and excited by realities, even when they were unpleasant or dangerous or horrible. Enviable, thought Oliver, if you wish to be happy; but impossible if you wish to do right, to make yourself and the world better. You are merely encouraging the fools to be fools, the rascals to be rascals, and the prostitutes to be prostitutes. It was all very well to sympathise with nature. You might fall in love with paganism, as Goethe did; but you mustn't condone nature's crimes, you mustn't become a pagan in your heart. That had been Goethe's mistake. In your heart you must remain a Platonist or a Christian, as the Vicar remained: not by any sentimental attachment to tradition or any flabbiness of thought, but because it was the very nature of the heart to choose a pure good, and to cleave to it. There was, there couldn't help being, a single supreme allegiance, a dedication to truth, to mercy, to beauty, infinitely to be preferred to this motley experience and this treadmill of bitter amusements. People like Mario weren't looking for the truth or for the best life: they were merely playing the game. In that sense Mario was more American, more modern, than Oliver himself: or rather he was what men of the world had always been, brilliant slaves of their circumstances. "I won't be the slave of my circumstances," the proud spirit in Oliver protested. "I will recognise them, because that is a prerequisite to changing them. I may even be their product, as far as my social person is concerned: but my social person is itself only a circumstance to be judged and altered by my immortal reason."

So confirmed in his spiritual self-reliance, Oliver had little confidence in the power of books or professors to give ultimate guidance: yet it was his duty to learn what the authorities might have to teach him; and he had bravely settled down in Germany to hard solitary work. He had read prodigiously in the major historians and philosophers, never with the joy of finding a great revelation, but often with satisfaction and always, he thought, with profit: because the wildest errors were instructive if you understood how people had come to embrace them. It was the living, however, that disappointed him most. What the Germans called *Wissenschaft* wasn't knowledge but theory; and this flow of theory, while it carried any amount of learning in its controversial currents, was absolutely arbitrary in its direction. It moved with the Zeitgeist in the direction of a trade wind. Yet this professional science, or fashionable theory, was proclaimed in a surprising tone of authority, with the expectation of brow-beating the world into accepting it until the Zeitgeist and the path of national consciousness should take another turn. If sickened by this spectacle Oliver consulted the independent minds—for they also existed—in search of the German freedom and inspiration of other days, the atmosphere was certainly purer, the outlook more unworldly; but in the end what did he find? Some myth concerning the birth of consciousness or its providential career. Could such fables be the ripe fruit of science and criticism? Couldn't the grammar of thought be studied without confusing it with cosmology? Wasn't this the radical illusion of theology surviving all the articles of faith?

He, at least, wouldn't flinch before the natural facts which we are in any case obliged to assume in our daily lives. A religion that supplemented these facts fantastically, or a philosophy that explained them away, was too obviously a self-deception. He at least wouldn't dope himself into believing in any other world nearer to the heart's desire. *Desire*, indeed! Could there be a more ignorant guide? The farther you pursued desire the deeper you sank into damnation. Not the heart's desire was the good to pursue, but the heart's health: a certain sanity of heart that should modulate desire to the key of possible achievement. That would also be the key of intelligence and of true beauty. To enlighten desire; to pick up the thread of salvation in this labyrinth of folly; to discern the causes of heathen bewilderment and the contrary principles of a pure life, wasn't that what Buddha and Lao Tse had done, but too soberly for the rabble? Wasn't it what Socrates too had done, only too late for the Greeks? Wasn't it what the early Christians had failed to do, because they were puffed up with fables, and the Puritans, because they were blighted by fanaticism? Might not we to-day in the ebb-tide of so many illusions trace the course of the last flood and learn to escape the next one?

That was the question to consider: and where could he consider it better than in Oxford, so near the centre of Babel, yet not altogether invaded, in this midsummer season, by the universal rush. Congresses and summer sessions had not yet absorbed the whole long vacation: and the occasional female tourist from the United States— how well he knew that younger replica of Letitia Lamb!—peeped in a little abashed, and turned quickly away again. The poor thing was in a hurry; she hadn't time to go all the way round the meadow; but at least *she had been in Addison's walk*. Oliver from his bench in the distance saw her flutter timidly, make a hurried note in her guide book and vanish: and by contrast he felt wonderfully at home.

Yet who could be more radically a stranger in Oxford than he was himself? Luckily in the Long Vacation Vanny and his friends wouldn't be there to distract his thoughts and tempt him to dally with them in Peckwater Quad, as they had during the last Hilary Term, when between his two German semesters he had made an escapade to Oxford. What a change of scene and music it had been, as in some fantastic opera-bouffe, to hear those voices and that airy talk, and see those fashionable or eccentric young persons flitting in and out

with the ease and casualness of butterflies, affecting to be wholly
frivolous in their studies and only half in earnest in their sports, and
giving you glimpses, by their allusions and habits, of a great world
beyond; a world great as the world goes, but really a medley of
smiling and calamitous littleness. Here at least the littleness was harmless and ended in play; but Oliver shuddered to think how easily the
same vanities could be prolonged and extended, to direct the State
and the Church and be the motive force in human affairs.

Peckwater: the one spot in Oxford where you might fancy yourself
in Rome or in Versailles, or at a stretch in the Escurial: the one place
where Mario didn't need to be Vanny (though Vanny everyone called
him) but might be Roman Mario with a sense of propriety and even
proprietorship. The spirit of this architecture was that of his own
deeper traditions; this society, with but a slight excess of horsiness,
satisfied his own instincts; and intellectually whether he turned to the
cathedral or to the library, he could feel more at home here, and a
truer child of Cardinal Wolsey, than the native occupants. Even the
ground had forgotten to be distinctly English and to become a lawn;
it had preferred to remain barren, a mere stamping-ground and area
between those brown façades, regular and conventional on three
sides, like a veteran regiment on parade, and majestic on the fourth,
as if for royal habitation. So perhaps the great world was on three
sides fashionable order and nullity, and on the fourth side experience, power, art, and magnificence.

Anyhow, this was no question for Oliver. He would return to America
and get down to business; but not quite yet. After the violence of
German theorising he needed to regain his mental balance, and to
look at things for a while at long range, under the form of eternity.
At Iffley the Vicar was always ready to receive him as a pupil. There
was a hidden Oxford that was deeply friendly to him, because it was
itself an exile in the world: not that perfect paradise for a rich young
man with pretensions to being a superior person; not the fashionable,
national, literary Oxford of a Dr. Jowett, but the Oxford represented
by the Vicar in his learned obscurity and metaphysical faith. Everything in Oxford that could offend a Puritan and an American, everything that could awaken an angry sense of inferiority, had now
receded into the background and become commonplace. The secret
of it no longer seemed very secret, or the greatness of it very great.
Oliver had now seen the ruins of ancient greatness at Karnak, at
Baalbek, at Rome. In Rome he had even seen greatness of a sort

actually surviving, when the Pope was carried into St. Peter's to the sound of silver trumpets. Here was still a man who believed he was the Vice-regent of God. Could such a pretension suffice to raise people to the top of the world? Oliver had also seen the Emperor William II reviewing his garrison in the Tempelhofer Feld; and if there wasn't much moral greatness in that, at least there were the stupid trappings and the suits of greatness. Most stupid, they seemed to Oliver's puritan mind; and it was with a certain sardonic relish that he turned from that spectacle to his collection of photographs, and to those vast rubbish-heaps in the East which he had snapped with his Kodak. Those ancient ruins gave him a grim satisfaction, because they were so thoroughly turned to dust, and such eloquent sermons against the greatness and madness of the builders.

The stones of Oxford, on the contrary, had crumbled only in the weather and had been lovingly replaced. They were a monument to the humble wisdom of the age that reared them against the folly of all other times. These stones had always been discreet in their elegance, and cut to the human scale. They were still sheltering and useful, and merited to be renewed indefinitely, as if nature had put them together and not the vanity of men. Half their charm lay in their homelike way of nestling amongst trees and gardens beside these rambling lanes and branching streams, so modestly navigable and so embowered. There was nothing dead about Oxford, nothing stark or outgrown. The most antiquated things in it were revivals. If the place seemed dedicated to recollection and fidelity, that was because here the seminal principles were still living which could give form to a wise mind. What can be more conservative than a seed? Unless you are something definite to begin with, unless you invincibly love something in particular, how are you to distinguish a direction of progress? How are you to choose a goal that is not capricious and delusive? What these low walls shut out was not the great universe. It was only a waste land of desolation and folly. Outside, not within, lay the real hopelessness and the real ruins. Within was an orchard of perennial fruits. These great trees carried the murmur of earthly labour almost to the clouds, almost to the veiled courses of the stars. Here was not the devouring silence of death or of the desert, rather a silence sustained by the music of nature and history, and scanned by the prosody of thought. In this air there was a placid tension, like the tension of truth; and this repose was only the equilibrium, at their centre, of all disputes and of all battles.

Seen in this broad light even the affectations of Oxonians began to seem less silly. If intellectual fops like to play with surfaces, it was perhaps because they were aware how inevitably the lights of things are refracted and how in any case the reality mocks us from beneath. Curious old customs were pleasant if they were honoured without superstition; and so was fearless reason, if you were loyal at heart to your traditions. There was true wisdom in qualifying your piety with openness of mind, your learning with humour and your wealth with unworldliness. Except perhaps for the humour, and a certain spright-liness that went with the humour, these were the very qualities Oliver valued in himself: only here they were combined with a larger knowl-edge of history and of human nature than he possessed, and a greater sympathy with religion and religious philosophies. Too great a sym-pathy, Oliver couldn't help feeling: because by cultivating imaginative reason you solved no real problem; perhaps you only prejudiced your mind and obstructed the only possible solution. Oxford philoso-phy seemed a compromise, a sort of lingering sunset: the classics and the poets, Platonism and Christianity, illuminating beautifully, for the old world, the approach of night. But it was the dawn that concerned Oliver, or any American, if dawn there was to be. He had no use for sunsets or for compromises. Better, far better, eternal night itself, without any atmospheric blue heavens or human mythologies. In that clear night, once your eyes were adapted to it, you might discover a whole universe of stars, distant and cruel, perhaps, but enlightening: enlightening and refreshing, like the sea, that he had always found, in its constancy and in its moodiness, the true friend of his spirit. And turning from the sea and the stars, without ever inwardly for-getting them, he might still live his appointed daylight life in the world, the busy cheerful life that everybody seemed to live in Amer-ica: simple spontaneous immersion in what happened to be going on: a perpetual boatrace; a perpetual football match; a brave strug-gle with no further purpose, yet not without moments within it of pride and satisfaction. This would not be a sentimental compromise between the world and the spirit or between tradition and truth: it would be an acceptance of both, each in its unvarnished reality.

The sea and the stars taught Oliver to expect no miracles, and to make no exceptions in his own favour: yet the world happened to have treated him, personally, remarkably well. Indeed, it had denied him nothing except the animal capacity to wallow, and to hug himself for joy at his private good luck. He couldn't do that; and he couldn't forgive the world its general stupidity and cruelty and disorder. Yet these evils, in a great measure, were open to correction. He would presently return to America, and return armed; not merely driven home, like his father and so many weary travellers, by the sheer discomfiture and shame of being everywhere else a foreigner. He would return to work, if not eagerly or with an instinctive gladness, at least deliberately and with a clear mind, like Senator Lunt and the heroes of Homer, beautifully accomplishing their destiny. If he asked himself in what direction he should exercise his influence, he might not be able to give a clear answer beforehand in words: but he felt that at each actual turn of affairs he would know what the right direction was.

> *Ein guter Mensch in seinem dunklen Drange*
> *Ist sich des rechten Weges wohl bewusst.*

The right direction for a *moral* man would always lead to ultimate order and kindness: an order itself kind: an order harmonising all sympathies, as far as such a harmony was possible, and not suffering the ignorant energies of men to waste themselves and neutralise one another, like the broad flat shifting currents of the Mississippi. Art must canalise nature, prevent disastrous inundations, and render those abundant waters nagivable and sweet.

The path, then, seemed to be clear before him. He was young, he was rich, he was strong; why wasn't he more eager and happy? Why, in particular, did his present holiday at Iffley seem somehow unsatisfactory? Odd: because everybody kept saying how particularly pleasant he must find it this year at the Vicarage. Hadn't Jim himself turned up between voyages, bluff and vigorous as ever, and carried his young friend off on daily excursions to Radley or Abingdon or Godstow? Naturally the jolly sailor was bound to make the most of his holiday ashore. Down he would plunge at ten o'clock in the morning into the garden, conspicuously dressed for boating, and waving a muffler. "You can't sit grubbing there all day like that. You'll get round-shouldered. What do you care what some old white-bearded fool may have written ages ago about what he didn't know?" And Oliver would find himself tilted out of his garden chair, or pulled out of it, and compelled partly by force and partly by friendliness to leave an interesting sentence half read, or a thought half formed. No doubt the exercise was good for him: it was disgraceful to be out of condition. Yet why must they always halt on the way to have luncheon or tea at the King's Arms at Sandford? Couldn't they have stopped just as well at the Island or the Tandem Inn or the Harcourt Arms? But no: Jim was obstinately attached to his old haunts, perfectly unconcerned and at home in the place and still apparently on the best of terms with Bowler and Mrs. Bowler, and even the kitchenmaids. Oliver's little friend Bobby wasn't there. Just as well, perhaps. His presence might have been embarrassing. Perhaps it was always just as well when you missed something that might have given you pleasure. And better for Bobby. An anonymous benefactor had made it possible to send the child away to a good school. Nevertheless Oliver was thoroughly uncomfortable. Jim's talk, too, when they were alone, had lost its old vividness and variety. The world no longer stimulated his wits or his cynicism: it had become an old story. He was interested only in his rather muddled private affairs, and kept repeating what an ass Smith had been and how outrageously Jones had behaved. Everything was a swindle, and he was always the innocent sufferer. His tone had become that of a discarded prime minister writing his memoirs. Everybody was to blame except himself; and other people's incredible continual stupidity had robbed him of the fruits of his clear genius, when they were hanging ready to pick from the bough. Glints of the old Lord Jim would come now and then to the surface, to reopen Oliver's wounds and make it impossible for him to become altogether resigned and indifferent; and it was a melancholy relief when the sailor went off to sea again.

Jim scarcely gone, Rose had come home for the holidays. She was finishing her education (at Oliver's expense) at the Abbey School in High Wycombe. Their childish betrothal was never mentioned and was well understood not to count; yet in Oliver's mind the idea of some day marrying Rose lay in reserve as a possibility that helped to give some shape to the distressing vagueness of his future. The girl, he liked to think, was like the Sylvia of Shakespeare's song, holy, fair, and wise; at least there was an intangible serenity about her that might suggest those epithets. Perhaps there was more disdain than holiness in her wisdom, and a certain coldness in her beauty. She moved about silent and open-eyed, as if a flower could walk; and her industriousness took nothing away from the obviously passive and providential grace by which she bloomed. She seemed all observation, all expectancy; there was no telling what she might become: and Oliver, who was himself maturing rather slowly, could afford to wait and see how she would turn out. As a sort of heraldic symbol for an ideal lady-love, this tall and ethereal child would do admirably for the present.

Especially in her absence; for when she appeared in person he was less at his ease. Not that she insisted on excursions: she was as silent and discreet as a ray of sunlight, and as impartial. The rooms, the furniture seemed to be burnished up and cleaner; there were fresh flowers in the house; there were little dainties for the table; and there was a slender white figure and golden head of hair shining in the garden, or moving lightly through the house, with the great grey-hound beside her that Oliver had given her. She never intruded, and they seldom spoke to each other directly. Yet somehow he was always aware of her existence, of her nearness. Her quiet ways, through no fault of her own, acquired for him the quality of stealth. His eye couldn't help following her movements. She charmed him and she troubled him. Why was her mere presence somehow reproachful and ironical? Why was he more reconciled with himself when alone? Could her pride be secretly offended because he helped her father and paid for her education? Did she remember that years ago they had played at being engaged, and did she expect him to make love to her now? Had she heard of Edith and was she jealous? Did she know that Edith had jilted him, and was she laughing at him? Did she mean to jilt him herself? Did she hate him? No: she showed in a hundred little motherly ways that she liked him, never forgot a word he said; turned to him first for suggestions; secretly looked after his clothes and sewed on his buttons; read the books he recommended; seemed always to agree with him, and to like what he liked. And yet all this friendliness seemed in her a matter of course, as if she had been a child's nurse or a fairy housekeeper. She smiled at him as if he were a baby, and seemed positively to pity him. Never mind. Perhaps she was merely accepting him as a member of the family. Very likely sisters were always like that; he meant nice sisters. His cousins, the daughters of Uncle Harry Bumstead at Williams-town, who were the nearest to sisters that he possessed, were not nice in the same way. They were clever and honest; but their manners were odious; their tone cheeky, caustic, provocative; and they talked through their noses, always with an exaggerated emphasis on the word *I*, which began every sentence, and on the word *vurry*, which went with every adjective. They would have been horrid sisters: as cousins it didn't matter, because he need never think of them or see them again. But Rose was a lovely sister to Jim, at once like a little mother and like a little child, never complaining or seeming to criticise, yet tremendously observant, divining his inmost secrets, and suffering silently with him when things went wrong. And she was rather like that to Oliver also, except that she evidently trusted and respected him more than she did Jim: and she was rather like that even to her father: patient, devoted, appreciative, yet secretly sorry for the old man, secretly laughing at him a little, because she thought he was harmlessly mad. Perhaps she thought Oliver harmlessly mad also.

In any case, much as he liked thinking about her, her material presence was too troubling a stimulus. He couldn't read, he couldn't think out an argument, with that preternatural magnetism in the air; and if he knocked off work, and took her out for a walk or on the river, he was not happier. Not only did he miss his books, which after all had more to tell him than his young companion, but he was ill at ease with himself in her company. He felt *de trop*, as if he were an intruder tolerated and smiled upon for his generosity, but not loved or wanted for himself. And piling up the gifts wouldn't mend matters: it would only make the strain greater and the mysterious latent discomfort more intolerable. Was he in love? But then why not say so, why not play the lover openly, be accepted, have all the privileges and foretastes of a future husband? Or why not be married at once? Rose was young, but she was perfectly marriageable and amply old enough in her mind. No: he evidently wasn't in love, since that prospect didn't attract him. He might like to marry her some day, but not now. Now he wanted to study.

Accordingly, with the pretext of being nearer the Bodleian, he moved into the town. For a lodging he chose an inn by chance with the same name as the ill-omened one at Sandford, the *King's Arms*. It stood precisely at the end of The Broad; it was modest, frequented by commercial travellers, farmers, clerics, and impecunious Americans. From his large low square room in the corner, which with its four many-paned windows reminded him of Emerson's room in Divinity Hall, he commanded a long view down The Broad, and a sidelong glimpse of Radcliffe and St. Mary's tower. His walls were decorated with engraved portraits of bishops and deans of Dr. Johnson's generation; and by simply walking downstairs into the private bar, he could descend a hundred years to the age of Dickens, catch the fumes of the steaming punch, note the desultory phrases exchanged by the tapsters, and admire the comely landlady amid her gleaming tankards. Oliver would sometimes sit there, on a deep black leather sofa, and have his tea, or even ask for a glass of shandy-gaff, deliberately evoking in his own mind echoes of the past, and deliberately defying them. He didn't like shandy-gaff, and he didn't much care for tea: the tapsters and landlady were perfectly indifferent to him, but he was inclined to ruminate on his own experience, thoroughly to digest and to disenchant it, with a sort of cruel sentimentality.

Every morning at nine o'clock he climbed the long staircase up to Duke Humphrey's Library. There was something symbolic in those broad easy flights of steps, turning and turning in their square tower. No knowing how many storeys you might be passing: hardly a door, and that barred and bolted, at any landing on the way. It was like his life, easy, promising, almost sumptuous, yet without outlets, without happy choices, only with a perpetual compulsion to go on. But here, at least, you came finally to the top. Near a window overlooking the garden of Exeter he found his pile of books, safe and complete on the long oaken reading-desk. His name on a slip of paper, stuck in the top book, sufficed to reserve them all. That alcove, like a cell in a beehive, where you worked silently and alone, but under the eye of the community and in its service; that glimpse of a cloistered garden; that roof with its wooden skeleton exposed to view, and become a picturesque decoration; that musty smell of the old books, bound in calf, which he was reading—all this intimately transported him into a by-gone age, into a world of pathos and duty, of love and war. Where was it fled, that enchantment, that courage, that merriment, that splendour?

Sometimes, of a late afternoon, to avoid the set dinner at the inn, he would walk to Iffley by the tow path, to share the bread and cheese and the nice fresh bit of lettuce that Mrs. Darnley would certainly have for supper: because in his absence this lady reverted to her old economy, except that now she could have a joint or a steak for her early dinner, and was more often seen quietly knitting in her corner, with a new air of gentility and pious resignation.

Then, after supper, with the upper air still broadly lighted by the sunken sun, he would draw the Vicar out for a walk through the fields, and a theological discussion. Mr. Darnley treated him with a mixture of patriarchal authority and apologetic deference, as a hermit might treat a young prince. On ordinary occasions his manners remained as brusque and awkward and as self-conscious as on the first day: but as their talks rose from the inevitable scraps and commonplaces of the moment to speculative themes, the Vicar would forget himself, and become the mouthpiece of pure intuition, speaking with a transfigured severity and a discriminating love, that separated sharply the gold from the dross in all human affections, especially in our affection for ourselves. Oliver at such times would endeavour to apply the purge to his own feelings, first stripping off the ecclesiastical myths and rhetoric in which the Vicar couldn't help clothing his moral philosophy: but the transposition was difficult. The Vicar was inspired: and when a man is inspired he can hardly help trusting his inspiration and mistaking what he invents for a reality that he simply discovers. Yet when the afflatus is past, that supposed reality loses its consistence: we see that it was a product of our mood, a symbol for our passions, as poetry is; so that far from guiding us wisely, inspiration cheats us with some mirage. If we were moving in the right direction, where reality might fulfil our hopes, we shouldn't need any visionary ideals to beckon us. Events would open out before us congenially, and would call forth our innocent interest and delight, gradually, concretely, in ways odder and more numerous than we expected. Why, then, is this not so? Why does experience leave us so desolate, so puzzled, so tired, that like Plato and Plotinus and the Christian saints we must look to some imaginary heaven or some impossible utopia for encouragement and for peace?

The Vicar certainly had a secret solution for this problem, but he was no missionary, no ambitious prophet, and he would gladly have left his wisdom unspoken. With Oliver he couldn't help thawing a little, the boy had such keenness, such spiritual intelligence, and behind all that such a fund of tenderness. In all their talk, master and pupil were aware of Jim in the distance, somehow the source and centre of their concern. Why was Jim a failure? Merely bad luck? False principles? But if Jim's principles were false, what were the right principles? What was there in the very nature of things that condemned nature? Plato, Plotinus, and the secret force of Christianity drew all their poignancy from that question.

It was agreed that these systems had no historical or cosmological truth: their ground and their justification was only human and psychological. They expressed mythically the revolt of man's moral nature against the actual world. But if man's moral nature contradicts the world and runs counter to it, ought not that moral nature to be transformed and made harmonious with the reality? Why nurse this unhappy moral rebellion with all sorts of fables, and sentimental regrets? Oliver's integrity could not stomach any double or ambiguous philosophy: and the poor Vicar, conscious of an invincible moral resistance, was cut short in his confessions and reduced again to figurative ways of speaking and to a traditional eloquence through which, as if through stained glass, there transpired a tantalising esoteric wisdom beyond Oliver's apprehension.

II

In Oliver's philosophy there was no principle, astronomical or vol-canic, to mark that particular summer for catastrophes; and he counted on the normal clemency of the weather to allow him placidly to read in the garden and punt or row on the river, as his studious fancy might prompt. But that summer happened to be the summer of 1914.

He was in the habit of perusing the newspapers with an American eye, noting the weather-reports, the accidents, the sporting events, the marriages and deaths, and sometimes, when the headings an-nounced a panic or a boom, glancing at the financial columns. But politics for him meant a periodic presidential campaign less interest-ing than the football championship; and the murders of Sarajevo, the German rearmaments, and the ultimatum to Serbia had crossed his mind like so many *faits divers*. It was with a kind of irritation passing into bewilderment that on the last day of July he received the following telegram from Paris:

"War on. Crossing to-night to join. Engleford thinks he can get me a commission in the Flying Corps. Must see you at once in town. Address St. James's Club. Mario."

Bewildered and irritated Oliver travelled the next day to London, left his things, with his instinctive fidelity to habit, at his father's old lodgings in Jermyn Street, and walked up the steps of St. James's Club almost somnambulistically, asking quite correctly for his cousin, but conscious only of the sunlight in Green Park, the tall railings and the long sweep and gentle descent of Piccadilly toward Hyde Park Corner. How sane, how proper, how splendidly steady everything was in the material world; why should these currents of groundless passion, of perversity, of rhetorical nonsense, sweep so devastatingly through the minds of men?

But here was Mario at once at the door, looking grave, somehow taller, paler, curiously radiant. "Come away from here," he said softly, much as one might speak at a funeral. "This place is full of old fogies spouting platitudes." And taking Oliver's arm in the old school-boy way, he drew him out again into the sunshine, and soon down into the bowels of the earth, to a little table in a corner at Hatchett's, where he ordered luncheon with his usual discrimination. Then, as if calling the meeting to order, he slapped both hands down on the edge of the table. The two young men looked at each other, and after a moment's pause Mario began.

"It's the chance of our lives. The Germans think they're sure to win. They have foreseen everything, prepared everything. This is to be their third Punic war. When it's over—and it won't last long—there's to be nobody of any consequence left on earth but themselves. Still things may not turn out quite as they're planned. The rest of this world may be blind and slow and divided, but it will prove stubborn. It's a question of fighting or being kicked, and even the sleepiest coward will fight then."

Mario seemed transformed, his eyes grown darker, and yet brighter, fixed on the vague distance, as if seeing something invisible. At the same time there was a ripple in him as of boyish merriment; he had become Vanny again, English in his sporting way of thinking of war; yet not altogether, because he wasn't humorous about it, wasn't minimising the occasion or the danger or the cause; was quite Italian in a sort of speculative glorification of the facts, a dash of cockiness and personal challenge, as if he had a feather in his cap and were drawing a flashing sword from the scabbard. He was serious, yet secretly happy, deeply elated, as if never so much alive before. That must be the way he looks, thought Oliver, when he is making love. But these were not thoughts to be uttered, only undercurrents in the mind destined perhaps to reappear long afterwards in some unaccountable swirl of the surface. Now it was only well-formed, rational, impersonal convictions that could find utterance.

"What are they going to fight about?" he asked coldly, almost with a sneer. "Is it Serbia, or is it Alsace-Lorraine? And what are Alsace-Lorraine and Serbia to you? Aren't you an American? What have you got to do with this dog-fight?"

"Being an American nominally won't be an obstacle—not in my case. I've been an Eton boy, and I'm at *The House*. Besides, if they make a fuss, I'll turn British subject. I might join the French army; it's really more France that we're fighting for, and I was born in Paris. But for this sort of business I'd rather be with the English. They know how to take hard things easily, how to rough it like a gentleman, how to suffer like a man. And they keep their mouths shut about their disappointments, and religious feelings, and the dear girls at home. Of course, they haven't the least notion what they are going to fight about. No more has any true soldier. You think it stupid, do you? Your philosophy requires you to find a reason for everything? But do you know why you were born? Do you know what you are living for? Are you sure it's worth while? It just happens. Is anything in this world arranged as anybody would have wished—the mountains and rivers or our own bodies or our own minds? No: but we have to make the best of them as they are. And sometimes it's glorious work. So is war. But it's horrible, you say, and stupid, because very likely at the end you'll be worse off than at the beginning. Yes, very likely: and you might say the same of love-making. Nobody would choose and plan it in cold blood. It's a silly business, a sad business; and I know what I'm talking about. Yet love-making is in the nature of things, like childbirth and death, which are horrible too; and no decent person would have put any of those things into human life, if he had had the say about it. Yet there they are: and where would the human race be without them? So it is with war. The world is always full up with people, hungry people, pushing people, barbarous people: you've got to crush them or be crushed. Suppose you escaped to some desert island or to some mountain top, and refused to touch anything that is actually going on: what would you find to do there? Fiddling? Sitting and finding fault? If you're a man you must be ready to fight every other man and to make love to every pretty woman."

As he listened deeply dissatisfied to his cousin, Oliver thought of Homer and of the living guide that Senator Lunt found in the *Iliad*. That was a picture of war, no less irrational and tragic than Vanny painted it, but how much more charitable, how saturated with religion! On both sides the Homeric heroes, if not faultless, were noble: they might all have been comrades and friends together. But the gods—the irrational forces of nature—whispered madness in their ears, contrived misunderstandings, and foiled good intentions. Yet these gods were truly gods: sometimes they also gave good counsel and inspiration; and in any case they ruled the world and the hearts of men. But Vanny was hot for the chase, warm with suppressed excitement, and in no mood to float on that stream of contemplative wisdom. Another train of thought in Oliver's deliberate mind meantime came to the surface and took shape in words.

"You talk as if we were savages," he said. "The savage may still exist in us, at bottom; but he's all wound round and held down by civilisation. This war that you're so eager for won't be a duel of individuals. You won't be boxing with William II; and you probably wouldn't care to rape all the women in Germany. This will be a war between Governments. And why on earth should you back one blind and helpless government against another? Do you want to give up your life to be ruled by Mr. Asquith or M. Clemenceau rather than by the Kaiser? I should think with your principles the Kaiser would suit you best."

"He would. He happens to be an ass, but at least he's an emperor," Vanny replied warmly. He had friends among the *Camelots du Roi* and had adopted the politics of Charles Maurras. "As for the governments, who cares a fig about them? What are they but a clique of politicians, Free Masons and Jews, more than half of them, parasites of the parliamentary farce, paid to cover up the facts with hollow phrases? Let's hope they'll all be bombed out of existence. We should be pretty well sold if after such a first class row we were still saddled with the same piggy-wiggies, and the same parties, and the same elections. One thing this war will do—*speriamo*—is to clear parliaments away for ever."

"And what will you have instead?"

"Soldiers, Cardinals, and engineers, people who know something in their own line, experts, administrators, and poets. But there's one thing I will say for your cabinet ministers. This war isn't their doing, as the opposition press will tell you. There were wars before there were governments. The wars produced natural leaders. But when kings became tame and sleepy, a lot of little parasitic ministers wormed themselves into office. Perhaps this war may bring us our natural leaders again."

Oliver felt vaguely that something great, something ancient and fundamental, lay behind Vanny's slap-dash sentiments. He felt entangled in a nasty spider's web of convention. He felt helpless and disinherited. Why couldn't he see things from above, like Vanny? Why couldn't he too be chivalrous and sure of his heart? A wave of profound distress rose within him, and half choked him; but he was too proud to regard it as distress about himself. *He* was safe: *he* was rational and master of his fate. It must be distress about Vanny. And the crest of the wave broke sadly into words.

"You will be killed."

"I don't think so," Mario retorted coolly, as if weighing scientific probabilities. "I sha'n't be killed; but if I were I shouldn't know it, and another chap would take my place and see the thing through. What does it matter who's there at the finish, if only it *is* a finish and we kick all this modern civilisation downstairs, where it belongs? And perhaps it's better that we ornamental johnnies, who hang on to the old order, without any right to exist, should be first swept out of the way. Nothing that we are good for will count any longer. It will be a different world."

Oliver, who though he wasn't very happy or useful in modern society, couldn't conceive of any other, thought this talk rather fantastic. "You expect everything to be smashed," he said, "and you don't seem to mind. You laugh, and slyly enjoy the prospect. And a rancid conservative like you can't wait for war to be declared, but must rush forward and enlist in order to smash everything."

"My dear Oliver, you don't understand these things. You read a great deal, but you don't perceive anything. I'm no conservative. I don't want to preserve myself, or things as they are, nor to move backwards and restore the past. It's impossible; and if we could do it by miracle, it wouldn't be worth while. The past was rather nasty, the present is horribly mixed, and I'm not perfect myself. Away with us, then, and a good riddance. But why are things, how can things be, imperfect and mixed and nasty? Because—and this is the first principle of everything which you don't understand—because they might be, and naturally would be, perfect and sweet and pure: they might be, that is, if ever since the Garden of Eden a horrible worm of a dragon hadn't been crawling all over the earth. At this moment your fire-breathing venomous Germany is the mouth of the monster, but his claws are stuck deep into England, his slaver is drooling all over the United States, and as for France, poor thing, she was swallowed whole by the beast at the Revolution, and has become, officially, nothing but the red cockscomb bobbing on its ugly head. The Devil, the Tempter, the Father of Lies. That's what we're up against, what everybody has been up against who has ever done anything beautiful. We can't kill him, but we may scotch him. Luckily he has so many fangs and so many tentacles that he often gets mixed up with himself, and bites a few of his own heads off. That's what's bound to happen now. Lovely! All the governments and all the parties and all the financiers and all the industrialists will smash one another, and the poor natural man will have a chance to breathe."

"Yes," said Oliver bitterly, "and how many poor natural men will be killed and tortured in the process?"

Unconvinced, unreconciled, he left his cousin to his own devices, and returned to Oxford. But now the morning paper, and the evening paper too, had a new meaning for him. He began to read them with European eyes. They began to make his moral philosophy seem rather distant, rather empty. He couldn't fix his attention on those verbal questions. Germany was sweeping everything before it. Germany was prepared, organised, scientific, determined. Wasn't that admirable? And this wealth of resource and invention, this tireless enterprise and perpetual success, wasn't it all a proof of German superiority, of the manifest destiny of Germany to lead the world? Then why did his stomach rise at this thought? Compared with the French and even the English, weren't the Germans very near to him in spirit? Hadn't he been brought up on Goethe? No! It had been only an expurgated, verbal, ladylike Goethe that Irma had set before him: Goethe the lyric poet, Goethe the maxim-maker, Goethe the connoisseur. But there was Goethe the vitalist, the heathen, the super-moralist, venerating power, fawning on success. That was the Goethe with real sap in him, blooming again in Nietzsche, in Bismarck, and in this war; the greedy Goethe that had inspired so many greedy professors and doctors and sycophants of to-day. The professional soldiers were probably not greedy—Oliver had not often come across them—and doubtless they liked war professionally, or sportingly, as Mario did: but they were old-fashioned, and were only hired servants or figure-heads for the greedy industrialists and greedy philosophers. Revolting, Oliver began to think it all, all this worldliness and optimism, flaunted by a profound, an incurable mediocrity. Just the things that Cousin Caleb Wetherbee had blamed in America: but how much uglier, how much more aggressive, they were in Germany! In America these vices were childlike, unconscious, easily yielding to kindness and good-will; but in Germany they rankled, nursed by centuries of envy, hatred, and deliberate self-praise.

Meantime the casualty-lists began to appear; Vanny had got his commission and gone to the front; the walls everywhere were covered with posters urging you to join; and Oliver, neither able nor willing to join (being a neutral and, at least in this conflict, a pacifist) became daily more uncomfortable, more distressed, more incapable of deciding what to hope for or what to do.

He had been sitting one morning restlessly in his wooden chair in Duke Humphrey's Library, taking notes mechanically at intervals, and at intervals gazing at the trees and grass in Exeter garden, when he became aware of somebody standing behind him. The Vicar was there waiting silently for him to turn his head. A yellow envelope trembled in his hand, on which Oliver could read, printed in bold type, *"On His Majesty's Service."*

"We have had bad news," Mr. Darnley said softly, and laid the official document, open, upon Oliver's open folio. The top seemed to begin—

"Sir, I regret to inform you . . ." and at the bottom, before the illegible signature, were the words, in large Gothic letters, *"God Save the King."*

"Jim's ship has been sunk," Oliver heard the Vicar saying. "He is reported missing. He isn't among the survivors that have been picked up. He must have been drowned."

Oliver had stood up on seeing the Vicar, and now he rested his hand heavily on the back of his chair, exactly as seven years before he had clutched the gate of the tow path bridge near Sandford, when Jim had first told him that Mrs. Bowler was his "wife." His head swam in the same way, and he had the same indescribable sensation of collapse, of despair. But that was only in the weak, uncontrolled upper parts of his brain; his hand held firm, his legs didn't give way, and in a moment his head, too, was clear. Without a word, he closed his folio, piled his smaller volumes and notebooks upon it, inserted the slip of paper with his name on it into the top book, and followed the Vicar out of the room, who fumbled a lot in trying to get that official yellow envelope back into his pocket.

As they walked slowly down the broad staircase turning in its square tower, he once or twice stopped to add a word or two. The news, he said, was also in the *Daily Mail.* An interview, it seemed, with one of the survivors. One boat had been picked up by a trawler. The sea was quite smooth. There hadn't been time to launch the other boats, or they had been drawn in and capsized in the whirlpool, when the ship finally plunged, head first, with the screw still turning in the air. One other boat was found floating keel upwards. Perhaps Jim had been in that.

This suggestion aroused Oliver, who all that time hadn't spoken a word. "No," he said quickly. "I think he must have dived from the deck, and never come to the surface."

"Why do you say that? He was a powerful swimmer. I am afraid it was a long struggle.—His thoughts may have turned to God.—May he rest in peace."

The Vicar swallowed his emotion, and they walked on in silence. They were in Grove Lane, leading down to the meadows and the barges, where a boatman would ferry them across. It was Oliver's favourite way of going to Iffley, avoiding the town as much as possible and keeping among the green fields.

"Mr. Darnley——"

"Well?"

"You'll think I've gone mad, but I must ask you a question. Is it possible for us to perceive the future, to be affected long beforehand by something that's going to happen?"

"It's an old belief; there are scattered evidences. It might be the devil. But how does it concern us? Why trouble about it now?"

"Because eight years ago, on the first day I ever saw Jim, when as yet he meant nothing to me, I had a horrible feeling that he was drowning, and I went through all the agony of it, as if it were happening to myself. It was only that he had dived from the deck, and I had no notion what a good swimmer he was, or how long a man can swim under water. Natural enough that I should have been surprised or even a bit alarmed for a moment. But why that terrible experience that seemed to last an eternity? It almost looks as if what has happened now, and what I ought to be feeling now, had been conveyed to me then by a vivid premonition. I say what I *ought* to be feeling now, because it was the full physical horror of the thing that reached me then, what an eye-witness might feel, a blind overwhelming oppression. Now that sense of physical anguish is very faint; it comes to me as knowledge not as experience; and this is a larger sorrow. I can see what it must mean to you and to Mrs. Darnley and to Rose. I can see that for me it means the end of a chapter, the end of youth. He was so marvellously young, though ten years older, that he lifted me continually out of my ruts and made me run free in the open. Yet then, when I was a boy, when I had just seen him for the first time and knew nothing about him, all this weight of loss, all this tragedy, all this passionate grief seemed to fall on me without a reason. How did that happen? Why did my feelings then exactly fit what has happened now? Is it possible that visions and sufferings should be transposed miraculously, so that one moment of life can bear the burden of another moment?"

"Who knows? The words in which we say these things may be inappropriate altogether, and to assert or to deny may be equally misleading. Yours is a large soul, Oliver, and a delicate soul: you may be sensitive to influences that escape gross observation. Perhaps magic correspondences and harmonies, vicarious punishments and penances may cross one another in the world. And what do we know of Time? In the spiritual sphere Time may not be so single and simple as we take it to be in our material concerns. It may not be a rigid succession of moments; there may be reversible circuits in it, intuitions in seven-league boots, or echoes endlessly repeated. Does not the mind of God survey all Time, and may he not infuse prophecy into us as well as memory? Yet I would not build on these possibilities. Let us leave the economy of Nature to God. In this case I suspect there is nothing miraculous. Didn't I say just now, by a mere chance, that the ship had gone down *head first*? That was hardly the right phrase, I should have said *bow* first: and perhaps that wrong word awakened in your mind the image of Jim diving, and brought back the atmosphere of that remote moment, when you had feared he was lost."

"But why should I have cared so much then? It is now that I have reason to care, and now I am calm, now I don't feel that anguish at all, now when the thing has actually happened I am indifferent. Isn't it because it's an old story, because I felt it all, exhausted it all long ago?"

The Vicar smiled, glancing at Oliver's pale face and drawn features. "My dear boy, you are not indifferent. You are deeply moved. You are not quite master of yourself for the moment. You are not hardened to such blows. We old people have suffered so many, that even the worst and the most sudden is deadened, merely sends a new tremor through the dull mass of our soreness and ancient grief. The force of that old impression of yours—which you may exaggerate in retrospect—might be explained in a lad as sensitive as you were then. I daresay Freud could explain it. And what you call your indifference now is like my own resignation, not indifference but despair though perhaps we shouldn't call it despair, but renunciation and conformity with God's will. Jim has made you suffer a great deal for years—don't think I have not perceived it—and you have been wonderfully patient, admirably faithful. No doubt it is in your nature to be constant, charitable, considerate; yet you are austere too; and how could you forgive so many faults, disregard so many disappointments? You were more deeply attached to Jim than you have ever suspected."

They were now in sight of the Iffley tower and the roofs of the Vicarage. Oliver walked on for a while, lost in thought; but just before they reached the gate he turned to the Vicar and said slowly, with painful distinctness and difficulty:

"Yes. That is the truth. I loved him from the beginning."

III

"Ah, Mr. Oliver, what a house you come to, all in ruins. My only boy, my first-born child, why should the curse have fallen upon him? How was he ever to blame? The sweetest child as ever was, the strongest child. He would tear his new pinafores to pieces, and his boots never lasted him a month, even with nails in them. Such a lovely midshipman, too, as he made afterwards, such a gallant boy, with his brass buttons and dirk and white gloves, and his white cap cocked over one ear. But the curse caught him there too. What fault was it of his if he obeyed orders and joined that *Thunderer* ship in that one voyage when there was foulness in the wind? And why should the mischief have been aired and punished then, and at no other time? It was an evil fate, Mr. Oliver, that pursued him, to drag him down to the poor man's level, to be a wanderer without friends, to work his way up from the very bottom, and when at last he got his honest standing in the Naval Reserve, and now with this dreadful war in the Navy again, which was the dream of his life, to perish at once, to be the first to go down, not to leave us even his dead body, that we might mourn over it and bury it. To float cold and stark in the green water, Mr. Oliver, and be devoured by sharks; it's the poor sailor's end. He should have lived like a gentleman and died like a gentleman; he had the right, because of his father. But the curse stood over him, because of me. He should have had another mother, he should have had another mother."

When Mrs. Darnley, on seeing Oliver, had begun her lamentations, the Vicar and Rose had quickly disappeared. They had heard those lamentations already; and poor Oliver was left alone to endure the strain and attempt to dry the old woman's tears. He had come to like her, to feel more comfortable in her company than in that of the rest of the household; her volubility relieved him in his habitual silence; it was picturesque; a simple sense for realities, a primitive honesty, underlay it. She maintained towards him obstinately the attitude of an old servant, persisted in calling him *Mr.* Oliver in spite of his protests, and allowed herself a certain crudity of speech, and certain innuendoes incompatible with playing the lady. In spite of his own delicacy, he was grateful to her for that. He could talk to her as if she were a man: the hard facts were common ground between them. Now when they were luckily alone, and she had worked herself up into a fit of sobs and of tears, he could go up to her and deliberately put his arm round her waist, as he had seen Jim do.

"But, Mrs. Darnley, consider for a moment. If he had had another mother he wouldn't have been himself, he wouldn't have been so strong or so frank, he wouldn't have known how to endure poverty and hardship, and he wouldn't have looked as he did, or had that ruddy face and those blue eyes under dark eyebrows. And what would have become of him in his troubles, if you hadn't been his mother? It was you he trusted, you he confided in, you who could understand his point of view, and could keep him straight without pestering him and moralising."

Mrs. Darnley was readily comforted. The least attention or kind-ness dispersed the clouds from her mind. She felt a warmth, a strength in Oliver's nearness which he himself was far from feeling; to his own sense he was merely groping, and trying to be as helpful as possible in a desperate case. Creature comforts, which he could command, seemed to him a dismal mockery: but to this battered old lady, who couldn't command them, they were the ultimate realities. She wiped her eyes, arranged her dress a little, picked up and slapped the cushions at one end of the sofa, to make his favourite corner fresh and comfortable for Oliver; and she sat herself down at the other end with a loud sigh, and looked like the last spurt of a shower when the sun is already shining.

"What a kind generous master your father was to my Jim," she whimpered, "treating him almost as a son, and remembering him so handsomely. Sad pity it was that you were such a young lad when that good gentleman died, and not your own master, or else in the kindness of your heart you would have kept up the yacht, with Jim for captain. You would have been so happy sailing about together, you were like two brothers, only that you should have been the elder and he the younger: you would have kept him out of a deal of trouble. It was those wicked females that ruined him, Mr. Oliver: women and gaming-tables abroad, women and the turf and the stockbrokers at home. I don't expect he's left a penny: not a farthing for his poor father and mother of all that mint of money that passed through his hands; not a farthing for his poor sister, not a farthing for that stray brat of his, as he had no business to bring into this world."

Sobs and tears, though less violent than before, here threatened to stop the flow of Mrs. Darnley's recollections: but she controlled herself, changed, as it were, the stops of her organ, and struck a new tune.

"At least you, Mr. Oliver, will be spared. There's that advantage now in being an American. They can't drag you into this wicked war, not with all their picture-posters and conscription that they say will have to come in the end. Our young men will drop like apples in a wet year in the orchard, some green and some ripe and some rotten and each with an iron worm in him. But it's a blessing that you're safe, and can live to enjoy your good fortune and to help and comfort us who are struck down, as I'm sure you always will."

Oliver hated allusions to his money and to his being an American, as if that divorced him from mankind; he was unhappy about the dubious privilege of not having to fight and not wishing to fight: and he wondered if he was really destined to live longer on that account.

"I may never live to be as old as Jim," he said, rising from the sofa, and picking up his hat and stick. "Besides, it's not those who live longest who enjoy life most, or who do most good. I should be glad to die now, if I could find something to die for. These poor recruits are told that they will be dying for their country. That's sheer cant. Nobody knows whether he's doing his country any good by dying for it, or whether his country is better worth dying for than any other. And what is one's country, anyhow? A piece of land? How is a piece of land in danger? Institutions and ideas? But institutions and ideas are always changing; by dying to preserve one set you will be creating another; and there will be less that you could care for in the world after you than there was before. It's a blind current that sweeps us on, we don't know for how long or to what issue."

Mrs. Darnley, who couldn't follow Oliver's thought, was impressed by his sadness, and pleased by it, because it was a tribute to Jim's attractions and ill-rewarded merits. "Indeed, indeed," she sighed, "it's too true. Isn't this house set in a churchyard? Young and old are struck down alike, and when it's not war, it's cancer and consumption and fever and ague. This is a wretched world, Mr. Oliver, a wretched world: and the worst of it is, that nobody can live in it for ever."

As he crossed the garden he saw Rose sitting on the grass under a tree, with her dog and a book, and he went up to her to say good-bye.

"You're not staying to luncheon?" she observed, noticing the stick in his hand and the determined air with which he looked towards the gate.

"Not to-day. It only rubs the sore to keep talking about Jim; and to talk of other things is worse: it's ghastly. I'm going for a walk." And he nodded in the direction of the river.

"To Sandford?"

"Possibly."

"You know Mrs. Bowler isn't there?"

"Not there? How's that?"

"She has left the inn—has run away—is living with a young farmer at Bicester."

Oliver stood silent while several quick thoughts passed through his mind. How did Rose guess his intentions? How did she hear all this low gossip? How had she, so youthful and so pure in aspect, the coolness to repeat it? As to Mrs. Bowler, to run away with some young ruffian when she must be nearly forty, was just what he would have expected of her. Perhaps it was as well that Jim would never hear of it. But what was to become of Bobby? Then he said aloud:

"The King's Arms is closed?"

"No. Mr. Bowler is carrying on as usual. They say he is suing for a divorce, and will get the licence transferred to his own name."

"And who will have the custody of the child? The 'father'?"

"Presumably." Rose smiled imperceptibly: there was an expression of sly amusement in her eye, yet her air in general was serenity itself. She seemed no ordinary human being, no innocent young girl. She understood everything, saw everything, foresaw everything.

"You were going to ask Mrs. Bowler, weren't you, not to take Bobby away from his nice school; because the unknown person who had been paying for his education through Jim would now continue to pay for it directly?"

"No," Oliver replied a little ruffled by so much calm divination. "I was going to explain that Jim was my oldest friend, that we had had no secrets from one another, that I knew he had been helping her to send Bobby to school, and that in his memory I should be glad to go on helping, or even to be responsible for Bobby's education altogether, so that in a year or two, when he is old enough, he should be ready to enter a naval college."

"Quite so. We all knew that this was what Jim wanted, and what you wanted; but do you suppose that anybody believed those two hundred pounds, or little less, came out of Jim's pocket? And who could the anonymous friend be but you? So that the fiction about taking Jim's place and carrying on his kind benefactions is entirely useless; although I daresay Mrs. Bowler would have been pleased, and might have adopted it for her version of Gospel truth. But with Mr. Bowler you needn't mince matters. If you offered bluntly to take the boy off his hands, and make a gentleman of him, Mr. Bowler would jump at it; except that when he saw your interest in Bobby's future, he might require some slight compensation for losing his son's services, as very soon the lad will be old enough to drive a market-cart, or to help wash the glasses in the bar."

"But Rose!" Oliver exclaimed, forgetting Jim entirely, and Bobby and his own projects. "How did you ever learn about such things? How can you talk like an old withered cynic, like somebody tired of observing and dissecting the world for fifty years? Is this the sort of thing they teach you at the Abbey School?"

"Most of the teachers there are simple souls enough. I may have picked up something from the girls. But it's a great lesson, Oliver, to be poor, to be practically an only child, to have a mother who belonged to the humbler classes, and a father with a profound knowledge of the heart, and no fear of the world and no respect for shams—not even in religion. I have seen a good deal, I have heard a good deal, that most nice girls don't see or hear. It doesn't seem strange to me that things should be as they are. It seems sad, but natural."

Did he, or didn't he like this uncanny knowingness in Rose? Was it a canker in her, the blight of a too early frost, or was it a rare spiritual gift, a mystic elevation above those ordinary mechanical humble offices of life which she performed so willingly and with such exquisite simplicity? Perhaps it was a mixture of both, or some secret of nature peculiar to her person. He was about to leave her, while thinking so hard about her, when she detained him.

"If Bobby is to go into the Navy, don't you think it would be better to separate him altogether from the Bowlers, to change his name and to let him belong entirely to us? It would be pleasanter for him in the gun-room, and even in the ward-room, if he didn't figure as the son of a publican."

"And of a sinner," Oliver added under his breath.

"Yet it isn't possible for you to adopt him legally or give him your name. You are too young; your people in America wouldn't like it; and he would then become an American too, and the British Navy would be out of the question. What you would wish, I suppose, is that he should be exactly like Jim, only more fortunate. The suitable person to adopt the boy is my father. He would be glad to do so, and I would look after him: see to his clothes and manners and all that, when he came home for the holidays. He is a nice little boy, less like Jim than when he was younger; promises to be taller and darker, and very good looking: all he needs is a change of surroundings. And my father could arrange the business of adoption more easily than you. They would show some respect to his age and to his cloth. They would acknowledge his moral claims and the naturalness of his interest; but with you they would be grasping and suspicious, merely thinking you rich and not understanding your motives. Leave it to us. You needn't appear in the case at all—except to make the whole thing possible."

She saw as she spoke that Oliver's face became gradually blank, that the wind was taken out of his sails, that he no longer glanced intermittently towards the river, but was looking at vacancy, and his somewhat owl-like eyes seemed to be blinded.

"I am so sorry," she added, really pitying him, "I am so sorry if this disappoints you. Bobby will know that he owes everything to you. He is affectionate, as Jim was; he already looks up to you as a wonderful distant paragon, a sort of deity; and he will not be un-grateful. If you took exclusive charge of him, what would you do with him when he was not at school or at sea? You would send him to us here. What difference does it make? Here you will find him, if you care to see him."

It was not in the direction of Sandford that Oliver turned when he let the churchyard gate close of itself behind him. He walked absent-mindedly back to Oxford. What else was there for him to do? Only to return to Duke Humphrey's Library, re-open his Greek folio, let his eyes rest at intervals on the greenery of Exeter Garden, and wonder how long the war would last.

It lasted indefinitely; it became for the callous a sort of normal climate, as war has always been for a great part of mankind; but for the sensitive like Oliver, nurtured in luxurious peace, and taught to think of all conflicts and contradictions as unnecessary and perverse, this long siege—so much shorter than that of Troy—seemed an eternity. The strain, instead of growing habitual and unconscious, mounted into an agony. His own inaction became intolerable. He must do something, must take part somehow in the work if not in the quarrel, in the danger, if not in the victory, dubious and almost impossible as any victory seemed.

He tried going to France and driving a motor-ambulance. Mario's friends Boscovitz and Street were doing it. Mario himself had been wounded, had recovered, had gone back to the front, and had left his apartment in Paris at Oliver's disposal. But Oliver himself began not to be well. France was disagreeable to him, and the language refractory. If he spoke at all, he wished to speak correctly; his pride and his love of rightness rejected scornfully the grotesque approximations that satisfied his American friends, and seemed to serve their crude purposes. The native women he found sly, the men false, and both avaricious. Moreover, the constant sight of the dead and wounded, when it did not turn his stomach or make his head swim, cut cruelly into his conscience. He couldn't throw off the sense of indignation, the perpetual rebellion of his reason against so much folly, so much suffering, so much unmitigated wickedness at the source of this carnage. He became nervous, sleepless, emaciated. The doctors ordered a rest. He must retire somewhere beyond the sound of guns and Zeppelins, and recover his nerve.

He retired to Oxford or rather to Iffley, with that instinct for self-imitation, for repetition, which was so deep in him. He couldn't fight, he couldn't study, he couldn't be of any use. "Yes," Mr. Darnley had observed, "you may be of some use, even while recuperating your strength here. Court Place is to let. Take it and turn it into a home for convalescent officers who have no domicile in England, for Canadians, for instance. You can easily put up ten or a dozen; and you needn't live with them; you can live here in the Vicarage, and merely keep an eye on the establishment next door. Rose will help you. She is an excellent housekeeper."

Yes, he could do that. It was merely a question of money; and money, Oliver said to himself bitterly, which personally he cared so little for and felt to be such a burden, was really his only strong point. If he hadn't been rich, he would have been a cipher. What a wrong, what a shame, when his mind was full of sound knowledge, carefully sifted, and his heart bursting with the desire to do good, to abolish injustice, to diffuse happiness! Why this strange impotence? Ah, how should it be possible to do good when you haven't discerned the good, or to abolish injustice when you're not sure what would be just, or to diffuse happiness when you have never tasted it? Moralists and reformers were like doctors for the dying: they might have a good bedside manner, and write excellent prescriptions. But the future belonged to the healthy, who didn't need doctors. Poor Oliver felt that he wasn't one of them. His body might be strong enough, but his soul had been born crippled. He was like Cousin Caleb Wetherbee turned inside out.

The establishment at Court Place worked on like other war-work, clumsily, extravagantly, dishearteningly; yet a gap was filled, some good was probably done, and the tact and discernment of young Rose kept mischief within bounds, and brought some order out of chaos. The young men from overseas, took their ease in their inn: they had their bills for extra whiskey and brandy sent to the establishment; some, who thought themselves fine fellows, left their signed photographs, dedicated to Miss Rose Darnley: and one even wrote to Oliver to thank him for his hospitality. They reminded him a little of his friends at the Great Falls School or at Williams College: but they seemed somehow commoner and more rowdy: or was it that his own perceptions were sharpened, that he had grown supersensitive and over-critical? However, he wasn't obliged to frequent their society; and soon he lost sight of them altogether. The United States came into the war, there was conscription, and it became his duty to go home and enlist.

The months he now spent in America passed like a hypnotic interlude. He lived somnambulistically, calmer than before in spite of all the agitation around him, and content in his conscience, though now actually an accomplice in the crime and folly which his conscience condemned. For now it was a case of *force majeure*; he was carried along by the stream; and his own action and fate became a spectacle to his deeper mind, as unaccountable and unintended as the revolution of the heavens. Besides, he was too busy to think, too tired to dream. Whether it was his native air, more "bracing," as they said, than the softness of England or France, or a reversion to his adolescence, when earnestness about athletic training and team-work had possessed him as a matter of course, he threw off his "depression," as again they called it, and the insolubility of all ultimate problems ceased to be agonising.

When a private at first in the ranks, and soon in various more responsible posts, he realised how exactly war was like football. He remembered all the false reasons which his mother and other high-minded people used to give to justify that game: that it was good for the health, or for young men's morals, or for testing and strengthening character; whereas he knew by experience that after the playing season every blackguard was as much, or twice as much, a blackguard as before, every sneak a sneak and every rake a rake. So now the same outsiders apologised for this war, saying that poor Serbia had been outraged, or poor Belgium invaded, or the *Lusitania* sunk; all of which might be grounds for resentment. Yet the soldier feels no resentment—except perhaps against his own officers—and has suffered no wrong. He simply hears the bugle, as it were for the chase; endures discipline, when once he is caught in the mesh, because he can't help it; and fights keenly on occasion, because war is the greatest excitement, the greatest adventure in human life. Just so, in little, football had been an outlet for instinct, and a mock war. The howling crowds were stirred vicariously by the same craving for rush and rivalry, and were exactly like the public in time of war, cheering each its own side. Oliver, in his secret mind, perfectly perceived all these pathetic but normal necessities; and he could acquiesce in them with a smile, because the physical man in him was engaged healthily, and seemed to move in unison with the world. It was a comfort to run in harness, and to wear blinkers, fatigue shutting out the irrelevant prospect on one side, and public opinion shutting it off on the other.

His mother received him warmly. Never had she been so cheerful about him as now, when he was about to run an appreciable risk of death. He had come back to his duty: he was doing what it was right for every young man to do: he was discarding at last that fatal proclivity to waste his life abroad, as his father had done; and he would now disprove that ill-natured prophecy of his uncle Nathaniel's that he was destined to *Peter out.*

All old ladies, unless they were lachrymose pacifists, were furious patriots: and if Mrs. Alden's sturdy patriotism made things easy for Oliver at that moment, it made them unbearable for the unfortunate Irma. The war, so long as America was out of it, had filled her with romantic pride: how magnificently Germany had swept every frontier, even the sea, and what a glorious, pure, idealistic future awaited the world under German guidance. True, in America as in other places, some misinformed persons might not wish to be guided: it was because they hadn't yet developed their sense for spiritual grandeur; it would be awakened in them when their education and philosophy had been more thoroughly Germanized. But now, with the United States at war, and her own beautiful Oliver going to battle against the army of light, her distress was extreme. Oliver himself tried to comfort her, to reassure her. He praised the Germans, acknowledged how faithfully they had carried out the maxims of their philosophy: the categorical imperative, and the will to dominate; how manfully they had risen to what they believed was the call of Providence. But all this glory was impossible without enemies: the greater the opposition vanquished, the nobler the victory; and Irma must not take it too hard if circumstances had placed him on the side of the non-Germans. Most human beings must be non-Germans; and, if he had happened to be born in Germany, he would no less faithfully have fought on that side.

It was a terrible tragedy, Irma reflected: but in the very horror of it there was something sublime. She was draining the cup of conflicting emotions to the dregs, and touching the deepest depths and the highest heights of experience. What a privilege! In regard to Oliver, therefore, she found some hard, stern, bitter consolations, and could nerve herself, like him, to be heroic. But who could put up with Mrs. Alden? Not one lie about the Germans that she didn't believe; not one victory of theirs that she didn't minimise; not one presage of victory that she didn't ridicule. With America in the contest, she said, the issue was settled. Oliver would march up Unter den Linden at the head of his regiment; the Kaiser would be dethroned and a peaceful German republic would be established on the model of the American Constitution.

"Ignorant, selfish, bigoted old woman," Irma would mutter between her teeth, in unintelligible German; but the strain was too great, and she resolved heroically to punish Mrs. Alden by leaving her. It was a great sacrifice made in honour of her country, because Mrs. Alden would now revoke the legacy she had assigned to Irma in her will: but perhaps Oliver would pay it notwithstanding. Anyhow he would never let her starve; unless indeed the Germans on conquering the United States, deprived him of his property, or the consequences of defeat brought on a revolution and absolute communism. But even that risk was worth running. She was proud to be reckless in these heroic times, and she intrepidly sailed away to Göttingen in a safe Dutch steamer.

Mrs. Alden, indignant but not surprised at the ingratitude of foreigners, was compelled to ask Letitia Lamb to come and keep house for her. Poor Letita herself was far from young and not very strong: but she was single: the selfish girl hadn't had the devastating experiences that fall upon a wife and mother; she might still last for a few years, and at any rate she wasn't a German.

These feminine echoes of the war fell rather indifferently upon Oliver's ears: they only confirmed a mild despair at the bottom of his mind. But he had other peep-holes through the Leviathan's hide, as if Jonah could have looked out through the eyes of his whale. For one thing, he had letters from Mario, long and frequent letters; for Vanny had been wounded a second time: "seriously," as he had at first written, but the word *seriously* had been scratched out, and the word *severely* substituted. His arm—his left arm—was smashed at the elbow, not an accident when flying; he had never had trouble in the air; but a stray fragment from a shell dropped on the aerodrome. An amputation wasn't thought necessary; but probably certain movements of the arm would become impossible, and he might never be able again to pilot his machine. *Tant pis.* Meantime, as soon as he could leave the hospital, he was returning to England for a long leave. The wound had been nasty at first, but it turned out in the end to be a five-pound one, as they called it: one of the sort that you would give five pounds to get. It would be lovely to go home— although he hadn't a home—and sit lazily in the garden, hearing the larks sing and perhaps playing a little croquet. Like returning to one's happy childhood and chasing a large rubber ball, painted in such pretty colours. Yet he hoped to recover in time to go back to the front before the finish. If only they finished well, squarely and fairly, without any illusions about the future. This should be the third Punic war indeed, but with Prussia in the part of Carthage. Germany should revert to its natural self—a mass of free cities and small principalities, without a Kaiser or an army.

Not having a home, he would go to Oliver's establishment at Iffley for his convalescence. Pity Oliver wasn't there. They must go round the world again, a different world, after the war. In the leisure, not to say boredom, of Iffley, in the care of Oliver's friends and in his invisible presence, there was plenty of time and provocation for this correspondence.

Last night, Mario wrote in one letter, I went to a coming-of-age dinner at Magdalen, and your ears must have burned at the time: because there were two Harvard men there who sang your praises and said the professors thought you had a great mind. I suppose you made them think that you agreed with their opinions. There was also a very pale and sallow ghost with an inaudible voice, like a dead leaf stirred by the wind. They say he is a master of insinuation, and has invented a new way of writing history, by suggesting everywhere the nasty things that might have happened, only they didn't. He lives in Oscar Wilde's old rooms, romantically overlooking the Cher, as if it were the moat of his castle; but they warned me not to mention this circumstance, because the name of Oscar Wilde was taboo in that circle. "In that case," I said, "they dislike insinuations." "Good Lord," cried my friend, "it's not that. Nobody minds that nowadays. But they abhor Oscar Wilde's rhetoric. They consider *The Picture of Dorian Gray* mid-Victorian, middle-class, melodramatic, and worm-eaten with morality; just what Dickens might have written if he had known about bric-a-brac and Greek love and had had no sense of humour."

After dinner I stopped to have a half-bottle of soda-water in the coffee room of the King's Arms, where I was spending the night in your honour, as I couldn't very well get to Iffley at that hour. I had ordered my drink, when I spied at another small table, a rather languid and wriggly young cleric, having what looked like camomile. My eye couldn't help resting affectionately on the large round white pot, so like that in which my mother and I always had our *camomille* at the *rue de Saint Simon*. The youthful clergyman was also eyeing me, evidently not with disapproval: and finally he hemmed and hawed a little and then burst out in a suppressed gasp:

"*Would* you perhaps like a cup of camomile, better than your cold soda-water? It's such a *warming* drink."

"Really," I replied with *nonchalance*, seeing that he invited familiarity, "I rather think I should. Clever of you to see that I was tempted. It was always our night-cap in France when I was a child."

"But aren't you English?"

"Yes and no: I'm in the army, but my father was an American and my mother an Italian."

There was a long pause, and I offered him a cigarette which he accepted. Then he burst out again in an explosive way, dying down in a *diminuendo*: "But if your mother was an Italian, you must be a Cah-tholic?"

"Yes: but I'm afraid I've lost my faith."

"I'm sorry to hear that," said the poor young man gasping, pressing his joined hands between his knees, and gazing upwards in prayer.

"And you have become a Protestant?" he ventured less in hope than in fear.

"Sir," I replied, looking at him severely and trying to be as crushing as Dr. Johnson, "I said I had lost my faith, not my reason."

He wilted, squirmed, and at the same time chirped "Hee hee" in evident delight. He had theoretically convinced himself that he too was a Cah-tholic, yet he couldn't help knowing that practically he was a Protestant. It was a ticklish predicament.

"But do you mean," he added after some apparently hard thinking, "that you wouldn't go to mass to-morrow?"

"To-morrow? Is it a Sunday? No: I hadn't thought of it. I hardly ever go."

"But isn't it a *mortal sin*?"

"I suppose it is: or venial at least. But I have so many on my conscience."

"I'm sorry to hear that."

Again there was a long pause, an agitated pause, as my friend's mind was evidently divided between the pleasure of smoking my gold-tipped aromatic cigarette and the pain of contemplating my damnation.

"I say," he finally whispered desperately, "if I went to mass with you to-morrow, would you come?"

"Really, it's very kind of you. Certainly, I'll go if you like."

"Very well," he answered smiling, as if the heavens had cleared. "But where's the Roman Mission church? Shall we be able to find it?"

At least, though I didn't frequent it, I knew it was somewhere behind St. Giles: and we agreed to meet in the morning before breakfast, and find our way to it.

As we did so the next day, the poor dear man looked nervously over one shoulder and then over the other.

"I hope I'm not being observed. My Bishop wouldn't like it. He wouldn't know that I've been to our own Early Communion Service already!"

At breakfast afterwards, he having apparently escaped observation and I having avoided a mortal sin, we were both in a cheerful frame of mind, and became confidential. I explained who I was and my experiences in the army.

"I, too," he murmured, "am seriously thinking of going to the front. Oh, not as a combatant. Oh, no. But they have offered me a chaplaincy in one of the new regiments. I have nothing to do. I've no pay. My brother had given me a family living, but he has taken it from me. I am considering that chaplaincy in Flanders, seriously considering it. It's nineteen shillings a day, and the eyes of the whole world are fixed upon Flanders."

I advised him strongly to accept that offer, such a chance to do penance, to assist the dying, and to warn Tommy Atkins not to fall into mortal sin. I assured him that it wasn't in the least cowardly merely to do hospital work instead of actually firing guns or throwing hand-grenades. He would share the danger. Shells were almost as likely to hit him pottering about in the rear as if he were in the trenches.

"I'm sorry to hear that," he murmured seriously perplexed. I could see that those nineteen shillings a day had lost half their lustre.

When I left him he seemed labouring under suppressed emotion. "My name," he said hesitatingly, in his explosive and evanescent voice, "my name is *Fulleylove—Robin* Fulleylove—the *Reverend* Robin Fulleylove." On his feet he seemed taller and better built than you would have thought at first, seeing him crumpled up in a chair, wriggling and gasping: and we parted with mixed feelings of affection and hopelessness.

Another day Mario wrote:

Who do you suppose sailed into this garden yesterday, waving the white muffler he always wears draped as if it were a tartan, and shouting "Congratulate me, congratulate me?" Cooly—Lord Basil Kilcoole, you know, who has those aesthetic rooms over mine in Peckwater. This garden, by the way, is the Vicar's, and not Court Place; because your fair friend Rose has most kindly set out your own wicker chair and your own work-table for my benefit under your favourite tree, so that I needn't breathe the thick atmosphere of wounded heroism all day and all night on the other side of the hedge: and I always sit here, weather permitting. Here too, and even more pleasantly, I feel that I am your guest and under your shadow, profiting by your merits and being smiled upon for your sake. This is one reason why I can't help writing you these frequent interminable letters that perhaps bore you, all about trifles, when questions of life and death are wracking your strategic mind. I say strategic, because now that you have to be a soldier, I'm sure at least you will soon be a general. But my dear Oliver, life and death are always in the balance: it's tiresome to trouble about them, or to watch anxiously how the needle wavers. The way it turns wouldn't after all matter, if there were none of these pleasant trifles to fill our lives while we live. Therefore, drop your strategy, and listen to the rest of my silly story.

"Very well," I said. "I congratulate you. But what about?"

"It's a boy."

"Hello. I didn't know you were married."

"I'm not married. I'm too young." Cooly is always referring to his extreme youth, but I happen to know that he is forty-three, and dyes his long hair a bright coppery auburn. He has one of those scrawny bony frames which don't vary much with age; he goes about hatless in all weathers, is a great mountain-climber, and keeps his high complexion apparently quite youthful—at a distance—by dint of hard exercise and constant fresh air.

"Well," I said, "I didn't know you were in the family way."

"Don't be an ass. It's not my child. It's my brother's. You know he had only daughters; and as he was foolish enough to join in this absurd war, though we Irish are neutrals, just because years ago he had been in the Guards, of course he was killed, and the bally title would have fallen on me— Danduffy—they would have called me Danduffy, and taken from me this lovely name, Basil Kilcoole—by which I wish to be known to posterity. Because luckily my sister-in-law was expecting another child, and if it had been a fifth girl, Danduffy I should have been all my life long, through the tyranny of His Majesty's Office of Heralds. But the Lord has had pity on me and it's turned out a boy. That infant organism is now the Marquis of Danduffy; and if the brat lives, I am saved. That's why I say, Congratulate me, Congratulate me."

"But what difference does your name make, and how are you to be known at all to posterity if you never publish your poetry?"

"Publish?" he hissed in mock loathing. "How should I *publish* anything? My verse is never written down. To nail a verse down on a page is to murder it. Don't you remember your *Phaedrus*? And if no living philosophy can ever be found in a book, how much less any living poetry. Homer never wrote anything. Socrates never wrote anything. Christ never wrote anything. St. Francis never wrote anything. And why should I materialise my spirit, and spatialise my melodies, by vilely imprisoning them in a chain of letters? Letters are fetters. I breathe my inspirations, I utter them; and those who have ears to hear may retain and report my words. Or if they don't exactly report them, but fetch a new inspiration, as St. Paul did, from the mere echo of a rumour of the divine word, so much the better. They will sing their own songs under my name, and I shall be singing a new song through their throats forever."

"Very pretty," I observed, "but my throat is dry. Let's go and have some tea."

One of Cooly's peculiarities is that he is very stingy, and loves to be invited to tea. I suspect that his artistic treasures are of his own manufacture, because he is a painter as well as a poet, and a painter in various styles. He can do Corots to the life, and his Byzantine madonnas might be sold for genuine, while he frescoes drawing-rooms in the styles of Tiepolo and of Watteau, and his fans, indistinguishable from Conder's, fetch a high price in Bond Street. Yet ninepence seems to him too much for tea; and he wears the same rough corduroys and Norfolk jackets for years. The idea of tea at my expense accordingly put him in good humour and he moved toward the Isis Inn with a stride worthy of Achilles.

"If you never write down your inspirations, Cooly, aren't you afraid of forgetting them, or of getting them mixed up and spoilt?"

"Yes," he replied wistfully. "I often don't know whether something that's running through my head is a line of Shakespeare's or an early one of me own. For instance, at this moment I am inwardly hearing the words: *Perpetual liars that deceive us never.* Is that line anybody's I wonder?"

"Oh yes: you've cribbed it from La Fontaine."

"Why question who said it first? It's a chameleon. Perhaps it was French once. Now it is English. Perhaps it only meant that too much lying defeats itself: a copy-book platitude. Yet it has come to mean that our inspirations themselves, in the guise of endless illusion, may lead us mystically to the heart of truth."

You remember those two poplars at the entrance to that little tea garden? They were particularly solemn and graceful that afternoon, swaying in the breeze, now intertwining and now separating their branches, as if two green spires all composed of pinnacles, like Saint Mary's, had begun to dance, locking arms and touching cheeks in time to the windy music. "If my Latin weren't so rusty," I said to Cooly, "and my Greek so inadequate, I should compose an epigram about those two poplars. Quite classic, that straightness of theirs, that amplitude, that murmur, and that sadness."

Cooly tossed his dyed plumes, as a bird does when drinking, and showed for a moment above his loose low collar a prodigious Adam's apple, moving up and down. The man actually seemed inspired, only, for a lyric Apollo he is rather a barebones, and looks too much like Abraham Lincoln. After a moment he began chanting:

> "*Ambigua Zephyro Geminae dum fronde susurrant*
> *cedit ab immemori muta sorore soror.*"

"Hear, hear," I cried, "but please say it again. In Latin you have a slight English brogue. I'm not sure I've caught it all."

"Impossible, impossible. Not good enough. Not worth remembering. But I'll say it in English."

Again Apollo shook his ambrosial locks, again Adam's apple moved up and down, and the words flowed irresistibly:

> "*Poplars, twin sisters, whispering side by side:*
> *The winds unite them, and the winds divide.*"

"Really, *mes compliments*. But the modern version is not quite faithful. There is more and less in it than in the original."

"Inevitably," he rejoined, still liturgically and under the spell of the Muse. "Poetry can never say the same thing twice."

"Granted. But will you explain this. Why is your English epigram classical and your Latin epigram romantic?"

"Because," he replied without the least hesitation, "when we move upward from chaos, we aspire towards truth, perfection, and simplicity; but when we reflect and turn inwards from the highest achievement, we find sorrow and disillusion and a murmur of the winds."

V

When Oliver received these letters he had already landed in France with his regiment, and was completely enmeshed, not yet in barbed wire, but in the endless tangle of preparations and allocations and training. Sometimes he would be doing office work at Bordeaux; sometimes he would be superintending some movement of troops: or tracing lost supplies; or cutting down trees in the Landes; or soaking and shivering in a dreary camp; or waiting for orders in some stray village, and quartered among natives more or less friendly, more or less acquisitive. There was as yet no great hardship or danger, yet the constant worry, the constant friction, the constant discomfort had a cumulative effect on his nerves. He had been born, as they say, with a silver spoon in his mouth. His athletic discipline, though strict and persistent, had always had a background of luxury to relieve it; always plenty of hot water and clean linen and comfortable beds and good food and perfect accessories and every aid that medicine or money could afford. Moreover, his asceticism hitherto had always been voluntary: he had been, more than other boys, his own master from the beginning, and either captain in his games, or able to question his leaders, or threaten to retire altogether from the sport and leave them in the lurch. But now he was a slave: his superiors were strangers, older and coarser and more ignorant than himself. He was without friends and without enthusiasm. Moreover, he was accustomed to shine, to be admired, to be held up as a model: and here, though it was admitted that he did his work well, and was thoroughly to be depended upon, he seemed to be one of a thousand, a name with a number to it, less remarked, because less pushing, than many another nobody. A reason for this submergence of the young hero, who had always been on the top, was that he was no longer well, no longer strikingly young and agile and handsome. Weary, faded, slow, he seemed even to himself when he looked in the glass: and the authorities were annoyed at his frequent illnesses. He was always suffering from coughs and colds, sleeplessness, or dyspepsia; and it became a positive comfort when a bad bronchitis or diarrhœa, with an unmistakable fever, sent him to the hospital. There, in bed, he could wait patiently for the doctor, on his morning and evening round; for long intervals, between the spells of his malady, he could sleep or he could rest. He craved rest, a complete rest, a prolonged rest.

Yet rest, for the present, was denied him. He would recover, and would return to his post. During one convalescence, noticing how moody he looked, his superiors sent him to Paris, to amuse himself for a fortnight. The *ville lumière* then kept very dark vigils; even at its gayest it had never dazzled him. He could admit the truth of what Vanny said of it, that nowhere else were so many different things agreeable to human nature set before you with so much art and discretion. But Oliver did not relish delights: he demanded something to build upon, sound principles and sure possessions. Even in matters of taste, Paris annoyed him. He hated the Place de la Concorde and the Champs Elysées, the boulevards and the Opéra. He liked only the quays along the river, the long lines of slanting trees with the hanging screen of their branches, the barges, the shining water. It was an old story that he had a transcendental mind, like a duck's back: it shed and rejected everything that merely happened to flow by. Nothing existed for him save that which his moral tentacles were ready to seize. Now, however, he discovered that this vital principle had an unexpected corollary: not only did he scorn delights, but he found laborious days intolerable. Work when it was exercise, when it was art and free adventure, he loved and bloomed in: but casual, servile, imposed work was crippling and wasteful. It destroyed its instrument, it destroyed his soul; and he very much doubted whether the social engine that required it served any good purpose.

Little as he liked Paris Oliver was now glad to be there. After his walk from Notre Dame to the Trocadéro, or his quarter chicken and salad at a neighbouring Duval, he could sit comfortably by the fire at the *rue de Saint Simon*, reading or dozing. Vanny was again at the front, not with his old Flying Corps, because he was no longer able to use his left arm freely, but in Italy, as a *liaison* officer with Lord Cavan's British division, being marked as hardly anyone else was for the post by his fluent knowledge of Italian. There was comparatively little danger in that position, and much distinction and contact with commanding officers. Vanny was a lucky dog. That seemed to Oliver the one bright spot in the prospect. Unfortunately it shone at a great remove from himself, far away geographically and far away morally.

He had no need of ingratiating himself with superior officers or shining in the great world. He was merely waiting for the war to be over, so as to return to Great Falls, or perhaps to Williamstown, and become a professor of philosophy or of history: at least he supposed they wouldn't refuse his services if he offered them gratis. Evidently there were people born to succeed in this world, and people born to fail. Mario belonged to the first set and he, Oliver, to the second.

Lost in these melancholy reflections he wasn't sure, one evening, whether he had heard a knock on the door; but he said *"Entrez."*

The old *bonne* Félise came in noiselessly, shut the door behind her, and spoke in a distinct whisper, almost in Oliver's ear, so that he might understand her French.

"There is a lady who wishes to speak to *Monsieur*. It is the *Baronne.*"

"Who?"

"The *Baronne*, the *Baronne du Bullier*, they call her. A friend of Mr. Mario's, an old friend. I explained that Mr. Mario is absent. She seemed struck by lightning. I explained that the young gentleman here was Monsieur the cousin of Mr. Mario. 'What?' cried the Baronne. 'Another young man? A cousin of Mr. Mario? Announce me instantly. I must speak with the cousin of Mr. Mario.' And *voilà.*" The old woman shrugged her shoulders, cocked her head so that it almost lay on her right shoulder, rolled her eyes, and raised both her hands in deprecation. She knew the Baronne. She knew her only too well. She knew that the Baronne came to beg for money. Her dumb show was intended to convey this confession, together with her own helplessness to prevent such exactions. She would like to protect her young master, but how could she? In reality she had reason to hope that if the Baronne was satisfied, *cent sous* or even ten francs might percolate into her own pocket. The Baronne, when she had money, was not ungenerous.

Meantime the closed door had opened as if by magic and a beautiful person, in aristocratic black, had appeared on the threshold.

"Pardon me, Sir," said the lovely stranger, with a dignity that seemed to drape some unuttered sorrow, as she advanced and made room for the old *bonne* to retire. "Pardon me if I disturb you. I thought my Mario was in Paris. I counted on him. He is so good. Never, in all my misfortunes, has he failed me." Here the Baronne sat down unasked, and nodded to Oliver to resume his seat. "Of course," she went on, "he is *volage*. He is young, he is pursued, he is a man. Men are *volages* by nature. You flutter from flower to flower.

You are not faithful, as we women are; or at least," she added with a deep sigh, "as we would wish to be. Ah, how many troubles, how many miseries! If my good Mario were here I know he would help me. He would fly to my assistance. My dear mother, Sir, is ill, gravely ill. These are her last days. Is it not enough to lose her? Is it not enough to dread, as I sit here, that perhaps at this very moment she is expiring? Must I see her suffer? She requires a fire; and wood to-day is unprocurable. She requires a cup of broth, a bit of chicken; but who to-day can pay for chicken? As for the doctor's bill, that's not so urgent. He can wait. But the pharmacist, sir, the pharmacist, alas, must be paid at once. And where shall the money come from? My friends are at the front, they are dead, they are mutilated, they are prisoners, and if any survive, who knows? With that atrocious experience of the trenches perhaps their minds are deranged. They have developed strange tastes. They have had a vision. They have undergone a conversion. They have become chaste. Ah, Sir, it is deplorable. A poor woman no longer knows where to turn." During this tirade the Baronne had been seated on the edge of a chair, on the other side of the fire. She had loosened her furs, and disclosed her bare neck, with a string of false pearls, and laces running down the front of her dress, sometimes closed and sometimes open. She had been watching Oliver: but his eyes were fixed on the fire; and when she finished, and made a dramatic pause, he seemed not to notice it. Why didn't he look at her? Why didn't he say something?

Irritated, she rose and stood nearer in front of him, and spoke in a changed tone, the tone of business transactions.

"Sir, if you would be good enough to lend me a small sum—five hundred francs, two hundred francs, one hundred francs—I am sure Mr. Van de Weyer would repay it at the first opportunity and he would thank you for having rescued a poor old friend of his from despair."

Oliver too had risen, relieved at the thought that the woman was going, and they were standing together in front of the fire. At first he had only partly understood her palaver; but no phrases were more familiar to his ear than one hundred francs, two hundred francs, or five hundred francs; and the word *prêter*, which she had used, was also one that had recurred constantly in his recent experience. Finally, her change of tone had reassured him: these were no longer vague and endless lamentations, sprinkled with lies, but a plain business proposal.

"Yes," he said, "I have no doubt that if my cousin were here he would assist you. Félise says you are old friends. I shall be very glad to give you something in his name."

Oliver habitually spoke slowly, even in English; and he was careful in French to be correct and distinct. While he composed his answer he had plenty of time to see that her eyes, large appealing eyes, were wet with tears, that her painted mouth was a little convulsed, and that her half visible bosom was heaving with genuine trouble. Nothing was more likely in itself. Who was not in trouble? How many people in this world were like him, not cramped and worried and tortured for want of money? So long as this woman had been trying to impress him, feeling that artifice, that falseness which he so abhorred, he had remained indifferent, or rather annoyed and hostile: but now that she forgot her play-acting and showed her real distress, he was touched. The sight of suffering, the knowledge of suffering, was intolerable to him; and he was not used to feminine softness. Neither his mother nor Irma, neither Edith nor Rose had ever appealed to his compassion; none of them had ever melted or trembled, or hung on him for help. And the Baronne's face, as she gradually understood that he would give her the money, had changed like a child's. She had smiled through her tears; she had made a little gesture of gratitude, of relief, of affection. He had a strange feeling, as if he himself were trembling and melting. It was absurd, disgraceful: and in order to give himself time to recover, he turned away to his desk, opened a drawer, opened another, and finally took out of his pocket-book a thousand-franc note, which he presented, folded, to the Baronne.

She instantly unfolded it, without in the least concealing her intense interest; made quite sure of its value, hid it in her dress, and looked at Oliver while her lips formed the words thank you.

This lady was far more practised in recognising the symptoms of tender emotion than Oliver in recognising the emotion itself. She instantly seized his hand. "How good you are," she exclaimed, "you have understood. You have pitied me. You have done a good action."

There was no reply. He could not speak. He made an effort to say something, but failed.

She looked at him again, intently, questioningly, knowingly. "But you are moved," she cried, clinging to him with all her strength, which was considerable, "you are overcome. You love me. You desire me. Why not say so? I should be so happy. You are so good, so strong, so young, so beautiful." With this last endearment she applied a frank warm lingering kiss to his mouth, a kiss intended to be irresistibly voluptuous and overwhelming. To her astonishment, the effect was instantly decisive in the contrary direction.

That day chanced to be a Friday. Piety and economy had united to make her observe the rules of the Church, as she did on principle, when not contrary to the exercise of her profession; and only half an hour earlier she had made a Lenten meal exclusively of sardines and cucumber salad. Now in the ardour of her sensual embrace she had caused Oliver distinctly to smell, almost to taste, both those savoury substances. A shiver of loathing had run through his whole body. If any passionate impulses, without his knowledge, had been maturing within him, they were suddenly reversed. He became a statue of ice, a pillar of granite. Meantime his mind had quickly cleared, cleared completely, with a far-reaching clearness such as they say comes to ecstatic philosophers and to drowning men. His disgust itself was only instantaneous. It was swept aside, together with his incipient cravings, by this new illumination. As the Baronne no longer tempted him, so she no longer annoyed him. He was simply sorry for her, as for the infinite miseries of mankind, and for his own miseries; not with that tremulous sympathy which he had felt at first, a sympathy that perhaps had been only disguised lust, but with a calm, just, deliberate charity, understanding all things, forgiving all things, and willingly draining the cup of truth to the dregs, as it were in atonement for the blind sin of existence. A bottomless sadness, a bottomless peace, seemed to possess him.

The poor Baronne, seeing the total change in his expression, and feeling him grown cold and stiff as a corpse, fell back in alarm. But he was not offended or ill or threatening. He could now have listened calmly to her story; he could have considered calmly how far he could help her, and how far she deserved help, or would profit by it. Even his French now was at his command: he remembered the hints Mario had given him, when once or twice they had gone together to the *Moulin Rouge* or the *Jardin de Paris*, as to how to dismiss importunate women without being rude to them. He was to thank the little person for her amiable offer, and say he was sorry, but that evening he was expecting a lady friend. Then he was to say good evening simply and add that perhaps they might meet again another day. Of course Oliver couldn't carry the politeness so far: that was only Mario's exaggerated way of putting things: but he could transfer the idea to his own level, and get out of an awkward situation kindly and with dignity.

Standing firmly and civilly at some distance he now turned to the Baronne, and explained in his best French that he expressed himself badly in that language, and had led her to misunderstand him. He had just come ill from the army, and his emotions were easily stirred at the thought of any misfortune. He had been touched by her account of her troubles and of the illness of her mother, who perhaps at that very moment was in need of her attentions. He therefore would not detain her. As to love, the troubles of the times drove all thought of it from his mind, and in any case he was not free.

"Not free? You love another?" the Baronne replied with a sarcastic smile. "I have heard that before. I daresay you are engaged to be married. But what of that? Your fiancée no doubt is in America, a thousand leagues from here. She would be brutally exacting if she expected you to be faithful in anticipation; and if you think that women really like that sort of lover, permit me to tell you that you are mistaken. But let it be as you please. It's not my affair. I thank you with all my heart for your generosity. When I see my Mario again I will tell him how much his cousin has favoured me. Good evening, Monsieur. You are too serious for me."

She found old Félise in the passage and drew her into the dining-room. "Tell me," she whispered, "who is this cousin of Mr. Mario's? Is he very rich? Is he in his senses? These Americans are so droll. He gives me a thousand francs, and he asks for nothing! Explain that to me, if you please. He must be ill. He must be mad. Or perhaps he doesn't love women. Yet for a moment I thought he was quite mellow, falling like fruit from the tree. But no. He may be tall, he may be strong, he may be generous, but he has a heart like that!" And she struck the marble chimney-piece a resounding blow with her knuckles, proving that the love of expression made her indifferent to pain, or that she had a particularly tough skin.

"Ah, Félise," she continued, "what can we do about it? *Au revoir*, my good friend, and thank you very much. To-day I haven't any change, not one *sou*; but I will remember you at New Year's. If only the New Year would bring this war to an end! And if only they don't all come home perverted or converted or mutilated or asthmatic. This is the end of the world. At last I shall have to marry some old *poilu* without arms or legs. At least he will have a pension."

VI

Oliver's lucidity did not vanish as quickly as it came, or as that vital crisis and revulsion which had caused it. It faded slowly, like the effects of splendid music or religious eloquence. He retained that insight as a sort of point of reference and high-water mark in the receding past; he knew that he had understood himself for a moment, and seen in prophecy the path that he was destined to tread. But the concrete vision was gone. His organism was too ponderous, his little duties and habits too distracting, for him to live steadily in the light. He could not keep all his organs and all his knowledge running abreast. Only some single thread of thought would remain luminous in the confused twilight of his daily routine, some one wire ignited by the casual interests of the moment. Even to keep alive these trivial or compulsory lines of thought was increasingly difficult to his blinking mind. He became doubly scrupulous about his exercise and his diet. It was his duty to nurse his health for the sake of his work, and to keep very busy, so as not to ask whether his work was worth doing.

When he reported again at headquarters, the colonel and the doctor glanced gravely at each other. "Alden, my boy," said the commanding officer, "you haven't amused yourself enough in Paris, or you've amused yourself too much. The doctor here must look you over and see what you are fit for." Obviously he was thin and sallow and tired: but his organs, if a bit sluggish, were found to be all right. Nevertheless, he couldn't sleep well at night, and seemed to be half asleep and dreaming all day. After a while, they put him again on the sick list, and sent him to a nursing home at Arcachon. It was normally the cheapest of seaside resorts, with cardboard villas and cinemas and merry-go-rounds: but there was a dull blue sea, belying the bad reputation of the Bay of Biscay; and there were vast pine plantations, crossing in endless rows the furrows and crests of the dunes. The warm sand strewn with pine-needles, the blazing sun, the solitude and the sea air certainly composed a fundamental harmony to which an ailing life might be attuned: too gross, perhaps, and too monotonous, for so high strung a being as Oliver. He could sleep better and eat more; he could lie in the thin shade of the pines, or take long walks along the sea shore; but it was a slow recuperation. The February sun was beginning to mount the heavens and become too hot in that oven, his regiment was reported to be almost ready for fighting, and the Germans for a last push, before he could, at a pinch, be pronounced capable of active service.

He had had ample time for meditation; and even without any exceptional flashes of intuition, by threading and re-threading the labyrinth of his thoughts, he had managed to come to clearness about himself and his duty.

"I told that woman that I wasn't free. Was that merely a white lie, suggested by Mario, to help me out of an awkward position? I wasn't engaged to anybody in America, as she was ready to believe. I didn't love anybody else. And yet it was profoundly true, in some sense, that I wasn't free. I wasn't telling a white lie. I was expressing a radical fact. I wasn't free; because the sort of love she expected from me is something I am held back from by my deepest nature. You might say it was the sardines and cucumbers that did it. Nonsense. When a fellow is free—I have seen it a thousand times in the army, and when we went round the world—when there is nothing in him inwardly to check his lust, little accidents like that, and even greater obstacles, filth, ugliness, danger of contagion, don't turn him back; or if they turn him back, it is by reflection, by prudence, not by pure impulse, not by a complete change of mood, as it was with me. And not for the first time, not by chance. If it hadn't been cucumbers and sardines, it would have been something else later: the repugnance, the horror, the vivid conviction that I was hugging a corpse, contradicting my own choice, outraging my own aspiration, would have come upon me in any case; if not before, after; if not as repulsion, certainly as shame. Because it is not any prejudice or maxim or external prohibition that holds me back: it's my own will. And a proof of this is that it all happened to me before, ten years ago, almost in the same form, yet when no accidents were concerned, when it was a dream hatched in my own mind entirely, and expressing only my most secret feelings. The Vicar doesn't wish me to believe in premonitions. If I told him how once in a dream Mrs. Bowler had made love to me, almost exactly as the Baronne actually did the other day, and that I had repelled her with the same disgust, he would refuse to admit that the dream had foreshadowed the reality. Very well: let it be a pure coincidence. But then it is all the more evident that the same impulses in me fashioned both experiences and made them similar; so that I could vividly react ten years ago in imagination just as I was to react the other day in fact. A mere look from Mrs. Bowler, a mere suggestion of her relations with Jim, were enough to plumb me to the depths, and show me how little hold a thousand female hypocrites or Parisian adventuresses would ever have upon me."

At other times, from the same beginning, Oliver's thoughts would take a different direction. "I said I was *not free*: but if something held me back, there must have been something else in me that impelled me forward, something that, if I had been free, would have had full course. And isn't freedom a blessing? Isn't freedom happiness? Isn't spontaneous life, when it is harmonious and pure, the most beautiful of things, and the source of all beauty? Why then not be free? Why not unearth the radical force that troubles me and that I am suppressing not without bitterness and unrest? Why not disentangle that impulse, harmonise it if possible with all the other impulses which now contradict it, and become free without being dissolute?—I ought to be married."

On the table at the rue de Saint Simon he had found a thin old volume of more or less gallant verse by some forgotten old poet: and his eye had been arrested by the following lines:

> *Stripling, rifle now the rose,*
> *tempt the perils of a kiss.*
> *Sweet heaven were as hell to those*
> *who would count the cost of bliss.*
> *From some random love like this*
> *every human kindness flows.*
> *Stripling, rifle now the rose,*
> *tempt the perils of a kiss.*

Alas, he was now no stripling, but a heavy-hearted, puzzle-headed man, poor in the midst of riches, tethered and yoked in the harness of unprofitable labour. But the word *rose* startled him. It had echoes in his personal life that seemed more than accidental. There were those petals of red roses that had fallen on his pillow when he lay crippled in the Harvard Infirmary, yet free inwardly as he had never been before or since, and confident that in Edith and Mario he had found his natural companions, for an enchantment to all his days, and a supplement to all his limitations. Now Edith was estranged voluntarily, because she preferred fashionable pretences and simpering compromises to the cold air of truth: and Mario threatened to be estranged involuntarily, by being caught in the currents of European high life, where Oliver wouldn't and couldn't follow him. And even more appealing to him now, there was his white Rose of Iffley: not a rose indeed to be rifled, not heavy with scent or tempting to every wanton bee; but a true English rose, blooming in the country hedges, simple, open, washed by the rain, with a delicate fragrance to be inhaled tenderly, and a clear beauty that would never pall, never surfeit, but could be borne for ever like a shield over the heart. No; he wouldn't follow the counsels of that old pander of a poet of Mario's, probably an unprincipled rogue and without philosophy. He wouldn't tempt any vulgar perils. His one kiss should seal his happiness, clear his mind of all poisons, dissolve the cramp within him, and make him free.

Accordingly he resolved to spend the remaining days of his leave in England, to marry Rose Darnley, and to make a will leaving her his whole fortune. Then he could go to the front with a clean conscience. Duly to prepare the way, he despatched the following letter.

MY BEAUTIFUL ROSE,

I have been ill, I have been very unhappy, I have a sort of premonition that I sha'n't live long. I don't want to leave matters between us as they stand now. I am coming next week to see you, if only for a few hours. Our regiment is moving to the front. If I had been in better health and clearer in my mind, I should have come to you before, and given you more time. Because I am not coming merely to say good-bye. I am coming to say something else that has always been in my mind. I want to ask you to marry me. Yes, to marry me now, at once, for one day only, so that I may go away with the assurance that you are mine, that our lives are joined together indissolubly, and that if I fall you will be properly provided for. So don't be surprised to see me on Tuesday, and be prepared for the wedding that afternoon. I shall have taken out the licence, and your father can marry us. The least possible ceremony the better. Do you mind? I much prefer it so. The real marriage, the wedding bells, the miracle, the joy of union, the solution to everything, the sense of having touched the zenith of life, will all be in our hearts. Until then and for ever, Your Ⓐ

VII

The Thames was in flood. Near the Varsity boathouse the water covered the tow-path, and Oliver thought he might have to turn back, and make for Iffley by road. But his heavy military boots were guaranteed waterproof, and by skirting the fences, and wading a bit here and there or risking a long jump, he reached the comparatively firm gravel beyond the Long Bridges. Those were the thickest black days of the war; Russia had collapsed, and people were waiting sullenly for that concerted attack in the West which the Germans meant to be final. Fatigue, and the sense of having endured so much, seemed to deaden fear, and to produce a dull resignation, mixed with a vague confidence that all would settle itself somehow. The mere momentum and mechanism of war continued to move the body, leaving the soul in profound apathy. Oliver trudged along, not at all in the spirit of a soldier on holiday who goes a-wooing. The sky was as leaden in his heart as it was over his head. He imbibed almost sadistically, as he walked on, the breath of that cold damp dull afternoon. He noted the empty and devastated look of the fields, where hedgerows and fences, strangely dwarfed and foreshortened by the loss of their base, stood out of the grey water like rows of imperfect crosses in a cemetery at the front. A sadness penetrated him, too restless and bitter to be called melancholy. Behind the fear that the world of yesterday was ruined and lost, lay the suspicion that it had never been worth preserving, that it had been a cruel farce and a vulgar sham. In an inundated field across the river, standing high and looking enormous in that stunted landscape, he saw a black swan. Never had he seen a black swan in Oxford before. Where did it come from? Yet there it floated alone, homeless and indolent, plunging its red beak at intervals into the calm opaque water, and seeming unconsciously to mock Oliver's most sentimental memories, which had once been hopes. How proudly, after all, how regally and blamelessly, the *Black Swan* had floated on the top of the world! How wise and kind and unassuming his father had been: a confessed failure, yet, compared with Oliver himself, a serene success. And

Lord Jim? It was three years now since he had perished; and his unmarked sailor's grave had brought a sort of rehabilitation to his image, a solution to his not too glorious career. One could now think of him at his best: the common man on a pedestal, not as wooden-headed sculptors represent the private of the rank and file, a mere dummy in uniform, but living and jolly and selfish and not ashamed of the fleshly and criminal impulses which are in every man's heart.

"What power there is," thought Oliver, almost enviously, "in that unregenerate human nature, how it survives, how fertile it is, how all our admired refinements and heroisms hang upon it! What force but Lord Jim's is leading me at this moment along this slimy path, perhaps on a last pilgrimage before my own end, to take counsel with his father and to marry his sister?"

The low square tower of Iffley Church was now visible amongst the globular tree-tops; and as Oliver looked up, about to quicken his pace, something at once strange and familiar, expected yet not expected there, arrested his eye. In the garden of the lock-keeper's cottage, beside the tall upstanding rose-bushes, like little trees, that he had often noticed there, stood Rose herself, perfectly still, her yellow hair only loosely gathered by a black ribbon behind her ears, and her black dress accentuating the slim curves of her figure and the diaphanous fineness of her skin: truly a living rose in lieu of those dead roses.

"You here?"

"We live here now."

"What? In the lock-keeper's cottage?"

"Yes. After Father's death we thought it best to leave the Vicarage at once."

"Your father's *death*?"

"Yes, a fortnight ago. I wrote you that same day, and again later. But I knew you didn't get my letters. Even if not able to write, you would have telegraphed."

"I haven't been with my regiment. I haven't been well. They sent me to Paris, to Arcachon. The letters must have been forwarded late, and miscarried."

He had forgotten to kiss her. They hadn't even shaken hands. They met as if in the other world, and there was a long pause. It seemed trivial to ask questions or to give explanations. What did it matter how these things had happened, when they were upon you, when the issue in any case was desolation and death? Each was curiously conceiving what must be passing through the other's mind. He was thinking, "She is looking at me sadly, not because of her father's death but because I make such a sorry bridegroom. It's kind of her not to laugh. She feels I am very ill, very useless, sure to be the next to disappear." Meantime, on her part, she thought he was troubled, not so much by the bad news she had given him, as by finding her here, in this working-man's cottage, independent of him, not having pursued him with telegrams and anxious enquiries, so as to secure his assistance. "He is shocked," she said to herself, "that Mother and I should know how to be poor."

"Shall we go in?" he said at last. "Is your mother in the house?"

"Yes, but Mrs. Higgs is with her. Higgs the lock-keeper and his older son have joined the army, and she and her boys are alone, looking after the gates. That's how we happened to find room here. Mrs. Higgs is an old friend of Mother's."

"Then can't you come with me somewhere—for a walk, or into the church—and tell me about everything? The Vicar too!"

"He seemed to expect to die," she began, following him into the towpath, and across the lock. "Ever since Jim's death, he had been failing. You know he thought it was his fault that Jim was a black sheep, or not an altogether white lamb; that this was his punishment, and that Jim had suffered innocently; and he himself suffered far more and more innocently in consequence. But with Jim's career closed, Father felt that no more reparation on his part was required, that he might allow himself to die in peace. You know how little he ever ate. He took to fasting more and more, and to sitting up all night over his books. He wasted away to a skeleton, and it seemed that hardly any change had come over him when he lay dead."

"And how has your mother borne this loss?"

"Oh, very well. Of course she laments, and wonders what will become of us. But she was very willing, almost happy, to move at once out of the Vicarage, when it appeared that the new incumbent was to be a young man who had never kept house before, and would gladly take over our maid and most of the furniture. Here, where we have no servants, she bustles about quite happily: and though we are only temporary lodgers, she seems to be more at home than in her own house. She never liked living in the Church close; it was a graveyard. Mother has a wonderful vitality. You wouldn't think so from her querulous talk, but her love of life is absolute; and when people are like that, the death of others is almost a victory. Father and I have always been rather strangers to her and too ghostly, and perhaps heaven is the right place for us. Not that she doesn't love us in her own way. You saw how she bore up with the loss of Jim, and with all his early troubles—bravely, defiantly, almost proudly. Yet Jim was the apple of her eye, one of her own ilk, her idea of a true Englishman. When she said the most damaging things about him— because she always believes the worst—she was really most in love with him. He had a right to do as he liked, and his fine feathers mustn't be plucked. He wasn't fit to suffer, like the rest of us, but only to enjoy. And when things went well with him, she chuckled at it, as she chuckles when the conductor in the bus forgets to ask for her penny, and she slips it again slyly into her long pocket. When he was gone, at least he was safe, he couldn't be found out or disgraced. She could think of him, she said, as one of the heroes of poetry. But with Father it was different. He too was released by Jim's death from a lifelong anxiety. The child of nature had run his course and made his expiation; his troubles could now be offered up to God in atone-ment, as a sacrifice of the first-born. After that, Father walked about repeating *Nunc dimittis* and *Consummatum est*. The rest of his days passed as in a trance. He kept up his visits in the parish unremittingly, in all weathers, as well as his sermons; but his cough grew worse, and with the first breath of winter he dropped like a sparrow.

"The end was peaceful and his mind clear. He spoke repeatedly of you. 'Rely on Oliver,' he would say to us. 'God has sent him to us. Oliver will provide.' Not that we are really destitute; we could manage very well; but Father was vague about these matters, and liked to follow the evangelical counsels about travelling without scrip or staff and taking no thought for the morrow. 'A Christian,' he would say, 'receives alms gratefully and humbly. It would be an offence to God to imagine that we ever live on anything but alms.' And now here you are, the almsgiver, coming providentially, without knowing why you have come."

"But I know why I have come, and you know. Didn't you get my letter?"

She was silent.

"Of course I will provide," he went on, "but it won't be an alms— that's only your father's religious phraseology—it will be the antici-pation of a right, even of a duty. You all count me, don't you, as already a member of the family? And you know that you and I have always been engaged to be married."

Rose made a little gesture of deprecation.

"I know it was only child's play at first, but it was prophetic, destined to become dead earnest some day. Hasn't the moment arrived? It would be a great support for me to be assured that, if I never came back, nobody would suffer, nothing would be the worse, for my disappearance. On the other hand, if all went well, what happiness to know that I had something to come back to, that you were waiting for me here, that our whole future was irrevocably sealed, that we should live it, whatever it might be, together, that you would never be abandoned, that I should never be alone."

To avoid the flooded parts near the river, they had instinctively turned into a broad grass road that leads up hill behind the church. Where the path to Littlemore branches off, there was a comfortable stile, embowered in the thick hedge; and here Rose sat down, making room for Oliver on the step below her. It was very much on such a stile that they had sat at Radley watching the boys' cricket, on the second day of their acquaintance; and Oliver, with his sensitiveness to such recurrences, felt a touch of superstitious joy. He saw again the bright playing-field, and the little boys in white calling shrilly to one another and scampering over the green. And here, the same golden-haired fairy, grown into a grave young princess, a wonderful sibyl, was sitting by his side, ready to counsel him in his confused adventures. She was speaking to him in her gentle voice, so clear and pure in its accents, so simply and sternly uttering the truth.

"My dear Oliver," he could hear her say, "you are dreaming. You can never come back here, to the Iffley you have known. Jim is dead. You will never draw from him again that animal warmth which you didn't have, or that sea breeze for which you panted. My father is dead. The Vicarage is occupied by strangers. You will never sit again under your tree in your wicker chair, reading your Plotinus, or listening to my father's commentary on the difference between the heavenly and the earthly soul. All that is past and gone. You can never return to it. The influences that led you to think of me and seemed to lend me a certain place in your life, to make me as it were inevitable, have all ceased for ever. What am I, what can I ever be, to you, in myself, apart from that setting? Nothing. If you took me from here and set me in the midst of your home landscape, in the hard light of America, you would find me an utter stranger, a silent nuisance, a living ghost. You would end by hating me. Of course I know you would always behave towards me with kindness and generosity: you would force yourself to do so. But I should be only one more burden, one more commitment, added to those that await you there: perhaps I should be the sharp edge of your misery, and the clearest visible daily proof of your loneliness."

"Why do you say that? Perhaps we shouldn't be altogether happy. Is anybody altogether happy? Whatever element of bitterness might remain in my life, surely you would sweeten it as no one else could. I am an American, and much as I love England, it is my duty to live at home. I suppose I shall be a professor—I'm not fit for anything else—probably in my old college. It is in the country, among pleasant hills, far from any large town. We should have a comfortable house, just like an English one, since we should build it to our own taste, and motors and horses and a great many books. The climate is a bit severe but bright and healthy. You would like the months of deep snow. In summer we could come here, or wherever you wished. You have a placid nature, you would lead a placid life. A difficulty at first might be my mother. We shouldn't live with her or near her; we should see her only once or twice a year. But she is a woman of strong character and rooted views, and I foresee that she might antagonise you. She hated Jim, whom she had never seen; she hates Vanny, though she has never seen him; and while she can have nothing on earth against you, yet the fact that you are English, and Jim's sister and that, so to speak, he brought us together, will prejudice her very much. Her animosities are terrible, they seem to sweep the whole world; and I should be sorry that my only near relation shouldn't be your friend, when you are so friendless."

"Somehow I seem not to need friends. I have never had any. I think I could propitiate your mother; but that is a secondary matter. What I ask is: Would you yourself be satisfied? As you paint the prospect, it seems to fill you with unutterable sadness."

"Ah, that is only my health, and the war. I can't shake off the incubus. The clouds are so thick, they have hung about us so long, that I can scarcely believe in the sunshine beyond. But that will pass. It is morbid. If I tried to paint any other future, without you, it would look twice as black."

"You mean that if you had to marry somebody else, it would be even worse? But why marry at all? How often hasn't Father said that you were called to a religious life? You don't care for wealth, you don't like war or women or the ways of the world. Why not join some religious Order, like the Cowley Fathers—you frown? Well, if you prefer, like the Franciscans or the Jesuits."

"I frown because I don't like religion better than wealth or war: I mean, not mock religion, or unjust wealth, or war falsely justified or fought for a false glory. I would gladly devote my life to religion, if there were a religion that was true. But Christianity and all the other religions are so childishly false that I wonder how sane people can put up with them. I used to ask your father how he could continue to use the language of the Church, while he silently interpreted it in a sense which the Church had never dreamt of. And he would reply by very deep considerations about the symbolism of all thought and language, and even of the images of the senses; how it could not be a literal truth that was proper to ideas, and how they were all nothing but symbols; so that it was legitimate and inevitable to use them figuratively. I granted all this: nevertheless it would remain utterly repulsive and impossible for me to read the Bible stories in church in an emotional tone, as if they were true, or to preach about Judgment Day and heaven and hell as if they were facts, when I was sure they were nothing but myths and poetic apologues. Your father fully appreciated my difficulty, and said he would have felt it himself, if his education had been different. To him the language of the Church was native; and it still seemed to him that the facts of moral life could not receive a more penetrating or adequate interpretation than that which the Christian fable supplied. But to me, brought up practically without religion, only the images created by science and profane history were native and spontaneous; and I could not honestly use any others. He dissuaded me from becoming a clergyman, even of the most modern stripe. Those were accommodations temporarily inevitable in certain circles; but I was a privileged being, I could stand alone, I could survey the scene impartially; and if that solitude was desolate, it was also ascetic, religious, and an act of worship to the true God. So that, you see, in order to lead a religious life, supposing I am called to it, I must absolutely renounce being a Jesuit or a Franciscan or even a Cowley Father. There is no occasion, then, to give up marriage or money, or such a place as I might fill in the world. If I did so, I should not be living more religiously. I should merely be living without a wife, without means, without a function in the world, and at the same time without a religion."

"You wouldn't be without a function in the world," Rose said in a changed voice, that sounded like her father's, "if you could understand the world or even yourself. Can anyone do anything better in this world than to understand the world and perhaps to reject it?"

"You are an ascetic without faith."

"Isn't that rather what *you* are?"

"Shouldn't we make a nice pair?"

"Like two drops of cold water," and Rose, smiling, brushed away two drops of rain that had fallen on her hand.

"Mightn't the water turn some day into wine, and the wine into blood?"

"I don't believe in miracles." She glanced at the threatening sky from which more stray drops were falling, and stood up in her place with a slight shiver. In silence they walked down the hill, a glimmer of amusement shooting through their sadness.

"Come into the churchyard," she said, "I will show you Father's grave."

There was no stone as yet to mark it. They had been waiting for Oliver to decide how expensive the stone should be. But the mound was already half overgrown with young grass, and two or three withered wreaths and bunches of dried flowers still partly covered it.

The drops of rain were turning into a drizzle, and as they stood before the grave, not wishing to hurry away, Oliver threw half his military great-coat over the shoulders of his companion, who was lightly clad. She didn't repel his embrace; it was too little dangerous, and there was some material comfort in it; it kept off the chilling damp wind. But Oliver himself, how uncouth! She was sure this embrace was deliberate, like his plan to carry her off and marry her that very day without her leave. He had decided in the train that an embrace would be in order. How could he help embracing her sooner or later, when he had their marriage licence in his pocket ready to sign? And why must his uniform be so mean, so scanty, so badly cut, and the cloth so unpleasant to the touch, like canvas? Luckily the great-coat was lined with chamois: the inside at least was soft and warm. But that stiff tight little collar must be dreadfully uncomfortable. She was glad he had taken off his little hard cap worn pulled down well over his eyes and leaving half the head sticking out behind unprotected. A soldier might be a bit rigid, if he was smart and resplendent; or he might be frankly loose and sporting in the modern military style, comfortable and workmanlike: but this prim wretched ugliness without a function—who could have invented it? And how seedy poor Oliver himself looked, in his graceless clothes! His eyes were still clear and beautiful, if a little tired, and his smile had all its old sweetness and purity: but he was growing skinny and thin, his wrists showed ugly bones and tendons; the skin was muddy and blotched; and the strands of his lank sandy hair, dampened by the rain, were beginning to part in places, and show the white scalp. He would make a gaunt old man, and prematurely. He looked as if he had suffered from poverty, overwork, or prolonged hardship: he, the pet of fortune, to whom the whole world was open, and who didn't know where to lay his head. As a young lover, he was too ridiculous. He couldn't even feign love, supposing he had had any reason for feigning it. He thought, like Don Quixote, that it was his duty to be in love. She was his Dulcinea and Iffley his El Toboso. Certainly he was a superior young man, or ought to have been; but how much less free and determined than she was herself? In her desolation she felt a certain cruel superiority; she was compensated for all untoward accidents by her inward clearness. But he? He was the victim of a congenital disease; he suffered from a moral cramp, a clog in the wheel of every natural passion. He was ashamed of his plight, and wished to outgrow it; but he never would. He would die as he had lived, with lead in his wing. In sighing over the fate of her virtuous friend, Rose sighed for her own sorrows; thought of her father, of Jim, also handicapped and defeated by contrary circumstances: and a great pity for the world possessed her.

"Father too," she said softly, "ought never to have married. Take warning from his life, because you have a like spirit. Marriage crossed his natural vocation; but he was faithful to his responsibilities, and they were a terrible trial to him, especially with all those children to bring up—for I had brothers and sisters who died young. His nature demanded something different: a rapt dedication to impersonal things. Yours does the same. Why force your inclination?"

"But what impersonal things? Inclination to what? Philosophy? A philosophy that is not a religion is only a vague science or a loose eloquence; and religion we have excluded. Science, then, or art? If you had been at a university and seen the professors at work, or seen the artists at work in Montmartre or in Montparnasse, you wouldn't speak of dedication to impersonal things. It is a horrible drudgery: and if you look at the inner springs of the work, at what might be ideal, you find the meanest, smallest, most accidental, most absurd motives. Science and art are prodigious shams. As to my inclination, I would rather live in the backwoods, and fell and haul timber. Or, if Jim were alive, I would give nearly all my money back to my mother, who expected to inherit it, and keep only enough to build a perfect sailing-ship, a modern clipper. Jim should have been captain, and I owner and super-cargo: and we should have sailed round and round the world doing an honest man's job, a genuine necessary business, yet, except for short intervals in port, far from the world of men, with only the wind and the sea to wrestle with, honest and useful enemies, and only our honest and useless thoughts to exchange, without the least reticence or hypocrisy. But I am not strong enough alone. I wish to do right, to be brave and independent, but as you told me long ago, I don't know how. That is why my friends have always meant so much to me. They gave me a lead which I am not clever enough to take for myself. They solved my problems for me by not posing them, and sympathy carried me forward where reason stood stock still. There was not only Jim, there was Vanny——"

"Why do you speak of him in the past? Your cousin isn't dead?"

"No, no. He is in Italy. But I needn't speak of him. You know him. He has been here."

"Yes. He used to make love to me."

"To you?"

"Not openly, not intentionally. He didn't propose marriage, as you do. He made love without meaning to. Shall I tell you how he did it? He entirely forgot himself. He circled about me. Interrupted himself in whatever he was doing—reading or chatting with the other officers—the moment he spied me, as if I had been his first interest, and all else secondary and instantly obscured. He played with my dog and taught him new tricks. He asked me what flowers I preferred, or what I liked best for a present; and the next day, if the thing was procurable, I would receive it in a lovely parcel from London. He would say and look compliments that seemed sincere because they were sincere. He praised you to the skies, praised Jim, praised my father, understood all about my mother. He complimented my French, made me feel that I had lost nothing by spending all my time in a country parsonage, that I had gained a great distinction and exquisiteness in consequence. When finally he said good-bye to all the family in order, he returned to say a word to me especially, and to shake hands once again. When you consider that he was a young man of five-and-twenty, of such striking appearance, wearing his uniform with so much ease and dash, wounded, but panting to return to the front and to resume his bombing excursions into the heart of Germany, I think a very young girl might be forgiven if her own heart panted a little. Yet he didn't know he was making love: he was thinking of you; merely being civil to your particular friend."

"Naturally. He knew that I hoped to marry you. He expected to be an intimate old friend of the family, he was preparing the welcome he should receive in our house. And why shouldn't he receive it? Not often, I am afraid, because his lines are going to be cast in other waters: but sometimes, perhaps, and at least always in spirit. It is you that must be my last friend, and the dearest, bound to me by ties that with men are impossible; one not to be divided from me, as men must be from one another by separate homes and separate interests. I'm not making love to you, as Vanny did, or as he does to every pretty woman. I'm not flushed with emotions that may last an hour or a month or a year, as if a drug had caused them. Perhaps I am not capable of what novelists call love, and describe to us at length, so that everybody thinks himself obliged to feel that interesting passion. I don't think my father and mother were ever in love. It's not in our blood. But I am sure you and I might live far more happily together than apart. We understand each other, we trust each other, we can never forget each other or cease to live in one another's life. You are a marvellous creature, so perfect, so serene, so intelligent, such absolute adamant. You will always seem to me a princess won by enchantment, and still radiant of some other magic world. Everyone will say, What a beautiful lady, what a noble mind, what exquisite manners, such are not got by training but must come by nature, like the step of the peacock. And I shall reply, Yes, this is my Rose, that I found standing amongst the roses of her little garden and have carried away with me, to set up in the midst of my house, to be the beauty of it, and the pride of my heart. There are tendrils that this rose will wind about me. There will be rosebuds some day. Come with me to-day to London. Let it be agreed between us that we have been married here, now, before your father's grave, married by him in spirit. He would have wished it. I must leave for France to-morrow evening. We shall have just time in the morning to go to the Register Office and to the Consulate, to sign my new will. At least we shall be legally married. My mind will be at rest. If anything happens to me, you will be provided for—No? Why not? You don't trust me?"

He had pressed his cloak a little closer about her, but now she shook herself loose.

"Not trust you? Who would ever distrust you?" she said smiling; but her smile had nothing reassuring about it. "Being trustworthy is your shining virtue. Do you think me a fool? What difference would it make, before or after? Indeed, if you were concerned for the proprieties, we could have taken my mother with us to cover the elopement—But it's cold here. Let's go back to the cottage."

With twice St. Martin's charity he compelled her to keep the whole of his cloak; and while they picked their way through the muddy paths and over the lock-gates, she spoke in short snatches, as if picking her thoughts out one by one from an accumulated store.

"Oliver, what you say is poetical, kind, chivalrous. But let me repeat, you are dreaming. I can't warm you because I am cold. I can't give you a direction in your perplexities, because I have no direction. I am content to live in suspense, in disbelief, in solitude. You are not content. I can't help you. But perhaps it's not that. You aren't asking for help, though you need it sorely. You, too, are willing to tread the winepress alone. But you are kind, you are all kindness, and you wish to help me, to protect me, to leave me rich, if you should have to leave me. Ah, I don't refuse that! I don't refuse your charity, your kindness, your generosity. To rely on in my extremity, instead of my helpless father and my useless brother, you are a tower of strength. But why spoil your magnanimity, why confuse your own mind, by asking me to marry you? You don't love me in that way, and in that way I don't love you."

"You don't love somebody else?"

"No: I have no other lover. But there are others with whom I might imagine myself in love. For instance, your cousin; only he banishes me from his thoughts, because he thinks I am mortgaged to you."

"You bear me a grudge for it? And you would actually prefer to marry him, even if he didn't love you?"

"Even if he didn't love me more than he might any other woman; even," she added blushing a little and looking Oliver defiantly in the face, "even if we were to be divorced the next day."

"But this is monstrous! When I have chosen you and put you on a pedestal all these years, and looked forward to the days when we should be married."

"It is nothing to be chosen, or put on a pedestal, or introduced into a programme of life. That is sentimentality or at best partnership. Love is something else; and to be worth while it must be happy love, natural, irresistible, unreasoning love. Love will never make you happy, Oliver. Don't marry. Live with your old governess, Fräulein Schlote."

Oliver perceived the irony of this, but somehow he felt no sting. He had been accustomed to endure his mother's sarcasms, and live them down. What difference did they make in the end? So this tiny spite. In his flood of troubles it was like one of the drops of rain pricking that swollen river. He disinfected it, he forgave it, he even saw the truth of it. In his immense generosity of mind, he thought of Rose as a sort of Iphigenia in Aulis, a prophetess, a healer of his soul; for he was like Orestes, distracted not by his own crimes but by the crimes of humanity; and she was a priestess of Diana, and knew the medicine for madness. But Iphigenia had followed her brother, leaving her temple and its cruel mysteries; and so this girl ought to follow him. Their spiritual relationship was not incompatible with marriage. Indeed, marriage was the only possible means of establishing that relationship firmly, of making her for ever the physician of his soul.

Very gently, very modestly, he tried to convey this idea, saying that perhaps marriage was a holier thing than love, as she conceived love; that perhaps she was still too young; that he would wait; that after the war, when he might have recovered his health and spirits, he would return for her; that perhaps her feelings would have changed, and she would be willing to follow him.

But she was obdurate, hardened still more by a persistence on his part which she thought stupid and a bit tyrannical.

"No, no," she said. "Quite apart from love, we are not made to live together. We are too much alike, both of us too independent, too solitary. Neither of us has enough light to guide, or enough humility to follow. Here you are, exposing your life you don't know why or in what cause, without belief and without hope. And when the war is over you will be caught in another trap, in America, and stretched on that wheel, till you die of the strain. That is the life you wish me to share? No: I would rather teach in the village school and live in a lock-keeper's cottage with his wife and children. They work and suffer and worry, but they know their wants. Perhaps the parson helps them to put up with their lot, sweetens it a little, blurs it a little, in their dark minds. But you, who are all enquiry and criticism, who ought to be all freedom, you are entangled in your knowledge and in your riches, far more painfully than they in their poverty and ignorance. Your deeper darkness is a terrible thing, because it is conscious. Can't you see that I would rather die than marry you?"

They had reached the little riverside garden and were about to enter the house. Oliver, as usual in his extremity, remembered his trump card. "One word," he said, "before we go in. In my will, which I am to sign to-morrow, it would be better, both on your account and on my mother's, that I should state expressly the reason for leaving you the sum I do. I had hoped to say: To my wife, or at least to my affianced wife, Rose Darnley, so much. But now, what shall I say?"

"The truth."

"What is that?"

"To Rose Darnley, sister of my late beloved friend, Lieutenant James Darnley, R.N., and daughter of my late revered friend, the Reverend Austin Darnley, Vicar of Iffley, in Oxfordshire, so much."

"Very well. But with one addition. I will say: 'to Rose Darnley, whom I have long looked upon as my future wife.'"

She bowed her head a little as she passed in before him over the cottage threshhold, humbled but not shaken by his magnanimity.

VIII

When, half an hour later, Oliver left the lock-keeper's cottage his head was so high that he never noticed whether the path was still flooded or not. His thoughts were in the clouds. His earthly person had been rejected, his earthly plan defeated; but by that defeat and rejection his soul had been wonderfully liberated. Whom the Lord loveth he chasteneth; and more than once in his sermons on that text the Vicar had magnified the blessings that come to us disguised as misfortunes: if only we do not look backward to the burning city of our vanity, but walk resolutely into the wilderness with God. "How glad I am," Oliver thought, "that I came to Oxford and cleared up this whole mess. Now I have given Mrs. Darnley a cheque for a thousand pounds. She will take it to-morrow morning to Barclay's Bank and open an account, to cover their expenses for the present: and they will look for a decent little house to live in until the war is over, and we can make final arrangements. I don't need to draw up a new will at all: the old one will do nicely. They are provided for in case of my death amply, not extravagantly. So is Bobby, so is Mario, so is Irma. I can sleep late to-morrow morning."

With the air of closing a fair bargain, and settling a business matter for good, he drew his marriage licence from his pocket, tore it to bits, and let the wind and the rain scatter the fragments in the darkness.

"What?" he asked himself, a little shocked at his own melodramatic action, "am I glad she has refused me? Am I glad the Vicar is dead? Was I glad when Jim went down and was lost? No: it was terrible. Nothing worse could have happened to me. And yet it all seems a solution. The strain is relaxed. The play is over, the doors open, and after all those unnecessary thrills and anxieties, I am walking out into the night, into my true life, into the inexorable humdrum punctual company of real things. I am falling back upon my deeper self. I may hardly be able to see the stars, after the blinding light of the theatre, but there they are; and gradually they will become visible again, I shall recognise them, I shall call each of them by its old name.

Yes; but with how much more understanding, with what a clear sense of the circumstances that have created me, and of what they mean to that immortal part of me which they have not created! It is this self-recovery, this self-knowledge, that exalts me. I may have made a mistake about Rose, as I did about Edith, but I've made no mistake about myself. They may not have been the right women, but they were the right symbols for me then for the thing I needed, for the thing I must find.

"Is this another woman? Possibly, by chance, but I don't think so. At bottom it can't be any one woman or any one thing. It must be all perfections and all beauties and all happiness. Now I see why I was wrong in my old thesis about Plato, and why the Vicar shook his head when I read it to him. Plato was talking poetry about a love that is an inspiration, a divine madness; whereas I was talking dead prose about general benevolence, friendliness, and charity. Now affection and kindness are all that I have felt or ever ought to feel about the real Rose, or about the real Edith; just as it was all I could rightly feel about the real Jim or the real Mario: but where I have added a touch of love, where I have allowed them to bewitch me or to make me suffer, then I was not seeing the reality in them at all, but only an image, only a mirage, of my own aspiration. They may drop out, they may change, they may prove to be the sad opposite of what I thought them: but my image of them in being detached from their accidental persons, will be clarified in itself, will become truer to my profound desire; and the inspiration of a profound desire, fixed upon some lovely image, is what is called love. And the true lover's tragedy is not being jilted; it is being accepted. What a predicament, if thinking I had married *my* Edith or *my* Rose, I had found an entirely different Rose or Edith that I was tied to for life! I have been a conscript all my life: a conscript son, a conscript schoolboy, a conscript athlete, a conscript soldier; at least I am not a conscript husband. Or not yet. For the present, I am free. And not in respect to women only or to friends or to dreams of personal happiness. I am free also in respect to this war, to my life afterwards in America, to rival systems of philosophy and to rival religions. Towards them, towards my wife and children, if I ever have them, natural affection, tenderness, sympathy; but no expectation that they can ever fill my whole being, or make my true happiness, or entrance my soul as only divine love could entrance it.

"How old-fashioned I am, how clerical, how rhetorical, talking about divine love. People would laugh if they heard me. I have read too much Plotinus. That idea of a divine being, the real object of all loves, is like my false Edith or my false Lord Jim, a mirage, an idol of the mind, an impossible object. Granted: yet the falser that object is, the stronger and clearer must have been the force in me that called it forth and compelled me to worship it. It is this force in myself that matters: to this I must be true.

"Old-fashioned: no doubt I am old-fashioned. *Weh dir, dass du ein Enkel bist.* I was born old. It is a dreadful inheritance, this of mine, that I need to be honest, that I need to be true, that I need to be just. That's not the fashion of to-day. The world is full of conscript minds only they are in different armies, and nobody is fighting to be free, but each to make his own conscription universal. I can't catch the contagion. I never could do anything in football except at full-back, never anything in rowing except alone or at stroke. I was born a moral aristocrat, able to obey only the voice of God, which means that of my own heart. My people first went to America as exiles into a stark wilderness to lead a life apart, purer and soberer than the carnival life of Christendom. We were not content to be well-dressed animals, rough or cunning or lustfully prowling and acquisitive, and perhaps inventing a religion to encourage us in our animality. We will not now sacrifice to Baal because we seem to have failed. We will bide our time. We will lie low and dip under, until the flood has passed and wasted itself over our heads. We are not wanted. In the world to-day we are a belated phenomenon, like April snow. Perhaps it is time for us to die. If we resist, and try to cling to the fringes, as I have done so far, we are shaken off rudely, or allowed to hang on neglected and disowned. If we attempt to live apart, as my father did, we wither early into amiable ghosts. There is my uncle Nathaniel. People jeer at him. Yet what just intuition he has shown all his life, what a brave loyalty to his breeding. Didn't Aunt Caroline say I was like Uncle Nathaniel? I am, and I'm proud of it. Of course, there's sixty years' difference in our ages, and he is an extreme survival, a mummy that somehow has kept itself alive. I shan't shut myself up in Beacon Street or mince my steps or wear black gloves. But I can keep my own thoughts inviolate, like Uncle Nathaniel, and not allow the world to override me. We will not accept anything cheaper or cruder than our own conscience. We have dedicated ourselves to the truth, to living in the presence of the noblest things we can conceive. If we can't live so, we won't live at all.

"It's no use looking backward or attempting compromises. There is Mario riding this storm almost merrily, as if he enjoyed it; but he hasn't any conscience; he doesn't care what happens or what is true; thinks it none of his business to inquire, but only to lend a hand, distinguish himself, laugh, and kiss as many girls as possible. His new friends have persuaded him that a beautiful jolly Christendom can be recreated, simply by force of discipline and of false eloquence; that they can and must dragoon mankind into being decent and cultivating the arts, and fighting one another at suitable intervals to see which is the most cocky. But the most cocky will be the most calamitously self-deceived; and the end of that competitive cockiness will be seven times worse than the beginning: as we see to-day in this war. The mind of the world is content to potter about with surfaces and numbers and machinery: it has been caught in the wheels of its own inventions, and its lovely motor has run away with it. The optimists call it progress. But I won't keep repeating things that are false and producing things that are useless and promising myself things that are impossible. Either the truth or nothing.

"But am I not perhaps rebelling against the truth by refusing to be a decent ordinary bee buzzing round the hive? What do I gain by kicking against the pricks? Nothing: and materially I have never kicked, I am not kicking now. I have submitted to all their conscriptions. I have played all their games. I am playing their horrible game now. I am going to fight the Germans whom I like on the side of the French whom I don't like. It's my duty. Yet in my inner man how can I be a conscript; and how can I help denouncing all these impositions and feeling that such duties ought not to be our duties, and such blind battles ought not to be our battles?

"What battles, then? What duties? To please my own mind, shall I decide what ought to be the world's business? Shall I get up an imaginary programme, and say, like Cousin Caleb Wetherbee, that the world's real business is something that the world neglects and has never heard of, something miraculously revealed only to me or to the sect I happen to belong to? Isn't that like the Pharisee hugging his own melancholy madness and calling all merry people mad? Theirs is the less painfully maintained, less artificial folly: the humble, browsing, sleepy, miscellaneous madness of the world. If I tried to do better, I might do worse. Enough if at all times I practise charity, and keep myself as much as possible from complicity in wrong."

So thinking, he bundled himself into his corner in the railway carriage, and prepared for his dismal, solitary night journey to London. He wasn't allowed even to look out of the window into the darkness. All the blinds had to be tightly pulled down by order, on account of Zeppelins. But he had fortified himself in the refreshment room with some sandwiches and hot milk. He wrapped himself warmly in his great-coat, the very coat he had wrapped an hour before round his ungrateful sweetheart. Perhaps in this warmth, in this softness, there lingered something of her cheek, something of her bosom. He turned the collar up over his ears, and closed his eyes.

IX

"No, sir," said Mrs. Higgs to the gallant officer who saluted as she came to the door. "Mrs. Darnley and the young lady don't live here now. We don't take lodgers, sir, not ordinary: only last year to accommodate when they was in trouble, and my husband and son away. They've moved to old Mrs. Tubb's. The first little white house, sir, at the turn of the road. You can't miss it, sir, with *Hawthorne Lodge* written on the gate."

Although a bereavement was the occasion of Vanny's visit to Iffley, he was no bearer of ill news. Those ladies had long known of Oliver's death, and to-day they were to hear only a more accurate account of his last will and testament, calculated to soften their regrets and to increase their happy veneration for their lost friend. The multitude of the fallen during those years had made death so familiar, that it was almost without pain, with a sigh of resignation at foreseen inevitable evils, like bad weather or taxes, that people bore the loss of their sons and brothers. There was even a touch of grandeur, almost of triumph, in a life finished roundly, that seemed an action and not a succession of involuntary predicaments. Short and commonplace as was the soldier's career, it had a beginning and an end, and a brave jollity; and if the only triumph in it was in death, such is after all the fate of all action, which necessarily perishes in being done. And the worst of it is, as Vanny in those days often had occasion to observe, that with the passing act, as for instance with this war, the purpose it might have had, or might be supposed to have had, passes also and becomes irrelevant. Every human achievement is submerged in the general flood of things, and its issue soon grows ambiguous and untraceable. We must be satisfied to catch our triumphs on the wing, to die continually, and to die content. Oliver at least hadn't had his young life cut short cruelly, as the old ladies were sure to say in their letters of condolence to his mother. He would have gained nothing by living to a hundred, never would have found better friends, or loved women otherwise. His later years would only have been pallid copies of his earlier ones. He had come to the end of his rope. He was played out.

Hawthorne Lodge was a modernised cottage, clean and comfortable, when once you overcame the oppression of its tiny windows and low ceilings.

"And so you were with him at the end," sighed Mrs. Darnley, half-smiling, when she had recovered from the flurry of receiving a superior visitor. "Ah, to think we have lost him, that good young man, that true friend of everybody, that sweet kind spotless creature, that needed indeed to go to heaven to find the likes of himself.—Do see about getting tea, Rose dear.—It shakes one's faith in Providence, this cutting down of the green bough, when there's so much dead wood in the world, ready for burning. Why didn't the good Lord call the Kaiser to his reckoning, or this great wooden Hindenburg of theirs, with all the gold nails hammered into him, instead of our poor young Oliver, who never hurt a flea in his life, and they guilty of the dear boy's blood, and living on in health and plenty in their wicked old age."

"Whatever the Germans may be guilty of, they didn't kill Oliver: and in a literal sense there was no question of blood in his case. It was several days after the armistice. All firing had ceased, but the troops were advancing rapidly; and somebody on a motor-bicycle, who thought all danger was over, came round a curve without warning on the wrong side of the road. Oliver, in trying to avoid a collision, ran into a milestone. His car turned turtle; he was caught under it and his neck broken. There were no external injuries, hardly a bruise. The fact that it happened after the armistice enabled me to get to Dijon in time to see the body, and have it properly buried, in a remote and quiet spot: but I expect it won't be allowed to rest there. His mother will have it removed to America. His face in death recovered its old aspect. You remember, don't you, how he looked as a boy. It was possible to take a photograph. I have one here."

"You were always taking his photograph," Rose interposed coldly, as she continued to pour out the tea. She looked at the photograph for a moment in an attentive melancholy way, and passed it on to her mother. Mrs. Darnley hadn't her glasses by her; she seldom had; and she might as well have seen the likeness upside down. But she had perceptions of a social sort. Vanny wore the uniform of a staff-officer. She was deferential, and knew what she ought to feel.

"Ah, yes," she murmured, "he was a noble-looking young man, if only he hadn't worried and burnt his eyes out reading all night and all day, like a poor pale scholar, with all that wealth they have lying idle in America. He needed rest and happiness, the poor dear lad, and he has found them now, sir, I do believe." Here she wiped her eyes with a distinct satisfaction at how well she was behaving.

Vanny smiled sympathetically at the old lady and quietly put back into his pocket the photograph which he had intended to leave with the Darnleys. Then he turned to Rose with a polite air, as if resuming a casual conversation.

"This time, as a matter of fact, it wasn't I who took the photo. I hadn't a camera: never had such a good one. It was a young doctor at the American hospital, where they had carried him: a Dr. Piper— Tom Piper, they called him—who appears to have been an old school-friend of his. At least, I assure you I never knew any army doctor so affected by a casualty."

"Indeed, they are hardened," sighed Mrs. Darnley, offering the bread and butter. "But it's no use knowing that it's the way of all flesh. When it comes to our nearest and dearest, it smites the heart. You find us twice stricken, sir, since you were last here. After losing our Jim, to have the Vicar too fading away and dying of hunger, I might almost call it; though it wasn't any fault of mine if everything was rationed; and then to learn that Mr. Oliver was cut down too. All three together, it's terrible. Yet as for him, sir, I'm sure he must look beautiful in heaven." Mrs. Darnley again wiped away a tear, shook some crumbs from her lap, and helped herself to a little more tea.

"You too have been wounded again," Rose observed, counting the little tabs of gold braid on his sleeve. "There were only two before."

"Yes, a flesh wound only. I wasn't so much exposed in Italy, merely rushing with despatches from one head-quarters to another. My wings have been clipped. They don't let me fly any more, and I'm about to resign my commission."

"Then you'll be in residence again at Christ Church?"

"No, no. I've taken my name off the books. The day comes when we have to give up childish things. For the moment I'm returning to Paris, until the sky finally clears. Eventually I expect to live in Italy. It was my mother's country. In one sense it's everybody's country who is conscious of the past, or who believes there is a future for Christendom. All our roads still lead from Rome, as well as to it."

Rose made no reply, and he took a large paper out of his pocket and turned again to Mrs. Darnley.

"I have brought you a copy of Oliver's will, which has now been proved. There are bequests in your favour. Shall I read them? Or I had better tell you the substance, these lawyers' phraseology is so ridiculous. He leaves you separate annuities, £500 a year for you, Mrs. Darnley, and £1,000 a year for your daughter, not only during her life, but in case she should have children—evidently not Oliver's—who survived her, to them conjointly until the youngest is of age."

There was a silence in the room for a few moments.

"I confess," Mario said dryly, "that considering his large fortune, the absence of all heirs, except his old mother, who is already very rich, and the fact, as I understand it, that you were tacitly engaged to be married, these provisions surprise me a little."

"Not at all," Rose retorted: "We were not engaged. The provisions are most generous: and that last, about my imaginary children, is very characteristic of Oliver. He shows himself absolutely unselfish and magnanimous; doesn't grudge me a husband and children; but he feels a scruple about detaching any part of his capital. It must all revert eventually to his people at home."

"Not in all cases, because he leaves me, who don't really need it, a very handsome round sum."

"Aren't there also some bequests to Universities or Art Museums?"

"Yes, precisely, to the Boston Art Museum, that's in memory of his father, who was a collector of curios; to the Great Falls Hospital for the Insane, that's in his mother's honour; and to Williams College for scholarships for needy but deserving youths—I suppose that's in memory of himself."

"He did seem sometimes," said Rose smiling, "as if he were suffering from some kind of want. And don't you see, you come under the same head as the Art Museums: you are to be preserved as a relic of extinct civilisations."

They all laughed, in spite of the melancholy occasion, but Vanny was not at his ease. He was astonished at these sallies. Why such bitterness and such ingratitude? Surely the Vicar, surely Jim, would have been otherwise moved.

"And is there no other bequest, no other annuity?" Rose inquired, as if sure of the reply.

"Yes. Also £500 a year to Mrs. Darnley's ward, Robert Bowler-Darnley."

The motherly, or rather grandmotherly, heart of the old lady was more elated at this bequest than at the one to herself.

"The goodness of this young man," she cried, "was only fit for a better world, where there are saints. Bobby, who was nothing to him but a wretched waif, to take pity on, remembered and made into a young gentleman with five hundred a year! God bless the charitable giver, and reward him in the other world, for in this he was too pure and good to endure our wretchedness. And a thousand a year for Rose is more than kingly bounty, all for nothing but having acted a children's play with her once, and been Cinderella to his Fairy Prince: because as you may conceive sir, there was nothing ever between them except that jest, when she was a little girl, and didn't know what marriage meant; for later, she couldn't expect him to look at a poor clergyman's child, when he might have married a duke's daughter, or some heiress in his own country."

"No, Mrs. Darnley, that wasn't his view of the matter. I can assure you that many a time, when we talked of love and marriage, he said he had his bride already chosen; they were like Paul and Virginia; only she was as yet too young. That was before the war; and of late, naturally we haven't talked much of that, nor in fact of anything, for we have been constantly separated. But after I had been your neighbour at Court Place, and so often your guest in your charming garden, I wrote congratulating him on his good taste and his good fortune; and he took my compliments quite simply and seriously, spoke of the home he hoped to make for you in America, and even—so much did his fancy run on the subject—of the children he hoped to have."

"Yes, he always thought of the children. I was only a necessary pre-requisite. They were to be boys like Jim and Bobby and perhaps one little girl, like myself idealised. I should have thought, as he said you were his best friend, that he would have preferred them to resemble you."

"Oh, he looked upon me as a sport of nature, an international hybrid, to be tolerated and perhaps smiled at. I think he sometimes admired his own broad-mindedness in being willing to be my friend; but mine was not a type to be reproduced. Your brother, on the contrary, seemed to him the perfection of manhood, as you of young girlhood, Nordic and unspoiled. You know his German governess and I used to call him Siegfried: the humour of that rather pleased him, he almost took it seriously: and you were to be his Brunhilda, only you didn't yodel or wear wings on your helmet."

"Yes, I know. He liked to deceive himself into thinking he was in love with me, because that protected him from other women. I should have failed sadly in my function if I hadn't also protected him against myself."

"Do you mean that you refused to marry him?"

"Yes."

"Nonsense," Mrs. Darnley broke in, reddening and putting on a scolding voice. "How dare you give yourself such airs before Mr. Oliver's friend? Do you expect him to believe you? As if the best that ever was weren't good enough for a poor penniless orphan? You left Mr. Oliver free, because he was so scrupulous and true to his word that perhaps he might have married you on account of that silly babble of yours when you were little children. You were too proud to take advantage of a thing like that. After all, you are my daughter; you aren't going to catch a young man unawares. You knew very well that he didn't love you. Nobody ever will. You are too cold and haughty on nothing a year; and it was only Christian duty and common decency to let the young gentleman go."

While her mother was still speaking Rose had left the room, not to be seen in tears.

"I am afraid your daughter had a deeper attachment to our friend than she likes to confess. Her sarcasms are only a feint to conceal her feelings. I am truly sorry. There must have been some misunderstanding between them. When people are reserved by nature their words often do their hearts an injustice. The fancy I knew Oliver had for your daughter, as for a wonderful rare child, made me particularly notice her when I was at Court Place; and I thought she showed signs beneath her calm caustic exterior, and in spite of her youth, of having a deep womanly nature. She was thinking of Oliver when she spoke to me; I could feel the secret agitation beneath her serenity; and I was thinking how great one day would be his happiness when I spoke to her. If fate hadn't cut him off, we should yet have seen them happy together. But he foresaw the end, and he felt keenly this curious mistaken estrangement. There are some verses of his found in his pocket—I never knew before that he was a poet— but they say we all are, once in our lives. I have a copy here. Would you like to hear them?"

Mrs. Darnley couldn't say no. She didn't expect to understand poetry any more than sermons or psalms; but the sound of many words was pleasing to her and familiar, and she settled herself in her comfortable chair by the fire, reconciled to undergoing even a whole canto.

Mario began to read slowly, in a low measured voice:

ROSE DARNLEY

She stood above the flooded stream,
Alone amid the ruin there,
Stood dreaming as a rose might dream,
Half open in the sunless air,
If once the salt sea wind of fate
Had touched her beauty with despair.
Look, child, your lover's at the gate.
See, 'tis not death that knocks to-day;
He's come, he's come, for whom you wait.
Have you no tenderer word to say
To one so faithful to his troth?
Duty has doubly hedged his way,
And sweet foreknowledge bound you both,
Silent and strong, this many a year.
Is it your youth that makes you loth,
Or his home-coming that you fear,
Had he but plucked this whitest rose
To lay a white rose on his bier?
If in your heart, before he goes,
His heart could shed one drop of blood,
Your trembling petals, as they close,
Might bloom, and be a crimson bud.
At last she spoke: "Our spirits move
Like snake-weeds writhing in the flood.
Men marry as their fortunes prove.
The times have laid on our two hearts
The pity, not the joy, of love."
She folds her hands, and he departs.

The monotone of these lines had soothed Mrs. Darnley; she had closed her eyes; she had peacefully taken the forty winks in which she usually indulged at that hour.

Vanny lifted his eyebrows, folded the despised verses, and silently slipped them into his pocket, next to the despised photograph. He was amazed at the indifference, at the ingratitude of these women. He buttoned down the flap of that pocket with a certain satisfaction in the solitary possession of his affections; and with the same satisfaction, from the other pocket he extracted a cigarette-case that had all the look of a present from some exalted personage. "Charming world," he thought. "The manners of the future. You may doze or smoke no matter when, no matter where, and make no pretence of feeling what you don't feel."

The scratch of the match awoke the old lady, who smiled vacantly and tried to look as if she had not slept. She had quite forgotten the existence of any verses.

"I must be off," he said rising, to break the spell and bring them both back to the commonplace. "May I say good-bye to Miss Rose, or will you do it for me?"

The rooms were few in that little dwelling and the partitions thin. Rose was not far away, and on hearing the unmistakable sounds of a visitor leaving, she came forward towards the sitting room.

"It is very kind of you," she said, "to have come in person to bring us this report. You might have let your solicitors send us the documents."

"I'm not merely an executor of Oliver's will, I am his representative. I wish to honour his feelings. Who could do less, when those feelings were so noble, so delicate, and so unrewarded?"

"Yes," she replied, quite unruffled by this reproach. "He wasn't very successful in his love-affairs. Not like you, if one may trust all one hears. He used to represent you as a terrible lady-killer; but I see he did you an injustice. Like almost all other men, you really care for your friends more than for your victims."

He was on the point of saying that there is a love that passeth the love of women; but he restrained himself. Why punish a poor girl who by her bitter words is trying to defend herself against her sufferings? The gallantry in him came to the fore. He took her hand with a certain friendly warmth, which meant that beneath their bickerings they were of one mind; and he spoke with a characteristic smile, humorous and self-depreciatory, yet redolent of subdued pleasure and strength. This smile was one of his best weapons in lady-killing.

"How unfair you women are! We all adore you, we hang on your least wishes, we are your slaves for life. We can't help it; it's a debt we owe to nature. And then, with a most groundless jealousy, you grudge us our revenge, our scattered moments of freedom, our poor melancholy old friendships!"

"You don't seem to be the slave of anyone yet."

"I assure you I am always in love. It has become a habit, and I am a slave to that. Poor Oliver didn't allow himself the comfort of habits—not in important matters. He kept revising himself, and never considered that if he had allowed himself to be as he naturally was, he would have been perfect."

"Certainly he wouldn't have improved himself by acquiring more virtues."

"You dislike virtue? That comes of being a clergyman's daughter. You are fed up with virtue, and with talk about it. But wild-flower virtue is the most charming thing in the world. Who could help loving it in Oliver? When was there ever such sweetness and such integrity?"

She saw a certain moisture in Vanny's eyes, as again he shook hands silently and turned to go. It was hopeless to struggle with these foolish men. They were so sentimental and so strong.

Vanny had a great tolerance for human frailty, and a positive love for variety of temperaments, especially in women. He could have undertaken the taming of the shrew; spirit and originality attracted him more than oddity offended him. Even to vice or to deception practised upon himself, he was full of good-natured indifference. Yet that evening, as he walked back to Oxford by the deserted river— for those were the Christmas holidays—he couldn't throw off a certain disquiet. He was profoundly surprised and aggrieved at the reception he had met with. What could have attached Oliver to this family, that proved so unworthy of his affection? Even the brother apparently had been a bad sixpence; and one might like a parson's sermons without wishing to marry his daughter, and without handsomely providing for his illegitimate grandchildren. What morbid fancy could have fixed Oliver's hopes upon this nominal sweetheart so scornful of his love, so ungenerous to his merits? Strange proud girl; no heart; couldn't possibly bring herself to love anybody, and was desperate in consequence.

Suddenly a new thought flashed into his mind. He stopped short, and looked back towards Iffley Mill, still faintly visible beneath its poplars. "Didn't she look at me rather steadily, rather oddly," he muttered, slapping his leg with his light military cane. "Didn't she count my wounds? Didn't she ask if I was returning to The House? Didn't she revert to me at every turn, instead of talking about Oliver? By Jove, it's that! She loathed him, not for himself—who could have loathed him for himself?—but because he was interposed between us, because even his memory will keep me from making up to her. *Que faire?* Go back, and begin a concerted attack? Say I had forgotten to ask if she didn't want to see Oliver's verses—which I should jolly well keep her from seeing? And when she says no, or shows indifference, open the offensive? And it could be an *Ueberfall,* because I'm sure of my ground. Well, and what then? *Marry* her? *Jamais de la vie.* I can't marry a woman without religion or family or money. It would be a crime against my children. True she now has a thousand a year, but it's only during her life. You can't found a family upon a life-annuity. Yes: but marriage being out of the running, there's an alternative. Seduce her? I can't seduce her. I never seduced any woman—not intentionally. I might tell her frankly that I can't marry, and make love to her on those terms. She is good-looking, she is intelligent—too intelligent. For a country girl, she is strangely distinguished. Yet hasn't she rather a fishy eye? It would be play-acting: a tiresome farce. I may have kissed a girl now and then out of pity, because she was a dear sweet thing and in her tears I really loved her; but to take up with a woman of this calibre, in the grand style, out of pity—what an absurdity! Her lover ought to adore her, or at least admire and venerate her, as poor Oliver did. But I know she's just like other women at bottom, only she walks on stilts. If I asked her to come with me to Paris for a fortnight, would she be offended? Would she jump at it? By Jove, I think she would. She's modern, she has no prejudices. Probably doesn't care whether she's married to her husband or not. She would be developing her personality. She would be gathering experience. She would be living a crowded hour of life." Here Mario added several strong expressions, French and Italian, turned on his heel, and resumed his walk towards Oxford at a great pace.

After a little, however, without knowing why, he stopped again, stooped, and carefully chose from the pebbles in the path, a suitable flat flint, and sent it fiercely skimming over the surface of the water. It was a small boy's diversion. He hadn't indulged in it since that remote time when, still unconscious of woman's charms, he had walked on feast days along the canal at Brussels with his little school comrades, two by two, in their black uniforms with brass buttons. Throwing stones was forbidden, but could be done when the young priest in charge was looking the other way. He was an amiable young man, and sometimes looked the other way on purpose. Ah, in what foolish things we take pleasure, things foolishly loved and foolishly forbidden! That bit of stone sent flying over the smooth face of the water was a perfect symbol to Vanny for all the mysteries of passion. It expressed, it relieved, and it dismissed with boyish derision, his momentary impulse to play the libertine. He had had, in imagination, his childish lark; he had had his fling; and he had utterly outgrown his desire to have it.

As he hastened on, with a joyous stride, swinging his stick and knocking off the heads of any too tall wayside grasses, the tag of an old French comedy kept running in his head: *Je ne vous aime pas, Marianne; c'était Célio qui vous aimait.*

Meantime, at Hawthorne Lodge, Rose had shut herself up again in her own small chamber; but this time, with no indiscreet visitor to overhear her, she didn't restrain her emotions. "Rose dear, don't cry," said her mother softly, stopping at the door, opening it a little, but not going in; for Mrs. Darnley stood in a certain awe of her daughter, and didn't wish to intrude into her private sorrows. "No need breaking your silly heart over a young man who's dead and gone. Hasn't he left you a pretty penny, and can't you marry somebody else? After all, he was a stranger to us, and no ladies' man. Yet for all that," the old lady mumbled, dropping into a cockney whine, like those poor women who sell matches at the street corners, "he was a *kind gentleman.*"

EPILOGUE

EPILOGUE

*F*iteen *years and more had elapsed since Mario Van de Weyer had first urged me to write this biography. We were still almost neighbours, but no longer in Paris. Different motives had prompted each of us to shift his centre to Rome, he more than ever in the current of the world and I more than ever out of it. We seldom met. Our acquaintance had passed into that serene crepuscular phase in which nothing more is demanded, and every past episode is affectionately folded in the cedar-chest of memory, to be shaken out on occasion together with the fragrance of time long past. At length I was able to send him a rough draft of these pages, composed at odd moments in the intervals of other work. He knew that, like the Pope, I accepted no invitations and paid no visits; but I asked him, after he had had time to dip into my manuscript, to come some fine day to lunch with me at the Pincio and tell me his impressions.*

Accordingly we sat one early afternoon, basking in the oblique warmth of the wintry sun, yet sheltered overhead by evergreen oak and ilex from the naked glare of the sky.

In respect to this novel, as I called it, I explained how insecure I had felt all these years, like an old schoolmaster for the first time in the saddle, at one moment innocently elated, and at the next in total distress. This wasn't my métier. However, I had got back alive to the stable, and safely dismounted. I stood again with both feet on my own ground; and I could laugh with him at my foolish excursion, if he pronounced it ridiculous.

My friend smiled amiably, looked about as if in doubt which of various observations to make first, and then said nothing.

Naturally he couldn't tell me outright to put the whole thing in the fire; but I was curious to know the grounds of his judgment.

"For instance," I said, "what of the characters, and in the first place of your own? Are you satisfied with your portrait?"

"It's no portrait; or so flattered that nobody would recognise it. You exaggerate enormously my favour with the fair sex. I wasn't different from any other young spark."

"You were more of a Don Juan than you now choose to remember. But you needn't disown your past. You are all of a piece, and your evolution has been

natural. *Don't you remember saying to Oliver that you wished to be a Knight of Malta? He thought the notion whimsical, but you have done even better. Gallantry in a gentleman passes easily into chivalry, and chivalry into religion."*

"With my father-in-law's position at the Vatican," he replied colouring a little, "the thing came of itself."

"No, no. It wasn't mere nepotism; rather the outward sign of an inward grace. Your modernness sucks in all the sap of the past, like the modernness of the new Italy; and any future worth having will spring from men like you, not from weedy intellectuals or self-inhibited puritans. Fortune will never smile on those who disown the living forces of nature. You can well afford to let an old philosopher here and there anticipate death and live as much as possible in eternity. The truth cannot help triumphing at the last judgment. Perhaps it cannot triumph before. Perhaps, while life lasts, in order to reconcile mankind with reality, fiction in some directions may be more needful than truth. You are at home in the grand tradition. With the beautiful Donna Laura and your charming children, you will hand on the torch of true civilisation; or rather, in this classic Italy, you have little need of tradition or torches. You have blood within and sunlight above, and are true enough to the past in being true to yourselves."

"Yes. We are frankly animal—But to return to your book. Besides overglorifying my peccadilloes, you almost turn me into a clever chap, which I never was. You put into my mouth a lot of good things of your own, or of Howard Sturgis's, or of other friends of yours. Moreover, in general, you make us all talk in your own philosophical style, and not in the least as we actually jabber. Your women are too intelligent, and your men also. There is clairvoyance in every quarter; whereas in the real world we are all unjust to one another and deceived about ourselves."

"Granted, granted," said I delighted that at last the ball was rolling merrily. "I hardly see anybody, and I don't know how people talk. But that doesn't matter for my purpose. If I had been absolutely true to life, half my possible readers wouldn't have understood me. I wasn't composing a philological document in which future antiquarians might study the dialects and slang of the early twentieth century. I have made you all speak the lingo natural to myself, as Homer made all his heroes talk in Ionian hexameters. Fiction is poetry, poetry is inspiration, and every word should come from the poet's heart, not out of the mouths of other people. If here and there I have hinted at a characteristic idiom, it's not for the sake of the idiom but for the sake of the character or the mood. Even in the simplest of us passion and temperament have a rich potential rhetoric that never finds utterance; and all the resources

*of a poet's language are requisite to convey not what his personages would
have been likely to say, but what they were really feeling. So with the characters
themselves, I am not photographing real people and changing their names.
On the contrary, wherever discretion permits, I keep the real names and the
real places, just as Homer does. Real names have a wonderful atmosphere.
But I recast, I re-live, I entirely transform the characters. They are creatures
of imagination. Imagination! We are of imagination all compact. You know
how energetically I reject the old axiom that sights and sounds exist in the
material world, and somehow cause us to perceive them. Sights and sounds
are products of the organism; they are forms of imagination; and all the
treasures of experience are nothing but spontaneous fictions provoked by the
impacts of material things. How foolish, then, should I have been in my own
eyes to reject the images which you and my other friends have excited within
me, when I have no other pigments at my disposal with which to paint
mankind! Yet though an image must be only an image, it may be more or less
suitable and proper. And if we were not all clairvoyant at bottom, how should
we ever recognise clairvoyance in others? How much poetic truth, for instance,
is there in my picture of Oliver himself?"*

*"More than in your picture of me. You knew him well. But you idealise
him, and make him too complex. You introduce something Freudian into him
which I never saw a sign of: fixations, transferences, inhibitions, or whatever
else you call them. To my mind, he was perfectly normal, only a little vague
and undeveloped. He required a lot of time to mobilise his forces."*

*"Yes," I interrupted, "because his forces were very great and drawn from
a vast territory."*

*"Perhaps: but then why do you make him so much more intelligent than he
seemed? You endow him with altogether too much insight. In reality he was
simply bewildered. There was a fundamental darkness within him, a long
arctic night, as in all Nordics."*

*"But isn't the arctic night very brilliant? And after the aurora borealis
isn't there an arctic day, no less prolonged? I think there is no great truth
that sensitive Nordics don't sometimes discover: only they don't stick to their
best insights. They don't recognise the difference between a great truth and a
speculative whim, and they wander off again into the mist, empty-handed and
puzzle-headed. As to moral complications in Oliver, you must allow me my
diagnosis. He was the child of an elderly and weary man, and of a thin-spun
race; from his mother he got only his bigness and athleticism, which notoriously
don't wear well. A moral nature burdened and over-strung, and a critical
faculty fearless but helplessly subjective—isn't that the true tragedy of your*

ultimate Puritan? However, suppose I am wrong about the facts. Shall I tear the book up, or will it do as a fable?"

"As a fable you may publish it. It's all your invention; but perhaps there's a better philosophy in it than in your other books."

"How so?"

"Because now you're not arguing or proving or criticising anything, but painting a picture. The trouble with you philosophers is that you misunderstand your vocation. You ought to be poets, but you insist on laying down the law for the universe, physical and moral, and are vexed with one another because your inspirations are not identical."

"Are you accusing me of dogmatism? Do I demand that everybody should agree with me?"

"Less loudly, I admit, than most philosophers. Yet when you profess to be describing a fact, you can't help antagonising those who take a different view of it, or are blind altogether to that sort of object. In this novel, on the contrary, the argument is dramatised, the views become human persuasions, and the presentation is all the truer for not professing to be true. You have said it somewhere yourself, though I may misquote the words: After life is over and the world has gone up in smoke, what realities might the spirit in us still call its own without illusion save the form of those very illusions which have made up our story?"

THE END

EDITORIAL
APPENDIX

LIST OF ABBREVIATIONS

The following abbreviations are used to designate the sources of readings:

MSpref Holograph manuscript of the preface to the Triton Edition of *The Last Puritan* (New York: Charles Scribner's Sons, 1937, vol. 11, vii–xv), used as copy-text for the Critical Edition text of the preface.

TSpref Scribner's typescript of the holograph manuscript of the preface to the Triton Edition.

TS Typescript of *The Last Puritan* used as copy-text.

TSGS Typescript marked with alterations by Santayana.

CP Constable page proofs (second proof) used as copy-text for those pages missing from the typescript.

E The English edition of *The Last Puritan* (London: Constable Publishers, 1935). Unless subsequent states or impressions are noted, the *E* will stand for the entire edition.

E^b The English edition, first impression, second state.

E^c The English edition, first impression, third state.

E^2 The English edition, second impression (London: Constable Publishers, 1935).

EGS Santayana's personal copy of the Constable 1935 first impression, first state,

with his annotations and corrections.

A The American first edition of *The Last Puritan* (New York: Charles Scribner's Sons, 1936A). Unless subsequent impressions are noted, the *A* will stand for the entire edition.

A^1936 The American first edition, second impression (New York: Charles Scribner's Sons, 1936).

A^1936b The American first edition, third impression (New York: Charles Scribner's Sons, 1936).

A^1937 The American first edition, fourth impression (New York: Charles Scribner's Sons, 1937).

A^1952 The American first edition, final impression during Santayana's lifetime (New York: Charles Scribner's Sons, 1952).

A2 The Triton Edition of *The Last Puritan*, in Volumes XI and XII of *The Works of George Santayana* (New York: Charles Scribner's Sons, 1937).

O "Oliver Chooses to Be a Boy," an excerpt from *The Last Puritan*, appeared in *The Saturday Review of Literature* prior to publication of the novel in the United States (12 [1935]: 3–4, 16).

CE The present Critical Edition.

SHORT-TITLE BIBLIOGRAPHY

The following short-title bibliography includes the works most frequently cited in the Notes to the Text. Annotated books and books referred to only once or twice are cited fully. Citations for works by Santayana, both published and unpublished, may be found in *George Santayana, A Bibliographical Checklist, 1880–1980* (Bowling Green, Ohio: Philosophy Documentation Center, 1982).

Egotism	George Santayana. *Egotism in German Philosophy*. New York: Charles Scribner's Sons, 1915; London: Dent, 1916.
Faust	Johann Wolfgang von Goethe. *Faust*, The Original German and A New Translation and Introduction by Walter Kaufmann, Part One and Sections from Part Two. Garden City, New York: Anchor Books, Doubleday & Co., 1963.
Harvard	Samuel Eliot Morison. *Three Centuries of Harvard*. Cambridge, Mass.: Harvard University Press, 1936.
Interpretations	George Santayana. *Interpretations of Poetry and Religion*. William G. Holzberger and Herman J. Saatkamp, Jr., eds. Cambridge, Mass. and London: The MIT Press, 1990
Life	John Francis Stanley, 2d Earl Russell. *My Life and Adventures*. London: Cassell, 1923.
Persons and Places	George Santayana. *Persons and Places: Fragments of Autobiography*. William G. Holzberger and Herman J. Saatkamp, Jr., eds. Cambridge, Mass. and London: The MIT Press, 1986.
Poems	William G. Holzberger, ed. *The Complete Poems of George Santayana*. Lewisburg, Pa.: Bucknell University Press, 1979.
Poets	George Santayana. *Three Philosophical Poets: Lucretius, Dante, and Goethe*. Cambridge: Harvard University Press; London: Oxford University Press, 1910.
Santayana	John McCormick. *George Santayana: A Biography*. New York: Alfred A. Knopf, Inc., 1987.
Scepticism	George Santayana. *Scepticism and Animal Faith: Introduction to a System of Philosophy*. New York: Charles Scribner's Sons; London: Constable & Co., 1923.
Shakespeare	William A. Wright, ed. *The Works of William Shakespeare*. 9 vols. New York: AMS Press, 1968 rpt. of 1891–1893 edition.

NOTES TO THE TEXT

4.8–9 Aristotle . . . history] From the *Poetics*, 1451b 6–7.

5.14–16 the early . . . accident.] [See Note at 518.3.]

8.5 Stoics . . . Spinoza] A school of Greek philosophy founded by Zeno of Citium around 308 B.C., Stoicism's fundamental injunction is to follow the law of nature. The physics of the Stoics is identified mainly with their theology; that is, God is the formative power that makes each thing what it is and that harmonizes all things. Living according to the orderliness and benevolence of the universe, one can achieve the ultimate desideratum of spiritual peace or *eudaimonia*. But, in contrast to Epicureanism, the Stoic must do more than seek his own happiness; he has a duty to promote the cosmopolis in reflecting the rationally ordered physical world. This is a duty of service to mankind based on the recognition of each person as a rational, creative being. The Stoicism found in Cicero's *De Officiis*, for example, emphasizes logical reasoning, self-discipline, temperance, and philanthropy.

Baruch (or Benedict) Spinoza (1632–1677), a rationalist metaphysician of Jewish descent, was born in Amsterdam. Spinoza's philosophy finds its fullest expression in his work *Ethics* (*Ethica Ordine Geometrico Demonstrata*). Breaking with Cartesian mechanistic rationalism and with Hobbesian empiricism, Spinoza maintains one cannot understand the world without understanding it as a whole, a single system that has two names, "God" and "Nature." The unity of this system lies in the deductive and geometrical character of substance which is capable of the two primary attributes of extension and thought. Spinoza's unity of substance is counter to any dualism: mind-body, God-world. In addition, the empiricist-rationalist controversy does not arise in Spinoza since these views represent different levels at which the mind operates. As with the Stoics, Spinoza's moral philosophy depends upon his metaphysics. However, neither he nor the Stoics believed in a God who rewards and punishes; thus the Universe-God they believed in "inspired but did not sanction" their moral philosophy. Strikingly individualistic, Spinoza has exerted considerable influence on modern philosophy since his rediscovery by Goethe and Schelling. Together with Plato and Aristotle, Spinoza is one of the chief sources of Santayana's philosophic inspiration. At the time of his graduation from Harvard College, Santayana published his essay "The Ethical Doctrine of Spinoza" (*Harvard Monthly* 2 [June 1886]: 144–52). Later, he wrote an introduction to the *Ethics* and *De Intellectus Emendatione* of Spinoza (London: Dent, 1910, vii–xxii). In his autobiography, Santayana acknowledges Spinoza as his "master and model" in understanding the naturalistic basis of morality (*Persons and Places*, 234–35).

9.6 Babbitts] Taken from the main character of Sinclair Lewis's novel *Babbitt*, the name has come to stand for a person who conforms unthinkingly to prevailing middle-class standards, who makes a cult of material success, and who is unappreciative of artistic or intellectual values.

10.1–4 *On . . .* ALAIN.] Alain, pen name of Émile-Auguste Chartier (1868–1951), a French philosopher and essayist best known for his *propos*, or short essays on well-known aphorisms. The quotation may be translated: "It is well said that experience speaks through the mouth of older men: but the best experience that they can bring to us is that of their salvaged youth." In *Persons and Places* Santayana emphasizes how much he has enjoyed his own youth and the youth of others in his old age, in recollection, and refers to *The Last Puritan* as one of the books which has allowed him to do this (535–36). For a linking of this motto with a specific characterization in the novel, see Note at 145.15.

11.2 *Mario Van de Weyer*] According to *Persons and Places*, Santayana's precocious undergraduate friend Ward Thoron was one model for Mario. Half-foreign in parentage, Catholic, rich and from New York, his "verbal sparkle and easy manners" betrayed a jolly cynicism that in everything "he was playing a farce, and there seemed to be nothing else for him to do." Santayana reports that Thoron once authored a college essay about the *"Art of Lying"* (221–22).

    Daniel Cory remarks in *The Later Years*, "In regard to Mario . . . I had reason to believe that I was one of the prototypes Santayana had in mind in creating him" (143). Another possible inspiration for Mario, as suggested by McCormick, may have been Robert Collier, wealthy son of the founder of *Collier's Weekly*. Collier also was a Catholic, from New York, "and a great sport" (*Santayana*, 331). Santayana met him in 1896 and described him in a letter to Guy Murchie dated 12 March of the same year: "My friend is living with his mother at the Empire, and deceives her into thinking he is at Harvard College, while he only comes out to Cambridge to see a friend of his and lounge about, until it is time to go to dinner and to the Hollis Street Theatre where one of the troupe is his present flame. This pleasant youth has been at Oxford, knows something of the lighter contemporary literature, and is lavish with invitations." (For more on the character of Mario, see notes at 145.15 and 287.5–9.)

11.3–4 *Left . . . Germain.*] Situated on the Left Bank of the Seine is the Quartier Latin and the University of Paris; to the west lies the fashionable residential suburb of the Faubourg Saint-Germain. The eastern area of this suburb is the residence of artists and literati. Santayana's long-time friend, Charles A. Strong, maintained an apartment at no. 9, rue de l'Observatoire in the Faubourg Saint-Germain, where from 1920–1927 Santayana spent part of every summer. He recalled in *Persons and Places*: "My nominal headquarters, as well as my books, remained for some time at Strong's," and "in the evening, I could remember that all Paris lay at my feet, behind that screen of green trees, and I would go to the Boulevards or to the Champs Elysées for a stroll and for dinner" (525–26).

11.15–17 *Windsor . . . Sturgis*] Howard Sturgis was the youngest son of Russell Sturgis, brother of George Sturgis, Santayana's mother's first husband. Howard Sturgis lived on the outskirts of Windsor Park in a house called Queen's Acre, near Eton College. A minor novelist, he was a friend of Santayana's from 1889, when the two men met, until his death in 1920. (Also see Note at 278.38.)

12.34–35 École . . . *Julian's,*] The *École des Beaux-Arts,* France's national school of fine arts in Paris, has departments of painting and graphic arts, sculpture, and architecture. Drawing and painting were taught at L'Académie Julian, founded in 1868 by the minor French painter Rodolphe Julian. It had an international reputation, particularly attracting many American students. Several of Santayana's friends studied at these institutions, Robert Potter and Lawrence Butler at the *Beaux-Arts,* Howard Cushing at Julian's (see *Persons and Places,* 350, 381–82).

12.37 *Lampoon*] Harvard University humor magazine, established in 1876. In his freshman year at Harvard, Santayana began to contribute drawings to the Harvard *Lampoon.* (See *Persons and Places,* 186–90.)

13.17 *mother*] Maddalena Van de Weyer, Mario's Italian mother and a fine mezzo-soprano.

13.34 *Lapérouse*] This Paris restaurant at the Quai des Grands-Augustins above the Seine had a star in the 1888 Baedeker. By the 1890s it was on the same footing as the Tour d'Argent and Foyot. The restaurant is located in the Latin Quarter, in the same area as Santayana's Paris residence at his old friend Strong's apartment on the rue de l'Observatoire (see Note at 11.3–4).

13.35–14.6 *the young* . . . PURITAN] Though the character of Oliver Alden has no single source, Santayana identified four friends of his youth who contributed attributes to the hero. Edward Bayley, an early friend and the original model for Oliver, was handsome, broad-minded yet committed to his Puritan roots, and possessed "perfect integrity" (*Persons and Places,* 178). Another prototype, Lawrence Butler, was a good sportsman who never married, and, more significantly, was plagued by indecision that ultimately left him "petered out": he could become neither an atheist nor a Roman Catholic, and in singing he tried "to coax and simulate emotions that he didn't feel" (*Persons and Places,* 382–83). In a letter to Alyse Gregory (10 November 1938), Santayana points to Scofield Thayer, editor of *The Dial* during the later 1920s, who "didn't seem spontaneous and natural; he found life difficult, and wasn't at home in this world." He adds that Thayer's hometown in Worcester, Massachusetts, almost became Oliver's birthplace, but its "topography" was wrong for the novel (see Note at 62.26–27). Finally, the puritan Cam Forbes, wealthy but ascetic, provided three traits: though he did not drink, he assumed it his duty to be sure someone provided drinks at parties he gave (*Persons and Places,* 348); he inspired the bootlace which Oliver uses instead of a watch-chain at 131.36–37 (Santayana to Boylston Adams Beal, 23 December 1935); and his father, William Forbes, was a self-indulgent and perhaps listless man (*Persons and Places,* 347). (For more notes on the characterization of Oliver, see 131.3–13 on Oliver and duty; 192.26–28 and 313.8 on Oliver's being likened to certain Biblical figures; 97.1–2, 223.6–33, and 287.5–9 on Oliver and Hamlet; and 518.3 on Oliver's "petering out.")

14.17–18 *Then* . . . *conscience*] This actually happened to Santayana; he alludes to it briefly in *Persons and Places* (133–34).

14.36–38 *people . . . singlemindedness*] An allusion to Matthew 18:8–9 (in the Sermon on the Mount): "Wherefore if thy hand or thy foot offend thee, cut them off, and cast them from thee: it is better for thee to enter into life halt or maimed, rather than having two hands or two feet to be cast into everlasting fire. And if thine eye offend thee, pluck it out, and cast it from thee: it is better for thee to enter into life with one eye, rather than having two eyes to be cast into hell fire."

17.1–2 *old Calvinists*] Here and at 307.7 Santayana makes a connection between Oliver and the "old Calvinists" who "hadn't been puritan enough."

21.2–22.40 the State House . . . King's Chapel] Nathaniel Alden lives in a very circumscribed world, as his brother's relief at learning that Beacon Street is not "the whole world" perhaps indicates (47.37–38). During the nineteenth century, Beacon Street, facing the 48-acre Common and with the seat of the Massachusetts State Legislature near its highest point, became the chief residential avenue for the Boston brahmins. The Mall and the Frog Pond are parts of the Common. Whenever Nathaniel walks up Beacon Hill (22.3–4), he passes the front of the State House and comes to the juncture of Beacon and Park Streets, where across from the State House sits Ticknor House, which gets its name from the eminent occupant George Ticknor (1791–1871), historian of Spanish literature and friend of the younger historian William Prescott (see Note at 183.9–10). Continuing on past Park Street, Nathaniel will come across the Boston Athenaeum, which maintained a library for the use of its members and also an art collection until 1876, when the collection was moved and became the Museum of Fine Arts. At this extremity of Beacon Street he will also encounter King's Chapel, one of the oldest churches in the city; Tremont House, the most luxurious hotel in America when built (29.9); and the Boston Museum, a theatre successively billed as the "Lecture Hall" and then "Museum" to allay the fears of respectable citizens (25.31–32). In the 1870s the Somerset Club, located on Beacon Street, was the club of clubs in Boston (61.23); and, back in the residential area near where Nathaniel lives, are Mt. Vernon Street (61.26) and Mount Vernon Place (185.4–5). When Nathaniel walks *down* Beacon Street, he is pointed toward the Back Bay, where land-filling is creating new growth for the city and ultimately a new center (see Note at 41.35).

21.7 twins] This is a description of Santayana's mother's house at 302 Beacon Street (see *Persons and Places*, 137–41).

22.3 Mr. Nathaniel Alden] Santayana wrote to his editor, John Hall Wheelock, "Mr. Nathaniel Alden is a recognisable caricature of two real persons, long since dead, & both old bachelors" (27 July 1935). In later letters to George Sturgis (12 March 1940) and to Rosamond Sturgis (8 February 1948), Santayana noted that Nathaniel was also derived from Dr. George Parkman: according to the second letter, the Parkman modeling included "some traits of Mr. Thomas Wigglesworth." He also based the murder of Nathaniel's father on that of Parkman in 1849, which was the crime of the century in America. Cleveland Amory relates the details of the case in his *The Proper Bostonians* (207–27), to which Santayana refers in the 1948 letter. Like Nathaniel's father, Parkman, elderly and respected but not liked as one of Boston's wealthiest men, was killed by a debtor, and was also "chopped up" for easier disposal by his murderer (see 166.6–7). In Parkman's case the killer was a professor of chemistry at the Harvard Medical School, John Webster White, who had been hounded mercilessly and personally by Parkman once the latter had perceived that White was not likely to pay back a debt. After the murder and trial, the Parkman family went into hiding: Parkman's son, who had been a merrymaking bachelor, moved his relations (including an invalid sister) to a new residence (on Beacon Street) and lived there for half a century in reclusion.

24.8 Julia] Nathaniel's mad sister Julia might have been inspired by Lizzie Grew, a member of the numerous Sturgis family (*Persons and Places*, 60).

24.33–25.6 The music . . . nations.] The Unitarians emphasize the unity of God as opposed to the doctrine of the Trinity; they minimalize doctrinaire principles and stress individual freedom of belief, the use of reason in religion, a commitment to advancing truth, religious tolerance, universal brotherhood of man, a creedless church, a united world community, and support of a vigorous program of liberal social action. After moving from Spain to Boston as a young boy, Santayana was exposed to Unitarian worship by his Brahmin relations. Reflecting on this experience in *Persons and Places*, he defines the appeal of Unitarianism as "the charm of religious nothingness" which allowed one to "feel religious without any intellectual consequences" (62). Elsewhere he criticizes the classical vocal music for its pretensions and obsoleteness, and recalls "the perfunctory, inaudible pretense at keeping up with the paid quartet that was really performing." He then gives a description of churchgoing similar to the one in the novel: "It seemed a little ridiculous, all those good people in their Sunday clothes, so demure, so conscious of one another, not needing in the least to pray or to be prayed for, nor inclined to sing, but liking to flock together once a week . . . and glad to hear a sermon like the leading article in some superior newspaper calculated to confirm the conviction already in them that their bourgeois virtues were quite sufficient and that perhaps in time poor backward races and nations might be led to acquire them" (160).

26.19 Mr. Tom Appleton] Probably Thomas Gold Appleton, 1812–1884, an essayist, poet, artist, and member of the literary coterie for which Boston was famous in the mid-nineteenth century. His presence among the literary society was not due to his artistic achievements but rather to his brilliant talk and flawless social graces.

27.14 Roxbury] Suburb of Boston where Santayana's mother lived during his graduate student days in the late 1880s.

29.9 Tremont House] [See Note at 21.2–22.40.]

31.18 Latin School] Santayana attended the Boston Public Latin School, a public high school founded in 1635, from 1874 until 1882, when he entered Harvard (see *Persons and Places*, "*The Latin School*").

32.24–25 vice . . . grossness] Edmund Burke in his *Letter to a member of the National Assembly* (1791).

35.25–27 Mr. Papanti's . . . ladies] Lorenzo Papanti, an exiled Tuscan count, established himself in Boston during the 1830s as dance instructor to young and old and introduced the ball into this puritan enclave. Mr. Papanti's "Friday evenings" afforded the matrons of Boston society an opportunity to bring their daughters into the company of rich Harvard freshmen (*Harvard*, 420).

37.5 Back Bay] Santayana lived near the Back Bay on Beacon Street during the time he was at the Boston Latin School (*Persons and Places*, 137–39).

41.35 Trinity Church] Built in the new Back Bay on Copley Square in the 1870s for Phillips Brooks (1835–1893), rector of Trinity Church for twenty-two years. The eminent and influential Episcopalian clergyman (ultimately a bishop) and Harvard overseer was a staunch supporter of the Union during the Civil War and one of the first to champion the rights of black people.

42.23 Associated Charities] Annie Fields, wife of the Boston publisher James T. Fields, was the founder and director of the Associated Charities of Boston.

42.36 Phillips Brooks] [See Note at 41.35.]

43.33–34 prophesied . . . some Irish Catholic might be mayor of Boston] Probably a reference to Patrick Fitzgerald, John F. Kennedy's grandfather, who was mayor of Boston, 1906–1907 and 1910–1913.

46.33 'The last shall be first.'] Matthew 19:30.

48.1–2 India Wharf] One of the largest wharves on the Boston waterfront during the nineteenth century, and where the East Indies and West Indies trade concentrated.

48.4 Richard Dana] Richard Henry Dana (1815–1882) wrote *Two Years before the Mast*, a narrative of his trip as a common seaman around Cape Horn to California.

48.19–49.9 the boy . . . Ishmael] The relationships among the three characters are thus: Nathaniel and Caroline are stepbrother and stepsister (no parents in common) and exactly the same age (49.1); Nathaniel and Peter are half brothers (same father, but different mothers); Peter and Caroline are half brother and half sister (same mother but different fathers). Peter's identification with Ishmael, Abraham's son through Hagar the Egyptian slave, is apt. Ishmael and Hagar were sent away into the wilderness when they became a political problem within Abraham's family after the birth of Isaac to Abraham's wife, Sarah (Book of Genesis 16:1–18:16, 21:1–21). In Nathaniel's eyes, Peter Alden, though the younger son, is an outcast like Ishmael. He sees himself as the legitimate heir, and Peter—offspring of a Southerner—as a usurper. (For an identification of Oliver as Isaac, see 313.7–9.)

49.19 petered out] In letters to Rosamond Sturgis, Santayana noted that he gave
Nathaniel "a younger brother, Peter, to peter out," and later told her that Peter was
"an amiable type of failure; there were many such in my day" (8 February 1948
and 5 February 1936). One possible model for Peter may have been Santayana's
own father, who, like Peter, was well-travelled, had married unwisely, and doted on
his own health (*Persons and Places*, 27, 424). Another possible model for Peter could
have been Andrew Green, who not only cruised the rivers of China in a junk (see
57.7–34), but also, according to Santayana in *Persons and Places*, possessed a "strong
satirical sense and . . . strong aesthetic sense," yet lacked "singleness of mind" (385–
86). Another inspiration may have been Colonel William Hathaway Forbes, who,
though wealthy and successful, was in Santayana's eyes "a man in whose life there
was something vague and ineffectual" (*Persons and Places*, 347; see Note at 13.35–
14.6). The prophecy of "petering out" is also referred to at 518.3 where its application to Peter's son Oliver is made explicit.

50.21–22 Elsa . . . Schwan.] The heroine of Richard Wagner's (1818–1883) opera
Lohengrin, Elsa is the victim of an unscrupulous attempt by relatives to deprive her
of her hereditary lands. She demands trial by combat, saying that she has seen her
champion in a dream. On the appointed day he comes, in a boat drawn by a swan,
nameless but in the outcome victorious. They are betrothed, but after further
troubles and his final slaying of her enemy, Elsa's champion reveals that he is
Lohengrin, a knight of the Holy Grail, and declares that he must leave. Yet Elsa is
consoled somewhat when the swan transforms into her brother, long before subjected to black arts by Elsa's enemies.
    Santayana had a life-long interest in opera, and, during his residence in Rome in
the 1920s and 1930s frequently attended performances at the Rome opera. His
greatest opportunity for experiencing Wagnerian opera, however, was during the
first year after his graduation from Harvard College, 1886–1887, when he and his
friend, Herbert Lyman, lived in Dresden and regularly attended performances of
Wagner's works at the Royal Theatre. He recalls these occasions, with comments on
the singers, in *Persons and Places* (254).

51.24 St. Anthony] St. Anthony the Great of Egypt (*c*.250–350), generally accounted
the founder of monasticism, was noted for the demonic temptations to which he
was subjected, including those of women and family life.

54.5–8 He . . . class] This desultory existence resembles Santayana's own in school (see
Persons and Places, "*The Latin School*"; "*The Harvard Yard*"; and "*College Studies*").

54.15 Montaigne] Michel Eyquem de Montaigne (1533–1592), French philosopher
and man of letters. His most important philosophical work is the skeptical essay,
"Apology for Raimond Sebond," in which he claims that humans can have no access
to truth or reality except through the grace of God. Santayana claims, in a letter of
7 October 1947 to William Elton, not to have read Montaigne very much, or to
have been much influenced by him.

54.15 *Don Quixote*] For Santayana's opinion of *Don Quixote* see "Cervantes (1547–1616)" (Charles D. Warner, ed. *A Library of the World's Best Literature, Ancient and Modern*, vol. 8 [New York: Knickerbocker Press, 1896], 3451–3457) and "Tom Sawyer and Don Quixote" (*Mark Twain Quarterly* [Winter 1952]: 1–3).

54.20–21 now . . . die] This echoes Keats's "Ode to a Nightingale."

54.26–55.38 There . . . country.] Peter's misadventure apparently had a real-life counterpart in the experience of a male member of the Forbes family. In a letter to Boylston Adams Beal dated 23 December 1935 Santayana wrote: "I hope the Forbes's won't mind the story about the college Bible. I tell it as it reached me, or as it shaped itself years after in my own mind. Perhaps it is transformed enough not to be recognisable, and in any case it is such ancient history now that I suppose it may be printed without offence." Samuel Eliot Morison originally identified the secret society at Harvard as the D.K.E., "Dickey" or "Deeks" (*Harvard*, 424), but he later wrote Santayana that it had been the "Med.Fac." and that the watchman had not been killed (Santayana to Hamilton Vaughan Bail, 20 February 1950). The Med.Fac. specialized in playing pranks and was periodically supressed (*Harvard*, 205–206).

55.39–40 Cunarder . . . tons] A passenger ship of the Cunard Line, one of the two chief transatlantic voyaging companies. During his lifetime, Santayana made just over forty transatlantic crossings and kept a map noting the route, dates, and ship of each crossing. The *Samaria* was the steamship on which Santayana first came to America with his father in 1872 (see *Persons and Places*, 128–29). In September 1893 Santayana made a crossing from Southampton, England, to New York on the *Kaiser Wilhelm* (see 252.35), and in July 1901 his twenty-second crossing was from New York to Queenstown and Liverpool aboard the *Lucania* (see 312.36). Santayana crossed the Atlantic on the *Lusitania* in 1909 and again in 1910 (see 320.4–5).

57.7–34 married . . . men-servants] Peter's travels in Japan and China echo those of Andrew Green and William Sturgis Bigelow. In *Persons and Places*, Santayana relates that Green bought a junk and sailed the rivers of China, and, when he finally settled down (in the West Indies), married a "negress" and had children (385–86). Bigelow studied medicine and worked with Pasteur, but did not practice his medical profession. Rather, he journeyed to Japan, studied Buddhism, and, along with his fellow Bostonians Edward S. Morse and Ernest Fenollosa, collected Japanese art. The collections of these three men gave Boston the core of one of the largest collections of Japanese art in the world. Bigelow became a Buddhist, and, when he eventually returned to Boston, published his only book, *Buddhism and Immortality*. (Van Wyck Brooks, *New England: Indian Summer 1865–1915* [n.p.: Dutton, 1940], 358–60.)

58.3 Museum of Fine Arts] Built in Copley Square in the Back Bay about the same time as Trinity Church (see Note at 21.2–22.40).

59.20 *gemütlich*] "Cozy, comfortable."

59.24 alienists] Physicians treating diseases of the mind. (Today the term implies a specialist in the legal aspects of psychiatry.)

59.39–60.3 Nauplia . . . remains] Santayana is drawing on his own 1904–1906 travels in the Near East and Europe for descriptions of Peter's wanderings (see *Persons and Places*, "*Travels*"). Peter stays at Nauplia, an insignificant town in antiquity, because it has grown in the intervening time to be the chief city of the region. Tiryns and Mycenae were in Peter's day ruins only recently excavated by Schliemann. The latter polis once commanded the road leading to and from the Corinthian isthmus, and was accordingly a powerful metropolis of Mycenean civilization; its acropolis is where Schliemann found the famous Royal Shaft graves. Epidaurus is across the Argolis peninsula on the Gulf of Salamis; its theatre, virtually intact today, was accounted the most beautiful in Greece. Santayana found this same locale "the most inspiring" in Greece during his tour (*Persons and Places*, 465).

60.5 Homer] In *The Iliad* and *The Odyssey* there are several references to the "black ships" of the Greeks.

60.20 Charcot's] Jean Martin Charcot (1825–1893), neurologist famous for founding a clinic in Paris, used hypnosis in the treatment of hysteria; Freud studied under Charcot. Peter's aversion to Charcot echoes Santayana's own response to the philosophical currents in the Germany of 1886–1888, where he studied on the Walker Fellowship from Harvard. In a letter to William James dated 3 July 1888 he refers to "the German school" of "psycho-physics," and castigates Wundt, for example, as "a survival of the alchemist." Altogether, Santayana found himself "oppressed by the scholasticism of the thing and by the absurd pretension to be scientific." Santayana, like Peter, came home to Harvard from Europe to complete the doctorate.

60.28 Mr. Morgan] The banker J. P. Morgan (1837–1913) was an avid yachtsman, twice winner of the America's cup.

60.38–39 Tavern Club] A Boston male dining and social club, founded in 1884. Its members, primarily Boston and Cambridge business and professional men, artists, and professors, were (and are) elected. Santayana was elected in 1894, together with Justice Holmes and fourteen others; in *Persons and Places* he calls it "the only club I ever belonged to in Boston" (70). The club often hosted visiting dignitaries.

61.6 Physician, heal thyself] Luke 4:23.

61.23 Somerset Club] [See Note at 21.2–22.40.]

61.26 Mt. Vernon Street] [See Note at 21.2–22.40.]

62.13–14 New London . . . broad river] New London, Connecticut, is on the west bank of the Thames River. Santayana knew the area well (see Note at 471.2).

62.26–27 Asylum . . . Hill] In a letter to Alyse Gregory dated 10 November 1938 Santayana sardonically remarks that he invented Great Falls for its "topography," so that "between a cemetery and an insane asylum my hero might enter this best of possible worlds, in the best of ages, and the best of countries."

66.10–11 I don't . . . peace.] Santayana translates this line from La Vallière: "*Je ne suis pas heureuse, mais je suis contente*" (*Persons and Places*, 428, see Note at 170.2).

68.15–17 *Hesperus*. . . . mother] The poetess of Lesbos is Sappho (early 6th century B.C.), whose works survive mainly in fragments. The full text of the fragment Peter alludes to is: "Evening Star that bringest back all that lightsome Dawn hath scattered afar, thou bringest the sheep, thou bringest the goat, thou bringest her child home to the mother" (*Lyra Graeca*, J. M. Edmonds, ed. [Cambridge: Harvard University Press; London: Heinemann, 1952, rev. ed., 3 vols.], I:287–88). There is no mention of wine in the original text.

73.11–16 Browning . . . all.] Societies centering on a poet were a staple of the "genteel" American culture which Santayana later castigated; he delivered the original form of "The Poetry of Barbarism," partially a severe critique of Browning, before the Browning Club of Boston (*Interpretations*, xvii). Several other pieces of the common high-cultural furniture (sometimes literally such) of late nineteenth-century American life make their appearance in the novel; these are distinctly domestic and frequently native to New England. At 73.20 appears Gilbert Stuart (1755–1828), Rhode Islander who, after studying in England under Benjamin West, became a famous portraitist in England and later in America. To have had an ancestor's portrait painted by Stuart is a rare and prestigious thing for an American. At 75.18–19 we learn that Mrs. Alden is a Daughter of the American Revolution. At 75.35 Henry Wadsworth Longfellow's famous *The Courtship of Miles Standish* is alluded to: Longfellow (1807–1882) was himself a literary institution of New England (and America) until after the turn of the century; at 217.42 appears *The Illustrated Life of Washington*, which Mrs. Alden does not read but nevertheless retains as token of her cultural rectitude; at 219.17–18 appear *A Scottish Shepherd and His Dog* and *View of the Yosemite Valley*, probably Edwin Landseer's *The Old Shepherd's Chief Mourner* and Albert Bierstadt's *Valley of the Yosemite*. The English Landseer and the American Bierstadt were both very popular painters, and these often-reproduced works were typical decorations.

74.17–20 Whatever . . . home,] In a letter to Bruno Lind dated 29 November 1951 Santayana identifies "the absence of affection" among Peter, Harriet, and Oliver as reflective of the relations among his own parents and himself.

74.22 Oliver Optic] Oliver Optic was the pseudonym of William Taylor Adams (1822–1897), a prolific author of stories for boys and girls, and one of the writers Santayana read as a child (*Persons and Places*, 142).

75.13 Mr. Bernard Shaw and Mr. Bernard Berenson] George Bernard Shaw (1856–1950), playwright and Nobel laureate, whom Santayana probably never met. Bernard Berenson (1865–1959), Lithuanian-born art critic and connoisseur of Italian Renaissance art, was a year behind Santayana at both the Boston Latin School and Harvard College. Their friendship, while sometimes strained, was of long standing.

75.18–19 Daughter of the American Revolution] [See Note at 73.11–16.]

75.31 Krafft-Ebing's] Santayana substituted the name of Richard von Krafft-Ebing (1840–1902) for "Freud" in his typescript of *The Last Puritan*. Krafft-Ebing was an Austrian physiologist who authored *Psychopathia Sexualis*, one of the many Viennese pre-Freudian formulations of human sexual deviance. Santayana went to Germany in 1886 and was probably familiar with Krafft-Ebing's magnum opus, published that year. For Santayana's personal response to the psychologizing prevalent in German philosophy at the time, see the Note at 60.20.

75.35 *The Courtship of Miles Standish*] [See Note at 73.11–16.]

80.3–82.20 The child . . . night.] Santayana's letter to Daniel Cory dated 12 November 1934—when the novel was complete and at the typist's—indicates that Santayana had been reading Heidegger for some time. Santayana wrote "Cp. the psychology of the infant Oliver" in the margin of his copy of *Sein und Zeit*, at the place where "Heidegger discusses space and the extension of Being-in-the-world" (*Santayana*, 332). (See Martin Heidegger, *Sein und Zeit*, 2 vols., 3rd ed. [Halle: Niemeyer, 1931], I:110.)

82.35–36 Fuzzy-Wuzzy] From Rudyard Kipling's poem "Fuzzy-Wuzzy" in *Barrack-Room Ballads* (1892).

84.10–17 I should . . . day.] By "pure" Santayana evidently meant non-regionalized, non-vernacular and rather British pronunciation. Elsewhere in the novel he connects purity and Britishness (95.14–16), and in *Persons and Places* relates that Lady Stanley of Alderley declared that he spoke "like Queen Victoria" (134–35). Daniel Cory once told William Holzberger that Santayana's accent was more British than American. See also a letter dated 14 March 1945 in which Santayana half-whimsically castigates Daniel Cory for "debasing my pure and legitimate English to conform to the vernacular," presumably in connection with Cory's supervision of the publication of the first two parts of *Persons and Places* in America during the Second World War.

85.20–21 Crete . . . excavations] The excavations at Knossos and other sites in Crete began just after the turn of the century. While in Athens during his tour of the Mediterranean and Near East (1904–1905), Santayana heard Sir Arthur Evans (1851–1941), most famous of the excavators in Crete, describe these discoveries (*Persons and Places*, 456).

87.3 Göttingen] Santayana began his graduate studies there in Germany in 1886.

87.4 Lotze] Rudolph Hermann Lotze (1817–1881), German philosopher who, conceding that the physical world is governed by mechanical laws, explained relation and development in the universe as functions of a world mind. Lotze was professor of philosophy at Göttingen from 1844–1881. Upon returning from Germany in 1888 Santayana wished to write his doctoral dissertation on Schopenhauer, but his dissertation director, Josiah Royce, advised him to write instead on Lotze, under whom Royce had studied. Santayana later called the result "a dull thesis" on a philosophy he characterized as "still-born" (*Persons and Places*, 389), which may explain the reference to "tepid philosophical currents" on 87.3–4.

Although Santayana nowhere acknowledges it, several people have written that he owes a certain intellectual debt to Lotze. John McCormick and Jerome Ashmore both see the influence of Lotze in Santayana's *The Sense of Beauty*, and Paul G. Kuntz is convinced that much of what was later refined in *Realms of Being* was already visible in the 1889 dissertation, "Lotze's Moral Philosophy"; indeed, Thomas Munson feels that the criticism of Lotze expressed in the dissertation could equally well apply to Santayana himself. (See *Santayana* [83, 126]; Jerome Ashmore, *Santayana, Art and Aesthetics* [Cleveland: Western Reserve, 1966, 26]; Paul G. Kuntz, ed., *Lotze's System of Philosophy* [Bloomington: Indiana, 1971, 4]; Thomas N. Munson, *The Essential Wisdom of George Santayana* [New York: Columbia, 1962, 88].)

87.6–7 Frau . . . boarders] While undertaking graduate study at Göttingen in 1886, Santayana actually boarded at the house of a "Frau Pastorin Schlote, whose elderly daughter . . . knew English and gave the foreign boarders lessons in German" (*Persons and Places*, 253).

87.17–24 *Eierkuchen . . . Aussichtspunkt*] *Eierkuchen* may mean either "omelet" or "pancake"; *Aussichtspunkt* is a "scenic vantage point".

88.13 Williams College] Santayana's connections with Williams College were few. In *Persons and Places* he says that he visited there only three times; however, his "first real friend," Bentley Warren, graduated a year early from the Boston Latin School to go there, and he and Santayana maintained a correspondence subsequently, at least until Warren's graduation, which Santayana attended at his own expense (174–75). In a letter to George Washburne Howgate dated 31 May 1933 Santayana reveals that it was because of Warren's having gone there and the "lively correspondence" between the two boys that he decided to send Oliver Alden to Williams. (See 216 for Oliver's decision to go to Williams.)

88.27 Lotte of *Werthers Leiden*] Charlotte, called "Lotte," is the chief female character in Goethe's early novel, *Die Leiden des jungen Werthers* (*The Sorrows of Young Werther*). Werther, a sensitive artist, is hopelessly in love with Charlotte, who is married to someone else. Ill at ease with the world and dissatisfied with life, Werther commits suicide. The work was a huge success throughout Europe. Young men adopted Werther's style of dress—blue coat and yellow breeches; perfumes were named after Werther; and the novel was said to have caused several suicides among young German Romantics at the time.

88.31–32 Goethe's *Entbehren sollst Du, sollst entbehren!*] From *Faust*, Part I, line 1549, this line as translated reads, "You must renounce! renounce your wishes!" In Santayana's personal copy of the book at the Houghton Library, Harvard University, this line reads, "Entbehren sollst du! sollst entbehren!" (*Goethes Sämtliche Werke. Mit Einleitungen von Karl Goedeke.* [Stuttgart: J. G. Cotta'schen Buchhandlung] 1883). For Santayana's treatment of Goethe see *Poets.*

88.33–34 *Es . . . sein!*] Both German tags are poetic refrains. The first—"Es war ein Traum" ("It was a dream")—is from Heinrich Heine's (1797–1856) famous short poem "In der Fremde," in which the poet laments his exile from Germany, personified as a woman. The second tag, from Victor Nessler's hit opera *Der Trompeter von Säckingen,* is the refrain to the last song in Act II, "Jung Werners Abschied" ("Young Werner's Farewell"): "Behüt' dich Gott, es wär' zu schön gewesen! / Behüt' dich Gott, es hat nicht sollen sein!" ("God be with you, it would have been too delightful! / God be with you, it was not meant to be!") In this scene the bugler to the old Baron von Schoenau, Young Werner, having just asked the Baron for the hand of his beautiful daughter, Maria, is banished for his pains, and must now bid his love farewell. The libretto, by Rudolf Bunge, was based on Joseph Viktor von Scheffel's 1854 verse narrative by the same name (the song quoted from is originally from Scheffel).

90.22–23 *Eva . . . Hans Sachs*] In Wagner's opera *Die Meistersinger von Nürenberg* (1868), Hans Sachs, by far the most accomplished of the Meistersingers, acts as the presiding genius of the action, and makes sure that Eva, prize to the winner of the singing contest, gets the man with whom she is already in love.

95.13–14 *"I . . . perfectly."*] The joke here is on the syntax (or word order) of Irma's sentence. "I speak also French perfectly" is German syntax ("Ich spreche auch Französisch ganz perfekt"). A native English speaker would say, "I also speak French perfectly." Also, of course, she is somewhat fatuously self-complacent about the compliments on her good English. Santayana is poking a little good-humored fun at her easily forgivable vanity and German "Egotism."

97.1–2 *He . . . well.*] This is a play on Hamlet's "To be or not to be" soliloquy, "And makes us rather bear those ills we have / Than fly to others that we know not of" (*Shakespeare,* III.i.81–82).

Santayana was keenly interested in *Hamlet,* and he comments on this scene in "Hamlet's Question," an introduction that he wrote to the play (*The Complete Works of William Shakespeare* [New York: Harper and Brothers, 1906–1908], 15:ix–xxxiii). Also, in a letter to Robert Potter dated 21 December 1922, Santayana wrote that the action of his novel (then in its early stages) will be "conceived from the hero's point of view, everything merely as it enters into his own experience, and transforms his Puritanism into a Hamlet-like perplexity." Oliver discusses the play with Jim Darnley at 229.25–231.36. (For other *Hamlet* echoes, see Notes at 223.6–33 and 287.5–9.)

97.9 *wunderschön*] "Beautiful."

97.35 *Kapellmeister*] "Conductor."

102.2 sign] Libra ("the balance") is the seventh sign of the zodiac, from approximately 22 September to 22 October.

106.39–40 dead . . . wind] In the *Iliad* vi.146, Homer says "Like that of leaves is a generation of men."

110.26 Adams's of Quincy] A reference to the Adams family of Quincy, Massachusetts, which produced two presidents of the United States and three historians, and which is foremost among the First Families of Boston.

111.37–38 *pommes soufflées*] Potato slices soaked in ice-water, then deep fried until they puff up.

113.1–2 those . . . Association] Peter refers to the exercise of swinging "Indian clubs," popular for both men and women during the latter half of the nineteenth century in the United States.

113.34 *confitures-à-surprise*] "Preserved fruit; preserves."

113.42–43 *Verweile doch*] ("Do linger.") This phrase occurs in a key passage, wherein Faust is agreeing that Mephistopheles will rightly have his soul if he ever wishes to remain in any situation—if he ever says "*Verweile doch.*" (*Faust*, line 1700).

114.5 Dante] Santayana's extensive analysis of Dante Alighieri's *The Divine Comedy* (1321) appears in the third section of *Poets*. Santayana also discusses the philosophies of Dante and Shakespeare and T. S. Eliot's interpretation of them in an essay entitled "Tragic Philosophy," (*Scrutiny* 4 [1936]: 365–76).

114.9 Arabian Nights] [See Note at 197.1.]

114.35 *Unsinn*] "Nonsense."

123.38–124.3 Chiron . . . old.] The centaur Chiron trained many heroes, including Achilles, who, it was prophecied, would not live long.

128.25–26 Cyrus Paul Whittle] Whittle is based, at least in part, on Mr. Byron Groce, Santayana's teacher of English composition and literature at the Boston Latin School (see *Persons and Places*, 151 and 153).

128.33 Emerson] Santayana's interest in Ralph Waldo Emerson (1803–1882) is not surprising: both were poets and both commanded rhetorically powerful and poetically rich prose styles. Emerson's "Divinity School Address" bears some remarkable similarities to Santayana's views expressed in *Interpretations*, particularly in terms of the psychology of religion and the origins and historical development of religious doctrines and institutions. In chapter seven of that book, which is devoted to Emerson, Santayana notes similarities in Emerson's thought to that of the German romantic and idealistic philosophers, which he calls "remarkable, all the more as he seems to have borrowed little or nothing from their works" (133). In this novel Santayana has Oliver stay in Emerson's old room in Divinity Hall at Harvard (399). During his own senior year at Harvard, Santayana unsuccessfully submitted an essay entitled "The Optimism of Ralph Waldo Emerson" for the Bowdoin Prize.

131.8–13 All . . . turn.] Oliver and "duty" are inseparable. On page 332 of *Santayana*, McCormick records that Santayana wrote "Oliver" next to this passage in his copy of an anthology of thoughts by Thoreau: "We consult our will and our understanding and the expectation of men, not our genius. I can impose upon myself tasks which will crush me for life and prevent all expansion, and this I am but too inclined to do" (Henry David Thoreau, *Paragraphs* [n. p.: n. p., 1933], 5).

131.36–37 tied . . . bootlace] [See Note at 13.35–14.6.]

134.31 Schopenhauer] Arthur Schopenhauer (1788–1860), German philosopher born in Danzig. His major philosophical works are *Die Welt als Wille und Vorstellung* (*The World as Will and Idea*, 1819) and a collection of aphorisms, *Parerga und Paralipomena* (1851). His philosophy, influenced by Eastern thought, was a major contributor to Santayana's philosophy of mind and aesthetics. Schopenhauer develops his philosophy in opposition to the Cartesian primacy of intellect and to the then prevalent mechanistic model of nature. Following Kant, he rejected metaphysical theorizing based on rational deduction; nevertheless, for him humans are *animal metaphysicum* who cannot avoid metaphysical wonder. For every human being the will is evident as the "in-itself" of individual being. Without ultimate purpose or design, the will is an arational force. There is no dualism. Will and body are simply different aspects of the same thing viewed from different perspectives, and all aspects of nature are captured in a meaningless struggle for existence characterized by stress and conflict. Consciousness does not reveal the underpinning biological forces of human behavior and is "the mere surface of our mind." His "instrumentalist" view of human thinking was a precursor of the American pragmatist school.

The only human activity that is not determined by the will is aesthetic contemplation, wherein the world is viewed without reference to any aim or desire of the will. The objects of such contemplation are not particular things or events, but the "permanent essential forms of the world and all its phenomena," which Schopenhauer called the "Ideas" (*Ideen*). In a letter to Milton K. Munitz dated 2 May 1938 Santayana writes: "Schopenhauer had a great hold on me for a short time and you might trace to him the relation I admit between spirit and nature, (i.e., Idea and Will) and the 'denial' (not destruction) of the Will in intuition." Santayana also agreed with Schopenhauer's view that the tenets of religion could only be accepted as allegorical explanations, and that to treat them as literal truths about a higher order of things is mistaken.

134.34 wicked Mephisto passages] It is difficult to identify specific quotations of Schopenhauer that Irma might have considered "Mephisto" in content. The difficulty is due primarily to the large quantity of highly critical passages relating to religion, priests, philosophy professors, and women. For examples, see Schopenhauer's essays "On Religion" and "On Women" in *Parerga and Paralipomena*.

137.4 LIESCHEN] Diminutive form of "Lise" or "Liselotte."

138.26 Priscilla costume] An invocation of *The Courtship of Miles Standish*.

138.28 *Backfisch*] "An adolescent girl."

139.28–29 Because . . . psalm-tunes.] [See Note at 24.33–25.6.]

140.6–18 hotel . . . Monument] Fräulein Irma's change of residence follows the path
of growth in nineteenth-century Boston: the Hotel Victoria was located in Boston's
new and fashionable Back Bay, whereas by the turn of the century Beacon Hill was,
despite its pedigree, "backwater" and long superceded, as well as closer to the
waterfront. The first two items on Fräulein's itinerary were in fact located in the
Back Bay on Copley Square: the Boston Public Library, the first sizeable library of
its kind and housed in a building distinguished for its architecture; and (kept in the
Boston Museum of Fine Arts) the Ludovisi Throne, a large marble sculpture alter-
natively known as the Boston Throne or Boston Relief, counterpart to a similar
relief exhibited in Rome and known as the Ludovisi Throne. The next item, "Mrs.
Gardner's Venetian palace," was also an artistic landmark, a house built by Isabella
Stewart Gardner (1840–1924) and intended to be a posthumous bequest to the city
as an art museum. Usually known as Fenway Court, it was the site of many formal
dinners and celebrations; Santayana himself frequently visited Mrs. Gardner's home
at her invitation.

The last three items on the list are Revolutionary memorabilia. Faneuil Hall, built
and then given to the town by the merchant Peter Faneuil in 1742, contained in its
upper story a meeting hall where significant political meetings were held during the
1770s, during one of which the Revolutionary orator James Otis proclaimed the
hall "Cradle of Liberty." The Old North Church (Christ Church), erected in 1723
for the Church of England, probably provided the steeple from which Paul Revere
signaled with two lanterns, and its common name "Old North" derives from Longfellow's poem, "Paul Revere's Ride." Finally, the Bunker Hill Monument, an obelisk
of 220 feet located in Charlestown, was dedicated in 1825 to commemorate the
fiftieth anniversary of the battle.

140.34 *Erlebnisse . . . Erinnerung!*] "Experience" and "memory."

142.7–8 *Black Swan*] [See Note at 156.18–157.34.]

143.5–13 Oliver . . . cabin.] In a letter to Robert Potter dated 21 December 1922
Santayana, thanking Potter for information about yachts, explains that Oliver's
induction into nautical mysteries resembles his own when he visited for a day
"William Forbes's yacht in Buzzard's Bay" (see Note at 13.35–14.6). The reference
to Jonah is at Jonah 1:17–2:10.

145.15 Lord Jim] Jim is actually connected to aristocracy on his father's side (148.7),
and his character is based primarily upon the personality of Santayana's long-time
friend, Lord Russell (John Francis Stanley, 2d Earl Russell). This similarity between

Jim and Russell lies primarily in their psychological makeup and gradual deterioration. To Santayana's delight, the similarity was perceived by Russell's third wife when she read the novel (see letters to Daniel Cory [31 October 1935] and Boylston Adams Beal [23 December 1935]). Santayana also linked Russell to the novel's epigraph: "Here is a real justification for the *motto* from Alain about '*jeunesse sauvée*.' Lord Jim is a bit of my youth preserved. I am much more partial to him than to Mario, who is a compound of several other friends of mine, all less important" (Cory letter cited above).

147.7–8 *wundervoll! wunderschön! herrlich!* and *grossartig!*] "Wonderful; beautiful; magnificent; and splendid!"

147.17 Joseph Conrad's] The Polish-born Conrad (1857–1924) became a novelist after retiring from the British merchant marine. *Lord Jim* (1900), his best-known novel, is, like much of his work, about the sea and sea-travel to distant places.

147.20–23 long . . . station.] The British Navy scandal (pages 157.36–37 and 161.20–163.33) is analogous to Lord Russell's Balliol College, Oxford, scandal involving Lionel Johnson as described by Santayana in *Persons and Places* (308–309). Russell was sent down by Benjamin Jowett.

150.10 Dick Dana] [See Note at 48.4.]

153.31 to the pure all things are pure] Titus 1:15.

154.24–155.2 A . . . observation.] Santayana wrote "Cf. Oliver when he thought Jim was drowned" in his copy of *Sein und Zeit* next to the passage about one's fear for another person who is himself fearless (*Santayana*, 334). (See Martin Heidegger, *Sein und Zeit*, 2 vols., 3rd ed. [Halle: Niemeyer, 1931], I:142.) (Also see Note at 80.3–82.20.)

155.11–13 swim . . . Leanders.] The mythical Hero and Leander were lovers separated by the Hellespont, which Leander would swim at night to be with her. He was eventually drowned when a storm overtook him during one of these swims. Byron, in imitation of Leander, executed the same feat and wrote a poem about it.

156.18–157.34 "She has . . . damn.] In all this explanation by Jim the classical allusion in the name *Black Swan* remains unexpressed; Peter likewise does not mention it in his elaboration on the name (176.15–39). The reference is to lines 161–83 of Juvenal's sixth satire, *Against Women*, in which the poet describes the ideal Roman wife of good family, pious towards her ancestors, full of public virtue, and chaste—whom he likens to that "rare bird," the black swan (165)—only to reject her as a horror of pride. Thus, the ship's name may well be an unadmitted ironic statement on Harriet. (Also see Oliver's sighting of one of these birds at 537.25–538.7.)

157.1–2 old Samson in the treadmill] Book of Judges 16:21.

157.28–29 Doge's . . . Adriatic] Beginning in 1000, the Doge of Venice sailed out on Ascension Day and in a nuptial ceremony wedded Venice and the Adriatic Sea. The State galley with which this was performed was the bucentaur, or "golden bark."

157.29 mirabolous] First Peter here and then Harold at 305.29 use the exclamation 'mirabolous', evidently a coinage based on the Latin *mirabile* ("wonderful").

159.30 Pindar] In the *Olympian Odes*, I.1, ἄριστον μὲν ὕδωρ may be translated "water is best."

161.39–40 Eton . . . Dartmouth] Eton and Radley are British public schools (see Note at 278.32 on Eton). Dartmouth, Britain's Annapolis, is on the Devonshire coast.

162.25 Bloomsbury radical] Bloomsbury, a residential section of London containing the British Museum and the University of London, was the home and center for a group who began meeting there around 1905. The Bloomsbury Group (including, among others, Virginia and Leonard Woolf, Vanessa Bell, John Maynard Keynes, Lytton Strachey, E. M. Forster, and Roger Fry) was in revolt against the artistic, social, and sexual restrictions of Victorian society.

162.38 Hyde Park oratory] A reference to the free speechifying traditionally allowed in London's Hyde Park.

165.8 Nietzsche] Friedrich Nietzsche (1844–1900), German philosopher and poet for whom the will to power is the source of all human action. *Also Sprach Zarathustra* (*Thus Spoke Zarathustra*), written between 1883–1885, is widely considered his magnum opus, and *Beyond Good and Evil* (*Jenseits von Gut und Böse*, 1886) and *Toward a Genealogy of Morals* (*Zur Genealogie der Moral*, 1887) are also significant philosophical works.

In *Egotism* Santayana criticizes Nietzsche for turning his back on truth; it "did not interest him; it was ugly; the bracing atmosphere of falsehood, passion, and subjective perspectives was the better thing" (128). Nietzsche makes up 'truth' to suit our purposes and his romantic egotism is compared to "the swagger of an immature, half-playful mind, like a child that tells you he will cut your head off" (134–35).

166.6–7 the old . . . up] [See Note at 22.3.]

167.2 alienist] [See Note at 59.24.]

170.2 Nirvana] The final state of beatitude that transcends suffering. In Buddhism, nirvana is achieved through overcoming desire and individual consciousness. According to Van Wyck Brooks, "nirvana" was a watchword among many pessimistic scions of New England in the late nineteenth century (*New England: Indian Summer 1865–1915* [n.p.: Dutton, 1940], 359–60). (Also see the Note at 488.4–21.)

170.19–20 transcendentalist] In a letter to Herbert W. Schneider dated 5 November 1930 Santayana writes: "Nevertheless, Emerson is much nearer to Oliver than

Franklin: and I am a bit troubled at the thought that perhaps he (Oliver) was the last transcendentalist rather than the last puritan." Transcendentalism (in America) was a mid-nineteenth-century intellectual movement originating in Boston and Concord; Ralph Waldo Emerson is acknowledged as its leader, although he never described himself as a transcendentalist. Having its beginnings in the Unitarian reaction against pessimistic and constrained Calvinist religion, the movement emphasized individualism, moral idealism, and freedom of conscience. To the transcendentalists ultimate reality resided in the unseen spiritual world which transcends the empirical and is discovered through poetry, philosophy and religion. In *Interpretations* Santayana writes that "To reject tradition and think as one might have thought if no man had ever existed before was indeed the aspiration of the Transcendentalists" (132).

170.35 Noah's Ark . . . Deluge] See Genesis 6–8 for the Ark, the Deluge, and Noah, the only "just and perfect" man before God in a "corrupt generation."

175.32–34 like Lazarus . . . goggles] Lazarus, friend of Christ and resurrected by him as recorded in chapter 11 of the Gospel of John. Dr. Alden is described similarly in Oliver's dream on 264.40.

175.40 Salem] On 23.40 Santayana makes a glancing reference to Nathaniel Hawthorne's *The Scarlet Letter*. Here the description of Salem resembles Hawthorne's prefatory sketch to *The Scarlet Letter*, "The Custom-House," which strongly evokes the sense of degeneracy evident in Santayana's own portrayal of "puritan" New England.

178.12 Walt Whitman] Santayana's attitude toward Walt Whitman (1819–1892) was complicated and ambivalent: he admired Whitman's genuine poetic sensibility and rhetorical power, while simultaneously deploring his primitivism and crudeness. Three of Santayana's own poems, "Had I the Choice (After Walt Whitman)," "With husky-haughty lips, O sea," and "You tides with ceaseless swell (After Walt Whitman") are directly inspired by Whitman's poetry (see *Poems*, 404–405, 410–11). Also, see Santayana's discussion of Whitman, "The Poetry of Barbarism" in *Interpretations*.

178.17–18 "But . . . American.] Jim Darnley's enthusiasm for Whitman is commensurate with that of Lord Russell, the model for Darnley. Russell visited Whitman during the latter's retirement in Camden, New Jersey (*Life*, 119). Russell also gave Santayana a copy of *Leaves of Grass* (*Persons and Places*, 475).

178.28–179.6 "I confess . . . involuntary."] Peter's view of poetry here is similar to Santayana's own as developed in *Interpretations*, particularly in the chapter, "The Elements and Function of Poetry."

179.12–14 *I . . . God.*] From stanza 32 of "Song of Myself," this passage reads:

> *I think I could turn and live with animals, they are so placid and self-contain'd,*
> *I stand and look at them long and long.*

They do not sweat and whine about their condition,
They do not lie awake in the dark and weep for their sins,
They do not make me sick discussing their duty to God.

In his personal copy of *Leaves of Grass* in the George Santayana Collection at Georgetown University Library, Santayana made a vertical mark next to the first eight lines of section 32 (Philadelphia: David McKay, 1891–1892, 52). He notes the appeal of this passage "when we are weary of conscience and ambition, and would yield ourselves for a while to the dream of sense" (*Interpretations*, 114).

179.18 lilies of the field] From the Gospel of Matthew 6:28: "Consider the lilies of the field, how they grow; they toil not, neither do they spin."

179.31 Rousseau] Jean Jacques Rousseau (1712–1778), Swiss-born French philosopher, essayist, and novelist. At the foundation of his thought lies a dichotomy between contemporary society and human nature. Modern society replaces the natural demands of man in a state of nature with the necessary artificial uniformity of behavior requisite for society. The natural self-love of man (*amour de soi*) is replaced by pride (*amour-propre*). Alienated from his true nature, man seeks to acquire items that separate him from others. By comparing himself to others, man takes pleasure in their misfortune or inferiority. This dichotomy is presented in his *Discourse on the Origin of Inequality* (*Discours sur l'origine de l'inégalité*, 1755) and *Letter to d'Alembert on the Theatre* (*Lettre à d'Alembert sur les spectacles*, 1758). In *Interpretations*, Santayana claims that Rousseau missed the point of evolution, i.e., emergent characteristics not only arise from previous states, but their evolution beyond those states makes returning to their previous form impossible (112). Further negative judgment of Rousseau is found in *Egotism*, where Santayana calls him "intensely unintelligent" and his attitude "foolish, incoherent, disastrous" (135).

179.37–38 Marie Antoinette] The queen of Louis XVI, famous for her love of pleasure, acted the minor role of a shepherdess in a theatrical she sponsored.

182.34–35 Benedictine Monastery] Caleb Wetherbee's Benedictine Monastery at Salem may have been inspired by the Anglican monastery of Father Waggett (of the Cowley Fathers) near Oxford that Santayana visited and described in *Persons and Places* (496).

183.9–10 Prescott . . . Parkman] Two New England historians of Protestant heritage. William Hickling Prescott (1796–1859) wrote *History of the Conquest of Mexico* and *The Conquest of Peru*; Francis Parkman (1823–1893) wrote *The Oregon Trail* and the series of histories *France and England in the New World*.

184.38 Benjamin] [See Note at 192.26–28.]

185.4–5 Mount Vernon Place] [See Note at 21.2–22.40.]

186.8 Charley . . . James] These men were Santayana's colleagues at Harvard and are described in "Official Career at Harvard" in *Persons and Places*. Charles Townsend Copeland (1860–1952), member of the English department at Harvard (1892–1928), is described by Santayana as "an artist rather than a scholar . . . a public reader by profession" (407). Barrett Wendell (1855–1921), taught English from 1880–1917 and was one of the founders of the Harvard *Lampoon*. He developed the idea of the "'daily themes', . . . a voluntary exercise in writing, feeling, and judging of all things like a gentleman" (406). William James (1842–1910), who taught first physiology and afterward philosophy (1872–1907), was Santayana's teacher and mentor, and later his colleague (401–405).

189.38 the Unitarian Church] [See Note at 24.33–25.6.]

190.5–7 French . . . everything.] Jean Baptiste Massillon (1663–1742), French bishop and famous speaker noted for his gentle persuasive appeal.

190.37 the Napoleon of letters] In his autobiography, *Dichtung und Wahrheit* (*Poetry and Truth*), Goethe describes his one meeting with Napoleon. Both men had great respect for one another.

190.37–39 But . . . invertebrate.] Many in the nineteenth century, including the transcendentalists, were fascinated by Goethe, yet repelled by him as a moral teacher. Voltaire (François Marie Arouet, 1694–1778) was the principal figure of the French Enlightenment and a prolific writer who fostered an extreme rationalism and skepticism. For Rousseau, see Note at 179.31.

191.3–7 Faust . . . hallelujah.] The reference is to Goethe's Faust, the aging scholar who promises his soul to Mephistopheles in exchange for the fresh experiences of youth. At the end of the drama, Faust is saved by a choir of angels and makes the *Himmelfahrt*, or "Ascent into Heaven."

191.8–10 Walt . . . I!] Cousin Caleb oversimplifies Whitman here, for the poet acknowledges his own elements of corruption (as in "Crossing Brooklyn Ferry").

191.11 Western-Easterly Divan] This is an allusion to Goethe's *West-Eastern Divan* (*West-östlicher Diwan*, 1819).

191.29–31 Rathskeller . . . Egmont.] Mephisto (Mephistopheles) and Gretchen (Margaret) are principal characters in Goethe's *Faust*. Mignon, a young girl in *Wilhelm Meisters Lehrjahre* (1777), sings her own songs and is representative of poetry. Rescued from a wandering group of dancers by the hero, she becomes passionately attached to him and eventually dies of hopeless love and longing for her homeland. *Götz von Berlichingen* and *Egmont* are dramas by Goethe.

191.33 young Daniel] [See Note at 192.26–28.]

192.9–22 *Himmelfahrt . . . Prologue in Heaven*] In the *Prologue in Heaven* God and Mephistopheles debate about which of them Faust will ultimately follow. (Also see Note at 191.3–7.)

192.26–28 "Who . . . shame?"] This likening of Oliver to the youthful Christ is the culmination of a series of biblical metaphors applied by Caleb to Oliver. At 184.38 Caleb refers to Oliver as "that green sprout of a Benjamin" and at 191.33 as "our young Daniel."

192.35 Professor Norton] Charles Eliot Norton (1827–1908), American author and educator, was a Dante scholar and professor of art history at Harvard (1873–1898). Norton was one of Santayana's professors when he was an undergraduate and later was one of his colleagues at Harvard (see *Persons and Places*, 399–401).

192.38 *Kulturgeschichte*] "Cultural history."

197.1 *Arabian Nights*] As a boy, Santayana read an expurgated version of the *Arabian Nights* by E. W. Lane (1840 English translation in three volumes). He later read the 1899 sixteen-volume French translation by J. C. Mardrus (see *Persons and Places*, 142, 462).

197.1 *Don Quixote*] [See Note at 54.15.]

197.3 Saint-Simon] Claude Henri de Rouvroy, comte de Saint-Simon (1760–1825), early socialist philosopher and intellectual, collaborator of Augustin Thierry and later Auguste Comte. Theorizing about history as well as politics and economics, he believed that human affairs should be investigated as well as managed in a scientific manner. He is the historical father of French socialism, and Karl Marx owed a significant debt to him.

197.19–198.2 He . . . gentleman.] This passage is a reflection of Santayana's essay, "The Higher Snobbery," in which he says, "I call snobbery, when people approve of it, the higher snobbery" (*Soliloquies in England* [London: Constable, 1922], 50).

198.20–200.11 "You . . . in."] In *Interpretations* Santayana views religion as an idealization of experience, not a description of reality; "the excellence of religion is due to an idealization of experience which, while making religion noble if treated as poetry, makes it necessarily false if treated as a science" (3). Caleb's literal belief in Catholic dogma distorts the aesthetic character of religion and falsifies it as statements of fact.

198.28 Caliban] The villainous part-human slave of the magician Prospero in *The Tempest*.

198.35–39 An . . . show] In his 1886 essay, "The Optimism of Ralph Waldo Emerson," Santayana comments on Emerson's extreme serenity, his gentle contempt for men and things, his "least respectable side—the mystic turned dilettante. When this half-seriousness, this supercilious satisfaction betray themselves, Emerson loses our confidence." (*George Santayana's America*, James Ballowe, ed. [Urbana: Illinois, 1967], 83).

199.40–200.1 catechism . . . thirty-nine articles] These are the Church of England's statements of belief, the latter being the equivalent of an Anglican creed; they both date from Elizabethan times and are found in the Book of Common Prayer.

200.17 Yoga-like exercise] In two letters to Daniel Cory the author reveals his own practice of breathing exercises to relieve coughing due to bronchitis (13 November 1929 and 4 December 1929).

205.16–23 Jim was . . . rare.] This description of the friendship between Oliver and Jim Darnley is very similar to the description Santayana gives of his friendship with the young Lord Russell in *Persons and Places*. Santayana describes thus the growth of their comradeship while exploring the rivers of Burgundy aboard Russell's yacht in June 1888: "Two men in their early twenties, eating and sleeping for three weeks in that same cabin, seeing the same sights and living through the same incidents without one moment of boredom, without one touch of misunderstanding or displeasure, could not but become very good friends" (313).

207.22 gnädige Frau] German idiom of respect equivalent to "Madam."

207.30 barcarolle . . . *Tales of Hoffmann*] The "Barcarolle" ("Boatman's Song," sung by gondoliers) is the most famous melody from Jacques Offenbach's three-act opera, which depicts three nemesis-crossed love affairs of the poet Hoffmann. At the beginning of Act II, Nicklausse, friend of Hoffmann, and Giulietta, Hoffmann's Venetian flame, sing the duet "Belle Nuit!" ("O Night of Love!").

214.30 *il gran rifiuto*] As Irma phrases it, Peter Alden "abdicates his rights and avoids his duties." The Italian phrase derives from Celestine V's refusal to accept papal office, but has come to refer to refusal of any honor or office. In Dante, Celestine is placed at the gate of hell, to suffer with other souls who had refused to take a stand for or against God (*Inferno* III, 60).

215.4 JOHN SARGENT AND HENRY JAMES] John Singer Sargent (1856–1925), the American painter famous primarily for his portraits, and Henry James (1843–1916), the American novelist and younger brother of Santayana's mentor, William James, were both Europeanized Americans. In *Persons and Places*, Santayana tells of meeting Sargent at Gibraltar during his tour of the eastern Mediterranean in 1905–1906 (450) and of having lunch with James (287).

215.18–20 *Lehrjahre* . . . *gelehrt*] *Lehrjahre* ("learning years; apprenticeship"); *Wanderjahre* ("travel years"); and *gelehrt* ("learned"). The first two words are references to two of Goethe's novels: *Wilhelm Meisters Lehrjahre*, often known simply as *Wilhelm Meister* and the original *Bildungsroman*; and *Wilhelm Meisters Wanderjahre*, its sequel.

217.7–10 Baalbek . . . islands] Santayana's travels of 1905–1906 began in southern Italy and took him through the Near East, Greece, and back to Rome. He was especially struck by the ruins at Baalbek (*Persons and Places*, 451–67).

217.42 *The Illustrated Life of Washington*] [See Note at 73.11–16.]

219.3 *Rathhausgasse*] "Town-hall Street."

219.17–18 *A Scottish Shepherd and His Dog* . . . *View of the Yosemite Valley*] [See Note at 73.11–16.]

220.7 *Aberglaube*] "Superstition."

220.12 *dévote*] "Devout."

223.6–33 A . . . sea.] This description of Oliver's *somnambulistic* existence in his last year of high school is analogous to Santayana's description of his own *somnambulistic* experience at high school and later during his Harvard career (*Persons and Places*, 147–48). More significant, however, are the echoes from *Hamlet* which anticipate Oliver's viewing of the play with Jim and their discussion of it (see 229.25–231.36). The passage here refers to Hamlet's response to Guildenstern that he's mad only "north-northwest," that when the wind is southerly he knows "a hawk from a handsaw" (II.ii.398–400). Earlier in the play, Hamlet refers to his father's ghost as the "old mole" in the "cellerage" (II.i.150–63). Another Shakespeare echo is the extended stage metaphor of the "world as a stage" from *As You Like It* (II.vii.143). (All references are from *Shakespeare*.)

223.32 yawping] A reference to the famous line from the conclusion of Whitman's "Song of Myself": "I sound my barbaric yawp over the roofs of the world."

224.23 Manhattan Hotel] [See Note at 371.37–372.1.]

227.10 Rome after Cannae] In 216 B.C. at Cannae in southern Italy there occurred the third of Hannibal's three great victories during the Second Punic War. Outnumbered by the largest army ever fielded by the Romans, Hannibal effected the annihilation of his enemy. The immediate response in Rome was panic proverbial in its intensity.

227.25 hoist with their own petard] Concerning Rosencrantz and Guildenstern's plot against him, Hamlet remarks in III.iv: "For 'tis the sport to have the enginer / Hoist with his own petar" (*Shakespeare*, 206–207).

228.1 Forbes-Robertson in *Hamlet*] This was one of the most famous roles played by Sir Johnston Forbes-Robertson (1853–1937), eminent actor of the British stage during the late nineteenth and early twentieth centuries. He first appeared in *Hamlet* in 1898 and was knighted in 1913.

229.12 *monsieur le père de monsieur*] "The father of the gentleman."

230.20–21 Ophelia . . . nunnery] In III.ii, Hamlet commands Ophelia: "Get thee to a nunnery: why wouldst thou be a breeder of sinners?" (*Shakespeare*, 122–23).

232.18 Radley—St. Peter's College] St. Peter's College, an English public school, takes its name from the village of Radley and is three miles south of Iffley. Nearby is the town of Abingdon, at the confluence of the River Thames and the River Ock.

234.5 Rose] In a letter to Robert Shaw Barlow dated 19 October 1935 Santayana writes: "[Rose] . . . is a picture of what I imagine my mother to have been like when a young girl." His mother, at the age of twenty, finding herself suddenly orphaned on the Philippine island of Batang in the society of natives only, began exporting hemp to Manila and did so well that she ignored the offers of relatives to take her in. In the letter Santayana explains that during this period she evidenced "a wonderful coolness and courage, and a quiet disdain for what she didn't feel was quite up to the mark. For that reason she wasn't very affectionate to her children: we were poor stuff" (also see *Persons and Places*, 35–36).

238.5–6 the advanced woman] Santayana's description of the "new woman" of the 1890s.

238.9 lover of gardens] Mary Annette Beauchamp (1866–1941), Countess von Arnim-Schlagenthin, later became the third Countess of Santayana's friend John Francis Stanley, second Earl Russell. She was herself an accomplished writer whom Santayana had first heard about in connection with *Elizabeth and Her German Garden* (her pen name was "Elizabeth"). (See *Persons and Places*, 479, 578.)

239.12–13 Even . . . exist] Santayana himself regularly made brief stays for over twenty-five years at No. 87 Jermyn Street, Saint James's, a house which took in boarders. See *Persons and Places* for a description of his stays at this location and his sudden discovery one day that it "was no longer an hotel" (270–71).

240.5 Boucicault's plays] Dion Boucicault (1820–1890), an Irish-born actor and prolific and successful writer of popular plays, spent most of his professional life in America.

241.3 *Rigoletto*] [See Note at 263.17–266.31.]

241.11 Oxford] In 1896 Santayana studied at King's College, Cambridge, and during World War I he again lived in England, primarily at Oxford. He was an inveterate walker and became intimately acquainted with the surrounding area (see his chapter on "Oxford Friends" in *Persons and Places*). Buckinghamshire is the shire due east of Oxfordshire, and the Chiltern Hills are southwest of Oxford. In 1896 he wrote Guy Murchie that his three favorite walks around Oxford were "one to Sandford and Iffley, one to Marston, and one to Wytham" (13 August 1896). During the war he wrote to Mrs. Frederick Winslow, "I am now in love with a new walk and tea-garden—in the direction of Nuneham and the Harcourt's park" (6 April 1918).

South of Oxford along the Thames, one encounters Iffley, then Sandford, and eight miles out, Nuneham Courtney, with Radley close by.

241.24–25 the Broad . . . Magdalen tower] [See Notes at 277.18–278.4 and 495.28–496.11 for descriptions of Oxford.]

242.11–15 He . . . himself.] In his biography John McCormick links Mr. Darnley to a Mr. Dickins whom Lord Russell mentioned in his autobiography, *My Life and Adventures*, and whom Santayana probably had met through Russell (*Santayana*, 330). McCormick reports that Santayana wrote in the margin of page 7 in his copy of Russell's book, "Mr. Dickins loved R. very deeply. He was a man with a broken heart & a high resignation. I doubt whether he *believed* anything, but he had a spiritual nature. He was gaunt, poor thin & not very clean; eaten up with a slow inward fire."

243.8 Saint Augustine] Saint Augustine (354–430), Bishop of Hippo in North Africa, is best known for his autobiographical *Confessions* and *City of God*. Santayana's review of Jules Martin's *Saint Augustine* was reprinted with changes in his *Reason in Religion* (1905) as part of chapter 9.

245.11 church] Iffley Church was built by the Norman family of St. Remy soon after 1160, in the reign of Henry II, probably while St. Thomas à Becket was Archbishop of Canterbury. Very few additions have been made to it since that time. The rights of appointment are shared by the Archdeacon of Oxford and the Dean and Chapter of Christ Church. The doorways, with their zigzag patterns and carvings of beasts, birds, and fish, the arches which support the central tower, and the great square font of black marble, are among the details which give this church the reputation of being the best Norman work in England.

246.23–247.37 "Do . . . shed."] Here Mr. Darnley is talking about the sermon he has just given. His description of "*soul*" is similar to Santayana's concept of the "*psyche*" or vital principal of each living organism.

247.10 ἀνὴρ πνευματικός] "A spiritual man by nature" as Mr. Darnley defines the term.

250.13 Sandford] About a mile down the Thames from Iffley, the village of Sandford was a popular area for pleasure-boating in summer.

251.5 Sandford Lock] To ensure a navigable waterway along the Thames to Oxford, a series of locks and dams began to be built in the seventeenth century at the villages of Iffley, Sandford, and Culham.

251.7–8 King's Arms Inn] Both King's Arms inns mentioned in the novel, at Sandford and Oxford, actually existed during Santayana's time in England.

252.35 *Kaiser Wilhelm*] [See Note at 55.39–40.]

254.14 Nuneham . . . Radley] [See Note at 241.11.]

261.5 Wenus] A joke based on the distinction between classical and church Latin in the pronunciation of 'v'; in classical Latin the 'v' is pronounced like a 'w'.

261.40–262.2 *Childe* . . . Oliver] The line is from *King Lear*, III.iv.185; the poem by Robert Browning takes its title from this line. The Oliver who died young was the faithful companion to Roland, nephew of Charlemagne, and doomed to die with him in the military disaster depicted in the anonymous medieval epic, *The Song of Roland*.

262.29 *ad libitum*] "Liberally."

263.17–266.31 So . . . spectacle.] Oliver and Jim have just seen a performance of Verdi's *Rigoletto* in London at Covent Garden—Verdi was Santayana's favorite opera composer. Rigoletto is the deformed court jester of the libertine Duke of Mantua, who has embittered members of his court by seducing their wives and daughters. Rigoletto openly ridicules them, but the most recent sufferer, Count Monterone, responds to this callousness with a father's curse. Rigoletto broods upon this curse, despite the assurance that his own daughter, Gilda, remains safely hidden. He is, however, mistaken; the Duke had noticed Gilda in church, and later, disguised as a student, made overtures to her. Soon afterward, a group of the courtiers manage to beguile the jester long enough to carry Gilda off to the ducal palace. Rigoletto hastens there, only to be jeered at by the courtiers and to find his daughter dishonored. He plots revenge. Rigoletto has arranged with Sparafucile, a professional assassin, for the murder of the Duke—with Sparafucile's comely sister, Maddalena, as the bait. Disguised as a young man by the order of her father, Gilda overhears Maddalena, who also has been taken with the charm of the young Duke, plead with her brother to save his life. They agree to murder the next person who stops at Sparafucile's inn, put the body in a sack and pass it off on Rigoletto as that of the Duke. Gilda decides to sacrifice her life for love of the Duke, knocks at the door (263.38–40), and is fatally stabbed by Sparafucile. At midnight Rigoletto claims the body of his enemy from Sparafucile, but his exultation is short-lived when he hears the Duke in the distance singing the famous aria "La donna è mobile" ("All women are fickle") (265.28–29), and then, knowing that the body in the sack cannot be the Duke's, discovers that it is his own beloved daughter. Rigoletto and Gilda then sing the final duet of the opera, "Lassù in cielo, vicin' alla madre" ("Up in heaven, near my mother")—"that last lovely duet" (265.23)—in which the dying Gilda tells her father that she will join her mother in heaven where both will pray for Rigoletto's soul. In an agony of despair, Rigoletto cries out the final words of the opera: "Ah, la Maledizione!"—"Ah, the curse!". Oliver's dream incorporates the final Act, with Oliver as Gilda, Jim Darnley as Sparafucile, and Minnie Bowler as Maddalena.

264.40 Lazarus] [See Note at 175.32–34.]

269.11–12 Who . . . good?] Mrs. Darnley's comment to Oliver, "Who of us would be in trouble, if we knew our own good?", expresses Santayana's philosophy exactly.

Santayana agrees with the Delphic injunction γνῶθι σαυτόν ("know thyself"); for him self-knowledge is the essential foundation for real happiness or personal success. In *Persons and Places* he opines that the requisites for living rationally "may be reduced to two: First, self-knowledge, the Socratic key to wisdom; and second, sufficient knowledge of the world to perceive what alternatives are open to you and which of them are favourable to your true interests" (542).

277.18–278.4 Oxford . . . Bullingdon Club.] The Mitre Hotel, directly across the street from All Saint's Church, was advertised as a "well-known Hotel for Families and Gentlemen, which is situated in the centre of the finest street in Europe . . ." (Edward C. Alden. *Alden's Oxford Guide* [Oxford: Alden & Co. Ltd., 1919]). Woodstock, a small village just northwest of Oxford, began as a royal hunting lodge, and later Blenheim Palace was built there. The Cher or Cherwell River flows from northeast to southeast through Oxford and empties into the Thames. The Isis is that part of the Thames which flows by the University to the west. The shore is lined with barges which serve as club-houses for the rowing clubs of the various colleges. Another Oxford sporting club, the Bullingdon, was connected with fox-hunting and served as the centre of Oxford's small plutocracy. While visiting Oxford, Santayana wrote to Conrad Slade that Magdalen tower was the "gem of Oxford" (11 August 1896). Peckwater Quad is one of the quadrangles of Christ Church, the largest of the Colleges comprising Oxford University. The gardens at St. John's College are on the East front of the library and occupy about five acres. Open free to the public, they are a favorite spot for visitors in the very heart of the city.

278.19 Let the dead bury their dead.] Matthew 8:22.

278.32 Eton] Eton College, largest of the English public schools, was founded in 1440 by Henry VI. It is situated on the Thames across the river from Windsor Castle. "Public" only in the sense that anyone may send a child to any public school, these schools are not part of the state system but are independent entities and self-governing. Seventy of the boys are King's Scholars who live in the original college and whose fees are paid by the foundation set up by Henry VI. These boys traditionally wear gowns and are known as tugs. The other boys live in town, in twenty-four houses named for the House Master who is referred to as "My Tutor". These boys are known as Oppidans. The students are divided into numbered classes or "forms" according to their degree of proficiency. When a larger number of classes is required, these forms are divided into "lower" and "upper," the "lower" form accommodating the less academically advanced boys. Forms may be designated by letter, A, B, C, etc., or by number, sixth, fifth, etc., with the Sixth Form being the highest. The three school terms and accompanying sports are: Michaelmas—soccer and rugby; Lent—the Field Game (a mixture of soccer and rugby peculiar to Eton); and Summer—cricket and rowing.

278.38 Windsor] Santayana was quite familiar with Windsor and the surrounding area. From 1890 to 1920, he made almost yearly visits to Queen's Acre, Howard Sturgis's home near Windsor. The White Hart Inn was a well-known stopping place in the vicinity. Santayana writes in *Persons and Places* that he first viewed Windsor Castle "not without profound emotion" (296). Windsor Castle has been a residence of English rulers since William the Conqueror. Many English kings are buried there in the vaults of St. George's Chapel, one of England's finest churches and the location of investiture of Knights of the Garter. The Long Walk, made in 1685 and planted with elm trees, extends three miles from the castle to the equestrian statue of George III (the Copper Horse).

280.37 σίδερος] The word means "made of iron" in Greek, but if transliterated into Latin script, the stem (sider-) means "star." Mario is thinking of the Latin word "*sideris*" or "star."

280.39 wet-bob] A wet-bob is a boy at Eton College who devotes himself to rowing, the sport at which Eton has always excelled.

281.10–11 the year . . . Lent half] [See Note at 278.32.]

281.18 *chez ma mère*] "At my mother's place" (in Paris).

281.36–37 *Cherubino* of Madamoiselle Favart] Cherubino is a "pants role" for mezzo-soprano in Mozart's *The Marriage of Figaro*. Marie Justine Benoîte Favart (1727–1772) was a French singer, actress, dancer and dramatist whose later career was entirely in the Comædie-Italienne. Her insistence upon costumes suitable for the characters she portrayed and upon realistic scenery and situations brought about a revolution in theatrical dress.

282.37–39 Bacchus . . . Orpheus] In Greek mythology Ariadne, daughter of King Minos, is abandoned by her mortal spouse and loved by the immortal god Bacchus. Orpheus, son of Apollo and the muse Calliope, is presented a lyre by his father and becomes the most famous of musicians, magically charming mortals, beasts, and even stones.

285.17 fagmaster] In English public schools, a fag is a junior who performs special duties or tasks for a senior (fagmaster).

285.20 Fifth Form] [See Note at 278.32.]

285.21 M'Tutor] [See Note at 278.32.]

285.23 Sappho and Anacreon] Both Sappho (*c.*mid-seventh century B.C.), a poetess from Lesbos, and Anacreon (sixth century B.C.), Greek lyric poet, wrote extensively on the subject of love.

286.18 forest primeval] An echo of the first sentence of Longfellow's poem *Evangeline*: "This is the forest primeval." Vanny is poking fun at late nineteenth-century American culture, of which Longfellow was a significant part.

287.5–9 Why, there . . . to be!] Oliver's series of self-condemnatory epithets is perhaps reminiscent of Hamlet's self-condemnation in his soliloquies, "O, what a rogue and peasant slave am I!" (II.ii.576) and "How weary, stale, flat, and unprofitable / Seem to me all the uses of this world" (*Shakespeare*, I.ii.133–34). (For more on Hamlet, see Note at 97.1–2.) Yet a more certain source has been identified by Van Meter Ames in his article "The Zenith as Ideal" (*The Journal of Philosophy* 49 [1952] 201–208). According to Ames, a passage in William James's *The Principles of Psychology* (1890) provides the sentiment and some of the wording for this comparison of Mario and Oliver. In the section "The Explosive Will," James contrasts the uninhibited and lively character "so common in the Latin and Celtic races" with the more sluggish temperament of the English peoples: "Monkeys these people seem to us, whilst we seem to them reptilian. It is quite impossible to judge, as between an obstructed and explosive individual, which has the greater sum of vital energy. An explosive Italian with good perception and intellect will cut a figure as a perfectly tremendous fellow, on an inward capital that could be tucked away inside of an obstructed Yankee and hardly let you know that it was there. He will be the king of his company, sing all the songs and make all the speeches, lead the parties, carry out the practical jokes, kiss all the girls, fight the men, and, if need be, lead the forlorn hopes and enterprises, so that an onlooker would think he has more life in his little finger than can exist in the whole body of a correct judicious fellow. But the judicious fellow all the while may have all these possibilities and more besides, ready to break out in the same or even a more violent way, if only the brakes were taken off. It is the absence of scruples, of consequences, of considerations, the extraordinary simplification of each moment's mental outlook, that gives to the explosive individual such motor energy and ease; it need not be the greater intensity of any of his passions, motives, or thoughts" (Cambridge, Mass.; London: Harvard University Press, 1981, 2:1144–45).

288.10 Mr. Rawdon-Smith] According to John McCormick, this character is taken from Shane Leslie's 1922 novel about Eton, *The Oppidian* (*Santayana*, 333). Santayana wrote, in a letter to Daniel Cory of 4 June 1948, that he drew heavily from Leslie's novel for details about Eton life.

290.17 *École des Beaux-Arts*] [See Note at 12.34–35.]

290.18–33 Groton . . . *Peab'dy*] Santayana is having fun with the Peabody name, so closely associated with education in America. The Groton School for boys in Groton, Massachusetts, northwest of Boston, was founded in 1884 by Endicott Peabody (1857–1944). The "Rev. Peabody" was Francis Greenwood Peabody (1847–1936), Unitarian theologian and pastor of First Parish Church, Cambridge (1874–1880), who also taught at Harvard (1881–1913). George Peabody (1795–1869), an American financier and philanthropist who made his fortune as a broker in London, contributed to educational institutions and funds both in England and America.

291.3 Winchester] Winchester College, an English public school founded by William of Wykeham (1324–1404) who was Bishop of Winchester and also founder of New

College, Oxford. A Wykehamist (or, as Santayana writes, Wyckhamite) is one who is or has been a student at Winchester.

291.11 Lionel Johnson] Santayana knew Lionel Pigot Johnson (1867–1902), the Welsh poet, and referred to him as "a spiritual rebel, a spiritual waif who couldn't endure the truth but demanded a lovelier fiction to revel in". Johnson composed a poem in Santayana's honor, "To a Spanish Friend." (See Santayana's discussion of Johnson in *Persons and Places*, 300–308.)

291.15–16 Kipling and Stephen Phillips and Sir William Watson] Kipling, Phillips, and Watson were all well-known poets at the turn of the century. Rudyard Kipling (1865–1936), English novelist, poet, and short story writer, was born in India and established his reputation with stories and poems set in India, including *Departmental Ditties* (1886) and *Barrack-Room Ballads* (1892). Stephen Phillips (1868–1915), English poet and dramatist, was compared to Sophocles and Shakespeare after the publication of his poetic drama *Paolo and Francesca* in 1900, but his later plays were failures. William Watson (1858–1935), English traditional romantic poet, gained recognition with *Wordsworth's Grave and Other Poems* (1890) and *Lachrymae Musarum* (1892, an elegy for Tennyson). But his later work was verbose and derivative, and is largely unknown.

291.19 Robert Bridges] Robert Bridges (1844–1930), Poet Laureate from 1913, was a personal friend of Santayana's. They saw one another frequently during Santayana's residence in Oxford, England, during the First World War. (See *Persons and Places*, 489–92 and 505–507.)

291.21 Henry the Sixth] Henry VI (1421–1471), the "baby king," became King of England in 1422. Zealous about education, he founded Eton College and King's College, Cambridge, and laid the groundwork for the English public school system.

291.32 Harrow or Rugby] English public schools. Harrow is about ten miles from London, and during the Victorian era the Eton-Harrow cricket match was a main event in the London season. Rugby is at the very center of England and is originator of the sport of Rugby football.

295.9–12 Curious . . . hobbies] [See Note at 200.17.]

295.40 *idée force*] In French, an idea or thought considered as a real factor in behavior and thus in the course of events.

299.33–34 *kunst-historisch*,] German for "art-historical," here emphasizing the scholarly, scientific approach to art.

300.23 *tug*] [See Note at 278.32.]

300.32–33 *beau monde*] Literally French for "beautiful world," it refers to the world of high society and fashion.

301.22–23 Squeers's School in *Nicholas Nickleby*] In this novel written by Charles Dickens in 1838–1839, Wackford Squeers is the vulgar, conceited, ignorant schoolmaster of Dotheboys Hall who steals money and clothing from the school boys, half-starves them, and basically teaches them nothing.

302.20–21 the vision of Jacob's ladder] In Genesis 28:12 Jacob has a vision of a ladder extending from earth to heaven.

302.35 Plato] Greek philosopher (*c*.427–347 B.C.), born in Athens or on the island of Aegina. He was the student of Socrates and the teacher of Aristotle. In about 387 B.C., Plato founded the Academy at Athens. He wrote approximately 24 compositions employing primarily a "dialectic" whereby a questioner and an answerer discuss or debate a thesis. The Theory of Forms is a central aspect of his philosophy and provides the basis for the Platonic unity of knowledge and action. All dialogue on specific issues relies on general concepts or universals. These universals or forms are immutable and timeless (justice, fearlessness, beauty), and they are the objects of knowledge providing certainty when genuinely known. Furthermore, the forms are the ontological basis of all particular occurrences in the changing, physical world. In the *Republic* the good life for the individual and the state is founded on action governed by knowledge of the forms, a sense of both the ideal and the individual that had a major influence on Santayana's philosophy. Platonic forms, stripped of any ontological or moral status, provide a basis for understanding Santayana's notion of essences that he developed as a part of his later naturalistic philosophy (see *Scepticism*).

303.32 a Pop] Pop is the Eton Society, a very prestigious group of boys that deals with disciplinary matters. One is elected as a Pop by current members, based upon personality.

303.38 Nietzsche] [See Note at 165.8.]

305.7 *Floreat Etona!*] On the seal of Eton College is the motto "Floreat Etona, Esto Perpetua" ("Let Eton flourish in perpetuity"). *Floreat Etona!* is also found in the song "Carmen Etonense" by A. C. Ainger (1837–1904). Peter recites the first lines of the poem, "Sonent voces omnium / liliorum florem". The escutcheon, assigned to Eton by Henry VI, was "on a field *sable* three lily-flowers *argent*, intending that our newly-founded College, lasting for ages to come, whose perpetuity we wish to be signified by the stability of the sable colour, shall bring forth the brightest flowers redolent of every kind of knowledge." (Sir H. C. Maxwell Lyte, *A History of Eton College* [London: Macmillan & Co., 1911]: 54).

305.29–33 was . . . hereditary] Here and at 315.11–14 in his personal copy of *The Last Puritan* (*EGS*), Santayana has drawn a vertical bar next to these lines of text. He often uses this technique to mark a passage for further consideration. No other mark appears in the text or in the margin at these places.

305.40–306.1 Ruskin . . . Browning] John Ruskin (1819–1900), English writer and art critic, praised Gothic architecture in *The Stones of Venice* (1851–1853) and was a champion of the Pre-Raphaelites (see *Persons and Places*, 138). The poet Algernon Charles Swinburne (1837–1909) achieved recognition with *Atalanta in Calydon* (1865), which was praised by Ruskin. He also was associated with the Pre-Raphaelite Brotherhood (see *Persons and Places*, 292). Robert Browning (1812–1889), who based many of his works upon Italian Renaissance subjects, was the focus, along with Walt Whitman, of Santayana's essay "The Poetry of Barbarism" in *Interpretations*.

306.9 *fioriture colorature, sfumature*] Italian terms used in the art of singing, and effectively rendered in English two lines later in the phrase "traceries and filigree"; they imply the singer's capacity for ornamentation and nuance in the effortless execution of usually rapid and complicated musical passages and scales.

306.13 Mater Dolorosa] Latin for "sorrowful mother", generally referring to the Virgin Mary.

307.7 old Calvinists] Oliver's sentiment is echoed in a letter from Santayana to William Haller dated 21 May 1939. To Santayana a literal belief in hell-fire is "gratuitous and insane." Oliver "had no such notion (as Emerson hadn't); it would not have shown true severity."

309.4 Hume] David Hume (1711–1776), Scottish philosopher and historian. His epistemological skepticism and his concept of natural belief provide a background for Santayana's skepticism and his concept of animal faith. In *Persons and Places* Santayana notes that he "studied Locke, Berkeley, and Hume under William James" (238), and that in his first year as instructor at Harvard he was invited to teach the course on Locke, Berkeley, and Hume because "James wished to relieve himself of his course" (390). Hume's significant works include *A Treatise of Human Nature* (1739), *An Enquiry concerning the Human Understanding* (1758), and *Dialogues concerning Natural Religion* (published posthumously and probably written in the 1750s).

312.36 *Lucania*] [See Note at 55.39–40.]

313.8 young Isaac] The Isaac story is at Genesis 22:1–14.

314.10 *Impayable*] French for "priceless" in the sense of a capital joke.

315.11–14 his self-possession . . . things.] [See Note at 305.29–33.]

318.38 one-horse shay] In Oliver Wendell Holmes's poem "The Deacon's Masterpiece: or The Wonderful 'One-Hoss-Shay'" (1858) the "shay", an open two-wheeled carriage drawn by one horse, represents the dogma of Calvinism. As Holmes describes it, the "one-hoss shay" was "built in such a logical way / It ran a hundred years to a day," and then suddenly disintegrated, "As if it had been to the mill and ground!"

319.16 Socrates] Socrates (*c*.470–399 B.C.), Greek philosopher, born in Athens. Socrates himself left no written record of his thought. Our conception of this extraordinary personality derives from the descriptions of him in Xenophon and particularly in the dialogues of Plato, Socrates' pupil. Socrates' teachings were essentially ethical, emphasizing self-knowledge and right action.

319.18 Asclepius] The Greek god of healing and medicine. Snakes, symbols of renewal, were his emblem, and the cock was commonly sacrificed to this god.

320.4–5 *Lusitania*] [See Note at 55.39–40.]

321.29–322.35 Thackeray Hotel . . . Paddington] Santayana wrote to his editor at Constable, Otto Kyllmann, on 26 June 1935, "I have a weakness for real names of places, and should like to keep the reference to the Thackeray Hotel if possible." The Thackeray Hotel, located on Great Russell Street, was a 'temperance hotel' where no alcoholic beverages were served; such establishments were generally less luxurious than the best West End hotels. The main building of the British Museum is an impressive structure located at Gower and Great Russell streets in Bloomsbury and houses some of the world's most famous collections of antiquities, coins, books, manuscripts and drawings, as well as reading-rooms for users of the library. Phidias (also spelled Pheidias) was an Athenian sculptor (*c*.500–*c*.434 B.C.) and ally of Pericles, celebrated in antiquity for his statues in bronze, in gold and in ivory. Enemies of Pericles charged Phidias with sacrilege for depicting himself and Pericles on Athena's shield; this shield is now housed in the British Museum (the "Strangford" shield). Long's Hotel was located in New Bond Street and well recommended at the turn of the century; Bond Street has been known as a luxury shopping district since the eighteenth century. The Burlington Arcade is a covered lane built in 1819 linking Piccadilly with Burlington Street and containing a variety of small shops. Santayana's Harvard friend, Charles Loeser, lived in London during the 1890s "in the Burlington Hotel, behind the Arcade" (*Persons and Places*, 218). Paddington Station, on Eastbourne Terrace, was the terminus of the Great Western Railway for the west and southwest of England.

323.2–4 Getting . . . Latin] Oliver may be thinking of "Festina lente" attributed to Augustus by Suetonius (*c*.69–*c*.130 A.D.), which means "Make haste slowly."

323.10 Slough of Despond] From John Bunyan's *Pilgrim's Progress* (1678), indicating the state or condition into which one may sink under the burden of sin.

324.37 Daughters of the Revolution] [See Note at 73.11–16.]

327.19 5, RUE DE SAINT SIMON,] 3 rue de Saint Simon was the Paris address of Santayana's close friend Robert Burnside Potter in 1896 (*Persons and Places*, 379–81).

327.28 *ça va sans dire*] "That goes without saying."

328.8 *épaté*] "Amazed; dumbfounded."

332.5 Thomas Aquinas] Saint Thomas Aquinas (1225–1274), Catholic theologian and philosopher. His thought is principally a rethinking of Aristotelianism with considerable influence from Stoicism, Neoplatonism, Augustinism, and Boethianism. *Summa Theologiae, Summa Contra Gentiles, De Pincippiis Naturae,* and *De Aeternitate Mundi* are among his major works.

337.21 *Tom Brown at Rugby*] *Tom Brown's School Days* (Thomas Hughes, 1857), was a famous book for boys portraying life in an English public school (Rugby). A sequel, *Tom Brown at Oxford* appeared in 1861.

341.10–11 *cum quibus*] In the ablative case, the Latin word '*quibus*', standing alone, signifies "means" ("by means of which"). Vanny's deliberately ungrammatical addition of the preposition '*cum*' ("with") provides the comic touch.

342.34–35 Snobbery . . . back yard.] [See Note at 197.19–198.2.]

347.13 *de contemptu mundi*] "Of (or about) contempt for the world."

348.30–31 from Schopenhauer . . . fault] This sentiment is sprinkled with characteristic acerbity throughout Schopenhauer's writings: see, for example, I.359–60 and II.80–81, 462–63, and 603 of *Parerga and Paralipomena* (E. F. J. Payne, trans. 2 vols. [Oxford: Clarendon, 1974]). Moreover, Oliver is using Schopenhauer to reemphasize his socially responsible "higher snobbery" (see Note at 197.19–198.2).

354.7 Lord Basil Kilcoole] In *Persons and Places* Santayana notes that he based the character of Lord Kilcoole upon his Oxford friend Gratten Esmonde (498).

354.20–21 damnable . . . Carlo] Lord Russell, principal model for Jim Darnley, evidently lost a good bit of money at Monte Carlo, as he hinted once to Santayana (*Persons and Places*, 313).

355.14–26 Oliver . . . now.] The young Lord Russell once gave vent to an "inexhaustible flow of foul words and blasphemous curses" which evidently left a lasting impression on Santayana (*Persons and Places*, 297–98). The observation about Jim and women also suggests Lord Russell. In a letter to Boylston Adams Beal dated 23 December 1935 Santayana says that "Jim's attitude towards women is absolutely" Russell's, and that the women whom Russell had known, including his wives, would recognize this. Santayana suggests that Russell, who had never known a mother, was seduced by Lady Scott (who later became his mother-in-law) in part because she showed him motherly kindness and understanding (*Persons and Places*, 317). (For more on Russell and Jim, see Note at 145.15.)

360.9–10 *Folies Bergères* . . . Montmartre] [See Note at 528.15.]

366.39 Manhattan Hotel] [See Note at 371.37–372.1.]

370.35 *giovanotto . . . cousin*] "Young American" and the "wicked (or naughty) cousin."

371.37–372.1 Manhattan Hotel . . . Brevoort House] The Manhattan Hotel, opened in 1896, stood at the corner of Madison Avenue and 42nd Street. Santayana sometimes stayed at the Manhattan Hotel when in New York. Built in 1854 the Hotel Brevoort, at Fifth Avenue and Eighth Street, was noted for its distinguished intellectual and cosmopolitan clientele.

372.33 Sherry's . . . *Martin*] Louis Sherry opened his first restaurant in New York City in 1881 and catered to the wealthy and elite of the city. Delmonico's famous restaurants have had many sites. The ninth, on 26th Street between Broadway and Fifth Avenue, was erected in 1876 and later became the Café Martin. It was demolished in 1914.

373.11 *comme-il-faut*] "Just right; in perfect taste."

375.6–7 Cloudcuckooland . . . Barataria] "Cloudcuckooland" is the mythical utopia in Aristophanes' comedy *The Birds*. "Lilliput" is the imaginary land in Book I of Jonathan Swift's *Gulliver's Travels* (1726), whose inhabitants are only a few inches tall. Barataria alludes to the fanciful monarchy in the Gilbert and Sullivan opera *The Gondoliers*.

375.7 *blague*] "Humorous banter."

375.29 *pagliacci*] The clowns in the traditional Italian comic theatre or *Commedia del' Arte*.

375.31 *Réparateur . . . porcelaine*] "Mender of crockery and china."

377.3 *le dernier cri*] "The latest fashion."

377.3 *stylisé*] "Modified; stylized."

377.5 *femme faite*] "A mature woman."

377.33 Claverly Hall] [See Note at 398.18.]

377.41 one of the professors] The professor is Santayana himself, who describes these stand-up breakfasts in a letter to Mrs. David Little (16 March 1952).

378.8 Boscovitz] Santayana's description of young Boscovitz resembles the description he gives of his Harvard friend Charles Loeser in *Persons and Places* (217). Santayana also notes that the "Boscovitz family is drawn in part after the Homers." His sister Susana became close friends with the Homer family in Boston (*Persons and Places*, 83–84). The name Boscovitz is probably taken from the Boscowitz family in Josiah Royce's only novel, *The Feud of Oakfield Creek* (1887).

378.20 *Bref*] "In brief; in short."

378.22–23 Professor Barrett Wendell] [See Note at 186.8.]

380.19–20 Mr. Stillman . . . Infirmary] The Stillman referred to is James Stillman (1850–1918), American banker and capitalist, among whose philanthropies were extensive donations to Harvard. The infirmary was procured in 1901. His son, Charles Chauncey Stillman, was a member of the Harvard Class of 1898 and a student of Santayana's.

387.10 Groton] As a young instructor at Harvard in the years 1893–1895, Santayana visited Groton, Amherst, Concord, and the surrounding area with friends and students. (Also see Note at 290.18–33.)

388.5 wall-game] The Wall Game is a peculiar form of football unique to Eton. A free-for-all sport, it is actually played against the wall of the playing field.

388.19–20 Old Manse] The home in Concord of Ralph Waldo Emerson and later of Nathaniel Hawthorne. (Also see Note at 387.10.)

388.39–40 *hors concours*] "Outside the official competition."

389.30 Longfellow's] [See Note at 73.11–16.]

389.34 Milesian tales] Originally a Greek collection of witty but obscene short stories; similar stories also are referred to as "Milesian Tales."

389.35–36 Evangeline and Priscilla] Evangeline is the heroine of Longfellow's poem of the same name (1847). Priscilla Alden, of the Mayflower Company, was poetized by Longfellow in *The Courtship of Miles Standish* (1858).

389.37 Excelsior] Excelsior means "ever upward" in Latin. Longfellow's "Excelsior" appeared in *Ballads and Other Poems* (1841) (*The Complete Poetical Works of Henry Wadsworth Longfellow* [Boston: Houghton Mifflin Co., 1893] 19–20).

390.1–2 *She . . . keel;*] From Longfellow's "The Building of the Ship," *The Seaside and the Fireside* (1850), lines 337–39, (*The Complete Poetical Works of Henry Wadsworth Longfellow* [Boston: Houghton Mifflin Co., 1893] 103).

390.17–18 *Do you ken John Peel*] This song is taken from the poem "John Peel" (first line "D'ye ken John Peel with his coat so gay?") by John Woodcock Graves (1795–1886).

390.18 *Bring . . . Boast*] [See Note at 397.18.]

390.18 *Gentlemen Rankers*] This song originated with the Whiffenpoof Society, a branch of the Yale University Glee Club, and is known as "The Whiffenpoof Song." The lines of the song are an adaptation of Rudyard Kipling's poem "Gentlemen-Rankers" from *Barrack-Room Ballads*.

390.21 Eton Boating Song] Mario is singing the second verse of the "Eton Boating Song". In the *Academy Song-Book* the chorus of the song is "Let us see how the loving cup flushes / At supper on Boveney meads" (Charles H. Levermore [New York: Ginn and Company, 1918] 108).

391.25–28 Professor Simpkins . . . subject.] Professor Simpkins's remark is a restatement of the same remark made to Santayana by Henry Adams; it is quoted in *Persons and Places* where Santayana describes his meeting with Adams (224).

392.33 rue de Saint Simon] [See Note at 327.19.]

392.34 *goûter*] A "snack," the French equivalent of English afternoon "tea."

392.36 *mezza*] A mezzo-soprano, the middle woman's singing voice: darker in timbre than a soprano but lighter than the lower contralto.

392.37–38 *Quis est homo*] "Who is this man?", the duet for mezzo and soprano, is from Rossini's *Stabat Mater* (*The Mother is standing*). This medieval Latin hymn which describes the suffering of the Virgin Mary at the foot of the Cross has been set to music by many composers.

392.38 the letter scene from *Le Nozze di Figaro*] The duet for two sopranos, "Che soave zefiretto" ("What gentle zephyrs will swell tonight"), is from Mozart's opera *The Marriage of Figaro*.

393.14 barbaric yawps] An echo of Walt Whitman's *Song of Myself*. Santayana's personal copy of *Leaves of Grass* (Philadelphia: David McKay, 1891–1892) is in the George Santayana Collection, Special Collections Division, Georgetown University Library.)

393.15–16 tear a passion to tatters] In Hamlet's speech to the players, he admonishes them not to "tear a passion to tatters" (*Shakespeare*, III.ii.11).

393.17 *Caro nome*] Italian for "beloved name," and the title and first words of Gilda's second-act aria from Verdi's *Rigoletto*.

393.17 the Queen of Night] The female villain in Mozart's opera *Die Zauberflöte* (*The Magic Flute*), who sings two arias which are so difficult that only a small number of sopranos—those possessing voices of exceptional agility and range—attempt the role. The arias are, first act: "Zum Leiden bin ich auserkoren" ("To sufferings am I destined") and second act: "Der Hölle Rache kocht in meinem Herzen" ("The vengeance of hell boils within my heart").

393.20–21 *du bout des lèvres*] "Barely touching the lips."

393.23–24 *Un bel maschio*] Italian for "a veritable male." Mario's response—*Sicuro!*—"Certainly!"

394.19–20 Rossini . . . *La Cenerentola*] Gioacchino Antonio Rossini (1792–1868), Italian composer of *The Barber of Seville* (1816), *William Tell* (1829), and some fifty other operas. Rossini's opera *La Cenerentola* (*Cinderella*) was first performed in January 1817.

394.35 *Deh, vieni alla finestra*] From Mozart's opera *Don Giovanni*, "O, come to the window" is the delicate serenade for baritone sung by Don Giovanni (the legendary lover Don Juan) to the maidservant of Donna Elvira, a lady whom he has seduced and abandoned.

395.3–4 *sotto voce*] "In a soft voice."

395.6 *scherzo*] Italian for "joke" or "jest," and in music a light-hearted, lively passage or section of a piece.

397.6 ἀνὴρ πνευματικός] [See Note at 247.10.]

397.18 *Here's a Health to King Charles*] This song occurs in chapter 20 of Sir Walter Scott's *Woodstock* (1826) with the title "Glee for King Charles". "Bring the Bowl which you boast" is the first line of the poem, and "Here's a health to King Charles" is the final line of each stanza.

398.18 Divinity Hall] Several Harvard buildings are mentioned in the novel. Oliver's room in Divinity Hall closely resembles Santayana's undergraduate room in Hollis Hall in the Harvard Yard (*Persons and Places*, 179, 183–85). Divinity Hall actually housed Harvard's Divinity School when it became more or less a department of the university. Claverly Hall (completed in 1893) was one of several "private dormitories" built for sons of millionaires. These new dormitories, built away from the Yard, separated Harvard students socially and financially. Memorial Hall was built in 1870–1874 as a memorial to the men of Harvard who died during the Civil War. Santayana mentions taking meals in Memorial Hall (*Persons and Places*, 187). (Also see *Harvard*.)

399.5 Ralph Waldo's] Ralph Waldo Emerson was at Harvard, both as an undergraduate (1817–1821) and as a Divinity School student (1825). The son of a poor widow, he made a mediocre record in his undergraduate studies; he waited table to earn money to pay his college expenses. (Also see Note at 128.33.)

399.37 Faust] [See Note at 191.3–7.]

400.7–8 *Gemütlichkeit* . . . tailor's.] *Gemütlichkeit* ("comfort or coziness"). Santayana here refers to the drinking bout in Auerbach's Keller in Leipzig from *Faust* (Part I, lines 2207–40), where Mephisto and Brander sing a song about a flea going to the tailor. This song has been set to music by many composers, including Guonod and Berlioz.

404.35–405.6 Claverly . . . Memorial] [See Note at 398.18.]

407.24–25 That everything was made of water, or that life was nothing but the restlessness of fire] These are the philosophical positions held by the Greek pre-Socratic philosophers Thales and Heraclitus, respectively. Thales (*c.*634–546 B.C.) is regarded as the founder of the Ionian school of natural philosophy. Our knowledge of Thales' work is largely drawn from references in Herodotus, Plato, and Aristotle. From these we learn that Thales was responsible for the axiomatization of geometry. He was credited with measuring the height of the pyramids and the distance of ships at sea, and he predicted the possibility of an eclipse in 585 B.C. In addition, he proposed that water was the key to understanding the world. The earth originated in water, is sustained by water, and all change is a transition in water. As a part of his natural philosophy he maintained that the world is animated and that even inanimate objects possess the principle of self-motion or *psyche*. Heraclitus (*c.*535–*c.*475) compares the flux of nature to a river, suggesting that everything is in a constant state of change as with his basic element of fire. Applied to natural objects, this means that even apparently stable things are changing, although total balance is always maintained.

407.37–408.4 *Hei, Siegfried . . . himself.*] This reference is from *Siegfried*, the third of Wagner's four music dramas comprising *Der Ring des Nibelungen*. The hero Siegfried acquires the magical power of understanding the meaning of the song of birds. In act two, after young Siegfried has slain both a dragon and an evil dwarf, and has thus acquired ring and helmet—both with magical powers—he is called to by a forest bird (with a soprano voice) *Hei, Siegfried!* ("Hark, Siegfried!"). The bird tells him where he may find yet another treasure, the beautiful maiden Brünhilde (one of the Valkyries), who sleeps on a rock surrounded by fire, awaiting her awakening by a fearless hero's kiss. (In the second work, *Die Walküre* (*The Valkyrie*), Brünhilde is put to sleep by Wotan after defying his order not to aid Siegfried's father. (Also see Note at 441.14–29.)

408.9 Zeller and the pre-Socratics] German philosopher Eduard Zeller (1814–1908), in his *Philosopie der Griechen*, regarded the Sophists, as opposed to the Pre-Socratics, as subjective idealists, characterized by relativism and skepticism and a revolt against physical science.

409.13 Shelley] Percy Bysshe Shelley (1792–1822), English romantic poet. Santayana greatly admired Shelley's poetry, as he did that of Byron and Keats, and his own poetry was influenced by their work. Santayana's essay "Shelley, or the Poetic Value of Revolutionary Principles," first published in *Winds of Doctrine* (New York: Scribner's; London: Dent, 1913), grew out of the "poetry bees" or regular meetings of undergraduates for the purpose of reading poetry aloud that Santayana held in his Harvard rooms. During 1910–11, the group read "only Shelley, from beginning to end, except *The Cenci*" (*Persons and Places*, 345). Mario is undoubtedly referring to these "poetry bees" at 412.34 where he says, "I can see all I want of him [Santayana] outside."

410.21–22 North End . . . Hollytree] Of the *Napoli* Santayana says, "I preferred the Napoli in the North End which was more genuinely Italian" (*Persons and Places*, 70).

And, in a letter to Robert Sturgis, he notes that "the tiny Holly Tree" was "in the basement of the tiny Lampoon building in the middle of Mt. Auburn Street," where they served "beefsteaks and eggs on toast" (28 January 1946).

410.39 Berlin or Marburg] Santayana studied philosophy in Berlin, but mentions in *Persons and Places* that perhaps he should have gone to Marburg or another German university (259–60).

411.12 *Voisin's*] *Voisin*, at the corner of Madison Avenue and Sixty-fifth Street, opened in New York prior to World War I and was one of the city's finest French restaurants. It was named for the more famous *Voisin* in Paris. Neither of these restaurants exists today.

411.23 *Elective Pamphlet*] Santayana expresses his disapproval of the elective system, which made its appearance at Harvard during the 1870s under the presidency of Charles William Eliot. Santayana also talks about the elective system at Harvard in *Persons and Places* (229).

411.31 "Too . . . handkerchief.] A reference to Professor Francis ("Fanny") Bowen, Santayana's first professor of philosophy at Harvard. Santayana describes Bowen in *Persons and Places* (236).

411.33–34 *hospitieren*] "To sit in on a lecture or lesson."

411.37 Professor Woods] John Houghton Woods (1864–1935) briefly studied philosophy in Japan and India. He taught both Eastern religion and philosophy at Harvard and also edited and translated works of non-Western philosophy.

411.38 *chouette*] "Splendid; swell."

412.4 Professor Royce] Josiah Royce (1855–1916) of the Harvard philosophy department (1882–1916) was the leading American philosopher of idealism. He supervised Santayana's dissertation on Lotze. (See Santayana's description of Royce in *Persons and Places*, 234.) Royce's major works include *The World and the Individual* (1901–1902), *Philosophy of Loyalty* (1908), and *The Problem of Christianity* (1913).

412.11 *exquises*] "Exquisite; delicious; delightful."

412.19 "He's the best man going,] Through Oliver, Santayana is perhaps expressing his appreciation of Royce as "the best man going." Santayana discusses Royce in *Character and Opinion in the United States: With Reminiscences of William James and Josiah Royce and Academic Life in America* (New York: Scribner's; London: Constable; Toronto: McLeod, 1920). Additional remarks concerning Royce are in *Persons and Places* (233–34, 389, 444).

412.28 Plato . . . *Symposium*] Santayana was always intensely interested in Plato. During his year off from teaching at Harvard (1896–1897), he spent the year at King's

College, Cambridge, England, studying with the distinguished Plato scholar Henry Jackson.

413.32 Kuchenschloss or von Gipfelstein] *Kuchenschloss* ("cake, or gingerbread castle"); *Gipfelstein* ("summit stone").

415.13 *Quelle erreur!*] "What a mistake!"

415.15–16 *'Ah, cette enfant,'* . . . *'c'est une polichinelle.'*] "Ah, that child, she's a mere puppet."

415.18 *il faut des dentelles*] "One must wear lace."

416.28 Knight of Malta] The Knights of Malta, a Catholic military order, has its origins in the Middle Ages. After Napoleon seized Malta in 1798, the order was dispersed throughout Europe. Since its beginning it has served the sick and poor, and the renown gained by the order in this service moved the pope to re-establish it in 1879 by papal decree. The order retains certain diplomatic privileges and has several legations. Mario's desire to be a Knight is referred to again on page 570.1–2.

418.10–11 Gil Blas or a Casanova] The picaresque hero of the novel, *Histoire de Gil Blas de Santillana*, by Alain René Lesage (1668–1747). In *Persons and Places* Santayana said of him, "if I were looking for ancestors there is only one known to fame to whom I might attempt to attach myself, and he is Gil Blas" (12–13). In his memoirs, the Venetian adventurer and author Casanova (Giovanni Giacomo Casanova de Seingalt, 1725–1798), stresses his innumerable, and probably partly mythical, conquests of women.

419.21–420.23 Plato . . . philosophy.] In *Persons and Places*, Santayana describes this essay as "an imaginary fragment" of the kind of paper he would receive from his best students in Philosophy 12, the course on Plato and Aristotle which he taught for most of his career at Harvard (394). At 420.14, "Absolute Idea of the Beautiful," Oliver is commenting on Plato's philosophy of love versus desire.

420.7–8 *being in love* is a kind of madness] Plato tells us so twice in the *Phaedrus*: through the lips of Phaedrus at 231E, and through those of Socrates at 265A (pp. 436 and 473, respectively, of *The Dialogues of Plato*, Benjamin Jowett, trans. Oxford: Clarendon Press, 1892).

431.30 Orestes . . . *Aulis*] Santayana has mistaken the title of Goethe's play. He is actually referring to *Iphigenia in Tauris* (*Iphigenie auf Tauris*). Goethe's play is after Euripides' drama of the same name.

433.31 the A.D.] The A.D. Club of Harvard is one of several clubs which started as chapters of national fraternitites (Alpha Delta Phi). In the late 1800s these clubs surrendered their charters and became local clubs. The A.D. was one of those at the top of the "club pyramid" known as "final clubs" (*Harvard*, 424–25).

436.15 *Respiro*] "That's a relief!"

436.17 *Basta*] "Enough; no more."

438.29 *mio sposo*] "My husband."

439.40–440.4 The . . . level.] Aunt Caroline's comments to Oliver are another example of Santayana's notion of "the higher snobbery." (Also see Note at 197.19–198.2.)

441.14–29 Rhinemaidens . . . *Götterdämmerung*] The Rhinemaidens appear in both *Das Rheingold* (*The Rhine Gold*) and *Die Götterdämmerung* (*The Twilight of the Gods*), the first and last of the four music dramas making up the Ring cycle. In the first work the Rhinemaidens, in the depths of the Rhine, guard a hoard of gold which has boundless powers. The dwarf Alberich takes the gold and makes from it a magic ring. When the ring is stolen from him by Wotan, he puts a curse upon it. In *Die Götterdämmerung*, the curse is fulfilled: Valhalla, with all the gods, is destroyed by fire, and the Rhinemaidens reclaim the ring. (Also see Note at 407.37–408.4.)

442.3 *la beauté des laides*] "The beauty of the ugly ones."

442.33 *à la Cléo de Mérode*] Cléo de Mérode was a famous Parisian courtesan and dancer at the turn of the century.

443.5 *entr'actes*] "Intermissions."

443.5 the *Rheingold*] [See Note at 441.14–29.]

446.34 *Beatri-ce*] The pure heroine of Dante's *La Divina Commedia*. Dante Alighieri (1265–1321), born in Florence, met the Florentine Beatrice Portinari (1266–1290) twice, when he was nine and again nine years later. His idealized love for her was the inspiration for most of his works. He considers love for a woman as the first step in the soul's spiritual improvement toward a capacity for divine love. In the *Divine Comedy* (1321), when the poet (who is, himself, the somewhat unconventional epic hero of the *Commedia*) has achieved the top of the mountain of Purgatory, it is Beatrice, as divine revelation, who conducts him through Paradise to God. (Also see Note at 114.5.)

447.2 *senza speme vivono in desio*] From Dante's *Inferno*, line 42 of Canto IV, the stanza reads, 'Per tai difetti, non per altro rio, / Semo perduti, e sol di tanto offesi, / Che sanza speme vivemo in disio' (as found in Santayana's personal copy of *La Divina Commedia*). In another of Santayana's books, Louis How's translation reads, 'For such defects, being else a sinless crew, / We're lost, but with no further punishment / Than hopeless living longing ever new.' (These copies of Santayana's personal books are in Special Collections, The Library of George Santayana in the University of Waterloo Library.)

453.5–6 *Fais le beau!*] The command to a dog to "show off, strut, or beg."

457.22 *Sorrows of Werther*] [See Note at 88.27.]

461.5 *Wanderjahre*] [See Note at 215.18–20.]

462.6 St. Elizabeth] St. Elizabeth (1207–1231), daughter of Andrew II, King of Hungary, devoted her life to religion and works of charity, despite having been at first forbidden to do so by her husband, Louis IV, landgrave of Thuringia. She assisted in the founding of many convents in the north of Germany.

463.38 *Meno male*] "All the better."

464.4–7 "Grant . . . to it."] Aunt Caroline is recalling figures prominent in the political corruption of the 1870s. Roscoe Conkling (1829–1888), U.S. Representative from New York (1859–1863, 1865–1867) and U.S. Senator (1867–1881), leader of the Republican Party in New York and "boss" of that state's political machine, staunch supporter of President Ulysses S. Grant and leader of the Party faction known as the "Stalwarts," fostered the corruption of Grant's later years. He disputed with Grant's successor Rutherford B. Hayes over the occupancy of some federal offices in New York, but managed to place his underling Chester A. Arthur as Vice Presidential candidate on the successful 1880 Republican ticket. However, when President James A. Garfield, seeking to pacify a rival Republican faction, appointed Conkling's chief New York State enemy as collector for the Port of New York, Conkling suddenly resigned. Almost immediately he decided to seek re-election by the New York Assembly, but failed miserably. Garfield's assassination by a petty "Stalwart" shortly thereafter did not improve matters.

471.2 New London] Santayana had first-hand knowledge of the area around New London and of the training of a Harvard rowing crew. In 1894, he went to New London as a Proctor to supervise the examinations of the Harvard rowing crew who were preparing for their race with Yale.

478.10 There's no real authority except the authority of *things*.] A fundamental principle of Santayana's materialist philosophy as expressed in *Scepticism* and in his *Realms of Being*.

486.13 *bonne-à-tout-faire*] "Maid-of-all-work."

486.17 Christ Church] It was in the rooms of a young American friend of Santayana's in Christ Church about 1895 that Santayana met Harold Fletcher, then a student and member of the Bullingdon Club. Fletcher later introduced Santayana to Father Philip Napier Waggett, who ran an Anglican monastery near Oxford at Cowley upon which Caleb Wetherbee's Benedictine monastery at Salem may be based (*Persons and Places*, 493–97). (Also see Notes at 182.34–35 and 277.18–278.4.)

486.19 Bullingdon Club] [See Note at 277.18–278.4.]

488.4–21 A religion . . . one?] Buddhism is a system of philosophy and ethics based on allegiance to the Buddha, or Enlightened One, a title given to Siddhartha Gautama, who lived in north India (*c.*563–483 B.C.). The doctrine taught by Gautama was summed up in the Four Noble Truths: (1) life is permeated by suffering or dissatisfaction, (2) the origin of suffering lies in craving or grasping, (3) the cessation of suffering is possible if craving ceases, (4) the way to the cessation of desire is through the Noble Eightfold Path. This path to Nirvana includes right views, right aspiration, right speech, right conduct, right livelihood, right effort, right mindfulness, and right contemplation. Santayana's reference in this section is to the Buddha, who could lead "his fellow-men to perfection." Taoism is a philosophical system based on the *Tao-te ching* of Chinese philosopher Lao Tzu (*c.*6th century B.C.). The *Tao*, or Way, is the path natural events take, with spontaneous creativity and regular alternation. Man gives up all striving to follow the *Tao*, his highest goal being the escape from illusion of desire through mystical contemplation. (For Socrates, see Note at 319.16.)

488.30 *Addison's walk*] East of Magdalen College are the Water-Walks, circling an island meadow made by the River Cherwell, about a mile around. Addison's Walk, along the northern section, is said to have been a favorite haunt of Joseph Addison (1672–1719) while a student there.

488.36 Hilary Term] The academic year at Oxford is divided into three terms. Michelmas (mid-October to about the first week of December) and Hilary (mid-January to about mid-March) are both followed by a six weeks' vacation, whereas Trinity or Summer term (about the fourth week in April to about the third week of June) is followed by the Long Vacation of approximately four months. Much of an undergraduate's reading is expected to be done during these vacations.

489.9 Peckwater] [See Note at 277.18–278.4.]

489.17 Cardinal Wolsey] Cardinal Wolsey (1472?–1530) founded Christ Church College, Oxford.

489.33 Dr. Jowett] Benjamin Jowett (1817–1893), distinguished classical scholar and head of Balliol College, Oxford University. In *Persons and Places* Santayana describes the circumstances under which Jowett sent the young Lord Russell down from Oxford in 1886 (308–309). (In *Life*, however, Russell notes that he was sent down toward the end of his second year in 1885. He visited Santayana at Harvard in 1886.)

489.39–490.5 Karnak . . . Feld] Santayana describes his travels among the ruins of Karnak and Baalbek in *Persons and Places* (457–58, 464). The land that became Tempelhofer Feld in Berlin was held by the Knights Templar during the Middle Ages, and, in the days of the kaisers, it was used as an exercise field for the Grenadiers of the Berlin garrison. It was converted from a parade ground to an airfield after the first world war.

490.6–7 the stupid trappings and the suits of greatness] Hamlet, in I.ii, responds to his mother's request that he give up his mourning costume: "these but the trappings and the suits of woe" (*Shakespeare*, line 86).

490.27–31 What . . . delusive?] This is a statement reminiscent of Santayana's adaptation of Aristotle's concept of entelechy: every living thing has a potential ideal career that, except for accident and misfortune, would bring it to a perfection of realization. This idea is also connected with Santayana's subscription to Socrates' principle that happiness depends on self-knowledge. One must know what one *is* in order to pursue a path leading to self-realization and happiness.

492.13–14 *Ein . . . bewusst.*] From Goethe's *Faust*, the *Prologue in Heaven*, lines 328–29, with the Lord speaking: "A good man in his darkling aspiration / Remembers the right road throughout his quest" (*Faust*, 89).

493.32 Sylvia of Shakespeare's song] Santayana here refers to Silvia in the "Song" from *The Two Gentlemen of Verona* (*Shakespeare*, IV.ii.39–53). This "Song" was later set to music by Franz Schubert.

495.17 *de trop*] "Unwanted; out of place."

495.28–496.11 Bodleian . . . Duke Humphrey's Library] In 1896 and again in 1909 when he was at Oxford, Santayana read in the Bodleian, the great central library of Oxford University. Duke Humphrey's Library, named after its fifteenth-century donor, is the core of the Bodleian. The Library is famous for its collection of rare old books and manuscripts, its fine wood paneling, painted ceiling, and splendid stained-glass windows. Thirty yards south is the Radcliffe Camera, a part of the Bodleian Library system used as a Reading Room. To the west is Exeter College, separated from the Bodleian by its garden. South of the Radcliffe Camera is St. Mary's Church. Santayana said of St. Mary's tower: "The sunlight here does wonders with the towers, especially St. Mary's and Magdalen, the latter one of the most engaging and satisfying towers in the world" (Santayana in a letter to Conrad Slade, 11 August 1896). North of the Bodleian, at the intersection of Broad and Holywell Streets, is the King's Arms Hotel. Santayana described the King's Arms in a letter to Otto Kyllmann of 27 July 1935 as "[my] favourite inn at Oxford when I wasn't in lodgings."

497.22–23 Plato and Plotinus] Oliver thinks that "like Plato and Plotinus . . . we must look to some imaginary heaven or some impossible utopia for encouragement and for peace." (See Note on Plato at 302.35.) Plotinus (*c.*205–270 A.D.), considered the founder of Neo-Platonism, was probably a Hellenized Egyptian rather than a Greek. Born in Lykopolis, Upper Egypt, he became deeply interested in philosophy at the age of twenty-eight and went to Alexandria to study with well-known masters. Disappointed by several teachers, he turned to Ammonius Saccas, who made a pivotal impression and remained his teacher for eleven years. Later he settled in Rome, conducted a school of philosophy and eventually asked the emperor Gallienus for some land to establish a community governed by the principles of Plato. This was perhaps an effort to aid the emperor in an attempted rejuvenation of paganism. Santayana's interest in Plotinus is attested to by "Fuller on Plotinus," an 84-page handwritten manuscript contained in a notebook in the collection of the Rare Book and Manuscript Library, Columbia University. In 1913 "Dr. Fuller, Plotinus, and the Nature of Evil" appeared in the *Journal of Philosophy, Psychology, and Scientific Methods* (10 [1913] 589–99).

499.15 *fait divers*] In French, incidental items in a newspaper, such as accidents or scandals.

499.23 Jermyn Street] [See Note at 239.12–13.]

500.6 Mario began.] In his personal copy of *The Last Puritan* (*EGS* page 628) Santayana has written 'Cf. p 718' in the left margin next to this line (see Note at 570.5–20).

500.9 third Punic war] This war effected the complete destruction of Carthage (149–146 B.C.). The Romans laid siege to the city, and, with Scipio in command, captured house by house the streets that led up to the citadel. Of a population of over half a million, only 50,000 survived the siege. The survivors were sold into slavery, and the city was obliterated.

500.35 *The House*] Christ Church, Oxford University, named "Aedes Christi," the House of Christ, is always spoken of colloquially as "the House".

501.2–25 Of course . . . woman."] In his personal copy of *The Last Puritan* (*EGS* pages 629–30) Santayana has drawn three separate vertical bars in the right margin and has numbered them '1', '2', and '3'. Number 1 encompasses lines 2–6, 'Of course . . . happens.'; number 2, lines 6–10, 'Is anything . . . war.'; and number 3, lines 10–14, 'But it's horrible . . . about.'. He continues with three separate vertical bars in the left margin numbered '4', '5', and '6'. Number 4 includes lines 14–18, 'Yet love-making . . . So it is with war.'; number 5, lines 18–20, 'The world . . . crushed.'; and number 6, lines 23–25, 'Fiddling? . . . woman."'. In the top margin of page 630 he has written '*Philosophy of War*'. Cross-purposes in the dark. 1.—This world irrational 2.—Horrible evils involved 3,4.—Over-population one of them, 5.—Better to be in the push than out of it, 6.'

502.8 Mr. Asquith or M. Clemenceau] Herbert Henry Asquith (1852–1928) was prime minister of England until 1916, when he was succeeded by David Lloyd George. George Clemenceau, "the Tiger," was French premier from 1917–1919. His "Sacred Union" cabinet was instrumental in achieving Allied victory. (Also see Note on the Kaiser at 557.14–21.)

502.12–13 *Camelots du Roi* . . . Maurras.] During the 1930s the Camelots ("the street-hawkers of the king"), right-wing university students, organized to distribute the royalist daily newspaper *L'Action Française* on the Left Bank and also were involved in rioting for their faction. Charles Maurras (1868–1952), a conservative political journalist and literary critic, was founder and editor of the newspaper.

502.20–30 One . . . again."] Mario's anti-parliamentarian, anti-democratic sentiments partially reflect Santayana's own political perspectives as found in *Dominations and Powers: Reflections on Liberty, Society, and Government* (New York: Scribner's; London: Constable, 1951).

502.20 *speriamo*] "Let us hope."

504.8–33 Germany . . . self-praise.] This is the negative view of Germany similar to that expressed in Santayana's *Egotism*. (Also see Notes on Goethe at 88.31–32; Nietzsche at 165.8.)

517.1 *force majeure*] "Circumstances outside one's control."

518.3 *Peter out*.] In *Persons and Places*, Santayana says that "petering out" was common among the young men he had known at Harvard (382–83); and in a letter to Van Wyck Brooks dated 22 May 1927 he asks: "Why do American poets and other geniuses die young or peter out, unless they go and hibernate in Europe?" Santayana had known some young poets at Harvard who suffered this "snuffing out" by the American environment (letter to Victor Calverton of 18 November 1934). In a letter to William Lyon Phelps dated 16 March 1936 he says that "they hadn't any alternative tradition (as I had) to fall back upon"; similarly, in a letter to Rosamond Sturgis of 5 February 1936 he says that Oliver's trouble "was that *he couldn't be exceptional, and yet positive*. There was no tradition worthy of him for him to join on to." As identified in the Phelps letter, the young Harvard poets who served as models for Oliver Alden were Thomas Parker Sanborn, Philip Savage, Hugh McCullough, Joseph Trumbull Stickney, George Cabot Lodge, and William Vaughn Moody. In addition Santayana described Lawrence Butler, one of the chief models for Oliver, as having "petered out". (Also see Note at 13.35–14.6.)

518.36 Unter den Linden] "Under the Linden Trees," a principal avenue in Berlin. In recent history, this is the street on which the Brandenburg Gates stand, once the separation point of East and West Berlin.

519.31 *Tant pis*] French expression of chagrin: "too bad" or "so much the worse" approximate its meaning.

520.1–2 Punic . . . Carthage] [See Note at 500.9.]

520.15–27 very pale and sallow ghost . . . humour.] The "ghost" Santayana is most likely referring to is Lytton Strachey (1880–1932), the British biographer and literary critic. In *Persons and Places* he describes Strachey as "a limp cadaverous creature, moving feebly, with lank long brown hair and the beginnings of a beard much paler in colour, and spasmodic treble murmurs of a voice utterly weary and contemptuous" (501). Strachey studied at Cambridge; Oscar Wilde (1854–1900) was at Oxford. Both men aroused scandalized protest because of their writings and their lifestyles (each had homosexual liaisons). In the preface to his novel, *The Picture of*

Dorian Gray, Wilde claimed that books were neither moral nor immoral; they were either well or badly written.

520.31–32 young cleric] In a letter to Otto Kyllmann of 27 July 1935 Santayana describes the model for the young parson, a clergyman he met "during the Boer war, not in 1916," and conversed with in the coffee-room of the King's Arms.

521.12–13 Dr. Johnson] Samuel Johnson (1709–1784), English author, essayist and satirist. Santayana seems to be alluding here not to something Johnson actually said or wrote, but to his manner of speaking as described in Boswell's *The Life of Samuel Johnson* (1791).

521.32–33 St. Giles] St. Giles's Church, rebuilt in the thirteenth century, is situated on the northern edge of Oxford where from about 1120 a church dedicated to St. Giles had stood. St. Giles is considered the patron saint of churches which are situated beyond the gates of a town.

522.6 Tommy Atkins] The generic name for the British foot-soldier during World War I is from Rudyard Kipling's poem "Tommy," in *Barrack-Room Ballads* (1892).

522.22 Lord Basil Kilcoole] [See Note at 354.7.]

523.24–31 *Phaedrus* . . . St. Paul] In the *Phaedrus*, a dialogue by Plato, Socrates and his friend Phaedrus discuss conventional versus true rhetoric. The Apostle Paul (*c*.A.D. 10–*c*.62), putative author of over one quarter of the New Testament.

523.42 Conder's] Charles Conder (1868–1909), British painter, studied art and lived in Paris during the 1890s. He began in 1896 the design and painting of fans, the work for which he is best known. Isabella Stewart Gardner was a collector of his fans.

524.8–10 *Perpetual* . . . La Fontaine.] Jean de La Fontaine (1621–1695), French poet and author of *Fables*. Kilcoole is paraphrasing La Fontaine, Fable XVIII, Book VII, line 33: "Ne me trompent jamais, en me mentant toujours."

524.19 Saint Mary's] [See Note at 495.28–496.11.]

527.9 *ville lumière*] The French phrase "city of light" is traditionally applied to Paris, a city with which Santayana had a long-standing acquaintance (see Note at 11.3–4).

527.34–35 Lord Cavan's] Frederick Rudolph Lambart, tenth Earl of Cavan (1865–1946), was a territorial brigade commander in World War I.

528.10 *bonne*] "Maid-servant."

528.15 *Baronne du Bullier*] Santayana probably named the "Baroness" du Bullier after the Bal Bullier, largest of the dance halls in Montparnasse. Located on the Left

Bank in the Boulevard de Montparnasse, the Bal Bullier was a huge, Moorish-style building which, unlike some of the other balls, was fairly reputable. It catered to a colorful and socially mixed crowd of artists, students, foreigners, and others from all parts of Paris. A succession of costume dances, begun in the 1880s, was continued in the next decade by such balls as the yearly Bal de l'Internat (Medical Students' Ball), hosted by the Bal Bullier and nearly as raucous and libertine as the Beaux Arts students' Bal de Quatr'Arts at the Moulin Rouge. The Moulin Rouge, another famous dance hall, was located in Montmartre, an outer district on the right bank of the city. When the Moulin Rouge closed for the summer, its branch on the Champs-Elysées, the Jardin de Paris, served as an open-air café-concert with variety show acts. The Folies Bergères was the most famous of the cafés-concerts, providing the worker as well as the aristocrat with the best professional singers, comics, and acrobats, in addition to food and drink.

528.20 *voilà*] "There; that's that."

528.28 *cent sous*] In French, a hundred sous (pennies), or five francs.

528.39 *volage*] "Fickle; inconstant."

529.36 *prêter*] "To lend."

531.33 *Jardin de Paris*] [See Note at 528.15.]

532.39 *poilu*] A French soldier.

535.20 rue de Saint Simon] [See Note at 327.19.]

535.23–30 *Stripling . . . kiss.*] This poem, in the style of the seventeenth-century cavaliers, is probably by Santayana himself.

537.25–538.7 In an . . . heart.] [See Note at 156.18–157.34.]

540.19 *Nunc dimittis* and *Consummatum est.*] From Luke 2:29: "nunc dimittis servum tuum, Domine" ("Lord, now let thy servant depart"); and from John 19:30: "consummatum est" ("It is completed"), Christ's last words on the cross.

549.9–10 Iphigenia in Aulis . . . Orestes] [See Note at 431.30.]

551.6–7 Whom . . . chasteneth] Hebrews 12:6.

552.13–14 Plato . . . inspiration] Relates to Oliver's thesis (419.21–420.23).

553.3 Plotinus] For Plotinus the highest principle of everything that exists is the One, which is absolutely transcendental and is the object of universal desire. Through purification, and attainment of the virtues, the soul can again be united with the

One; the soul ascends to its original source and merges with God. (Also see Note at
497.22–23.)

553.9–10 *Weh dir, dass du ein Enkel bist.*] "To be a grandson is a curse" (*Faust*, Part I,
line 1977). At this point in Goethe's drama, Mephistopheles is mockingly sympa-
thizing with the burden of cultural inheritance felt by youth. Santayana quotes this
line also in *Persons and Places* where he is discussing three well-placed young men
he knew at Harvard, two of whom never married (348). (This line ends with an
exclamation point in Santayana's copy of the German edition, and, with a line drawn
in the margin, Santayana highlights this passage. His copy of *Faust* is in the George
Santayana Collection, Houghton Library, Harvard University. See *Goethes Sämtliche
Werke. Mit Einleitungen von Karl Goedeke.* [Stuttgart: J. G. Cotta'schen Buchhandlung]
1883).

557.14–21 Kaiser . . . armistice.] Beginning in 1916, huge wooden statues of German
Field Marshall Paul von Hindenburg (1847–1934) were erected as a money-raising
scheme. The German people paid to hammer iron nails into the statues, and the
proceeds went to the German Red Cross. Kaiser Wilhelm II (1859–1941), Emperor
of Germany, abdicated his throne as part of the peace negotiations ordered by
President Wilson at the end of the war. The Armistice ending World War I was
signed on 11 November 1918.

559.25 Boston Art Museum] Peter's collecting of art is reminiscent of that of William
Sturgis Bigelow (see Note at 57.7–34).

560.20 Paul and Virginia] *Paul et Virginie* (1788) by Jacques-Henri Bernardin Saint-
Pierre, a friend and follower of Rousseau, tells the story of two French children
brought up as brother and sister according to Nature's law. Living on a tropical
island, they are raised by their mothers in a simple, frugal life free of religious
superstition, social prejudice, and fear of authority. However, Virginia's aunt re-
quests that she come to Paris to be educated so that she may later assume the aunt's
fortune. Upon her return to the island several years later, Virginia refuses to undress
to save herself and is drowned when her ship founders on a reef in sight of land.
Paul and the two mothers die shortly thereafter of grief.

561.1–2 Siegfried . . . Brunhilda] [See Note at 407.37–408.4.]

562.7–35 ROSE . . . *departs.*] This poem by Santayana was written for the novel.

563.31–32 there is a love that passeth the love of women] "Thy love to me was
wonderful, passing the love of women." From Second Samuel 1:26, this is King
David's lamentation over the dead Saul and Jonathan.

565.7 *Que faire?*] "What to do?"

565.10 *Ueberfall*] "Surprise attack."

565.11–12 *Jamais de la vie.*] "Not on your life! Never!"

566.14–15 *Je . . . aimait.*] "I don't love you, Marianne; it was Célio who loved you" is the final line (II.xx) of Alfred de Musset's 1833 play *Les Caprices de Marianne*. (Also see the Introduction to this edition, xxxiii). He was a favorite poet of the young Santayana, who had translated into English passages from de Musset's poetry.

570.1–2 *Knight of Malta*] [See Note at 416.28.]

570.5–20 *colouring . . . yourselves."*] In the left margin of his personal copy (*EGS* page 718) next to line 5 Santayana has written 'Cf. p. 628' (*CE* page 500). In the following paragraph (lines 7–20) six vertical lines are drawn in the left margin and are numbered '1' through '6'. Number '1' is beside lines 7–9 '*of an . . . worth*'; '2' by lines 9–11 '*having . . . those who*'; '3' by lines 11–12 '*disown . . . let an*'; '4' by lines 13–16 '*possible . . . home in*'; '5' by lines 16–17 '*the grand . . . and your*'; and '6' by lines 18– 20 '*or rather, . . . yourselves.*'". In the bottom margin of the page Santayana writes: '*Lights on Fascism before the disaster. 1, 5, 6 point out the conservative side* of Fascism. 2. asserts that this must subsist in any *fruitful* movement. 3 risks a bit too much in saying *never* for never *for long*. 4. Admits that *illusion is normal* & perhaps necessary for vitality or an *inevitable consequence* of it.'

570.16–17 *Donna Laura*] The name is an allusion to Petrarch's Laura, the symbol of his aspirations. The name has been used by poets and writers since Petrarch to indicate similar idealized loves. Here Santayana suggests that Mario's wife is such an ideal woman.

570.24 *Howard Sturgis's*] [See Note at 11.15–17.]

571.7 *We are of imagination all compact.*] Santayana quotes from *A Midsummer Night's Dream*: "The lunatic, the lover, and the poet / Are of imagination all compact" (*Shakespeare*, V,i,7–8).

572.18–21 After . . . story?"] In *Platonism and the Spiritual Life* these lines read: "for after life is done, and the world is gone up in smoke, what realities may the spirit of a man boast to have embraced without illusion, save the very forms of those illusions by which he has been deceived?" (New York: Charles Scribner's Sons, 1927, 89).

Colophon

*This book was designed and set in Baskerville
by DEKR Corporation. It was printed on 60-pound
acid-free offset paper and bound in Holliston Roxite
B-51545 cloth by Maple-Vail Incorporated.*